The Blinding Walk

The Blinding Walk

K. M. Ross

First published in 2014 by

THE WAYWISER PRESS

Bench House, 82 London Road, Chipping Norton, Oxon OX7 5FN, UK
P.O. Box 6205, Baltimore, MD 21206, USA
http://waywiser-press.com

Editor-in-Chief
Philip Hoy

Senior American Editor
Joseph Harrison

Associate Editors
Dora Malech | Eric McHenry | V. Penelope Pelizzon | Clive Watkins | Greg Williamson

Printed and bound by
T. J. International Ltd., Padstow, Cornwall, PL28 8RW

To my sister Anne

ACKNOWLEDGEMENTS

Extracts from *The Blinding Walk* have previously appeared in a slightly different form in the magazines *Percutio* (from the chapters *Yehune in Matamata*, *Samovar* and *An Accident*) and *brief* (from the chapters *First Steps*, *Samovar* and *ONE*).

The author would like to thank his wife Janet, Philip Hoy, Simon Creasey, Tony Lawrence, Jill Scott, Jack Ross and Bronwyn Lloyd, and all the people who gave their time to read the book in manuscript.

CONTENTS

Contents

Sydney Evening

'Now, did I tell Mel the Yip? Think so, Yip and the Piano, but it won't be late enough yet, if not's not a worry. Yip yip yahoo. Might not even have got off. A huh, a huh-huh… shit what a clown, bugger me if it isn't.'

That was the form of words. It made small print tracks across street crossings, under the historic Coke sign, threaded in block-square letters through and around the solid metallic joints of scaffolding at the fag-end of the Strip past the King's Cross club and bar signs. Where the light died yielding to light. Cracked neon, red and specious yellow. Fail light, fall light; where the night draws down its brow. Beetly-nighto. Hey yeah good one.

'What did you say your name was?' the girl Neeomi had asked.

'Yehune.'

'Oh. Um, I'm sorry, can you say that again?'

'Yehune.'

'Oh, right. What sort of a name is that?'

'It's of Hebraic origin,' he'd said to her, face held enigmatic under the strip-lights of the bar before: yip-yip.

'Ah…'

Print Shop Tony put in in a stage whisper, 'He means he's Jewish, dumbo.'

'Oh, *Jewish*? Why didn't you say so? No need to be embarrassed, we love the Jews over here. This *is* a civilised country.'

Thees *eez* a see-vilised country. Seev, a seev-a. Words appeared to him again like shark's teeth carried on the many-lustred air, just as the tail of his eye was drawn to an unusual shape lying down in the gutter. What looked like the broken-off snout of a shark moulded in iridescent plastic. Why not? he thought for a moment incoherently: says he's Jewish.

Past the angles of pipes, the busker he'd seen took on line and detail, bobbing and ducking in the face of a small crowd. He was cadaverous in an orange raincoat, with a clown's deep-red mouth, working to a beat in the middle of a bombsite of strewn cups and paper plates and fragments of old food. A huh, a huh-huh; rubbish of a street-fest; Sydney Lighting Association. Banners hung from the trees. Just as Yehune drew in, the clown was making a show of offering kids the limp prophylactics of burst balloons.

Sucks, wouldn't you say? And: kids, so there are kids in fucking King's Cross, this hour; but those could be the parents just over there. Not those others. Three taller ladies stood off to one side, done up in careful plumage.

Unhesitatingly, Yehune broke formation. His workmate Tony was just then gassing discoursing print print on about something, the girls caught in different attitudes behind them. His first trip was to the gutterside to pick up the shark-end, then he had a job matching the soughing splintered edges roughly to the borders of his face. Got it – there – but can't see fuck. Next, he bore down, bore in, making a sort of noise in the back of his throat, *mm*-ooiiinn, *mm*-ooiiinn, which made for a strange discordancy with the tin-blip beat of the ghetto blaster. Shark warning; out of the water. Better get a wriggle on. A voice from behind him, Tony's voice, 'Ah... Yehune?' was lost in the logic of moments streaming back behind him, and broken into by a far louder shrilling from one of the transvestites,

'Owwwm, look what's comin' *our* way darlings.'

Near the last moment, the clown met his eye through a gap, and before the crescendo of his throat-noise turned to words Yehune was able to see just one time the sad apprehensive brow under grease paint, the eyes, the chin too long under the ruby smile: a real person, flawed and fallible, life not artifice.

He roared into the shark-mask,

'I – eat – clowns.'

The busker registered hesitancy. Well you might, after all, balloon burst... whaddaya. It wasn't possible to think too much in the moment-to-moment stringing of event, in the rattling on of moments. When the busker picked another scrap of balloon out of the small sprig under his left arm and held it out, his attacker could only think, got you now anus-head. He tossed the headpiece

10

savagely, bracing the movement over the short even stubs of his legs. The clown retreated, toe over toe. And from the ragged collection of bystanders was shouted,

'Hey! Whyn't cha leave 'eem alone?'

'Yeah. The keedies were liking 'eem.'

Resistance; but in the lull the shark had found a weak point, and he stooped to menace the velvet ruffle-hat that had been stood on the pavement to catch coins. The clown did confusion. *I'll* confuse you, sucker. But just then, a tall someone in tight lycra put her weight behind a cleverly-angled elbow. *Oouwff,* fuck it; he stumbled, shark-head dropped; though he managed to clutch it down to his side with a wrench of defeated plastic.

'C'mon now big-dong, give the *artiste* a chance,' sang out razor-edged like the cry of an Australian parrot over the cacks and gestures of the rest of the sidewalk flock.

So now he was in retreat, edging back from what seemed an army of advancing lady-men, and came up against the lowest transverse strut of the metal scaffolding behind him. He scrambled up, and managed to stay there, hanging on one stout arm. The clown-man dashed in to spend a few moments in loving reunion with his fluffy hat. Something, he couldn't have said what, moved Yehune just then to set his face jaw-out and jig-jig like an ape – *'Hoo! hoo!'* – and he pumped his right arm twice and sent the shark-head flying in a long arc nearly into the stream of cars beyond. The tallest of the transvestites fluttered and cowered back.

But already, the fun was over; he could see a purposeful figure walking out of the dark of the restaurant premises next in line; Tony and the girl from the aquarium moved in around him, and it wasn't long before he was being force-walked, to all appearances, between them on along the sidewalk, still hearing from the corner behind a voice that boomed out whining flexible spectra of vowels… 'gooiiin ooouurrn'… over the sand-whoosh racket of the cars. God, yeah, good one, just like old times. Freemans Bay. Pissing over the walls. Ruth the aquarium presently dropped back to join her friend, and Neeomi as well held herself on the edge of association, just to underline the fact that though she was there with Tony she wasn't actually, you know, *with* him; unvalent lattice; piss relations; and they were on their way to the Piano Bar, and whaddaya think will Mel be there or will he not be because well he might not even have got off the ferry yet

There was Tony, Tony from the Print Shop, with whom was associated Neeomi; and then there were the two girls or rather one he'd met at the aquarium, but two because she'd brought another friend to replace the friend he'd met her with; and himself; and Mel, who wasn't there yet. Yehune let figures and relations skim across the surface of his overactive mind while the first manoeuvring for position went on around the side tables. Neeomi's eyes were bright glowing pegs, always lighting on his, and she kept making pointed use of his name as if she was trying to make up for it... 'What're you all having?' he said, 'Oh, thanks... *Yehune*... um, mine's a margarita?' The others, he had to say, had gone a bit subdued since that thing with the clown. Even here; semidark; blue-light... even safe in the textured smudge-world of the Piano Bar, half a street and a perpendicular corner off Darlinghurst Road, they were self-shrunk units in a moving Chinese pegboard – Ruth a floating of eyelashes seen from the side, Guddie not much more than a hollow of shimmer-grey.

The bar. He'd said The Bar. He was sure he had. He could feel his lips move, saying it: Yip, and the Piano Bar. But as a matter of fact the Piano Bar wasn't even its name, it was just the way he'd always heard everyone talking about it. He could half-remember seeing a sign outside; must have; saying... what? Hohner's, Joe's, Frankie's? Just now he was out on his own again, making his way without a hitch through crowds of bar-goers, jostling when he had to, hearing someone's fingers cracking patterns of schmaltzed-up jazz out into the general noise. There was a clunky old upright with candle-holders standing in the corner nearest the street, which he could see from where he was, as well as the fingers of the amateur wombat-buggerer driving in at an angle of 45. A tinkly-tinka-tonkle-tonkle-crash... a *whoooeeeee*... shit me, Gershwin, don't forget to lick your finger when you do that or you'll be getting labourer's fingernail.

Tony nudged him, coming up behind with his revised drinks order. Yeah – OK – righto. Not going so well for you, is it mate? You need your spritzer. As if from another angle bearing out of the crowd came Neeomi, Tony's pickup, determined to keep herself aloof. It wasn't until Tony turned back that she sidled in alongside, ready to help with drinks.

He was at the barside, reeling off drink names... margarita? -arita?... having succeeded in catching a barman's attention against a chorus of competing shouts; he played with the ice-tongs; considered names for the figure in an outsize check shirt who was bending to pick a bottle out of a low fridge... Thomas? Goes all right, Thomas the bar. He asked him, butting in across, whether the piano was free for all. The massive shoulders shrugged. Then came the price, wheedled high in an Australian accent.

A fag. A fag. Nothing for it, mates, since I can't see Mel anywhere. What's that? Friend of mine, darling. Oh yeah? You see someone you know?

He took an inconsequent moment to reflect, coming back with the drinks with Neeomi, that it was a funny thing, how those currents set up in the blood, energies, twitching scarlet ribbons, lingered on in you; or took, you know, a while to run out to the end. Funny thing, that. Neeomi seemed to have it too. Cocked an eye at the piano stool: no-one. The bar to him was still a strut over a street side edging with cracked toy plastic while the head of a lorikeet fell arc-slipped to car level.

Neeomi asked him: 'So what was with all that with the clown?' 'Tryin' to make a point.'

But she seemed to be expecting something more. He lipped out, 'Us Jews have got a lot more militaristic since, you know, 1948.'

Negotiations were still going on around a long board to the side by the wall, draped with coats and fabric handbags, where a small party was either just leaving or not, and appeared to be sensitive about who crowded in on them. Neeomi collared someone hovering nearby even while she set down drinks: 'Is that *you* Brett? Gorrd, I mean to say...' Yehune's hands were free; he adjusted the cigarette, which had been held clenched between two rows of teeth.

He took another sighting. Still empty, shitboys, do me a favour. Well then, let's go for it.

That was how it happened that Yehune Trent, 22, lately of Auckland, New Zealand, came to ease his broad flat buttocks down over the well-compacted piano stool in a bar in King's Cross, somewhere in Australia; take the fag out of his mouth and consider positions for it, up there above the high notes, wedged into a joint of the swingdown music stand... then stretch back for a moment to get the feel of the atmosphere before moving his hands over and essaying a confident half-scale. God-*damn,* what's that noise. Chinese gongs behind a plaster wall. And how about that funny smell, oh it's my own fucking... gotta have your fag. Can't do without it. Well now, how's about a few popular favourites....

He launched into 'Click Go the Shears Boys', picking it for a crowd-pleaser, laying it on thick as you please with fingers that powered down into the keyboard like panel-beaters' hammers. Cross-cultural reference. *Click – cli-click,* he went as far as syncopation of the medial clickery; don't fool yourself, couldn't be bad enough. He was beginning to woo his public, he could tell; he could feel his eyes watering strangely, and associated it with the thread of smoke like a savage whisker of reminiscence hanging there between uneven struts. He intuited rather than saw a drift of the standing part of the crowd towards the source of noise. Fag toppled – oy my Marlboro – and tried to get itself involved in the agile spider-march of fingers. Bug, just missed it. Squash the fucker. Lost it down? People were craning around him, apparently just to get a look at someone doing that, making noises with his fingers on a piannah. Some were vaguely moaning, trying to sing. He finished with a few scintillating arpeggios, half-referring to the old jazz-masher before him, and only paused to reinsert his fag before beginning the next number... ah, what... 'Woolloomooloo Choo-choo', something like that? Hit it. Choo-choo choo-se me baby. And: shit God can you believe it, they're actually loving it; loving me; loving and loving and loving....

Lip-light love on the underhouse of oldish Sydney loves. Curling of smoke up above, into the continental gap, forking just above the woolly-haired blunt of the top of the pianist's head, so that it seemed it might have seemed to any observer among the bodies from about four metres away in the direction of the tables and barside that two branches stuck out, flagging, indeterminate, like aerials protruding from a point above each temple, sending quick glowing tags of thought and music, analogue waves, in lightning cavalries into the upper darkness.

Y-fork. Yip Yehune

The fork was on a beach, fork was in my mind, hesitancy of sun-blazed electricity, crackle across of worlds, while I felt the settling of my heels into the backed-up sand of each step down a stone seawall and trailed across a level surface to the tideline and the beginning of the rocks, sudden rippling tear of hemisphere across to hemisphere, with a glance up across the cut of the wind to see the white-painted iron bench at the top of the wall. And when I looked down at that rock that could have been home in Maeraki, it was like the mudstone back home sectioned by traced lightning-lines of a harder rock, primitive sedimentary, volcanic crystalline glint, couldn't help but feel the uninterrupted force of it through all the afternoons of my childhood playing in the sand and across endlessly-migrating streams from the sewerage outlets, but there are beaches and beaches, this one spread like a long scythe ground by the wind to a stinging flatness out in front of my eyes and as far as the minute heads with tussock and parked cars. Wandering, that was it, without any aim in mind, come down from the big house beyond the golf course and the road. And I kept thinking I could see him walking up there, above the bank with the harsh yellow grasses like flax and the concrete blocks collapsed in places set there to shore it up, taking tracks that I couldn't see from down here on the flat, walking and running in and out so that I saw him now and the next moment didn't, saw him racing in and out of the paths like a monkey-shape at the head and the tops of the shoulders; that crux, that branching, companion in dissidence, old Yehune. Which brought it back to my mind

Games on the beach. Thompsons. Rotted remains of old jetties. Up where the rocks had been resculptured. Concrete creek outlet already undermined. Making cities; a double-handed squeeze for a tower of sand. Different, that sand; it was finer, whiter, fracturing in sharp cliffs. Cities of the Dog Sand they were called and the Driers were the ones that stoned them, dry sand that was, names drawn out of mind and memory like a quick inventive slipway flight of that tongue, of the child's first jabber, of me and my brother and Mandy too in the end when she was finally allowed in the game, smaller version, dress hanging wet and dirty from the last level invasion of the waves up onto the sand. A boy as well. One of those from over Weimar Road, in the games even before Mandy was, can't remember the name, and he was nothing like him really, long straight eyebrows like two dashes, some reminder I suppose in that quickness of movement in a broad frame. He was nothing like him, to me he looks the same, as if all the faces were in the beach already, as if he was really there at a time before I'd ever met him or got in with him, even before the fights, when we were still playing games of damming the creek and building cityscapes across the dams and the buildings crept up the rocks as a kind of protection against flurries of pebble artillery

'*God,* Yehune.... I didn't know you could really *play.*'

That was Ruth. Ruth, Ruthie; right. He had to bring himself back to himself, from a sort of irrelevant dream, built on the association of the fag the old coffin-nail with stout wooden boxes and from there to cabinet-making in the outback and then to the discoloured wooden panel in front of his eyes, migrating sideways over a cloud, so that it had seemed to him, sitting there working his hands, as if the bar and the people had gone and there was only the piano brown and cracking at the sides, the one real object, superimposed on the lower right-hand corner of a relief map of the Australian continent.

16

… So Ruth had drifted up, where was her mate? Not there. He looked down. Estimated the progress of a white link. Picked another out of the packet in his shirt pocket, and took his time to light it from the glowing stub.

'Tell you what Ruth,' he said, addressing her in a low tone in the face of all those bystanders, '… here's a little something I wrote myself.'

Now for it. Yeah, yeah, yeah, giv'em a bit of fucking… *motorism*… but first, better rest it, virgin piece, lovely long light stick, different technique, see, calls for a different approach with the old inhaler… up there on the wood, that's it; right.

The first, or fugal section of Yehune's own three-part composition 'Œcophony for an Invaded Sphere', for piano and harsh whisper, had the effect of making the crowd disperse fairly quickly, building out of the deep bowels of the instrument, introducing rhythmic lines into the pub air like a new and questionable smell. In F, A, and C flat. Go, go, go: bibble a donk a, donk a, bibble a; fourth finger's lazy, no it's their bloody sticky E. Go on, *huh, huh, huh,* God, yeah man… that's just so good. The audience were unsure at first, only recognising that the singalong had turned a corner of taste where they couldn't follow; they milled around, readdressed their friends, and looked for places at tables again. It wasn't until the second section, this one unlimited by the keyboard, where the pianist seemed to have gone mad, forsaking his tools, indulging in free verbal imitations of water-buffalo or the Sydney Harbour container-machinery, that unrest began to show itself. Loud Australian catcalls broke in, so that the harsh whisper called for by the score came out as more of a breathy shout. But that section was a short one. The third was more a, sort of, spherical evocation, by means of huge fat rounded chords, dropped with the full weight of the arm, rests of unpredictable lengths here and there, time signatures all shaved or eked out to fit, a-*cruuuuuuuunnnnnngge!* a-*crooooooowwfff!* Jeez Christ what a poxy tone this old joanna's got, but that's OK, feel the old tide rising, poise the arm, full-weight drop, *whhhhhoooouuuffff.* Sounds like an anvil playing tiggy with a biscuit tin, but who the hell

17

cares, what I'm saying is, Hey! Listen, Aussos! Get a load of the fucking culture mate....

For a while it had been the presence of Ruth there at the piano side that had kept the crowd in check. Some unassailable bar-chic; the general Aussie rightness of her turnout. But still, there was something unstable, a flutter in the higher aether... people come here to drink, eh... and a few of the others, Neeomi, Brett, not without their own pub weather-sense, had taken the time to move up to the front just as a precaution. An older man with a younger woman in tow were standing one side of Ruth now, trying to reason with her, apparently reluctant to be first to interrupt the, er, the, mm....

Tony leaned in to put a hand on Yehune's shoulder, and before any popular movement could get off the ground he was induced to stand up – damn, so cool; eyes watering; half-chuffing, half-bent over – regretfully before the work had had time to wind down to its end.

Bugger it, so much left, so much to do, eh, so little fucking... yeah. Hey, wait, my cigarette! Na, OK, leave it.

And so, even in the artificial twilight of a King's Cross pub, a small light might begin to dawn. Crowd-rouser, self-advertiser, commentator by a kind of involuted jokiness on the affairs of the world around him, this man of parts, solid parts but none too high, under a curly crown of hair, was something else as well – a capable pianist, in his own eyes a composer, not without a claim to some seriousness of intention under the burlesque. His nose went before him, unexceptionable and straight as a woodchip, not seeming (though possibly you couldn't tell from that alone) to confirm anything like the racial history he claimed for himself. His eyes were lively but small, jaw scratchy, lines of the face growing fleshier as they proceeded downwards towards the neck, where despite the loss of definition they still managed to give an impression of fuzzy muscularity. And why stop there? You could go further, picking up indications as your eye drifted downwards, from the loose-necked well-ironed shirt with the cigarette packet in one pocket, the thickness at waist and hip, the preference for fashionably-cut trousers over shorts... all surely a wrong direction, all inessential, when what we really want is an outward tendency, the way the man projected himself through claims, lies, conversation, as the evening built in tone and burden there around their heads....

At the moment, it seemed to have entered a quieter phase. Behind a long side table on the opposite wing of the bar's L-shape, Neeomi's acquaintance Brett, there before any of them, had managed to wangle them a few seats together. Yehune was wedged in, then, either by accident or some subtle engineering on the part of Tony and the others, somewhere near the middle of the bench, with Ruth on his right and Neeomi on his left. Not one of those friends or acquaintances referred to his last performance, taking care to use language for other things entirely;

(though that turned out in the end to be something Yehune wouldn't stand for, so that later, Mel still not having arrived, he made a careful reference to his musical efforts... Ruth asked him whether he'd been making the last bit up as he went along, to which he replied,

'Mm – no. Seems that way sometimes though. That's polytonalism, you see, Milhaud and the greats. But I'm taking it a bit further than he does, I'm trying to give an impression of, you know, a kind of, ah... bipartite structure... for the universe...'

Neeomi on his left side, intent on picking a toothpick out of her drink, came back with,

'Oa, Ye-*hooooon*. Stop bollocksing us.')

in the meantime he had a Bacardi and Coke to contemplate, and Guddie, diagonally opposite beside a couple he didn't know, and the ice-blue backdrop of the drinks cooler behind the bar. There were bodies in continuous shuffle across the light, and the planes of faces, forever fading or shock-lit. Guddie's. ... Was dreamy, self-effacing, when you could see it clearly; with a haze of short hair over the right upper quarter and her right eye. Nice eyes, though. Could say the nose was a bit big. Guddie, what could that be short for? Gud, gud... Godiva? Godot? ...or a female version, Godette? Music was piped in, hate piped fucking music; a shicker-shicker invading the sub-recesses of the mind while voices surged and rumbled above it; Neeomi's chatting to Brett, who leaned in with a glass, Ruth's calling across to someone.

Now, a perception like Yehune's couldn't fail to be aware of the two separate bulges of female hip so close to his; one side and the other. Neeomi's was pressed in the closer, while her upper body leant away. To him, it was true, the necessity for action had faded for the moment, giving way to a private vegetative underpath of experience in time, tinted with cold blue, persistently irritated by the shicker-shicker shit they thought was music. A sort of objective occurred to him, with time on his hands, in the absence of Mel... with one girl, he thought it might be possible. But two? Two at the same time?... Everything fell together into the form of a whole mandala of priorities, dares, revisable on the point of a moment. Both Ruth and Neeomi, you could have said, had shown at one time or another what might (Ruth shifted here, white skirt interestingly articulating) – be called – an interest.

So then maybe...?

Ruth's response to the large but agile hand that took a position on her right hip was to stiffen a little bit, sit up straighter, falter in her conversation; unless it was that it had just then reached a lull. Neeomi, on the other hand, moved closer in. She was a taker of opportunities, Yehune could see it. Brett had turned to address someone else; even so, bloody hell – thank Go- Go- for the tableside. His left fingertips sensitively probed the loose folds of her dress, red with Turkish patterning of gold. That was the first site for an invasion, though of course both hands were supposed to go in together; only had one... brain... mm. There's something, he could feel some part of her thigh, and, what was that? Cloth on cloth, it was hard to tell; but his right hand in the meantime was trying to negotiate what was a more difficult entrance-way, where the white skirt happened to be pulled tight under Ruth's lower region. `

What's that?... caught it. Ah, now... *that's* what we're looking for.

The first to strike panties; and to do it he'd had to pull the skirt. A small pile of fabric, bags and a coat, was all that shielded him from Tony himself, the next in line. Something silk-like. Elusive fringe of scallops. On the other side, he found Neeomi's higher up, which gave him more territory to cover before the discovery; there was a soft but apparently muscular surface before the elastic strip: your classic, ah, sports-panties; couldn't imagine the colour – Ruth's by contrast were a sort of French style, he could see them grey like the soft grey radiance of Guddie's dress across the table....

Neeomi turned and looked him straight in the face, eyebrows lifted. It was disconcerting, when you'd just grabbed hold of her most private undergarment with some sort of he supposed unstated *romantic* intention... just us kikes don'worry... so you can imagine. He looked back at her, blandly aware, meeting the accusation with as bald a face as he could.

'Hmm,' said Neeomi, just audibly, and accepted an answer or an attitude, moulding herself into him in a way that might be almost too obvious to someone able to see more clearly than the darkness allowed, or, worse still, make a guess at what his other hand was doing.

Now Brett was off and making contacts, some group of hard-boys in shorts it looked like; and what's-his-name... Dennis. Good one. Left Neem-, left us free. In a private corner of time Yehune experienced a phenomenon where figures and dapples of colour and the sharp-edged bar furniture seemed to fall together into one neglectable screen; his vision wandered away; all his attention was gathered into the tiny sensory trigger-points in broad square fingers. Down across the lines of Neeomi, he searched, particularly insistent on and around the creases where fabric joined to flesh. And the flesh to flesh?... that's another thing.... While at the same time his right hand was savouring a slimmer softer kind of thigh, moving upwards for some reason, to challenge the unyielding stiffness that had come over Ruth. Amazing, the skin, how it was actually smoother than the silk... or silky-stuff. Why didn't she look round? Know your luck, you never, he drawled or jabbered inwardly; but Yehune did know it. It was that nervous reaction of Ruth's – trying to pretend it wasn't happening? Maybe even hoping he wouldn't stop? – that held the whole precarious moment up.

He couldn't leave it, he just couldn't be content. It was in the nature of a Yehune to find out how far he could go. He began to snake his right hand further round, experimentally, frontwards across the delicate structure of Ruth's hip, towards that fascinating tuck of the silk (as he saw it in his mind's eye, character-lit in darkness) between the legs and under. Some barrier in the intricacies of cloth gave way; did she relax there a bit?... can't be sure; either way he was going there; he was... in there, surely; almost round....

Now, in direct contrast to Ruth, Neeomi had let herself fall into a dreamy and languorous state of pure enjoyment, expressed mainly in motions of the body, realignments, cooing gestures of the lips up towards the nearer of Yehune's ears. She had a tendency to let her eyes rove freely, over bags and scattered gear, and even as far as the crotches of companions male or female. That was how she became aware. Something in a moving bulge towards the tightened front of Ruth's skirt, which was a white shape in the gloom, must have caused her to look again and hesitate for an explanation and make a scan of the exact set of Yehune's shoulders; and then she rose.

'Shit!' she said.

She upset coats and jackets, bumped the arm of a girl on the bench to her left, as she skipped sideways and along, trying to get clear of the seat and out onto the floor.

'You bloody bastard!' she called at Yehune. Her voice was loud. With one clean jerk, he swept his hand clear of the central regions of Ruth.

'Whatizza mumble mumble...' Brett turned to her where he stood not far away, and she addressed the world in a high clear voice,

'He's got his fucking hand under that bitch's... fucking... *skirt!*'

People were already beginning to collect. Some were smiling. Yehune quickly put both hands up above the table, displaying them; not that that really convinced anyone, or had any effect on the uglier expressions that were beginning to appear on faces here and there. Especially Brett's own. Tony had actually stood up and forged into the crowd, with an intention that will unfortunately never be known, because Brett had got away from him and was trying to rejoin his laddish friends in the back-depths of the room where the crowd and the levels of noise came to a local climax. Dennis; oh yeah.

Yehune chanced a look at Ruth beside him, sitting there deprived of the support she'd, you know, grown to.... Loosened up by the run of events, she let her head turn and consider him.

Further out on the floor, Neeomi seemed to be on the point of delivering some terrific speech. She looked around, possibly for Brett, didn't find him, and saw something might be Tony bearing down might be something else she saw; but she took one look and turned, elasticated haunches, flag waving, red with gold. Yehune could make out buttocks moving under cloth, then the standing ranks.

Piano behind that. Time to move, yeah, do something. Barside? No no, gotta extricate, extrapulate. Give 'em a chance to, you know, cool off, let it all blow over....

There were currents in motion, people swaying to and fro, and the stubby pianist as he launched himself out sensed rather than saw a jostling for position somewhere over in the other direction. Meantime he made a sort of pretence of trying to follow after Neeomi. 'Neeomi,' he even said. It was the work of a moment to shoulder aside the circles gathered to talk around the stool, gently, everything gently, and sit himself down there; nothing's happening here and nothing's ever even going to....

Whaddaya think? Something calming, Rachmaninoff, something... not the C sharp minor. Avoid the big noise, that's for sure. Try the Elegie, op three number one? OK, take it, let's see if this old clanger'll sustain a note....

The introduction slipped in softly, line of deadened individual banjo-plucks; until the first notes of the theme came sounding, cantando, downward-falling, défaillant. As a mark of defiance someone at the bar had turned up the canned music, coming in a rush. Then lilted, shaped and jangling, poignantly off the beat, those, several, clangs. Oh Ruthie Ruthie Roo. Soft double-notes went rising to a spire, falling again. Now see if we... who's that, was it Ruth and then to join her Guddie stood and working their way out over the floor, going up to Thomas, Tom? Could be, probably, hard to see; because by the time the theme came in stronger again or was it just a bit afterwards the noise in competition for a wonder died, or at least dropped down a lot. Great, good girls, gi's a chance. And – yipso, missed a couple there –

The pegs, the mask, the inter intertwig of Rachmaninoff's broad romantic tirade swelled out over the barside modern-blue and the clumping of human forms to drink and talk, oh voices tower'd, immense recursion, immemorially meandering march! and march! and ripple, clatter down! – with all the singing Yehune with his years of training on the instrument could shoehorn into it. Given that the scaly old goanna wasn't even remotely up to it; so you go out, drop away; or even easier try and imagine it's a *piano* you're playing. There was an effect, though, as if the air was altered in pitch or velvet consistency of darkness; currents in the crowd-drift smoothed away; even though the number of people must have been the same there seemed more of them seated, fewer to blunder and disturb each other out on the floor. Taint in the air of organism… oh yeah. A Russian onion dome in nineteenth-century coattails. Take care on those bloody doubles. Hey, I know; it's *Classical,* eh, background music, so you keep to your seats and talk. Well, good enough. Neither he nor anybody there could have denied it, the *atmosphere* there in that venue was growing again on the spot, some plant-effect; or could be he was just applying a bit of antifungus to mushrooms that were waiting in the murk to bloom again….

And time passed, time passed, past the central catastrophe, with a nice poised – locked – rubato on those uppers, and a fall, like turgid flopdown under pedal stacc and down right-thundering-down-into-the-depths; then three mighty notes to end it – wink… wink-wink.

Shit what a travesty. Hope I didn't break something there.

There was something missing; something white, light, long, with orange tidemark. Bug me, never did get a chance to light one. The instinctive twitch of the hand towards his upper pocket had to be restrained, no point now. Yehune swivelled instead with an energetic straddling movement of both legs to look out on the space he'd held for the odd few moments under his sway. There was a change, to him; a subtle difference in the shading and coloration and the clothes that struck his eye from this direction or that. Cutback. Static display. He stood up now, no need to be hustled off the stool, and threaded his way back in again.

On the lookout. Darling Harbour aquarium. … Little darlings; met 'em at Darling.

The fag was already pulled out and lit, the canned music turned up above the twitter, when he spotted Guddie turned back-on to him, a chair or two along now. He cruised up puffing, to take a space beside Ruth on the wall bench.

She mumbled something; didn't catch. But he began to apologise, just on the off chance, in case she still mightn't be aware of his simultaneous approach to Neeomi in the underbasis; or, you could say, where she lived. Why not eh? Give it a burl.

He was saying: 'I'm really sorry about that, Ruth. It was just Neeomi, she was sort of jealous... I guess she must have got this idea into her head...'

Ruth passed a significant glance to Guddie, who passed it back to Ruth. The falling half-curtain of her hair was dark and streaked with orange, yielding suddenly to that unbelievably soft texture of skin (skin; remember skin). And a contained little orange-crimson mouth, not like Neeomi's big snapper. Ruth. She reached up, then, to just touch Yehune's shoulder.

'That was so nice – what you were playing there.'

'Oh, right. The Elegie. Rachmaninoff. Famous, ah, Russian guy, from a while ago...'

'I wish *I* could...'

Just like that, he thought. Just like that, he was re-established, though maybe not with all his faculties intact. A famous Russian guy, right.... Careful with the hands now, careful. Just gently, no skin, back of the shoulder, like that. And he leaned back, taking a long draw on his fag.

My God though. I'd never've thought the Late Romantics were such a chick-magnet.

And he put it to them, 'What would you think about moving on, about now?'

Guddie put in a word from across the table,

'I'm easy.'

'Oh – but what about that Friend of Yours that's supposed to come?'

Ruth almost looked anxious, as if considerate for that unknown person. He had, Yehune might have admitted, become a bit of an icon, talking-point, and so inevitably was making his bloody presence felt even when he wasn't even present like just that time before when Neeomi was asking about

(Neeomi had said:

'Oh no, he sounds like a *real* wet blanket. You mean he crashes early and never ever goes out?'

'No, no, just tonight, I thought he might have, you know. He works till quite late. Then he has to get the ferry or something.'

'Fffff. I bet he's tall and got little weaky blue eyes.'

That had made Yehune shift radially from the waistband up. But being Yehune, he was ready with the persuasive spiel,

'Hell no, you've got him wrong. Mel's an absolute prince. At least, girls always think so. Something in his face, God knows, it always beats me. But as a *guy*, I mean – he's the best. ... Shit, would *I* be flatting with him otherwise?'

Neeomi mocked and laughed and mocked again, but he'd been able to observe the face of Guddie across the table with an expression of serious interest, taking it all in – silver-wafting, twilit lily. Contemplative, literal, tentative. And he thought, remembered thinking, 'That's for Mel,' as just then again now in the crowd)

The crowd Mosaicly parted in front to admit a sort of deputation, tightly meshed. People shuffled to make room. OK – could be Brett? Or *Dennis,* is that, standing shorter and bent bullishly forwards, with a black moustache like two bits of charcoal stuck to his upper lip.

Dennis came out with,

'Are you satisfied?'

That, as Yehune had learned over his years in various pubs and situations, was a proposition not worth answering. Are you satisfied. Oh no laddie boy. His experience was that you could sometimes turn away a fair amount of wrath by refusing to believe you could possibly be the person spoken to.

'Are you fucking satisfied?' the one with the moustache repeated louder. He was isolated in the front, the others hanging silent behind him. Brett was in there somewhere, doing nothing; but we're here – gotta hand it to us – back up our mate.

'Shit, I mean, what *are* ya?' Dennis prosecuted. 'Fucking old hoaries, coming over here, stealing our woomin...'

'Thinks he can play the piano…' someone added.

'And *you* shut your drain,' Dennis reacted, turning at head and shoulders and talking into the murk.

Now was the time to move, if ever there was one. Are you satisfied. Yep, sure am, thanks, armful of girl like yours isn't; but I can see how I might not be when you and your mates have corrected the situation. He glanced over towards the front way. Not much hope there….

'Well, what about it?' The spokesman's patience was nearly at an end; he barked again,

'Hey, you! Ki! I'm talking to you.'

Tony had come up, forming a sort of end-of-bench rearguard. Yehune made little whispers to Ruth, seeming self-involved, but always scanning the currents of movement. Was there a side-entrance somewhere? Yeah, surely….

And as it sometimes will, a complicating factor happened to intrude at just that point of a moment in time in the form of a chubby little guy about seventeen or eighteen who probably shouldn't have been in a pub anyway, skipping in from the direction of the shadowy rear doors, crucially dividing the challenger's attention,

'Den! Ah… Joicob sez he wants to talk to ya abeart the *bee* - .'

Or something, bee-oo, bull, bayo… not that it mattered, because Yehune was already on his feet, not minding the girls or the hands on drinks that might have interrupted the smoothness of his progress over Ruth almost and inboards of Tony, leaving them to find their own way after him, thrusting himself along past wall candles, boozers, and something oversized like a lit-up papier-mâché mask. To the deeper, the shadier wall, is it this…?

Yes. Out into darkness. A self-contained street, with small white tables. Doorman hanging there. The girls should be coming out. C'mon. Hear anything? The sound of a ruckus growing from inside, a breakout, maybe, of what? Equivalent of rednecks: brownface, brickiebum. He could catch more-or-less distinctly out of the layers of interior clamour,

'Where's the?… Shit, can't have…'

'Come on, we'll teach 'eem…'

And he had to wait. Was that them? No, damn and bugger. The

feeling of a division of worlds came down on him again; once in; then out; which brought to his mind the white humming machines of the Print Shop, set here and there in the vast sky past street walls; and surprising isolated pictures from Greville's motorcycle repair shop. Old Grev, he'd… well, fuck…

There was a guttural shout. Here they are now. Something like, 'Fucking Ooree!'

And passing the scattered white of tables he heard already dwindling behind him a casual interchange of strangers,

'What's that, Ooree?'

'*You* know. … A Maori dick.'

'Oh, OK.'

Then he was with Ruth, with Guddie, Tony a bit behind, making their way back into the larger street while Yehune thought about, remembered, swinging with the shark-head off a bar, Piano Bar, I did say the Piano. Coming after? *Blue-dog muzzle sabre teeth* not once. Lights were up against the blank of lightlessness, some breeze in the functions of man on sidewalks, and he balanced straight and upwards like a rail, a scaffold-piece, seeing a moment out of Sydney Zoo a crowd of schoolkids, *'what a gross monkey'*

And feeling Ruth's fingers tight against his side like a little clutching parcel of mice.

Hearing

ba-boon ba. Ba-boon ba. A huh a huh-huh

the warpaint face of an adult male baboon screeching full-voice and the grace of the limbs in intersymmetric arcs that thrash up and down in loose-to-vagrant motion follow motion arms thrown further than the legs a harrrnk *a* harr-harrrnnnk *where something catch something in the irrecoverably-foreign creases around eye and temple age-old knowing and enraged white rage and rage and rage*

the catastrophic roar of an open-throat Harley 1200 from one set of lights to the next. Congratulations, boys, you made it. Funny how I once. More Greville's cup of tea, or, I don't know, fucking mescaline, chuck up and start, chuck up and start. Now would you say that was one of them coming

ba

and shrunk down planed back like a computer simulation the face that huge schematic flatrun of the Australian continent out yellow like a map goes antitelescoped down and down and referenced under a frame of white serrations until there's nothing nothing boys but a postage stamp with a tiny wink at Sydney commemorating float to curl in an album god jeezyboys Our Nation

or not, got shorts just like them

piano's a floating box in the sea in oilpoint patterns lift of the w w

sampled just

with the sand in streaks slopes up from the low-tide and the shunt of the wind that nudges me on from behind, wandering this way out to the heads, where I took a quick glance back and was nearly blinded by the glare of the sun where that turreted effigy burned like a paling with the radiance green-pale and fading to red at the sides, like a fairy palace; oh yeah, the power station; two thin chimneys up to the sky. Turned back with a spectral rotor in the edge of my focus that clashed with the ripple of wet sand in the lee of the rocks there coated with green slime. Slime was the slime I used to see on the concrete pathway from Thompsons round to Piri where Mandy slipped one day and couldn't get up and I stayed with her while Geoff ran for help, how old, she must only have been three or four. So many of those, scattering of scraps along the way like strewn bits of rubbish in the runs of seaweed here half-dried and separating one colour of sand from another; there's splinters of wood I can see in there and shells and cardboard lolly-sticks and foam packing bits and red plastic ties washed up on the lift of waves. I can remember white foam pieces that we took for floating soldiers and played with all one Christmas holiday afternoon, and the next day they were nearly all gone and we scratched around finding one here and a cluster of three there trying to start the game again, and Geoff said he should have thought of collecting some together and putting them in a cleft in the rock above the tidemark. That's the difference. That's all the difference, the cut, the lightning cut, when you suddenly look back and see out of another time the moment of thinking that's divisional irreconcilable. Or maybe it's something that happens when you step into a plane on one side of the world and sit and sleep and wake up and trail out at airports and don't sleep and get in another and get out again and in the end you walk out somewhere else, another world, another planet, not having seen anything in between, ripple across of static, something missing in the head. So we decided to do it the other way instead, place to place to place, and in the end it's still the same. Sand sinks leaving footprints, one, another, sampled just. One one one, then another, one beach and another, Thompsons in Maeraki to Longniddry, Bents, never just now without that nagging movement past the wind to the right of me and a bit above of the guy that I can see thrusting on taking paths parallel and opposed through tussock up over the shoulder of the bank. Running man. Keeping up, Yehune the old and best, and I wish I could see what's going through *his* head, crackle of galvanic fires through slight horns out above the temples, I keep wondering what it was and can't help thinking about it here where there are no cliffs towering up into headlands but only the furze and leafless trees leaning away out of the shock of the wind

The Bondi House

He came through the shimmering, beast-infested Aussie darkness (not that dark really), through a shadowy crosscut of light effects from streetlamps and house windows and the October sky, in a seething whisper from the bushes and unmown grass, off the sidewalk, up the cracked concrete of a path, to the place where treeheads gave way to the shape of a Colonial-style roof. He was walking fast, nearly running. A stray flap of his shirt appeared behind him now and then, surprisingly, like the tail of a rooster startled in retreat. It billowed again as he flew up the two wooden steps in one, past the white verandah railing, and pulled himself up at the front door.

A dum-dum de da. Now who's left the fucking... oh right, Mel must be. About Jesus time too; um... my f'ck'n keys. Keys. Keys.

This house, which had been his dossing-place for three months now, was an ungainly hat and verandah in West Bondi crowded round with a maze of other temporary dwelling places, on a hillside that fell through the twists and turns of residential streets all the way down to Campbell Parade and the Beach. It was a thing of layers, of generations; leased by Kiwis, run by Kiwis, for an endless line of Kiwi travellers past and future, occasionally fixed or adjusted or (most often) repainted by the people who happened to be staying in it at the time, but in a way that was always makeshift, never seeing beyond the next few weeks of occupation. To keep any mental picture of it, to think of it in any way as *home,* you had to hold a lot of unmanageable detail in mind – reworked piping on the wall by the shed, the little touched-up patches in the paint around the door, incursions of jasmine and nasturtiums into the front path with paspalum and dock towering up behind it – which the pianist brought off without the need for conscious thought. He paused in front of the door, solid on his large feet, his shirttail dangling. He registered the halo of small insects around the outside light; different levels of grey in the shed wall; and most especially the difficulty of getting his hand in through the trapdoor *forwards* and then turning the key *backwards* while all the rest of the keys did their best to bugger up on something.

He saw the details, caught, processed and discarded them, as separate events in his progress through the maze of streets; the way back, back to number 24. He came poised on a headlong rush of movement, out of the Sydney traffic and the streets and bars of King's Cross, singing under his breath, 'Ape-man, ape-, ape-a man.' He had absolutely no claim to being a Jew. Yehune was not his real name.

His loud voice intersected with the crash of the screen door back on its moorings,

'Mel! ... Mel!'

and a moment later he was clomping along the bare boards of the hall. Without bothering with the doorhandle, he punched his way through the third door on the left, and was carried on by pure momentum. But he changed direction, turned away into the doorside – why? It could have been out of a kind of belated respect.

A body was lying supine on the counterpane of the bed; and he had a lightning association with bodies flung in dark earth ditches in South America, Nicaragua, El Salvador. Leavings of the death-squads. Only there the smell and the surroundings might be different – flies, and a dirt ridge, and another dozen or so bodies scattered around. Here he saw a piled-up shelf, a window propped open, and a pack on the floor from which all sorts of small possessions fanned outwards.

'Oh, hi,' said Yehune in a quieter voice.

What was on the bed stirred fitfully, struggling for life and movement. After about a second it managed to bring up its head.

'Shit, man...' it rasped, '... was asleep.' Then immediately afterwards, 'Was I asleep? Dunno.'

Over the face in the artificial light – small blue eyes, a nose broad at the base – came a look of disarmed self-study. For a moment; then gone.

'So where were you?' Yehune asked, leaning more easily against the wall beyond the open door. He was already drawing a cigarette out of the packet from his shirt pocket and fiddling around for matches.

'Oh yeah... I said I'd meet you, didn't I? At the – Yitz or the Bluegum or something.'

'Yip. It's a bar.'

'Uh- huuuhhh.'

That seemed to be all the body could manage; what strength it had ever had was already exhausted. Its head flopped back on the pillow. Yehune – the one who called himself Yehune – went through the deliberately calming routine of lighting his cigarette from a match wedged just above his palm, shaking the match out and replacing it carefully in the box. He enjoyed his first, deep, flavourful puff. With the easy detachment his higher energy level gave him, he cast an eye over the thing on the bed.

There was no barrier between them. Or at least, that was the ancient wisdom, formulated in a time when time itself was blindingly open to the long, long sunlight in the sky over the north-of-Auckland bays, when none of them knew anything, nobody knew anything, except whatever small items might have filtered in through the moribund grey curtain of their courses at Montgomery Secondary. It was surprising what massive, sometimes indelible misconceptions could arise between two school-age people, in the atmosphere of the small coastal district of Maeraki, out of haphazard talk and the desire to be – some word, some -ism – which then had to be mentally constructed on the spot out of bits and pieces of things they'd read. There were similarities between them, that was true, this Mel Seuchar and the self-proclaimed Yehune; they spoke alike, sometimes accidentally thought alike, or at least with the same external result, making the same dint or imprint on the earth's great busily-connecting fabric of scratches. On the other hand, they were fundamentally different. Mel – tall and slim and lightly detached at the head, with hair the colour of dry tussock in an early Southland twilight, no great physique, but a mind that was able to stretch out of itself so far as to write good essays, pass exams – Mel was both straightforward and a little bit shrinking in his approach to the world, and would get involved in small clashes and arguments wherever he went. Yehune, as we know already, a solid five foot five with a thatch of dark curling hair, was an extrovert, a funny-man, with an unusual amount of moral courage single-mindedly devoted to not giving a holy shit; and yet he was always sliding away from you, difficult to analyse or confront, as if his real self was set in some unguessable shape about two micrometres behind the exterior.

Mel had never been anything but Mel, born to a Scottish father and a fifth-generation New Zealand mother in the old National Women's Hospital in Auckland (since demolished), and had stayed in the same place being the same Mel Seuchar without swerve or apology throughout his school life and university years. Yehune, by contrast, had origins that were complex, overlayered, having come out of some mid-North Island small town at the age of ten, then through a succession of schools as his socially-ambitious parents had followed their star through the different areas of Auckland. It was in the last of those schools, Montgomery, that the two boys had met, broken apart, joined up again on the accident of their classes and the social mix, and an association had developed that was founded on – what? On some long-running legend of a similarity in aspirations. On music, on random clutter, books, motorcycles (not, yet, to mention their big mistake, that central sin against society that, knowing nothing, they'd managed to fall into before they realised how much it would end up setting them apart) – on a certain long talk between them and another boy on the muddy floor of E Block, on a later moment in a University Student Union refectory... an association that was allowed to grow as far as an actual mirroring of gestures and mannerisms between one and the other, a chiming of the timbres of the voice, at least to people who didn't know them too well, in the years after school. They 'thought together'. That was the easy phrase, those were the words, repeated without effort in the mind of Yehune behind the swirls and haloes the smoke made in the breeze from the open window, as he looked his friend up and down.

Thinking,

Jeez, Mel. Lying there covered in mud and shit. Gidday mate, I'm Joe Bloggs from the estuary, 'scusee, just crapped me waders. Can just see him walking into the Yip like that, doubt if he'd have turned a hair, hi Yehune, sorry, didn't have time to change. *Rufus!* Outski. Oh, but….

At the same time, he was remembering scraps of a more recent history: him and Mel, their plans to leave, the selling of bikes, the actual moment of buying tickets in Hueffer's Travel in the Bay. All of which hadn't done much in the end, it seemed, but drop them here, into urban Bondi – what he might call a far more Aussie variation on the fucking plot. Sourly he let his eyes brush over the shapes of two unmuscular lower legs, ending in khaki socks.

And launched himself away from the wall, taking a fierce sharp draw on the fag. A bag on the littered floor containing notebooks and more bags got in his way, and he turned, still moving his arms in gestures.

'Well, anyway, listen: this is what we've got to do,' he said. 'There's two girls I met tonight, they're at home, I mean, one of their homes, and we're going out to meet them again. One's just right for you. Guddie, her name is. Really nice, ash-blonde hair, nose is a bit big but excellent little eyes, ah…'

'Oh, right. Yeah.' The words came heavily. 'Thing is, I don't know, I seem to be utterly crashed out just now. Happened to me on the bus coming back. It's like, this punch-drunk boxer just came in and slogged me out of the sky. Chuuu-uuf. Dead…. Muh.'

'No no no. Shit, these are *girls*. Have you forgotten what those are? … Anyway I thought you came on the ferry.'

'Oh no. Not for a… working up round South Head.'

Mel's voice was already weakening; he was settling more comfortably into his new position, turned onto one side on the rucked bamboo-printed coverlet, so that fragments of dried something-or-other on his left jeans leg began to flake off and trickle away across the cloth.

'Don't go to sleep! I've been telling them all about you.'

It was painful how long the answer took to come. 'Oh, yeah. I seem to remember I did have some kind of intention of getting there… remember that distinctly… but it just seemed to dissolve into those pictures along the way, little red-brick hinterlands, watertanks, different coloured glows in the sky. Hit me.'

'You got tired. – Is that your workboots on the cover?'

'I've got newspaper.'

It was true, there were three double sheets of the Sydney Herald pulled up and distorted under the mud-caked pair of boots. Nor, really, was it any concern of Yehune's, when this room belonged to Mel at least temporarily, he himself having shifted across into the couples' room the month before when Gibby and Sheil moved out. Still, Yehune looked down at the bed again with a secret irritation, smoothed over the line of his own clothes, and discovered the untucked shirttail, which he began with precise movements to feed back under his waistband. Thinking: Time for a shower. Could do with a piss as well. I know who goes first though. Fucking scruffy bastard, but, I dunno, you never know....

Girls occurred in his head again – a bedroom, with a plastic stereo and some dim boy-wonder posters. It brought back his crowning moment, palpation of curves, intensest curves, under what looked like a bright-pink wallflower. He laughed.

'What?' Mel mumbled.

'Oh... nothing. Just, you know... stuff that happened.'

'What?'

Yehune squelched down on the side of the bed, feeling the springs give under his weight. He made a quick scan of the room; bike hung askew on two hooks hammered into the wall, Mel's books and notebooks piled on the bedside prop.

'Well – at one point I managed to get my hands up two girls' skirts at once.'

'*Aah,* huh. Good-good. ... Anything else?'

'Well, it wasn't that bad – that chaotic. If that's what you mean. Ah, let's see... I played the piano a bit in this bar, that was good for a laugh. Then I managed that with the girls – not your one, don' worry, it was a new one, someone old Tony's trying to wangle a job for. Then, you know, some of the Australians seemed to take a bit of offence at that, so we had these Aussie weight-lifter types after us...'

'Sounds about typical. Glad I wasn't there, I would've been the one who got hit by that bottle that flew past your head.'

'Anyway, this girl Ruth took me over to her place... not far from

here to there.' And recalling the ride out, the brief side-run into
Bondi, he added laconically, 'Shit, we need to buy a car though. Can't
run a life without one, in Sydney.'

'A car...?'

Mel had half-risen by this time, holding himself up on his elbows.
He seemed to be listening well enough. But his tone just then was
deadening, as if he was trying to kill a concept by nothing more than
a determined resistance to all vibration.

So fucking

'So anyway – mmf – you want to come out?'

'Oh, yeah... I mean, I would have.'

The words came slowly, in snatches, nasally drawling, then falling
back to silence.

'... If not for this... you know, been building walkways all day.
This guy there, Chris... knows all about the way to build them,
knows all the Aus native timbers, or I don't know if they're native,
all grow around here though. I mean, he was telling me quite a lot.'
Mel shifted his weight, held up now by only one elbow. 'Poor bastard
has this girlfriend with expensive tastes, he's thinking of quitting and
getting a proper job somewhere. Rache, her name is. Fucking pain.
You know, all that... expertise... just getting lost. Knows every bark,
every bud. I'd like to talk to him again. But that's the way of it.'

There was a pause, as they both considered the way of it.

'The others,' Mel went on, '... they'd be quite happy to stay
there till doomsday. I can see into their heads. They're, I mean... we
could've met them in New Zealand. Easily. There's this Maori guy
there, came over a month before us...'

'Old stick-in-the-muds, huh? Go off working in Sydney parks.'

'Yeah yeah, I know. Me, if I've got a job, I've got a job. You seem
to fly around like a, um, bloody chalk-fight, bike mechanic here,
Print Shop there...'

'Hm. So what about the Maori guy?'

'Oh, yeah... excuse me, brain's off on its travels. Peter, his name
is. He's a real laugh, he keeps talking about the kind of plants and
trees and all that, but he always uses the New Zealand name... I
mean, you know, he takes some New Zealand native that's sort of

remotely like it and calls it that. Gods, it's hilarious. Pisses the others off untold. I mean, I don't know what he's talking about half the time either.'

'Shit God. It sounds just like Matamata.'

Saying that, absently, not with the sort of commitment that would go to seem to make it true or not true, just exactly as if he was thinking of something else, Yehune stood up from the bedside again. He considered the fag, nearly burned away to nothing. Gasp or two to go. Looked down again at Mel.

Who'd just finished saying,

'Now that's an awful thing to say about anything. What makes you reckon?'

'... You're not referring to Australian trees in Maori yourself yet?'

'Yeah, I've picked it up a bit. Just for devilment. Or maybe 'cause I can see how his brain's working. I think he gets a bit of stick here. And it's work work work, for who, for what, and we're not even all that far away...'

Yehune felt no impatience. But the fag was finished, time for another, and he didn't especially want to break into the store in his breast pocket. Better his own room. ... Quick piss, then, and off to get 'em.

'Shall I ring those girls?' he said briskly. 'I've got Ruth's number.'

'Yeah... better ring and tell them.'

'Tell them. So you're not up for it?'

'No... sorry... swimming. Couldn't bolt another log. See the heads of trees... gum trees. Bark up close.'

Mel had fallen back again. His eyes were closed, and you could see the delicate but in no way feeble structuring in his face and head; bones there all right, the three dimensions picked out in light and shade. Without moving anything but his mouth, he began a strange and wandering monologue, not without spirit, not without the sort of mistracked concentration you might expect in a dream,

'You know, I came across this leaf, held it up to the light and you could see through it; go to skeletons; there's usually quite a few on the ground after the... skip it. But it makes, I don't know how to say it. A picture in your head. Something you can suddenly understand, like the spark in a plug. And there are so many, millions on millions. So I thought, you know, they're like pages, you could do something with that – an angling of the light. You'd have to draw, I don't know, cartoons... have to use something more than just text. But the sunlight, spilling across it all. That's the continuity. The swim, something that joins one indelible... thing... to another. That's what we're missing, something that's over and above the pages. Nothing like the black... block... texts in your Print Shop. It's like water, something flowing across it all. If you could only get *that,* what we're missing...'

His eyes twitched open, looked away to the side,

'because, you know that thing, we're always divided away from ourselves, moods come in and make us forget what we were feeling two minutes ago... pfauuugh...'

and closed, giving it up,

'Oh, shit... just tired.'

...

Through all this, Yehune hadn't made a noise, nor had he been really watching his friend or listening to the words he was saying; it was too far removed from what he'd call real to make any dent in his own way of perceiving the world. Instead, he was looking fixedly in another direction. He glared with something like intensity, something like suspicion, a contraction of the whole head and face that wasn't flattering to the set of his fleshy neck. ... At what? The wall, under the rear derailleur of a hanging racing-bike complete with decals and what he would have called the best tyres money could buy, flat as they were just then. There he was, standing in Sydney, staring at a wall. The Sydney, that is, of the casual layabout, labourer or bush-valet, the drifting backpacker whose aim was to get out into the burned interior or up and down the coast, see Surfers and the Reef, then bounce away to some other country. Not the cutthroat business Sydney; not the home of Sydney's residents. What was more, in Bondi, where Kiwis were known to rent houses on-and-off for months or years. Looking at nothing, at a tyre scuffmark on a pink-blancmange-coloured stretch of plaster. Something was beginning to creep up on him; an objective realisation, an abstract assessment, something that wasn't natural to his way of thinking at all, if you ignored what he said about himself and looked at his actual mental habits. It was moving up beside him, gaining ground. It was something about the two of them – something to do with Mel.

Yehune already knew that the choice of Bondi, West Bondi in particular, and of this house – who'd chosen that? – was something stereotypical. A sort of public declaration of the will to move. Because this was the direction everybody always went in, at least in Yehune and Mel's perspective, when they began the classic world adventure tour of the young Kiwi. Of which there were several versions they knew of – you might begin with the Trans-Australian, but from there the direction had to be upwards, for the run of South East Asia or the sub-Asian Spice Trail; either that or the big one, the major hoof, north through China to the Soviet Union and all the way west across the world's largest continent to break in on Europe through the back door. Consequently, there were Kiwis everywhere in Bondi, in that house, in the neighbouring houses, walking through the streets sporting equipment labelled Macpac and Fairydown, leaning together swapping notes in pubs, or even laughably trying to avoid meeting other Kiwis in an area that had reached something like saturation point, where the shopkeepers or lifeguards or rubbish collectors were as likely as not to have originated two hundred metres down the road from them in their own country.

OK so far. (Decals said *Hi-Sprite, Trundlegear, Shimano.*) ... But there was another West Bondi tradition, what you might call people-exchange. This was generally known to be the place where groups broke up, the die-hards left and blazed their trails in some direction while those who were more easily contented held down a job, got tired of it and drifted back across the Tasman, or else settled down with some Aussie guy or girl and converted to what you might call a common-law Australian. The red-faced guy who ran the corner milkbar, Larry, was it – he was a Kiwi; his two friends and his girlfriend had run on for Bali a year and a half ago and he was still making hopeful noises about catching them up... no. No. How could that be relevant? That was – someone else.

But what was it that made Yehune, fagless, pinned there under the monologue, begin to have suspicions of his friend? Mel hadn't wanted to change his unambitious Sydney job since he got it. He just plodded in every day. But more than that, some impression of pure fixation, an imaginative self-involvement growing free in the drift of all those words, as if, possibly, their speaker felt comfortable enough where he was, had begun to paint him in Yehune's eyes in the colours of a stayer – someone who against all expectation might turn out to be lacking in the real spirit of adventure.

He pushed himself away from the bed. He didn't see the hanging bike; only the swing past, to a window open on the insectile night.

'Fuck it,' he said.

Mel didn't react. So Yehune followed through; he squatted down, pulled open the lowest drawer of a chipped blue-painted chest of drawers, and began to root around among wads of loose papers.

'Fuck it,' he said again more harshly.

If he'd taken the time to glance to his left, he might have noticed Mel lift his head again and watch him with something around the lips that was… amused? Enigmatic. Prow-lipped in the light.

'You know,' Yehune was saying, 'it's about time we left. I mean, left Oz. We can get tickets to Hong Kong, should give ourselves a week or so though. Whaddaya think? Getting out of here?'

He didn't pause long enough to allow an answer, nor look up from his busy shuffling and sorting of what looked like sheaves of out-of-date junk mail,

'I was talking to a guy in the shop who reckons you can still get it all done in Hong Kong, but you have to go through the travel agents instead of the individual embassies now. Something Student Travel, it was. – Cas'll have something in that letter of his. – Said the advantage is they speak English there, you can get all your visas together in about a week… two at the most. So we'd have to budget for a couple of weeks there.' His large, efficient fingers were picking out shiny foldovers, throwing aside bills and sheets of typescript. 'I don't know that it's all that expensive.' With a loud rattle, he pulled the drawer out whole and deposited it on the floor. '*Feeuuh* – fuck-k-kin'. There's a sort of backpacker's place, isn't there, what's it called, Chongching Mansions? – We'd have to chart our route beforehand, get all the dates. Think there's a brochure round here somewhere. Got it back in Hueffer's, so it's probably all changed...' He pulled out a piece of printout, 'Shit, will you take a look at all these bloody currencies...' But the words had begun to run down, wind away to nothing, giving way to mumbled phrases with the occasional punctuating curse.

In the meantime, the other one in the room lay propped there on the crook of an arm. For lack of a free shoulder to shrug, he barely inclined his head to the upwards side.

'Yeah. All right.'

First Steps

Yehune appeared walking purposefully, his red Macpac on his back and a sleek black airline bag in one hand. Behind him towered and hesitated the fairer-topped head of Mel, upright at least, and committed enough to hold up an ex-army pack and a smaller backpack in the face of the crowds; but somehow questing, loose-jointed, as if he were being pulled along on an invisible elastic string.

The leader stopped for a moment to consider signs. The other, drawn up level, took it as an opportunity for conversation,

'Airport. Hilarious.'

'Yep. First and last flight though.'

'We hope.'

Ignoring him, Yehune slid off to his right, sifting and processing information, Qant-inental-El Al, peering through racks, terraces, human figures draped in cloth, searching for the right direction. Mel stood for a moment, then followed. Since they'd carried their loads through the self-actuating sliding doors, it was as if they'd been in some way personally negated, reduced to the level of the generic space they moved in, ground down, maybe, to small stipples in the texture of those perfect partition units that stood everywhere arranged by need. But of course, it meant nothing. None of this was real. It was a sort of in-between world, like something in a fairy tale; a space behind reality that was the same everywhere you went, that you only had to step into (and be worthy – have the money) to be magically conveyed to the corresponding space in Bombay, Belgrade, Hong Kong, anywhere.

They stood in a long untidy queue to check in for their flight, CX110. Another metre or two and there was no-one; here, instant ghetto. Mel was only half-committed to the business of waiting. He'd tend to straggle off looking at something else, relying on Yehune and his propped-up pack to keep the place for him.

Yehune said,

'Hey, don't leave your.... Wait. Mel. You don't leave your *passport* lying on top of your bag. Come on man, fucking use it.'

Mel came back and picked up a little dark-blue booklet with the coat-of-arms. He held it up in the air, presenting it back and front, as if to say, Who could be bothered stealing a New Zealand passport?

'C'mon, we're moving up,' Yehune said.

They came eventually to the bench-side, where they met a woman, old-young, with fair straight hair in a wigwam. What seemed young about her was her voice, which piped out formulas in the chirpy accents of recorded messages everywhere. To Mel,

'Did you pack your own bags, sir?'

'Uh-huh.'

'Did you leave your luggage unattended at any time?'

'Ah…'

Yehune told him, 'Right answer: no.'

'No.'

'Do your bags contain any poisonous or explosive substances or anything occurring on the list of forbidden items posted on the left side of the hall as you entered?'

'No.'

Here Yehune saw fit to add, 'Um, what about that little black thing I saw you slipping in this morning, man, could've been a bomb or something?'

'Yeah, right, thanks,' said Mel.

And after the woman had looked at Yehune's ticket and accepted his pack on the mini-conveyor under the bench, to both:

'Would you prefer seats in Smoking or No Smoking?'

'Smoking,' said Yehune, and 'No Smoking,' said Mel, at about the same time, and looked at each other.

'Oh… bbbb,' Yehune commented, not being able for that moment to come up with just the right swearword – 'OK, No Smoking.'

Mel put in, 'Can I get a window seat, by the way?'

'There are no window seats left at present in the No Smoking area, but we could accommodate you in Smoking.'

'Hm. Ah…'

'C'mon man, a bit of smoke never hurt anyone.'

'Except for that line of lungless half-corpses along the side of one wall in every hospital in the known world.'

'Still, it's nice to be able to look out the window.'

'I know. Ah… damn.'

'C'mon man, *aesthetics* or health?'

'Gotta suffer.'

'I know. Specially someone else.'

'I know. You bastard. What sort of seat do *you* want, anyway, could be there's none available in Smoking.'

'Don't care, mate.'

Yehune noticed that the lady had a human side: she was looking from one to the other of them, bemused, as if she'd suddenly been presented with an extempore cross-talk act. It wasn't the first time he'd caught that expression on the faces of people listening to them.

Mel was still considering the problem,

'Ah, I suppose… if we did get a seat in No Smoking we might be able to persuade someone to swap?'

They had two whole hours before takeoff time to look and look again at the sterile glittering shops, and consider and reject snacks at cafés, and think of things they hadn't done that it was far too late to worry about now; because once they were checked and passed and x-rayed there was no going back, they were in for the long corridors to their even barer amenity-free corral in that great human stockyard before the Gates. A number: 23, hmm. 'S what I thought. And the status? OK. And where's… shit not again….

Time and event were moving slowly in circles, persistently repeating themselves. Mel had been left behind again at a Books And Magazines partitioned mini-space, where he gazed at the rows of paperbacks someone had decided were suitable for people to read on aeroplanes, as if out of un-self conscious habit, searching glumly for what couldn't possibly be there.

Yehune called back,

'Mel, come on,'

while a family of voluble Greeks arranged and rearranged their bags around a row of seats, tripping him, forcing a change of direction, for what seemed the fourth or the fifth time.

Funny. Guy just drags on behind, like a…? Mouse, not quite wound up. Taller, head's away. Not like in school, he was whaddaya call, directional? Had, you know, determination, like a little dark shady bit round the eyes. … Squint back, what do you see? nothing; just a wall-eyed slope away from the upper nose. Abstracted. Behind it, the run down of light from a corner of the wall open on the glass roof, starkly points out the faceline. … But his mum. Ah yeah well.

After passing through a portal flanked by guys in shorts, they trailed on, ignoring the mobile walkways, watching people, people pass; people who even here in this behind-the-city limbo still looked comfortable and big-boned and spoke to each other often enough like Australians. Which is home, which is still here – screens just over there, a cig machine. It's hard to believe. All that's cut off. Greville and his Harleys and Tony and Corley at the Print Shop, Bondi, lapping sun-glaze, chop-chop – run out into Asia. For something, what? … Oh wow, will you look at that. Tight white semitranslucent trousers, bearing hip structure, plump-filled, what a darling. Must be comfortable for travelling in. Nice things you see. And looking back she'll see a pair of ignorant Auckland apes with unexpensive bags, fatty and skinny, short and tall. Deary me. Looks up at her hairy-goat pornstar boyfriend. Little does she know we're actually *artists*; one day she'll recognise our picture off a cover, tell her mum about it. Ooh, she'll say. If not mumless.

There's a rack: Flightways, Beastways, Heavy Neck, 'zines.

'You got something to read for the plane?'

'Thing or two, yeah.'

Yehune glanced down at the blocky weight of Mel's bag.

'Bet you do. … They sometimes give you newspapers, don't they?'

'Oh, yeah. It'll be in Cantonese, though.'

'No prob. I'll get my friend Mel to translate it.'

'Mm. Don't speak it. But I'll give you my best guess. For a small fee.'

'Mingy bastard.'

'… That's not the plane, I suppose?'

'Are you mad? It'll be at least four times the size of that with a colossal Cathy Pacific logo on the tail.'

'Must be somewhere. ... Cathay Pacific, what does that look like?'

Look like, look like. Something reminded Yehune for a moment of the exotic patterning on the dress of that girl Neeomi; panties elasticated at the sides; and the stippled heads of people sprawled there with nothing to do suddenly fell away with the swift meander upwards of his vision into the green....

'Shit,' he said. 'Flight's delayed.'

There in the bare lounge, strewn with bags and limbs and clothing, dominated by an overscreen, giving out on a huge field of runways where nothing much was happening to concern them, Yehune had the impression that the future ahead of him was reduced to a great inverted funnel of indeterminacy. An empty belling hollowness, in which the vision found nothing to focus on, no crease in the roiling uneventful smoke to fasten on and rest. They were neither properly in Australia nor out of it; Mel was uninvolved, going through the motions; all the sunny filmstrip of life and jobs in Sydney was cut off like a guillotined page. In whatever came next, whatever the two disaffected and very opinionated *artists* were throwing themselves into, he must have been aware that it was himself who would be the mover and shaker, arguer with officials, the source of energy and untier of knots; and like a physical weight that vision of future labour fell back to exhaust him before he could even start. Of course, it was true – he laughed at all that. Hassles? he loved 'em. But everything in the human psyche has a positive and a negative face: it's hardly possible to say anything about a person of which the opposite isn't equally true. Crushed, he enjoyed it. Teeth gritted, he throve on it. And hunting, careless, reaching out desperately for a side of anything to grapple on for purchase, he tried to think ahead through the series of blanks that could still be sifted and manipulated: to Hong Kong, Guangzhou, the train to Beijing, from there by the Russian or Chinese train through Manchuria or Mongolia to join up with the Trans-Siberian Railway at Irkutsk, and through to the Moscow they'd never seen and the eastern precincts of Europe... pulling currency rules out of his memory, the dos and don'ts of travel guides, but seeing for all his functional reductionism nothing real in it, nothing yet, but that slender reed-throat open on a titanic recess, on a roaring and evacuate hollowness.

A change in the engine note. An air-host, or whaddaya call them, steward, stumbled past on the way to his hideout under curtains. It was hours later (flight was 3:10, delayed to 4:45, eight hours forty minutes) when the entire floor-surface dipped away to the right like a boat capsizing, and out of windows open on the dark Yehune saw, Mel craned past to see, a dazzling constellation of richly-compacted lights.

Good old pilot, that'll be, giving us a look. Or no, idiot, he's only turning. Going for... whaddaya call it, *Kai Tak,* in Kowloon Bay. $30 American. And you take the airport bus to *Tsim Sha Tsui*....

'Hey man, that's cool – they must be showing us,' Mel said. A book and three sheets of scribbled-on paper were carefully laid out on his tray.

'Don't be a dick. We're turning right.'

'Oh, right. ... Hey look, there are guys actually closing their windows over there. Must not have a fucking shred.'

'Yeah. They could at least let other people... um...'

Again, inexorably, the floor or deck was tilting, this time the other way, while one woman in the centre aisle groaned out loud, and suddenly the cold black air just past Mel's head was printed with the vast complexity of Hong Kong, like crumpled newspaper barely out of the incinerator. It was Yehune's turn to crane past Mel. Who'd reached up, who was trying to force his window sash higher than it could possibly go, muttering,

'Fucking undeads.'

At the bus stop in the hot dark where they stood waiting for the airport coach that never came, Yehune was able to recall in a series of short shutter-bursts the dragon's breath or wind from an open blast-furnace that had met them when they came out of the plane; the thrust and crush of people in the big wide bus over the runway surface to the nineteen solidly-packed queues at Immigration; standing there in line, and standing, and standing, along with a huge variety of travellers of all races and nationalities dressed in what seemed to him every possible style of clothing; the official's dismissive wave when they got to him; baggage-carousels; Chinese faces; confusion; a waft of exotic smokes. Now, having taken the plunge, immersed themselves from the head downwards in this strange half-Western Orient, they watched anxiously every way around the cordoned-off access road, where taxis swung in and out, pedestrians were sparse by contrast, and the lower sky held a great eye-deceiving halo of refracted light; whether an atmospheric effect or some unthinkable sky-written exhalation from a city. 'Take the airport bus to Tsim Sha Tsui,' Cas had written. And here they were, under the yellow-and-white sign obligingly written in Latin letters as well as Chinese, TSIM SHA TSUI, along with a single lank backpacker who looked worn by hard usage, with raddled features, life-blasted hair, who was quick to introduce himself as Mickey from Ohio.

'No bus, eh?' Yehune said eventually.

'No,' said this Mickey. 'And it don't look like it's going to come now.'

'Might have left early?'

'Might have.'

Their letter, the 21-pages-long compendium of everything they needed to know to do the Trans-Siberian that had been sent to Mel by their one-time classmate Timothy Castor, turned out to be somewhere at the bottom of Mel's pack. Actual guidebooks (again on the advice of the oracle Cas) had been judged too heavy to take along. This Mickey, though, talked as though he'd been there before; he was holding a pamphlet folded open at a tourist map.

He announced, 'Me, I'm going for public transport.'

'Goodoh. Us too. Y'on for that, Mel?'

Mel said nothing, but his face reflected changing lights that must have been flashing somewhere in the heat-rashed distance.

The streets of the real Hong Kong were paved with people, people in perpetual motion, in vehicles and out of them, hurrying past or squatting in doorways or cooking up sizzling food in black woks in stands on the street, all walled around by the high towers of buildings and character signs like ornamental geegaws, as if this out-of-doors were one huge brightly-coloured sitting room in which any number of humans could feel completely at their ease. The two New Zealanders, with Mickey a little in advance of them, tramped along the footpaths with their packs, Yehune compact and super-alert, never letting an opportunity pass, jumping up to buses barely stopped and trying to talk to the drivers. They turned out a bit resistant to foreign-language conversation. He mentioned taxis; Mel reminded him of their financial limitations. Again and again, a Chinese gentleman of a certain age, one time a lady, would come up and stop them, ask where they were going and offer to help. That was how out of place they were. Once, in a progress so confused and alien as to become a legend in the memory, of which any precise detail was hard to pin down afterwards, they did get on a bus, paying with the smallest of the bills from their money exchange at the airport, though they never managed to work out whether that short hop took them any nearer to their goal. Mickey was the expert; he had the map; it was just three miles, round about, he drawled back at them, from Kai Tak to Chungking Mansions.

A block or so before they got there, walking southwards down Nathan Road, Mickey came up against a cadaverous dog-like tout, who took him by the arm, barking again and again a few phrases in English,

'Nice room, TV, you come see.'

'How much?' Mickey asked him, and again, 'How much?'

'You come, *nice* room, come see. *TV. TV.*'

Thus claimed, tugboated, they came to Chungking.

The Mansions turned out to be nothing but a towerblock, or rather four towers in one, squalid and threatening, in which a number of tiny backpacker-accommodators plied their trade, without any central organisation except by whatever shady operators they must have paid off for the right to be there. Seeing it, any illusions he might have built out of the name 'Chungking Mansions' swept away on the spot, Yehune actually smiled, baring his teeth in a kind of self-lacerating satisfaction. Two more touts

50

had peeled off from the crews that cruised or loitered around the bare floor of the shaft, facing up to him and Mel,

'*So* good room, *so* good, TV.'

Straight away the first tout, the dog-like one, was at them, shouting furiously in Cantonese. In the argument that followed Yehune couldn't, of course, understand any of the words, but some of the gestures were expressive enough. He and Mel were separated from Mickey by a scattering of bodies in short-sleeved shirts. At a certain moment when he must have thought the tourists' eyes were somewhere else, the dog-tout made a very quick upward swipe of the hand into an opponent's face, so that the boy bent away with his hands over his eyes.

Mickey put an end to it. He just walked towards them, and the canine spokesman had to face him with a smile and go through his whole spiel again. This time, Mickey refused to be led,

'How much?'

Someone moved between, their faces were lost, and Yehune could only hear, 'Too much'. By then he himself was beginning to negotiate with the second group, the *so*-goods; who it turned out wouldn't give him any prices at all until everyone had seen everything. But Mickey stepped up and divided their attention. He talked to the one furthest from Yehune – there was a mumbling back and forth – Mickey was satisfied. Their whole escort left the two New Zealanders flat while they bustled their new client away to a lift.

Ah, right. There's a chance gone. And good old Mick, God, I knew him more than half an hour.

And here comes dog-tout sniffing around again. Fuck this, eh. Where's

'Where's Traveller Hostel?'

'No' open. No' open.'

Not open. But

'But where is it?'

'No Travel' Hostel. No' open.' And he added with a broad grin of satisfaction, 'No place open now.'

Yehune's inner demon, embracing action and the sense of difficulty, mirrored that nod with an implicit facial expression not far different. Looked down. What's it, zero something – a bit past midnight.

'OK, man,' he said to Mel. 'You guard the packs. Stay right here, I'm off to look. Don't let any of these vampires shift you one inch.'

But Mel's whole attitude displayed his lack of intention of doing anything at all; he could have been staring from a pole, Yehune thought, still a bit surprised from when the axe had come down.

Pack off. To the lifts, A, B, C and D. Traveller Hostel? Taking its time. No, get off me, don't wanna know. Mel's still there, Mel's right.

On the strength of guesswork and blind instinct he managed to make his way to the long glass shopfront with its sign, Traveller Hostel, the one Cas had mentioned. He knocked, then pounded, then shouted, but no-one would come out. Scraps, dusters, noticeboards, all behind glass. A big operation. Side-door? No. Right, go down again. Everywhere he went, he passed 'Guest Houses', Happy Guest House, Lucky Guest House, London Guest House, each with its locked door and usually a portcullis of security steel.

So back he went, to find Mel practically besieged, though another group had arrived as well by now (nattier, with fat airline bags) and several of the agents had been siphoned off to work them. Yehune reported,

'Nothin' doin', the guy's right. Where is he now?'

Mel gave a shrug-like upturn of a hand, and Yehune went to find that snub-snouted jackal of the ground floor centre shaft. Then, by instants, away and up, to whatever luxury suite he was advertising. Mel came too. Dog-tout was sullener, drawn from other prey. But he led them right up to the high C's and into a nameless grotto, all got up to imitate the glitz of a real hotel, but badly, veneer peeling away from walls weeping with residual scunge, the *TV, TV,* in an ancient fishbowl-screened style. How much? was finally answered: 140 Hong Kong dollars for the night, which is… bugger. I don't know. 'Too much,' he said aloud. Lists in Cas's letter recurred in his mind, the details sharp-etched: $20 for a dorm? He left, pulling Mel on; the tout wouldn't let them go, he was arguing every step of the way and making up other propositions as they all rode down in the lift, in what sounded like half-English half-Chinese,

'En teu teng mong. You come me. Uh? En teu.'

It meant nothing to Yehune. But later a random mumble from Mel went some way to explaining it, as they were shuffling around their bags back down on the common floor:

'Couldn't afford his bloody entertainment.'

Calmer now and almost self-possessed, Yehune organised Mel. Each of them would take one shaft and get prices from whoever was awake enough to give them, and at one or earlier they'd meet here, right here, in the central tout-hall. The difficulty was they had to lug both bags and packs along with them. Mel chose A, with a level of equanimity that made Yehune doubt he'd even listened to what he had to do; so he explained it one more time. Then he waited for the D lift, but changed his mind when the C one opened its doors a few metres across the floor.

Endless landings – bizarre effects of graffiti painted out – High Guest House, Swallow Guest House – so many that two people couldn't cover them all in a night; and what was more they really were all closed. He had to batter and thunder, yell 'Open up!'; he was targeting the smaller houses with slighter grilles for their effect of amateurishness, defencelessness, though he told himself it was for the lower prices. He did eventually bring people out of some of them. Tightly-drawn Chinese faces, anything but reserved, inscrutable, kept shouting 'Closed!' at him. If ever he was let in, he had to do the full tour, hall, appointments, the room itself, answer all their questions, before he was allowed to know a price. It took so *long*. Twenty to already. Something in the low combat and brutality of the process did leave him obscurely enjoying it, in his own head kicking, kicking at doors, as if splintering all the obstacles in his way. He could imagine how Mel was doing; probably hadn't got in a single door. Scared he might wake someone.

Now what's this…? – Gerard Guest House, pinkish-grey and lime of a mouldy fish, not a single iron bar….

The lady in charge was small, with hair cut brush-style, and seemed anxious to please, once he got her past the 'Closed' routine. Ha, he thought, you don't know. Keep a Yehune out, when you can't even afford a grille? They walked past a row of doors along a hall pungent with a smell of old frying; she took him into a room so small that it could only fit the double bed (twin singles were unthought-of in Chungking) and the indispensable TV, miniaturised, on a high perch. A tinny coughing roar from the air conditioner. Squalid, but OK. The price surprised him: $70. That was 35 each, which was cheaper than some far less liveable-in places. On the spot, guessing that Mel wouldn't have got much further, he said he'd take it. Stood looking while she went to collect receipts, forms, whatever it might be. An inscription in ballpoint on the wall. 'Timothy and Meikle spent a wonderful night in this room.' On a shelf by the TV, *Chinese for Travellers*. Outside the window, the perpetual all-night charge of traffic up and down, the shouts of people, hurrying head to tail, in their thousands, their millions, boisterous, unsleeping....

Possibly tired, he had the impression of a rush of sand-grains, and behind or across them the enormous hollowness that opened up blank to the feelers of the mind. Trying to picture a future – a night spent in this room, in this bed, the day after that – he found himself groping in the unpainted, that vast and limitless torus of the undefined that seemed to bell out around him, broadly, irreducibly. Mel's still on the hunt, he recited carefully to himself. Hope he guards his money belt. And tomorrow we have to go and find out about visas, do the camera thing, look for. Ghetto blaster. Maybe a stereo. With plodding deliberate words, the application of limits, he tried again to reduce that overbearing blind recess, which was somehow built on the sense of their frustrated aspiration, on all the unforeseeable struggles to come; or maybe on the feeling that his life was on hold, all normal activity suspended, girls, work, music, while this trip wore out its way under their feet and was finally sent back used and scratched and delimited into the past. He stood over the red pack leant against one wall, and watched the grey smokes rolling, forever receding backwards out ahead. Held off, held back, till... what? Till. Till something – he might have picked out of the very vanishing point of vagueness – a pickup. Pickup by something larger. The beyond-quotidian, which was what? ... a tentative straining in the shrillest part of his hearing: a person? then, surely, a girl? his young mind rationalised... or something. Or something. Roar of universal noise. And time tracked by in gleaming droplets, trip-points on the surface of the vast; the commotion of the Hong Kong night out there beyond the window bars never flagged; and it seemed he was leaning far out against nothing, poised in the face of unknowing, straining, straining against the receiving hollowness, like a boy launched off a tree-branch, or a diver frozen in the perfect empty moment between the board's end and the air.

Yehune in Matamata

Somewhere near the beginning of his life, he saw down, far down into a network of diverging colours, lapped internal frieze of the cascading sunlight and trembling twigs and leaves casting spotlights of green, and was able to imagine that diminutive avenue laid open to admit his mummy and Brett and Aunty Clar and himself, like dolls or insects moving, held all together in a perfect bowl of time suspended. Though the location was immediately forgotten (where had it been? Not in the bush-walk behind their house, not in the park, maybe at one of the picnic sites further towards Tirau their father was always driving them to in the car), the experience was vivid enough to be looked for again and again, the same quality of vision repeated, random thickets and messes of undergrowth or even hedges picked out to look down into, deeply, with concentration and purpose, through the years that followed. It built a magic pause for him, an utter freshness for a few moments, when whatever apprehensions he might have been forming about life were smoothed away in the face of some fragile luminous power. He caught it again most often near the mottled trunk of a sycamore in the yard, less so in selected spots of the park area on Centennial Drive round the corner; and as the years went by he continued to apply the same process of vision to places further removed. The concrete drive of their house became a cityscape in miniature, the clipped lawn a forest. Even the corner of a brown-stained paling fence (on Tainui Street where he waited for the school bus) was a place where, if he happened to be alone, he could lean down, droop his broad head, and lose himself in a self-forgetful study of what was smallest.

That, the secret self built up in him in moments of diminution, never named, hardly ever thought about, had nothing to do with the course of his real life. It went on on another level altogether. An episode of crying and flailing his arms at the breakfast table. Coming to the house with his mummy, leaving the house with his mummy.

Airfix model parts left by his far older brother, Brett, on flat surfaces that he was always wanting to use himself. Brett retreating into his room. Some saw-edged, pervasive colour printed across it all, across the natural air and blue domelike sky of the small town that he didn't see yet as a small town: something that his inner processes uneasily identified with a kind of bright orange. What was that? He didn't know. He could only hear his own name repeated in his head, Johann, **Yo**-hann, **Yo**, **Yo**, in the inescapable tones of his mother's voice,

'Johann. Are you going to eat your egg? **Yo**-hann.'

At breakfast time, there were so many other things to think of. There were the scuffles with Brett, who usually managed to be somewhere else after a while; the familiarity of the colours of the plastic tablecloth and the shape of the dining-room window; and conversations that seemed to go on and on in the limitless spaces above that slice of the world he inhabited alone:

'Could you just step quietly, please, my head... *Andrew*. Quietly. ... How's your study going?'

'Oh, as usual.'

'As usual. That doesn't sound quite good enough; as usual. Considering how we have to sweat and slave, considering how every moment of my time's taken up...'

'What? Looking after the kids?'

'Well, you don't do it.'

'Someone's got to bring home the bacon. I mean, when I'm...'

'Bring home the bacon. If only you did. Sometimes I wish I'd stayed on full-time and just hired somebody in. I could make more than you're doing now.'

'Which is why the exams, you see. I don't intend to do this forever.'

'But can't you see how it puts everything else onto me? I just can't see the point... could you *please* stop clicking and clicking that spoon like that; I can't see the point, when there are all sorts of opportunities for a legal executive in the city.'

His father had a squiggle in his nose. Usually he was pale-faced, not symmetrical, shifting back and forward like a stocky ghost through the door to the study and out again. When the nose moved, the squiggle changed, and so the boy looked interestedly over at the window, source of that intense mid-North Island bale of light that lit up every surface down to the bare rough grains.

'All right, that's enough. I just came out for a weetbix or two, then it's back to durance vile.'

'You're not answering me. And will you stop clicking that… *Andrew*.'

The loud rattle of a spoon. 'There, finished. Have a good day at school, Johann.'

'And who's got to get him ready for school? … Johann, haven't you eaten that egg yet? … **Yo**-hann. Are you listening? No toys or treats today if you don't. Do you hear me, **Yo**-hann? **Yo**-hann.'

But the egg was funny, though he couldn't say that to his mother. On his plate it looked like a mountain of coagulated grease, barely tinted with the plastic orange-and-white that allowed it to imitate a fried egg. The impossibility of actually trying to fold that glistering object, that bulb of yolk, inside his body was something beyond him even to understand, let alone express; and so he fixed his eye instead on temporary details of the crockery and furniture. His old Winnie-the-Pooh plate for breakfast cereal. Flakes of dry weetbix that must have been tracked over by his father from the box there, which you could fold into robots. Brett's 'dollar scholar' diploma. A plywood frame for modelling on the sideboard, and a picture he'd done himself and his brother had defaced later on. He ticked it off, none of it implying much emotion to him. But there was an ill feeling still, a hateful thing, kept far enough away that it never actively engaged him; the **Yo**, **Yo**, that rising, cawing commotion of the air that blushed into harsh colours like a confusion of all oranges and scarlets, high over the air of the room, the town; a mysterious coloration; and more, an unsolid sense of nausea, building in back-waves out of the sound of that syllable, **Yo** – the **yolk** – first sound of his own name.

With Hone and Petie and Alex he played in the bushland round the corner where the horses clopped along, or up around the dusty railway lines, noticing the grains in things, the burning gritty overlay to everything that could be called real. Over that, their words to each other, like separate floating blobs. According to his mother, he'd been slow to learn to talk. So he thought of a long, unhurried gestation where nothing but shapes in primary colours moved inside his mind: the dream-time. After that, words beginning to dawn on him almost one by one; he could see himself learning *'Airfix'*, and *'byoo-ti-ful'*, the word that was made to describe his mother. She was also *'Austrian'*, which built a picture to him of a heraldic-looking feathered bird. Far later, when her long hair had been cut to shoulder length and he'd almost stopped seeing her features at all, he kept that assumption about her, that bird of fine plumage, in a kind of mental lozenge, unchanging, stamped in the colours of first experience.

'Your mum's *Austrian*.'

'She was born in New Zealand.'

'Oh yeah? What's her first name then?'

'Brigitte.' He pronounced it with a hard 'g'.

'That proves it. Doesn't it, Hone?'

Hone didn't even grunt. He might have felt a bit removed from the distinctions of Europeanness. Alex drawled out,

'So what?'

She was picking at her dress; she must have been bored. But the result was that Johann (named by his mother; Brett had been his father's choice) was able to accept it as a distinction rather than something to be ashamed of.

He always preferred to be away from the house. So he remembered looking forward to going to school; it must have seemed the ideal opportunity to him.

School turned out to be a room with wooden playthings and the most hideous glaring nursery-rhyme illustrations hanging on the walls. Jack Sprat with teeth; Miss Muffet with a purple-grey expanse of cheek. He learned quickly about blackboards, and coloured chalks, and cuisenaire. In primer one they were drilled in when to sleep and when to wake up.

He was expected to bring 5c for the milk-in-schools. His was a sixpence, with the Maori clubs. Gracie Waka was following him and happened to see the coin; she asked him for it. Some impulse made him give it to her. But another boy noticed; he pointed at her and started chanting, *'Big Grace Wokka-wokka, big Grace Wokka-wokka'.*

All the kids joined in. Johann as well, in the end, because it sounded good.

Another time, he managed to get in the fence that screened off the school incinerator. It was Out-of-Bounds. Even the standards kept their distance, and one shouted across to him that he'd get the strap. There was no way out that he could find. But a girl called Faye Sturkenboom, a primer four, saw him crying and boldly climbed in across a pile of crates; when she was in there she untwined the rusty wire from the gate catch. She told him not to worry. She never spoke to him again; but any time he saw her after that he was lost in depthless admiration.

Slow to talk, he was also slow to learn to coordinate himself. His arms and legs would move clumsily or go in the wrong direction. So he wasn't going to climb the few steps up to the junior flying fox. 'My mum told me I had to be careful,' he told the teachers, and stuck to that. He hadn't learned connection; he hadn't realised that notes on that and everything went straight back to his mother.

It was a year or two before he was accused of actual truancy.

His mother said to him, 'We were told you've been playing truant. Is it true?'

Johann said nothing.

'I think they call it "wagging",' suggested his dad.

'Andy, will you just stay out of it? – Well, Johann?'

That afternoon, he'd been sent to the school office with a message from Mrs McConnochie. He'd found the office door and knocked on it but got no answer, found no-one else to ask, and just sat down on a bench outside the door and waited for someone to come along. He must have waited for some time. Eventually someone had appeared, a teacher whose name he knew, Miss Kidd, in a big scarlet dress and carrying a clipboard and a box of colour-matched stationery.

She asked him what he was doing there. He'd told her about the message. Still rearranging the contents of the box, pulling out sheaf after sheaf and replacing it, apparently searching for something, she'd smiled into mid-air and said he should get back to his class. By then, though, the afternoon playtime had started.

'Is that a no?' his father asked.

'I might as well tell you, Johann, that we've been told a group of school-age children were running wild through the parks and shouting at around quarter to two. There were five boys, or four, and a girl. Mr Lovett in the town saw them.'

'It wasn't me,' he said.

But he thought: a girl. That was Alex. After the break he'd noticed she wasn't there; then later she and one other had come in.

'Mr Lovett says he saw you. He recognised your bright-blue tee-shirt.'

'It wasn't *my* bright-blue tee-shirt. I was at the office.'

'At the *office*,' his mother repeated. 'The school office? Curiouser and curiouser. ... Well then, there'll be someone at the office who can tell us you were there.'

But he didn't think so. No-one had seen him, Miss Kidd had been doing a thousand different things – some early instinct for the nature of people in offices told him that any one of them would be ready to swear he hadn't been there.

'They forgot about me.' He could feel his face glowing hot inside the skin.

His father said, 'Tell us what happened, Johann.'

But before he could, his mother: 'As far as I'm concerned, Johann, you were out of school, that's all there is to it. So – no races on Saturday, and you can stay in tonight and tomorrow evening as well and think about it. ... Of course, if someone at the office tells me differently...'

'How did they forget about you?' asked his father, looking at him carefully.

'I had a.... They forgot about me *in the office*.'

'Mm. Did your teacher send you there?'

'Yes. But she forgot too.'

His dad mentioned to the space above him, 'You know, old Lovett isn't always the clearest observer of the natural scene.'

'What *nonsense* is this?' his mother burst out. 'I'll get this cleared up, you can be sure of that. Mrs McConnochie will be able to give me chapter and verse, but as far as I'm concerned we have a positive identification already.'

'Well now, Briggie, you shouldn't jump to conclusions before all the evidence is in.'

His mum seemed to be straining against something. 'Oh… I'll just… and if you think I can listen to *you* coming out with all that…'

As words went on, battering back and forwards above his head, the boy ceased to listen, though possibly not to pay it any attention. It was like a stream, or the waves of a storm, brightly-coloured and upside-down, and you had to learn to thread the storm when you needed to. He became glass, in a practised and only half-deliberate mental motion: long cooled and hardened under the experience of rows. He fell back to the timeless, the apprehension of nothing at all through the accidental footfalls of things on the outside of his eye. He had rules for it, which he repeated if he needed to shut out the noise. Never move. Never think if it's fair. Nothing happened. Stop. Wait. Watch.

There was a time when both combatants flagged for a minute, his mother's face hidden as she leaned over against the bench with the breadboard, his father sitting in the chair looking preoccupied and a bit unguarded. So he said slowly,

'Dad… I *really* want to go and see the races on Saturday…'

The man's voice was different. 'Oh well, listen, Johann. We'll call everything provisional until we can establish the facts. We'll have to find your teacher and go right into this, and until then…'

That was the beginning of another outburst by his mother, who shouted fit to bring the house down, but not at him. Johann got out of the room. It wasn't even a victory, because he was almost sure his teacher wouldn't have the slightest memory of his errand. The class was like that, people constantly coming in and out and being sent all over and coming up to her with notes. He sat at the piano, watching the edges of the keys go up and down. It wasn't the first time he'd sat on the wind-up stool pushing notes at random. He was fascinated, living utterly at a remove. He heard the sounds across the crash of sound, knowing that somewhere inside the case those intricate wood-block towers were shifting, the softened tadpole-heads jumping forward to bang the wires.

There were the rules, the rules of conduct; only it seemed to him that parents were outside them, brawling away on a level over people's heads. They just used words instead of their fists and teeth. Naturally, Johann wasn't interested in criticising; his concern was to avoid any wind that might blow his way out of the constantly-brewing parental storm. His brother Brett had long ago learned the advantage of being somewhere else, and left the spiky and somehow breathless atmosphere of the inner house to him. His mother he could guess at best. She was likely to make up new rules and principles on the spot and apply them unevenly. But it was when his father got involved that you could forget arguing; you had to go away, either in your head or in full body.

He spent as much time as possible out in the streets. On their way home from school, he and the other kids would naturally drift to some point most convenient to them all: a meeting of fences, a hole in the ground, or the kerb of some pavement where their short-trousered legs could splay out onto the tarmac of a road. There, in the mid-afternoon, when the day showed no tendency to differentiation except by a pedestrian or two, the thundering past of a stock-truck that had missed its back road, the hours they spent in aimless conversation drew out longer and longer.

Johann walked backwards. His arms were out and tipping from side to side. An expression of concentration on his face and the way he placed one foot behind the other were supposed to indicate a tightrope hidden in the lines in the concrete. Lewis laughed. Alex hardly seemed to notice. So he made an effort to get her attention. 'Oh God, I'm...' and his stagger happened to coincide with the appearance of a wooden telegraph pole just behind him. Bang; instead of pretending, he really measured the pavement.

Alex looked down this time, smiling; though he could see concern hovering in the background in case he'd hurt himself for real.

He jumped up, grabbed his schoolbag and went on normally under the Broadway overawnings. He was well enough pleased with his effect. That was the good thing about being funny; anything unexpected happening usually made it funnier.

'You should'a *seen* it,' Lewis was saying to Hone. 'It was such a laugh, he sort of did this backwards, I-dunno... fell right on his back off the ropes, and old Gabby was having concussion. Then – then he was sent off to the *shars*. Weren't you, Yo?'

They were drawing up alongside the Bakeroom Café. Johann modestly acknowledged his day's success, though Hone's face was immobile, like some dramatic sculpture done a bit too young. When he glanced at Alex, she was looking somewhere else.

So they came to the gash of the roadworks. It was a dirt hole that would have been over his head if he'd gone down into it, but it was cordoned off by white-and-orange striped ribbons held up by looped wire pegs. Johann personally could have sat staring into it for hours. He inched up as close as he could go, passing his bare feet beyond the limit the tape made; the others were more interested in talking.

Deep down, in the nameless streaks of a darker substance by two bared water-pipes, monsters crawled. But there was layer on layer to be seen – tentatively, gauging the different makeups of the dirt, he brought out two large earth-moving machines onto the ledge that looked like a long road leading up,

'Backing – hoy! Beep – beep – beep – watch out for that edge, Dickie.'

'OK, Mr Foreman.'

'Right, we'll have to level that. Push the dirt to that side and we'll bring up the crane.'

'Right you are.'

His mum had got permission to take him back to the bush confidence course after school hours. At that early time, the small Johann had refused point-blank to go on any of the equipment, not just the flying fox. So she drove him up on it, taunting and cajoling, in the face of all his resistance, holding him up to catch the rope, dropping him, pulling him up where he lay in a heap and wailed, holding him up again, dropping him. She was tall enough to do it, big-boned though slim, her blonde hair pulled back in a wedge. No matter how much he shouted, begged or tried to get away, she was always there, talking. There was a sort of fever in her look as she put up with what he must have given back to her; because no matter what happened she wasn't going to give up. So eventually he had to catch the rope. After which he panicked, let go, and hit the mud again, which was followed by more wails and another burst of words. That kept on happening day after day. It was only a few weeks before he was tentatively inching along the narrow wooden beam, to her repetitive rebukes and suggestions: 'Yo-hann, no, not that way. Try your right leg, there, no, *there*. You'll twist over and fall if you do that, look… no… there, I told you so. Try again. All right – that's better. And again. Come on, now. I know you don't want your friends to think you're *afraid*.'

Afraid was no longer the word. He hated that stretch of bush; he had dreams about the horrible gap where you had to jump from a tyre and catch a knot of rope. It was all mixed in with the solid streak of colour in the bush-heads, the red overarc of the afternoon sun through leaves. For a while, even trees and leaves looked scarred or tainted to him, and especially the ground below them, reminding him inescapably of those great stagnant wet patches he kept falling into, one under each of the swings, but the worst under the three-rope walk the big boys went on. He could see his own head coming out of that like a serpent rising. When they trailed back to the car through the failing light at the end of a session, he seemed to feel something dark, mud-fecal, closing in to choke him out of every uncertain patch of shadow.

The sun cried down. You couldn't see, in its glaring collision-points with the clay and mud of the under-road, the place where a group of tiny people shouted and waved their arms, uncertain of the solidity of their foundation.

'I'm *foreman, and* I *say go on.*'

'*I'm the one who has to drive it. The engineer's reports tell us we'll go right through.*'

'*Who'll back Dickie? – Me! And me!*'

'*You lot'll be down the road right off if you don't obey the Company's orders.*'

Down in the earth gash, the argument went on, while Hone and Alex kept their own conversation going somewhere towards the broad immobile sky,

'A hairclip. It used to be green.'

'Shit. … I find any, I use them for soldiers.'

His resistance had been broken down in the end, as it usually will. But only physically. What strange transformations of the soul might have begun under the shell of his young boy's body were unguessable to parents and adults, but lay gestating there, ready to startle them all one day. But by a sort of accident – either that, or some internal toughness – things were flipped around on them. At school Johann obeyed the new order from mother through teacher, and participated on the confidence course. But his initial fear had become a sort of haunting; he had to be lifted up, white-faced, to the smallest height to do the slightest thing; then he closed his eyes and usually fell off again. It was hilarious. All the other kids thought so. After a while he could see himself that his turn had become an event, with everyone standing and watching and ready to laugh. He was expected to fail; and at one point, never really pinned down in time, he began to choose his moment. Little by little, over a period of years, he built up a repertoire. It was then that those hours of obsessive training under what amounted to test conditions paid off, in a perverse and negative way. They could force him on, but they couldn't make him succeed. In the meantime, the growing certainty that he was playing to the crowd was grating more and more on the teachers who were there to build a healthy attitude from the primers on to out-of-doors activities; he was told off, sent to the showers, condemned in teacherly orations. He only gained the greater celebrity. And he learned: foolery, it could be *against* them. It was an alternative path, a bending with the wind, an elusive technique that by its nature never forced you to a direct clash. The school authorities stopped consulting with his mother; some perceptive spirit must have worked out that it wasn't the best idea. But her work had been done. In the end, they could have forbidden him the confidence course and that whole school-owned patch of valley bushland, and he still would have turned up, working his way along the queue and preparing his act.

It was obvious by now that Petie wasn't going to come. The other three had been discussing it for what seemed like forever, while nothing moved on sky or earth, and the feeling of dusty heat along with the stench from the roadworks seemed to clamp tightly around the top part of his skull; something like an on-site helmet.

After adventures, mutinies, problems and resolutions, the crisis had come. Someone had bravely driven the heaviest bulldozer out onto the ultimate flat, which was just a false surface of grains compacted by drying. He and his whole crew had plunged through – aaaarrrgh! – to the festering mud-bottom, by the domes of giant pipes – where monsters writhed, where dragons swam.

'**Yo**-hann. Is that you? **Yo**, **Yo**, **Yo**-hann…'

Jerked suddenly out of his dream-world, he seemed to see the gaudy stripes of corralling tape expanded in wide beams across the heavens' white and blue: impossibly high contrails of an intensity of colour only chemically attainable, like the dye in a plastic toy.

'**Yo**-hann, what are you *doing* there, are you completely mad? Have you forgotten it's a Tuesday? Miss Petchell and I didn't have a clue where you were, I've been giving her cups of tea, how can you have forgotten your *piano* lesson? I honestly don't know what I'm going to do with you. Get up now, at once, and come with me…'

Which made the colours settle down with a smooth habitual movement; high lines of wires burning across the atmosphere of the small town that he'd long ago recognised as such. Just another incident in the weaving of the day. He got to his feet clumsily, matter-of-factly, like a small bear in school clothes, and was reaching for his bag when it was snatched away and higher up. Alex didn't embarrass him with a glance. He said 'See ya' to the two boys, and the next moment was following his mother up the road, managing to give the impression that following was the last thing he was thinking of. In his mind, his scale books and an old *Hours With the Masters* in worn oatmeal had replaced the carnage of death in the mud, by a process unnoticed, automatic, and in a primitive way reassuring.

They up and moved to Auckland when the boy was about ten, when his father had qualified as a Barrister and Solicitor. They couldn't live where they wanted to at first, but they had to be within commutable distance. Johann was deprived at one blow of every place he knew; his secret sites of diminution, all the ancient, worn-out scenes and corners. He was thrown into other settings instead, and others again, as the family kept upgrading, shifting house from one district to another. He knew they weren't really all that far away. But everything here was painted in different colours. Even that electric taint was almost gone – his mother's voice, though insistent, failed to draw the same huge, sky-collusive resonance.

'How are you getting on in maths?' she said.

'All right.'

'Wasn't there a test today?'

'Oh… yeah.'

'What mark did you get?'

'Nineteen, som'ing like that.'

'Out of what?'

'Can't remember.'

'**Yo**-hann, you know I like to write it down, don't forget to find out tomorrow for me. Is there anything you're not understanding? Maybe I can help you with it. And by the way, find out who got the best mark in your class. Come on. You're good at maths, you always have been…'

Moved from school to school, he wasn't thrown completely on his own resources. Instead he learned quickly about appearances and the way to involve himself with a group of friends. He was determined not to stay alone. He developed a feel for it: buffoonery in the right places was important, and a ruthless response to anyone who tried to put him down. Girls you could forget. You had to be in with a whole lot of others to start with, then you might possibly get somewhere.

'Ah, let me introduce the new boy in our class. Class, this is Johann Trent. Now say, "Good morning, Jo…"'

'It's pronounced "Yehune".'

'I beg your pardon?'

'Yehune. That's my name. Yehune Trent.'

'Are you sure? It's spelt, ah… J, O, H, A, double N.'

'Yes sir. Yehune. My dad told me the registrar spelt it wrong.'

'Spelt it *wrongly* – please. Well, then, class, this is – Yehune? – Trent.'

There was the usual titter, along with exaggerated belly-laughs from the desks nearest the back. Feeling not at all embarrassed, but somehow tired, having lived through something like the same scene in every new school he'd been in, he stood and waited for it to be over. At the same time, he was letting his eye cruise over the boys who laughed the loudest: potential allies or enemies in the weeks to come. 'Hoon, hoo-oon,' one crooned softly to him when he finally got to take a seat.

Yehune only moved the edge of his cheek slightly, trying not to let any sign of his approval show through.

Some extraneous scene was with him as he turned, dipped down, and started to bring a folder up out of his bag. It had nothing to do with the chalky interior of that classroom. Instead, it was something like a skateboard park, too detailed, diagrammatic, richly coloured to be anything he could have seen in day-to-day life. A dream… or TV? In that setting, a carrot-topped individual with a cap backwards on his head was turning in the foreground, saying to someone out-of-picture something like,

'Ya hoon, eh?' or

'Oa, ya *hoon,*'

which must have been his laconic response to another boarder's sharp piece of navigating. The clack-clack of lines in moulded surfaces under wheels. Someone's laughter dying away. 'Ya hoon'… not that even he would have claimed that this was any sort of origin. Origins are hard to find. But along the irrecoverable *coulisse* of the development in him of his name of fantasy, that grunt or inward noise that didn't depend on the baggage laid on him by time or town or circumstances or most especially his parents, that was the frame that stood out, a single dream-stick somehow including everything else, giving him an excuse or logic for something that was his own, self-generated, a separate tag of meaning. *Yehune* (he thought): remember it. – And as for you, crooner, I'll see you later.

…

He might have moved ten thousand miles away. At Maeraki on the sea-shore, he started out in yet another secondary, Montgomery High. The weather, the tides of things couldn't have been more different, there by that chopped and undulating northern coast. The air swirled into aethereal formations, lived on the updraft, built chimeras that changed and changed again. He didn't feel that baking central stasis, the endless repetition of things around backgrounds that were always too familiar.

Now he was standing on the front quad where the school driveway took a turn.

' 'Course, it was boys-only there,' he said. 'This one's better by a *lot*.'

Some of the boys around him nodded. The idea of a single-sex school was ridiculous and unthinkable to anyone who went to Monty.

Someone asked, 'Did you shift house?'

Just then, a tall and straight-built individual put his head up and over,

'Don't listen, he's bullshitting you. He's some hick from down country, just got off the truck.'

By that time, Johann-Yehune was stocky and imposing, with dark edges to his features that might have indicated strength of character. Untried, of course, in those surroundings. One of the boys mumbled,

'Thought he's from Westlake.'

'Yeah,' said the aquiline one, warming to his theme, 'he's one of those big cow-pats from Wai-kick-a-moo-cow way.'

Yehune lashed back like a whip,

'Why fuck you up the bum, green-snot features?'

That drew a laugh. The tall boy, though, was of the sort that might have attracted followers. He moved closer, now, to where Yehune stood four-square and planted – not built for a hero, always the faithful dwarf.

'Do you want your dirty face punched in?'

Instead of answering, he turned with apparent ease to the circle of smaller and more nondescript boys,

'Mm. Well, looks like *he* won't be coming along.'

'Whaddaya talking about?' the tall one asked.

He turned. 'Us guys're all doing something, you're not coming. Have you got that?'

'Stuff you, cow-pat, I'll go where I feel like.' But by that time the speaker must have been feeling the way the others were editing him out. Sloping away, with an implicit embarrassment or reserve. '... Coming where?'

70

And that's you done, Alphonse. Things like that you've got to nip in the bud. Yehune was fully conscious of himself at that crux of moments, taking chances. Despite the fact that he had about one minute or less to come up with something daring and original they were all going to do, he felt only clean, uplifted, his criminal inventiveness woken and alert. Cars, car-stealing occurred to him, and the look of a certain teacher's old Ford that he already knew wasn't locked, and that might be likely to respond to more than one shape of ignition key. 'You know old Routledge, you know his car?' he was saying to whichever of them showed an interest. He could see a joy-ride, nothing worse, then choosing a parking-place for the old heap on the other side of the road from where it had been to start with. A girl passed by; he saw her out of the corner of his eye. Grey skirt, decorous, unrevealing as any old school-ma'am could want; only she glanced in his direction, or in the direction of the whole guilty group. Blue plastic hairclips, the delicate whisk of forehead to nose. There were teeth inside him, locked into a grin, and a new thing, a substance, nothing bottleable; dark exhilaration, the feel of a bent saw suddenly whipped back the other way. 'Yeah, and we could all wait by the crossing and watch 'im when 'e comes out,' a smaller boy said, looking almost ridiculously young. It was going in his favour, and Yehune had grown taller, maybe, than the leaders, those emaciate towerers that drew men to their call; for a moment he saw himself running and running, irrelevantly, running over a piece of grass somewhere

and the two Bruces were with him on his left side and another boy and then Alex behind them all as they came around the corner into Firth Street and took a run across the railway line to the corner of Bedford Park where the rugby matches were played out, shouting and hooting, swearing and having short playfights, in the blessed hour, the moments when good little boys and girls were sitting at their desks stultified under the early-afternoon monologue of teachers' voices. And Bruce and Bruce started fighting the Rawhiti Ave kid and laying him out on the grass and punching him gently while Alex in passing grabbed Bruce Vernon's schoolbag up – what the hell did he need his schoolbag for? – and threw it over for a good kicking. That had started the rugby game they all kept up, with the Bruces both flat out to get the bag back and him trying to stop them and old Rawhiti whining that now was the time to get back to school because it'd soon be playtime and they could come in without the teachers noticing; but nobody could give a damn about that. And Johann was the one who picked out the old codgers standing around in bigger numbers than he might have liked, the Thomson guy and the wattle-like red underjowl of Lovett with his offended look at the ruffianly nature of everything he saw, and heard authoritarian shouts beginning; and got them all together and restarted the run shouting again and howling over the broad tree margin that goes into Centennial Drive, but taking good care to run right over Rata and on down and left on Hohaia Street towards the next available grassland and never go anywhere near his own house, which was on Tamihana at the corner with the red Firestone. So Alex was at the end then and there was no-one else. There were five of them and Alex. He braked back, watching the others lope on past, and went to take her hand, then saw it was useless, he couldn't tug her on faster. But the others were sticking to the route and hanging back for him still, whoever had been following wasn't in sight and might possibly have given up or found something better to do; and there under the meaningless blank of the long unchanging concave sky with her hand in his hand he felt the strange weave of dimensions outwards-inwards as if the earth was shrinking under him, he was seeing the plan of small-town streets under his feet where concrete gave way to weeded edging and the whole world receding to a curved ball notched in relief; and he was gigantic, expanded, running beyond time and beyond the lipless imperceptible shrill gurn of cicadas or the process of the afternoon, the boys ahead like crickets in a miniature racetrack running to his plan; and that new swelled and indefeasible Johann in the bright-blue tee-shirt stopped, and let go of her hand, and stood for a moment – at the level of the broad sky – listening.

Hong Kong

'Yes. Can do. You stay Hong Kong coul' be six wee'.'

'Six *weeks*? Did you say six weeks?'

'Coul' be no' so long.'

A cheek in fine eggshell, shaded and contoured to the small high nose. Beside a structural strut of bone were two eyes narrowed and elongated, lively, almost too alive, calling up a memory in Yehune of guys he'd known from university. Box structures in white and grey made up most of the background, and posters, and straggling interminable queues of people backed up to the walls.

'Look, we can't... Mel, can we afford to spend six weeks here?'

In Hong Kong Student Travel, in Star House near the ferry terminal, Mel was all but inert, staring morosely at the floor or underbench, only moving his mouth when he was forced to it – when Yehune's Kiwi and the travel aide's Sinicised versions of English completely failed to mesh.

He jerked his head once to the side.

'OK then... could we book from Beijing?'

The eyes grew even more alive, beaming approval of the good student.

'Book Beijing ver' good. Three wee' there. Have to get visas, right ord', ticke' first. Apply So-vie' visa, transit, if you wan' touris' visa can be buy all ticke', go book all excurs', visa denie' then. ...'

Hong Kong, for Yehune, had turned out to be torrential, sudden, never-ending, alive with incident and accident and misapprehension, a place where almost anything could happen at any moment. It was seedy, people-clogged, paved with layer on layer of shit and detritus, yet somehow magnificent too with a duplicitous clarity, a splendour of coloured lights. It all depended on where you happened to be standing to look at it. Personally, he approved of it; it filled some need he had for the fast and racy life. Trying to sum it up, he'd come to the conclusion that there were several views or sizes that all but contradicted each other. There was the outlook from the plane; that was some billion-winking perfection spread out rumpled against the dark, what he'd seen as the ash of a burned newspaper racing with pinpricks. Then there was the impression he still held from their Sunday evening excursion to the peak of the Island, Shan Teng: like an impossibly large showcase taken out of some sky-built jeweller's shop, containing – what? – something like a crouching jet-black cat, and crowned at the top with neon capitals. FURAMA, BANK OF AMERICA, THE MANDARIN. Against those two, everything he experienced of the actual life at ground level, which was imperfection doubled and redoubled, shady deals and a crush and jostle of people and grit and rubbish trodden together into the street hot as an oven, where you trudged in a light patina or oil-bath of your own sweat, peering at maps and the street signs, to the jungle caw of the vendors: 'Come see, come buy, very cheap, watch, watch, calc'lator, you come in!'

Three levels; maybe more. And they weren't the only contradictions. In everything Yehune tried to do there – and there was quite a lot; as well as the organisation of visas and tickets there was the standard insurance scam he was running on a lost camera, and an integrated stereo system he wanted to buy and ship on to Mel's brother's address – he kept coming up against difficulties, unspoken pacts, a twisting of language and implied meaning.

He said, 'Thought Cas told us it's good to book in Hong Kong 'cause everyone here speaks English?'

'Yeah, he wrote that,' Mel admitted. 'Meant everyone *thinks* they speak English.'

Their travel assistant returned, then, from the higher platform or computerised holy of holies behind him.

'Yes, we got num' three train, Chine' train go through Mon-gol-ia, take I thin' one day less, you need Mon-gol' visa, So-vie' train num' nineteen, through Man-chu-ria, 'course you have extra day on visa some time blizz' on line.'

'What's that? Some time what?'

'Blizzards on the line,' Mel muttered.

'OK – but then – what I want to know is, say we want to take the extra day' (he laughed) '– just say there's, you know, no blizzard…'

That face: chiselled, friendly. Faces spreading away to the left, to the right, a semicircle of uniformly-dressed young Hong Kongese, swivelling on their seats, and the rattle of keyboards and bursts of twisted syllables, all the final consonants left off, which wavered strangely in and out of synch like an expression of cyborg logic, *tak-tak-tak-tak-tak,* or a row of miswired teletype machines.

Mel was sinking bit by bit into a black torpor.

'… but we were told – I was sure they said we could take the extra day. Mel. Hey, Mel. Could you check that in the letter?'

So he was forced into action, in triple-slow motion. The travel-aide said, 'Yes, yes, 24 hour', 24 hour' for connec'. Wait, I as' Mu Wu.'

A rapid stream of Cantonese into the unseen upper level was followed by a long wait, then another stream, and their own advisor stood up and dropped in a moment out of their lives.

And there it is. Nothing to do but wait. The crowd behind stirred ominously, crackling with voices.

'You got it man? Can I just see…?'

'Ah… had it here. I'm sure it was. Looks like… nope. I was sure it was in the bottom of this bag. Put it in deliberately. Ffff-f. Wouldn't you just know it, stick it in, hour later, there it isn't. Complex thing, reality.'

'You *didn't bring* Cas's letter?'

'Yeah, 'course I did. Just that it isn't here now. Sorry.'

Mel's participation certainly came from a distance. He was fagged, at one remove, or possibly as energetic as the next man but lost by no fault of his own in a dimension of time-space just one partition away from day-to-day processes. He didn't sleep much – though he'd never said a word about it, he seemed more put off than you'd expect by having to lie under the same covers as Yehune's own stocky male form in boxer shorts. Natural enough. But you've got to put up with these things; Yehune did; and Mel's near-nonexistent buttocks were encased in a more clinging confection altogether. Hairy bugger.

In the mornings, getting up to the glaring bar-imprinted lightstream and the roar of Hong Kong close outside their window, they always found themselves in a struggle to begin or put off the action of the day.

'C'mon. 'S Tuesday, gotta do the Insurance today, get to the airport again, check the lost property, go out to Commercial Union and screw them out of a bit of cash, go to a bank, organise a few things...'

'What? ... Fuck.'

'Mel. Mel boy. Mel-Mel-Mel.'

'God shit willya lea'me...'

'Brekkie first, eh. You need green tea, man. Never seen a more likely candidate. We'll just get out to a café and...'

'Meuu-*urrh*,' he bellowed, stretching. 'Well... you're not bringing that fucking Pentax, I hope.'

Yehune shook his head with tolerant cheerfulness. That camera was the theoretically lost item he was claiming insurance for. But he knew, just as well as the next artist (Mel, of course, excluded), that he could turn up for all the interviews jauntily swinging it from his shoulder and not once would anyone say, Hey, that camera there, isn't that the one you reckon you left under the seat of your Cathy Pacific flight CX110 and never saw again, lost property number BUL 9898? They might use it to *compare* with the lost camera. They might ask how recently he'd bought it and what the going rate was. Not that he was actually going to do that; and not that, the mêlée of Hong Kong time-management and imposed confusion being what it was, the whole thing would in the long run even come to anything: they'd be dumped off the bus in some nameless remoteness of Ma Tau Wai Road and take nearly two hours to find their way from there (a jet airliner large as twenty houses looming barely above the overbridge for a moment with an ear-negating shriek, an effect of planets brushing hideously close), and eventually thread their way from floor to floor of the Wing Lung building (a sign on the lift said: 'The Irresponsible For Accidents Caused By Overloading'), and, Yehune having suddenly remembered that the banks all closed at twelve noon and he needed money to finance his stereo that same day, they'd hoof it for the nearest Hang Seng, knowing they wouldn't hit another branch of Commercial Union until Western Europe. But still....

But still. It was the mindset that mattered. Look 'em straight in the eye and dare them to say anything. Mel, on the other hand... well, he was....

'Six *weeks*,' he was saying. 'Can't see we can stay here six days. Bamboo curtain countries're cheaper. Can't tell exactly how much money's running out, but we're riding on it... we're riding on it.'

'Oh, yeah. It'll arrange itself, eh,' Yehune remarked.

'No, it won't. I wish I knew, could work out exactly... I need a little thingy. One of those...'

'OK, OK. When are you going to finish that Coke or whatever it is and let me out to Peking Road?'

'Not a Coke. Some disgusting iced tea thing. One of those...'

'Eat at Fairwoods Fast Foods tonight?'

'Oh no, not again. How 'bout looking for a real Chinese place, probably won't cost as much either? ... A calculator.'

'A *calculator*. For God's sake, is that all? You're in Hong Kong.'

Shopping was the other serious business in hand, in Yehune's view at least; and he could never quite take Mel's voice of prudence seriously, though it had become the one subject his friend was able to rise to his normal levels of vehemence about. They had about $1200 NZ for the whole trip, originally the money from the sale of their motorcycles in the pre-Sydney era – a sum of which Yehune's part had been three-quarters squandered, Mel's a little bit increased in the meantime. They'd sat down and worked it out, assuming limited amounts of time in each country, and relying completely on their friend Cas's estimates of daily expenditure plus some Trans-Siberian prices they got out of a pamphlet. Of course, Cas had done the trip around May of the same year, which was the Northern Hemisphere's spring; of course too, prices seemed to have jumped in the intervening five and a half months. But still – Yehune couldn't stop himself thinking – what was it all about? They were in Hong Kong, a stereo system was something you had to get, and as many Walkmans and alarm clocks and calculators as you could carry or freight ahead, at prices you'd never see in any Western country. Budgeting was OK. But in things like this you had to take the *long view*. Mel, now, he'd go sniffing around the Bureau de Change-s like a fucking IRS inspector, he was incapable of letting a penny go out of his pocket, and, hilarious irony, he couldn't even bring himself to buy the calculator he thought he needed so desperately. He'd dither around Ocean Terminal and Canton Road shopfronts and question terrier-faced young salespersons for minutes at a time about this model or that, and whether their price was really to be considered their price, until they gave up on him and went off to sniff out better prey.

It did do one thing though; it woke him up. More than anything else, the money question managed to unplug him from that twilight world of his of tiny notes on bits of paper and language paperbacks and oceans of scribble in a green hardbacked notebook. Otherwise Mel might as well not have been there; he was no help in even the minor planning, bus-routes, eating places – to Yehune he stood like a black felt shock-absorber between him and the livingness of it all. And that, you might even say, was understandable. After all (he thought to himself, waiting in a queue, buying tickets, standing outside the slowly moving cages at the foot of the Peak), who'd made the decision to leave New Zealand? He had; he'd dictated their choice of moment, grilled the travel agents, even lumped his bike together with Mel's to make sure of getting him a sale.

And even Yehune was finding that the experience of the trip, especially all the extra activities, organisation, shopping, freighting, his standing brassily in the face of all the world's attempts to fuck them, forced him into a sliding mental state where no sort of interior contemplation was possible. An extra-time – slipping away under his feet, like the water of Waidoleiaa Harbour in the evening. He saw it, at that moment, as a crinkling surface of ricepaper impressed with Chinese scrawl. Rocking motion of seats under a roof, as pieces of the lit-up city seemed to break off towards him. Seeing pictures in the cryptic surface – thousands upon thousands of people sitting on newspapers eating lunch in a blocked-off road. In a subway tunnel, a glimpse of a prostrate beggar in rags. The scenes around him forever shifting, disappearing, changing, like an emptiness in which everything was sure to happen at least once...

and beside him (because now, as he thought it, they were slipping up in the cable car towards the heights), Mel, gazing out over the heads of pine trees, noting something down.

At least *he* had time to pursue his... what, his thing, aspiration. Though he may not have had the slightest idea what the fuck was going on.

'Um... OK. But, would you mind – that one just up there, in the black case – no, above the orange box, could I just...?'

Yehune put in, 'How many places have we been to now?'

'Thanks, that's it. Does it have auto-power-off?'

'Shit, Mel, couldn't you just *buy* that thing?'

'Does it have an instruction sheet? Instructions? In – struct...'

'I mean, how much is it anyway?'

'I sometimes wonder if it's just the way we talk, you know... never really open our mouths. They sort of can't get a handle on it, it just comes out like a slurring – boneless – mumble to them.'

In an overlit ground-floor retail palace on a street off Nathan Road, Yehune found not much to lean against, little to see, nothing at all to do, while Mel harried the usually predatory salespeople for tiny bits of information about one pocket calculator or another, sending them on missions to find an expert or a better English speaker or the manufacturer's instructions, and missing them when they came back; that is, if they ever did come back, that particular tall fair-haired Westerner having been tagged as a hazard by the hunters of the Electronic Goods shelves. Yehune had long ceased to register the shapes and colours of blow-driers and home shaving kits, or, on the other side, small ghetto blasters graded up to mini-systems that were piled in a blocky arrangement like the Hong Kong skyscape; his mind was wandering, creating its own loops and inner commentaries on the past, the present, and the course of the Trip to come. He saw, vaguely, Jim, the other one of the three, following head-down after a stampede of muddy rugby players through a school corridor. He saw figures stumbling across a landscape of fire-flushed craterwork that distantly resembled the shelving of the shop... he caught again, for an instant (as Mel turned to address a person he thought was the salesperson, but who was only another shopper, though Asiatic in appearance and neatly dressed) – he caught that illusion of the elastic rope stretched invisibly from his own hand to the incorrigible Seuchar neck. Pulling him out. Pulling him out, getting him away, drawing him on... after. On after. ... In any case, how much could the damn thing be? About twelve dollars?

Mel said, 'Let's try over there. I think I saw the guy go through that door.'

'How much are we talking about, Mel? Twelve dollars?'

'The last one? Ah, 'bout that.' He glanced at Yehune with an expression of transparent cunning. '... But I want it for *eleven* dollars.'

A new salesperson was drawn in, after a bit of waiting around while he dealt with another customer, and Mel's process of rapid-fire questions followed by tortured indecision began all over again. Yehune started a game of looking at the other shoppers and trying to guess where they were from. A jostle of fat ladies spoke broad American, there were two young Brits in football shirts with sharp fox-noses, one Chinese face at least was *venerable*, hardly any specially *inscrutable*.... Mel was biting his nails, probably unconsciously, with the strain of the forces wrestling one way and then the other inside his skull. Buy; don't buy. Salesperson glanced at him, the companion, as if for a clue.

Yehune's eyes had fallen on a group of Chinese girls in possibly their mid-twenties, neat and dark-haired, heights varying around the five-foot mark, who were picking out electronic goods by the handful, joking and laughing. They had a kind of uniform on, thin black jackets trimmed with gold lamé. Their voices twittered out against the canned music, small-Chinese, something like birdsong. Their faces were uniformly beautiful, though some possibly less good-natured than others. Sure do pick 'em. Wonder what airline, that is if it is an airline....

Suddenly, in a neat twirl finishing with perfect poise, one of the girls had turned and was holding something out towards Mel. Yehune's eyes went to her face: wide, kind-looking, with eyes that seemed to bulge forward for the very slightness of the eyebrow-ridge.

She said in perfect English, 'You can borrow mine if you like.'

Mel looked down; she was holding out an expensive-looking sliver in a black leather case. Calculator.

Three of the girls twittered with laughter. Mel looked surprised, then made a gesture with his hands.

'No, please take it, it's no trouble,' said the girl. One of her friends was swaying, bending one way and another at hip level with her appreciation of the joke.

'It's OK. … I'm just trying to decide, you know,' said Mel lamely.

'Are you air hostesses?' Yehune asked the nearest girl with studied casualness. Inside, he was almost mooing with frustration. Silly bugger got action from nothing but standing round dithering, then didn't know what to do with it when he had it.

But the chance was gone, the game was over; she looked at him blankly. A shiver seemed to pass through the whole attractive school, as if they'd seen or intuited something; and a moment later they all fluttered away in another direction among the standing shelves.

It was later, far later that evening that Mel brought himself to the point of buying his calculator. Yehune showed no emotion. But all the way out and down to the fast food palace at the five-way traffic lights, he was asking himself what was stopping him jumping on the guy and mashing him.

Mel wrote in his diary:

Aus × 1.3014 = NZ   HK$ ÷ 3.8157744 = NZ   US × 2.0429 = NZ
US × 3.6849 = FEC   FEC ÷ 1.8174164 = NZ   (*real:* 1.79)

Not bad, this. It's got a little card with all the functions slipped into the cover. The rates they post are never what you get, I should maybe work out two lots of ratios, one based on the real no-bullshit amount of crinkly stuff they actually put into your hand. Only it'd vary of course depending what twinkle-eyed Shylock fleeced you last.

No sleep. Money change Hang Seng Bank $600HK, Hankow Rd branch. Swedes in the lift. Bus 2K to the station, waiting for it we saw an old workman on a site, ancient and emaciated, in the sweltering sun bending down to pick away half-heartedly at a hole, like that all day every day, seems kind of a waste of humanity, or is that how people are supposed to be? Social work-ethic. There y'are granddad, pick in your hand, job offer was there. They scuff hock into the pavement with a foot. Seem to produce an awful lot of phlegm, Chinese types, and get rid of it too, which is healthy. A whole sublanguage you can imagine, phatic communion, hawks and glottal grumbles, tonsils have it, spit right, spit left. You'd think.

Then rushing around looking for the train to Lo Wu. Hot, misted, sunny. $4.10 HK stamps, tried to get change and couldn't get the right amount, only put $1.60 on the card to Geoff. On the train, air conditioned, silent, downward-bearing, sword of heaven. Great super-squalid apt blocks. Rock walls. Chinese through the speakers. Suddenly a tunnel, everything black and a light – light – light flitting backwards. Past tower after filthy tower, housing for five million. Makes Chungking Mansions look like the Intercontinental Hilton. The shape of towerblocks ritzy forward-thinking and falling down around the living population, unmaintained, with macro-scars of discoloration and the leaves of hung washing. Faster through the tunnel – and faster. Bamboo scaffolding on concrete skull-shells, and suddenly, titanic glossy buildings: the latest. Tai Wai. To the right a hillside lush green dotted with hovels and blocks indiscriminately, cloud's bearing in now. Huger, greater, out of some Atlantean duck-dream, with the grey rock mountainside behind. She Tin. Green sticks like spears from the windows, to hang the washing on. Standards, people-flags. The mountains through mist up ahead, 'University Station': a city on the hill (could be the University?) High-roofed buildings under a lowering white-dark sky. Shanty-towns of concrete boxes, then estate, estate, estate.

Change HK $850.04 to FECs. Abacus. Rate per 100: 47.08 ~ 400.20.

23.4¥ FEC to Guangzhou.

God my Mandarin must be bad. You can't read a thing, it's all characters, as you might expect, and hundreds and hundreds of hungry-looking down-at-heel people in clothes all cut from the same length of cloth. This after 'Immigration', gaudily-dressed officials, going into rooms to fill out forms. Foreigners, Seamen and Overseas Chinese (and garbage-dump attendants, turds, criminals) all channelled one way for a Health Inspection. The rain pouring down. Walking miles through the mud with mobs of people pushing endlessly the other way. I keep going up to people asking where the trains leave from, Y points them out for me, I never get anything but a hand gesture or a quick babble in return. They don't even know what language I'm trying to speak. Just shows. Harder than you'd think to learn pronunciation from two phrasebooks and the memory of a Chinese professor talking back in the uni.

Now Y's learned the words and he's asking for me. 'Where, train, go, Guangzhou?' Even less result.

We found it eventually. Clearly posted on the wall, if you can read it. Contrast with the Hong Kong train, this is clattery, fazed, a carriage half full of bolted empty racks. We're strange beasts, no-one'll sit near us. Y's what? Gone to sleep? Outside, rice paddies, low hills, light-green stands of bamboo, their peculiar-looking cows and the yellow mud-brick houses. Wide coolie hats to keep the rain off. The mud's red and orange. There's a group of young guys a few seats ahead playing music as loud as they can, one of them tattooed all over his bare back. Looking around with a dangerous lipless face, skull-nosed, simian and alert. Nowhere to rest, not really. Flickering forms in heat, that catch you up like gorse bushes. You see yourself as you pass through them. Mud huts deserted in the bare green. And heading for what at the other end, a scattered square. Where do you go? Cas's letter. Greasy racchinose smells burn in through the windows. Guy's looking round, laughing. No air to hold us, log to sleep on, or corner of a room to call or that I always did call my own. But how can you believe being here? Got there. Cathay, not Pacific. Have to find somewhere to stay tonight, for not too many yuan. They always keep a different price for the foreigners.

I can remember sitting in the oldest of the Anglias with my father driving me to Maeraki Primary, seeing kerbs, at the age of God-knows-what. Kerbs, imprinted like speaking selves of themselves in the light and past the backwards window-frames. That's what this is. They tell you the beat of identity goes by the shifting of worlds around you, the Ontological. Ont. Onat. Seeing yourself as you go. So who was that that got onat the ferry and onat the runway and onat the porch, that stilled fledgling immaculacy, radiance before I knew it? The kerbs up at the top of Rosedale Rd, which were the vision beyond thinking or regret. Now where is it? Fresh. Here. Me. Lightfilled colourless single stab of purest inapprehensible silence in the word:

(interrupted)

How to Write a Story

Yehune couldn't work it out, he just couldn't work it out. Having caught the bug himself, having given up on sports talent and his early flair for maths and thrown all the weight of his aspirations behind that idle tendency he had to tinker with sounds and harmonies at the piano keyboard, having finally, in the last year of school and even more as their university life began, *agreed* with Mel, he couldn't bring himself to accept the guy's lack of any noticeable impetus. He didn't understand why he couldn't just pick up a pen and *do* it. It surely wasn't for lack of time. While Yehune started undergrad English, stuck it out for nine or ten months of the first year despite his parents' furious resistance, gave in and took Law by correspondence, let that gradually tail off while he did other things, looked into the job market, began an association with a garage-and-car-showroom and moved to a West Auckland flat, Mel did nothing but stick to his BA course; nor did it seem to cost him too much in the way of assiduous study. So baffled had Yehune been that he even began to turn out a few short pieces of prose himself, with something like the aim of showing old Mel how easy it could be if only you went about it the right way.

As far as music went, he thought he was doing well enough. He'd gained the standard piano diploma late in his seventh form year, and was feeling more and more at home in his own style of modern composition. So this writing wasn't something he *needed,* exactly, for himself; only he thought there was no harm in developing it as a kind of second string. And now, of course, he had the background – could remember texts he'd read, assignments he'd handed in, in that fleeting stub of an English course – despite his lack of any deeper interest in what a bunch of fogeys could have extruded onto pieces of paper in some era before the invention of the word processor.

He could remember; not with the legendary vagueness of the

far earlier image, but with precision, immediacy; sounding the horn of his old Chrysler Valiant in the tree-shadowed bit of a road behind Mel's parents' house. Or more a hut, you could call it, on a crumbling edge of the headland that divided Thompsons from Campbells Beach. Where they'd all lived, the Seuchars, until the mum's demise.

He saw, pointed out in the one-sided light of moon and stars, one broken-off statue stub, and a jagged edge of fibrolite at one end of the house wall.

Mel had come wavering out.

'Hey man. Where's Ange?'

'She's off up north. You coming?'

' 'Course. Where?'

'I dunno. Maeraki Valley?'

'Excellent, I'll just get... wait on a sec, I'll get us a couple of...'

There wasn't much in the look of that dark smudge in jeans and jacket trailing its way back to the house to remind Yehune of the image he kept in his mind of the same person long before, not long after his own arrival at Montgomery Secondary. He could call it back any time he liked, unchanged, though fudged a bit at the edges, creeping like an unfinalised emulsion or one of those trick-photography oil patterns they show on TV. It was the picture of a single boy, stooped and driving forwards, seen on one of the rear fields that descended in two broad steps towards the school's lower gate – someone built tall and thin, but bent over just then as if in expression of a furious purpose, all long arms and legs, shoes kicking back the grass, with only the rectangle of a bag to give any impression of a central bulk. He might have asked someone who it was; he didn't remember getting an answer. But that grey-draped vector had continued to impress him afterwards as the essence of fixation on a goal. There was someone who *really* wanted to get home. Later, he'd got to know who the boy was: a fellow fourth former by the name of Mel Seuchar; and after the incident of the shoulder bashing in their Geography class it had even happened that a tenuous connection sprang up between them....

Where was that *direction* now? He meant, then; when the dark clink of bottles signalled the return of Mel from the house; a light at the side went on and then off again.

Not long afterwards, a space was cleared in the mess of junk beside him, the car door crunched shut, and they were cruising noisily down Clifftop Drive towards the Coast Road.

'Would have come on the Triumph,' Yehune explained, 'but you said the Laverda's…'

' "The Laverda's not going." '

'Yeah… anyway… I've never believed in drinking and motorcycling too much myself.'

'Both dangerous and antisocial.'

'Fuckin' A. You could break a rabbit's neck.'

Up beyond the main artery of Westborough Road was a long, gentle decline, usually called the Maeraki Valley, which in those days was covered with farmland and scrub forest and some of the best loose-hooning tracks you could skid a car around. It was one of the places they went to when they wanted a way of escaping from their lives or courses. Yehune retained memories from that actual occasion; a quick image of Mel wrestling with the bottle-opener down on the car floor; and later, a time when they must have stopped – where trees soughed mightily, pine branches moved against the vast trough of the sky.

They talked of many things. Among them, Yehune:

'Got a letter back from *Solilquooz*.'

'Uh?'

'You know. About the story I sent in?'

'Oh, right. They accept it?'

'Ah, well, not as such, but the guy wrote quite a lot of garbage back, must've really put his back into it. Almost better than an acceptance.'

'Right. … You got it there?'

There was a pause, in which Mel adjusted the top-of-windscreen light and tried to screw himself into a position in which he could make out words.

'I mean, you liked that one, didn't you? I called it "Spooning at the Sea".'

'Ah, can't remember if I've… I can remember one about a duck.'

'Fuck, man. That's the first one I wrote, "The Duck That Wasn't". It's not *about* a duck.'

'Oh, right. I seem to have remembered some duck though.'

'It's not totally *unrelated* to a duck. Mind you, there was a tern in one of the others, what was it, "Honest Men". That's a sort of water-bird as well.'

'… This looks promising.'

'But you didn't like it. The story.'

'Yeah, I like 'em all,' Mel had said lightly, handing the scrunched paper back to Yehune.

'So – hey' he couldn't restrain himself from delivering, '– when are you going to get going and produce a few of your own?'

'Oh, I dunno. … I did do one.'

'You never showed me anything.'

'Na, well… I have been, you know, working on something.'

'Oh yeah?'

They drank again, by turns, setting their lips to the bottle and sloshing upwards, swearing loudly when anything spilled, each screwing his fingers beforehand around the bottle-mouth in a token attempt at hygiene.

Yehune felt unsatisfied with the vague answers he was getting. He said,

'Shit man, I dunno. It's not like it's all that hard. I've shown you how you go about it. You get hold of copies of all the main magazines, preferably a few issues of each, then work out which ones you're going to target. Write a couple of stories for each, in some sort of area you think might tickle their gonads. Send 'em off. Start collecting a few "We regret to inform you"-s.'

'Have to get some more of this Waimauku cider. The shop stuff's fucked.'

'I'll go on the bike some time. Laverda's not going.'

'Could zip over in the car, I s'pose. – Na, fuck it, that'd defeat the purpose.'

'… I mean, the great thing is, you can put down *anything*. It's not like there's anyone standing there timing you with a stopwatch.'

'That's the great thing,' Mel repeated, but without commitment, not as if he was really saying it. 'What about all your piano stuff? How's that going?'

'Not much. I find… it's weird.' Yehune, crouching on the seat, sent his forearm back to support his neck on a tilt, 'I only seem to be able to do one or the other.'

Despite all that encouragement, it had never really happened that Mel got down to it. The two small fragments of open-ended narrative he came out with in the end seemed to have been written less for any purpose of his own than in some kind of effort to get Yehune to stop. He hadn't sent them off anywhere, had seemed reluctant even to mention them after Yehune had been allowed to look at them once (and they were *different*, Yehune had to admit, in a way that made him wonder what or how or why or whether he'd been going about it all wrong)…. But it wasn't till some time later that year that he woke up to the idea that Mel, against everything he'd always assumed, in fact against what everybody in Maeraki openly talked about, didn't see himself as wanting to be a *writer*. What he *did* want – it was too hopelessly fragmented, disturbed, self-contradictory, never mentioned except in the unguarded moments when the dizzy bastard was more than three-quarters drunk and well on his way to collapse, to define exactly. More than that, it fluctuated wildly at different times. But basically,

(… and here the scene shifted, memory after memory in a series of loops unfolded to represent to him the common room of his own shared West Auckland flat, a TV blazing back over their gentian-coloured Bremworth pictures from a black-and-white vampire movie) …

'I heard of someone,' Yehune's voice was saying, in a tone more subdued than usual, 'I heard of someone – woman I think she was – who went to sleep… when she woke up, there was all this stuff she'd written down… turned out to be music by Beethoven, you know, but nothing Beethoven'd ever actually written…'

'Oh right. Spirit dictation.'

'Yeah… yeah. You think that really… I mean, has that ever, something like it ever happened to you?'

Mel had looked at him curiously. He could still remember the look of that face, those eyes, reprinted like a stamp in and through the flickering TV lines.

'Not all that much music paper lying round our house.'

After a few more swallows, Yehune had taken it up again, '... So when are you going to haul off and write something else, dog?'

'Oh, OK.' Mel had turned stretching for something out of the rubbish stacked on the seat of the hairy old sofa that neither of them sat on. 'Gi's the back of that envelope... I'll do it now.'

But the upshot had been that he hadn't left it there, had worked his way up by degrees to the full ramble, a bit later on, while vampire lovers attended to each other onscreen,

'I'm not going to be, you know, what you'd call a *writer*.'

'Not what you'd... not what I'd... not what?'

'Not what,' they'd repeated back and forward, in different tones of voice, milking the expression for every drop of inanity.

'Na... writing's, black on white, just words.'

'OK. Just words. Better words than not-words, though, wouldn't you say?'

'By hell, you bring up some perplexing issues.'

'Ah, fuggoff.'

But Mel had seemed to gather what faculties he had, and given Yehune the first inkling of something almost as peculiar as their state of mind at the time (which was built on large quantities of freezing cider over a foundation of gin),

'I mean, I can see something... a person might want to *do*, I s'pose, but it's all mixed up. I can see it sometimes – just now. There. It's a great big... bellying... drum-tight sort of sail, spiring up out of my head and just barely higher than the telegraph poles when I go walking down to Thompsons Beach... comes out of my backbone, might. Yeah. A backbone extrusion. Kind of sewn together out of patches and bits of stuff, scraps of this and that, comic-book divisions, divisual sort of... what's it. Zivisual. Coming out in clumps of pictures. Gotta have the words and the other thing, something. Whatever the hell, and it might be, picitorial. Picinuary. Pici-ninny...'

'Ah, Mel. Not quite sure what the fuck you're talking about, you stopped speaking English a while ago.'

'English, that's just it, this can't be *English,* you know? There's a huge triangular sail-piece thrusting up and fingering all over the sky, can't get rid of it, cruises along with me, keeps it blowing, 's all built up out of bits of patchwood, mood, thought, memory... keeps pace. That's what it is I thought I might maybe gonna do. One day. Can't see exactly how...'

'So it's a sail. And you talk about something...'

'Some thing thing thing thing thing.'

'Something outside yourself, you mean?'

'Outside; well, 's outside, but 's inside, you know? I'm not sure yet, you get painters who work with mud on cardboard or scratched marks in the sand on the beach. I just haven't found... a combination.'

'A *combination.*'

'Any more of this cold.'

'I've... completely lost me.'

'I mean, in the fridge.'

'Oh! Right. Got two more in the freezer, probably congealed about five minutes ago when you were blowing to the moon.'

That was all it amounted to. Though they didn't mention it often after that, though it was far from becoming any sort of talking-point between them, the odd reference by Mel at around that time and later, right up to the beginning of his mum's illness, tended to confirm it: instead of aspiring to any recognisable occupation, the sandy-haired Aucklander got along on that weird personal delusion he called 'the Sail' – an image no doubt suggested by all the broken-down sailing tackle that had lain scattered at various times around and under the Seuchars' house. Disappointing as that answer might have been, Yehune at least had profited by his short dip into the forces directing someone else's head – he'd managed to master a practical approach to knocking out a short piece of prose. Written, if he counted them all up, fourteen of them by the time they both left the country, though so far none of them had been accepted by a magazine. Which was twelve more than Mel had done. So his friend's problem remained his own; one way in which the minds of the two of them certainly did work differently. But in any case, Yehune decided, you had to be generous – who could say but what that rising mainsail of tacked-together snips and fudges, webless accompanying spanker, might turn out to be productive for old Mel in some way? Though to himself it might seem a shaky enough thing to catch the wind with.

What Happened in Guangzhou

From the rectilinear two-stepped plinth under the second of two poles on the crowded square outside Guangzhou Railway Station, panning slowly right to left – Sanyo; Seiko; squat buildings flanking the main road; long overhead bridge soars and declines like the concrete neck of a swan; the people, people everywhere in single-coloured suits with a bias to the dark blue; bicycles swooping to and fro like black mechanic flocks of birds; a plane moans overhead, causing a quick skip and refocus of the picture; now looking back again, past minibuses and on to sparser ground; tall fences, walkways, fences again; an empty stretch of asphalt blanched with dust. C. A. A. C. C. I. T. S., as far to the left as you can go. Begin again. And begin again. Oh Gong-jow, Gong-jow, how I love your fucking station square. ... Ahead and three yards to the right of him, a stack of wooden pallets more than head-high. Behind that, the bicycle-hire man inexhaustibly jabbering, repeating and repeating certain syllables.

Single dropped chopstick down on the coarse asphalt. Cracked in places. ... Lacked in paces. ... Unreal.

He was looking at two stumps of blue-clad leg ending suddenly at the knee. His own hand holding a matchbox: Beehive. And the stick of a fag, unlit, grown indistinct as it drew in under the arches of his eyes.

He couldn't bring himself to credit this. Who could have expected it? That it would be *Mel* who stood up, bulging at the breast and covered in spikes, armed with two newsprint Mandarin phrasebooks, and went into battle to resuscitate their dying adventure. Not himself; Mel. That was what got to him. Could get to anyone, stay long enough out here. While Yehune Trent, the man who got things done, was left to cool his heels by one of these two featureless Poles of Future Progress and Prosperity, looking after the packs.

Give it up, man. Pull back, throat open, for the comforting cool-blue stream right down into the lungs. Watching the red glow eat back through brushwood; a double halo for the end of your nose.

The whole thing had begun with their arrival in Gong (Yehune had never even tried to pronounce it with the sort of exaggerated voice whine Mel did, *Guuuu*-ang, Ge-*eeaaaung*; nor were they apparently allowed to call it Canton), where nothing could be seen but a frantic and buzzing crowd of people stretching away into the far distance; with occasionally, bobbing over the sea of heads, the topknot of an isolated Westerner. Though signs were everywhere, they'd of course had no way of knowing where to go. But a determined hunting down of some of those Caucasian-looking people had left them with two pieces of news: there was a backpackers' hostel across the road from the White Swan Hotel; and there'd be no getting out of Gong for two weeks at least because of the world-famous Chinese Commodities Export Fair, which was just then in its sober but very, very crowded full swing. How could they have known that? Yehune wondered, pulling again nervously, restlessly at his fag – for two babe-in-the-wood New Zealanders unbothered by travel agents, never having heard of that or any other Chinese trade fair, and lacking even the budget guidebook everyone carried with them, bulky as two bricks and put out by a company called Orbital Stone, stuff like that was something you found out when you got there. He remembered the Hueffer travel agent: 'You can't just go up to Communist China and knock on the door.' Though his own reaction back in Maeraki had been a determination to do just that and fuck his eyes, thus saving them about two thirds of the price, it was just now that he began to understand there might be some inconvenience involved. Like the nights in an unventilated hostel where the arguments about whose bed was which were just getting going at about two a.m. Like the three long, dragging days in which the two of them had used every ounce of their persistence and cunning to buy or beg a way out of there, haunting the overcrowded station, badgering the snooty white-shirts of the C. I. T. S., trying and trying again for ticket office number nine, which was where foreigners bought their tickets, and which seemed to be the only ticket window that was permanently, hopelessly, dustily closed. Getting any English-speaking person they could find to translate the signs for them, 'Trains Full', 'Standing Room Only', 'These Services Cancelled' – and especially in Mel's case, worrying, tapping figures into his calculator, wondering whether there was any way at all they could find a passage, by oxcart or agricultural tricycle if they had to, because, as he stated often to the world at large, they couldn't afford to spend two weeks in Gu-*uaauuung*-jow.

In the end, in pure desperation and not really knowing the score, Yehune had managed to wait his way to the head of a queue and pay the foreigners' prices for what they had: two 'hard seat' tickets to Beijing, leaving on Thursday at eight p.m. for the thirty-six hour trip. Only a bit later did he fully realise what sort of trip it was likely to be. The Orbital Stone book (which a Scandinavian girl from the dorm next door obligingly lent to him) pronounced anyone technically insane who would think of travelling *long-distance* standing up in the fugged, stifling, ever-harassed space between other people's elbows where they smoked and fought and were flung from side to side with every judder of the carriage, and spat a collective goop-ocean onto the floor, and took every opportunity to display their hostility to one not of themselves; while what seats there were were occupied in a rota strictly excluding all non-citizens of the People's Republic. That, for thirty-six hours… with no sleep, no rest, no surcease from battering, and not even a free patch of the evilly-stinking floor to sit down on for a moment – Yehune could see it – was going to be an experience. The girl kindly explained to him that what he wanted was a *hard sleeper*, which to be fair was exactly what he'd been trying to get hold of ever since he got to Gong; she also gave him the fruits of her wisdom on the Chinese social question, theorised on the general rise in income which just at that time was making it possible for ordinary people to travel in their own country; and revealed the existence of a *soft sleeper* as well, more comfortable, and ideal for visiting foreign dignitaries or Texan oil millionaires or anyone with far more money than they had a use for. But Yehune was putting the finishing touches to his pack – organising Mel to catch bus 5 again – so they had to run.

Was that Mel, up there ahead? … Could be. He'd caught the blue of a jacket, the shape of someone taller, a bit slumped at the shoulders ... hidden at moments by bicycles. Earnestly motioning to someone out of sight. The next moment, two boys carrying four wooden cages suspended from a long pole over their shoulders moved right into the way. Identification uncertain. There was a frantic twittering of small birds; now the cages had been dropped near him and a boy had parked his bum on one of them. Mel? Gone by now. Ought to be over just about there... no, there, by the rock... in conference with a certain Mandarin-speaking black market racketeer. Laying their plots, tying down details, agreeing mutual safeguards against a double-cross. Mel. You just wouldn't believe it.

Half-heartedly, he turned his head back towards the station building to check the time. A well-knit girl flashed past his eye. At the same moment the boy on the cage started banging viciously on the upper slats, shouting out something to the crammed-together birdlife inside, *Yong yong yong yong yong yong yong* – shut up in there; give up and die. That whicker of high-pitched racket distracted Yehune; his eye went trailing off after the girl. (Fag was shorter now, burning near the lips.) She looked oblivious, clean-living, with the fresh-faced integrity of the groups of heroic workers depicted on the FEC bills. ... World alternative. ... Collective struggle. ... Mel there with them, grown to hero size.

On this, the Thursday, the last day before their ordeal, they'd paid their hostel bill and then spent an unpromising morning trying desperately to swap their hard seat tickets for anything else at all. Yehune had even gone to the C. I. T. S. with his Visa card, prepared to put himself into debt for the price of two soft sleepers; but they'd informed him (in their perfect, accentless, always completely unhelpful English) that all exchanges had to be made at the station, and anyway they didn't take Visa. Mel had had his face sunk deep in his phrasebooks – just a few degrees worse than useless. Because by then, it seemed, that towering brain had managed to spot the fallacy of his assumption that everything would change to the National Language as soon as they crossed the border. In fact, given that they were in Guuaaanng-jou or *Canton,* mightn't it be possible that everyone was still talking *Cantonese,* like back in Hong Kong?

That had been a bit astonishing to Yehune. Given that close study of the pronunciation – that practice mouthing – those syllables he'd been forced to learn, 'Where, train, go, Gong-jow?' and reel off to passers-by… but, there it was. A day or two before, Mel had presented his new idea to Yehune with a sort of contained inner fury, a glow of self-vindication – so *that* was why no-one had bloodywell understood him.

Yehune's response might have been a bit stony. Perversely, he couldn't see it as proof of his friend's sound grasp of the whole Chinese language question; rather the opposite.

They'd bought lunch, two cheap foam boxes of rice and bony meat, and sat on the plinth under the pole beside their packs to eat it. There was nothing doing in Gong-jow station square. Or, you might say, all too much. Every now and again a massive 1930s-looking black automobile would bear down at full speed on the mass of people and bicycles, insistently parping its horn: get out of the way or get crushed. It was impressive how people did, usually, manage to get out of the way, given that there was nowhere to go. Only twice now in Gong had he seen bloody accidents involving bikes under a motor vehicle. He'd tried to talk to Mel, but Mel was working away at his words again. Everything was wearily imprinted, move as it might; there were the concrete overbridge, the squat and unimpressive buildings, the bike-riders' feet that cycled slowly, slowly, seen through others, meshing and morphing into strange collective shapes.

The two Westerners happened to occupy one face of a general resting-point. Young people, blue- or orange-clad, would constantly sit down and stand up and hold long conversations on the plinth steps. Birds would streak by, shrieking, vying with the car horns. There was the constant underlying jingle of bicycle bells; something you didn't even notice after the first day or two. A slight man shifted in his place on one of the perpendicular edges, crowding Mel's book elbow. Mel must have looked up.

Next, the man had addressed him with a phrase that sounded like, 'N'how'.

Mel took up, 'N'how.'

And so they kept on for what seemed a considerable time, 'how'ing back and forth like a couple of Red Indians.

Some far more laboured gibberish followed. Yehune started to get impatient, seeing how much time his zoned-out companion had for chatting to total strangers.

Until Mel had turned and said,

'This guy's just asked if we want to buy two hard sleeper tickets to Beijing.'

Later, given leisure to think, Yehune supposed the correct answer would have been 'Are you *sure?*' That is, are you sure he hasn't just told you how much he admires your punk-look army bag? His respect for Mel's attainments in *pu-tong*-whatsit or the National Language after about four hours of looking at a phrasebook was admittedly at a low point; and what was more, hard sleeper tickets were clearly on Mel's mind. When you thought about it, how likely was it that anyone would suddenly plonk himself down beside two Westerners in a station square and start talking to them in Mandarin? The whole thing was nothing but a matchstick castle of shaky suppositions. But, then, to set against that, there was the logic of the scam itself, which Mel picked up bit by bit and retailed to Yehune across the plinth-side....

By official decree, foreigners had to pay a good deal more for their tickets. Therefore, if a genuine Chinese person went up and bought a ticket, at *his* price, and sold it on to a foreigner at a mark-up, the Chinese would make on the deal, and even the foreigner would end up getting the ticket at a discount. It was so blindingly self-evident that Yehune even wondered for a moment whether it had been built into the laws, whether those polite shinybums in the C. I. T. S. had it all under control and received a regular cut... but no. 'Course not. Unthinkable. They were the Chinese Government.

So it was that instinctive inner acknowledgment, the 'that'll be how it works', that in the end made Yehune agree to let Mel take off with the tout (who was thin-faced, with a tiny black moustache, and had a permanent twist to his body) for the first of several stages of the deal. He himself stayed back to keep an eye on their things. The tickets still had to be bought from the station. Mel had already tried his contact in every other language he knew, but Mandarin was the only one they had in common; in fact, Yehune learned afterwards, the tout had even commented on their good luck, apparently dropping something like, 'No-one round here speaks it.' So that was how it happened that it was the dynamic one, the Trent himself, who'd sat watching them move away towards a corner of the station building, strangely aware of his own uselessness like a kind of added physical weight. The stump of an amputated limb. Someone who – goddamn! – hadn't even studied a Mandarin phrasebook.

A little bit after that, he started to take out and review the very good reasons he had for worrying.

He looked down at the fag-butt. Gnawed, mate. Better work on your lip skills. Again and again, he asked himself whether there was anything he could be doing with the time. But no. Wait. Do nothing. If there was anything the Yehune physical and emotional setup was badly adapted to, it was inactivity. Single points in the scene in front of him expanded monolithically when he forgot to move his eyes off them, suffusing visible China with their own especial shape and colour. Then shrank just as quickly into specks unimaginably small. His thoughts seemed to loop out strangely, and out again; following nearly the same chain of thinking to a conclusion, then, for lack of anything else to do, starting off at the beginning again. ... Old Mel. At some point, either ten or twenty minutes since they'd left (but time had lost reality, short and long durations mingled in a confusing way), Yehune thought he'd identified Mel and his new friend, crossing the square to a point where bikes and crowds and a minibus blocked them again. Chatting, or so it seemed. Now, you wouldn't have thought anyone could actually *chat* in a language he'd studied for four hours out of a phrasebook; even that initial 'N'how', Yehune thought, must have used up a large proportion of Mel's vocabulary. That was one thing to worry about. The second, though, was worse....

He allowed a picture to form in him of the Seuchar clifftop house, or fibrolite hut, an extravagant display of white plaster statuary standing or lying around it. Inside was a wall-to-ceiling crush of every book ever written by man, in stacks where the shelves wouldn't hold them, and a bit of run-down furniture. Mel – he just wasn't the one to shine in a scenario involving action. For him to bring off an operation requiring alertness and cunning and sensitivity to a possible swindle, illegally, in broad daylight in a very foreign country, for *Mel* to do that, Mel….

Birds atwitter broke into the run of his thoughts. Brassy music had been building in the square, as something like a parade disturbed the crowds. Yehune held his eyes to the ground. His friend's dropped chopstick. A clutter of fag-ends, including three of his own. … And what was more, he fretted, how in hell was the guy going to work out what they were saying; at what point was he going to decide to hand over real money; how could Mel be expected to recognise a hard sleeper ticket to Beijing if he saw one…?

Three flags ran ahead; then came a group of marching men in pseudo-military green uniforms, and a block of young women following in contrasting yellow. When he thought about it, it was the most *unreal* thing he'd seen that day. Even a car, unprecedentedly, was forced to slow to a stop, honking all the time, to allow the whole sweeping, articulated mass of them to pass. It was incredible to him that they could find a way through. But he had to admit, the crowd had got sparser at that point of the afternoon. Involuntarily, he glanced behind him at the huge dinner-plate clock on the station-front. If there were hands on it, he could never remember afterwards where they'd been. He forced himself not to turn and look again; nor did he pull his sleeve back over his wrist. How long… how long, he kept wondering, did this have to go on? He fumbled for a fag, for matches, then realised there was one already in his mouth. So he dropped his head again. Fixated on details. Chinese sweet-papers there by the cracks of the asphalt among the dropped cigarette-ends. Mel's foam box, a fuzzed near foreground, and the chopstick lying down there among flittering specks of black. The time… it bared you somehow. Time, and anxiety, and the cool blue-tinted smoke. Nothing could be real about this. What had made it? Those were flies, little crawling specks of mischief among the lolly-papers. What are they? Read the Chinese characters. Gobstoppers, fizzee-mates, wogglies. With a harsh violence of panicked noise, the bird-cage was suddenly lifted away from beside him. Opened you up… to other influences. Tickle-legs of something. Mel's doing it, Mel's all right. Far away mate, nothing to do with. *Bzzt. Bjjaauut.* And the black car finally surged its engine apoplectically, built up speed, and charged away like a huge black cigar-shape awash with the surreal echoes of old noise….

The flies. He saw the flies. Dirty little bastards. And – *aaachd aaaaauuull* there was a picture or something sensation right in the blocked confines of what he'd thought he'd *Ah no ah-ah*

Eeaaeeeiiiikkkaadii aaachd aaaaauuull into my house, for the house, into my house; on the antitragus pauses vibrating fast at the halteres stalked drumsticks, beating and beating at the mesothorax; the head (holoptic, mobile) poking in at the external meatus that opens from the concha, bears the whisks of scape and pedicel and flagellum, and *Aaaaiiaaaauunnntdd* and it's heading now for the fibrocartilaginous tunnel and looking as it mops with the great exaggerated sponge of its labella for the cerumen sweated out of bone walls and tripping with the five-segmented tarsus at the inner deep sock headfast with the head into the head, I FU- it's going for the house with my tympanic membrane's up in the attic and the stirrup's in an oval window, secret, intent, advancing, -UU- seeking for the vestibule semicircular canals and cochlea of the inner ear but first descend -AAU- where the roof comes down ahead and is it *Cyclorrhapha* and of that the *Calypterae* and of that the *Muscidae* -UULLK- and there because no hypopleural bristles chitinous plate on the side of the thorax though bristly enough anyway with extensible proboscis and the crinkling wing with veins in sweeping abstract I oh Jeezuzz -KKKKK to the tympanic membrane door's closed scratches and scratches at the drumskin could it conceivably be a little *musca domestica* AWAWEEEIIIIGH *I'll fucking no get out of me* you bastard little creeping jeezling Nazi Satan garbage-sucker

---

He must have flung himself off the concrete step, knocking the foam box away, and tossed his head violently from side to side, then thumped hard with the heel of his hand at his left ear while awkwardly holding the right one down towards the asphalt. Still feeling it, danced in a small circle. Roaring and swearing all the while, get *out,* get out, out, out. – Look at that, Ling Wu. I can see, Yin. Foreign devil, acting like a fool. – With an extreme galvanic collusion of all his forces, Yehune did everything he could think of at once to dislodge the unspeakable invader from his ear.

At the end of which (he saw later the packs were still there, a bit out of position; a dozen people at least had gathered to watch the show) –

something did actually seem to leave him; ascending without haste above his head like a floating light.

E-Block Floor

School was long, it was more than life-long – a morass of oceanic time slowed almost to a standstill, to be lived out by each young sensibility between grimy walls of tedium and constraint. Alone, hardly anyone could have endured it. But by a side-effect of the system (probably something to do with limited space for classrooms and money for teachers' salaries), a large number of inmates were forced in on top of each other. The result was a kind of melting-pot of free association, where the ideas of friendship and acquaintanceship were pushed to a limit of flexibility, where you might find yourself talking to the most unlikely people on the basis of nothing but who happened to be there at the time. And so, Yehune remembered Mel – at first no more than a grey image of thrusting purpose on one of the lower fields, then labelled as a swot by rumour; and later (after the moment in Hodgey's Geography class when the Trent shoulder had felt the sudden impact of his fist), allowed to develop some of the detailing of an actual person. He had features, if you cared to notice them: the eyes close together and let down by the stub of a nose, a prominent jaw something like the frame of a bedstead tipped outwards from the general contours of the junkyard, or face. Hair clipped at back and sides that was the colour of dirty honey in the sunshine, darker under clouds or rain. He had a way of looking straight down out of a height, real or imaginary. As the months drew on into summer he kept the winter uniform of grey woollen shorts as long as he could, and was known to wear a jacket on the most scorching days, possibly from force of habit. Also, he did well at English and the Arts. That was something Yehune spotted as an opportunity even back in those early fourth-form days; he managed to set up a trade, his own maths answers for the odd poncey-sounding essay, as part of his struggle to gain any sort of advantage in the war of marks.

The arrangement dropped off soon enough. But it wasn't what was important. The truth was that it was just such interactions, cross-pollinations between one view of life and another – links broken and renewed, it might be, over the course of years that seemed to expand into half-forgotten ages of the world – Fourth Form, Fifth Form, Sixth Form – that could end up changing the whole tendency of a person's thinking. It was in the conversations, rootless and undirected as they were, that a light might begin to shine... though it could be a deceptive light coming out of a very mistaken corner. Both Yehune and Mel, as it happened, had a lack of embarrassment about using words that looked like similarity to them. Mel was more abstract, unengaged; Yehune the conductor or impresario, especially if there were a lot of other people around. Words flowed, ideas expanded, and their ignorance gradually gained new books of commentary. Looking back, it would have been hard to chart any direction to it; only overall a light distortion might have been achieved, a lens effect in the nature of their separate thinking, that would never have come about in either without the influence of the other.

One of the greatest of the conversations, the one that stood out in Yehune's mind – subsuming the tendencies of all the others in itself, like an avatar of a thousand casual moments – took place one winter lunchtime on the scuffed and muddy floor of the corridor of E Block. He could remember the gloom of the setting, marks of violent collision along the walls, and the light coming in the door that led out onto the western or 'back' field. Mel was there, in the school jersey with two stripes at the neck, sitting cross-legged on the floor. The other one, Jim the Excise, was leaning in an uncomfortable-looking position between a heap of shin-guards and the corner of a radiator. There were probably lunchboxes, a waft of crushed tuna mingling with the stench of disinfectant from the toilet blocks – most of the details had flown away, replaced long ago by whatever he'd decided was most likely.

He did, though, vividly recall a sudden rush, a stampede of furious hunched bodies through the passageway, forcing the three of them to pack themselves back against the walls. A confusion of rugby boots; the voice of a male teacher bellowing high.

'What was all that about?' Jim asked.

Yehune (possibly resmoothing an edge of grease paper over a strayed sandwich):

'Practice. 5a prob'ly, they've got a match Friday afternoon,'

or at least those were the words he put back in his mouth, standing far outside it. He wasn't even sure whether the whole thing had fitted into a lunch hour; there may have been a free period attached to it. Nor could the talk itself be remembered very easily. It had wavered and twisted from this subject to that, moving effortlessly on the pivot of a word or phrase; it had guttered out, built up again from an accidental sentence, taken wrong turnings, followed no rules he could ever work out. Certain highlights stood out clearly, favourites of his memory not always in the most important places, which he thought he could have quoted word-for-word a long time afterwards. But more than words, or even subjects (Mel was an introducer of *subjects,* bringing up one area of study after another, some of which Yehune had never even heard of), he remembered the feel of it, a frustrated striving for expression... as he struggled to come to terms with something overriding in him, a vision of hopeless driven mediocrity. What was the purpose of it? he tried to ask. The *point* of school – if it even had a point.

Jim had the standard answer to that question,

'... to explain the world around us.'

Mel laughed loudly. 'You're shitting me.'

And Yehune, 'Na, think you got it wrong. Aren't they trying to make us apemen into useful citizens fit for their so-*ci*-ety?'

Mel said, 'Yeah – that's closer – actually I reckon they're just trying to keep us out from underfoot.'

'Then why give us maths and science and fucking languages and stuff?' Jim objected. 'Why *exams?*'

'Something to occupy the enemy. Exams are thin air, they're... I dunno... like "points" for your "house".'

'Oh, rubbish. You can say that easily enough, you breeze the bloody languages,' said Jim, who for some reason had been named The Excise. Then he added after a moment's silence,

' – Like it or not, they matter, the ones like School C do. We'll have to live with those marks all our lives.'

'Shit, eh?' joked Yehune. 'Might as well just limber up my toilet-cleaning brush and save myself the trouble.'

Mel, detached, turned a set of owllike eyes. 'You think they matter?'

That was the first inkling Yehune had that Mel Seuchar might have been as casually cynical about the whole school and even social setup as he was himself; and from then on, if he had any conscious purpose in it at all, it was to draw him out, to make him confess his leanings to the *revolutionary*.

As for himself, he needed to say something, but he didn't absolutely know what. And later on he got his opportunity. For some reason, the conversation had turned to their fathers; it might have been with some idea of judging the results of all this education. And their fathers all turned out to have shortcomings. Jim's was a dark-haired, beetle-browed automotive engineer, Mel's, a greying medical researcher who walked with a stick. Yehune's... well, he gave the impression of always being tired, but he must have posed and rationalised well enough on the floor of his midtown court.

'*Your* dad's OK,' Jim told him. 'That's an example, eh. He got good marks. Now he's got a good job. Makes a lot of money.'

Yehune said, 'My dad's fucking *what*? – You just look after your own family budget.'

Mel remarked vaguely, 'Dads. Usually steer clear.'

Then Yehune launched out, just halting his way,

'I was... you know, there was this time my dad took me to the stockyards. Ah, selling breeding heifers mostly, one by one, lot this and lot that – they might have brought up a bull.' Had there really been a bull? He couldn't remember, but saw the solid reeking hide and flesh of them, brown flanks trembling with each hooffall, and the auctioneer in shirtsleeves and the farmers and sales agents clustering against the bars of the fence. There might have been something bull-*like*? ... or what the fuck.

'They just... I mean... my mum wasn't there, I remember that, so it was just him and me. He kept sending me away to buy drinks. He asked for cups of tea, and I got Coke. He was always standing with some mate of his when I got back. ... God, I can remember him, you know, looking at me. He's just been talking to this old cobber, and sees me there, and he looks as if… as if he didn't know what to do with me, y'know?' He tried to hunt through his vocabulary for a description – half-knowing he wouldn't ever find it – still living in the country stench among the leathery sides of bull-flesh-mountains.

'Like… sheepish.'

Jim laughed exaggeratedly, '*Sheep*ish?'

'Oh fuck off.'

But now he made an effort to bring it to a conclusion, make some sort of larger point,

'I don't know, it's like, those cows, …they breed them, show them, and what for?… We know that well enough, for meat, they kill 'em. And my dad… I dunno…'

Jim put in, 'He's just out of place there. He's a barrister.'

'You don't get it.'

'Maybe *you* don't get it. Bet he was sent there by his firm, eh, for a whatsit, client? What's so weird about that?'

'OK, OK. Right, Jim.'

Jim the Excise was precise-minded enough, but couldn't be expected to get any message that was so abstract, indefinable, that its originator himself wasn't sure what he was driving at. So the current of things moved away. Again, it was hard to build it all around a strict chronology; Yehune might have been skipping whole sections before the next clear memory. By that time, Mel and Jim had got onto ground that was more familiar to them: arguing away about the relative merits of the art and science subjects.

On this occasion, Mel happened to take the position that arts and sciences weren't parallel in any way; therefore there couldn't be any rivalry. But Jim seemed to suspect that by that he meant the arts were so toweringly, celestially above him and his mere rooting in the physical that he didn't even present a threat. He started to get a bit heated. Yehune, in the meantime, only sat there, biding his time and trying to manage the flow.

The Excise, rubbing with his finger and thumb both sides of his nose (which was on the long side, descending to a bulb at the end):

'Try making any *money* with French-Russian.'

'Right. Get a good degree – get a good job – make money.'

'Yeah.'

'So it doesn't matter what you take, does it? Just what you get out of it in the end.'

'Ah…'

'Just remember. Study something you hate, you'll spend the rest of your life slogging your guts out at something you hate.'

'But I *like* Physics and Chemistry.'

'OK. And that gets you what, a BSc?'

'Fuck of a lot better than a BA, you ask me.'

'Maybe. They're both pretty good ways to end up unemployed. – You do what you do out of interest. Don't you, Y'une?'

Yehune wasn't really sure what the argument was about, and was only waiting for a chance to bend it in with his own thought processes.

'Dunno,' he said at random. 'I guess it's true that an arts ticket is hard to get a job with.'

Jim said, 'See?'

'But you do know the choice isn't just one or the other?'

'Yeah, it is. It's Arts V Sciences. Ask any teacher.'

'Shit,' Mel said softly. He'd been looking suspiciously at a sandwich, possibly trying to gauge the smell of it above the general context of disinfectant and dried mud. '… Neither of them are doing what they're pretending to be doing.'

Yehune saw that opening, and provoked him quickly, 'What d'you mean by that?'

That was when memory failed in him. It couldn't find a foothold in what Mel said next, the curves and swells of his casually-flung-out apologetic for his own way of thinking. A well-placed microphone might have picked up the actual words, but nothing Yehune could do left him with more than a lame paraphrase. Surely, though, it all turned on something like the question he'd asked himself: on the *point* of it all. Unless he'd missed something. It was all about the *reason* behind the seemingly spontaneous impulse in the academics to 'explain our world', the reason not in art, not in science, but from the point of view of some primally-conceived central unit, some single personal spark, which was pictured for some reason in the act of walking down the street, in the complex and radiant interweave of the fall of light and shadow, among trees and the angles of buildings. *That* was what Mel reckoned to be the point: the very thing that was usually ignored by the theory of any actual discipline, and that according to him was the ultimate motive behind what anyone ever did, including monkeying around with arts or sciences. That self... that pure – universe-inclusive – vast, unlanguaged gap. That was as far as Yehune understood him. It wasn't hard to see how such a point of view might put old Mel at odds with the assumptions behind school thinking.

'Where did you get that?' he asked, with his hand raised to hold off a stammering Jim.

He didn't get much of an answer. So he asked (breaking in on another comment by the scientist among the shin-guards),

'Whaddaya call it?'

'Nothing. ... Oh, well, the Aesthetic.'

'The Es-...'

The Aesthetic. First time Yehune had heard the word, which was to be taken then and ever after in its distorted sense, like most of what they discussed then and later, like the conceptions of 'existentialism' pieced together by Mel from the mystical writings of one Gerhard Schaeff, like his theories about the relation of metabolic speed to the optimism or pessimism of certain writers, footnotes about the Russian 'plodder' and 'superfluous man' (which Yehune privately dismissed under the category of 'Russian Background'); ignorant, tangential, and sometimes not without a sort of half-baked originality. It seemed that years before, Mel had happened to catch an old black-and-white documentary on television, all about a group of writers or artists at some time or other in some English university he couldn't remember the name of; people with slicked-down hair centrally parted and dressed in ribbon neckties, light cutaway coats; from which he'd gathered only one piece of actual information, the name this group had given themselves (– what group had it been? When, and why? Yehune was left without a footing in detail to save him from the same void of abstraction that had probably attracted

Mel): 'the Aesthetes'. He'd taken over that name, as a general noun, for his own Mel-ish way of looking at things.

Yehune listened, and tried to understand, though without committing himself either way. He had a large statement of his own to get into the air, and was only hampered by not knowing what it actually was.

So a bit later, he found himself involved in a second personal narrative, rambling on in search of a message:

'I saw a good thing once,' begins Yehune. 'Sort of short film... leadup to a movie, it was, in one of the theatres on Queen Street. Could've been the Classic?... Or the Odeon. Anyway, there were these rugby players, going in slow motion. All full colour and that. Down-country New Zealand teams they might've been; I couldn't recognise the jerseys. They were all playing rugby, eh, and in the background, they had this soft music, it was like a string quartet. It was like...'

The great sides of them, hulking thunderous fall and grind under weight of others falling. Slow-motion flap of the folds of a jowl in the moment of impact, tremulous under hoof. The bulls the bulls and the strings that cut them what was what was the

'... music – it was something you'd expect to hear on a film, y'know. But then after a while I sort of began to guess it was actually something real. You know, something... I kept wondering who it was who'd done it. Then right at the end it was shown up on the screen, "New Zealand Film Commission, music by Tschaikovsky."

'Tschaikovsky...' He shook his head, turning his finger and thumb on the air, somehow not able to grasp or come to terms with the fact that it had been Tschaikovsky.

(– Two boys and a girl were drawing up, either then or out of another time, past or future; clopping along the length of the shaded and narrow corridor, and just as they passed Yehune one of them murmured,

'Beethoven,'

then glanced quickly back, as if he hadn't really intended the owner of the tag to hear him. It was a nickname the pianist had picked up from the times he had to play at the school assembly. Eyes unfocussed, Yehune addressed the skinny grey-wool back – absently correcting the pronunciation, which had been 'beat' when it should have been '*bate*' – and repeated, gabbling it in his head in automatic litany,

'*Beet*-hoven, *Beet*-hoven, late-Beet, Beet-late.')

And that, of course, had nothing to do with anything. It was no more than a random impulse of the mind, what Jim would have called spontaneous electrical activity in the cortex. But that was how it was, trying to remember this; episodes were added or shifted around, de- or re-emphasised according to the need for a sort of coherence. As he was building it now, the Mel-view seemed to have got the upper hand; and so it wasn't hard to skip ahead to another moment, when he'd started to ask Mel about what he was thinking of doing himself:

'I mean… so, I guess you're going to do writing, are you?'

'Uh…?'

'You know, or whatever. Like that poem you put in the old Polly-whatsit.'

Surprisingly, Mel had sworn a few times and completely dried up, and from then on nothing could be got out of him about the whole subject, 'the Aesthetic', or any future intention he might or might not have, or the poem itself. It did exist though. Yehune could remember their English teacher maundering on about it for almost half a period in such detail that he'd actually found it a problem to blank it all out. For the record, or for the purposes of this narrative, we can state that a poetic effusion by Mel had in fact been included in an issue of the school magazine *Polymnia,* which for some reason or other wasn't looked on in the same way as all the usual metreless stuff by the other pupils in the same year. It was on the long side, 'free verse', if old Guillemot was to be believed. But there, a later memory came to the rescue. It was from some time after the E-Block floor; in the changing-rooms of the school swimming pool. That time, in a different mood entirely, Mel had rubbished the teacher's opinion with a contemptuous 'Shows how much he knows'. He'd gone so far as to admit lifting the loose six-beat line from a translation of the Odyssey he'd seen, though he had modernised the content… jazzed it up quite a bit, really. Something in his face that might have

111

hinted at self-satisfaction had made Yehune go straight at him with the nearest water-bearing object; a wet sponge or a scrubbing brush.

After which, the relations between them had mysteriously died down. They'd stayed practically at zero through the whole of their sixth form year. Yehune was occupied with his rugby, despairing of what had once seemed a bit of a talent for maths or calculation; and in any case the two of them were in different form classes. It wasn't until the later epochal moment in the University Student Union refectory that things had started up again, on a completely different basis this time.... Until then, know it or ignore it, the seeds had been laid in both of them, to die and fester in the silent soil of the undermind. Well, at least....

At least that was how it seemed to Yehune, a product of his summary, valid only for the moment he stood in. Another time he might have traced their talk in another direction entirely, forgotten whole aspects and replaced them with others, fixated on what happened to occur to him as important. It was like a cloud, unfixable, streaming through the long school corridor where light in split columns fanned away into the distance, a cloud that formed real edges at unexpected moments, sending crystal-clear formations to his eye. But school – school was dull and motionless. Here were clouds that billowed quickly. Rushing through a channel, making large inchoate gestures, moving, always moving, across the long continuous streamer of the formation of himself. And out of the cloudland – suddenly congealing – piling back now, in the footfall of the moment's crush,

he saw the return of the rugby players, maddened with adrenaline, covered in dirt and sweat, drumming and skidding through the corridor, while Yehune and Mel (Jim, for some reason, had gone) fell back with a practised motion to the sides of the walls – a hulking mass of brutes in streaked torn tee-shirts, hammering and hammering on the hard tile floor through darkness, flesh flanks a-tremble, driven by ones and clusters through into the courtyard on the other side. – And the lunch hour must have ended.

From Mel's diary:

… Falcon, not the Anglia, mum used to say faull-con, driving out on the Westborough Rd on the way home from Waiwera. Me and Geoff and Mandy in the back. Times when we weren't carsick. Sometimes you'd look over towards where the sun was setting and see the amazing cutout of hills against the light, in a shivered sudden frame, like a cartoon world. <u>Frost</u>, it made me think of, or somewhere where impossible stories could happen in the day-to-day. And past you go. Sound of the windscreen wipers when the clouds overhead burst down into rain, that sickmaking <u>wheek-wheek-wheek.</u> Driving on to tedium in the sub-guts. And building to all the colours of vomit in the prismed surface of drops running down the window glass. Time freezes on you. In the lip-lip from side to side over the grey plastic of the upholstery. And everything goes running past. Tackatack, tackatack, the rhythm of metal wheels over the joins of track, rice fields outside moving back against the solid state of hills. Which is the place you can never get to. But you see it, it lights something up in you… a fuse?

I've got the middle bunk, thank God. Everyone sits on the lower ones, and you can't look out the window from the upper. You lie there watching two pictures endlessly unreeling, head stuffed up, breathing through your mouth. The cold everyone catches in Guangzhou. Last night my bloody notebook-bag disappeared on me, I searched for about half an hour before I found it deep in the mattress of the bed below me behind a row of seated conversationalists. There's no-one but Chinese people in this whole carriage, they smoke and chatter to each other all day and blast music out on one tiny transistor radio they've got. Yehune's standing up at the window, braced himself, seems happy enough, smoking in self defence. They all accept us completely, meaning they ignore us. No-one questioned our tickets. It's only now I realise that those were <u>Chinese</u> people's hard sleeper tickets, 10pm train, foreigners leave at 8pm someone said, so it could be we're supposed to be not only in a different carriage but on a separate train. Luck! The amazing luck we must have had, to have got away with it at all.

For the money it cost, I can't see how our benefactors thought it was worth their while. Yehune prob. wouldn't believe it if he heard me saying that. Two hard sleepers to Beijing, 200¥ FEC. We paid 157.60 for the hard seats, and Yehune managed to get almost the whole lot back, 139.60, which means we paid 218.00 overall, which isn't far off the normal price, a touch below. HK$ ÷ 2.123136 = FEC. FEC ÷ 1.79 (real) = NZ.

My vocabulary in putonghua must be about 100 words, if that. I could never work out how to pronounce the consonants. So this guy with the bony face and the Hitler job must have really wanted to catch my attention. I kept repeating, Ni hao, ni hao, just to let him know that I was still interested. He went into this whole long speech about his family and how it happened that he spoke that language and what his sister was doing out in the country, the odd bit of which I sometimes thought I picked up, but I just gave back a word or two while frantically trying to work out the next functional sentence I was going to have to say. It was over by the rock when he came back and rejoined me with the merchandise that I had my bad moment. This gaping half-doltish stringbean guy suddenly appears over us while we're on the point of doing illicit deals in the open street, at the exact moment when there's a blast of military music and what looks like the Red Guard or whatever they have now crawling all over the station yard. Well, how the fuck do I know? He looked like a policeman or some military thing, with epaulettes and braid edges and all of it. He stands there smiling right at us, possibly drooling a bit over the stubble, just making his presence felt.

So I dry up, start talking about the weather if that, not saying much at all I suppose, and Mr Hitler's going on about something to do with foreign relations and how they helped to keep the wheels of economy turning, if I got it right. He wants to show me the things. I resist. Just sunning myself here. He gets a bit pissed off, wondering why I'm not keeping up my end. Dolt-boy's just standing there. Finally I lean in to the ticket-holder like a long-lost uncle and whisper one of those laboriously constructed gems: 'Who – he?'

'Oooh!' Light dawns. 'Pengyou! Pengyou!'

Which just happens to be one of the words I got from the back of the book, meaning friend. So he's a friend. Well, I'll say again, how the hell was I to know? I don't know what their prisons are like over here, but going on general likelihood I'd assume no better than ours and probably a whole shit-load worse. So we all have a good laugh, then he hands over the goods for me to check.

Which naturally Yehune took up with me later. How in the living fuck, says he, did I think I was going to tell what was a hard sleeper ticket to Beijing and what wasn't? The guy gives me two tiny rectangles of white cardboard, home-made looking and not especially presenting the appearance of tickets as we know them. But I look carefully at the characters: 4 spikes and a TV set with a hat on: Beijing. Man about to suicide and multiple people falling down cliffs: Guangzhou. 30/10, the date, 22:00 for the time, and most important, 'sleeper', a brick wall with a hoe beside it. Fine. I hand over 200¥ FEC, and thanks a lot. What else could I do? What other options, in particular, did we have?

Actually, old Yehune didn't make as much of it as I thought he would. He goes on for a while about how much cheaper it'd be for them to print up these bits of cardboard in any back room where there's a Chinese-language typewriter rather than bothering to buy real ones at the ticket office, and how given that Mr Moustache didn't exactly inspire confidence by his appearance we could safely assume he wasn't in it for anything except the money. But all in all he seemed far more concerned with some fly he reckoned had got into his ear. Me, I couldn't get that great drongo out of my head, hanging there like the clang of official nemesis in all the pseudo-military gear. Heighth of local fashion. He really shook me up, all right. Y might have thought I was going on about it a bit. But why – will somebody tell me why? these Guangdong bastards have to buy all their fucking clothes at the army surplus?

A Chinese Train

Some sweet flavour in the pervasive smoke put Yehune off the idea of trying one of theirs. He only hoped he'd brought enough Marlboros with him from Sydney. The interior of the carriage was stifling, everyone sprawled talking or eating on every possible surface. And sweet smoke, which seemed to rise up outside as well in great translucent masses – train fumes – into the measureless volumes of air behind them and overhead. Diesel, that'll be. Sprinkled into China. Good one. Or: Sinitally atomised. Yeah yeah. Words, they slip away. Gi's a keyboard any day. I mean, a *piano* keyboard – better get that straight. I notice keyboard's begun to mean a sort of toy polyphonic synthesiser.

Managing not to be too bothered by the fact that he was a walking resonator for his own culture, barging through what might have been ancient air, the long-fermenting sweetness of a contrary sense of things, Yehune turned round in the space between the fixed table and the (occupied) side of the bottom bunk.

He saw Mel stumbling towards him from the direction of the toilet.

'*Shit* – their toilets.'

'... You got it,' Yehune responded vaguely.

' 'Christ I can't smell a thing.'

Yehune swept his arm out expansively in the general direction of the window. A smoker with a wispy sort of beard just missed catching a hand, and fired out a few syllables.

'China,' said Yehune, generously presenting the whole view to his friend as if it was something he'd just created. Mel, in the moment before climbing up again to sink himself into his notebooks, looked out. Until then it might have appeared that he was beginning to be a little bit jaundiced about the whole place; now, he hesitated, and looked back with a sort of acquiescent half-smile.

It must have been somewhere between Changsha and Yue

Yang; they might have been seeing fields set at different levels, half-submerged spikes around the tiny haystacks. The smoker had looked somehow offended; he'd climbed to his feet and griped his way off towards the rear of the carriage. More words might have followed between the two – and actions – but they seemed colourless, ghosted in, when the moment, and that particular location on the track, had already run away behind them in the headlong flow.

a bababa a bababa a baba

fl

There was a ceaseless and resistless flow, and within it some remarkable continuity, tide and grain and blown beach old Yehune, stitched roughly, patched in across the musculature of the world's surface, *a brum-ba-ba,* like something like the diagram of a caveman picking up a flint superimposed on the half-circle bisected of the sundial of the earth's whole history, sky blue above and black above that and all the elliptical movements of heavenly bodies tracing out *a bum babum babum babum* the incredible logic of duration; who rattled aside by the endless battery of the ill-fitted sleeper carriage walls looked out a window, braced fag in hand between a bed pallet and the side of a table, stared out across the beaming sunwashed real and flat-earth-sculpted scene of actual paddy fields and the bent-backed men and women never looking up and behind them the tiny earthen huts, banks now and then towering above the swell of rivers, covered suddenly by an uncountable multitude filling a breach with single sandbags, some with those peculiar one-man two-handled agricultural machines, otherwise only the cattle to help with their strange horns, and villages suddenly bared to intimacy by the cut of the railway line in all the improbability of the detailed positions of their houses tallied bright with paint across the jut and swoop of a hillside; and that thing, the continuity, the ape-head, stretched relayed by time through point-pass point-pass of the shift of particles the matter's exchange and peaceable air's vibration, was thinking that anyway by God you had to say it was a far cry from Matamata. *A thaka-thunna a thaka-thunna a thaka-thunna a thaka-thunna a thaka-thunna...*

Beijing

It was the sting that woke him; some searing intolerable pinpoint somewhere deep in behind the right nostril, making him heave over to one side and bring his hand up to his face. He saw rucked greyish sheets, a diaphanous curtain of white in front of an already blurry window ledge. Bright light. No blinds. Another point of pain drilled into his head about an inch above the left eyebrow, and under that was the rawness in his throat. Oh shi – shi – shai – sheee – e – ... *Sheeeeff!!*

Shit. Qiao Yuan Hostel; die, die, die. Where's my fuckin'...?

Beijing burst in on him; an awareness fully-formed, before his hand groping along the side of the dormitory bed could come on his handkerchief. Beijing: a network of false streets, embassy facades, impossible directives, in a chilly wind of dust. The buses mobbed by thousands. Dustbowl parks, nearly empty, for which even citizens had to buy a ticket. Young females in uniform with their hands out, insistently whining an order, *'Pyow! Pyow!'*; bad maps, headache and frustration, under the glare, the depthless alloy-tinted glare of the sky. And it was all for visas, all for their tickets and visas – the complex official posturing of the Visa-dance.

The process of getting visas in Beijing had turned out to be a kind of sadistically-planned mouse-maze, everything having to be done in a particular order at breakneck speed during the brief opening hours of the embassies. As well as the visas, there were the various stages of ticket, which always had to come either before or after something else, according to whether you needed the ticket for the visa or the visa for the ticket, or the ticket for one visa for another visa for the ticket. If you were unlucky enough to take any extra time, or had it wasted for you, as it might be, by a longer queue than usual or an official on a coffee-break, the place could well close on you before you completed your application, which might delay the pickup of some emergency-express visa or other by as much as a week. That could put all the tickets or visas you already had out of date, and you'd have to start all over again minus a large chunk of your money. What was worse, the regulations changed every few months, so the information in any travel guide, though interesting as an anthropological case study, might not have very much to do with reality.

Three weeks, they'd been told – three weeks to go through all that. They'd budgeted for it. But partly as a result of Yehune's dynamism, partly from certain conditions of the dates on the tickets, they seemed to be on the point of doing it in one week. Fingers crossed. In fact, that morning they'd actually managed to get their East German and their Russian. Yehune had brought it off, not by studying guidebooks, but by talking to the people on the spot: there were travellers of every nationality at the Qiao Yuan Hostel, some of whom loved more than anything else to sound in-the-know. And yet, it had been far from easy. There was a sort of demon of mismatch and inattention ruling the Beijing air, a spirit you could almost see, sneering down at you through the cold two-dimensional sky. Failures, falls, Mel's dropped glove, the hostile glares of passers-by if you tried to ask them anything. The inability of the bicycle-hire people ever to hire out any bicycles. The representation on the map of the whole intricate warren of Sanlitun Compound as an empty purple square. The crowds at the bus stops, pushing and elbowing their way onto a bus that was as likely as not to break down after two blocks and disgorge them all without refund or apology into the street again. The apparent collapse of Mel's pretensions to any knowledge of *pu-tong*-whatsit, or of spirit or belief or whatever it was, coming right on the tail of that moment of linguistic heroism in Gong-jow. … The hassle. … The hassle.

On the other hand, it did seem to be working. So far, he meant. Snorting his nose, watching another gout of steam whiten the air around him from the vent directly under his bed, he found pictures from the recent battle coming back to him. Taking the 113. Getting lost in gridlike factory streets. Short snips of Mel's conversation in the teahouse that morning: 'Are you sorry…?'

Morning, this morning; then what's the time? Not bothering

with his glasses, he put his forearm close to his face to peer at his watch. – Four o'clock.

His sudden swing up out of the sheets had him swooning again, seeing, for a moment, crows with bloody heads perched in a line; a bath of indefinite colours... frail echoes of the dream he'd been having only a few moments before.

When he got his glasses on, three sinister-looking shapes leaning together became a group of Asiatic travellers sitting on another bed. Mel...? Nowhere. Above the specific pains in his throat and nose, he felt the headache rise triumphant.

– The steam-vent, that'll be. But why? Feels warm enough to me.

He glanced down across his physical self, dressed in all his crumpled outdoor clothes. The money belt made an uncomfortable bulge under the jut of his belly and to one side. Must've gone to sleep. Not like me, eh. ... When he looked down to check for the packs, he saw his own smaller bag there, but not Mel's. The map was lying there discarded, that useful Beijing map that must have been made when most of the streets were called something else.

Straight away, he could see it: Mel wandering alone through the wind-whipped caverns of Beijing without any sort of a map. He'd be sure to lose himself – get arrested – wander into the nearest Party Headquarters and insult the government. Old Mel. For God's, fucking....

As he thought it, he was already fumbling his boots on. With clean, deliberate movements, trying to ignore two simultaneous stabs of pain in his left forehead and mid-ear, he got to his feet – took one look back – and almost as an afterthought, bent to grab up the map.

Beijing teahouse. Newsprint for tablecloths. Mel had been sprawled on a chair on the other side of the table. Now, what was it exactly they'd been talking about? ...

'I reckon this is the right way to do it all right,' Yehune had said. 'We'll just have to watch our money, not eat in the dining car.' (Mel muttered noises that sounded like 'a-*gone* sto-*ran*'.) '...We'll take a whole sack of food from China. Tinned stuff, mandarins. Have to watch out it's not spoilable, Cas reckons they put it under an x-ray at the border.'

He was fixating, as usual, on the details of the thing, transactions, tariffs, ways and means. Dim specs went circulating in his head. The Trans-Manchuria was more expensive, but it left earlier, and saved you the Mongolian visa. Two photos, $18 American, your Russian visa. Leave your passport. ...

It was all there, clear and detailed, from the morning that had just unrolled behind them. Their mad dash through the security of the East German Embassy. Before that, the nail-biting half-hour wait when a massive Russian lady informed them that their visas and any trace of an application had been 'mees-plessed'. The face of the friendly Aussie who'd suggested they try bus 113 to Chongwenmen, which was quicker eh, since they were hoping to get to the C. I. T. S. while there was still some chance of it being open. The disastrousness of that choice – escape from the bus so far from where they wanted to go that they ended up wandering lost in the streets – Mel's eyes screwed shut to stop dust from getting under his contact lenses – leading him (none too gently) by the slack of one sleeve whenever there was a road to be crossed.

He remembered at one point passing a line of tiny Beijing children being led the other way, each holding a ring on a long ribbon. One was dressed in a miniature Red Guard uniform. One other in an American-style camouflage jacket. All of a piece, he'd thought to himself, and screwed his fingers into Mel's sleeve, possibly a bit more forcefully than necessary.

And after tramping on and on apparently for hours, they'd stumbled on this shopfront – dirty yellow-grey, with a crude painted picture of a teacup.

Yehune had said, 'Quite funny what he says about Cher-*noble*. You're supposed to avoid leafy veg and dairy products – but there ain't no leafy veg, and nothing to eat but dairy products. You remember…?'

'Mm – think so. What are you thinking of having here?'

Yehune looked up and saw the proprietor standing near him like a casually-placed wall.

'Ah, just some green tea or something,' he said. 'We've still got some bread back at the hostel.'

'Thank God for that. I'll just... er...'

Mel attempted to order by the simple process of pointing to lines on the menu and mumbling in New Zealand English. The answer was always *'Meow'*. Even Yehune knew that meant something like 'fuck off', 'get out of here', 'you must be joking'. It was the Beijing word, one of only two he'd learned since coming here (the other being *'pyow'*, ticket).

'You wanna have a try?' Mel asked colourlessly.

'Come on man, you're practically one of them. Remember those hard sleeper tickets.'

'Yeah... thing is... I hadn't quite realised back then how much I didn't know.'

More noises followed. The waiter swayed silently off towards a rear door. Mel seemed to have no idea whether he'd ordered them anything or not.

Yehune ploughed on, 'I just hope the fucking C. I. T. S. is open for a change. No point in getting there around lunchtime. An' in the arvo they'll probably be on some national siesta or something. I mean, it seems right to you, doesn't it, taking the... Russian, you know. Manchuria... saves four days... suppose it balances...'

He stopped talking and put his head back. There was a long pause.

After a while he heard a loud 'clop', and what sounded like someone in complex glottal difficulties. Yehune forced his neck to move. One of the other diners had finished, tipped his plate over on the table, and spat with every evidence of appreciation on the floor.

Mel said,

'Are you sorry you came this way?'

'Huh? Am I *sorry*?'

For the first moment, Yehune hadn't really registered what he'd been asked. He said,

'Just, um... brain shut down there for a second.'

Am I sorry. Fuck's sake. Am I sorry. Some people would, y'know, not me. Would Mel? Edith Piaf. Non, I don' rrregret nothin'. Peanuts: Lucy, I regret everything. Mel, his ol' fishhook....

Now, as he strode past peeling whitewash in the corridors of Qiao Yuan Hostel, Yehune experienced a return of that quick flight of impressions in the form of moving pictures – a blacked-down Parisian woman on a stage, smooth cartoon lines, a brightly-coloured yacht rocking by a jetty. Am I *sorry?* Am I sorry. Sorry we came *this* way, s'pose he must have meant, which means overland, in the spirit of Cas, instead of just springing a thousand bucks on a plane ticket. But it wasn't so much what Mel had asked him that he was chewing on, as what was implied, hovering unsaid in the dark skirts of the question; an acknowledgement – could it be? – of what Yehune had actually done for him back then in New Zealand. Choosing their moment, selling the bikes, taking on Asia and the Old World, with Mel dragged on behind. Ghosts: a ghostly recognition. A sneaking hint there... gratitude, or even guilt? Not that anyone could really say it was *his* fault....

But pictures brought distractions in themselves, chiming and clashing with the sensory imprints of the front lobby, with its scattering of human heads and coloured posters in Chinese and English. Soon afterwards, he was in the outside air. Enough, thank God, to stave off that insidious strain or taint in his thinking that might have, could have, smudged the clear relations between them. – After all. Once you started noticing things like that, where were you?

And so his thoughts plunged on in an easily-substituted narrative, bringing back something that must have happened... seventh, was it, late seventh?... at one of the many parties they'd both been at around the end of their seventh form year.

Something like:

Funny how you pick these things up. Mel, regret – regret-Mel. Something he told me about, was it, yeah, that party at Jody's. Jody's parents' place, one of those parties around the end. Can't exactly remember about the little snippet of conversation, 'Yeah, that was regrettable.' But you gotta put yourself into the fuckers' shoes. Shoes. Something else he told me. In any case I've only got Mel's....

I s'pose you could call it a classic case, Mel getting all tangled up and bamboozled by Jim's Jody. Female takes off the prizes, always. And what for? Probably no doubt for some jealousy or revenge thing she was trying to lay on her regular boyfriend, who was just then as I remember away in Tongariro on a ski trip. Imagine old Jim on skis. The ex-essential ski-man. Jody: picture of a darkness round the light face auntie-nosed and the body that'd lately grown out of fatness into a shape a lot of guys were regularly dreaming about; eyes nice enough, side-elongated, mouth a bit too small. I think I was mixed up with someone else at the time in Jody's parents' kitchen. Small girl, Patsy, was it Shapiro? Incredible the names you don't remember. All tangled up with her; later Mel called her 'insignificant', but that was later when he was roaring and feeling jerked around by it all and thinking of ways that if only this or that it might not have ever happened, i.e. someone else's fault. 'Course he failed to see her hidden depths. Little breast under that blouse-front like a pale fish.

From what Mel tells me, *I'm* supposed to have mentioned to him at some point before all this that Jody said she liked him, which is not even completely impossible with the proviso that I don't remember a fucking thing about it. Things can happen, y'know, messages pass your lips, words fall. She might have said something, who knows? Which nobody would ever interpret in the vaguest way as serious, because – Jim and Jody, there's not a question. Two years or so established. – So anyway, from what Mel says, she comes up to him in a crowded hall and asks casual-like whether he'd be interested in having a look at her dad's boat, which is a twenty-one foot Phoenix or something with an inboard and sails. Not totally implausible, you see, given that Mel's dad was always a kind of academised sailor-man manké, and Mel looks around, says he'll think about it, there's something he's got to talk to old Yehune about first. She says she'll meet him there. So he comes steaming in to get my advice, finds me in the kitchen sort of tied up, Patsy, leant back against the kitchen bench and arms involved any way so that I didn't even bother with a wave of the hand to warn him off. Away he goes to meet up with Jody. Not thinking, as any normal thoughtless dolt of the age of seventeen might've, it's all perfectly innocent and she'll have about twenty friends on deck with her, but in some peculiar Mel-oid upper compartment, holding all the strings, confident of his ability to make a totally objective decision if and when it might be needed as to which of the available courses of action was the one, sort of thing, and act on it without regret or second thought. Ruthless: carry it through. Word we used in those days. Impeccable was another. Got that from Castaneda.

So there they both are. Mel in a kitchen cuddy-area with small pans dangling and clinking around his face, no-one else there of course, just him and Jody in her pulled back and cut away green top and with that supreme chassis tightly wrapped in white jean-pattern trousers talking to him in sympathetic tones about her deeper feelings and problems, as a girl knows so well how to do, with the lift of unsolid basis below them rocking the whole world on its hinges, as it will, as it will. He tries to talk about the buckets, he tells me, and the technical aspects as far as he can remember them of the management of bilge in a boat this size, sub-keeler class. And so in the end she seems to be getting a bit fed up and just slinks on up to him, and says, something, changes every time, Mel puts it in the words he likes to remember having happened to him: I want you to… whatever it might be in the given moment of invention. So Mel makes his choice. Warm girl just sinking into his arms, unbelievably vital and alive and blood-activatingly there, cloth tight on the limbs and contours, breathing up at him, her face with that unknowable self gazing star-like through the eyes; old Mel makes an informed decision to throw everything to the winds and just ignore any trickier aspects of the whole thing, and… in short, they consummate their passion on a red plastic squab covered with a yellow cloth, probably half-dressed, I can just see it, and whoever had a condom I can imagine it wouldn't have been Mel, it just wouldn't have occurred to him. Nor would the whole thing. Should have talked to me about it, eh. Not part of his conceptions. … He just didn't realise *the power*.

And a bit later, proceeded separately back to the house, by mutual agreement, and here Mel admits that Jody seemed unkeen on further contact after the great jismatic consummation and anxious to avoid discovery; which could mean second thoughts, or just the next stage of her so-female plan to score off her boyfriend or secure the prick of some guy for later dissection, whatever. Which is when Mel's already begun, you know, to *regret* it. Never again is he able to look old Jim squarely in the eye, or Jody more especially, what's more he's constantly at me with his latest discovery about minute breezes of change in the attitude of one or the other towards him: Jim's always supposed to be a tiny bit standoffish, Jody after the initial reaction all too matey, given that a word from her could so fucking easily wreck Mel's whole social orbit and start a blood feud on the spot. But that's all bollocks. Excise man's oblivious. Anyway he never heard it from me. And anything up to two glances from Mel in the direction of Jody's fine curvature could have caused a suspicion like that, or even better, Mel's imagination… and then coming in to the house

Or some other house, some time later or before – never did get straight exactly when and where it's supposed to have happened – Mel hears

'Yeah – though – as far as selling off our land to a Taiwanese conglomerate…'

'Aw, yeah, that was regrettable. But the situ-a-tion might've been more complex than we can see.'

'This is right. Try putting yourself in the government's shoes.'

Shoes. Regrettable. This is right. Three older people, or two and an aspiring young economist, standing round a small table not far inside the back door in indolent attitudes as if waiting for their taxi, talking over the incidents of the day, not sure if it was Muldoon or Lange just then. It's just the tail end of a conversation he heard, coming into the house again. Or could be some other time. But Mel being Mel, just then the tidal wash of an idea goes flooding through his head, all built around that one word, 'regrettable'…. It's this picture. The picture, if I've got it, of a tiny little fishhook swinging out ahead from some decision you've made ever so lightly, expanding forward into the run of time, building, building, living alongside you, grown to the size of a claw, then a meathook, then an anchor, shading the whole world – to scythe into you at some unpredictable moment in the future and take your guts away with it. *The Regrettable,* he called it. Mel being Mel, having to have a fully-formed theory for every shift of the way he might happen to be feeling at the time….

What's doing here now? Bike with a brown fleck; carriers on them. Someone to ask? –

But there was more came into it. Remember that story he told me. Electric lawnmower, wife switches plugs – guy loses four fingers. And ever after, the *wild regret*, eh. Yep-yep. Could never have happened with a Masport....

In a small square surrounded by shrubberies a little way down the concrete-channelled river, there were usually a few young people waiting around to change FECs for renmenbi. But now, at ten past four on a weekday afternoon, only a cyclist or two charged through, some passers-by hurried forward with a blinkered look. The sky was overcast, with what felt like a light mechanical buzz. Try the ol' mandarin stall back the other way? As he retraced his steps, Yehune tried to construct a mental diagram of the streets around him, even stopping once to check it with the map. All this, possibly, was *You'anmen*... so the road might be *You'anmen Dongbinhe*...? Everything else a paper blank. Goodoh, economy of brushstrokes. And o'course when you think of it the guy might even have grabbed a bus....

The lady at the mandarin stall (which was actually nothing less than a complete fruit and vegetable shop under a squared-off canvas awning) seemed nervous to be seen talking to him. She was slight, wrinkled at the cheeks, and had always seemed friendly enough. Now, she was all at sea, as if she didn't want to admit to understanding anything. He questioned her with slow loud phrases, and tried to mime Mel's looks and walk to her. After a while she presented her shoulder. 'Spose we all look alike. Could buy a few mandarins, just while I'm...? Well, na, another time.

Businesslike as ever, but somehow disconsolate, Yehune found organisational phrases running at random through his head – train-information, Saturday not the Wednesday, money-change at Manzhouli – as he took a few turns in the streets. His nose was stinging, head throbbing out of time with his bootfalls on the pavement.

A boot-repairman, sitting in the street sewing leather on an ancient hand sewing machine, looked up as the foreigner passed. Pockmarked face, a broad jowl.

Here there were blocks of flats or offices rising to medium height, and the sun had come out, peering lustreless through layer on layer of smog. Some semi-residential wasteland. Wherever he walked, his feet stirred up the swirling, fine-spun particles of dust. Dust, he thought to himself, dust and steam-vents, no wonder we all... all... aaa... aaaauu... a *tcheeecch!!* Fu-fu-fu. He groped for the crumpled square of linen in his jacket pocket.

Damn that Mel, he could've left a note. Could he have gone to Tiananmen? The chocolate slug pastry-shop? Then he'd have to have got the 43, which'd be from the next street up....

Almost as he thought it, his feet reacted, turning left in a shortcut through an alleyway that looked as if it might connect the major roads.

Straight away, he wished they hadn't. Residential, did he say? The little alley was a residence in itself: people were living openly out on the concrete, lying on plastic bags as a protection against the mountains of dust. The bricks lying everywhere had been painstakingly piled up in places to make walls; he saw dirty faces staring out from compartments like makeshift rooms. Two small fires, yellow, in careful rectangles of bricks. Not good, he thought, not good. The thing was, once he was in there, he didn't especially want to turn back. Just sail on, casual as hell. Wouldn't want to make any move that might be interpreted by the locals as an *unfriendly action*....

As he got deeper into the shaded part, he seemed to catch bizarre or impossible sights out of the corner of his eye. A withered man, staring fixedly, missing one eye and an arm. A woman in multiple wrappings of cloth bent over something that was surely too small for a baby – something his imagination rebuilt into the form of a rubicund foetus, alive and stirring. Wary eyes looked out at him from every direction, and just then no-one was saying a word. These were down-and-outs, no question. But, he babbled to himself, how could there be down-and-outs under the happy Communist system? Thought they all partook of the common, you know. Shadowy patches, human sized, amoeba-variable, were moving barely out of sight among the textures of the stucco walls and dusty brick partitions. Yehune fixed his eyes on the small opening at the other end of the alleyway.

Of course, the patches drew in and arranged themselves in front of him, becoming shabbily-dressed young people, four of them across his path.

Don't look back. There'll be another three pulled up behind. *Unsuspicious* is the ticket; and good God, can't understand a word you say mate.

A young man set off from the rest, lean, almost noseless, stood on back-locked legs with his hand held out,

'Wu-ge kuai!'

Something something kuai, was that? 'Kuai' was some amount of currency, so the man, or boy, must have been demanding a toll. How much Yehune didn't know: could've been something like five cents. But he was aware of the slack bulge of the money belt under his shirt, which held a fuck of a lot more than a few kuai. His opinion was that they'd be getting round to that pretty soon if he was dumb enough to give way.

He moved straight in, friendly and open-eyed, as if he was about to go into a confidential huddle. The spokesman took one step back.

'Thanks, sorry I can't understand, but where I'm trying to go is just up there, see, around the end of the street – looking for a bus 43. Bus, you know – 43.'

'Wu-ge kuai!'

'Thanks so much. I don't know what I would have done without – just up there, see, at the bus stop.'

There was a hanging, dangerous moment. Yehune objectively knew he'd have to lunge out and make a run for it, and was bringing himself to the point. But then, the boy turned side-on and bared a mouthful of broken teeth. Pretending to the good will that was so obviously expected of him. He spoke a line of words, lost on Yehune, but which could have been something like, Oh, you want to go *there*, that's all right then, you walk straight up the alleyway and turn…. In making a small motion at the neck, acknowledgment or thanks,

Yehune could see two faces poised around a glowing flame, looking on non-committally. The line broke up, the other young people taking their cue from their leader.

And he sailed through, innocent as all-get-out, money belt intact, in his Western red jacket with the map in one side and jeans pockets not even plumbed for the odd small kuai, seeing a strip of the street with passing bicycles like a yellow-bright projection expanding in his upward-tilted eye, floating to him, without a connection with the rough concrete he was walking on. Not a worry in the world. Shit, eh? Pretty amiable thieves they've got in Beijing. And when you think, it's a good thing I didn't know a fucking word, or I would have had to be sure and not use it....

A few moments later, he was hesitating between a rightwards and a leftwards course, having decided to forget the bus stop after all.

Thinking:

'Bloody Mel, eh. Ought to keep him on a leash. ... I bet he's sitting waiting for me back in the dorm.'

The next day, both of them were in the front-but-one seats of the minibus for the official tour of the Ming Tombs and the Great Wall Badaling. They breathed in second-hand fumes from the cigarettes of the driver and a female official. Driver and official were swaying, swaying and crooning, as they doubled the voice line of the shrill Chinese pop songs coming over the radio. Yehune was in a low state, struggling to control his cold. Mel occasionally came out with a word or two.

At one point, they swerved wildly past a group in the road: what looked like two black bicycles caught under the wheel of an ambulance. Their own minibus barely missed barging into a whole flock of cyclists coming the other way. Most of the passengers crowded over to one side for a better look.

But it was already printed on his eye. A howling man bathed in blood up the length of one leg; and onlookers who seemed to pat at him, wafting small compliments over the reddened haunch.

'Some driver, huh?' he said.

From behind them came a robust voice, *'Mondieuje-je...'*

Though Yehune didn't understand a word of it, he had Mel on hand. It was the voice of the negotiator he heard, the man who, the day before, had taken it on himself to hire their own minibus for an *un*-official Great Wall tour. The idea had been to leave out the Tombs, which were supposed to be uninteresting and a mere money-spinner. The man was a burly, loud Canadian, non-French, though he was just now speaking French to his seat-companion and another woman across the aisle.

'What's he saying?' Yehune asked.

'Who?'

'Mr Big.'

'Oh, Mr I-Speak-Money? Hang on a sec... ah... he's explaining to those girls that he learned French so's to talk to girls.'

The evening before, Mr Big had driven a hard bargain with the Chinese minibus drivers. He'd got so pushy that he managed to push his way right out the other side. Yehune had stepped up, but by then the drivers had lost interest. Yehune had tried to get Mel to translate. Mel, magisterially, had refused to have anything to do with a conversation involving specific numbers in a language he didn't know.

... Just now, Mel was talking again,

'Mind you, this is a bloody new section of the Wall. We should've gone to Simatai.'

'...'

'Yeah, did you know – 's quite a good laugh. This bit of the Wall only comes from about fifteen or sixteen something. ... Anyway, the thing was started out by the *Qin* some time back in the BCs, to keep the Mongols out or something. Then the Mongols got in anyway, got kicked out later by, I think it was the *Mings* – which might've been when this Beijing bit was made – to keep out the *Manchus*, from Manchuria, who, guess what, got past it as well – and funnily enough those guys couldn't really seem to see very much need for a Great Wall.'

'Uh.'

Should have gone to Simatai. Yehune tasted it on his tongue, immune as he was just then to the flavour of anything much. Should have gone. Should've.

He groped in a hurry for his handkerchief, a bit too late to catch the full effluvia of his next sneeze,

'Kaaaassschhh!!'

Soon afterwards, Mel said,

'Oh, shit, man. You really gonna put that thing back in your pocket?'

Outside the window, Yehune could see the long snaking road, and broken hills that grew eventually into mountains, all of which irresistibly reminded him of something else. There were huge upthrusts from ground level, clothed at the foot with green or khaki vegetation, then rising in linear columns the colour of pipe-clay to a series of little knobby peaks. Those peaks were what were different. High, neat, and almost symmetrical. Like some alien, some many-centuries-civilised version of what he saw inside him: the rough power, the rain-wet savagery of his own New Zealand hills. China, he kept reminding himself. We're in China. Don't start comparing. And yet, something had already communicated to him out of that single swerving line of the crag horizon – a memory, an evocation that he couldn't have changed or cancelled if he'd wanted to. High country. Where was that...?

'Ahnonnon mais,' the big-boned Canadian rumbled on behind him, and the music like a solid wall went battering at his eardrums. Mel said something, but it was defeated by the noise and Yehune's blocked head.

But, he was trying to tell himself, you have to remember. New Zealand, it's not all like that. Not all that extremest punch at the air of the pre-human geological... you know.

Peculiarly, paradoxically then, the memory sequence that came to visit him was set somewhere in the lowest flatlands of Maeraki, in the layout of streets behind Campbells Beach, where there were half-hearted suburban earthworks on the edge of Glen Road – shovels, a stationary engine hard up against a wall of the gutted house that had been taken over by the E. C. B. B. C. for a P. E. P. hut.

...

Like this:

Stood for a moment looking at the Trump. Blue-silver metal: one trickle of burned oil on the leftwards exhaust. The bike was leaning away from him on its side-stand. Jim's head appeared just over it, at the hole where a door should have been.

'Yehune. What the fuck are you doing here?'

'Hi Jim. Slacking off?'

'C'mon into the hut.'

Outside against the wall, the stationary engine throbbed perpetually, monotonously. He sat down at the table and accepted a cup of the classic P. E. P. Scheme tea: stewed there day-in day-out in a huge charred pot. Two other members of Maeraki's unemployed were draped against another wall. Through a large broken space in the window, Yehune could see the ridges of upturned clay, a few buildings, and over a flat, dead space, the footpath by Glen Road.

'What about that guy Cas?...' Jim had asked. For a while they discussed him desultorily: Timothy Castor, who was about to take off on a backpacking tour of the whole world. Incredible, who'd have thought it: old Cas. And they might have put in a word about Mel, who was away on his bike in the South Island. Then the discussion died away for lack of a subject.

At the same time, over the grinding, single-toned racket, he could pick out the conversation of the two layabouts standing by the shovel rack. One was *Wally*, as he found out later; the other *Peter*.

Wally: 'I s'pose you know we've only got two or three years left?'

Peter: (Interrogative noise.)

Wally: 'Yeah, times are comin', man. I read all about it in this book, *Braille of the Earth*. The vultures've been laying three eggs to every nest over the past two years. Normally they only lay one. That's it.'

Peter: 'Unscientific.'

Wally: 'Like fuck. I told you it's in this book.'

Peter: 'That book's got it wrong. Look, don't you know about frions? Living electrical stabilisers... they're invisible, but they live in the Earth's atmosphere. They're all over the place. Everything we do, all the power we use, comes off of these frions. They wouldn't let the world end. They're, like, the secret force for con-*tin*-uance. Electric motors, you name it... fuck, that generator out there...'

Wally: 'That's crap. You should read this book.'

Jim had been listening as well, and made a comment,

Jim: 'Frions' – sounds cold, somehow. Isn't that some chemical?'

Peter: 'Someone prob'ly stole the name. ... Ever felt a fizzing in your head? I mean, mate, whatever you do, you just can't get away from them.'

Wally: 'Na, na. Your fry-os wouldn't have much of a chance against the real live Holocaust, that's for sure. If you think the book's got it wrong, it's all written up in the Bible.'

Outside, there was a brief incident involving a passing well-dressed lady carrying an elegant shopping bag. She might have gone down the wrong road, or been on her way to somewhere else. A couple of the guys had whistled at her; one hooted a few obscenities.

Yehune saw her turn her head. She seemed to recognise one of them and walked over to him; he could almost hear the inconsequential chitchat: she knew his dad, hadn't he done a course in the Tech, how was it going? ...

By that time, he'd gone some way towards thinking of something to say. He wanted to set a few people back on the right track, nothing more. He stood up and took a few steps towards the shovels.

Yehune: 'Tell you, I can't buy this frions stuff – but I can sort of see where you're coming from. Isn't it, like, something extra, something that isn't in the readouts from their particle analysers? ... But I can't help thinking, you know, you're looking for it in the wrong place. It's not that fucking would-be scientific claptrap... it's – *experiential*. You have to look for it in the arts – which is like, a universal atmospheric relay, all around us like a steam-bath, pokes and prods us all the time, gives us the fuel to make us go. ... Read Thomas *Aq*-uinas. Or better still, look for it in music or in a certain kind of books...'

Peter: '*Books?* You're saying frions are in *books?*'

Yehune: 'Na na, not frions. That's just some bullshit. It's something real that you can see and hear. But it's a matter of perception – you have to, you know, tune yourself in. Take me... I'm an artist...'

Wally: 'A what? An ar*tiste*? You mean, like a cage dancer?'

Peter: 'Na, you know – paints pictures.'

Yehune: 'Yeah, something like that. Play the piano.'

Wally: 'Fuck. ... An' you're playing the *piano* to make all this stuff happen?' (Works fingers in piano-playing motions.)

Yehune: 'Ah, well, yeah, and compose a bit... and even write a bit, y'know...'

Which was when *the look* had passed between them, or at least Yehune had seen it clearly enough on Wally's face, aimed past the top of his head to where Peter stood behind: that big-eyed look suppressing a laugh, saying as clearly as words: We've got a right one here. Humour him while you can and keep a clear run to the exit. Yahoo, boy. Takes all sorts, or what?

Not too long afterwards, the two left the house, not on any Scheme duties, but on a special mission to the pub. Peter had his official P. E. P. green overalls on. Wally was poking and prodding him from behind as they went out the door, chanting, 'Little green Peter'.

'C'mon Yehune,' said Jim, alone at the table. 'Don't you believe in frions?'

'Don't fucking start. ... How's the old C15, by the way?'

Jim sat back comfortably and spread his feet out.

'Not going. I've had it stripped down in the garage for about a year. But I've ordered some bits from this mail-order place in England... not BSA. General specialty.'

'Gods, that'll take forever. What with that and Mel's old SF...'

Jim seemed offended. '*SF*, huh. You're not comparing that with *my* bike? Shit, it might as well be Japanese.'

'Ah, it's from Italy. I think that's in Europe.'

'... Anyhow, it's OK for you to talk. Some of us have got to work for it.'

'You're not talking about *me*?'

'Didn't you get given a brand-new Bonneville for your birthday or something?'

'Not exactly.'

Yehune didn't know how many times he'd told him, and he didn't feel like repeating it now. His parents had given him just over half, supposedly for his nineteenth birthday, really on condition that he stuck to the correspondence Law course he'd been doing at the time. Through the hole in the window he could see its front wheel, leaning off to his right.

And as a matter of fact, he didn't feel much in the mood for talking. The real effect of Jim's dig had been to remind him of his mother and father, who he almost never went to see. Perched up there on the Westborough Road at the top of John Downs. There was a restless, high-strung demon of argument hovering around them. So here he was instead; he'd come all the way from West Auckland to this, Maeraki dregs, to this sea-edged bottomland between a couple of ridges, just to talk to Jim. The flatlands. Though there were a few hills here and there. But still – flat as ditchwater. Where any possible idea, he thought, was admissible except the right one; by which he meant the one he'd happened to fix on in those youthful, ignorant years of seeking in a vacuum, before the voice of the social norm had got its verdict across to him. Not done, not talked about. Not here. Then, where – where? ...

The bike caught gleams from the sun at the steering head and well-chromed front mudguard. Standing, poised for flight. It struck him that it was maybe about time to take off. ... You could call it a pity, in a way.

A Russian Train

It might have begun in Beijing, but it didn't end with Beijing. Even when the train, that oblong secondary-Russia in the heart of the Chinese capital, slid back its doors and the black-moustached *provodnik* leaned out to take their bags, spouting cheerful Russian, surprised and overjoyed when Mel managed to answer in a simplified version of the same tongue, even when they sat in the neat four-berth compartment that was to be their home for the next six days watching northern China pass by outside the window, a grey cloud seemed to have settled in over Yehune's internal systems, soaking up good cheer, draining vital signs, siphoning off into its unresponsive heart anything that looked like enthusiasm or interest in the world around him. From his careless good cheer was left – uncaring; from his lively black humour – blackness. It might have been a function of the nagging strain of responsibility for the whole trip, his sense of burden where Mel was concerned, frenetic activity all suddenly cut off – because for the next six days until Moscow (or seven, depending on blizzards), as they forged across the breadth of the Asian steppes, Yehune didn't actually have to *do* anything. Mel was the one who had to consult with their Slavonic hosts about the reliability of drinking water, arrangements for money changing, how to obtain food in the short stops at frozen Siberian stations along the way, because Mel was the only one who could even begin to communicate. He himself lived on, superfluous, in an isolation chamber rattling with a rhythm in nine-eight time, *a drmmp-a-drmm… a drmmp-a-drmm,* organising nothing, talking to no-one but his one English-speaking travelling companion, with not a thing to worry about – except his place in the queue for the tiny toilet cubicle in which everyone had to try and wash themselves – as if that soul-sucking greyness were nothing but the hole, the gap in air, from which the volume of his earthly cares had suddenly betrayed him by disappearing.

They missed the money-change at Manzhouli.

Two compartment-mates got on at Zabaikalsk: a hulking well-fleshed couple travelling from there to Riga, where he was something in the military.

Mel was kept occupied by multi-lingual conversations with a young Yugoslavian kung fu specialist from the next carriage, and what sounded like formal conversation classes with the military dame. He also had a million or so books with him, among them some basic readers in Russian, which were riffled through with suspicion by the wall-eyed border guard. – 'Your lityeratur! Lityeratur!'

Yehune had cigarettes.

Outside – after the border post flanked by Soviet soldiers, overtopped by a massive banner with pictures of square-jawed heroic labourers – the casual enormousness of the steppes crawled by them, bringing with it a sense of pulling desolation, the alienness of the infinitely-extending space. In spite of the tiny villages with their crazily-designed houses, in spite of fields, fords, and individual wrinkles in the land, it evoked a sadness that he couldn't believe he'd brought there with him. And he had all the opportunity he needed to consider it, standing alone – or as much alone as he could be – out in the corridor, gazing through the double-glazing, smoking one fag after another. Marlboros were nearly out. He didn't care, or at least he didn't feel like going back into their little burgundy-upholstered cave to break open another packet. ... Without any outward sign, any real poaching of space, it had somehow become the domain of the bear-like military husband, with his wife as helpmeet and Mel as a sort of unevictable house-guest.

So he stood there, staring out at a body of water, wrinkled, horizonless, with broken-down timber sheds along the shore. Strange sharp-nosed boats lay lashed together in clumps. He seemed to remember a phrase from his isolated year of third-form Russian – 'Sharp-nosed barques'... did something. And 'Glorious sea, something-or-other Baikal...'

Mel appeared beside him. ... So what? Suck on the fag. Gasp in, draw it all in slowly and blow it out again. One red coal hovering out beyond the scratched-over window.

Mel didn't start out by saying anything. 'God for small mercies.

Yehune contracted his focus, trying not to hear the occasional sniffs and careful phlegm-management to one side of him. He could see a page of newsprint, violet-coloured print smelling of cyclostyling fluid. *Stenka Razin.* ... Mel hadn't been in that class with him; he and all the other fourth formers were already up in the next year's course. There'd been an absence of Mel. ... Which, he thought, would have been welcome just now.

'God! Yeah – can just see it,' commented Mel over the top of his green notebook.

Don't say anything. What's that out there, seen it before – big white heaps on the pebbles. Salt, alum? ... Jesus, no, must be snow.

He waited till his cigarette had burned down to a minimal stub, just about singeing his lower lip, before asking,

' 'Fuck are you on about?'

Mel said, 'Just this – God! – idea. Shit, it's just so...'

And after a while, Yehune having come out with nothing more,

'See, what I'm thinking is... you know the Sail?'

Yehune pulled the fag out of his mouth, felt for another – pushed his lips out in the direction of all that water and bizarreness.

'Nope. Heard you telling me about it.'

'Mm. Oh. ... Well, it doesn't matter.'

There was a distraction when the young Yugoslavian, slick-haired and well-built at the shoulders, politely shuffled his way past them. The corridor wasn't wide enough for two people to pass abreast. Mel mumbled words in Russian. Now, as Yehune commented inwardly, the Yugoslavian's English was probably as good as his Russian – Russian wasn't actually the same as his native Yugo-whatwasit – so why did Mel have to struggle on in a foreign language? Guy'd known a bit of Mandarin, he probably would've tried that. *Talk English,* Mel....

Mel went on with:

'God, though – you know, I'm thinking, why don't I take it out there? I mean, out into the world? Not so much write things, or not mainly, but be a sort of, *(sniff-iff)*, entrepreneur... teacher, inspirational... something? I could get it all worked out, then really go for it, build a team, conduct seminars.... 'Course I'd have to get it all off the ground somehow...'

'What's all this for?'

'For my – you know. For what I'm going to *do*. That, ah...'

'Arrr-hh.'

There *was* another fag. Hallelujah. Bit limp from his pocket. Yehune took it carefully in his hands, stroking it, trying to restore the body to its battered length, before eventually bringing it up to his mouth. His head, he noticed, felt something like a steel boiler full of compacted gravel. Mel, in the meantime, scribbled with a clawlike hand, stopped and scribbled again, as if he was struggling to catch the precious thoughts an instant before they melted away into the hot carriage air.

'Well, I don't know why,' he went on conversationally, 'but it's just suddenly occurred to me, came to me first at breakfast, actually, when Mr and Mrs Bear were nice enough to give us all that tinned fish and stuff...'

'Yeah, and I cut my finger on the can...'

'Hmm... hmm.' Mel didn't actually say Yehune was a hilarious whinger, but implied it by his tone. '... Well, if you have an idea these days you don't sit on it, you get it out there,' he said. 'I thought I could do travelling lectures, you know; *(eccchhht)*, of course I'd have to make a name for myself first. Write a few books... I mean, guidance stuff *(hoorrkghk)*, pamphlets at least.'

'Bloody tins of fish. For bloody breakfast. I can see why they both have about twelve dozen extra layers of fat, probably need it to survive out here.'

'Yeah, though they live in Latvia.'

'Fucking cold country, Latvia.'

They were interrupted again, this time by the fat female night-provodnik shoving past on her way from somewhere to somewhere, uttering a string of what must have been imprecations at the stupid foreigners who didn't even know how to stand in a corridor. Fucking, bloody, buggered, foreign capitalist dog-shit extrusions, die strangled in your own entrails – good one. Mel might even have understood it. In the meantime, the droplets of rain on the outside of the window-panes had become flower-textured ice; there were pines among the birches, then more pines; a black crow with something in its beak braked in the air to avoid the upper edge of their carriage. ... Mel. Die strangled. Mel. Die strangled. Doesn't work.

Somewhere further on into the developing pine forest he saw a thick-set woman trudging slowly along a track of snow, carrying two bags and a bucket full of something; where nothing was, from nowhere, on her laborious way to nowhere.

Mel had loudly blown his nose, and was dabbing at it now with a piece of pink toilet paper.

'So I mean,' he said, 'whaddaya think? Everyone tells me I have to get it out there, I have to *project*, at least Mandy used to say that… well, here's a sort of last word in projection, all sewn up. All I have to do is…'

'… How is she, by the way? Mandy.'

Now, that enquiry after the health of Mel's sister wasn't as casual or innocent as it might have seemed. Because at one time in the past, Yehune might have been more qualified to answer the question than either of the girl's mere brothers. He and Mandy had once, potentially, been an item – had stood shyly on the border of exploring a blossoming mutual esteem; or even more than that. Mel was well aware of it. So the question coming just then was more than anything an expression of Yehune's inner state, his built up and compacted bile (both literally and figuratively: his head was a sinusless lump in which the headache beat on and on like a stable wave); where any directer way of putting it might have seemed out of place to a companion so unusually upbeat.

Rather than the textures of her skin and hair, the words that had passed between them – the usual shutter-points of the memory – Yehune saw the neglected roadside clearing in the Kauaeranga where the crisis of Debs had occurred. It had been no more than the beginning, the pre-beginning of contact between Mandy and Yehune. But it was that intense flame-imitation, New Zealand bush at near-vertical, a living riot of leaves and stems and trunks upwards towards the sun, that he couldn't help picturing whenever he thought about her now. The break of the bank to the track; white water roaring below. His own mum's blue Toyota four-by-four standing at a distance on the flat scrub grass. Accidents, interactions, which taken together had had some never-to-be-understood effect on the perception of Mandy, Mel's sister – where a person who held a simple position in another universe (old Yehune, her brother's friend) had been allowed some sort of possible connection to herself. Something must have caused it, though Yehune couldn't have said what.

The few words they exchanged on that occasion had been astringent enough:

'I can't get forward, and I can't get back,' Debs was complaining.

Mandy's voice broke across her, 'You mean we've got to go to the *right*? To that big tree over there? Just don't assume I know *anything*, Yehune.'

'No, no. I can't even see which tree you're pointing to... look, try going north, in the direction of the river.'

'Stop northing me. I don't know where north is. Do we go along this little clay bit here, or not?'

'*Mandy. Mandy.* Can you get me unstuck, please?'

The two of them were down the bank; he could barely see Mandy's head like a furry dot bobbing among branches. He stood at the top, on the edge of the flat bit, feeling the small creases etched by grass blades in the sides of his feet. Behind him, Mel was just beginning to untie his boots. Yehune's, by contrast, were already laid neatly side by side on the groundsheet to dry.

Bootless, he couldn't do a thing. Send Mel down to give them a hand? That crouched, oblivious figure...? Hmm.

Yehune was the one who was supposed to know the ground. It was a spot he'd found out about two years before on a seventh-form class trip: the point where two separate tracks came very close to meeting up, so that – with a little bit of scrambling and a head for heights – you could get from one to the other. Yehune had done most of the coordination of the two parties; the Seuchars with Debs in their old Holden, and himself and his mother in the Toyota.

He and Mel had just done the longer track. The idea was that the girls would be brought to the spot by Yehune's mum (Mel's parents being off looking at a logging museum), and the boys could help them get onto the shorter track, which started lower down. Then the Seuchars would come up and help transport everyone back to camp. As things turned out, Yehune had drastically slashed the allowable time for their track, and it ended up taking them half an hour longer than he'd thought. They got there to discover the girls already gone – they'd got tired of waiting and started down the precipitous bank by themselves. His mother sat alone in her all-terrain vehicle, fuming, no doubt, at the way her good advice had been ignored.

'I can't see your clay bit,' he shouted down. 'North, north… which way is the river running?'

Mandy answered him with an unladylike word.

Then came Debs's vocal self-assertion, her great moment, as the possibilities began to dawn on her. She gave a rising scream like a siren, a breath of the city in that tree-covered wilderness, breaking into recognisable words,

'I – can't – get – *out* – of – here!'

Mel ambled up to see what was going on. Yehune was looking around him, trying to assess the situation. The Toyota, blue-square, under a massive twisted totara. Their dark-grey groundsheet. He could hear Mandy's voice making reasonable suggestions, like isolated chirping sounds over the river noise, and Debs's panicked answer,

'I can't, I can't. … I'll fall!'

With a minimum of fuss, he sent Mel over the grass to alert his mother to a possible problem down the bank. Then he made a dash for his boots.

A little later he heard the roar of the Toyota as it started up and swung away into the road.

Mel ran up again.

'Didn't you tell her?'

'Yes, I bloody told her. She gives me this polite smile and goes, "Thank you Mel, I'll see you back at the camp," and drives right off!'

Not that it really made much difference. Because by then Yehune's boots were loosely tied around his feet and he was on the way to beginning his impromptu descent. The Toyota was a four-wheel-drive, and had a winch on the back. It was hard to think how that could have helped… but still. But still. He could hear Debs's vocal efforts like an eccentric backing track: it was amazing to him that someone could really wail like that. Low, then shrieking high, then undulating down to a moan again. As if on another channel, bits and pieces of Mel's steady rave came through, as he stomped around on the flat and swore away at Yehune's mother, the – better forget what – who took off at the exact moment she was needed.

His boots were flapping on him, loose around the ankles. He gripped handfuls of tough hook-grass and toatoa. Fire-banks, flame-banks… an upward-reaching fury of leaf sails. Closer to the eye were exaggerated details of the undergrowth: flat earthborne leaves, sprigs of bracken, a single stalk that beaded into tiny light-blue flower things. Swaying slowly, in mimicry of the blue of the sky. Which didn't seem to be above him just now, but somehow to the side and behind – while immediately in front of him all the plant life cut out, in a short brutal drop to the streambed.

See how she might get a bit panicked, eh. Pays not to think about it. But you get to feeling kind of responsible. …Weird, but you do.

And *there* was their bloody clay bit. To the north…?

He slid down towards the huddle of two slighter bodies, taking grips on whatever he could get hold of, lowering himself to the point where one of his thick ankles was within reach of Debs. He told her huskily to grab hold of it. She turned out hard to persuade. Luckily, Mandy was there to wrench one of Debs's hands off the sapling she'd fastened onto and shift it to Yehune's leg, then beat with a small fist on the other one until it let go. '*Debs*, will you… bloody hell. Be *sens – i – ble*!' But once in position, Debs latched on with a surprising convulsive strength, while her siren-song rose to a climax again. Yehune started trying to lever himself up. Holy shit, – it – was… God. Go for it. Powerhouse. Apeman. Give it all you got. Owwf – treetrunk, you inconvenient *bastard*. Skinned my bugging wrist. He had to drag her living weight along behind him, sprawled over grass and the thick dark mud, catching at random on any stray root or clump of vegetation. 'S that boot coming loose? Fuck – don't

want to lose it down. Could be her gripping-point? Dun' 'ink 'o. ...
Good tramping boots – hard to find.

All the while, Debs was crying and screaming; twisting a little bit
on the hook, but not actually resisting; and Mandy did valuable work
boosting her by her broadest region from below. More – Yehune
couldn't do, he realised, in a final, absolute crisis of wind. But did
manage to moor his living burden in a more-or-less secure position
about a metre and a half above the last real danger point. And lay
there gasping for air – *phew,* fuck that – with his head against the
uneven side of a tree-root.

And so it happened that in the course of time Debs was delivered
safe to the top of the bank, Mandy and Yehune having cajoled her
up between them on a kind of sling of two arms, her left, his right,
which left their outer hands free to grip with. At just about that time,
Mel's parents' battered Holden came lumbering to a stop over the
grass. And Mel? – Mel. He hadn't even begun to get over the Trent
parental slight; he was crouched over, looking in the other direction,
mumbling explosive little phrases to himself. ... But, there you go.
When you thought about it, he didn't know the ground, he wasn't
likely to have been a whole lot of use anyway.

Not much more had happened during the remaining – how
many? – days of the two families' collective break in the Kauaeranga
Ranges; though Debs had been shy of going out on any sort of
track at all, and Yehune's mother had privately mentioned that she'd
never again have anything to do with (the phrase came from later
on) those awful Seuchars and their *Holden.* Mel seemed to get over
it. Mel's mum was broad and comfortable and always unruffled, his
dad ponderously humorous, leaning on his stick. But something had
happened, something Yehune never managed to account for – could
it have been admiration on Mandy's part for Yehune's handling of a
crisis; or some personal recognition in something he'd said; or just a
side-effect of the coordination of their bodies, the touching of arm
and arm, where male and female were nothing but living electrical
polarities, helpless in case of contact...?

In any case, Mandy had subtly shown herself responsive to

being asked out, and Yehune had naturally obliged her. She was a young seventeen, and had barely started university at the end of her sixth form. He'd taken her out on the back of his then brand-new Bonneville, first to a movie or two, then to parties and gatherings. Mel at that time had been unsettled, unpredictable, either communicating by grunts or flaring up into sudden rages. In fact, relations between them had been at a low for four months or more. After which the whole thing had fizzled out, come to nothing; and (here Yehune was fairly sure of himself) no-one except the principals had been allowed to know the real story behind that breakup, or how much or how little had ever happened between the two of them, though more-or-less misleading pronouncements had been given out to string along Mel and the outside world; where, of course – if the facts were known –

'... How is she, by the way? Mandy.'
'... OK last time I heard.'
Mel's voice was flat. So it seemed to Yehune that he'd at least succeeded in taking the edge off that heart-warming good cheer that the guy had contracted from somewhere. Russian thing, probably. He hadn't noticed it before the train. It was amazing: sometimes the fuckeder-up you were, the sprightlier old Mel'd get. Yehune was still hoping, hoping against hope, for a favourable outcome; anything, whatever it took, as long as he could be left in peace....

But Mel made a sort of abandoned pirouette in the tight corridor space, gesturing with his pink tissue towards the scene outside the window,

'But, you know, this could be *it*. The call. And here, right here –
in this place, Asian railroad, under Lake Baikal…

'So, I mean, whaddaya reckon?'

Yehune was actually forced to consider it. A scene sprang up in
his mind's eye without his doing anything to encourage it: Mel,
addressing one of the gatherings of his little flock. Mel shaking like
a leaf, fumble-fingered with embarrassment, dropping all his notes
on the floor. Fainting at the altar from dehydration and the last
three sleepless nights. Caught, in decaying slo-mo, in the angelic
arms of several young women wearing snowy white robes, heavenly
ministrants, and ascending with them slowly up into the air.

… He said,

'I think I missed something. What exactly is this revelation you're
s'posed to be delivering?'

Mel looked at him for a moment, head held a bit to one side. 'My
findings.'

'Your findings.'

Some germ of madness had surely infected the guy, either from
the overheated carriage or from that interminable Slavonic desolation
outside. The idea sucked; it was a drug-dream rather than anything
that could possibly happen in reality. But if he said that – then Mel
would surely come out with logical arguments, and that would be
the end of the lugubrious peace of his discontent, smoking and dying
there alone.

One other thing stopped him from coming out with as strong a
negative reaction as he could. Not even his mention of Mandy had
been enough to deflate Mel. There he still was, spinning nonsense,
babbling incoherently about his findings. Which meant – could it
mean? – that his mind was off it, the master-plan had worked, that
the Mel inner self was beginning to recover from the shock of the
very recent death of a female parent?

In which case….

'Good, Mel. … Good.'

Samovar

Drawing into European Russia.

Houses now without that topping of bright white snow deeper than the depth of visible house. Dotted around in places. Houses with inspirationally-carved window frames, patterns of curves and half-moons. Or crazy woodwork: blocks in a fishbone V.

In *Danilov* at nine in the morning, all the station kiosks were closed. Yehune and Mel made a foray into the streets, and came across a tiny shop that sold loaves of black bread for 14 kopeks. Sour-wholemeal taste.

Beautiful *Perm*. Mel just had to get out for some exercise. They piled on jerseys, jackets, coats, double socks with their tramping boots. Forged up and down a couple of hundred yards of dirty snow between two trains. They were late getting back. Carriages already rolling – the provodnik bawling gibberish.

Over the bridge across a vast and imposing river to *Yaroslavl*, accepted almost into the arms of a factory that spewed out white smoke from no fewer than seven chimneys. Crusts of ice at the edges of waterways. Two workmen, on a siding deep in the industrial area, warming themselves by the red tongues of a fire.

Past another train: *Yaroslavl-Leningrad* (Mel read the words out loud). People sitting at their tables in secret haloes of orange light, vectored away at 90, double-lit by the dusty beams of the sun.

A huge palace at *Zagorsk* with gilded domes. As against the rows and rows of broken-down shacks, still with their gingerbread window frames. Weird shapes, barnlike. An A-house steep as a thorn.

They were getting closer and closer to Moscow. They stood in the corridor with all their gear, looking out the windows. Mel held dialogues with anyone he could find: always a rapid garble on the other person's part. 'Information-gathering', he called it to Yehune, though he admitted he never caught more than a phrase or two.

Suddenly, the train had stopped; suddenly, everyone was piling out; suddenly they found themselves floundering in a sea of moving passengers without too much of an idea where they were or what they should do next. Yehune flashed a look of enquiry. Mel seemed to deny all knowledge. But he looked around and quickly found someone to ask – one of two big-boned men in dark suits and red armbands who stood there monitoring the flow.

Straight away, both the suits clustered round him, looking all too interested and not the tiniest bit friendly. They only spoke their Russian-accented English, which allowed Yehune as well to get the force of their utterances, and, incidentally, feel the waft of pure threat.

It turned out they were suspicious of Mel's basic Russian. '*How duss it come about* that you speak Russian?'

Mel began a laboured explanation, not in Russian this time.

One thrust his pudgy hand nearly into Yehune's face. 'Permit!'

'Ah… "permit"? We've got, ah, our passports, if that's what you mean. And tickets. Visas, they've got an extra day, you know, because of the blizzards. But when it comes to…'

But already the fleshier one of the two had looked his utter contempt at Yehune's passport, given his companion a glance in which the Lubyanka seemed to float vestigially, fascinatingly, in the middle distance, and made a decision:

'You will take the Metro.' (Pointing.) 'You will go straight to Belorusski Station. You will take the next train to Poland. You will go now.'

They shuffled off with their packs on their backs, letting the crowd carry them away.

At the head of the Metro steps, Yehune glanced back.

Mel: 'Those seemed serious customers.'

Yehune: 'Yeah. What made you go and talk to them in Russian?'

'I mean... I dunno. On the train...'

'I mean, fuck Mel. Where do you think you are, the capital of Russia?'

Great overhead signs in Cyrillic script gave notice of destinations, or the nicknames of the different Metro lines, it was hard to tell which. Out of the line of sight of their two fairy-tale ogres, Yehune was suddenly a good deal happier. He couldn't believe they'd been let go – without a 'permit' yet. Down in the underground milling-space where thousands of people went about the laborious business of being transported to somewhere else, he tried to picture himself and Mel as they walked along, two bundled-up clods with towering backpacks. Obvious station dossers. Overstayers. Better get those stashed then, ready for the next KGB task force they met....

Everywhere he looked, there was a fair proportion of young people trying to look fashionable, in jeans, always jeans, with a variety of jackets and footwear. Mel's huge fur hat swayed in the foreground of his eye.

'So where do we go?' Mel ventured.

'You asking *me* that?'

'I mean, if it's to Belorusski Station... I don't see where the hell...'

Mel turned round, wobbling with the counterweight of the pack. He scanned the signs, then looked down to crowd level,

'I'll just ask those people over there.'

'What people? Mel, be...'

But the fur hat was already bobbing over to two neatly-turned-out girls, one in a black coat, and a tall, slightly effeminate young man.

Well... OK, he grudgingly allowed. Can't be the government, unless their disguises are getting pretty damn good....

Just like that, in an instant, in a movement of handshakes and bright greetings, Yehune and Mel were introduced to the retail face of the free-wheeling Soviet black market. The young Muscovites all seemed interested, talkative, and amenable to almost any suggestion from a couple of snuffling backpackers they'd met twenty seconds before. Tall Ruslan would have liked to take control. But

Mel naturally preferred to talk to the two girls, who introduced themselves as Gelya and Irina. They knew very well how to get to Belorusski Station, and all the detailed rules for the depositing of baggage; and even offered to escort them there in person.

Gelya seemed fascinated by the Russian-style fur hat that Mel had brought from China; she kept putting her fingers up to stroke it. 'You look like one of us, and yet' (touching the pack) '– a tourist!'

They couldn't believe, positively couldn't believe, that Mel had learned his Russian at school in some unlikely Western country called Novaya Zelandiya. Of course, he refused to switch to English when he was given the chance. Every now and then some phrase he came out with would bring gusts of hilarity from the girls, to his never-failing surprise.

Mel walked in the front rank with Gelya and Irina. Yehune was left behind with Ruslan in his tan cowboy boots. (Thinking, Yep, boy. Fucking hell… why didn't I think to buy one of those bloody dogskin hats?)

But he took the opportunity to confer with Ruslan about the feasibility of doing what they were just about to do. He explained about the visa dates. He asked whether people really did sleep in Belorusski Station and spend the extra day in Moscow –

'*No problem* sleep in station,' was the answer. '*No problem.*'

Ruslan even totted up the figures in his head, lagging behind holding Yehune's papers, mumbling to himself in deep liquid Russian. 'Two days to border,' he pronounced. 'You will be one day over. But two days, even three – *no problem.*'

It didn't agree with Yehune's understanding of the situation, which was that they wouldn't be a day over, and if they were it would very much be a problem. But the youthful, long-drawn features, with the strong forehead and small hooked nose, gave an impression both of dreaminess and a businesslike certainty – subject closed.

Ruslan went on with a self-directed discussion about how *free* people were in the Soviet Union, where in Western countries they were *enslaved*. It was a point of view Yehune had never heard of or suspected, never come across even in the rosy paragraphs of his Russian Background texts.

'So you mean...' he ventured to ask, 'you'd be allowed to leave this country if you wanted to?'

'Leave this country? Why? We do anything we want here. But in America – ha. There people are starving, they are oppressed by system, small number of oligarchs control all food, transport, distribution...'

'Oh. ... Ah, right.'

'You find this, yes?'

'Mm – not sure. ... Never actually been to America myself.'

In an interior hall of Belorusski Station, an important motive behind the young Russians' interest suddenly came up. Ruslan asked them, 'You have anything to sell us – jeans, music cassettes, any *modni* thing?' There was an unmistakable look of appeal in his eye. By that time, Mel had positively bonded with the two girls, probably had a complete knowledge of their university courses and career prospects and current boyfriends – unless it had all gone out the other ear – and was disposed to be helpful. As for Yehune, he started rummaging through his pack as well, under the very strange influence of a sense of obligation.

He found a couple of dress shirts he could spare. Mel in the meantime had hooked out a pair of very long slim Levi's.

'Might be hard to get anyone to fit these,' he warned them.

'Ah. No problem. We sell them on. That is...'

'You have hard currency, American dollars?' one of the girls broke in. 'We can change them for roubles. Have night out in Moscow, go to restaurant, or buy whatever you like...'

That, of course, was the hitch. They had roubles now, which had a high exchange value. But you couldn't change them back when you left the U.S.S.R.

Luckily though, Mel had already thought of something he might want to buy,

'Um, I was wondering – if I could get a samovar somewhere here. A samovar... that'd be a pretty amazing thing to have. Do you have any idea where...?'

'Ah! Samovar,' Gelya said, smiling merrily. 'You come with us, we show you.'

So began one of the most dismal and bebollocksed portions of the whole trip, for Yehune; probably one of the more pleasant ones for Mel – the search, the very, very prolonged heraldic quest through the streets of Moscow for a samovar. *Of course* they could get a samovar. This was Moscow. Of course, naturally; and yet for some reason the things seemed devilishly elusive. Mel wasn't interested in the standard tourist product, those little gilded toys on sale here and there for American dollars only; he wanted one that worked. Yehune wouldn't admit out loud that he was extremely vague about what a samovar was; he had a dim idea that the Russians used them to sleep on during the winter, or something equally fantastic… but as he watched and listened, as the group flowed and reconstituted itself, from street to Metro to street again, the idea gradually filtered back to him that the idea was to make tea. That, and of course to be able to point the gleaming curvaceous artifact out to visitors, Oh yeah, that's the *samovar,* y'know, we picked it up when we were last in Moscow… Trans-Siberian Railway… bla bla bla.

It turned out that Gelya knew of several good shops, all in different districts. The three Russians and Mel were all packing into the front row now, taking up the breadth of the pavement. So Yehune found himself trailing endlessly on behind in a stupor of semi-exhaustion, watching darkness fall over streets that had little in common with the domed Tartaric weirdness he might have been expecting. He caught echoes or snatches of sound that seemed to bounce back off the streaked, pilastered walls. In that state of mind, half-asleep, tormented by motion, he could pick up meanings from the very smallest indications, unless he was only dreaming it….

Mel: 'Something something GUM?'

Irina (with a dismissive wave): 'Ne something something f'GUM.'

Don't bother with the GUM. Or something like that. The GUM, the GUM…. Yehune knew what that was: the Whatsit Whatsit Magazine, the biggest department store in the world. So why, he asked himself, was it such a hopeless idea to go looking in the GUM? It was as if all the values of his third-form Russian Background were being contradicted, attitudes he didn't even know he had – the economic heroism of the Five Year Plans, the brave endeavour to pull

Soviet Industry into the twentieth century. He was almost offended by it. But the reality that met his eye just then failed to carry his point for him. Here in the weeping, cur-haunted streets, everything was a deception, nothing answered to plan. Such basic things as the location of a toilet or a place to buy food had acquired the status of secret information known only to the few. Once, Ruslan seriously pointed out a door with a sign above it, M-something: you can go to the toilet here. Far later, driven by an uncomfortable insistency, Yehune would remember that moment, look for the place, dragging Mel behind him, retrace the paths they'd taken to get there – only to find the door, of course, locked – after hours – do not shit.

For now, though, the samovar question was in its infancy. Shops were still being tried out in a spirit of happy optimism, as if Mel might be able to find and buy the perfect samovar right here and now... after which they'd all go off and do something else. The night had hardly begun. The young Russians seemed to give of their time with unbounded generosity, almost as if (Yehune speculated) the principle of self-interest that ruled every exchange in normal places might have only dimly begun to filter through to them. When you thought about it, there was nothing else for them – not a pair of jeans or a music cassette or a fucking *modni* thing. So then, why bother? Why not leave the bedraggled Westerners to their own half-intentions, give it all up, blow them off... let Yehune drag his sorry arse back to Belorusski Station?

Behind a stretch of yellow wall bare of any sign, someone was selling fat globular objects like 1950s toasters. They looked more like tea-urns than samovars. Mel pronounced them not traditional enough.

No matter, Gelya knew of another place....

Again and again, they cut back and forth through Moscow and environs on long sad trains, Mel talking and arguing, always paying the few kopeks' charge for all five of them.

A fat lady was trying out the circuits of electric samovars: the very cheapest. Bent out of well-fatigued tin. Doesn't work. Doesn't work.... Ah! *Vot!* One that works. A battered body, legs splayed out in all directions, surely used for a ball in street games between

156

Moscow children. ... Gelya anxiously consulted Mel. He decided against buying it.

Trailing behind, cut out of the line by the accident of their number, Yehune felt the novelty of being pulled on not where *he* wanted to go, through a fathomless urban dusk in which the signs were unreadable (that is, unless he stood puzzling them out for hours), districts irreconcilable, the Metro something like a mechanical giant standing at every street corner ready to slash across any sense of orientation as soon as it was born. Mel at least must have been enjoying himself – Yehune watched the fur hat wobbling on ahead in a sort of drunken alter-world. *Two* personable young women to talk to, and a foreign language to blunder about in. Sardonically, Yehune let himself think that if that was all it took to bring him back to life, they might as well not have left Auckland.

... And thought again: no. Not really. You never knew how it'd affect a guy like.... Never knew. Mum got dead. He recalled a sort of *lost* look, a sense of the dimming of all commitment – which could have been what had spurred him on to take on the organisation, force the sale of motorcycles, even to the extent of refusing buyers unless they agreed to take Mel's Laverda as well.

And now... now look at him. The action of time, was it? Places, scenes progressing past the eyes...?

From there, Yehune had only a short way to go to wonder what was in it for himself. What could be his own direction here – was there something he was *going towards*? Pounding on behind through the filthy, cavernous streets, glimpsing the faces of hunched and pallid passers-by, he found his mind revolving around questions like that, hopelessly, repetitively. He'd fallen back into a nauseous, recurrent cycle of experience, something like a marijuana dream. He saw himself in his mind's eye trailing endlessly under the rain, stoned and freezing, somewhere on the edge of Auckland City, trying to hitch a lift back over the bridge.

Where were they now? Blagoveshchenski? ... Didn't he recognise that name? Hadn't they been here three, even four times in the last hour...?

Gelya fell back on purpose to talk to him. She couldn't believe that such a thing as a proper samovar wasn't to be found in her home city. 'I am so em-barrassed!'

Her broad cheeks, and that delicate, far-away look in the corners of the eyes. A residue, maybe, of some epicanthic fold far back in the bloodline.

Some time later, he noticed the lofty form of Ruslan pacing silently beside him. Disgruntled about something. Yehune preferred to stay in his reverie, letting his eyes catch up on accidental details of the darkness as they passed by. *Of course* there was a direction. There must be. But then, what could it be? A shape, a familiar spirit, keeping pace? ... Na, doubt it, that's old Ruslan in his cowboy boots. But rather (as they stopped at a kerb to wait for an antique truck to rattle past, flanked by two Dniepers with sidecars)

– red dot. In the bubbles of the interstitial tar between flat blocks, caught in the halo of a street light, a snip of bright-red ribbon.

How the *fuck* did that get there? Where you couldn't buy a ribbon for love or...? Gone dirty on one side. Discarded, minuscule, lying, as he looked at it, against two dark crater shapes of what to an ant might be about dog-kennel size.

Some peculiar micro-insects, might be, bred in Slavonic countries. Going out, anto? Take your dog.

The party moved on then, Yehune lagging a bit behind. Naturally some woman must have dropped it there. He could see women, in extreme expansion, walking up ahead. With Mel. ... Left out, you can be, cut off by the accident of size. To damnation and hell. It was already obvious to him they were never going to find a samovar; they'd used up their best chances. But not to the others. Still they slogged ahead. And yet, it seemed....

In the red red red red. Magnified in the globules of the tar, insects, those Slav-bred dogs.

...

Again

... it seemed that somewhere, someone, close, there was a shape. Whispering. On the outside. On the outside, must be – somewhere outside himself. Angelic. Cataclysmic. Peopling emptiness; focus in the universal gorge

Then God willya oh God hurry up and
...

Was it hours later, years later? that Mel turned round, secretly taking time out from some exchange or other, and shrugged expressively – 'What can I do?'

An extract from Mel's diary:

At 6 we gave up trying to sleep, Inturist wasn't going to open till 9. Creaked out the station doors. It's freezing on the street, frost-blown. I wound the tartan scarf round my neck. We got into a roadside kafe for something to eat. A huge queue, stand-up tables. We got what we thought were two teas, but they turned out to be coffee. So I went back for what looked like a glass of milk. Sour cream. Yehune spooned sugar into his coffee. Salt.

Reservations, and Ruslan was wrong (alliteration). We arrive on 16/11 at 9 or 10pm, so our visas will be OK after all. Ha!

Out, half-dead with the pain in my legs and my mind in inertial lag. You move, it catches up. It's all a <u>trestle</u>, see, carrying the unbelievable fabulousness of this experience like a magnesium flare at the top, finally coming up close to the Khram Vasiliya Blazhennovo with its orange bricks with white, a dome swooping up above us like a titanic convex belly of corrugated plastic. We went over a deeply-worn stone doorstep through an ancient door. Queued up for a ticket. Displays, crazy ancient Russian manuscripts, shields and chain mail, heavy decorated gold plates and big keys and painted wooden chests like props from 'Ivan the Terrible', the shadows of the boyars falling over us. Also some paintings of the Khram in various former eras. We sort of half-attached ourselves to a tour group, there are a lot of them here. She drones, drawls out the Russian syllables with a little upwards catch at the end of a sentence, projecting boredom, I learned this by rote, eh, and can't wait till lunch break. Delivery, how not to. Just wait till you get me to a podium, if or whenever such a thing might occur, then you'll see fireworks. Crashing! Quick-thunder topple of phrase!

I did a bit of translating for Y.

To a monk's cell, age-old arched brick roof, a window narrow and melancholic set into the wall. Like an arrow slit. Imagine living there... just imagine it! Then everyone up a long narrow staircase in single file.

Up there were the most amazing rooms of all, starting with a central shaft going up the whole length of a tower. I wandered off by myself, past windows with displays of ancient Russian this and that, old murals for walls, chewed corroded brickwork, corridors leading off into space, a huge door blocked by an iron bar. Trying to avoid the others, forced here and there by the currents of tour groups abreast and ahead of me and parallel to another wall. Schools of shuttle-fish. Catching Y, meeting, disappearing. Drenched with tiredness, hungry with it. This whole notebook wouldn't be enough to describe the detail, or half a dozen more. And it's all in a single building. It seemed to go on without an end, and yet some time we found some other steps down and out the side of the Khram, onto worn uneven cobbles. Krasnaya Ploshchad' again.

Some sort of climax. That cathedral to me was more amazing than anything I've seen along the way, strangeness embodied, golden and cracked. And it's all wound up with slogging up old high steps in a stupor of suffering, beating on the trestle, the purest unreality somehow made real.

We got here through a tunnel – the tunnel of the train carriage, shaded and white. Posters I saw through the windows: Honour and Glory to the Soviet People the Builders of Communism. Slava Trudu: Glory to Labour. Clatter of wheels on the rails. The darkness, that feeling of not knowing, never knowing. Staring out on the incredible fragile beauty of the breaks of birch forest, leafless, like ghost trees. Lakeland, the picture on the coloured pencils. Can remember all those books and teachers going on about the Siberian steppes, endless space, 60 below, not one of them ever said it was beautiful. But that, all that was like the clutter towards, full of dialogues misunderstood. All a framework. For this – the culmination. You can feel your body aching and stumbling, moving on legs, all to transport your head and seeing eyes onwards through space. Framing you up. And if

(Nothing. Interrupted. I thought that if I saw something incredible in the next minute, then it'd all work out, my idea, and saw… gibbering old man against the steps. The high bright contrail of a jet.)

Here, you can't do anything but focus on the <u>now</u>. It's hilarious, tramping the streets, going in the wrong direction. We tried to find a toilet again, and met up with some more young junk-buyers, who showed us where to go to get into the Kreml'. Still no toilet. A shutter opened for a matter of two minutes out of a blank wall, we managed to buy 2 pastries and some glasses of apple-juice, before it closed – bang! – queue trailed away leaving nothing.

Fatigued, but it's nothing but mechanism. You have to keep it in mind the amazing thing is that we managed to <u>do</u> this – stay the night in the station – see Khram and Kreml' and Krasnaya Ploshchad', without even having to pay the price of a hotel room.

We've still got roubles to spend. But it's a real job paying for things, you have to get the sour old salesperson interested enough to hook it down for you, then trail off to get a ticket, then take it to the kassa, then come back, then…. Even harder to find anything any undistorted human could want to buy. The GUM. Ha! Samovar.

And so we wandered off to the Kreml', past a white wedding going on in front of the Tomb of the Unknown Soldier, through the park and up to an overhead walkway, where a dead-faced soldier stopped us, mumbled something and pointed to our bags, and we had to crawl down and deposit them and then crawl up again. They let us in, without a ticket yet. I lost track of time for a bit, as if I were caught in some loop – had we really gone in? Everything so ordinary, street-layout much as before –

To one of the most extreme moments of heightening, through burrs of my systemal decrepitude: the sight of the vast golden-domed cathedral blazing against the sun, towering off balance, the trail of a jet at that moment streaking overhead not quite touching the outermost tower as we walked towards it, intolerably white in clarity, after that the whole array (around a square) of intricate churches, fresco-painted woods, a whole man-made Volcanovia of gilded domes, with little tricked-up crosses hovering on

…

In the Refectory

Hearing syllables repeated – *bark*-ba, *bark*-ba – in the strident voice of the cleaning lady pulling a bucket and mop behind her, he came to himself, reconnected, gathering together small shards and fragments of himself blown widely over wends and countries. Where she was too, maybe, far away… a greyscale Russian cleaning lady, leaning somewhere among all the galleries of shades.

He coughed and gasped for air. Nose was blocked up. Saw he was on the floor, spread out between two fixed rows of plastic chairs.

Aah… fucking shit. You woke. But….

Now he'd worked out where he was. In a medium-sized waiting room in Belorusski Station, where several dozen other travellers or tramps were sprawled in inventive positions all over the seats. Oh Go-od. A weird part of the tape… strange place to wake up in.

You fucking carping old cow *bitch,* will you *shut… up?*

But by then, all the other people were getting up and trailing over to the other side of the room. A cascade of 'zh' sounds conveyed the command. Or rather didn't, to him; but something in the general consensus of direction had Yehune climbing to the level of the hard chair tops.

And I'll never sleep again. How 'bout that.

Better carve myself a bit of floor. Where's M'? Oh, OK….

Uh-huh. So….

He knew he didn't stand a chance, now, of getting back to his diffuse and wonderful state of self-forgetfulness. Somewhere, though, in the fuzzy byways of his thinking, strangely universalised just then, he thought he could see another story playing. What was that? … Another time. Institutional seating. Some pass across, pass across… in a room far larger, among dabs of half-defeated sunlight….

In the Ref, was it? in the Ref the u u U

…

The University of Auckland Student Union temporary refectory. That was its proper title. It was something set up on one floor of the big Student Union building, late in their sixth form year. Not for them of course, but a visiting group from Ghana. On the third floor, was it, or the fourth? Yehune could remember the deep 'thunk-thunk' of electric music vibrating on a level somewhere below them, where some daylight student orgy must have been going on. As for the hall itself – because of the modernistic, cast concrete, room-within-a-room construction, where vertical slits of windows opened onto a length of corridor, even the full summer sunlight outside was filtered down in there to a sort of seething and constricted twilight, so that in theory the lights had to be kept on all day. In practice, they weren't; or not for a group of visiting sixth forms from the northern area secondary schools. Further, the long trestle-construction bar along one side of the room was empty of snacks or bottles. But it gave the teachers somewhere to sit and pass each other cups of tea; and the pupils had their lunchboxes.

The grid of tables and chairs could have provided seating for hundreds of sixth formers. In fact, though, only a few groups were still there to occupy that deep-light-pollinated crepuscule; most were out in the grounds (with orders to reappear at 2:30 on the dot), either in the quad or across the road in Albert Park, watching with their astonished sixth-form eyes the activities of university students moving back and forth in what must have seemed to them a purpose-built earthly paradise. And as they watched, drinking in the message: why not come here? why not get a bursary? why not do a seventh form year...? Why not? Why not?

Yehune and a group of sporty cronies had just come in the door. They gathered at the back wall, leaning or sitting, scorning chairs of any kind. Thoroughwell was there, the dark all-rounder, as well as Rhat (rugby) and Mickey, who was predominant in tennis and badminton. For them, the elite, the popular, this was a pointless farce, since not one of them was going to do a seventh form year.

So there he leaned, in idleness and tedium. He could see Mr Peele behind the trestles checking them out with a wary eye. One other large group was using the room: probably less of a worry to

164

the supervisory powers. The high marks getters, the school pariahs, scapegoats of everybody's discontent, had a table to themselves close by one of the inner windows.

Beside Yehune, Rhat took items out of his lunchbox one by one, making little noises of protest.

Thoroughwell asked Mickey (small, red-faced) if he had his racquet and if he was coming tonight.

Mickey answered with a grunt. He commented on the venue's layout and the elasticity of the surface.

'Oh yeah,' said Thoroughwell back.

In a small bright Tupperware lunchbox, Yehune had six sandwiches cut in a perfect wedge of triangles. He remembered looking upwards from the red lid.

He saw a strange tableau. It was like a group of statues. Not strange for that time and place and the unusual properties of the light, but... strange. Lesser mortals, he'd have said. On and around their table, Mel Seuchar and his friend Templeton and some of the other academic successes, the girl Bicklespear, others, along with a few hangers-on like Locke and Timothy Castor, stood in the banded, luminous jut and shadow of filtered and refiltered sun's rays; some, like Seuchar and his friend, actually raised up on chairs or the tabletop so that they formed slim masts, a sort of irregular summit to the array; others flanking them, stilled for just that moment in supporting attitudes. There was something striking about the accidental contrast of dark and light, visible to him from where he leaned against the facing of the wall, different, he supposed, from any other angle – upward spars, imposition of light-haloes – and the word fell into his head: 'alphas'. This was just a sampling, Seuchar and Templeton, Kathleen Bicklespear too; the swots, the goodlets. But the ones who he supposed in the course of things would go on to dominate the social pack. In the future, that was... that nearly unthinkable stretch of time after the yellow sludge-end of school.

It struck Yehune that that future was just about to start. There was the rest of the year and the summer holidays. ... And after that? He didn't need to give it much conscious thought, he'd been aware of it for some time. Games, for him, were played out. They'd been good enough for school. But he knew, his body told him with the occasional twinge or awkwardness, that he didn't have it in him to be a champion, something like an All Black.

Which meant that the ones he'd be competing with were standing right up there. Idly he cast around for any other possibility. Maths? No. Music...?

He was far from feeling any sort of desperation; because at his age, with the breezy irreverence of his mid-teens, Yehune naturally felt he could take any risk, throw his future prosperity to the four winds and laugh. More on a whim, it must have been, with an air of conferring a favour – a movement of acceptance, probably, of weird futures never dreamed of, possibilities he might be refusing just by standing against that wall – Yehune took it into his head to cross the floor.

Someone might have looked up; at least he heard the exclamation behind him, 'Hey! Trent!' Not in Thoroughwell's voice. Tables moved by him scattered with school possessions, mostly empty otherwise. He was aware of the momentousness of the break with tradition, and in fact gloried in it. Fuck it, fuck them – fuck everything in fact. In the meantime, creases of drapery began to shift minutely in the stand of figures presented there; heads revolved; the whole composed, light-centred frieze of it grew more alive as his eyes moved onwards.

Mel Seuchar wasn't facing in his direction. But Cas was down on a chair below him, and Yehune knew Cas fairly well.

'Cas.'

'Oh, hi, Yehune. What's going on?'

'Nothin' much.'

(Strange snips of conversation could be picked out of the gloomy space above their heads:

'But, you know, if you take the axial centre of gravity, um, independently of the weight...'

It might have been something about bikes. He was interested in bikes.) He grabbed a chair from one of the neighbouring tables, screeched it up to the tableside, and was established.

A few more words with Cas followed. But Yehune was impatient. He didn't bother to wait for a gap in Mel's conversation,

'So, Mel! Hey, Mel. Ahh-m... what sort of stuff are you thinkin' of taking in university, then?'

The features of Mel Seuchar appeared above. Spare, eyes close together, the jawline sculpted and a bit prolonged.

'Oh, Trent. Don't know yet, I haven't got the Calendar.'

'You mean you're not doing English?'

'English, why English?' Mel Seuchar let his eyes turn back to Templeton in apology for the distraction. Templeton's face was even more chiselled, his framework taller, as he stepped down to the tableside.

'Oh well... no, I doubt it. You don't take English if you're...'

If you're what? Bursting to take over, still Yehune forced himself to wait. Polite – like a winning sportsman on TV – who never shows a trace of condescension.

Mel looked away into space for a moment, then said,

'You know... Solzhenitsyn said the best thing he ever did was not getting a literary education.'

'Oh. Soldier Nitsin said that?'

If the comment had meant anything to him, if it might have conveyed any sort of message (the syllables 'Soldier Nitsin' being vaguely familiar to him from a years-old residue of Russian Background), the thought process was quickly interrupted by a younger boy at the tableside, who piped up just then about Yehune's *mighty* performance in last week's match, and how he'd got them two tries. He felt obliged to mumble, 'Only one, but it got converted.' In the meantime Mel had bent to the tabletop, taken hold of a large schoolbag, and was rummaging for something.

Rugby – always rugby. Not normally averse to that kind of hero-worship, Yehune felt it as the wings of an older world brushing by him, deflecting him from new intentions.

Now Templeton from the side had started a conversation with the Bicklespear girl – once over-tall, now what you might call statuesque, and Mel's main rival for dominance in the arts subjects. Mel seemed to be listening and not listening, while he snagged out a crushed Woolly's supermarket bag that must have had his lunch in it.

Yehune caught his eye, and gave a shrug.

'What about you,' Mel asked, 'you going on to the seventh form?'
'I'm not charging straight on in here, if that's what you mean.'
'No, I just didn't know if you…. Maths was your thing, wasn't it?'
'Used to be. Now it's music.'

Now it's music. Yehune might have been surprised to hear himself say it, those expensive lessons and his hours of experimenting at the piano keyboard having been taken more-or-less for granted until then…. But he went on,

'Remember when you used to write essays for me and I'd slip you all the maths answers?'

'Oh yeah… I can vaguely remember scribbling some stuff.'

'Right. So now I can give your music the old master-touch too.'

Mel laughed. 'There isn't any.'

They'd drifted by then to the top of the table, seated, along with a few others, in a position where the indirect sunlight waxed and waned on them, leaving them most of the time in semi-darkness. Yehune had a clear view of his line of cronies at the back of the room. For some reason they'd all stood up, and were going with bangs and crashes for the door.

Damn, Yehune thought. Nothing stays still. What, what in the world, had made him head over here? Free flow. Something in him resisted boundaries of any kind. Must be his nature. Now he was stuck with it, with the alphas on the hill.

So he went on,

'Come on, you must listen to *music*.'

'Well, you know, only rock, and a bit of blues… is that the kind of music you…?'

Music. Music, is music, is music. … As he thought it, his eyes were looking with a kind of guilty fascination at the half-squashed, unappetising lump of food Mel had extracted from the Woolly's bag.

He said,

'You like Zappa, the Mothers of Invention?'

'Ah, I think so… I usually listen to older stuff though. You know, Clapton and Led Zeppelin and that.'

'Oh, right. "In Through the Out Door".'

Mel's voice came muffled by brown bread and elderly sardine,

'That's the last one... I haven't actually heard it yet.'

Now, Mel must surely have come round once or twice to Yehune's place, to the bright, well-ordered bungalow on the corner of Macclewell Avenue. Yehune could clearly picture the run-down clifftop shack the guy lived in himself.

'I've got it at home,' he said. 'Come round and listen to it some time, if you can be bothered.'

'Wouldn't mind.'

Suddenly, a very loud voice crowed out from somewhere near them,

'Bugger my arse, they're married!'

Mel Seuchar looked around sharply, a flush beginning in his cheek.

Yehune, for his part, took a little bit of time to study their surroundings. And found a possible sense or purpose to it all further down the length of the room,

where Templeton and Kathleen Bicklespear were walking together towards the door, two arses under trousers and a grey skirt.

An Accident

Again and again, on the floor of Belorusski Station, where the fluorescent lighting blinked and stabbed and pinned him down between the seat posts, Yehune changed position, trying for some sort of truce between his upper and lower body. Shoulders were too big. Then there were the hips and bum. He unwrapped his left leg from round a metal upright, and strained his neck to the point of cricking.

Mel's head, in the extreme foreground. Stripes of dirty-fair hair radiating from a central well.

Anything else…? Couldn't quite see. He had to fumble his glasses on for a proper look. (And a long, bellowing moan sounded out from another Station dosser a few seats away.)

No, no, it was nothing. Just Mel's old jacket wrapped most of the way round his neck. And yet, there seemed to be something strange about the set of that body, limbs folded in and clutching… what? Sky-blue nylon corner.

Was that his bag? Jeez Christ, when he could've stashed it….

Yehune lay back again. He delicately folded his glasses and set them near his head.

Lying awake, casting around for something to think, he happened to fall back on the train of pictures he'd been following in the drip-dark streets. Strange intimations of an emptiness ahead. What would come to fill it…? A girl, of course, smooth limbs, girl… or… the inner darkness, burgeoning into life. Behind your eye: entoptic forms. Those white-yellow haloes of red and green. Fold your eyes up, go floating back into the brain. You can see people walking. Not grails… not doggie-leash. Only. Only. There was something. What? In the what not known. That we'll live, somewhere… sim, simwhere, simhoop. Or

His eyes opened. Saw Mel's hair again, a cascading tangle of strips. Sandy. What could *he* be dreaming…?

Sandy, in sand is sand is sand-sand falling. Sifts towards... and out... until in the macroscope (his eyes were closing again) it flats out, sands out, to a tidal spun infinity out towards v, towards vanish, vanishing p p poi

To who, wha'...?

(And here we have to report an episode from the European spring five months later, when the two of them had already crossed from East to West Berlin, made their way to England and Mel's brother Geoff in Essex, shot out again nearly as quickly, taken his beaten-up Austin Chevalier to drive down in through France to Spain and Italy, found jobs in a dive restaurant in Tuscany, connected by the gift of Yehune's personality with a Signor Freibrecht who owned an art collection in Florence, spent the rest of the winter as guards or caretakers in Signor Freibrecht's vacant house; then started back up the length of France again towards Luxembourg and the north of Germany, and after that, who knew, possibly Scandinavia…?)

There was a grubby mark on the wall just under the official timetable. Like a hermetic sign, repeated dwindling, different with each imprint, until it drew down into the black line between plank and plank. Yehune fixed it in his eye. After what seemed a long time, he grudgingly cleared the SNCF of the charge of uncleanliness. Stained in, he thought. Couldn't really avoid that. But all along the platform (which opened out to him as he turned and caught the light in his eye, staring back along the line of planking under a light-blue sky) there was an effect of grainy blackness; railway oil mixed with the airborne sediment stirred up by train after train.

'So, basically…' he said.

He gestured at the boardwalk under a partial awning – doors to the station waiting room – the toilets for Hommes and Femmes – and the sharp brink before the rails. Beyond them there was only a walled-off embankment and the side of a stone bridge.

'Aah, yeah.'

Mel sat slumped on the side of a flatbed luggage trolley. For the moment, empty of luggage. Just as there were no other people, nothing – unless you counted two heads behind the stationmaster's office window; which if you waited long enough were joined by hands gesticulating.

'Here we are then. But fucking where?' Yehune went on.

'Coigny.'
' "Change at Change-y". '
'OK, OK, I'm sorry, all right? For the millionth time.'
Yehune (who was shorter-haired now, nearly clean-shaven, dressed in a slightly rumpled Italian dress leather jacket) took his time to answer. He scrounged through his pockets for a fag and matches. Took a few steps up along the station platform, then back again, looking around him. He began to light up, hands cupped for protection against the wind.

'That's all right,' he said, shaking his match. 'Though I've gotta say, all this foreign words shit, I generally leave it to you…'

Mel said, 'Well, you were the one who burned the car.'

Burned the car. Burned the. Fucking what… how long ago was…? The total non-sequitur put Yehune off his stride, giving the initiative back to the figure half-sprawled on the trolley. But Mel failed to take it up. Just then he seemed drained of all energy, a touch less lively than his own pack.

Yehune just stood and blew smoke.

Sure enough, eventually Mel came out with:

'I mean, how can they *possibly* have two stations with practically the same name, on near enough the same…'

Giving him the opportunity to say, 'Though it's not actually the same line, since I've no doubt you were on the beam enough to notice we *did* come up through Borgen-Bross.'

Before Yehune could finish his sentence, Mel hove to his feet. It looked as if life might be coming back. He took a step, even a few steps, weaving along the breadth of the platform as if he was considering the layout of track and buildings to some purpose or other. He knelt down near the edge. Peered down with intensity into the space below. A sort of wave, backwards to forwards, convulsed his whole body; and violently, far-reachingly, he chucked his guts.

A stir behind the office window. A door opened; presently a small man in uniform came up the platform towards them. He burst out with a torrent of French, excited, declamatory, as if some pot seething there in the slowness of the changing moments in Coigny had suddenly blown out in a passionate and unbroken steam-voice. Nor did it mean any more than that to Yehune, who watched him with detachment. After a while, the stationmaster, or whatever he was, must have realised he was having no effect. He made an upward-tossing movement of his hand into the air, and turned on his heel – thinking (Yehune guessed), These foreigners, *mon doo* – decadent student chunderers.

A voice from behind the window trebled weakly, 'Gaston?'

That day they'd come up from Nice, travelling on railcards after the demise of their car. Neither of them had particularly studied the routes. It was only in the vicinity of Lyon that any confusion could possibly arise, where their chosen course drew near and either converged or didn't converge with the main line northward to Paris. Paris: they'd done Paris; but somehow it always seemed a problem to travel in France if you didn't want to go there. But, no matter. They were aiming for the more north-easterly line through Nancy, Metz, Luxembourg; easy enough to connect with if you went straight through to Dijon; only requiring one change if you took the train that went via Mâcon.

They sat on either side of a table scattered with bags, bottles, pamphlets, books and loose possessions, while rich rolling countryside sped past outside the windows. Mel seemed to be going to sleep, collapsed against the corner of the seat and carriage-side. There was the whisk of a line of discontent around the upper ridges of his mouth. Yehune reflected that he hadn't been ticking well all day.

Just then, that slumped frame stirred a bit, head turning, to look out at the station signs streaming past.

Coigny. Coigny. Coigny...

'Hey!' Mel called out. The change of expression was almost comical: his eyes shone like two little bright pebbles through straggles of hair. 'That's it – Coigny! That's our station! Quick, we'd better...'

He began scooping things back into his bag with a feverish energy that wasn't matched on the other side of the table. Yehune watched the hands actually grabbing small items of his own, a pack of cards, a black glasses-case.

'Are you sure? Is that the name? Gotta say, I wasn't expecting...'

'Yeah! Yeah, hurry up! I remember, see – if we miss it, where'll we be?'

Then Yehune started catching things together as well. They pulled their bags shut, not bothering to check for anything they'd dropped, scrambled for the packs that lay in the suitcase rack further towards the door, and hit the button at what seemed like the last possible moment; when Yehune could have sworn the wheels were already turning, heaving irretrievably into motion again. And hit it again, and another time for good measure.

Other passengers stared at them impassively.

Mel was babbling,

'See, I remembered. That guy who made up the tickets for us, he told us all about it, you remember me saying to you? There are two trains going out this way, one you have to change at Coigny. I remembered it, "Change at Change-y," I said. This is it. Change at Change-y.'

They were out the door, having successfully negotiated the train exit, and could feel the solid platform under their shoes.

Yehune said, 'Change-y doesn't sound all that much like Cwanyee.'

'No,' Mel returned almost gaily, 'but there was another name I wanted to distinguish it from, there's a Ch and a... well, there was a name a bit like it in the index, something like... or... no, it can't have...'

Yehune only looked at him. His pack toppled clumsily from the right shoulder, and he caught it and let it down easily. Something was apparently percolating in the Seuchar head. Nobody but them had got out. Just then, the train was flashing past them, carriage after carriage, heading off into infinity on the iron rails of south-to-eastern France.

Mel's eyes were dull again, and he seemed frozen, waiting for Yehune to say something.

He let him stew.

'Oh, fuck.'

Chagny was the name, in distinction to *Cagny,* another name to be found in France though not in that particular area; whereas the all but non-existent provincial station they'd ended up in was *Coigny*; and furthermore they wouldn't have had to change at all since the train they'd been so comfortably ensconced in was the one that went through Bourg-en-Brosse and so was set to proceed directly to Dijon and the north-east. The hugeness, the perfect avoidability of the mistake seemed to point to a mentality so unattached to anything earthbound that Yehune actually made the connection, even in the mood he was in, with certain things he'd noticed earlier in the day: a listlessness in the Seuchar actions, bad colour in his face, a lack of appetite at breakfast. He'd gone so far as to ask, 'Are you OK?', to which the answer had been 'I'm absolutely fine'. Now, Yehune was well enough acquainted with the version of English Mel used to know that as often as not 'I'm fine' could mean 'I'm not fine', depending on the circumstances and who he was talking to and the state of his inner self. He seemed to recall a dead fish-eye by a slab of greenish meat that had done duty for Mel's eye, the left side of his face, under the lights of a railway eating hall. More than that, he had inside knowledge, as the Coigny stationmaster didn't, of the itinerary of Mel's life over the last few days, which didn't include any real debauchery. So his conclusions were different, reactions more sympathetic, when the explosive vomiting-fit occurred, spattering the edge of the platform with a crescent of orange and turquoise unspeakableness; drawing groans, whimpers, sometimes actual tears between gut-driven bout and bout.

He looked back towards the station office window, which was empty now.

Breathing carefully through his mouth, he approached the body.

'Prob'ly a virus,' he remarked cheerfully. 'Either that or something you ate.'

But he did fish out his handkerchief, white and crumpled but recently washed, and put it within reach of Mel's hand.

'Here.'

'Aaaaah – aaaah – …what's 'a?' gasped Mel.

'Wipe your mouth. The stink's appalling.'

It wasn't as if they were actually *going* anywhere. That much had changed in Yehune's attitude during the past five months, especially after the brief stay with Geoff in Essex. That had been somewhere he'd thought he was *going*. But the aim of a trip, he thought, was surely tripping; looking around you, living in a sideways-slipping kaleidoscope of strange scenes while you plotted routes and dossed here and there and sometimes got stuck in one place for a matter of months, generally as a result of some scheme to get you money to go further. The scents, the signposts, the flavours in the air were different here, whether you were moving or stationary, miserable or having a whale of a time. And it was only now (he thought vaguely), now, when you were young, that you could live with all the obvious discomforts and still get up every day full of the determination to go on – only now, in fact, that you were likely to have the chance to try. In any case, an unspoken set of rules seemed to have been agreed between him and Mel: that they'd go where they wanted, find casual work wherever they could, and never retrace their steps unless it was absolutely necessary. Mel had said something about Austria. Nothing had especially grabbed him in that, historical or family interest as it surely ought to have held for him; and since he hadn't gone for it it hadn't been mentioned again. But both of them had been impressed with Monaco, possibly in different ways (Yehune, unlike Mel, having no particular objection to overrich people swanking around on their motor yachts), and from that they'd developed a hankering to see another small state, Luxembourg – which was part of a general drift northward, north and north again, with perhaps a dim vision of mountain inlets at the end of it – Grieg and the misted precipices – Fiordland overturned…?

Now that Mel had caught this bug, even that illusion of forward progress was put in danger. But Yehune was already plotting ways to pick up where they'd left off. The smoke was whipped away from his mouth and fag-end both by the cool spring wind. He was thinking about Dijon, travel times, anywhere at all they could pick up a train. It was four and a half hours, as he reckoned it, till the next one came through here. Again, he looked towards the office

177

window, where the side of a face had appeared and disappeared some time within the last three minutes.

Leaving Mel lying there (Yehune had an irrational impulse to give him a pat on the head in passing), he strode over and loudly rapped on the door.

That was how they came to be slogging along a nearly-deserted country road with their packs on their backs, through the dust and scattered grasses of the edging, along lines of hedge that protected frameworks of laced vines, woody-leafy and bare of any fruit. Mel was pale as dough, labouring on behind. Yehune shouldered the responsibilities of keeping an eye out for cars and holding his hand loosely stretched out, as well as worrying continuously about Mel and how long he'd be able to keep this up. 'Bien soor,' the stationmaster had said, 'Bien soor,' when he finally allowed himself to understand Yehune's perfectly clear questions in English about whether it might be possible for them to get to Dijon by road from there. 'Ma bien soor,' or something, and a wave of the hand to indicate where the road was, and a direction, laboriously checked later by Yehune against the general direction of the sun.

Incidentally, he'd found it was really no problem to communicate without a language in common. Here that little guy in the hat had already confirmed his reading of the French station timetables, and managed (though without showing much commitment to the conversation) to second the idea Yehune already had: that they could do a lot better for themselves than waiting four and a half hours till nightfall for the next train to trickle by. After all, he reasoned, a bigger town, more trains – including the one they would have changed to if they actually *had* come by Change-y. Mel, for once, wasn't there to interpret the accompanying garble; Yehune had worked most of it out from the gestures.

And so he found the way to purposeful action. In Yehune's system of belief, you had to move, then things happened. The things could be either good or bad, but most likely good. He was jittering with inward frustration and the desire to be somewhere else, in any perverse and laughable scrape rather than this one. So he set himself a series of tasks; the first (and by no means the easiest) being to get Mel on his feet and persuade him that he had it in him to walk with a pack.

Now he was telling himself that he'd been right, damn it, right. Four and a half hours to wait – too much. When there were roads, he had a thumb. How could he have known that this particular road, neat and well made, snaking all over the undulating countryside for all the world as if it had some aim in mind, was pretty much empty of anything? Some nearby autoroute must be channelling away interest. In all the time they'd been walking, only a few cars had passed – and passed was the word. In the meantime, the sky was beginning to wink with interesting atmospheric colorations in preparation for going dark, that cooling breeze had become a frigid blast, and Mel was looking worse – his skin, whenever Yehune happened to see it, giving the impression of a thin white paste applied over some abysmal rot.

How long could the guy hold out? Somewhere, some time, Yehune had learned a simple clockwork view of human progress. He couldn't let him stop. Stop properly, that is; Mel had already paused three times by the side of the road and attempted to empty his stomach through his mouth, in which he'd been successful once. He kept taking long, despairing pulls on Yehune's water bottle. Have to get that washed, then. But Yehune's idea was that once Mel was allowed to cease motion entirely, take his pack off and sit down or collapse on something, whatever scrubby bit of roadside shoulder they happened to be on would turn out to be their bed for the night. Neither of them had a tent or a bivvy-bag; it hadn't been thought necessary when travelling over one of the most built-up parts of the earth's surface.

Dijon, Dijon, he thought with a punchy, subvocal violence, almost strong enough to bring the place to him or him to the place. He didn't *want* this – he didn't want to be dossing with a vomity Mel by the side of a road. And yet – he cast his eyes back again, forward again, upwards to the all-embracing, gloriously-lit-up sky. A way. A way outa here. No lifts. A… give us a….

It might have been their rock-bottom necessity (as Yehune saw it) that produced the conditions for change; or just the fact of their having thrown themselves completely on the mercy of a world that really did move, scatter and reform in random patterns; where nothing, particularly on a road in a large European country, was ever still for long. Whether or not, a minivan came trundling doggedly over the rise of the hill behind them. Yehune by that time was already facing backwards, thumb set in the hitchhiker's hook, having picked up the engine note over bird and cricket noise a matter of fifteen seconds before.

And whoever it was stopped. Only – as the man himself told them later in a slow argotic monotone that Mel occasionally stirred himself to interpret – only because he could see they'd never get a lift from where they were. Which for Yehune was as good a reason as any. Their driver was black-haired, rascally-looking, with five o'clock shadow like a grey stain covering his large jowl; he could have been cast as an extra in one of those Napoleonic films if there hadn't been something a whisker ill-matched, not-quite-handsome about the modelling of his eye ridge, nose and chin. Out of proportion, or *de*-proportioned. A devil's emissary, maybe; an advocate of darkness. And the promise he brought was short-lived; he was local, only going a short distance among placenames that he rattled out hardly bothering to break them into syllables.

In a spirit of friendly admonition, their benefactor gave them a short speech before dropping them off at a crossroads that looked emptier, bleaker in the dying light, more utterly forsaken by man and beast and car than the road they'd started out on. Yehune tried to stall, asked the name of the nearest settlement (was it 'Le Verne'?), did his best to imply that even a little bit to east or west might be better for them. But the driver pushed a sinewy arm past him and opened his door. *Ov-war,* and *bon* something-or-other. They tumbled out, in Mel's case almost literally. He couldn't lift his pack. While Yehune dealt with it, the old sickie stumbled to the side of a red stone wall and delivered himself of all the chunder that must have built up in him during the car-ride, held back, possibly, by some charmed psychological floodgate or politeness of the internal organs.

'Wha'did'e say?' Yehune asked after a while.

There were three directions from there, four if you counted a private farm road on the other side of an iron gateway. Of the three, one was hidden by the brow of a small rise; the other two were open enough, winding through laid-out fields of irregular pastureland, which hesitated now between dark green and grey as the sun began to give up on illuminating anything in that particular corner of the earth. Except for the wind, everything was still; no living animal could be seen in the paddocks.

They were on a fair-sized grassy triangle, broad enough at one side for Yehune to stride back and forth on. His pack lay at one corner. Mel, after his initial purge, had utterly given up.

There you have it, eh. What I said. Stop, and you're screwed.

'Hey. Mel. That driver guy. Wha'did'e say?'

But he was if anything more wide-awake, alive with plans and schemes, reconciled to their stay in the French countryside, after the car-ride than before it; possibly because he'd had a chance to light a cigarette, or was relieved of the burden of driving them on and on.

'Mel. *Mel.* Wake up. I'm asking you a question.'

'Aaaa-aarrrgh.'

'C'mon. You can't be *that* out-of-it.'

'... Aah... right. I just don't feel...'

'Right, yeah. Sorry about that. ... Did you get anything of what that guy burbled, there at the last?'

'Oh... aah. He said... said we'd never get picked up, better to try a farmhouse... farmhouse? Oh I... fucking...'

'A farmhouse? What farmhouse? What?'

That raised another line of thought entirely. Yehune reflected comfortably, watching a tenuous slug of smoke blow away on the chilly air, that it was a bugger not to be able to talk languages. He wasn't too worried by the fact that the driver had thought they had no chance at all of a lift. Non-hitchers were always pessimistic. But it seemed they might have been dumped on this deserted corner of grass for a reason after all, and that reason had nothing to do with the three possible directions of road. A farmhouse – if Mel was right. Couldn't it be that the Napoleonic brigand had meant not just any farmhouse, but some actual real-life farmhouse they might conceivably get to from where they were…?

Or not. He could be assuming too much. But almost anything was worth a try.

A sort of gaiety of enterprise was creeping into his eye-corners as he turned to consider the gate and the driveway behind them. The gate was iron, standing a little open, not far from an outcrop of the ground that was scarred by repeated openings. It was starting to go rusty in streaks where the whatever-coloured paint (just then deepest black) had worn away. Beyond it was a hard clay roadway.

He took care to grind his fag out in the moist grass. Avoid forest fires.

'Packs up. Hike, man. … Fuck it, I'm taking yours.'

It had no battlements. Otherwise, in some other time the tall, square, inward-facing building or mass of buildings might well have done for a fortress. Walking up the primitive rutted road, Yehune had begun to feel he was back in the world of living creatures: there were shaped lumps in the darkness that must be cows, and the odd moan or murmur came from other farm animals. Mel was a vague presence or sense of movement behind him. He was coming near the outer walls of the farmhouse, which gave back a blank, unfriendly impression. He only stopped when he came to a second gate – possibly not secured, but he didn't feel like trying it – and he let both packs flop heavily down on the ground.

There was a high, antique bell fastened to a chain that dangled down. Yehune grabbed it straight away and pulled hard.

The frighteningly-loud peal caused a ruckus in the inner courtyard, a shrieking of poultry, barking of big dogs, and eventually a drawn-out, wuffling monologue that seemed to come from a male human being. Still no-one appeared. The proprietor, if he was that, might have been more concerned with calming down his menagerie than in going to answer any bells, deafening and traditional as they might have been. But a gruff shout a few minutes later, *'Allay, allay'*, might possibly have been meant to apply to the visitors. Yehune assumed it was, and started to puzzle out the gate clip.

Having made it across the cobbled courtyard, to a renewed clucking and bounding of wildlife, they came to the main door – wide open, and blocked by a peculiar figure, holding a stout fire-iron in one hand and with two very large dogs beside him. He was dressed in a long light-green shirt that could have been his version of pyjamas. He was balding, and what hair he had was white and shot up at unruly angles from different parts of his head. Some sparse streaks of the same white hair proceeded triangularly downwards over his chin, to converge in a point somewhere in front of the neck; and there was a ragged moustache to match. Two eyes looked wildly out from inside two red hollows. Yehune was uncomfortably aware that his own hands were empty; everything they owned had been left at the gate.

He began by trying to explain. After failing with English (the man's face stayed rigid; the dogs stared and growled), he fell back on signs. He'd got as far as the first three – pointing to himself, a hitchhiker's thumb, and a wave of the hand down towards the road – when a woman appeared behind the man, far shorter, done up in a mauve dressing gown. Her face, you could almost say, was as mobile as her companion's was unchanging.

She bypassed any contribution he might have made, and with bustling gestures and an unstoppable flood of words appeared to invite the two strangers in.

'Ah, non, Mathilde...' the farmer started to object, but his voice sank down to join the other background noises, as Yehune passed into the farmhouse interior, taking care to give his shoes a wipe as he crossed the threshold. Mel came on after him, and the man of the house fell in behind, still grumbling. The dogs were let free. They stood outside the door and barked energetically. A period of confusion followed, in which the travellers were guided to wooden chairs around a huge kitchen table, while being asked something that might have had to do with their choice of refreshment.

All the time Yehune kept trying to explain what they were

doing there. Without much success so far. The room was dominated by the dogs' background racket, the clinking of cups and pots, intermittent streams of words in two languages from three directions, and a fug of herbal and earthy smells.

He finally resorted to asking Mel the word for 'sick'.

'Malade,' was the answer.

'Mallard,' repeated Yehune, pointing with a vigorous stabbing motion of the forefinger back at Mel. 'I'm really sorry, but that's why we're here, you know, my companion – *companyong* – mallard.'

The whirlwind started again then, Madame throwing up her hands and expostulating noisily and insisting on taking Mel away somewhere else where he could be better looked after, with suggestions and arguments from the man (who was later found to be her husband, a Monsieur Quay-rear). After another few minutes of chaos, she and Mel had left the room.

Leaving Yehune at the table, behind a pot of villainous black coffee, looking sideways at the wonky-haired old gent and wondering what was going to happen next.

'*Un* – something something. *Ang?*'

Something had lit up in the old man. He crossed the room and hunted up a blackened old bottle, out of which he poured a dark-brown liquid into two tiny glasses. The immobility had disappeared from his eyes. He hunkered together with the unknown traveller while clinking glasses with him – and about then, Yehune began to feel that everything might turn out all right.

One more time in the course of a day he was given the impression that all this language business was really nonsense: people who wanted to communicate could always communicate. As the fug deepened, he tossed off his second or possibly third small glass of the farmer's pungent spirits (something he'd never tasted before, mouth-shrivellingly bitter) – a long, animated, sometimes laborious conversation developed between him and the farmer and, when she came back in, the farmer's wife. Props were needed, and a lot of benevolent guesswork. M. Queyrières began by picking up framed photographs of what Yehune supposed must be the couple's son and daughters, and giving detailed accounts of the lives of each of them, what they had done and what they were doing now, deconstructed in the very vibrations of the air as the words left his mouth and reconstituted by Yehune from the gestures and sound effects the farmer never failed to provide. Madame took no part in the drinking (and in fact, the bottle had disappeared by some sleight-of-hand a moment before she came in); but she added her two francs' worth to the conversation, pronouncing certain words over and over quite slowly, with a pronunciation so distortedly, exaggeratedly French that it occurred to Yehune she might have been trying to speak English. Mel was deeply asleep, she mimed to Yehune, and it followed of course that he also (pointing, making yawning motions, sleeping head on her hands) had to spend the night with them. The hospitality. The kindness. Somewhere behind the lightly extraresonant state of his ears, the altered sense of balance in his forehead, Yehune was touched, and tried to express it in his own version of sign language. Of course, he'd have to go and get their packs from the gate. *Non, non*, Monsieur would do that, *a cause* of the *shing*. The *shing*. Monsieur pretended to be a huge dog ferociously barking. But – hang on a moment – Yehune held up his hand – just in a spirit of enquiry, you know, of general information, if you get what I mean....

He tried to ask about the lay of the land. More especially, of the roads thereabouts. The action of those stiff drinks on his cogitative machinery, as it happened, hadn't calmed him down, but spurred him to new enterprise, breaking down what inhibitions he might have had while leaving his instinct for trouble wide awake. Monsieur quickly located a map of the immediate area, and a conversation began that had placenames as its most useful currency: *Plaine de Brosse – Doms – Chazeaux* – which that wispily-whiskered mouth always formed with a special emphasis or respect. They were somewhere in the region of a creek called the *Solnan,* Yehune gathered (understanding it to be a creek by the rolling motions of the hand M. Queyrières made every time he talked about it). There was a large n-road not far to the east, in the opposite direction from *le Verne*. M. Queyrières had picked up the idea that what was wanted was a way to rejoin the railway lines. At that point, Yehune was made to realise that his faith in the stationmaster had been completely misplaced. Getting to Dijon on all those little roads was a job for a car; to a hitchhiker it might as well have been impossible. A more practical solution, the farmer reckoned, would be to follow the green route nationale to the north through *Cuiselles, St Âme,* as far as a larger town called *Lons-le-Sauvage,* from which they could catch a train to Dijon through places like *Mouchard, Dole*....

He meant, of course, in the morning. But that wasn't what Yehune was thinking. He displayed his intention of going out then and there, to see if there was any form of transport to be got that night. His hosts were horrified. He couldn't go. Already Madame was in the process of making up a nourishing soup for them all before they went to bed. Yehune was effusively grateful, and of course he had to go and get the packs anyway. But wouldn't he wait for the soup? The soup! Yehune remembered a word, and repeated it as he found his way back to the door and as he passed through the door, bringing Monsieur back to his side to help with the dogs. Mercy. Against all the emphatic protests of his hosts: 'Mercy – mercy – mercy.'

He had a feeling of freedom. Now that he had an idea of the geography, he was happier walking than not, pushing on to get something done, through the cool night, along roads that were reduced in his mind to the size of the line drawings on the farmer's foldable map. Muzzled; made harmless. Carless too, of course – but the effect of desolation was always relieved by some little detail: a marker like a cat's headstone; whirring of sudden wings in the blackness of trees overhead; a shape like a bloody cup built out of colourlessness and moonlight. It was true that normally and in his right mind he wouldn't be doing anything that involved hitchhiking, at that hour, in such unpromising conditions. But something seemed to have woken him up. And Mel was being looked after. As he'd gone past the two packs at the gate, he'd pulled a light rain-jacket out of his own; and only regretted the tramper's water bottle.

He came to the n-road, crossed over, and established himself under a road light on a small strip of edging grass. Cars were passing, all right; but with that impression of single-minded determination you could sometimes get from the straightness of a headlight-beam or the tightness of a shift in direction. These drivers weren't for stopping. Unconcerned (seeing his pack in his mind's eye silent and untouched at the top of the farmhouse road), Yehune took up a position where he was most visible, where he'd seem to be looking each motorist directly in the eye.

After an hour, he moved around and sat down. He had matches on him, but searched in vain for a fag. Then he got up, with the rain-jacket added, and held his thumb out again.

A car pulled up with a grinding of gravel on a wider piece of shoulder about forty metres along from him. Straight away he knew that it hadn't stopped for him. It was an old Citroën, dark at the windscreen. Presently a light went on, and he saw a couple of heads whose outlines suggested they were female. He made gestures to indicate that they should go on with what they were doing and not bother about him. Girls, at the side of a road. Might be paranoid, eh. He had to keep pushing down the small, barking head of his optimism, reminding himself that there was absolutely no chance of getting a lift from anyone who hadn't stopped for that purpose.

Was that guy...? He might be, might be... no. The car swooped past him, cruising on steadily into the north. And of course if anyone did stop... then the explanations would start, which would be sure to bring it all to nothing. It was a bit like fishing without a worm. (Yehune had never done much fishing.) In the small island of light behind the Citroën's windscreen, he saw the two heads move closer together, and a foldout book appeared spread against the lower part of the glass.

Were they looking at him? He supposed so. He began to mime a whole story, doing his best to be reassuring. I'm just a hitchhiker, see. Weirdly, I've got this friend lying in a farmhouse across the way. We missed our train, or rather, got out of a train we should've stayed in – don't worry about me. Just go on looking at your map. Not dangerous. No, no, no. Now this friend of mine.... All this he tried to get across with stage-size gestures, making sound effects for his own benefit, putting on expressions he believed were innocuous, smiling, dipping, waving his arms around. Trying to explain away his presence. After all, he thought, who'd be hitching at that hour, except a loony or an axe-murderer? And given the low frequency of cars around that time, he didn't have much else to do. From time to time he saw a miniaturised face like a little shining coin, looking up at him. The two heads moved; pages were flipped forwards and back.

Another ten or fifteen minutes might have passed. He'd come to the end of his act, and only added a gesture of self-deprecation every now and then, to remind them. The flighty spring rain didn't bother him; but the wind was getting colder and colder out there. No-one had even looked like stopping. His thoughts began to hover around the farmhouse again: would the packs be getting wet? What time, do you think, would they turn the lights off and give up on him? ...

The Citroën's engine started. The yellow headlights shone on raindrops. Bye, girls. Hope you get where you.... But it only rolled along the forty metres, and crunched up beside him.

The driver's window rolled down, and a girl sang out – *in English* –

' 'Scuse me, would you mind having a look at this? We think we're on the wrong road, we're trying to get to Paris.'

She had a high voice, with a clear, lilting music in it. The head he saw when he came round the side of the car was small and youthful, with short dark hair, large eyes tending almost to the rectangular (probably from some carefully-applied makeup) – giving a general Southern European impression, until you got as far as the nose and lower jaw. Those didn't tend to protrude, as they did in so many French and Italian girls he'd seen, but drew in with the curvature of a vase, not especially symmetrical, to a well-moulded chin. There was some self-containment in the angling of her head, character showing through the qualified prettiness – possibly a capacity for warmth – but by then Yehune was reaching, inventing the qualities that he would have liked to see in her. The car's other occupant was a shape in the darkness, big and obviously female.

He couldn't help starting out by asking how the... how, he meant, the girl had managed to guess he was English-speaking. She didn't answer him, but directed his attention straight away to the big book of maps. But later on he got an explanation out of her, and by then some hint of the flavour of her personality had got across to him, so that she was already more than just a face on a squally night asking directions. She had to think about it. It was his body-language, she told him, and the way he dressed. (The way I *dress*? I got these clothes in Italy, what's wrong with how I *dress*?) It was obvious he wasn't French, and since he was hitching he must be a traveller, and English was the first language you tried on European-looking travellers in a foreign country. ... And that was her, the nature of her, the closeness to humans, the flitting of an unconscious intuition. That was Mairi.

Mel would have got the basic story a matter of twenty minutes later when he was roused up from his warm and comfortable bed in the farmhouse and told to get dressed, there was a car outside with two girls willing to take them on out of there. Only going to Paris; but there you are. Only, would he hurry it up a bit, otherwise they might give up and abscond. They'd been coming from Geneva (Mel would have heard, shivering and only barely awake), and had nothing but a car compass to keep them right; the French one had started by taking them the wrong way out because it made her feel funny to look at maps in a moving car. (... Made her feel funny... Mel didn't even laugh, fumbling in a kind of horror-dream with the belt of his black jeans.) Anyway, Yehune'd worked out a good route for them, what they need was the what they needed needed was the

'... ah, this one, the N5. So, well, you'll have to keep on this road right up to, um, joins page... excuse me?... this one, page... right here, till you get to Lonse-l'Savage. And you can see how you go from there.'

'Oh. ... And so...'

'I mean, the N5's right there – so you turn off just here, no name on it, then run through on the D-whatsit-whatsit, sweep right round, you can see it crosses the autoroute twice...'

'Right. So that's how we get there? The N5?'

'Yeah. It's not a problem. – I can mark it out for you if you've got a pencil.'

'*Google google google, Celestine?*'

Her companion answered back in French.

The dark-haired one had turned to him and said, 'Look, would you mind very much, I know you're hitching and it might be out of your way – if you could just ride along with us you could show us the places to turn…?'

At that the French girl had moved over into the light, trying to assess him for danger, the look on her round face growing sourer the further he got into his explanation:

'Oh. Yeah. Hm. That's a really good idea. The only thing is…'

… was Mel, of course; was Mel collapsed and moribund in a stucco-walled castle somewhere in the boondocks, and both their packs, and a couple of very long-suffering would-be hosts for the night: all of which Yehune managed to dismiss with the help of a very self-directed outlook on time and space; it can be done, or if not it can be ignored; as the tottering but now fully-dressed thing himself was bustled through the bedroom door, remembered he'd forgotten the water bottle, claimed weakly he didn't know what else he'd forgotten, and bundled on into the cold darkness to the protests of Madame and the clamouring of one or more of their Cerberus-sized watchdogs.

The car trip began, with Yehune in the front seat cradling the book of maps while Mairi drove, her larger friend Celestine in the back seat with Mel. At some point or other, he wasn't sure when, Yehune had given up on the idea of trying to get back to their original direction. There was that electrifying but aimless feeling in the air – some unacknowledged spice in the interplay of personalities where male related to female, all contradicted by the hitcher's bland assumption that this was nothing more than a way of eating up the miles. And they were doing that; the small French engine was howling and rumbling and shunting them on, if only in the direction of Paris. In the meantime, he had nothing much to do except practise his technique, asking Mairi question after question about herself, keeping his mouth shut as much as humanly possible while she answered – and the third part (so often neglected even with the best of intentions): trying to remember what she'd said. That was with a view to further chats. Which pretty obviously would never happen here. He looked out on the right side-wall of her hair, which gathered to a floating point at the end. There was something in the way her legs in jeans controlled the pedals, hand gripped wheel or gear lever, something definite, reserved, expressive in her sweeping changes from one lane to another, like an underlay to her short but vivacious catches of words.

He'd worked out that her pronunciation was Scottish a while before she divulged that she lived in Edinburgh and was something she called an 'artistic secretary'. Celestine, by contrast, had a flat in the 10th Arrondissement in Paris, which was where they were all headed at the moment. Not information that ought to have concerned him too closely, you might have thought – but something in the act of renouncing his own destination had freed him to any possibility, opening bets again, building a speculative logic that he could always reset to zero whenever he wanted. ... Either that, or there was something prophetic in it: something that told him that a chance meeting by the side of a road in the sticks of France could go on to decide his choice of country and means of living and a lot of other things besides; reset the currents in new eddies; harden and change them all; and send them hurtling towards their respective fates... something in the moment-to-moment apprehension of a personality, where the complexity was of an order far beyond physics, beyond the refinement to a sum of unities, where it seemed that messages true or false could be gathered from the tendency of an eye, an affinity in speeds of vibration, or the feather textures of surfaces seen through the premonitory air that whistled around them in the cabin of a moving car.

This girl Mairi was quick enough to ask about him in return. Yehune gave her a few details, along with some more upbeat anecdotes of his recent travels. And she surely couldn't have been putting on that appearance of a deep and natural interest in what he was saying. ...

'Mont-something? Chauvier...' she broke in.

'Oh, right, Montchauvier. Sellières. Swing on left.'

'Right here? Or...'

As for Mel, early on he'd begged some of the water in a net of plastic bottles floating around under the back seats, and after that hadn't said a word or made a sound that Yehune could remember. Nor was Celestine very talkative. Yehune might possibly even have spared a thought for what it might have been like for his friend, sandwiched between packs and car-rubbish and a stony Celestine in the rushing dark, seeing hills and lights pass backwards in a disjunct world of sick fatigue. He did happen to wonder how long the guy could hold out, drinking all that water. The answer to that was, not long. The crisis came after a while, Mel piped up, and they stopped a few miles after that at a roadside café. By some agreement between the girls, the drivers were swapped at that point, Mel allowed to flop in the passenger seat, and Yehune and Mairi left to their own devices in the back. She was tired after driving. His shoulder served as a warm support. Which was only the beginning (– they'd long since passed the last junction at which his advice could have been useful, and were drawn into that inexorable whirlpool leading to Paris or nowhere) of their exploration, tentative feeling out of a new affinity, settled back there among the packs and a residue of wrappers and books and mats and bent umbrellas, while the dark cruised over them, lights passed like gigantic praying-mantis elbows in the sky, side-forces continually pushed and thrust at them so that no way was noticeably up or back or forward; and hardly a sound came back to them out of the front seats.

What did he find in her? Or she in him? From his point of view, a kind of luminosity in features drawn dark against a pale skin, movements quick but understated, which gave the effect of a positive calm she managed to keep up through any disruption: the jolting motions of the car around them, the sliding uncertainties of a relation just begun, and the gradual toppling of assumptions in both of them about where they were just then and where they were headed. When she talked about herself, her occupation of 'artistic secretary' (which turned out to mean girl Friday for an Edinburgh arts millionaire), she only managed to reinforce the impression he had of a very businesslike and committed child or waif. It was when she talked about other people that her context broadened, building her into an ever-expanding pattern of people she'd known or heard about, until their stories branched and rebranched far beyond his ability to follow; and something came into her face, sympathetic and impassioned, rising to a scent, sounding the straits of the personal through history…. That's funny, he thought. A specialist, carried away by her subject. And though everything came across in words, those vowel-modified and sometimes quaintly-put phrases in the accent of the West Coast of Scotland, it was something outside the words he had a hint of, accompanied by something spearing and bell-like from the sounds themselves – so that she almost became herself that expressive clarity, newness in the lilting of a voice; her unseen self called out, you could say, through interconnected tunnels of the real-life narratives of other people.

On her side…? The picture she had of him must have come partly from his anecdotes, partly from the physical lump right there in the seat with her. In her world, where human interaction mattered so much, he might have seemed someone undefeatable, the sailer over knots, able to negotiate anything and everything through the simple strength of his self-persuasion. She couldn't have failed to see that this was no practised attempt at deception. He was joky and attentive, and all he could do by way of inducement was to stand up (so to speak) and say: this is me, take it or leave it. Stories he told about his travels were less interesting to her than his vaguely-imagined South Pacific origins, and the name itself, 'Yehune', which at that early stage took the form to her of some outlandish fruit in tropical yellow-orange. Physically, he had breadth in every direction except the vertical, big shoulders, a big midriff as well, and black hair like raw wool to the touch. His mouth tasted distantly of smoke. His hands, despite all that bluntness, were graceful and moved gently but surely to the point. In that twilight place where she made her decisions, she must have been aware that other girls were likely to fall prey to that effect of easy strength. But after all, there was danger everywhere; every movement you could make carried the seeds of destruction; and in any case they were only going together as far as Paris.

You might say they got to know each other too quickly. It was all innocent enough so far, and yet with a spur of uninnocent excitement.

They were thrown into a world where the conventions of personal distance had suddenly been balled up and chucked away, where the sexual was there like an acknowledgement, a scarlet-tinted cloud rushing them on headlong into decisions. So far, everything they'd done came easily under the heading of what Mairi would have called 'romance'. They wanted to find each other out, through fingertips and shapes of lips and textures of the face, encompassing the other person by something so simple as holding him or her at the shoulder. … But when you came down to it, who or what was Yehune? Mel might have had some idea; Mairi none at all. That was the danger, which spawned the excitement. And as a result, they were well-versed in the physical side of each other – those little characteristic turns of arm and leg and set of the head that had been part of them since their earliest childhoods, now taken over into bodies that were matured and in a sexual prime – long before they came to anything to do with their habits of thinking, their longings, tics, their sadnesses, and whatever it might be in the silence of the mind that drove them to do or think or imagine what they did.

As the stream of cars flowed along in the dark, crucial decisions about turnoffs had to be made. They were even discussed a bit. The two New Zealanders obviously hadn't intended to arrive in the capital of France late at night, or even go there at all; and what was more one of them was ill.

Mairi took the view that they were there as a personal favour, and they'd changed their destination to suit her. In a series of fluent exchanges with Celestine in the front seat (who drove with a sort of blinking abandonment, unsure of herself, without any of Mairi's grace with the wheel and gearstick), the idea grew up that the two of them could stay that night with the girls at the flat.

The city outside was built in cold lights. It was all industrial bulk and edges up and down; occasionally they glimpsed a human figure at the last moment at a junction. The French girl seemed to have withdrawn into herself, and surely still had serious reservations about their passengers. But she couldn't ignore what Mairi so obviously wanted; and it was agreed without much more being said.

194

Celestine might have had the idea that the two of them would go and hunt up a hotel in the morning. But it didn't turn out that way; and already Mairi might well have been looking at the next three days as a sort of test period, where the first euphoria could pass off, any incompatibilities be discovered, and the second, less important New Zealander be given a chance to get back to his normal state. ... Celestine was due back at work on Monday, after which Mairi would be going back up to Edinburgh.

'Mel. Mel. Where's that guy?'

What had looked like the remains of someone's night, an unzipped sleeping bag lying on top of sheets and a lilo, sinuously flowed, and Mel's head appeared from behind the rear-upwards corner.

'Where would I be?' he grizzled.

Mairi, beside Yehune, held out something folded in a napkin.

'We brought you something to eat. See?'

'Oh, right. Thanks.' He levered himself higher. 'Ah... you really think I'd be able to...?'

'Have a try.' She braced one knee on the faded antique couch and passed it down to him. He was boxed in there behind its four spindling legs, maybe trying to create some illusion of privacy.

Yehune: 'Fuck, man, can only kill you.'

The item turned out to be a crêpe; not a cheese crêpe, but smeared on the inside with sweet jelly of some kind. Someone's traditional French wisdom had proclaimed animal products to be bad for his condition. Mel took it, looked it over, and let it fall a few centimetres in his hand – while he glanced towards the round red basin pushed back in the obscurest corner.

He said, 'Damn, you know – I am bloody hungry.'

A pattern had established itself for Mel during the first full day and night of their stay in Celestine's flat: he'd feel far better after eating something, then progressively worse and worse over the next four to five hours, to the point of abject misery; after which his body would gather itself for the next major, tear-squeezing, gut-wrenching chuck. The cycle would start all over again when he got interested in what there might be to eat. In the meantime, everyone else went about their business – Yehune and Mairi were off out most of the time, while Celestine silently occupied herself with small bits of cleaning or domestic economy, naturally with the intention of guarding her property from what, for all she knew, might be wolves in human form, for all that one of them had risen to the temporary status of Mairi's boyfriend. Every now and then the two principals would burst in with the tales of their adventures, as well as little bits and pieces of food they thought (so far wrongly) that Mel might be able to keep down.

Celestine appeared now, pallid and substantial, from just behind the door of the main room.

'Salut Celestine,' said Mairi, approaching for the kisses on the cheek.

' 'Allo. Where 'iv you bin?'

Mairi looked back at Yehune, on the way brushing her eyes past Mel lying on the floor, then back at Celestine. For a moment her eyes became even more good-natured, having perceived certain insubstantial threads of logic.

Yehune answered for her,

'Oh, just down the Canal S'nt *Mar*tin and a few streets round there. God, it was pretty amazing though. You should've been there, man. We met these guys who lived under the bridge, I think the main guy sells drugs or something, they've got, like, a whole setup. Anyway, we just happen to be hanging round there and I ask him for a match, and he seems to take a liking to us, so he showed us all over. An' there was a girl too – what was she called, Mairi?...'

The girl had called herself 'Zizi', Mairi couldn't remember her ever giving a real name. She was slim, and could have been considered quite attractive, only a bit marbled around the eyes as if from a few nights' clubbing too many. By contrast, the gang-leader type was dressed in strange rags and didn't admit to any name at all. He reacted to Yehune's advance with a tooth-baring familiarity – he had a habit of constantly blocking one side of his nose and sucking violently through the other side. *'Les anglais',* he loved them, he kept on saying – though that word couldn't have been said to describe either Mairi or Yehune. So they were given the tour, taken down under one of the overbridges to where a few big pieces of house furniture blocked off a little dossers' paradise; where a fat boy sat impassively in the frame of an armchair, a man with patchy hair leaned smoking against the bridge foundation. There was a narrow path left for people to walk past. Nobody ever bothered them there, they said; and Yehune had no trouble believing it. The ringleader did suggest a few deals – but half-heartedly, jokingly, as if his long-lost cousin *Yé-une* and his girlfriend *Marie* (who stood to one side with Zizi in a strange, illusory bubble of feminine decorum) were somehow exempt: *les anglais*. After some scratching around, it was admitted that no matches were to be had... in the end Yehune's cigarette was lit off the stub of the wall-leaner's home-rolled. Everyone made protestations of mutual esteem. Yehune promised another visit... in his mind, maybe, already comparing this germ of a shanty-town with the Beijing version, which was built on genuine poverty rather than mere crime; where, in fact, serious crime hadn't quite managed to get off the ground. And as for Mairi....

Mairi was quite likely thinking about the kind of situation Yehune managed to get himself into, that insouciance that had made him go up to an obvious criminal and ask for a light. He seemed to flow along untouchable on a personal wave or current, there in Celestine's down-at-heel district by the two grubby railway stations and the canal. It certainly didn't reduce the excitement for her. He could be theatrical, silly at times; and yet she could recognise another side to him, a fine judgement in weighing up circumstances, and always that monumental confidence that brought things off. After all, there they were, free in the streets, hunting up a shop she remembered, to see if they could buy some snack or salad to bring back to the other New Zealander.

Yehune's spirit of adventure had actually been expanded by the new romantic, now sexual, connection. Closer contact with Mairi hadn't disappointed him at all. Though her face was more unique, imperfect, less generically 'pretty' than he'd thought at first, she was snakily built, curving attractively back at the hips; and she was a perfect companion in the outlying streets of Paris. She had the trick of defusing the rudeness of strangers and shopkeepers, always taking exactly the right tone to get behind their guard. And in a foreign language too. None of the minor adventures he'd had in Italy compared with this; and he was already wondering – without, of course, any thought of pressuring Mel – how he might suggest a return to the good old island nation without seeming to betray any of their new free-wheeling rules....

While Yehune talked – Mel breaking in with a question now and then – in someone's memory someone might have said,

'Dis, Celestine. Je voudrais drais drais dr'

and the two women left the room for a chat; at any rate they seemed to have disappeared into the second of the two bedrooms.

Leaving Yehune and Mel. Yehune looked down at the sickie, huddled under the long water-marked wall under the antique end-piece.

'How've you been?' he asked in a lower voice.

'Flopped out. Too exhausted. Looking at the back of this... couch.'

'Ah, well. You'll get better. Get that crêpe in you, build yourself up...'

And he started to walk around, under the high walls of Celestine's sepulchral living room, rambling on in words either to Mel or himself,

'God knows how they make a living, really. I *think* they sold drugs. Pity he had to do that, just for money. – It's all money, eh. But shit, when you think about it, how else...?'

Money, in fact, was the tough question, and it was carried over into their journey to the north, where Yehune speculated,

'I s'pose I'll be able to get some sort of job or other up there?'

Och, don't worry your head, there's sure to be something – Mairi didn't say. Instead, she eyed him slantwise from her position just beside him at the small table in the train.

'Eh, I'm not sure. Do you have any A-levels?'

'Oh. ... Hmm, dunno, really. What are they, Mel?'

'Some equivalence. Bursary and Scholarship or something. You got a Bursary, didn't you?'

Mel was all fixed, got up in a crisply unironed tee-shirt ('Moto Laverda Breganze') and jeans, with his old blue jacket flopped down somewhere near his elbow just in case the British Rail carriage temperatures got out of hand. He was cadaverously thin; Yehune could see the bones in the side of his face as he kept turning his head towards the scenes speeding past outside the windows. Gazing at vegetation, back yards, the odd abandoned piece of agricultural machinery. Green, he might have been writing in his notebook. Green, green, light green and not-so-light green, it's all so unbelievably, verdiferently green....

'Ah, she'll be right, we'll make out,' said Yehune, with the airy confidence of someone in a dress leather jacket with a girlfriend beside him. 'Mel'll get some job shovelling dung twenty hours a day or something. And, ah... I'll just find the one thing – you know – no-one's ever quite noticed you can do. Get contacts. Work between the lines...'

Mairi was looking at him oddly, as if to say, 'Just wait till you get there'. He ended lamely,

'... That's what we always do, usually.'

Various castle-like formations appeared as if in anticipation out of the hillside, as the train slowed to a walking pace and a voice through speakers announced, 'Edinb'rr'h Waverrleh'. Without realising it, Yehune had been expecting some sort of anticlimax after the sunburned, historical cities they'd seen in Tuscany. Now he thought confusedly, Edinburgh, doesn't that have a castle? Could one of these be...?

Until they drew in under the lid of a Victorian-age hangar, and slowly threaded their way out of the train; to come on Mairi's parents almost straight away in a broad bay under a noticeboard.

He was taken aback; she hadn't said anything about it. As if it were the most natural thing in the world – to be met.

Her father was small, white-haired and hatchet-faced, from a place called Paisley, as she'd already told him. In the beginning he could hardly understand a single word he said. In her mother he thought he could make out some of the lines, scored in and weatherbeaten, of Mairi's face: a long-lost indication of gentleness round the eyes.

Yehune and Mel stood off during the ceremony: a 'Willsuy'r*ba*'' from the father, an easier 'Hello dear' from the mother, and hugs, and confusion with the bags.

'These are some friends of mine I met in France,' Mairi threw out.

'So nice to meet you.'

'Frêns, y'see?' Mr MacFarlane looked askance at her from a set-back world of canny deliberation.

'I hope you'll all be joinin' us for tea,' her mother offered.

'We've only got time for a biscuit or two just now,' Mairi told her. 'We've got to be getting over to Nicky's.'

'Nicky's? What are you wantin' wi' her?'

'Oh, it's for Yehune and Mel. I said I'd introduce them.'

It seemed the calls she'd been making on phonecards from boxes all around Paris had mainly been to this friend of hers; it was easy to see that her parents knew nothing at all. Yehune imagined he could feel the assassin's smile of the father burning into him as they waited for a taxi to be free – and waited, and waited – and finally lumbered in a group up the slope, with the two packs and Mairi's three suitcases, to stand at the bus stop.

For the first time, then, Yehune saw it: a single-sided street in the misted rain, with the ornate stone buildings, obelisks and monuments, and the *real* castle, bearing up overhead like a natural outgrowth of the torn black rock of the cliff.

He looked at Mel, and got a smile and a slight shake of the head.

'Z'is the main street?' Mel said.

And so for Yehune the eye not open was focussed again, somewhere in the great prevailing sickle-curve of that emptiness a point was dotted in; the point, a point, or any point... a girl. A girl was Mairi. That might have been it, all right; they might just have been toppled and caught up in the moment's turbulence of that raging supercelestial void as it gathered itself for the leap into future time –

And yet. There was a ripple of colours, dimpling and changing at the back of his eyes, and something out of time, dictating, all-eloquent, existing somewhere in the limitless wash of a sky spread out in pastels overhead. Deep in the recesses of his mind at rest, he felt memories stirring, a line of hills – not in Belorusski Station in Moscow this time, but in the unplaned high country of Nelson National Park – a point or point or

pointpoin

A Walk in the Hills

That time, he'd hitched down as far as Wellington, and been struck again with an impression of whole lifetimes lived through in a day, one for the mentality and speed of living of each of the car drivers that picked him up. It was as if he sealed himself into a particular state of the air every time he slammed a car door shut, some collective miasma put out by the shape behind the wheel and whoever might happen to be sitting round the other seats. Shaded again, of course, by the character he chose to put on in response. Would he start out by telling the truth, or lies? If lies, how would they make him describe himself? ... He met a marketing executive in a light-blue Camira speeding on youth and caffeine and everything he was 'achieving'; a middle-aged couple who were thinking of renewing their piano and welcomed his advice when they heard he was with the NZSO; and others, slow, taciturn, vicious, or bitten by inner insects, in the little upholstered capsules that drew the environments of their lives along with them; all running together in the end in an effect of different filmstrips crossing and parting, spliced in at pickup, run away at dropoff, to be lost in the anonymity of the roads around State Highway One.

And that was what he wanted. He felt he'd been stuck with the personalities of his workmates at Rumbus Dispatch for far too long. His simple theory was that you could dump all that any time, just by stepping up to a road and putting out your thumb. In fact, he found the transition took a bit longer than that; the ghosts of problems back in Auckland, career questions, the jump he was about to make to OTextil on the grounds that you couldn't run a serious dispatching company out of somebody's front room – those dim harassing creations of his mind rode not very far behind him, occasionally coming close enough to stick a claw into his dream-shoulders. He was aware that this Easter weekend of 1985 was probably the last time he'd be able to get down there; the last of a series of breaks he'd been taking almost at his whim. OTextil was a different sort of firm entirely, established and conservative, and unlikely to care too much about the hobbies of its workers.

On the ferry across Cook Strait he felt he'd almost got away from it; especially when he stood at the rail with dozens of tourists around him, watching Queen Charlotte Sound in the breathless early-evening clarity creep slowly by under boas of grey mist. He was visited again by voices on the bus from Picton, the interpersonal politics of Shar and Ange and Toddy at the Dispatch; but of course he was tired by then; and he easily dismissed them into the run of the landscape outside, the hulking beginnings of big hill-masses by the roadside. Instead, he thought about the routes he might take. As he saw it, he had just three days to walk the perfect loop, using a survey map and his general knowledge of the terrain to try and pick out the best places. It might turn out a bit of a rush. He knew that he was really only dipping into it, sticking to the northernmost extremity of his superhuman playground for no other reason than that it cut down the travel time. Which was why from the very beginning he was stretching out of himself, determined to make the change, outrun the twittering in his head and the sense of tight constriction left over from months of working in the city.

Far from being a prosaic necessity, a sacrifice of time, that period of passing through other people's lives from the moment he left Auckland until his late arrival at the St Arnaud hostel the same night (– the manager grumbled that he was too late to check in, Yehune said nothing, looked sympathetic, searched in his eyes for a gleam of answering life) had seemed in a way to wash him clean. However much he might have thought of himself as aloof and consistent, Yehune's own sense of himself did go through phases. He was probably unaware how much he hated being in a room with his parents, or sitting stuck to a telephone receiver while his workmates tried to involve him in their feuds; passive acceptance was one thing he wasn't very good at. Now, in spite of the alienness of this temporary reality, with its functional sinks and board corridors painted white, the subtle taint or smell of objects that had never been cared for in a personal way – despite it, maybe because of it – he was once again free and clear, able to find the version of himself that operated not in sameness, but in the charge and accident of passing moments.

In the kitchen, two Kiwi-foreigner couples asked him separately where he was going and where he'd come from – one Sheila with a boyfriend name of Johann, and another the other way round: boy-New Zealander and girl-foreigner. He went so far as to tell them the truth. He noticed he was able to maintain a perfect friendliness while at the same time blanking out the hostel manager, who loitered meaningly by the housing of a cupboard.

'Ex-cusse me, are you using the scribber?' 'The what?' 'Oa, he means the dushmop, down there, floatin in the worta.' The worta. 'Oh, sorry, no, help yourselves.'

The manager was glowering around them, impatient to get to his bed.

'Thanks – vot voss your name again?' asked the other Johann. Yehune fixed him with a steely eye: 'Ye-*hune*.' 'Oh, I just thought, could be – ha ha ha.'

Since he'd made such good time, he had to accept the conditions in his dormitory as something to be expected; five beefy guys had set up a howling party based on some square bottles of something like Jim Beam they had in a plastic bin. Asking them to be quiet only made him the centre of their attention for about the next hour and a half. After that, they went back to their normal subjects, shouting 'Albatross!' to each other in gutsy voices, tailing off to murmurs at one point, only to be stirred up to life again by the arrival of another of them, even beefier, with two little yapping rat-catcher dogs. Yehune went so far as to try and move to another room, not bothering to rouse the manager out and tell him; but he was met with indignant shouts and diatribes wherever he went. So he gave up, and returned to the party. By about six a.m. most of his room companions were unconscious, and he did drop off. He didn't wake up again till about eleven o'clock, when he pulled a few things together for a shower, then went clattering around by himself in the big empty spaces of the kitchen.

As a result, he was ready with his pack by about midday. Two yellow earthworking machines were arranging themselves ponderously on the road outside the hostel, to antiphonal yells from the drivers. Round the head of Kerr Bay he walked, and began a southward trek along the eastern side of Lake Rotoiti, suddenly stepping into silence, exchanging the noisy rectangular spaces for treeheads and the bowl of the sky. He walked through young beech forest, over a rotting cover of leaves on the dark ground, with glimpses of the lake past treetrunks. When he got to the lake head, the ground began to slope upwards, and he followed the track, the valley drier now and shaded with autumnal browns. There was always water on his right side, waving or rippling at its limit under the air, sending unusual sense-impressions to him of a clearer, colder region of the world. He took the footbridge over the Travers River. Then his boots dug into mud, the red pack began to feel heavy, as he followed the Hukere Stream up the steep ridge beside Mount Angelus. The trees were growing more and more stunted as he climbed. Then there were none; though he could see another line of mountain beech to the north of the clearing. There was a breeze in the air of quick strange insects, biting on the back of his hand; he tried to wave them away. They were crystals of snow, wafting gently downwards through stillness. Snow was something he never thought about in Auckland, somehow out of keeping with the great rumbus of human affairs, which he associated now with an incessant noise of hot-rod engines plying their way up and down Queen Street.

It wasn't long before something different in the gathering of the clouds, the buffeting of the wind around him, made him try to walk more quickly. But he couldn't do that very well; not uphill on that track. The snow was rushing down now, in what would have been a cloudburst if it were rain, fluffy and unpenetrating, and still not exactly harmless. The light had dwindled. The hut was still far away; but he did see a rock overhanging the stream about a hundred metres or so to the north of the path. He left his pack and went up a track through rapidly-whitening tussock grass, wondering if he could shelter under there if the worst came to the worst.

Closer up, he could see how steep and rocky the ground was. Not hospitable; nope, boy. He took a look back to his pack, and saw two keas perched on it, predatory and self-satisfied, pecking hard at the flaps and pockets.

He ran back shouting. He checked it over – no serious damage – while the keas shrieked and circled round his head. At that point, there was nothing to do but go on.

The path had gone icy and treacherous, steeper by just enough to force him to keep a constant watch on the placing of his boots. There were deep sharp fissures in the line of the rock, giving him some purchase for the treads. Wind came suddenly from behind him, nearly blowing him out of the position he'd set his feet in: a raging Southerly that didn't let up from then on. Visibility had gone, and strangely, so had his energy. Left behind, he supposed, in that unwelcoming dorm, with the cries of Beam-y yobbos. For long moments they seemed to have become the bearers of a peculiar doom: shouting faces, bawling people, hurtling on with him to deliver parcels through the streets of Auckland, to the rumm-rumm of a huge van engine. But far away. He discovered he was half-stepping, half-ploughing through snow that came up to his calves, though the ground had begun to level out. There was still no sign of the hut.

When he did come on it, it was almost by accident; it appeared like a dark mirage through a haze of blowing snow not long before the real dusk began to fall. It was set on open ground by Lake Angelus, and through a sudden break he glimpsed rock slopes rising to the east. He got through the door and found no-one inside, just a cast-iron stove and a system of lines to hang clothes on, and the bunks braced up against the wooden sides. He let his pack down. It was as if he was suddenly shifted again from one side to the other: in a dull-grey space of calm air with the wind raging outside it. Outside; thank God. Only then the sensory levels of his surroundings winked in one by one, like lines of music in some symphony his head was composing for itself. Bangs of a small high window, the coldness at his face and hands and legs – his clothes were all wet. Sitting on the side of the bunk, he vaguely patted a pocket for matches. Then remembered everything was in the pack. Stupid idiot. The symphony was bursting on, at one of its climaxes, built in his inner ear by all the real and imagined frequencies in the roar outside, with loud untimed percussions – bam! … bam!

If he'd been looking forward to a peaceful night's sleep, he was disappointed. First, he couldn't get the stove to light; possibly, or possibly not, because the wind and snow outside had built in strength and fury until you had to give it a name – it was a fucking blizzard, B. L. I., and not one of your playful little blizzards either. His clothes were hung up neatly, but without the stove to warm them he wasn't sure how much use that would be. He'd discovered the window swung up and outwards – and swung, and swung, having no catch; nothing he did to try and fasten it would hold for more than a few minutes. The unattached personas of certain girls he'd known came into his head to visit him, when he hadn't had any intention of thinking about them. Angie (not Ange at Rumbus); Charlie; one other whose name he couldn't remember but who was a gathered softness of curves in some other darkness; along with the narratives of breakups: those painful memories of our good and bad actions that we all carry with us. He thought he might have been *in love* with…. Uff. Unusual thought. But her face in surrounding hair, the way she'd turned to him, wide-eyed after drinking cider. And there was the other one….

His sleeping bag supposedly worked to minus forty; but the air in there was freezing enough, and whenever he took a breath it rushed in through the gap around his nose and mouth. Like being continually splashed with ice-water. He was drifting, floating with them, feeling inconsolable loss – bam! Yeowwff! Fuckinbloody… oh shit, shit. Then the whole bunk shifted distinctly to one side, and he sat up with a shock-pattern dwindling across his chest. Had that happened? Can't have…. But a few minutes later, haah! – it happened again, like the sideways lurch of a ship in the trough of a wave. It wasn't only the bunk: the whole hut had moved. And would continue to heave from one side to the other, unstable in the wind, through all the miserable, storm-haunted hours of the night to come.

The next morning, it was all gone. He struggled into his clothes, parts of which had frozen overnight, and painfully pulled his boots on. The sun was shining when he went outside. That was the first time he noticed the stout twisted-steel cables that came down from each corner of the hut and drove into the ground, tethering the whole frail ark against the open winds of God.

So he crunched around in the remains of the snow, shallow now, and carved here and there into peculiar shapes. He had breakfast, and washed and emptied his pots. He was able to see things clearly, appreciate the massive structure of the topography around him, for maybe the first time since he'd started up the Cascade. There was still a bite in the air. In his imagination it answered to the single, razor-sharp bead of the mountain ridges at their meeting with the sky – where other, aerial mountains started, especially to the south. Huge rising cloudbanks that seemed to continue the convolutions of the ranges underneath. What with the size of things, it was hard to tell… but, no matter. He took the pots back into the hut and started to pack everything up.

When he came out, the sunlight had died again; yielded to that bright flat greyness of the sky that you sometimes get in the mountains. At first, it wasn't anything he saw, more a sense of something, a quality of the breeze, a heightened tension in the air, that warned him there might be something more to come. He looked towards the southern cloudbanks, which had reared up much higher, making an ugly clump far up into the side-wall of the sky. What was more, the wind was coming from that direction. With the inhuman openness of everything, he found it hard to get any sense of scale and distance. Hard to work out how fast he'd have to move, to get off the exposed ground before the whole lot came down on him.

He chugged and grunted under the weight of his pack towards the treeline, which he couldn't see, but which he knew must be there somewhere. He was racing it, racing something invisible and incalculable, something that wasn't even substantial in the way the broken schist was substantial under the clattering of his boots. It was more like a spectre, a size, a dread, toppling down on him out of the atmosphere at a rate that could have been anything; bike-speed, train-speed, moving in proportion to the speed of the heightened wind that whipped at him as he stepped – hopped – slipped on broken chips of rock. Gingerly, but quickly. Wouldn't do to break an ankle just then. Nope, boy. But in fact, it was the memory of the night before that contributed the larger part of his sense of impending disaster – by now he knew deep down, knew in his gut, that insubstantial as it seemed, the effect would be devastating enough.

And so it loomed down on him, as he ran in the absence of any other down over rocks and scrub, as if the hills and rivers and fault lines around him and the trees ahead and the sky over him had a single mouth, had formed in it a dark and misshapen word, and had barfed it out to him, like an immense ink-blot of doubt, over all the certainties of his life. To him and no-one else. Because he was alone here. Even the other trampers had deserted him – why? Any other time he would have expected to meet them coming and going, find different faces in every hut. Could it be that they had more sense, or had maybe all listened to the same weather report...?

He reached the treeline, and was suddenly among tall beeches with a cushioning of leaves underfoot. Above him, over the roof of the treetops, he could see nothing but an inert and leaden sky; but still he felt a building of pressure, heard something deep-voiced behind the whistling and tearing of the wind. He raced on down along the track, jumping over roots. He was thinking about weather reports. Phrases bounced in and out with the rhythm of his boots. Weather, weather, rep-, port. Unscientific, of course. After all, there was Chaos Theory. What was it Mel said? Instance of modern fortune-telling... all memory of the... prophecy, was it, cancelled out by the event. Now he was revising that knowing, city-dwellers' attitude. They could maybe have their – *val*-ue (he dodged branches, ran up against a mound of roots to break his speed) – in certain circumstances. Though the larger movements of the sky were invisible from where he was, he had a sense of them, built partly on the sound effects and the swaying of the trunks and branches. Rain was drumming hard through the leaves. And there was a point when he could almost feel it, something standing overhead, ready to collapse on him with an irresistible weight. But then it swung aside (as he built it in his head) with a sort of unheard *whoosh* and the trampling of monster feet; and seemed to take another path; east or west of him, he couldn't have said. Though he couldn't see much, it was almost as if something that big couldn't go uncommunicated. And sure enough, it was about then that the noise started to fall off, the rain stopped its furious rattling and died down to a patter of drops from the treeheads above him.

He didn't slacken his pace. The forest grew more and more golden as he ran, over ground with very little undergrowth, through foreground browns and russets backed by dazzling shots of sunlight. Thanks, eh? Thank God, God. 'God he was on the other side. Experimentally, he replayed the conversation from one afternoon at the Dispatch: Ange had been trying to badmouth Toddy, who'd gone out on a date with a friend of hers. And *she* said to *him*… all somehow shrunk now, reduced, like the small tracks of insects living on the forest floor. Here everything was on a larger scale. Here, as it was coming home to him, there were no easy lifelines: no delivery vans, dispatch routes, or system of telephone wires running backwards and forwards to the farthest corners of the earth.

By the time he came to Lake Rotoroa on the other side, all trace of the storm had gone. A low plane of water reflected light in flashes past the black of treetrunks. He stopped and dropped his pack, and stood rather than sat, pulling out his packet and matches; because everything he could have sat on was either spiky or soaking wet. He smoked a fag, then, in the immense and unencompassable mountain air, relishing it as he seldom had before. Breathing, feeling the pounding of his blood; wafting the flavour inwards. Seeing the thin slight curls expanding and disappearing, like a more pungent freshness into the freshness. And when he'd finished, he trod out the fag-end, carefully wrapped it in an end of Glad Wrap, and put it in a pocket of his jacket. … Wasn't going to be any danger of *him* burning up all that shit.

He followed the river as far as the next hut. There, he rejoined the world of human beings; there was a whole chattering family from Oamaru way just getting ready to do the walk to Lake Constance. What the hell? he thought, and decided to leave his pack at the hut and go on with them. He kept his own pace, either leading or trailing, occasionally responding to a comment or two. By that time, it was truly cold again, the snow up to chest height in the drifts. And everyone talking normally. But he was under the spell of

210

a light disorientation, remembering the clouds, always aware of the extremity of sizes above them, barely over the tops of their heads. As if any ordinary scale of things was lost in an immensity of space and distance, the sunlight falsely reassuring on the foreground snow and rock – beyond it, that; the implacable slow face of a tidal wave, the mushroom-cloud of nature's force bending down on him.

The effect was even stronger when they came to the lake, which was frozen, a side of crystal under drifting giant-breaths of mist. The woman stood beside him, telling him a long story about something that had happened to their van. But moved away quickly enough when he lit another fag. Seemed quite huffy about it, the old bat. Just puttin' a bit of white in the clouds here. He looked past and above her, into the boiling perpetual motion of the sky, and humorously tipped the cigarette to something or someone behind her back.

The greatest effort came the next day. He had to get over to the other side of the range again, then climb to a certain hut he'd picked out on the map, which he'd thought might have good views. But he hadn't quite allowed for the slow gruelling climb up to and over the Travers Saddle: nothing but the ground in front of his face, and work, and work, his hands numb and sore as he used them (the gloves were all right, but tended to abrade with the constant gripping), and the fragility he felt in his knees. Even when his body was younger, in the days of his rugby playing, those knees had given him trouble. So he was more careful than he thought he had to be, since he couldn't imagine two men with a stretcher appearing to take him off the hill. At least not for the first six or eight hours. Views, he was thinking: they were one thing. But the view in front of him had become nothing but a dazing sequence of shapes in dirt and rock and tussock, caught in his eye and gone again, while his legs slogged on somewhere else, half-numb and unassociated. One close-up view looked like three dwarfs' faces on top of each other. Then another, like a minute landscape invaded by a flat bit of yellow rock. Underneath it, thigh muscles tensing and relaxing like pistons in an engine room.

Once he looked up in the buffeting wind, to see whether the bumps and ridges ahead might have got any closer. On an exposed head far above and to the left of him, he saw a chamois standing, almost motionless, quivering at the flank. Watching his slow and solitary crawl. He had to switch his eyes back to the ground in front of him; when he looked up again it had disappeared.

The climb had become endless, a state of life; the pattern of knobs above him that he identified as the head of the pass was frozen and unchanging. More worrying to him than his knees, or than the process of questioning in his mind which never shut off – why had he come this way? What was the point of it? – was a tendency of his lungs and windpipe to take short breaths. It was as if there was nothing to fill there but a shallow pan, and once it had bottomed out he was left gasping like a caught fish. He couldn't remember ever feeling that before. He had plenty of air, eh. Just not the re*sources* to as*sim*ilate it. In the meantime, his heart was pumping faster and faster, so that he had to stop now and then to give it the chance to slow down. Was it the effect of the fags? Could be. … He could see himself, lying corpse-grey there by the side of the track, waiting for the next tramper, with a little flag coming out of his chest. 'Smoking Kills'. Could even be a relief – he huffed and wheezed at that, wasting the air he had in him.

The head of the pass did come. But as if in another age of the world, with little relation to the lifetime that had gone before. He felt that he'd become another person, spat out reborn on the brown-and-grey stone of the hilltops like something perhaps not innocent but unknowing; completely at the mercy of the rock and sky. His chest was rising and falling so quickly by then that he absolutely had to take a break. But first, there was the problem of getting out of the wind. After some experiment, he found a tiny space he could stand in at the junction of two vertical surfaces. He struggled his pack open. Everything he did seemed unreasonably slow; his muscles just wouldn't move any faster. He hooked out some silver-covered packets. He was mainly surviving on muesli bars during the day; in the evenings he had his trampers' dry meals. He let his jaws do some of the work. Now, finally at the top of it all, he didn't want to look at the dirt and grass, but only upwards. The distended bowl of the upper atmosphere was its own world, alive with the movement of clouds, blue behind, only finding a limit where the humps of the ranges around him – Mount Travers, was it, to his left? – made dark occluding cutouts. Long after he'd sat down on the pack, he was still finding the air hard to get into him. He had food to eat, plenty to drink; but he felt he needed something else – what? Patted his pockets. ... Oh no, that's right.

For the next four hours of walking, adding up to about eight hours by the time he came to the foot of another long rise, his heart did slow down to something like a normal rate. What faced him then was a climb up beside the Cupola Creek to the hut he'd picked out to spend the night in. If not for his work over the map, he wouldn't have thought of doing any more that day. He paused, as much to take stock as to give himself a rest. He wasn't sure how long it would take him to get up there. He felt the air; it was still cold, but not with the biting, lacerating cold of the Sabine tracks over the way. But he was weary, unsure of his essential fitness, and somehow lost to himself, cut off from the chattering voices that made up all the normal context of his life. He'd have preferred to strip off and lie down on the root-woven, leafy ground. Which naturally he couldn't do. A quick look at the map showed him an alternative hut, about three quarters of an hour away along the flat. But....

That beginning of a trail did have a sort of fairy promise, disappearing upwards in an irregular corridor of moisture-laden trees. And then of course there was the plan – the plan.

So he did it; he started all over again. Trudging upwards, back up towards the crest of the range. His legs were serviceable enough, aching, working away under a veil he built in his mind. The forest was colder in the shadow; the slope slanted slightly away from the light-beams that fell in from the east and south. Even now that the wind had died down, the trees would never stop whispering. There were cracks of sudden noise, inexplicable crashes not far away from him: could be possums? Either that, or some very fat birds. The biggest noise, though, came from his own progress, including the loud *ouff, ouff, ouff* of his breathing. He'd felt it coming short again almost straight away. Each inhalation was taken at a cost. Even so, Yehune refused to stop or even pause. Some slow alchemy of the long day in the hills, and perhaps of the two days before that, had accomplished something in him: he was one with it, whatever it might be; or somehow self-evidently aware of it, as if this dank New Zealand black or mountain beech might have been the only real and natural home for him. A spear of sunlight passing by the notch of a ridge shot down, lighting up black-blotched trunks and the aerial fill of leaves. Brotherly, almost expected. He felt a sudden sharp pain in his chest.

Oh, aaau*uuu*, God. He had to stop then. That was a sp... spea. That was a spear all right. Funny, man. Very funny. He puffed in and out very quickly, limiting it to the top part of the action of his chest; it was the only way he could keep the air coming. His hand was forced hard up against a treetrunk.

Gradually, the pain died off, and he tried a normal breath or two. Seemed to go well. Right then.

He took his hand off, brushed it on the thigh of his trousers, and started to walk on.

The way he moved was different. Because now, as well as the shallow breathing, there was always the threat of pain, a pain which lurked like a glow of metal in the barrel of his chest, and occasionally – not too often – flared up into red-hot life. He watched the toes of his tramping boots moving out in front of him, one, two, like the lift of a conductor's baton. He tried to make them regular, coax the movements of his body into a sort of frictionless glide. He wasn't sure whether it was working or not. The trees around him had been thinning out. Just like that, the trail had become steeper and more rocky. He saw the black of a ridge, stark and unbelievable, surely far higher above him than it ought to be. It almost stopped him walking. A saw-toothed extremity of mountain upper edge... and then it came again, *aaaahh*, Cricchsss....

He stopped, barely for long enough to let it pass off. Then he started to take steps again. The trees with their soughing voices were passing behind him, but he hardly noticed; his thoughts were fixed on the threat of danger in the fall of each boot, and on what was up ahead – that inspiration of black cruelty, the saw ridge topping everything. Of course, he had to go on. How could he have stopped?

214

That thing he saw above him held all the concentrated power of his days of walking: it was a flight, a shout, an upper sine-wave. It was the unattainable made real. He couldn't remember seeing anything remotely like it. He would have surmounted any obstacle to get nearer to it. And he almost had to, working all sorts of respiratory gymnastics to try and escape the quick stabs, the twinges in his chest that made him think of hearts, heart attacks, though he told himself they couldn't be that. He could never quite escape from them. It might even be that the constant upward trudging wasn't the best thing for his body. Often, quite often, he had to stop – and was always drawn on again by the sight of the exceptional; that cock's crest of simple asseveration set against the dwindling light of the sun.

In his wandering mind his experience resolved itself into a song, a melody of slow anticipation. He was hauled upwards on the painful rhythm, one-two, of his own boots. The contours of the hill and land-masses all around him were the rolling harmony of it, the sweep and fall; and the idea, the point behind it all, that ridge. Dead or alive, he had to struggle up. That kind of determination made him push a little too hard, and every now and then the pain in his chest came again – though it seemed to him he was learning to manage it. Wasn't he getting used to the way it worked? Two intersecting hill-forms at different distances were very gradually moving into line with each other, the sky was opening out. The sky. The... he had a sort of unearthly premonition.

Then he twisted over onto the ground, falling clumsily, with his pack on one side of him. Something struck him like the kick of a hoof, or the touch of a golden wand, and he curled in on himself without making a noise.

The sharp rocks under him were nothing: some lost, unspiritual point of basis. This time the agony of his inward self was serious, seeming to suck him up and out past silent ranges of black and gold. Beyond him was some large thing filling a brasier, beyond and further out; though he knew in some part of him that he wasn't anywhere near that yet. He was a tiny, motionless insect, lying still on the side of that hill, pierced with a silver bolt. Time had left him, struck away. There were roads or trails that whipped around in front of him, dozens

215

of them, back and forward, squirming with the forward process of his inner eye, and which one would he go on, which one...? Then they were gone, the vision snatched away, and by chance he was left back on the earth again.

He had to remember everything bit by bit. He was a tramper lying at dusk, ridiculously, on the unforgiving stones and base rock of a hill track. His chest blurred in in red. The first thing he really knew was that he had to get up.

First, he had to clip off the straps of his pack, then get to his feet. Then he had to struggle it all back on. He did manage the first two. The third he thought he'd never be able to do. But the ridge was there, more enormous than before, inhumanly challenging. He tried some other ways, dragging the pack or trying to carry it. They always turned out even more difficult than trying to get it on his back. In the end he used what looked like a step of brown wood, but was really upwardly-striated rock – a treestump, maybe, from the ancient forest – to lean the pack on while he got into the straps.

And stood up. Right. Now take a step. Take another step.

Barely past the next slope, he saw a very small hut, clear in the dying light of the day. And something else was there. He went on, stepping right and left and right again, onto the big exposed field of rock and tussock; when he came as far as the hut side he clipped his pack off gingerly and let it fall. He wanted to go on: the ridge was still there ahead of him. But his wishes were somehow struck aside. The kernel of him was... where? Was burned; or had in a sudden shift of ascendancies ceased to matter.

Already during his ordeal on the hill he'd been aware of certain extraordinary colours building in the sky. Now the whole canvas was open in front of him, and no matter where he looked, how much he tried to take in at a time, his field of vision always limited it at the edges. The gold-edged cumulus he'd seen had built to impossible tracts and regencies layered across the breadth of the sky, white bending through yellow-green to a pulsing strain of caramel. In the short time that he'd been watching, the luminosity of the partially-hidden sun had died by about three quarters. The ridge ahead was still that wild combative shout, all details of the hillsides themselves smoothed away in a wash of the tinctures of the dusk, so that the jagged upper limit was isolated, pointed out sharp as crystal against the half-light. It stood to the west of him; and all the way across through north and south and east was a blend and graduation of shapes out of the psychology of a madman, fabulously coloured, sublime or grotesque or elemental, leaving only patches of the lead-grey remoteness of sky bare behind it. It appeared to him, standing where he was, as if everything was progressing from the heartland of a crumple of hills somewhere outside the valley and to the east, aflood with a warm brown or ochre that must have come out of the original furnace, and spread out from there into the colossal fretwork of the sky; as if a lion's long molten-golden forepaw had been forgotten there on the ground and the grandeur and savagery of it had spilt over into the world's atmosphere. Whatever expressions he might have thought of, the quality of the light wasn't describable by any of the words we use for colours. It was like the momentary revelation of the eye of a sleeping beast, saying, here is the glint, the heartlight, before it recedes again among the physical contours of ragged-coated head and sprawled leg. And he was the only one to have seen it, it had winked for him alone – no other face could have been turned to it from quite the same angle in that formidable hillscape.

But there was still more to it. Whatever views he'd thought he was going to see (hitch down on the Friday, he'd thought, do a few walks in the area), he couldn't have been expecting such a literal message. It went far beyond the familiar feeling that all this was apart from him, placed immeasurably above him, remote from his own loves and pains; uncaring, implacable, extramundane. The simple volume of the air and the relations of sizes would have been enough to have that effect. Nor was it beauty, or colours, or cloud and mountainscapes, that were doing it. He seemed to have been levitated to a position where he felt the breathing of the breathless Other, one brush of the paw of that lion, not in the mountain line now, but up above, in the origin of light, in the original sounding, in the white inceptive roar. It was as if he'd suddenly been given an inkling of a cycle distinct from his own uncertain heartbeat; there was a tide, there was a face, there was a clock on being. Something was aware in the wind, and not a thing on the scale of mountains or continental plates or the wheeling planet itself, but as much greater than those as they were greater than him, and that strain, that mouth, that lion, knew him in the thought and quick of him as well as it knew his pack and the hut and every leaf of the lichens and alpine flowers among the rocks heaped up to his right, knew every tiniest aspect of all that revolving radiating ephemeral packet of half-lives all around: knew him and saluted him with the Light. It was in the light that it had come, the knowledge – and all through that night when he would lie breathing in the small hut with its big flat window (some indication that the builders of the hut as well had been aware of the power of that local sky) in the presence of thousands or millions of visible stars like a frigid rash above him, he would know; and far later on when he tried to tell the story to Mel, he would know: that in the light was the recumbent lion, brush of the hairs of a paw, intangible connection with an existence outside him, not part of him, un-Yehune, piercing him again and again with a renewable though now really superfluous sense of his own insignificance, and more, half-justifying him by the fact of it, the knowledge of the presence of... of....

Of what, he couldn't know or guess. That was the proof, really, and the distinction. Or so he reasoned it out, when reason had become an available resource to him again – the next day, hurrying to retrace his steps to catch the bus to Picton, and then again while crossing the Strait in a grey overcast over the lift of waves. He'd seen – *whatever*. Some brush of the tip of that almighty face that roosts out there beyond the individual, *whatever* it might be; not just an idea to be filled in in the detail by his own suppositions or imagination, or worse, religion. Which made it as enigmatic as any scoffer could want, proclaiming, like a shout, presence, position, but never a particular shape. Identity? It was his. That was Yehune's part of it. The knowledge was all tied up in him with the memory of trees and the roots lacing the ground and the glinting of the stream beside him as he ran down with his pack; small details of washing mess tins in the freezing water of a creek, and finding a place to relieve himself among the holy incendiary light-threads of the standing forest. Nor could Mel, or anyone, ever be made to see the point. After a few tries, he gave up on it entirely. And so the moment, the arc of outside-self to self, was singular, personal, unrepeatable, and so... absurdly bound to him alone, so... moving on as he would, job to job, person to person, through all the stock confusions of his life... and s

And so

And so

To Edinburgh

Nicky had a flat in Balcarres Street, near the foot of the long slow rise of Morningside Road. That was where Yehune and Mel found themselves staying, on the strength of Mairi's many phonecalls from Paris. So they'd made it to Edinburgh, all the currents had come together; though whether it could be put down to unknown developments in the relations of Mairi and Yehune, or the winds of change, which blow strongest where no real plan exists, would have been hard for an outsider to say. Nicky was capped by black-and-maroon striped hair, attractive around the brow and eyes, and fell off from there, by way of thin lips tinged with blue to unbraced shoulders and something a bit sacklike about the hang of the body. She was rarely up before ten, so she missed the crisis of activity every morning when Yehune pulled on clothes and flung himself out the door for the morning papers – 'You gotta get in early,' as he told Mel. He pulled the pages apart with expert hands, then sat at the kitchen table with a drying felt-tip pen, circling ad after ad under 'Flatmates Wanted'.

Every evening, if they could spare the time from flatmate interviews, they made the trip to Mairi's parents' flat in Marchmont, either a long walk or walk-and-bus-ride to the north and east.

Mel was cautioned,

'Just, I mean, be careful what you say. Around Nicky, I mean. She's had a hard time.'

'Oh…. Careful what I say?'

'Yeah. Mairi told me.'

'… Can you give me a clue? What subjects to steer clear of?'

'Ah… well…' Yehune tried to think, then gave up on it. 'Just about anything, really.'

Mairi's voice, once it had begun to run through Nicky's personal woes, had quickly become an objective phenomenon of the air that he could have reached out and touched, licked for its bright refreshing flavour, held to his chest and played with, but never, never followed for its sense. It all seemed to centre around or at least begin with a cousin of Nicky's, Bernie, who'd been killed on a Munro that autumn, only he was really a kind of brother considering the way they'd been brought up; then there were her two real brothers and the effect it had had on one of them especially, along with various complications caused by boyfriends of Nicky's and girlfriends of her brother's and their two guardians-in-lieu-of-parents. And all of them had names. Yehune might, possibly, you'd imagine, have *wanted* to understand, given that Nicky was likeable, and in any case someone who'd put them up on the mere say-so of Mairi had to be respected for her loyalty and good sense. But he kept coming up against clauses like,

'… whose father – eh – Roberts, not the real father, that was MacConnochie, but the one Aileen had found through the paper, had this testicular cancer that he never let any of them know about until her sister Emma the little sister found out from the patients' computer records in a clinic she was going to for some post-natal hormonal thing…'

and his attention fell back onto her features, seen through the diffuse light-rays in her parents' Marchmont kitchen. Determined – mobile – lightly glinting around sclera and iris.

He asked her once, not about anything in particular, whether she ever watched daytime TV.

'Soaps, you mean? No. … That's bad art,' Mairi said,

and looked at him once, speculatively, as if he might be implying some distant meaning. Then let the suspicion fall back into the many levels under her eye's bright surface, to co-exist with a thousand other hypothetical scraps she'd picked up in the course of her day.

Morningside Road was a slow-moving upward causeway, crawling with double-deckers and weighed down with shops, and if you were keen you could walk the length of it up to Bruntsfield at the crest of the hill. After all the walking they'd done that day, Mel must have felt it was a strain on his muscles too many.

'God, there are about a million buses – couldn't we have hopped one?' he asked.

'Na. Use our legs, eh. Who needs transportation?'

Mairi had never stopped apologising for the fact that she lived with her parents and so couldn't house them herself. On the other hand, Mel might have considered – might even have written down in his diary – it did say something about her, that she seemed to have friends in every European city so devoted to her that they were willing to take in two New Zealanders at the drop of a hat.

'All this stonework,' Yehune commented absently. 'Someone had to lay all that.'

'Suppose it must have kept the economy alive, back in 1502 or something,' said Mel.

And on they pounded, making small detours for queues, slow walkers, and a whole family loaded down with white plastic shopping bags.

'… You think that's why their shops are so small?'

It was at the top of the hill, in Bruntsfield, that they were delayed on one side of the road while an endless stream of cars wove up and down, some grinding along in first gear behind cyclists that seemed in no hurry. A large truck had begun to manoeuvre half-in, half-out of the entrance to Viewforth; cars were backed up there, ready to duck past when they could. Yehune leapt out suddenly between one fender and another. In a moment or two he was on the other side of the road, gesturing, two-dimensional in full face, like a squat cardboard cutout of himself.

'Hurry up, man – Mairi'll be waiting!' he called across.

With a lunge, Mel made it to the traffic island – just barely. But he couldn't get any further. For every second he stood there, Yehune's attitude of bumptious superiority became more pronounced, his strength, quickness and success with women, while car windows reflected the grey and moody sky.

There was an impersonal flash of carnage. A picture out of their past: Geoff's old Chevalier, on fire by the side of the road somewhere on the outskirts of Turin, the green paint blistering, flames like quick red-tipped reminders on panels that barely seemed to be burning at all. He and Yehune standing, or rather dancing, on the edge of the street, along with a few delighted bambini, before the *polizia* got there. ... Yehune had been under the car, doing his best to fix an ignition problem, 'I'll just try...' and he touched two bare wires together. Mel had laughed, 'Shit man, you've set it on...' But Yehune was more aware of his danger than that; he scrambled out of there more quickly than he'd ever moved on a rugby field.

Who needs transportation...?

Mel: 'Look, I'm... sorry for the hass, but, do you think I could get an aspirin or something?'

Mairi: 'Are you still under the weather? I'm sorry about that.'

Yehune: 'Na na na, he's as right as rain. Just from pounding pavements a bit. It'll blow over.'

Mairi: 'Mum will have something. – Mum! Mel's got a headache.'

Mum: 'What kind of headache, dear? We've got the generic paracet 500ml, but if it's something more per-*sis*-tent you'll be glad of a Co-codamol or even Veganin – here, come away with me and look.'

Mairi's parents' kitchen. Light tried desperately to make the leap from the forever cloudy world outside, through four metres of walls and floor of the laundry or 'utility room', to the spot where people usually gathered around the rustic wooden table. There Mairi and Yehune were sitting, with big mugs of tea, under the dominant display: a set of three Grecian-looking earthenware vases draped tastefully with a grey cloth. They hardly dared move any closer together, or acknowledge each other by anything more than quick looks or shifts of the facial muscles. Someone could have come up at any moment.

'You haven't got any more interviews, then?' asked Mairi.

'Oh yeah. Another one at nine thirty, it's for a place in Easter Road. Apparently they had a couple lined up, but they cancelled at the last mo. So we've got a chance.'

'Easter Road – it's not just round the corner.'

'Mm.' (Slurping tea.) 'See, nobody wants two guys. Nobody even wants one guy. To get a shared flat you generally want to be female, young, not too large, good-looking – hey, somebody just like...'

'Oh aye. Will I do the interview for you, and we'll switch over when it comes time to move in?'

'Yeah, not a bad idea. Given that, you know, we'll probably be frequenting the old establishment both.'

'Are you… are you both getting on all right with Nicky?'

'Oh yeah, she's cool. I've been kind of careful not to mention anything.'

'O-hh, I didn't mean that. I'm sure she wouldn't mind having you there a little while longer, specially if you bring her a bottle of wine now and then…'

Which, if it was a ploy of Mairi's, couldn't have been in any way conscious. Mel had noticed since they'd come up north that language could be as difficult here as in Russia or Italy – maybe not China – and passed that finding on to Yehune, who'd immediately put it out of his mind. Language, up here, was a process of dipping and probing, angling for a reaction, then withdrawing quickly. It was lightly handled, feathery soft, nothing so crude as a vibrating string stretched between two tin cans. Because Mairi was speaking here against her own interest, inviting catastrophe as the price of reassurance. It was almost certain that Yehune's persistence in looking for flats, never thinking to take the easy way out and stay on with Nicky for a while, was doing a lot to confirm him in her good opinion.

So Yehune and Mairi went on with their conversation, with a little byplay of stimulations: a touch of hands past a cup, the slightest brush of fingers over the material of a blouse-back. Both in their different ways might have been wondering how to get away from parents and well-meaning friends – a club, a pub, anywhere outside.…

When Mel appeared again, walking steadily, remembering not to trip at the place where the two floor levels joined.

He sat down, looking pale but undaunted. He shouted into his tin can,

'Shit man, I'd swear they actually *make* the pills in there.'

One of those massive, archaic black taxis swung them in a U-turn from one side to the other of Gorgie Road, tumbling all their possessions in catastrophic slo-mo over to the left. Mel went with it, though Yehune managed to get a grip. Seatbelts were there, but neither of them had taken any notice of them. There were their two packs and several smaller bags, a box, a wicker clothes basket, a single wooden chair, various pieces of electronic paraphernalia including a second-hand ghetto blaster – all the things they'd somehow accumulated in the short time they'd been staying with Nicky.

'What the fuck made us bring this *chair*?' Mel grumbled, trying to extricate himself from over and across it. Yehune was screwing his body round while he fished for change in one pocket.

'Dunno. Useful thing to sit on.'

'Useful thing to stick…'

And the driver: 'Five forty-five, please.'

'Sure thing. Jus' sec… ah… could you just hold on while we…'

'Nae problem. Y'look like y'could do wi' a hand.'

Near the overbridge and on almost the same level was a grimed-up window in a black side of the tenement, flanked by others behind shutters. 'Escorts – Models – All Your Party Fun' was painted all over the very-bright-purple lower storey. But it wasn't for that that Yehune and Mel had come. They had a better reason. Their new flat was behind that window, halfway up a stair that began at a chipped white side-door. It was one of those doors you barely noticed, run-down, slyly elusive, with an impression that if you looked a second time it might turn out not to be there.

'Fuck, Mel, will you give me a lift? … 'Scusee mate, just unloading here…'

Their whole collection was quickly transferred to the wall-side of the pavement, the driver was paid, and with a cheery 'Bye jus' now' he piloted his taxi like a monstrous rumbling beetle out into the road again. Mel was happy enough to stand beside the evidence of all his work. But after a while, he righted the chair and sat on it, looking out on the street vista, showrooms, a small betting shop and the white panel-sided bridge. The passers-by hardly gave him a glance.

Yehune looked hard down the street and then up it, and presently

225

began to cruise up and down the gutterside like a questing setter, in search of something or someone.

'Doug said she'd be here at... God, what's the time...?'

It was half an hour, or nearly that, before a girl in the most peculiar of costumes ambled along with two bags of shopping to somewhere near the same bit of pavement. She wore one of those Elizabethan ballooning arrangements at the hips, with tights below it, ending at a pair of long pointed shoes. From the middle upwards, there was a leotard-top partly covered by a nondescript jacket; her hair bulged out around a face streaked around the eyes and upper cheeks with rainbow-coloured grease paint. Nothing in her suggested the slightest self-consciousness. In fact, she came nearly to an intersection with Yehune at the chipped door before she seemed to notice he and Mel were there.

Then, 'Hello!' she said in a home-counties accent. 'You're not the new flatmates are you? ... Would you like me to let you in?'

'That'd be great.'

'Oh! Ha ha ha. I remember you're from Australia, aren't you? I *was* wondering for a moment if you really were Yahoo-n and Mike.'

'Yehune. Mel. Think we must have got the time wrong.'

'The time?' she repeated vaguely. And a few moments later when Yehune and Mel were struggling up the curved staircases behind her, carrying their full packs and several other items, 'You see, I just had to get a bit of shopping in after the class, and you know how time *does* fly. Look, I've got the bags. So sorry; but you know.'

Two flatmates Yehune had already met; this was the one who hadn't been present at the interview. Mel had been there. But he'd kept so quiet in the face of Yehune's flow of talk that he might as well have been wandering in the landscapes of the moon.

Now he asked hesitantly,

'Are you an actor?'

'Ha ha ha. More a student, really. ... Oh, you mean these?'

The girl arrived at the flat door, opened it and stood back for them to go in, then set her plastic bags down just inside the door. She seemed on the point of going out again straight away. Yehune held her up,

226

'I think we'd better give you some money. And get keys and things.'

'That's right, that's right,' with a dazzling smile. 'How would you like to do it?'

Mel mumbled, 'I've, ah, I've got a chequebook. But not a cheque card yet; it's coming on later.'

'OK, Mike, we'll just have to trust you, won't we? It all goes off to our landlord, you know. We haven't got a proper lease or anything. You *will* both have a cup of tea?'

'Oh, yeah, thanks,' Mel replied. Yehune was more interested in throwing himself down the stairs again to pick up more of their junk.

The girl was saying, 'So – after that, I'm offski. I haven't got too much time to get to my rep meeting. I think I've got a set of keys... or was it two...'

She searched in the handbag strapped diagonally across her body. Mel mentioned,

'It's Mel.'

'Uh?'

'My name. Mel.'

'Oh. I'm Susan.'

'Pleased to know you.'

So after another twenty minutes or so, the two New Zealanders stood by a toppling pile of objects in the larger of the two rooms they now occupied; unlighted because of a lack of bulbs, with a single too-small window giving on the grey street scene and the side of the bridge. As for the interior, a thin sacking material had been stuck to the walls at one time in place of wallpaper; there were blue-flecked gaps in it where the posters had once been; the carpet must once have been orange, and still was in places, but had mostly faded to uneven waves of sulphur-yellow and a staining of something that looked like human blood. A door on one side led to the second room, windowless, and only big enough to fit a single bed.

'Here we are then,' Yehune pronounced.

'Yep, sure are. ... Why, exactly?'

'Shit, man, thought you liked it. If not we can always go back to Doug again, call the whole thing off.'

'No, I mean... not "why this flat?" It's excellent, brilliant, I can't believe the amount of self-determined fucking labour you went to to get it... cupboards. Hilarious. Everyone must totally get their own meals. And a little roster system for cleaning.'

'Mm-hmm. So why what?'

'Edinburgh. I mean, are we here just 'cause Mairi is?'

Yehune was shielding his fag, poising the match and drawing.

'There's a lot to be said for it. Females, I mean. You ought to keep your eyes open, y'know.' He shook the match out. 'I must say that Suze seemed to light up when you started to tell her your details, you've got a sure one there...'

'OK. Funny. ... But I was wondering. Whether you, you know, might have some sort of idea in all this.'

'Well, strange you should say that. – This bed's not super-hard.' He seemed to consider his friend out of the side of the eyes, calculating whether or not to begin, in a way that seemed out of keeping with his smash-and-grab approach to life.

'Come to think of it, I s'pose you could say there is something, sort of, at the very back of my mind.'

He only developed the conversation in brief statements. But they were unguarded ones, each giving a part of the picture that had to be caught immediately, because it would certainly never be repeated. He gave the impression that this was no casual motion of the back of his mind, but a well-prepared plan, soon to be carried out in this city which by the grace of chance and Mairi they'd ended up in. It must have been hard for anyone to pull the central idea out of those scraps, divergent and unexpected as they were, building pictures in the eye that seemed to rise out of the mysterious line where one thing ended (the wooden bed-stanchion) and another began (the carpet's frayed edge) in the melancholy afternoon absence of light on their first day in the Gorgie Road flat. Mayan; Aztec; Tenochtitlan; king-band. Those were ideas that rose up out of the air, dissolved, and were woken again with a mention. A crown of gold. A Mayan crown (though whether there was such a thing as a *Mayan* crown, whether the Mayans used gold for crowns, was something only borne out by dim memories of an old literature of ducks).... All the more confusing for the fact that the speaker apparently identified it with a complex cage-system of glowing tungsten heated by some remote source of electric power: an element, or in fact, The Element; all positioned in and around the top of his own head. In fact, that turned out to be the word for all this, 'The Element', leaving only speculation to decide whether the gold of one version did duty for a yellow-hot glow in the burning mass of spokes; or whether a crown could be so strangely designed as to look like a bulbous wiry circuitry actually disappearing in places under the curled lawn of the hair. Mel was careful not to enquire more deeply into it, aware, as not many people might have been, of the danger Yehune was running in even talking about this. The other-view – the action of someone else's eyes and mind – could generally be relied on to sicken and destroy any concept of the sort, not immediately but soon afterwards; and must have been the death of many a momentarily-glimpsed idea which could otherwise have secretly lightened someone's inner burden or provided some way out of the trap of their thoughts. – 'The Element'. A Mayan crown. All right.

From the tone of it all, Mel must have guessed at a period of planning beforehand, of the sort that might have been done in pictures on a series of scraps of paper, with slogans carefully lettered in over the Masonic symbolism of the wiry headpiece in the whole and the parts. Because that was what could have produced any system of the sort in himself, inveterate scribbler and illuminator as he was. But he was careful not to let anything like that pass his lips. When he did ask questions, he kept it as far as possible on a practical level, taking the weird double-image shimmering on the air between them as read and understood,

'So it sits up in your head, this thing?'

'Yep. Sort of a mechanism.'

'Wire bits.'

'Round, frizzling… you know.'

'And won't let you do… what?'

'It's what I *will* do. Though I admit there's a certain number of restrictions involved. Because I can't just be living casually like I did before, eating any old thing, enjoying myself, spending money, going to pubs and clubs…'

'You can't. And instead, you'll be – what you call working?'

'Mm…. Yeah. That's it. I have to…'

'Yeah?'

'I've just…. You remember Connolly?'

'Connolly? Who's Connolly?'

In fact, Mel must have been well enough aware who Connolly was, though the name held him up for a moment by its apparent irrelevancy. But now, he felt, it was coming: the reasoning behind the heraldry, the idea under the Idea, introduced in a typically roundabout way and in down-to-earth tones intended to bypass any hint of the *fanciful*: you remember old Connolly? Oh yeah, how's he doing?…

Connolly was a tall, thin musician they both knew, who'd lived in a tiny converted office off Victoria Street in central Auckland. He owned almost nothing; nothing but a few guitars and some amplification and recording equipment, and possibly some music paper and a pencil or two. A bed? He must have slept somewhere. He did have a chair, Mel remembered that, and one of those tiny classical-guitarist footstools; anyone who visited got to sit on the chair while the host parked himself on the amp.

'It's *purpose,* just that. He lived by teaching – played the guitar – wrote his stuff, I suppose.'

'Yeah, I guess he must have. There was nothing else he could do.'

'Because he'd cut everything else out. Everything. That's the way to approach it, you know? If you're going to do something, *do* it. No distractions, no books, no pubs, no bloody great televisions… bare boards.'

'It's… ah, hmm. It's *a* way.'

'My fucking way. No compromise.'

Mel might have been remembering Connolly as he really was, no very impressive figure to him, a jigsaw of bones and elbows always done up in a black suit (so there must have been a drawer or clothes hanger somewhere), who did in fact doodle little sounds on a variety of guitar-shaped objects.

'That's what you have to do if you want to get something *done*,' Yehune insisted.

'Yeah. Though I'm not aware that Connolly ever really did anything.'

The other's eyes were sharp through the pall of smoke and lightlessness. Eventually, he said,

'… True. But I'm not Connolly.'

He was petting his fag again; holding the butt of the first between his fingers and thumb even while he smoked a second, rolling and lovingly half-crushing it, turning it round and beginning the process again.

Mel had taken the chair that looked most likely to be comfortable. 'So, just to get this straight – will you be, for example, buying a motorcycle here?'

'Hell no. Precluded. Element'd fry my brains.'

'And are you going to be, you know, going out with chicks? Or sticking with Mairi?'

'Mairi.'

'Are you thinking of getting, I dunno, a job, in the near future?'

'Doubt it. I'll need a piano, of course. … I can't be sure. But I think Mairi's on for it. After all, all this working business takes up an awful lot of time.'

'Yeah, I know… we'll need money.'

'Yeah.'

'I'm thinking of going out and getting something myself,' Mel mentioned, unbrushed by time and the objective. Nothing at all to do with what they were talking about, while Yehune looked past him.

'Oh.'

'Yeah… don't know what yet. I thought, delivering papers, if I could get the work, which might tide us over till I can find something better.'

'You always go for the most…' The fag was squeezed, almost separated from its filter. Yehune stopped and said, 'You mean, *you'd* work, I mean, to…?'

Mel leaned back, to a strange many-voiced wail in the wicker chair he sat on.

'Yeah, well... I'm thinking of you right now as being something in the nature of an invalid, Yehune, with all that fucking ironmongery in your head. It must be pretty heavy. Possibly, um, partially restrictive of the mental processes, being as how it's right up there in your brain; so it looks like for the moment at least it might be up to me...'

'Shit, man. You're making me feel guilty.'

Anything less guilty-looking than Yehune as he sat there on the double bed behind the smoke from his active cigarette (Mel had to wave at the air sometimes to dispel the poisons, despite all the philosophy he'd developed for living near a smoker) could hardly be imagined. He looked four-square and elemental, something rock-like with human limbs, and with nothing particularly glowing about the upper region of the head – it could be that was supposed to come later. But Mel – Mel was remembering the Trip. He remembered all the trips, including everything that had happened after their short stay with his brother Geoff, and the way Yehune had acted as the single buffer between them and the world, organising, worrying, obsessively scraping them jobs and tickets. Signor Freibrecht and his art collection. Wangled, like everything, by Yehune with his power to fascinate; and where would they have finished up if he hadn't got them that? Somewhere in Toscana, maybe, dead under a bush. Mel may or may not have been aware, back then, that something was keeping him from the call to action; a dullness; a sort of wet cloth, he might have called it, between the Desire and the Fruition. But now he was back to normal. At least enough to do a sort of Sydney again, take up easily-found and badly-paid jobs, assuming there were any. The rent – it was sixty-six a month each, plus bills. Then that was what he'd have to make. If there was any chance for Yehune and his aspirations to artisthood (in the field, he was supposing, of music and composition), it was for him to supply the means. The mention of Mairi somehow encouraged him as well, indicating that she might be involved, have given it her approval; or at least had had the idea fully spilled to her before it was spilled to him.

At that point, everything seemed very theoretical and not at all threatening. To Mel the equation must have been as obvious as it could be, appearing to him as lines of red and white and gold in structured intersection on the crosshatch of the surrounding air, with something like the personal reality that Yehune's imaginary crown had for him. Connolly was no more than a kind of ideal, a precedent. But brought up like this, he almost proved the pianist's seriousness of intention. No two lifestyles could have been more different. So there it was: out of the shadowy geological forces of Yehune's private character the path had come, the challenge, direct as a notification of draft: you will do this and this. And though the real internal logic might have been a mystery to be forever sorted and resorted, Mel had to believe that, given his head and a piano and a means to live in Edinburgh, his friend might be capable of following that path as far as the glowing and hypothetical *oeuvre* he thought he needed.

'So, anywea-*eeii-eegh*,' Mel said. He was standing, stretching his limbs to the extreme, like an insect in rigor mortis. ' – Who gets the double bed?'

'This thing? I'm sitting on it, aren't I?'

'Na, come on man, this is a serious matter. What say we toss for it, every Sunday, six o'clock on the dot?'

'Hmmf. F'you want. Though I've gotta say, if you did something in the direction of girlfriend-development you might have more reason to get it away from me...'

Nothing was hanging down from the centre ceiling but a bare wire. Mel went from one to the other of the three old lamps, clicking their triggers back and forth.

'Is there any way of getting a fucking *light* in this place?'

...

A light. A light, an indication – appearing out of the twilight, fugitively glowing. Some faint, self-illumining halo, flickering around the smoker's head whenever the redness of the fag-end died away. Could it have been burning from the headpiece of a man who'd come to his vocation? Maybe; or then again, maybe not. Young men of around 23 have a bit of a reputation for heroic resolves, a small proportion of which are actually carried out; a week or a month later we might even find that Yehune had dropped this one and invented and discarded several others in the meantime, or more likely, gone back to his normal spur-of-the-moment basis for deciding his own actions, avoiding anything that smelled of a *routine*. And yet, for now the principle had been laid down, the tubing set up in the rafters; and knowing Yehune's habit of purposeful directness we can at least assume he didn't take it lightly. A sort of mental goad, it might be, ready to shock him when his lifestyle got too free; or a pickup for whatever strange and alien voices he thought were mumbling in the aether around him. It certainly gives us a clue to the tracks he was thinking in, and through that to the shape of the mentality underneath – that unseeable compound of predisposition and habituation which might in theory, given a similar situation, the same accidents of surrounding and opportunity, have brought him to this conclusion again. The inner Yehune – there must have been such a thing. Nothing comes out of nothing. And yet to chart it on the basis of anything better than the wildest guesswork might turn out to be impossible, using the only process we can, which is to take small photographs or exemplary moments out of what was really a continuous run of history from the moment of his birth, and on down the sequence of the years that stand one by one in a row; first; second; third; like towering shadowy ledgers. ... Who was he? And can we do that – reduce the stream of *character* to a frame?

No-one who knew his parents could have been in any doubt about the shape of his childhood. Brigitte and Andrew Trent (especially Brigitte) had been behind him, pushing and pushing and pushing all the way; though the result must not have been what they were expecting. The ethic of success had gone awry in him, that much was obvious to anyone who knew him in more than the most superficial of ways: nor were the tortured processes, the formative ordeals, anything he would have acknowledged to himself or anyone else. To Mel, the closest friend he had, he always claimed that he remembered nothing at all about his childhood. It had become a blank, performed its operations and distortions on his secret innerness and disappeared, leaving that broad face topped with curly brown hair as his single interface with the world.

But it isn't hard to imagine the course things must have taken. Yehune had a brain about as good as anybody else's, which had unfortunately managed by the earliest channelling of his interests to miss the call to the subjects he'd later have to compete in. At school, he was forever struggling, a little behind the rest; though he did what he could, plotted and copied and worked one thing against another – anything short of applying himself to the hard study his whole mind and body rebelled against. His parents, those two professionals, were always demanding *the best,* which wasn't something in his power to give. Nor was their own example much of an advertisement. Hardly a day went by without some major row between the two of them, with thumps and shouts and harrowing insults; while he kept away, haunted other rooms, toyed with the keys of the upright piano in the sitting room and made soft chaotic noises to himself. The pressure on him never lightened, and of course it all had to go somewhere. An *eye* must have been pushed up in him soon enough: one single bulb on a long stalk that advanced periscopically up above their noisy raging, looking coolly around for an escape-route. It was direct, pragmatic, not to be influenced by any amount of emotional charging. He found there was almost always some manipulation that could buy him time, if not get him off scot-free. He became wily, not to be read. And this wasn't even an aberration. It was a natural writing, given the constraints of his environment, to what we have to assume was the basis of him, his inner makeup, that glistening spiral lattice of the genes (– and in the *genetic* connection, it shouldn't be forgotten that both his parents were ruthless and self-directed and unlikely to give up at anything at all). He'd learned well enough by then that open opposition was useless. It could even have ended up breaking him; and Yehune was one boy very unwilling to be broken.

And so the *eye* kept seeking out his advantage; in which, you could say, it was only imitating those same parental values. But in him they were misapplied, seeking round the back, looking for the alternative, through buffoonery, or contacts, or a game of appearances. And he looked for something else as well: some subject or idea that he could call his own. That turned out hard to find. But some of the attempts survive, for example in his name, Yehune, which if he'd known it was more Ethiopian than Hebraic; but which he took as an early seal of individuality, a sort of trusty flannel duggie to comfort him against the endless battering of voices from outside. While in his environmental training he was the true son of his parents, straining every nerve towards some kind of visible success, it was a given that that success should have nothing to do with anything Brigitte (especially) or Andrew Trent had ever wanted for him. Still, strangely, to their credit stand two directions, two small scams or escape-routes which really were gifts of their solicitude. His sports ability, which in its backhanded way originated in those training-sessions on the confidence course equipment; and music, the gift of their expensive and so-bourgeois private lessons. Against them, almost everything else. The dwarfish comedian in him; the naughtiness that came near and sometimes passed the boundaries of the criminal; his sampling of drugs; the glamour of fast motorcycles and the clothes and attitudes associated with them; frequent experiments with girls (which among other things were a proof of something, a staking of the claim of his personality) – even a vague, undirected anti-Germanism. That last one had flowered at one point in a plan, never carried out, to go to Israel and join a kibbutz, on the basis of information he'd picked up somewhere that anyone could get in who had the slightest real or bogus claim to Jewish blood.

We catch him travelling just now, partly to help the kindred spirit Mel out of a period of inner paralysis. But for himself, unstoppably scanning to the side, always searching in the great hollowness for a sign. It might have come, in the person of Mairi; in any case he'd made an exception to their makeshift rules of travel and settled down in Edinburgh for a while. And in the meantime, that perpetual spyer-out of the main chance was nagging away inside him: angling for another excuse, since (try as we might to sort them out for him) all the tangled string-ends of his motives had never quite come together. So: Connolly. Pragmatic art. The direct and only chance. He *was* an artist, after all; he'd discovered that peculiar form of creative rebellion; and he thought he might as well start now as later. To Yehune, the arts were free and flexible, the graceful opposite of school. There were no marks, no standards, no teachers sitting there with an answer page – more specifically, no mother crowing high-voiced behind him, reddening the broad vault of the sky, subsuming all existence in a yolk. – Any advice *she* might have given him would have been in the opposite direction.

So it seemed that through a series of small rebellions Yehune had come to strength. He'd started with a habit of tinkering at the piano keyboard, developed that into a form of composition, then accidentally opened up the field of writing when he tried to show old Mel how it should be done. And he'd defined a way for himself; the one and only path in life, possibly, in which the better he succeeded the less his parents would like it. 'Self-expression', the educational theorists had called it at the time he was going through school. He might still have been considering it that way, like gestures, like the expressions of a face; automatically his own because he himself had made it. If 'good', that would have been an accident, the free transfiguring touch of some force outside Yehune. It was an outlook that entitled him to ignore himself, and the elements that made him up, with the same happy insouciance that he enjoyed in real life.

And yet, for others looking in, there might still have been clues. What were his gestures? What brashness, sensitivity, wry humour, yearning or regret, could be read in the movements of his face? Why did so many people like him, when his self-certainty and occasional extreme behaviour might have made him seem pushy or abrasive? Where was he? What – and who?

Yehune. He was first of all a physical body. We can see him broad and stocky, low to the ground, about five foot five in his bare feet. Some hulking effect of the join of neck to shoulder gave him a mistaken appearance of thick-necked brutality, of muscles tightened and bulging, especially when you looked at him in back three-quarter view. And yet the head was always mobile, as if it hinged at a point just above the neck and swivelled freely on some unrelated plane. He never stopped looking around him. That made the contrast with his solid torso, which fell from fleshy shoulders to a midriff that only ever turned as much as it had to. After that, the legs, growing down from hips that were slightly on the broad side, taking away any grace or neatness from his walk and leaving only functionality: the necessity of pushing one leg forward and then the other. His arms dangled down alongside, barely swinging when he walked (which made them seem longer than they were); each coming to an end in a large bear-paw. It might have been something in his piano training, or just more characteristics out of the bloodlines of Andrew or Brigitte Trent, that gave those backward-dangling extremities their appearance of sleepy power, like two machines that were switched off just then but might spring into activity at any moment. When they did move, it was with deftness and precision, as if every finger was meeting every other perfectly centred at the tip – and paradoxically, sometimes with clumsiness as well, or even a little bit too much relaxation. It has to be admitted, Yehune dropped things more often than most other people.

Then there are facial expressions: the body's giveaways. Yehune's expressions were appealing and alive – so Mel would have said, or someone else he knew and trusted. But to others, it would happen that there was a sudden look of blankness, a freezing of the outer self, something that could be taken for a passing absence or wonderment, while his thoughts went away on unseen paths. When someone amused Yehune without intending to, it could seem that the whole middle of his face was set apart like a mask: the setting of feature to feature was polite and free of commentary, while the area round about, the upper forehead to the hairline and the periphery from cheekbones down to the region of his chin, seemed to move to its own rules, expressing all the silent laughter he felt. Likewise when he was angry, his face usually held still. But then you could just see the edges appear to cloud over, crawl with a brewing of potential storm, reflecting in the graduation of the cheek a darkening that threatened to take the mask and throw it aside and reel to its own strains; to break out like a disease across the eyes and mouth and the flanges of the nose. And it was that same face that could be caught in a variety of quirked or humorous sets throughout the course of any day; especially when the days contained something interesting, new scenes, or foreign countries. We might mention Yehune's habit of opening one eye wider than the other and somehow broadening out one side of his face, while raising the same eyebrow, sucking his mouth in a bit and dropping his chin at the same time, in acknowledgement of the passing of some thought. At other times, for no apparent reason, a formation of extra wrinkles came into being, etched like an insubstantial *moko* across his brow and at the corners of his eyes. He was mobile, un-self conscious, energetic and willing to experiment; and all of that lay lightly on him, like a *modus operandi* deeply inherent to him and never questioned from the inside. Action was what he cared about, the control of appearances, a sportsman's timing of everything he did; along with a readiness to punch or jab or break something when he had to.

From his own point of view, he must have lived inside a sort of glazed screen: simple consciousness. All his inner processes and characteristics were hidden behind that static shield, that depthless sheet of paper. It was the silent engine, the process of moments through time, unstudied and uncommunicated. We would have to go far behind it, deeper and deeper in, to try and catch a glimpse of the heart of him, which is nothing isolable in space; nothing, maybe, but a quick and blinding fragment always moving away from the eye that looks for it. The part of us, of me, and you, and every other person, which is really the life and the miracle – he being like all of us, in the deepest recess, that shrinking animal, beautiful, diminutive and unobserved, curled down on itself and chanting in the inward silence, 'Don't hurt me'.

Which leaves us...? Yehune; or Johann Trent. ... A monkey-cage in orbital swing, intersecting the courses of the planets in a long unarrested curve. And in the cage no monkey, but a human baby or boy child of around one-and-a-half to two, naked, his face frozen just at that moment in an expression of conscious naughtiness. The cage as bullet, flinging itself at high velocity through the dark emptiness of space; then seen again from further out, in a graceful dance with asteroids and tumbling debris. The cage with a velvet cover, hidden under a curtain dusted purple-black; hooded for the night the lidless night which will which has to come. Suddenly, a rush and cannon back of violet and orange billiard balls – which is the action of the mind, unfixable, always supplying its own motion and colour. And when we apply our dream-eyes to the child itself, we see a face bulbous and smooth as glass, shading and changing, each feature vast, slow-moving, ponderously animated, as it seems to stare up with a mixture of unguessed apprehensions – and further in past the flash of a stubbly jowl, we can make out the flesh under the skin, the bone under the flesh, and deeper again, far down amidst the throb of organs – heart, liver, pancreas, kidneys, lungs and stomach – we catch astoundingly the inner self, like a short bright-scarlet flash of ribbon stitched among mounds of tissue… and moving outwards, out again from that glaring quick, we pass barely below the swinging of colossus arms, two long-haired monkey-arms, stretched out and out to encompass heart and mind and wind and stars and whatever else we might happen to be looking at – which turns out to be space, the black and cartoned universe, blazing of interplanetary wicks – and steadily, sideways, rushing away again, we seem to observe over a bulging midriff the shy preemptive root, the slip and substance: the short stub-end of a monkey penis.

. . .

Yehune! – Himself! – The inward nature summarised!

In the Car

–

Mairi said:

'It changes. Seems to change.'

She was right: it changed and changed. Just as the streets swung past in an endless variation of colours and reflections, down the hill and on to the Pleasance; when it was the same route, the same city... you could maybe say. He opened his mouth,

but Mairi's head was turned to an intersecting street. She went on to list a few differences in her clear, vowel-shifted voice. One moment he was writing words; then it was music he was writing; then the piano he was playing; now there was all this hiring of halls and churches....

'Oh yeah. But he's still sticking to the same thing basically. You know, it's the wires in his head.'

The girl seemed absent, fazed, possibly, from the stresses of the day, talking at random. She made a small 'Mm', changed gear, and said,

'He sticks at it... and what about you?'

There should have been some awkwardness there; something to do with the strange sub-culture of the lift, where two people, male and female, had to sit isolated together in a moving space. By that time, though, he'd got used to Mairi. No matter how personal their conversations got, he was aware her focal point was always Yehune.

'Oh, I'm OK, taking the old English pupils an' that. So, you know... as long as Yehune wants to hang around here and do his thing...'

'You mean as long as his friend Mel wants to. You're the stubborn one, after all.'

'Me?' He was a bit surprised. There was another in-car silence, as Mairi either dealt with problems in the traffic or took her time to register that he hadn't agreed; hadn't seen it.

'Oh, come on, you must realise – he always looks to you for a lead.'

Mel had laughed. Looking back later on, he would remember the sun on the upward-rising red-orange barrier of Salisbury Crags above the buildings, gashed in, like a lurid and crumbling cliff of sand.

'No no no. It's just The Element.'

He had no sense of her understanding him, so he went on. The fact that Mairi, Mairi of all people, could have got it so completely wrong was one of those curious surprises the world kept coming out with, defying all expectation. Never boring. Not for a moment. The rumble and shuffle of cars was bringing them slowly to the intersection with Hope Park Terrace and their right turn.

'Look, Mairi, I know you two are together and all that. But that's not the way it is at all. My God, you should have seen us when we were going through China and Russia, I just… I really don't even know…'

He didn't know, to that day, what had been happening in him; all the reasoning and raw feelings were sunk so far down that he had no way of accessing them. But the way Yehune, Yehune alone, had faced up to every decision and made it and then single-handedly fought for the outcome, doing his best not to bother a person obviously too far gone to help in any way or even advise, still formed a prominent, even an epic picture in his head. Mairi hadn't been there, that was all. He kept trying to put it into words – marvelling, at the same time, at how closeness and personal regard could destroy all objectivity about a person. And in *Mairi*. She was probably thinking about something else; the birthday present for her father, or how her mum would cope with the dinner to come.

In any case, he could tell, as her small Renault took the long curve of Melville Drive, in spectral sunlight, past ashes and sycamores stippled against the sky, that all the words he said were doing nothing to convince her.

–

ONE

And when I came down from the big house not possible to say what was in my head, not that we are heads, but eyes and necks and feelings and perambulatory digestive systems riding on the air pushed at us *crump-ra-rump* past windblocks at the peak of the driveway, where the cop car stood like a new bright-painted toy. Seeing in the eye of my mind the little group of them in uniform with Pom and the cap off one of them, a hair wisp flying, the one who'd told me vunc vunc a-*vunc*ularly I'd best wait my turn somewhere nearby. They'd be half an hour. Both of which can mean anything you like, nearby and half an hour, in the language ordinary people use down here, untyped, unlitigated, and I might have wondered where there was to wait, in my tiny slope-roofed bedroom with the print of Chamonix, or maybe on a heap of planks in the half-finished conservatory over on the golf course side.

So it must have happened that I fell out the front door and rolled away past the greenhouse and the shock of blue-and-yellow stripes and the topiary bushes to the wall's edge and Gosford Road beyond, all without anything in mind or head or heart but the vacuum suck of that which isn't there when the trick of the wind pulls the air out of your nostrils. Where leaves had barely finished falling. Stark cut of the branches against a milk-deep sky, clashing with all the residential neatness, where every hedge was perfect, footpaths swept down in places, and I went trailing on past houses, Harmony, Shangrila, to the 40 signs in the bay of two roads. I could see the wall over the other side running on for mile after mile and changing in sections red to grey, and the heads of trees in someone's private parkland. Don't they love their walls. With those weird stone stanchions, the ones that always reminded me of New Zealand letterboxes. Down, further down where the sky opened out again past breaks of sea buckthorn and you could see the shore and island and Cockenzie Power Station towards the edge, there was an interruption in the wall and a real letterbox, 'Ivantyr'. Porter's house: the entrance less grand. Beech leaves on the ground. Ahead, the cluster of signs like huddled sails that rattled day in, day out, bearing the assault, to inform the motorists: *Aberlady, Gullane, Cockenzie and Port Seton. Edinburgh* was arrowed back the way I came. When I could actually make out the hump of Arthur's Seat and a tiny Castle away off to my left, like a dream horizon past two smokestacks.

And in keeping with my lack of motive or understanding of persona or head or heart I turned left into the rippling gust. Why? Could be because that stretch was a killer, cars went hammering past and you couldn't hear them for the wind noise. Cross at the hawthorn, I must have been thinking. On the golf course (nettles, the blue-grey buckthorn and a straggling fence) – on the golf course the pine windbreaks were permanently twisted sideways, reaching south-eastward down the coast. Once beyond the bushes I could look up to pick out the back of our own B and B, and there was no-one on the course, and the wind unleashed into my face (trying to tell me not to go that way?) was like the undulation of the coast road left and right; and I waited a bit and crossed. The hawthorn there like a dark infolding twig-world, vegetative brain. Saw tiny flowers down in the scrub grass, even in November. Knew some of those: bloody cranesbill and, was it, marsh ragwort… and something that looked like an Alpine Buttercup or something-leafed Buttercup, but with prickles and tiny little pinnate leaves. Going on, to where, to the bench of course and the steps in the seawall; not quite feeling as if I was coming home, but near it, in the perpetual rumpling blast of the air of anywhere but, through grass with prints of horses' hooves.

To say I came to the bench and seawall isn't to say I thought of Thompsons and its darker seawall better defined in mortar, or splintering walls and pilings of Nga taringa, the ears, or a hundred dozen other barriers against the sea up and down another coast entirely; I never came here without thinking of them. Things looked rough here, battlemented. A big rectangular block in the same stone as the steps set on the left to mark the way. Above, a bench for golfers; wrought iron painted white. Looking out on the low flatness of the skyline, sand streaks and water streaks, the sad slock of the waves despite all the wind's force, I stood balanced for a single moment, beach and beach. With a minor effect in the bead of my eye where one became the other, and back and back and back again, fast wind-ripple, and I saw not with my eyes in the light-blue spaces over the hills a crackle of zigzag dividing fires.

Started to go down. It was funny to think it was possible to fall, when I was already, to myself and in a way, tumbling over and over in the open air past the edge of a cliff lost behind me, headless, groundless, even while I watched my feet plod step by step down to the level of the sand.

Caught there. Unopinioned. Dropped just here by the undirected shuttling of incident after incident. I let my feet walk this way and that way, chuffing into the soft rough sand in the low glare of the sun, until the rocks fell into my eye and brought back Thompsons Beach with such a shock of recognition that I caught the waft of a dozen events out of childhood as if they'd happened no more than half an hour before: Geoff and Mandy running with me at the lip of the waves; the big stone fights with the Torrance kids; epic journeys over the greenslicked tops of rocks from one beach to the other; and vertical wave explosions against the concrete walkway when the tide was just at the level. But here. I was here: Longniddry. One glance back, to convince myself, at the white bench at the top of the steps.

A red face Coca-cola What was that? Thought I saw a head moving further back – was there someone there? Turned, and couldn't see anyone. Back in the tracks in the grass, people could pass and cross out of my line of sight. But now my eyes were down again to beach level, and seemed to see traces of verbiage like old print-tracks snaking away across the contours of the sand, at somewhere around the height of my shin. Words and more words, making colours, loomed projections on the underside of my eye, Lip-lip, Y' Y' Yip, with a kind of apelike laughter sounding in the distance. My God, was I even *allowed* to think...? A shock of jagged lightning, split at the charge into the upper air, topped off a face I maybe oughtn't to've dwelt on, and I saw like a quick mirage those shoulders hunched in a baboon lift.

And when I glanced up and to the right I could see the monkey form of him running in and out on tracks through the grass, now here, now gone again. Hearing the *shoof-shoof* of cars on the road beyond. Should I go, set wheels in motion? … The bank to the right of me fell away south-eastwards in a series of sweeps and catches, making each slight promontory swell until the moment when you passed it. Sand and grass building up in my eye; then, suddenly, gone; and the sad tenebrous expanse of the beach was laid bare in front of me, like the attenuated shape of a scythe, to the tiny headland where people parked their cars; and there in the downcast state of the air and sky and the forward thrust of the wind it was suddenly hollow, an overwhelming hollowness drawing me forwards and on.

Ripples in the beach. You know… there was that kid, the Weimar kid. But that was, what? an exterior likeness, nothing more. Yehune in the egg, the **yo**. I could see him now side-on, in a hurry, behind the racing backwards stands of half-dry grasses up there on the flat, could see him and picture him all right, but it wasn't so easy to. Oh no. I tried to imagine, for a moment, Matamata, which looked to me like a flood plain by a ridge of hills, and old Yo stuck there, having to fight his patch, holding his own against the enemy (which must which had to be his parents)… coming out that cautious, predatory mix. Underneath it – what? Far-gone in naughtiness. Strong out of necessity. But you know if you want to see in any way deeper, further in….

There was a long spit bearing deep into the sealine past a mess of darker rocks. Beyond it, two ships out in the Firth, one shifting slowly but perceptibly towards the other.

I caught a quick reflection from the sea surface, a conversation of light. *Ricepaper, a Chinese scrawl* And after that there was one and one and then another; and I couldn't help thinking of the setting after setting, flying back and shifting metamorphosising in our eyes, shuffling in their effects on primacy, on the ont ont of the inner immaculate, cycling round from sea to shore to what-was-it

Fresh. Here. Me.

I'd written. Had I written? Something like that.

Just here there was seaweed, kelp or maybe wrack, making a long irregular heap between the dry sand and the wet. The dry was coarse, churned with footprints; wet sand was easier to walk on. So I did, adding the print of foot by foot behind the lift of my shoe's heel, in the wind that kept moaning on and on about something. Diaries, of course that was from my diaries, which made it more to do with me. And yet... (all the time I was wandering, looping, turning this way and that, and scuffing at the sand with the toe of my shoe, looking inside the bank at the tumbled blocks of concrete shoring it up...)

and yet you could say not completely beside the point. Because there was the, him on me and me on him, there was an influence. *My old black jacket; Bremworth in a flat;* a flood of pictures came suddenly rushing in in support, none of them really called up, none having to be any more than tweaked at an edge. We became *artists* – how, why? There was my Sail, patched up out of remnants. And all the time I could look up and see him, seem to see him, his face looking out from above the tussock with a peculiar smile, at me, or something else...?

Something, at something outside... the Outside Himself. Why outside? Maybe because he wanted to have it dictated. Or no, it was more than that. Look at it his way for a second, what's outside yourself you can't control, could be it might not turn out what you expected; or double, triple, come to a multitude; the jeezling little N – S – garbage-suckers, a jostling of forms, of things you can't quite catch....

Sssshzzzzh, the wind was cold. It numbed my toes and fingers, or rattled across the hollow of my ear a thaka thaka thaka thaka thaka

So what was I doing here? Wandering, only wandering. There was no point or purpose to it. I happened to turn back on myself around then, glance into the wind and low beam of the sun

And my eye was threaded   .

Seeing   .

Figment bathed in light, like a high turret two turrets burned beyond with green yellow purple fields in the utmost sky of spears beyond like a bearing ratcheted on courses of coiled-down orange never to be seen in the real, or never now, and

I was taken out of myself to a time before sense or knowing a
time when longing wasn't doubled on itself: to a fairy palace

Power station, of course. Cockenzie. Two tall slim chimneys
chuffing out smoke or steam into the partial white of the sky.

I shifted my line of sight. Skittering across sand-leavings, flecks
of ancient shells, with a spectral rotor-shape of emergent and
receding colours somewhere near the focus of my eye. Over all
the sweep of the beach that vanished on ahead, and over the road
sign just coming visible to the left before the hawthorn again, and
over the house with the orange roof on the other side of the road,
I could see it, an unhitched blaze of colours. Move, and it moved.
Or he moved – there he was – looking airy, colour-rich, as he
broke out through the grass and stood for a moment and loped
back again on one of the pathways in the tussock.

Mandy, fallen on the path from Thompsons round to Piri

Couldn't help but wonder where they came from, pictures,
images: just then there was a line of children led on rings on a
long ribbon. Maybe from all the heterogeneous rubbish scattered
here and there in the seaweed. I looked in closer, seeing shells
and stones and bits of wrappers, an old sock. Packing material,
in white and red and green. Shape like a fishhook, hills and flats,
down among the pods. And a fine scattering of white, something
like flour, or alum…? Couldn't quite see. Tyre tread of a 4 × 4. Red
ribbon, red, in the Moscow tar, and contrails of a jet; a greyscale,
to the *zhhh* of the wind, the greyed-down faces of a sculpture,
slava trudu…

Which was the difference, I could see it now; that was all the
difference: the cut, the lightning cut; hemisphere to hemisphere,
childhood to now; the fork or sudden crackle of the consciousness
of worlds divided. The moment of looking back to where you
can never be again. Which could have been that as well… the
fork up over his head, the Y; startling in the aerials fizzing wild
and sending unknown messages out into the aether. Yehune, the
running man

Keep up

Keep up, man. What was the point, for *him*? Going on...
to who, what? I could see him just then looking sideways into the
hollow, into the vanishing point of earth and air.

And so – I told myself again – you have to consider the point.
The point.

Well, it might be or anyway you could say it was when we
managed to lose ourselves in France and crawled through a station
and a road that led nowhere or everywhere in the vicinity of the
Solnan and Plaine de Brosse and my guts were bad and by laughable
and unbelievable chance happened to come on, you know... which
was a point, could be one, a girl, or, or

Or else the other, that walk he told me about so many times, in
Nelson National Park. Where it seems he fell by a process of teeth-
gritting labour upwards into the sky, on the day or building over
days a feeling charged and recharged and spilling over into certainty,
right or wrong: the certainty of a presence, transcendence, something
painted openly on the sky in unbearable braised extremity, an answer
spoken, that only later you or he might come to realise is unsayable,
so that

so that

So I looked up, to where the larger of two hawthorns was set back
towards the road. Hearing the cries from the seagulls, the sough of
the surf over the roaring in my ears. Thinking: he's there. A ribbon,
bearing into emptiness. The two ships in the sea were still distinct,
turned in the perspective the way my feet had wandered. Out the
same way, there was a wasteland of dark rocks.

Where one round boulder stood in the foreground, drawing my
eye. It was split in a single crack from top to bottom. And then,
despite myself, I thought of Mairi.

Home to the Gorgie Flat

It was coming up to their second Christmas at the flat. And here we have to make sure of the details, fix and clarify them and bring them back into the run of memory, to avoid confusing one broad phase or tidal level of a human life with another. At that time, Mel's run for home from work, from 'The Royal Edinburgh School of the King's English' on George IV Bridge, would have been done in the dark, in a tracksuit and his cheap yellow trainers, with a backpack to carry his work clothes in. He was varying his route from day to day, trying to bring it closer to his ideal twenty-minute run. His face, at that period, would have been on the bony side, with a small hollow below each cheekbone, though the side volume of his hair cancelled out any effect of thinness. If you looked at photos taken of him and Yehune then and at other times, they always looked more or less hairy, slimmer or fatter round the gills, sometimes with some unusual feature – an extra intensity in the eye, a shift in skin shade – which might have been an accident of light when the shutter fell, or the sallowness of a three-day illness, or the effect of some train of thought. And so the variations built up – running on layer after layer – keyed, we have to suppose, on an invisible timeline that must have included every floating speck of rubbish in the outward-spreading drift of the surroundings of their lives.

So then. ... He remembered pacing along in a light rain past Gorgie Bath Centre and the bookie's on the other side of the street, feeling the cold of the air on his head and chest and the upper front of his legs. Everywhere else was warmed by exertion. He was on the last stretch, pulsing hard. A quick pause to check his watch – heartbeat for ten seconds. 24; nobbad. The outer door was unlatched, no need to dig around for keys. Then he was trudging up the stairwell towards their door.

A large dog went pounding up past him, scrabbling with its paws on the wall-side edges of the steps. Get over, you... Jeez gods. Almost had me off there. As he turned on the stairs, he saw a tallish, brown-haired man receiving the dog at the open door,

'Good-dog good-dog – who loves you? Andy loves you.'

Andy, or Andrew. That was the new lead trumpeter. Who might or might not have noticed Mel, or recognised his claim on the flat; in any case, he and the dog faded back inside.

Dogs on the stair. Big mutt. Active too. It meant a meeting of Yehune's Ensemble. Or rather, not a meeting; one of his discreet pre-meeting gatherings.

'*God,* Mark, I mean a *tuba* case…'

The phrase came through to Mel while he was still in the flat's short common hall. He could make out piano noise as well, but too soft to be real, possibly from a tape. He came to the lintel and passed it. Four people were standing inside their larger room – three round the piano, the other beside the case of a large instrument.

Of course, they have to be in here. It's the piano. Dark at the window, ocean's darkness, invisibling the slight rain, out there by the bridge.

'Hi Yehune.'

'Mm? Oh. Hi.'

Something automatic kept him moving, maybe words or small flutters of the mind; picture of a bath; of his clothes in the bottom of the white chest of drawers he could see behind a collapsed music stand and someone's stonewashed jeans. And there were the job-forms, got to get. He was aware of Yehune leaning on the piano in the centre, discussing something that sounded more financial than musical:

'Now, as I was saying, projected receipts from the concerts should cancel out the amount you were talking about…'

'Assuming we can just do it like that, set one against the other – wouldn't we have to have the players' agreement?'

'Oh, no, that's for the management committee to decide. We could bring it up in March, though, that's only fair.'

'OK. So it's Italy first, you say, that deal the committee in Ventimiglia's offered you…'

'I thought you said it was Denmark first,' another voice objected.

251

Mel went into the ruck, pushed his way through, sweaty and panting, and bent down to pull out the lowest drawer. Just then, the tape clicked off. He heard impetuous doggy noises close behind him; a chuffing and scrabbling. He pulled out clothing, but found he couldn't do much useful sorting out just then. Best to go on into the boxroom, bypass the struggle. There was that paper he needed for his qualifications.

So there it was, the qualifications – he didn't have the certificate. So it must have been near the end of his job at the Edinburgh School, to pin it down again to a moment in the long receding landscape of time and space; in memory. They'd taken him on on nothing but his school and university record, which of course included his English marks. But the lady at the interview had practically forced him to claim he had a certificate; he'd told her it was being sent from New Zealand. Over other pictures from the time – paper decorations in the common lounge, and the dark wet streets, and the tinkling of Christmas music from behind the window of a shop – he could see Lammer: a pale, triangular face with a tic at the eye-corner. Lammer had been the one pressuring him to produce the actual diploma. However, the lady had signed some interim slip saying she believed he had the qualifications he claimed he had; and it was that bit of paper he was trying to put his hand on.

Out he came again, having at least established where the paper wasn't. Another dog, even bigger than the first, was snuffling with its nose in the pile of clothes he'd left on the floor.

'*Grendel!* Get out of that! – Careful boy, or you'll be catching something.'

Andrew the lead trumpeter gave him a smile of pretend apology: just a joke really. That doggy nose, down rootling in the clothes. Mel was about to say something, but decided, not yet. Wait. He picked out some underwear and a pair of long black jeans, and scouted round for a tee-shirt, any tee-shirt.

'… think we should be raising the subs though. After all, it's only fair.'

'Yeah, we all know you do all the work. Um… how much to, do you think?'

'Oh, um, twenty-five… no, let's say thirty a quarter. For just now. I need a bit of working capital.'

'Oh, that's fair enough.'

'That's fair enough,' echoed someone in a weaker voice. The others had gone quiet. Mel walked out with his clothes, to start turning on all the hot taps in the flat, which was the only way to force the combi boiler to start heating up the water.

Yehune called across,

'Mel! Oh, Mel boy – don't go in the bathroom just now, will ya? I'm about to use it, gotta get the whole show off on the road in three minutes. We're just waiting for Eber to arrive.'

He hesitated. And called back, 'OK man. I'll just run my bath.'

On the way out through the hall to the kitchen and laundry – 'utility room', as they called it here – he passed the open door of the lounge. The first of the brown dogs, like a huge leggy sausage, was chewing happily away at one of Susan's Christmas ribbons that had gone astray, trailing down the bookcase beside the lightable joke Christmas tree. Susan's ribbons; she'll love that. He passed the door,

seeing the shape exaggerated of a little Santa's elf by an upright log, genericised   bump by an upright.

Flushed red, redder as he passed on.

– In the mind's eye, trailing floater.

So it seemed Yehune was involved in the usual Ensemble politics, holding his meetings, or meetings before the meetings, trying to make things go the way he wanted them to. Such private little chats – usually without the dogs – were necessary, apparently, to keep down the intriguers, who were bound to come to the surface wherever money was involved.

Wherever money. Money. Mel had always supposed it was in aid of something else (he spun the kitchen sink tap, watched the stream splash minute droplets onto every surface) – music or something? Oh yeah, but…. Some dishes were left over from a Chinese carry-out Susan and her friends had had: won ton, prawn cracker remains. Better than I'll be eating. Have they gone out?

And as it happened, this was the first time he'd seen so much evidence all in one place that Yehune had motives over and above a general devotion to art and music. Specifically, that he was running scams on the Ensemble players by dangling overseas trips in front of their eyes. Denmark, they'd said, or somewhere in Italy. He could just imagine. Mel tried hard not to judge, realising that motives and priorities were different in each of us, and usually a long way from the easy stereotypes. It could be Yehune was holding his artistic ideal in his head at the same time as his other purposes. Or one might depend on the other. Or anything. Laundry tap on. Back to the bathroom.

Another bloody dog came jostling in, wagging its tail with a broad oscillation of its hind-quarters, just as he came out of the bathroom door into the hall. Stumbled just. Andrew there to meet it. Joy and delight! Wuffling, rough caresses! Couldn't tell whether it was the bigger or the smaller one. But at about that point, he did begin to wonder how long it was going to take Yehune to get his piss and go out, with players, horns, cases, smart-arses and especially dogs – great, huge, clothes-sniffing dogs – and leave him alone in the room that was supposed to be theirs, like private.

In any case, he thought he'd better establish his right to be there. He walked right into the centre of their larger room, where Yehune and the others were conferring in groups towards the edges, and stripped off his tracksuit top. No-one really looked at him; the two nearest to him were tinkering with the valves on some small brass instrument. Only the piano, tall and antique-looking, Yehune's new alter-ego or first cause, seemed to stare blankly at him from the rear wall as he modestly draped a towel around his shoulders.

It made him think back to Yehune's piano teaching. Now, that had been an intrusion on their space; this was nothing by comparison. He'd had to hang around in the lounge, at the mercy of Doug and Susan's friends, till all the lessons were finished. But in the end, Yehune had claimed he couldn't go on with it – the reason given: that he couldn't play without a fag on the go, and he'd found it impractical to smoke for three hours without a break.

On an ashy saucer to the right of the keys lay six or seven fag-ends, and smoke was rising invisibly from somewhere; whiff of forests smouldering.

A knock came at the half-open door.

'Oh, hi Eber,' said Yehune. 'Come in. Time we got going.'

The man who appeared was small and wizened, in his forties or fifties; he gave the impression of having been shrunk down out of a different scale. He was a percussionist. But his importance to the Ensemble had more to do with the van he owned, useful for transporting people and large instruments from one venue to another.

Andrew the trumpet seemed eager to break the news,

'Subs going up. Thirty pounds a quarter now.'

Eber took on an even jowlier look than before.

'It's fair enough though,' said Andrew. 'For everything Yehune does, his... professional services to the Ensemble.'

Eber's body-language indicated that he was putting it all to one side for the moment. He said, 'I'm double-parked.'

'Oh, Eber,' Yehune sang out, 'have a listen to this and tell me what you think about a percussion approach.'

He started to play something from a sheet of scribbled music paper, and suddenly there was the fag. It was at a point in the evolution of Yehune's style where he was using what sounded to Mel like traditional harmonies, but restlessly, seekingly, soaring away and never finding a place to pause. Eber listened, tapped uncertainly, while the notes went cracking loudly in the dry acoustics of the room, leaving aftertones clashing behind them. And on it lifted, on and up, and never stopped, and never looked like stopping, making an endless *dong do-dong* in the pans of Mel's ears as he hung there waiting, even when Grendel the dog raised a healthy voice to create a counter-tune, and the tuba-man rapped on his case, and the bath kept filling up, and time passed never to be recalled, and old Yehune hadn't even got near to leaving or picking up his shit or making a move towards the bathroom....

A self-assertive rapping came at the door. So there were three sorts of taps: the percussionist, the tubist, and by far the loudest, what sounded like an angry cop banging on the door panels. Anyone but Yehune, any lesser artist, might have stopped to see who it was; but no, he tinkled and meandered on – he wasn't finished – so that the last notes, possibly wrong ones, outlasted any of the three tappers by as much as a second.

'Ex-*cuse* me,' Susan's voice came at the opening, and she appeared behind it, hair tied untidily, shrewish around the eyes. 'There's someone's *dog* chewing on the wires for the Christmas lights, would somebody please come and get him away?'

Andrew, with the other dog, slipped past her. Shouts of *'Kriemhild! Kriemhild! No!'* were clearly audible, as Susan started to go on at length about her Christmas ribbons and the mess the lounge was in and how insanely dangerous it was to let a dog chew on an electric wire of any kind, and how it was only lucky it hadn't been on at the wall, otherwise she hated to think what might have happened – addressing mainly Yehune and Mel, but anyone else there if they wanted to take it that way, and in a voice loud enough to be heard by dark-haired chancers off in another room.

Susan, he remembered her. She was a known quantity by then, dressed at the time in a grey-and-brown panelled shirtfront with matching trousers. No grease paint. More her routine daywear. The promise of the first day's encounter had come to nothing – Mel having made a few social blunders, and then accidentally destroyed the wiring of her stereo with a beater-hoover. In any case, he knew enough not to get involved in a discussion with her; and of course it was nothing to do with him.

His bath must be nearly ready. He headed past her for the door, trusting to his sweatiness and the draped-over towel to clear the way for him. And it might have done. But Yehune moved faster, ducking inside him with a signal, finally going for his piss. Had to be off, he told Susan, not bothering to wait for a gap in the flow. Sorry for the mess, he'd talk to her about it later in the evening or maybe tomorrow; right now Eber was double-parked. A yelp and the sound of a slap from outside the room drowned out Susan's answer. Just afterwards came the confirmation of what Yehune had said, from somewhere out the window and down the street: the long, lonely parp of a car horn, repeating and repeating in the night.

So Yehune was out; then Andrew came in again with the dogs, making Susan retreat towards the door-jamb with what looked like elegant distaste. Bags and instruments were collected together. In a few more minutes, the musicians were out of there, away to their practice in the church, Yehune yelling 'Turned your water off!' before he slammed the flat door shut on the whole human-canine circus, which could still be heard crashing and shouting its way down the echoey stairwell. And still Mel couldn't leave the room, couldn't get to his bath, since by some process inexplicable but at the same time somehow natural he was left there in clammy tracksuit bottoms with his clothes cradled in his hands, explaining to Susan how it was, why there were dogs everywhere and the decorations she'd bought with her own money and hung up in her free time were chewed and scattered all over the room, and what was going to be done about the dog problem in the future, not to mention the problem of noise and muddy footprints through the hall, and when exactly Yehune was going to be available to answer her questions, in default of which her intention was to relay them all through him.

And that – remember, you'll remember – that was a time where the tide-drift changed. The beginning of the end of their acceptability to their flatmates of nearly two years; and incidentally, the last time he ever came home to the Gorgie flat in peace.

Derek

Because The Element, Yehune's dominating idea, had survived the first winter intact. Certainly it had changed, faltered, retreated at times, gathered its forces and advanced again along another path; but there, essentially, it was, curling and interweaving like pipes in a foundry, warming up the top half of his head. And that's a lot to say. Especially in the bleak winter days, when time achieved a hopeless, lightless monotony, ticking on and on while flatmates thumped and shrilled and lived their lives on the other sides of the walls, it might have seemed to him that any sustained effort of will was under threat. And there were other problems, not the least of which was money. No happy-go-lucky artist's lifestyle was possible in a city where you had to hug a radiator to keep warmth in your body, keep monumental stone walls between yourself and the sleet-driven streets, and pay substantial bills for gas and electricity. So far, Mel, slogging up and down tenement staircases all day delivering leaflets and newspapers, had managed to cover most of the utility bills and what was left of the rent after Housing Benefit. But there was still food, and booze, and their entertainment to pay for.

Having bought a second-hand piano, Yehune had tried out a bit of piano teaching. That didn't last long; the flat had been blocked up for hours while he took his pupils, his tobacco consumption had hit a new high, and even the piano itself had started to develop strange quirks and gripes. Some time later on, their money got so short that he'd been forced to take a temporary job set-building at a local theatre. That did help them on a bit. And yet, by the time spring finally rolled around, all his musical supplies were being paid for by cheques that appeared out of nowhere, signed 'Mairi MacFarlane'.

Cut Out Everything, Yehune had said. But it was hard. As his very serious efforts had tended to add up to large piles of crumpled music paper, but never a completed work, he'd thrown it all up and gone over to writing. Then he'd given up on that and switched back to music again. The rules shifted constantly, while he was slowly forced to realise that he did have needs, bodily and psychological, and the latter could even be the more important, given that that was where the spark, the determination, the spirit of that Mayan red-hot capital accelerator really lived. Pubs and clubs, of course, were banned. But he had to do *something* for relaxation. So lists, priorities, systems of a sort must have been worked out behind that mat of hair, squirming and adjusting in him from one day to the next. Sometimes he accidentally let one of his guidelines slip – like the time he told Mel he didn't take milk for breakfast, but allowed himself one piece of chocolate every evening, since they provided his body with the same thing. Mel's delight at that nutritional theory, his drawn-out laughter, jokes and further suggestions, made him wary of saying anything about it from then on.

But that, you could say, was an exception. In general his friends were sympathetic – it was obvious enough to anyone that he'd have to do a lot of wriggling around to prepare the bed of his life-routine.

Wriggle he did. His whole tendency and direction could so easily be changed, by a word or two he read in a magazine, a short flu, the failure of one block of wood in the action of his upright to connect properly with another; after which the Yehune state of mind could never quite get back into its former shape. It was that – the brutality of a single line of event – the intrusion of new thinking – the tenuousness (it sometimes seemed) of his first belief, that could break up the clear lines for him. Allowing, maybe, aspects of his deeper nature to take over; things he wasn't even aware of himself. Not laziness, exactly… but a sort of overstimulated exertion to no purpose. And alongside that, a bit too much interest in the outside world, in the financial, the entrepreneurial side of things… which always seemed to him to amount to so much more than scribbles on bits of paper.

When Mel looked at it, tried to find rhyme or reason behind the state things had come to, he could only see a continuity of event on event that twisted slowly upwards, like some paper Christmas decoration, or a model of a string of DNA out of a school science exhibition. But there were markers. If you looked closer, one particular face, or a group of faces at a table or in a street, might stand out for a instant, minutely playing a scene before it was pulled back into the swim. Small incidents; no more than accidents, a casual exchange or two – he saw a rising smoke, and the confines of Mairi's parents' flat… or that man Derek, remember him, the Slovak…?

Some time in the spring of their first year, around the end of the real cold, the three of them had left the theatre group minivan standing in a bay in Spottiswoode Street.

'Mum!' Mairi called out gaily. 'Have we got some – some string – what is it, Yehune?'

'Wire, some cord, or a bit of clothes line, anything like that?'

Three active, energetic bodies, thundering at foot level on the varnished wood, had exploded into the static airways of Mairi's parents' flat.

'Eh… I'm not sure,' said her mother. 'What's it for?'

'Oh, Yehune's got the minivan and we've been picking up all sorts of things, offcuts and things for building sets with. Only the back door of the van's jammed open, so we thought we'd come in to…'

Yehune broke in, 'And we could do with the loan of a saw or a Stanley knife… the biggest bits are mainly foam, you see.'

Janine had been doing something in the kitchen with two big pots. There was a sort of roseate fug in there, like the essence of a fruit-drop dispersed into the farthest corners. And something else as well – Mel picked out the strains, the fruit of drier fields. As if tiny devils were lurking under the benches, holding smoking bowls.

She protested, 'I don't know that it's safe to drive around like that. You have-n' got it parked on the street with the back door open?'

'Ah… yeah,' Yehune admitted, '… so we can only stay a moment.'

'O-hh no, you can surely stay for a cup of tea. I'll look out the clothes line, but as for the saws, you'll have to ask your father. He's in there with Derek – you know, from his work.'

Her tone dropped towards the end. Mairi gave no sign of having picked anything up; she was turning already, her jacket radiating a nearly-visible frosting of the outside air,

'Don't worry mum, I know where it's kept!'

They all followed Mairi to a storage cupboard off the hall. And there was the door of the sitting room just across from it.

Yehune said, 'Whole lot of stuff. If we can just get back before the pigs ticket us – 's your father in the lounge, front room, what-you-call-it?'

She didn't let her voice rise too high,

'Yes, with Derek. He's a Slovak; he's resource manager in my dad's work.'

'Should give them tickets to the show.' And he mumbled, 'Slide out pretty sharpish after this.'

Mel asked, ' 'S that cigar smoke I smell?'

Mairi, involved with boxes, said,

'They usually have cigars and malt whisky until it's time to eat. Oh, I know. We're sort of smoke-free, but that's mainly mum.'

Yehune leaned past her and made a grab. 'Got it. This'll do.'

Then the two New Zealanders wanted to head for the front door, which was a few steps further down the hall. But Mairi wasn't moving. Using only a facial expression, she indicated that they should go back for the tea her mum had offered.

Janine had left the kitchen. But three large mugs and a pink-lined porcelain teapot had been set out in a row, stately and remote. High-trunked. 'Here's my handle, here's my spout.' Now go giddying the yawn-os out. Or something. – Mel, tired and stuttering at the inner head, said,

'It's another world, their work, isn't it? What does it stand for again, Solveg PEERD?'

Mairi was pouring out.

'It's Pan-European Energy Resource Development,' she said.

'And they do what? ... No, no. Don't tell me.'

Yehune commented, 'Bit of a contrast with fucking penniless composers and... paper-deliverers.'

Mairi sat down herself. 'Well, it doesn't have to be. Wait till you get your big breakthrough, then you can buy yourself a mansion-house and smoke in it.'

'Fuck, Mairi. I'm set-building.'

261

'But I suppose you're managing something still? ... How's the music getting on?'

'Ah... it's not. But wait till this job's finished. It's only for a few weeks more.'

So they began their conversation again. It was one of the subjects that seemed to lie dormant between them, flaring up into life whenever they had a leisure moment. Mairi, who worked in the administrative side of the arts, could never understand Yehune's stoical pessimism about ever finding an outlet for his work. To her it was all straightforward; if there was a problem, it must be a lack of the right connections or the proper advertising. Either that, or a natural time delay while the artist worked away and got his portfolio together. But – that wasn't quite it. Trying to explain it once again, Yehune must have felt a soft void of frustration around him, like a truckload of sheared fleeces; beyond that the hard metal edge of the flatbed that put a limit to all movement. Mel beside him was aware of some of the reasoning, but felt it wasn't for him to put it across. And so the near-argument would spring up again and again, any progress in understanding made the last time being cancelled by the tendency of people's thinking to snap back into shape after a period of exercise.

Mairi hazarded, 'But you need the money, is that it? To get a bigger place, so you can work properly in it?'

'Well, it's not really...'

In those few minutes of rest, while the van stood out there vulnerable to traffic wardens, Yehune was due to be back at Church Hill, Mel to start his evening deliveries, and Mairi to come back and rejoin her parents, the whole subject began to be worked through again. (– In the meantime, Janine had come in again, stirred the pots, and started getting a few things together for the dinner.)

Mairi: 'I *know* there's a demand for composers. It's just a matter of finding the right contacts.'

Yehune: 'Well... look. You see, it's not possible to do what I'm doing – trying to do – and one day break into the "market".' He paused, reaching for words. 'I don't want no markets, I don't want no demand or supply or fuck-me-Harry. That's a different thing. The problem's not contacts, or work conditions... well, I mean, not much.'

Mel: 'Maybe a little bit. I mean, you're not even working on music at the moment, are you?'

The composer turned a bleak eye to him. And went on, mainly to Mairi,

'Mm. Not while this job lasts… the piano's on the blink, I'll have to get it looked at. In the meantime I was filling in with a bit of writing again. Not stories, but something bigger, about… I dunno.' His eyes turned upwards. 'Passing through places.'

'But what about your music?'

'Ah… it's hard to explain. There's a demand for *composers*, see. But we're talking someone who'll do, like, a theme tune for a Disney film, or a glockenspiel version of Ten Green Bottles to use in someone's advertisement…. It all depends on what sort of composer you are. I mean, you get something finished – *if* you get something finished – and then what? Who's going to be all that interested in going out and hearing Trent's latest opera, Opus 5,710…?'

'Oh, I dunno. I'd give it a listen,' said Mel.

'Not that I'd write an opera, y'know…'

It was then that the Slovak Derek appeared in the kitchen, bringing a tray with used glasses on it and a bottle. He was an associate of Mairi's father's, but a good deal younger; which might, in some systems of thinking, barely have put Mairi within his reach. But there was something a bit cadaverous about him – something about the hang of his body, which was slightly askew as if he was twisted around an upright pole. His face was dark, with deep-set eyes; a sharp nose carved the world in front of him into two equal halves. Just now, he acknowledged Janine with a courtly shrug, and started looking in the cupboards for something.

Mairi was saying, 'So what is your sort of composer?'

'God, that's a question.' Yehune leaned back in his chair and tried to think. 'I'm interested in writing… *music,* you know? Something different, something *event*-ful. Not just for solo piano. There's too much competition there already. Something for a group, an orchestra'd be all right, or some other, er, congregation of instruments… and, well, there's the problem. You end up with a score. Who's going to play it?' He groped at the air with particular fingers. 'You'd at least need something to try things out on. Keyboards, recording equipment, or at the best a group of lunatics who want to waste their time playing...'

Mel laughed. Mairi repeated, 'Lunatics...'

Derek put in a word, standing in his fawn sleeveless jumper under an array of cupboards.

'So you write music?'

Yehune looked up. 'Hm. Yeah, that's what I do all right. But not the sort of music...'

At that moment, Janine made a loud clatter with a stack of pots on one side of the bench, and Derek leant further in, the better to hear and make his points. And for Mel, that was the shape that stood out, came swimming out of the upwards-twisting sea of all that general motion: Derek, leant in over a table, keen-eyed, talking away in a thick Slavonic accent, with his strange mixture of old-world formality and what seemed like plain rudeness,

'I do not care what *sort* of music. Why do you not just find people to fulfil your requirement? You need contacts, somewhere to practise, a hall to give the concerts in.'

'Mm,' said Yehune, 'I've vaguely thought about all that. But where? Nobody has garages here; that's the place you'd naturally go to practise in back at home. No-one wants the noise, you see. Then, as to halls...'

'These things can always be arranged. Halls, try an old church. Too many of them here and people don't know how to use the space. As for a practice room, find contacts first. Some of them are sure to have, ah, access to a place. I'm sure Mairi can help you there.' He gave her a twisting smile from where he leaned, implying, possibly, some sort of gallantry.

Mairi stirred. 'Well, I don't know if I'd know the right people – I'm mainly on the professional side. But maybe you and Yehune...'

'Why not?' said Derek, standing up erect. 'You know people, I know people, I'm sure your friend – your name? Mel? – also knows people. But in the meantime, we talk, you tell me where you live, if you have any... special requirements.'

He pulled up another chair behind him. 'There. I take tea. Janine, if you would be so very, very kind...'

'I'll get it,' said Mairi quickly.

By the time they all got back to their van (unticketed, as it happened), with a coil of plastic-covered string and a long kitchen knife for cutting foams, the whole thing had been put together like one more theatre set built out of air and polystyrene. It wasn't that Derek's input had been very productive; he'd made a practical suggestion or two, none of which had come to anything at the time. But he must have nudged the whole weather-system just an inch or two to the south-east, and time, and Yehune's own dynamism, had done the rest; whirling off in a run of moments which changed, and regrouped, and ploughed ahead again, giving a real impression of accident. The 'Ensemble' was born, not then but a few months later. It turned out to be more the sort of thing the composer could get his teeth into, drawing on all his skills in budgeting, organisation, and people-management. It wasn't an orchestra, or a big band either, but a certain combination of instruments that as far as Yehune knew had never been hit on before, heavy on the brass and percussion, and perfect for a new style of composition he was thinking of trying. Players were drawn to it slowly, in ones and twos, by advertisements and word of mouth, and the common instinct of amateur music makers to find other people to make a noise with. And Yehune's personality must have played a part – and of course, the promises of overseas tours. By the time of the pre-meeting in the Gorgie flat, the group hadn't done more than a few impromptu concerts at street corners; but bigger things were in the air.

And though Yehune seemed to have given up on his old, ultra-serious style of composition, he was quickly engrossed in the nuts and bolts of a more practical sort of music; writing, arranging, and copying out parts; throwing together a repertoire that would suit a band. He had the piano fixed, and thumped away day and night, and hardly talked about anything except the musicians, going on and on about their 'expression' – Bill's expression was suffering, Louise just wasn't expressing today – which for some reason made Mel think of industrial pump-mechanisms placed over the teats of cows, milk delivered mechanically into canisters. As for writing, it was never mentioned at all; and by that time the artist must have forgotten that the identity of his muse had ever wavered.

All of which, more or less, was the state of things when the two of them were asked to leave the Gorgie flat, and Yehune worked out, on some basis or other, that they might just be able to afford to rent a place on their own – a haven of the arts and free thinking, or more exactly a miniature Kiwi crashpad somewhere nearer the centre, where they could doss in comfort and he could get his necessary work done without so many people around to complain about it.

Mel Notices

Just occasionally, the sky gave back connections. That blown-out expanse of cold pale blue, with heaped cloud-continents. Mairi... the European. And her boss, the arts millionaire Pascuale. Both Scottish, he by way of some Italian parents or grandparents; but (this is the point) both managing to put across an impression that was more Continental than British. Like a lot of Scots, they had an instinct to make their cultural alliances straight to the east and across the ocean, cutting out anything directly to the south of them. More so in Mairi – as well as her colouring, her clothes and hairstyles, her whole approach to life had some intangible dusting of the French or Italian, probably because she'd been travelling around in those places for so long. She had a certain independence of thinking, an almost fatalistic outlook on things that happened around her; and (hard though it was to pin down) a sort of extra awareness, you could even say an acceptance, of her own femininity. Mel and Yehune had met cousins of hers from Glasgow, and once, briefly, her sister; and found that none of them had her physical ease of approach, her habit of kissing a friend once on the cheek when they met; none had the same *range* – as if she believed that any variation in people was part of a great extended whole that spanned countries and cultures.

In her work as well as her life, that natural femininity was a key to what worked for her and what didn't. Her body was sensual, though small, with a sinuous shape at the hips; she had certain charming or dependent airs in a relationship; she approached things not from above, as the Great Lady, but from a level standing or even below it, wondering what this or that person 'might like', setting a huge value on accommodation and mutual respect. All of which suited her perfectly to a job of Personal Assistant. Meaning that her true talent, which was an inspired understanding of people's ways of relating to each other, actually had the effect of keeping her low down in the business hierarchy.

Nor were men always understanding. As things were at the time in Britain, any man not including her boyfriend could have interpreted her approach as flirtatious. But they were only mistaking the signals. Despite her youthfulness, her lightness, that vivacity or awakeness you could sometimes catch in the look of her face from side-on, Mairi was serious about her relationship, as she was serious in most things. And so men like Pascuale – Pascuale, her boss – and other men like him....

But these are generalities, the province of the broad dome of the sky. To understand the moment, it's better to turn to specifics, to the grouping of the tiny single objects caught here and there in the weed, or the knolls and dips of the ground at eye level. It happened that Mel had just got back from three days in the Lake District. He'd been guiding or overseeing two Swiss pupils of his on their last fling in Britain before they went back to their jobs in the home country. He'd been paid well enough for it, as he remembered. But he'd come home creaking at the seams with tiredness, having hardly slept at all the night before; and then that same evening Yehune and Mairi had seen fit to drag him out to a nightclub, the one which at the time had been called Tiger Jim's.

From which it can easily be seen that the rules had changed again. The first brave austerity of Yehune's Element was a thing of the past. These days, Yehune and Mairi would as often as not hit the pubs and clubs of an evening, either traditional establishments such as The Bell or The Wee Swalley; or somewhere like Mass Disturbance on Leith Street if they wanted to dance; or in this case, the closest and most convenient, just around the corner in West Tollcross....

Mel had gone wandering on along the Fountainbridge pavement to the lights. He was slow to notice changes of direction. Yehune called back from the head of a side street,

'Mel – over here!'

'Oh shit. Sorry man. Not totally used to these streets.'

' 'S natural. New flat – new stuff around you.'

Alongside Mairi another guy was walking, Richard, from her

work. As those two drifted back from the right-hand street to rejoin the party, he asked casually,

'Have you moved house?'

They had. After an extensive search, they'd found something for as much rent as they could possibly have paid, but right at the bottom end of one-room flats. It was something like a crude cave, roughly wallpapered over, sunk half below ground level in a cul-de-sac off Gardner's Crescent. There, Mel and Yehune had settled themselves, thrown their possessions any-old-where on the floor or flat surfaces, painted and curtained off a rough frame wardrobe knocked together out of four-by-four by some resident in the past. There, Yehune was free to smoke and scribble and play his piano, stare up at the old brown stain that deepened as the wall drew higher to the ceiling, and possibly seek for a glint of light in the two high windows that came out at about street level on the other side of the wall. Not only his location, but his appearance was different. Now he was the Bandmaster himself, with a little goatee beard and rectangular glasses under a clipped-down mat of hair. The ghetto blaster he'd always relied on for music had broken down, but in the meantime their stereo had finally arrived, from Hong Kong via Geoff in Essex, and been given pride of place on the wall across from the piano. It was already beginning to be submerged – both the speakers and the central units – under the accretion of new objects: a hoover, bags, chairs and stools, an electronic keyboard, books and folders in heaps, and papers like drifting leaves.

In that badly-managed space, their lives went on. Yehune was alone in there a lot of the time, as Mel took private pupils in houses or cafés around the city. The new address had turned out a godsend for the aspiring composer, giving him a chance to keep his private and his public lives separate. Now nobody turned up at the door to put a spanner in the act of creation… nobody, that is, except a few Ensemble women who were pledged to total secrecy. Women, or you might say girls. Mel noticed that some of them were on the way to becoming fixtures, popping in for tea or coffee at odd times of the day. Another thing he noticed was that Yehune was suddenly very interested in when exactly he, Mel, would be out. The conclusion was obvious – that some of those girls had become more to Yehune than just Ensemble contacts. But of course, there was no way of proving that. Even after the three days he'd spent away, leaving the flat to his friend like a kind of playground of the sensual delights, Mel didn't really expect to find any giveaways, ripped condom packets or items of feminine underwear, peeping out from the upper strata of the junk.

These days Mel usually tagged along with Yehune and Mairi on their nights out. He'd failed to develop much of a circle of acquaintance of his own. He had no girlfriend, nor anything approaching one – 'Leanne' was no more than a name to him yet. With the result that he was able to observe the way relations had changed between them; Yehune and Mairi had got to the point where, like an established married couple, their attention was turned outwards, looking for distraction in the personalities around them. So in any case he might have served a purpose for them, he thought; like a pet dog, or a mildly interesting conversation-piece.

For Yehune, managing Mel's progress must have been something like steering a B-movie zombie. They'd come up to the door of the club, where a large crowd milled around and waited for a chance to get in; there Mel had stopped, not facing any direction in particular – wound down, to all appearances, or tripping away inside the head.

Yehune said, 'What time *did* you get to bed last night?'

'Ah… about five thirty, six. It was the pub crawl they decided to do on the last night.' He looked around and blinked. 'The girl was OK, but that guy…'

'Hm, good one,' Yehune remarked. 'You should be just warming up then.'

Mairi had gone ahead into the ragged pack of people shuffling to get in; a thin stream of people leaving flowed out to the right. The Richard character – with a centralised mop of what looked like dyed hair – was dressed in a way that somehow answered to hers. Thinner fabrics, designer cut. For Mel, everything would move on for a moment, stop, and move again, then stop; the lights and roaring voices and the beat through external speakers acting like flashes of gunpowder on his overtired brain.

He saw, for a moment, Mairi drop back and press something into Yehune's hand. Crumpled bills. And she murmured something into his ear. Then the bouncer came into view; an imposing, bald man in a subfusc suit without tie – but short, remarkably short, barely above the size that would have qualified him for dwarfhood.

'One drink free wi' th'entry. Take y'r tickets tuth' bar.'

He could only hope there wouldn't be any sort of trouble. But maybe the guy was a machine.

They jostled around, getting their starter drinks and looking for a place to settle. Mairi and Richard ended up half-seated on the broad chairbacks of other people, while the other two leaned elegantly against a wall. When the band played, there was absolutely nothing to say. But

thoughts moved on, woozily underconnecting. Now, Yehune might like this, thought Mel. Guitar band just, but it is live.   Richard… mightn't.   Doesn't get to talk.

There were gaps, occasionally, between one song and another. Someone asked Mel something twice.

Mairi said, 'Are you all right?'

'Na na, can't you see it?' Yehune put in. 'He's just scouting the bar. Picking out the next victim of his charms.'

It might have been something about the stagey darkness there inside, the careful imposition of depth by light and shading, that sent the conversation up to less and less serious levels. Richard and Yehune tended to bounce off each other. The friend-from-Mairi's-work had beetling eyebrows under the topknot, which was coloured a sort of charred blond.

Once, during a longer break, he made an effort with Mel,

'So what is it you do?'

'Oh, private tutoring. EFL, that sort of thing.'

'I see.' He knitted his brow. 'A form of *salesmanship,* I can imagine – is it something like that?'

'Ah, they usually come to me… of course I've got an ad out.'

Yehune fell into a spiel, 'Oh shit, don't listen to him. He's a real entrepren-*oor*, is our Mel. He's just biding his time, eh. Gonna write all sorts of books, hold meetings, invent his own religion and get people believing in it. He told me all about it – ah – somewhere'r other...'

'Siberia,' said Mel.

'Ministering angels – imparting wisdom –'

'The cold must've been getting to me.'

Richard: 'Well, joking apart, that's not a bad angle. You could make a lot of money.'

There was a short pause, which didn't happen to be interrupted by any great rush of noise. Either Yehune or Mairi could have been remembering long tirades by Mel at various times in the past about money being a reason for doing anything – money in great gobs, that is, power money, fatcat lubricant – the great God, he claimed, of the modern era, and literally the only motive allowed for any sort of enterprise whatever from collecting rainwater to writing a fucking play.... So Mel had held forth. Though some people might have noticed that he was careful enough about it in smaller quantities.

Just then, one band was disconnecting its equipment, while another was making its cumbrous way onto the stage. Mairi said,

'Actually, I think you're looking quite good. I mean, considering...'

Yehune broke in, 'Considering what he looked like when you first met him, you mean.'

She laughed. 'Eh, well, you were a bit immobile. Sort of like... cataleptic.'

'Feel it now.'

Richard: 'Not at all. It's most attractive, I'd say. Not that I'd entirely *know*. But that bruises-round-the-eyes look, Gothic thing, it can be just what you need to attract women.'

Yehune nodded over to Mairi. 'Ah. It's the tall weedy ones the girls always go for. And as for the old Seuchar business enterprises – shit, when you consider the paper round he started out with...'

'*Paper round?*' Richard burst out.

'Where you goin', Mel?' Yehune asked.

'Off to the loos.'

Mel launched himself off from the wall, into a large dark space, like one of those hyper-barns he remembered going to for rock concerts in New Zealand. Smaller here, though. Less clogged with trendies standing and drinking. Richard's voice was dwindling behind him:

'Yehune, what's yours?'

And Mairi's, softer, 'Oh, it's my turn…'

'It's my turn' played back a few times in his head. It was Mairi's turn. It always seemed to be her turn. What's more, when he went to pay the rent and bills, he found often enough that Yehune's part had been taken care of. Mairi was the great financial lap. Not that it was any of his business….

He threaded his way through the standing drinkers, milling in different-sized circles, their elbows poised to be bumped. Lights, and the peaks of noise, were startling to him, like quick étincillant bursts. … Too tired. Shouldn't oughta've come. Uh-huh. … He was moving in a dream-state, as if the normal complexities of the waking world were far beyond him, the signals bearing directly on the nerve. While underneath it there was some other feeling…. Beggared. Disconsolate. He used what mental forces he had to try and get to it, as he forced his way past people towards the right-of-stage corner….

He'd been away. That always gave you a new way of seeing. It was some sort of parallel that had grabbed him: Marta and Dietrich were another girl-boy unit, a completeness, outside which Mel had been running around. Creating timetables, arguing with cashiers. Here, girl too: Mairi. M again. And nothing for em-em. Em…. Embrication, what's that?

Now that's funny, thought the loos were. Nothing but a fire door here. Yehune was right then. So he had to get

It was clear enough all right he had no *social group*. Whereas Yehune was building one – that was for sure. Things were different, now he was out of the School… no co-workers. Male, female, male, female: none. (Now he was struggling across the streams, on the most crowded part of the floor, trying to beat a path to stage-left.) So he was left endlessly on the outskirts of something, wanting what he couldn't have – which could easily sour things in itself. Go sour, for Y'une, for you, like currents in a conversation. That one they'd had just now. All the bla bla bla…. It was the tone, the tone of it, which flew up in spite of you to find its level, baa-ing up around the roof beams, over the heads of individuals, to something, what….

A sudden noise – *Feeiiiooooww!* – from someone tuning a guitar up on the stage cut into his eardrums with a downward-falling sourness, where he stood suddenly at a dead end between one group and another, nearly to the left. And at the same instant

his eyes gave bars of strange worms in colours appearing and disappearing, like luminous entrails.

contextual, con-nex nex nex

– some LCD readout, glimpsed through a slab of thick perspex just there

'Mel!'

Mairi's voice should have made him jump. Here, it was part of the general nightmare, people's elbows clothed and jagging out at skeletal angles. He turned (glimpsing an overlarge mouth in a man's face).

She asked, 'What were you going to have?'

She'd found him; how had she? He looked down at the empty glass his hand had been warming.

'Oh, hi Mairi. Ah… beer, thanks.'

'Lager you mean? Any special sort?'

He slowly considered it.

'Actually, make it a half of something, OK? Can't be bothered drinking much, not after last night.'

'Oh. What is it, are you feeling a bit off-colour?'

'Um… just tired, mainly. Thanks.'

She had a gift of making herself heard without speaking loudly. Something in the quality of her voice: a light soprano like an aethereal bore. She moved round to face him.

'Listen, Mel – I think we were all a bit outspoken, just now. I hope we didn't…'

His face broke out in a smile. 'Hell no,' he responded, 'you must be joking. It's, you know… legitimate piss-take.'

'Well,' she said. 'As long as you know, that's not the way we *really* think of you.' She laid her hand for a moment on his arm.

Like that, she was suddenly real, complete, extra-dimensional, full of grace and understanding, the only actual thing or person in the confused twilight of Mel's perception. Everything else had become a vague chirping at his ears and eyes. It was a reaction on a completely different level from her slight gesture, which was a characteristically Mairi-like effort to cancel out possible offence, she being the only one to have noticed or cared that that offence had ever been taken. But everything in Mel at the time was mildly disproportionate. So as it turned out, nothing in even Mairi's social perception could have foreseen the result of what she'd said, or of that touch on the arm. It was this: Mel noticed Mairi. There she was, standing in front of him in an understated light-yellow dress to mid-thigh, black shoes, her arms bare and thin as a pipe-cleaner, smooth as a plastic straw, to his distorting eye; her hair was a gelled chaos reflecting blue from some nearby wall light; her body was utterly, deeply, astoundingly female, slight-breasted and full-hipped, the promise of all life, fulfilment and a handle to dreams; her face was questioning, cuppable, clear, glittering at the black-lined eyes, contained around mouth and chin, somehow physically smaller than he might have expected of any human face. And *kind* – for which he was grateful out of all proportion – and also, at that moment, at just that moment…

the band happened to crash in with a disorientating block of electric noise.

… What had she been to him before? He couldn't tell. If he'd put his mind to it he might have worked out that most of his reactions to her had been tentative and completely sexless, as if he were dealing with some well-loved object in Yehune's vicinity which he had to work his way around to keep their friendship ticking. The piano, maybe, provided with nerves instead of strings, radiating human feeling in the place of sound. A political value – only distantly a person. But not any more. *Craa* – tak*ataa* – tak*ataa* – tak*ataa*… the band thrashed out a rhythm. Rage – rage – rage and thunder entered into him at the ears, and vibrated out at his chest and the tips of his fingers.

None of his reaction had been visible. Mairi seemed to catch from his face that her reassurance was received and understood (he'd felt it as a caress), and she slipped away between two taller people to go and get the drinks.

He was left in the crush, somewhere near the left of the stage. Thinking he ought to have offered to help her carry. But: too late. The loos – the loos, they were round here somewhere, given they weren't in the other place....

And all the time his electrically-awakened anger was growing, jarring him nearly to irrationality. Directed against Yehune. Yehune, and his philandering – those mysterious women he always had hanging on him, and who he more than suspected weren't all just mates. Which wasn't any of his business. But exactly what the *fuck* did the guy think he was doing?

When he had Mairi – *Mairi*. Wasn't she good enough for him?

Handkerchief

But of course, nothing came of that. Things fell straight back into the old routine of work and leisure and a mutual liking between the three of them. Mel, for his part, believing in any case that *liking* or *disliking* among real people was a superficiality, part of what he referred to as the 'exterior view'. He reasoned it this way: how could you *like* a universe, a single compendium of all impressions and all colours and all beauties, all boredoms and all horrors as well; how could that even be possible, unless you allowed yourself to think of it as nothing but a little stick of clothing ambling around the world, completely defined by its occupation, butcher, English teacher, Prime Minister or supermarket attendant; then let it appear abrasive, moody, pretty or likeable to you according to the accident of its outer layer?

He even discussed things like that with Yehune occasionally, in conversations that went something along these lines:

'What's supposed to happen when two universes meet? Do they – ah – implode, explode?'

'Wha'...? What's a universe?'

'You know. Theory of linked expanding universes. Wormholes, that stuff. You must know, you're the maths.'

'I dunno. I'm sort of more interested in getting a few notes to fit together in this one.'

'I saw it on TV, there were these two physicists talking on a train. One absorbs the other? Or is there some sort of weird meniscus effect?'

'... Why?'

' 'Cause the universes are people. You know. Like, I don't know, a guy and a girl – on the *in*-side, and then, they clash, grope, intersect...'

'Oh yeah, see what you mean. It's all good, Mel. You should go for it.'

'You're just saying that. ... I mean, there's no reason to *suppose* wormholes, like, any sort of real connection at all, so you're not joining. You're joining but you're not. The effect must be an illusion, which is interior, but it's an illusion we need... so, you know, we do it anyway.'

'Do it.'

'Yeah. ... Ah... I remember you wrote something like that yourself, didn't you? Dual universes, or two globes interpenetrating or something...'

'Oh – that thing for piano and whisper? Shhh-hhhh-*uht*, Mel. That's all old stuff. Not *gebrauk* enough, eh. But now that you mention it... there's something I've thought about too.'

'What's that?'

'Well, if you're walking down the street, and there's a girl walking in front of you...'

'Uh-huh.'

'Well, unless she's wearing a coat, you can usually see exactly where her panties begin and end...'

'Oh, right?'

'Sometimes you have to look closely. But the point is, they're never absolutely even, y'know. Now, this is it... have you noticed how they almost always ride up higher on the *right* side? Not always, it's not totally consistent. But often enough to prove it.'

'Well – I can't say I had – but mightn't it be that most people are right-handed and therefore right-legged and so the action of a girl's walk...'

'Yeah, given the, you know, shapes and forms involved. But would that really make her panties ride up to the right?'

'You could try it out, do an experiment. You get a very skimpy pair of female panties. Then you put them on, pull them up really, really tight into your hairy arse...'

'*Fuck* off, you dirty bugger.'

So the talk went on between them, so new theories were formulated – usually not tested – and gave way to other theories after a longer or shorter space of time. And all of it managed to bypass or ignore that effect of pure necessity: the way that ordinary sexuality, the self-evident basis of everything, could occasionally be lifted so far above itself as to become, miraculously, something else – with no apparent stop, no pause for breath or process of appeal. When suddenly the human subject might be forced into a sort of instant springtime of the emotions, a bizarre awakening, in the face of some suddenly-lit-up unit of the opposite sex. For years, it seemed, those emotions could be successfully pushed down, lie dormant while the subject led a serene existence on the surface – until one day the wizened seeds would sprout, the shoots wend their way upwards, and the whole entrancing, captivating, disturbing and tormenting process would begin again, drowning the poor defenceless centre-of-a-universe in forces beyond any human will to control.

By this time, Mel had an ongoing thing with a certain Leanne. She was a teacher at the Royal Edinburgh School of the King's English, where he hadn't been working for some time now. She had blonde hair, smooth and regular features, and the hint of something gooselike around the mouth and chin. Naturally she was in demand. Mel could never be quite sure how much the thing she had was with him, and how much with any male person of round about the right age she happened to meet. Partly because of that, partly because he found her almost impossible to read, things seemed to drag on for month after month without any sort of resolution – what was it about her? he wondered. It wasn't deceit, or even depth. It was a way she had of never seeming to suggest or imply anything beyond the words she was saying at the time. Which might have come from an uncontemplative way of thinking, or some strange insensitivity of the facial muscles, or just a great neutrality… as if that whole pneumatic exterior was a big limp cushion she stepped into every morning and blew up with a nozzle placed somewhere near her mouth.

He would have been surprised to be told how much he clung to the theory that this girl allowed him privileges she wouldn't have given to other men. And it was true that she didn't seem to; not while he was around. Leanne was known to be a free kisser, and a fondler to the extent and limit of the more innocent regions of the body; and that was all it took to keep that maddening sexual promise alive for him. When one time his hands had strayed daringly to the region of her buttocks during a good-night kiss outside the Gardner's Crescent flat (he found them large, feminine, not especially well-toned) she'd broken off at once and said, 'Careful'. But after all, that was far less than a slap in the face. He might even have taken it as an instigation to try harder. His friend Yehune must have had to listen to a good deal of agonising about the possible implications of it all, for month after month, mainly because no statement from that glossy pair of lips Leanne was so free with could really be believed… until later, of course, far later, in a sort of offset crisis

But no no it had nothing to do with and sticking to the general not to fall into the narrating of incidents where what was the use

my rock cleft standing heel

…

Until months later. Until many months later, in fact, jumping over well into the spring or even early summer of the next year. Not to pretend to be certain of a specific date, but he could say for sure that it was a Wednesday. That was the night of Yehune's fixed band practice. And surely it was better to take them one by one, one month and then another, charting the turns and accidents as they happened and staying true to the great Chronology that shapes human affairs, not letting the vision waver even for a moment to right or left….

Spring was a good time to be in Edinburgh. The dourness of monuments under a sky in mourning gave way to something brighter, more immediate: the clear play of sunlight on all those classic sandstone surfaces, sometimes with a dappling of leaf-shade. On St Mary's Street, which ran off at the connection of High Street and the Canongate, the shadows of posts and building-sides were like cuts of darkness stretching out to the north and east, and faces in the crowd were beginning to look harried or impatient as the day drew nearer to an end.

Mel walked, or rather mooched, along the westward and more shadowed pavement. All day he'd been working out of cafés, with a short visit to the School. His last pupil had stood him up, and he'd been in that café since before six and known that, however sure he was that no-one was going to come, he had to stay there till at least seven on the very remote chance of getting his fee. Now he was hungry, not being able to afford a café main course, and the only question in his mind (after scanning the street this way and that way and seeing no pupil at either end of it) was how long it would take him by hoof and bus to get back to Gardner's Crescent and whatever meal he could throw together in a hurry.

He noticed all the cigarette-ends in the gutter. There was a spill of people out of the side of a new gallery. A huge fat man was swaying with a tiny dog. Beyond him, a small woman in a fawn jacket looking towards a shop window: neat, constricted, self-protecting.

She recognised him first. The head, which had been something objective, became Mairi, a world expanding outwards in a rush. Her eyes were lit up out of strange recesses as she said, 'Mel'.

'Mel – didn't you recognise me?'

'Oh, hi. Not at first. … What are you doing here?'

'I've just been hunting for a present for my dad. You?'

'Working. Or I would have been, if the hound had bothered to turn up.'

'Oh, that's a shame. You must be hungry.'

He looked at her. 'How did you know…?'

'Oh, I don't know – you're not exactly going out like a house end.'

'Ah. Um…. Well, look, I have to be…'

'My car's just round the corner. Will I give you a lift back?'

So it was arranged that Mel should come round to her parents' flat for a quick dinner. They were going out later, she told him, to some concert in the Usher Hall. Though he was wolf-hungry, he still felt a bit diffident about barging in on them,

'Won't it be a bit of a shock?'

'No more than usual, Mel. … No, really. Mum likes to have someone extra there to try her cooking out on.'

Before they went, though, Mairi had to duck into a fabric shop, one which she thought stayed open till 7:30. She glanced at her watch, not looking at all like that stranger Mel had glimpsed in the street – more like a smooth-faced girl beset by adult worries.

Whenever it happened that Mairi and Mel were together on their own, they talked about Yehune. He was a safe and unlimited subject for them. It had begun quite early on, when Mairi, not bothered at all by the way her new boyfriend romanced and exaggerated, had wanted for reasons of her own to know which parts of what he said were actually true. Mel had been able to give her the broad lines – he wasn't Jewish; the Austrian connection was real and quite likely what had pushed him into his perverse pseudo-Semitism in the first place; he had ridden motorcycles but not really raced them (that had been more Jim's thing); and most of the unlikely-sounding things he claimed to have done he really had done, though sometimes for very short periods. Any claims of hobnobbing with internationally-famous musicians were lies. Mel never felt in any way like an informer in telling her these things; he was only clarifying points that Yehune doubtless expected her to pick up for herself, while sometimes forgetting to provide the means.

Back out of the fabric shop, Mairi had looked worn and a bit preoccupied, possibly by something at her work. But she was always easy to talk to. They fell back automatically on their old subject. Her parents' small Renault, metallic blue and flaking at the edges of the doors, nudged smoothly out into a gap in the stream of traffic, and they were moving down towards the dip of the Cowgate and the Pleasance that rose like a smooth wave beyond it.

She remarked, 'Yehune seems to be doing well with his music just now.'

'Oh yeah. He's always got plenty on, all right.'

She mused, 'It changes. Seems to change.'

By that time the New Zealanders had been in Edinburgh for three years; the decade had turned.

–

–

And south of the Meadows…

282

Her mum was more surprised than Mairi had seemed to expect. Her hair was raised in a complicated 'do', she was floating from place to place in a bathrobe while putting the finishing touches to the meal. That was nothing elaborate: there was a large pot of rice on the boil, some sort of fresh-water fish, and sauce from a plastic packet labelled 'Marks and Spencer'. Formal-looking clothing was spread all over the room on the cushions and chairbacks. Of course Mel was welcome; there was no doubt about that. And as it happened, though he might have had plenty of reason for feeling awkward, his need for food cancelled it out – there in the warmth and kitchen smells it had grown in his body and mind until it had become something like a baying empty corridor of light; ruddy light; with a taunting underbreeze of fish.

Janine asked, 'So you're standing in for Yehune tonight, Mel?'

'Mum – it's Yehune's practice night. Wednesday, remember?'

'Eh… that's right then,' she said vaguely. 'Don't you mind us, we'll be out of your way in two minutes.'

For a while, eating food, Mel felt both full and still hungry, while his jaws went on gnashing through more and more. So much so that Mairi became curious about what he'd had to eat that day.

He thought back. 'Ah… I had a couple of pastries. Around midday?'

The television was chattering on in the background about problems arising from the Abolition of Domestic Rates. Mel actually began to find a limit to his capacity – and he felt physically blessed, levitated to some unexpected state of grace. Saved all the treks and buses and fumbling with can openers, or else the long wait in a Carry-Out.

'H'wait raiss,' Mairi's father complained to his wife.

'It's not so long to cook, dear. And the veg is all organic.'

'Ay, orgunnuc. Tha's good.' He nodded over his tie.

Naturally, Mairi and Mel offered to do the clearing up. So her parents were free to leave the flat in their splendour. Mairi occupied herself with the arranging and the washing up itself, while Mel brought the dishes over, dried and then stacked them. He would have thought doing dishes was something that encouraged conversation. But she hardly said anything at all.

Almost at the end, she suggested, 'Come away to the sitting room. If you're not needing to get back.'

'Do you know, does he carry things round in the pocket of his coat?'

'Yehune? ... Like what, for example?'

Mairi was sitting on the three-seated yellow-to-cream coloured sofa, her head turned in the direction of the edge of the wall where it joined, on one side, the frame of the door, through which you could see a full-length mirror out in the hall reflecting other spaces and other doors.

'Well, tissues – I know he wouldn't carry tissues, would he? He's always used a handkerchief, that I've seen.'

For some reason, Mel got up from his perch on a sort of Queen Anne-style chair by the mantelpiece, and started to walk around.

He said, 'It's sort of a distant speculation – me, now, I'd carry things round, all sorts of things. Yehune, I s'pose he might be more concerned for the exact fall or outer lines of the coat, you know? I've heard of people who've got something against actually using the pockets God gave them...'

'But he doesn't use tissues, much?'

'Handkerchief. Definitely a handkerchief.'

She only sat there, her face alive but darkened, musing on something. Though he was glad to have been of some help, Mel wondered why she hadn't just asked him herself.

'So what's this all about, exactly?' he asked.

'Eh, well... I think he might have been going astray a bit. I mean, that he's been...'

'What? Unfaithful to you?' He knew straight away that he'd said it too quickly, and ploughed on, 'How could that be happening and me not know about it?'

'Will I tell you what happened? ... You're sure you wouldn't like something to drink?'

'No, that's all right, just tell me. That is, if you want to.'

Mairi looked past his head towards the lounge window and the view of other buildings facing. Her face was set and pale, not even pretending to any sort of casualness.

'Well, on Monday he came here to the house. We were both sitting here, where I am now. Or I was a bit further over, so I could see all the way to the door.'

'Hang on. By the door – you mean the front door?'

'Come over here.' She stood up, and waited while he sat on the high-backed sofa about where she'd been sitting. 'No, more to your left.'

From there he could see most of the hall mirror through the sitting-room door, standing like an abstract wing of different-coloured light. Incidentally, through it, the row of coats hung up along the nearer wall. He remembered that mirror then – the first couple of times he'd come into the flat he'd looked into it, and found it sliced his head off at about the mouth.

'Hmm. OK, I see.'

'Anyway…' Mairi started pacing up and down in front of him, 'he had to go to the loo, he told me. So he went out of the room, but he thought of something as he went through the door, and instead of going on down the hall he walked over to his coat.

'I saw him take something out of the pocket, a white bit of paper. He read something on it. Then I saw him rip it one way and then the other. It made almost no noise at all. After that he headed off for the loo, and came back after a while, looking pleased with himself. He sat down with me again and we started – talking, and all that. … Anyway, I asked him what he'd got out of his coat.'

Mel said nothing. It was like something out of a novel, this reconstruction of the crime. Which would make him the visiting Inspector Truffaut. It would have been an absurdity, if the look on her face hadn't been so serious.

'He said, "Some old tissues that were in my coat pocket." He told me he'd just thought of it, must have been carrying them around for a day or two. But you said, you agreed with me… that he never uses tissues?'

Ah. Now here was the crux. Mel thought hard and quickly.

'I don't know. He might, even if not to blow his nose on.' His hand drew a spontaneous wavy figure on the air. 'There's all sorts of things you could use tissues for.'

'Well. It doesn't matter.'

285

The idea, in all its perfect, bronze illogic, had only just fallen together in his mind. He couldn't quite decide what direction to attack it from. The defensiveness he felt seemed to take in himself as well as Yehune, and their tiny cluttered flat, and their whole three-year existence in Edinburgh. And the enemy was – a supposition. Just that. He looked at Mairi, who had changed before dinner into a light-blue blouse and maroon trousers, and was leaning against the fireplace surround, hip turned outwards. He decided there was no point in saying to her that a piece of tissue paper, seen through a mirror from a distance, might look the same as a solid piece of paper.

'I mean, just say it *wasn't* tissues, what then? It could have been anything. A receipt for, I don't know, something he's bought for you. A – note to himself to do this or that. Probably not that, but I'm just thinking…'

As he thought, as he spoke, he was already recalling Yehune's habit of leaving little scraps of paper everywhere, some of them dubious if not actually incriminating, phone numbers written in looping feminine hands, little bits of notes that he himself had got into the habit of turning over without looking at them. It struck him as close to certain that it really had been something of the sort that Yehune had discovered, there in the very girlfriend's house, and straight away ripped up and flushed like a good operative. Mairi was still looking at him, not with the scepticism he expected, but something more like commiseration – as if both of them were caught, there, trying to defend the same beloved person or idea.

'It's OK, Mel,' she said. 'I knew you'd want to stick up for him.'

He got to his feet. 'But I'm – ' He could almost feel it slipping away from him. 'Well, let's leave that for a moment.'

He had to repeat to himself that it wasn't the truth that mattered; it was what Mairi thought or believed. He started with,

'Yehune's… how can I put it? You sort of have to know how to deal with him. You know, you're already aware, you can't expect absolute truthfulness all the time.'

But her face had taken on a grey look, turned the smallest bit at the chin and the curve of the cheek, though she was still face-on to him. She was either crying or very near it. He moved in and laid his arm across her shoulders. 'Mairi…'

'I don't know… I just can't see how things can be right after this.'

It was as if suddenly, the moment she started to cry, the rights and wrongs of it had ceased to exist, and he was forced down to practicalities. He experienced one of those strange slides of personal foundation: what he'd been assuming about where he was, where they all were, the process of the evening and evenings after it, was suddenly gone. He'd spend the evening here – and it felt right, self-evident – instead of swanning around at the flat, reading a book and eventually going to bed. He'd be here, fighting for the continuance of a relationship which, when all was said and done, was central to all of them and the real reason they were in Edinburgh. Unless, of course, that had already ended – unless Mairi was just then seeking out the new channels her emotions were going to run in from that night onwards.

He drew off, just steadying her by the shoulders. He told her she ought to sit down, and asked if she wanted something to drink. She looked at him, a bit surprised,

'Oh, eh… it's a good idea. Just mineral water. With a splash of something.'

So he went out the door, glancing curiously once at the hall mirror, and on past doors to the step in the floor caused by some ancient subsidence, and opened various cupboards in the kitchen. He thought he knew where the glasses and bottles were kept. Gin, did that go with fizzy water? The whisky bottles looked too forbidding, like a parade of fat dignitaries. The knowledge that it was right now, this evening and the following night, that Yehune would be seeing other women if he ever did (he always got in late if at all from the Wednesday practice) made him as aware of the falseness of his position as the harshest critic could have wanted. Now, was there any cold…? Yep, a big bottle, Highland Spring. For himself, he only wanted an orange juice or something.

He asked himself seriously what his intention was here: was it to cover up for Yehune no matter what? And whether or not his thinking was good thinking, a whole makeshift system fell together in his head to justify doing just that. It went like this: he wasn't absolutely sure of Yehune's guilt, not enough to justify turning informer even if he'd felt that was the right thing to do. And he didn't. Something resembling a general human truth seemed barely graspable beyond the facts: he summed it up, swilling liquid into glasses, as the law of distancing through time. Things were more devastating the closer you were to them. However they looked just then, they might still be smoothable-over given enough time – if not, they were all fucked anyway. But now, so early on, Mairi was showing a tendency to take the cataclysmic view. As Yehune's only agent in the field, Mel wondered whether he might be able to guide her away from any irrevocable decisions – by doing nothing. Sympathising. Dropping in the odd word now and then....

Right or wrong. ... Right. That's it, give the fridge door an extra nudge to make the seal. Carry two. Watch the step – uh. Damn it. Didn't I say to watch...?

Mairi's position on the sofa hadn't changed; on her face the bad weather had set in. He juggled drinks, and put his arm round her shoulder again. He had to overcome a sort of trained-in delicacy to get so close to his best friend's girlfriend. The slightness, the narrow span of her shoulders under the blouse, was surprising a second time.

It seemed what she really needed was to talk,

'God, I was just talking to Biddy about something like this – that's my mother's cousin. She's got two daughters, both of them live in the Gorbals, and both of them have caught their men having affairs. In the space of a week. One's got a husband – had – the other was a boyfriend but they'd been together something like seven years. And all the time I was talking to her, I was thinking – you know, not meaning anything, but I thought, "That can't happen to me."...'

'But nothing's happening to you. Nothing's actually happened. I mean, what you've told me this evening isn't proof. Take it from me, I'm supposed to be an objective ear... well, I suppose not too objective...'

'I'm glad you're not objective. Who would I have to talk to then? As for "proof"...'

'Well, you know, I mean... the important thing is not to let it get to you.'

'It's a bit late for that.' She gave a quick double chuff of what seemed like laughter, and at the same time jerked her hand in such a way that a few drops of her drink spilled on the varnished floorboards.

'I'd better put this down,' she said.

'I'll get a tissue – I mean a – oh, sorry.'

He tried to move his arm away. Mairi laughed at his accidental choice of words, laying her drink down on a low wooden table that stood covered with reports and pamphlets of her father's. She nudged her head back in under his arm. Silently proclaiming her contempt of floorboards, at least in this crisis.

For a while, they only sat there. She seemed not to be aware of herself from the outside, not even able to maintain the front of normal people sitting beside each other in a room.

He said, 'Look, Mairi, I wouldn't give up on Yehune... I don't know what exactly's happening, but I know he really loves you. He's just going through some phase.'

'Oh, shut up, Mel. Just hold me for a bit. I don't have to be told whether he loves...'

And later, out of some ineluctable personal slump, she confessed, 'I'm awful miserable.'

He let himself kiss her gently on the cheek beside her mouth, feeling his sense of what was and wasn't allowed clear enough to risk it.

Out in the kitchen getting another drink, Mel couldn't help seeing them, Mairi and Yehune, as two forms a little bit larger than life, bearing in over the clutter of their lives and occupations, together, always linked together. He remembered their beginnings, that fortuitous brush together by the side of a road in France, the immediate meeting of... minds, or bodies, or whatever it might be, and the way the heavens seemed to have set a protecting hand over them. And the move to Edinburgh, surely as good a place as any for someone to get down to the serious business of his life. And now... now. That halfwit was chucking it all away, because he couldn't resist a pretty... right. Fuck. – It. –, he thought in two separate words.

There was no doubt about it: Yehune's fault was growing and growing in his own eyes even as he tried to diminish it for Mairi. Slowly but surely, a full-blooded Mairi partisan was rising up in him.

When he got back to the room, something had changed. They fell back into the same position as before on the sofa at the kitchen-end of Mairi's parents' sitting room. But it was as if their closeness, all correct and only for the purposes of consolation, had taken on some willed or headstrong quality. Mairi gave the impression of having come to some decision, he dreaded to think what. Nothing she said referred to it. She talked on in a rambling way about things she remembered from their short stay in Paris, cuttings of experience which appeared in some general way to centre on Mel: the tall familiar, the body in a sleeping bag. He knew that if you listened to Mairi's long digressions they always ended up making some point, unexpected as it might be. But what could the point be here – unless she was trying to say she was glad Yehune had such a mate? He wasn't acting the mate very well just then.

(And for a moment, Yehune was in his eyes, breathing into a girl's face in some squalid tenement room in Edinburgh.)

'… different,' she was saying. 'So there's something for Yehune to rest on. Me too.' She moved on one arm, possibly to avoid cramp, levering her head up higher from his right lower chest, and turned to look out of the window. 'You'll have to take care of him…'

That sounded ominous. Too ominous to leave alone.

'*You'll* have to look after him, you mean. Or we both…'

By that time, it was too late. He wouldn't have been able to say which one of them had started it, but they were kissing mouth to mouth, like the completion of a natural gesture, as if something as distant from them as the law of gravity had caused that tiniest adjustment towards each other. All that time, Mel had been struggling, trying to check his actions against the accepted norms for touching, which were freer with Mairi than with most people. But now – now they were interacting with lips and the ends of their tongues in a way that was all too educated; not yet absolutely deep-kissing. He had to bring in Leanne to make it make any sense. After all, he kissed Leanne in just the same way, and weren't they supposed to be friends?

290

Which gave the fatal justification that let him go on for just a few moments more.

His hands were holding her at the shoulders, one of hers was behind his back and the other gently resting at the hollow above his iliac crest. Excitement had already exploded in him, out of what had been physical weariness; biting into him at the groin and lower stomach.

He got his mouth free to say,

'God, Mairi.'

'Mel.' She looked up at him.

'You know, we shouldn't.'

'No. I know.'

He'd stood up to talk to her, and she was drawn up with him. Their bodies seemed to fit naturally one to the other, and no instinct in either of them made them want to break apart. After all: Leanne. He was comforting her. But why was *she*…? That air of having come to a decision: had she just decided to accept the same licence Yehune applied to himself? Of course, Mel was about her age, and didn't have any obvious physical defects, and they'd grown to know each other… all of which were potent elements, not at all the trivialities they might have seemed. Worse, there was an affinity of thinking between them. With all that, he tried to see it clearly. As for the events, they went on by themselves without any need for thought. They'd moved themselves awkwardly without separating to the wall on the door-side away from the window, and his jeaned legs were entwined with hers in a way that was obviously sexual for both of them. He did have the feeling that he wanted this for a tiny bit longer, to feel her lips touch his and the moving of their tongues against each other; aware of something breaking away and running free in that exact moment, that it was happening *now, now*… and would come to a halt somewhere. A cloud that slipped alongside him to disaster. And he saw Yehune….

In his mind's eye, saw Yehune smiling slyly along with him, ogling some girl just out of sight. Why not? Go on. She'll never, he'll never, find out, and it's fun, and it makes you feel like something's going right for you and that you might be something more than the useless little ashheap of your own aspirations. Go f'r it.

Mel pulled away again, this time completely. He said with a voice that was only barely under control,

'Tell you what, listen.... We'd better stop this.'

She said nothing. She looked into his face with a saner look than he would have expected, as if asking, Do you really mean that?

Seeing clearly won out. He took the few steps out of the room and round the corner, and rummaged for his jacket on the hall peg. She went after him, but stopped at the sitting-room door. He picked his bag up, and before he went out gave a sort of twisting smile, raising his hand to halfway as he pulled the front door open. No lifts home, he thought to himself, no hassling around.

She seemed to understand the intention. Her face was shaded against the back light of the sitting room.

Trip Again

Which, in any case, is not the subject; but times before, through times ahead, casting solid intersections of light. But the wash of time revisited, including all those things you just missed saying or couldn't ever say or haven't got round to saying yet. Like Poland, with its nostalgic, sepia quality of light as they looked out of the train window; the same sort of light, to their surprise, that they remembered from watching old European movies on TV late at night. Like passing across the Wall at Checkpoint Charlie, East to West, to feel the glittering glamour-parade of West Berlin explode on their eyes and ears after weeks of the Eastern Block; and sitting down crazy with sleeplessness in a bar at six in the morning and having a beautiful golden lager for breakfast with *Wurst*. Or the old *Mitfahrzentrale,* German organised hitchhiking, where Yehune excelled himself arguing and bartering on a pay phone across the barrier of a language he couldn't find his head or elbow in, occasionally demanding a word from Mel in 'some language, any fucking language'; in the end managing to link them up with two French female dancers who were driving a small car across Belgium. Later, crossing the Channel at strange and abrupt angles on a bucking ferry. And after another few things, getting to Geoff in Essex, and their first British culture-clash; which gave Yehune another chance to show his quality. The discreet word passed from Geoff's wife Jenny, through Geoff, to his brother Mel, that they'd turned up at a rather inconvenient time and in a typically happy-go-lucky Antipodean manner on their doorstep (in Orsett Green, near Stanford-le-Brave), and all that smiling hospit-*aah*-lity had actually been a sophisticated and very civilised sham; Yehune rousing them up at first light the next morning to get out of there, voting with his feet. After which Geoff turned up at the backpackers' hostel in London as soon as he got an address for them, and sold the car to them on the spot for ten quid – clearly by way of a sort of apology, and probably without the knowledge of his wife

Jenny. (It should be said that Mel and Yehune had actually sent a card ahead; but remembering the paint-flaking hole in the wall on the outskirts of a disused Belgian airfield they'd posted it in, Mel wasn't particularly surprised it had never got there.) And that was the car they took back to the Continent, the aging Austin Chevalier that Yehune later managed to set fire to. ... Later on, in Italy, the thing with Signor Freibrecht, which was another example of Yehune's skill at association, when the two of them (having missed the picking season) were working as dishwashers and roustabouts at a small restaurant and had no way either of getting out of there or surviving the approaching winter: where otherwise they would logically have had to ravel out to an end somewhere in Toscana. How had Yehune done it? Every night, around the tables chatting and telling yarns, this time in his own individual version of English, wooing the old art collector and amateur student of character to trust them with his precious Collection for the winter, and even go so far as to pay them for it. Pay Yehune, that is, so that each of them ended up getting half of a purely nominal wage. In Florence, *Firenze* – where there was nothing to do but read (but no books in the English language) and mope around wearing headphones and occasionally do things to the boiler and maintain the radiators and try to keep things clean. Which Yehune did with a demonic energy now and then; only now and then; the extreme activity leading often enough to a disaster which his general lassitude didn't allow him to try and put right – the boiler broke, and Mel didn't even pretend to know anything about boilers. Long months. No heating. The mercurial shifts of mood. Yehune at rest, facing the wall with his headphones on, too down and beat to bother getting himself anything to eat. The times when, paradoxically, it was actually Mel who insisted they get out of there, go off into town, find a bar, spend some of their precious *lire* on having a few beers and a good time; his friend pulled grumbling on behind. Could it be that it was Yehune's old bugbear: the lack of activity dragging him down? Possibly. But there seemed to be patterns in it, hidden waves of action and reaction; he managed to be down just when there was something very definite he ought to be doing, up for just long enough to make gains, establish relations, that he could later squash and destroy by an utter lack of response; a way of proceeding most people would have called distinctly un-Yehunish.

Since they had a bit of time on their hands, they had leisure to think about *art* again. Especially Yehune did that, even writing a few more stories that included the brick-red walls collapsing under flower pots and the roofs and windy marketplaces of the town they were living in. Once again, he started pestering Mel about what *he* was doing, and grew even more morose when he got no answer or a facetious one, again as if his whole motivation in writing words (which he did straight off, in a large, messy but legible hand with few erasures, taking a fixed amount of time for it like an Intermediate School essay) was to persuade Mel to do the same. Mel read his stories. And he liked them; he did. He liked them all the more for the errors in language and blindness to the basic inferences of things, as if to clean those up would be to ruin them; take away all their bold Yehunian punch and character. But (they had oceans of time, this was only one of the many, many things they talked about) Yehune would always ask him for his opinion, and seemed interested in putting himself up for serious competition. So Mel did get round to making a few comments. For one thing, there seemed to be climaxes anywhere and everywhere, or else the text was totally flat and without any apparent point (which had a sort of charm of its own, setting them off, maybe, in some ultra-modern hinterland not everyone could have got to). Mel gave him a map of proportions to try out: a slow rise, a climax or cutting together of strands somewhere round three quarters of the way through, then a dénouement. Yehune went on to write four or five pieces, one per day, each taking about an hour, that were formed exactly to that plan; so exactly that they gave the air of having been tacked like a quick word-blanket over a frame of four-by-two. In Yehune's music as well, after that, Mel almost always perceived the ghost of that innocent suggestion running under the surface like a forward-pitching wave, whatever relevance it might or might not have had to the point of the composition. He took care, back there in Florence, not to let any more advice out of his mouth, telling Yehune that anything he said would 'only mitigate the purity, sort of thing' –

which made the man even more short-worded and short-tempered than before.

(… Because there *was* a purity, Mel believed. And right or wrong, he himself only watched, felt, listened, played on a harp of shapes in the silence of his head, did nothing that wasn't in the unseen preprogrammed maze of his nature to do. … Of which, of course, nothing came.)

And so that night, after having dragged Yehune off to the principal streets of their own southward area of the town, and found a Caffè-Bar with music and sat down, and actually seen a group of girls of about the right age and not completely self-involved at a table across the way….

The notable thing was how bright and jocular Yehune was there at the start, using his very foreignness, his distance from any ideal of tall good looks, to trick his way in. Self-mockery, and the choice of the perfect tone in approaching three unknown girls at a table, and above all a flow of un-self conscious words, were what did it for him. It was all about cigarette papers at first, showing the girls how to roll their own; while Mel managed to carve a niche for himself by agreeing with the one non-smoker about the horrors of a table full of busy puffers. Mel was attempting a sort of pidgin Italian, which tended to block communication rather than help it, but the music was so loud most of the time that they couldn't hear each other anyway. He got up to dance with the girl who didn't smoke, who was small and dark with two large and carefully-pencilled eyes. But it turned out she was on a curfew, and presently she left. So there were Mel and Yehune and the two smokers. About then, Yehune dried up, barely bothering to extend his hand to pass the shag and papers over when asked, staring into space, or rather at a point near the bottom of the glass-mounted door, sluicing down beers and later limoncello with thick stoicism as if following some cure for dissipation or the screaming devils. Mel had to prod him for a while to get him to produce the money they'd brought. The girls – one probably-false blonde with a cute and symmetrical face until you came to the undercut chin; the other a very tall brunette with a marked lower bulge to the body (so: not a man dressed up) – seemed to fasten on Mel as the lively one

and the one who dispensed the money; and after a while either Mel
or one of them suggested they go for a walk outside.

Then nothing would persuade Yehune to get up. 'His' girl, the tall
brunette, went so far as to try and heave him up by the shoulders,
giving him very rapidly in Italian her views on men who wouldn't
stir themselves from a boozy seat; or foreigners, curly-haired ruffians,
or just men in general; but Yehune only lurched and stared as if he
really was on the verge of catatonia. Mel wondered whether he was
all right. He reminded him, speaking low in one ear, that these were
girls. Had he forgotten what those were? His two companions were
on the point of taking off by themselves, and Mel was about to let
them go, to give up the pleasure or at least relief from monotony that
accompanying two ladies along the banks of some local watercourse
would have been for him; but just at the end Yehune did give voice,
slurring out of the side of his mouth like a character in a corny
Western,

'Can't be arsed. – Fine. – Lea' me alone.'

And that was the last Mel saw of his friend until far later that
night, all the way back at Signor Freibrecht's. So Mel did in fact
stroll along a bank with the girls, giving up on Italian but keeping
up a lively enough conversation in English, and tried to memorise
their names (Lucia and something that might have been Marignetta
or Marzonella), and walked them like a gentleman to their different
homes, without good-night kisses or any sort of amorousness; which
turned out to be one of the most purely enjoyable experiences he'd
had not only in Italy but throughout the whole trip since the single
high point at Moscow. He even learned a lesson (whether or not he
went on to apply it afterwards): that it could sometimes be better
to fall back on English than keep on bashing away in a language
you were really only pretending you knew. ... But all the while, he
couldn't get Yehune out of his mind. Back at the house, he was careful
to leave the door unlocked, and still he couldn't get to sleep for several
hours, as if his blood was jumping and sparking with stimulants. In
the end he must have dropped off. He wove around in inconclusive
dreams, which of course were absorbing enough at the time; and so
naturally he was only shocked and exasperated when, at about four

o'clock in the morning, that uncoordinated body did lurch in the door with a flood of broken words and a loud metallic rattle. Leaving Mel relieved, exhausted, and again unable to sleep. For the rest of the night, and even long afterwards, it stayed with him, the feeling of leaving his best friend alone in a bar like that, like a dream of losing some all-important thing that you never manage to get back.

TWO

I thought of Mairi. And something slipping away – something she said in the car. What was that? They change, they change; they change and change. A fat boulder-shape, split cleanly from bottom to top, grew slowly in my eye as my footsteps wandered up towards it: standing proud against the whole spread level of the tidal pools. I could feel my feet chuffing down into sand as I came nearer, it grew bigger, I came nearer. What is it she said…? Something without rhyme or reason – as if it might be at the very edge of the graph, the boundary point on Mairiness. Talking about changing, and said… that he looked to me for a lead. To me. Couldn't have been much wronger there. The rock was broader now, the light cut brighter at the outline. Of course she wasn't there; and who can see the whole picture? Who ever can? A wind-weathered stone face bulging sideways, the split drawn round to one side now by the direction my feet had taken; neat, defined, with chiselled flecks at the edges. All the perspectives falling out of true. It was as if the closeness cancelled out all feeling for line and proportion, all sense of him, at the level of the expected; and now I was even closer, seeing dimples and accretions, surface chips and grains in all their clear complexity in the side of the rock, like Neolithic scoremarks. Some little splurgy bits of vegetation masked in cradles of stone. All symmetry lost. The beach lost. And yet you had to admit she *was* Mairi….

Mairi she was. And if, just for a moment, you could conjure up a world where what she said was true….

If you could, just for a moment. Then being Mairi, I'd guess she would have meant something in the bone, something deeper down than just the normal systole and diastole between any two people. Which meant… what? That from the earliest times he'd have to have been following the shape *I* gave to things… which is just. Which isn't….

If you looked at the beach from here it was an endlessly-varying series of stripes, the leavings from one tide and another. All coming to different levels. Turned to look back, letting my eye brush past the cracked rock. So small, it barely came as high as my knee.

Just think if the stripes were times, extents. Levels of the history of us, him and her and me. From the tussock grass downward was the dry sand, all fluffy churned with footprints; then wet sand in different stages, bounded by seaweed in long untidy clumps; rock then, glistening with diamond-flat surfaces; and then the lowest, hidden under the cold dank waves. His face across it, or more the back of his head. What was that, then? Talking and arguing with marks. The Ensemble: fiddling money and telling them the tale, the foreign trips, what was that – how – out of the run of time in circle....

Slow fold upwards, twisting. A small twig, there, settled in seaweed – bump by an upright.

Glowing red and redder in the eye's brink hidden

But you know it isn't hard to see the way it happened. There are always faces that stand out. Old Derek, in knitwear leaning in over a table, building up the set; and having no money, and writing or music? And girls, his girls, were – what? For a moment I let my eyes fall upwards, rolling up into the blue above us.

Sometimes you can catch them in the sky: connections. Great hazy clouds were lying up there, ruminating. All the bowl of the air, blue and smoothly graduated down towards the edges, broken by nothing except those white uncertain buffers and the angle of the light. To where it connected with the earth; the green of hills, the Firth.

Now over to the right of me the beach was coming to a lip again, a turning. Stark edge of humped-up grasses, knolls and dips, and closer in and down were all the little things that were caught in the weed. Appearance. Remember the appearance. Everything was appearances for a time; I could see those small rectangles over the eyes and a sharp little beard, that was him building his set again, and you have to admit, man, that under the crust of an appearance any fucking thing...

feeiiioooww of the wind noise rattling in the cup of my ear, finding its resonance; his girls, what was that for; or what was any of it –

And so past the outward bend in the tussock to the right of me I wandered on, imagining now in spite of myself: girls, a slow kiss. Leanne, it could be, outside the Gardner's Crescent flat. My fingertips snaking down. Or something else or something more, lips not so full, cheekbones like fired contours....

Where suddenly sprang full-formed into existence the house with the orange roof and the roadway meandering away past two hung-out road signs seen from the back, and the creek now, winding down out of a wasteland of blackberry and dead nettles, and the sweep of perspectives to a vanishing point again as I came as I walked round the corner. With an itch at the left heel. Not that, the something else. Oh no I should never think of that when what's the fucking use

One other, something that had nearly sucked the breath out of me, no not thinking of or even the next spring summer never to think

(it had nothing to do with and not to fall into the rehashing of event on event where what was the use)

... later, it was spring or early summer, and he was away somewhere and she picked me up and we went in the car through trees and she said that thing she said, and afterwards invited me into the lounge. And. And water, flowing mirror of the water over pebbles. Stop looking. Look at the sky instead. ... For the mirror, myself looking back at myself, out of drenched white-shaded clumps and the pale blue lost or hankered after somewhere behind.

... So eventually I looked down again. The creek was there, shallow and going fast, bashed down at the edge by footprints. The sand here rough and tawny, not like the sand back home. Someone had put a plank down so you could walk over it.

Picking or stalking my way across the seaweed line to the plank washed down by water. There were sandcastles just before it, a series of mounds some kids had built. Like a distant copy of Arthur's Seat on the horizon? ... Or a lopsided question mark.

But in any case, that wasn't even the subject, what was the subject, I suppose all the things in my head that hadn't been touched on; the dusty hollowness of the train clattering on through Poland; the places in Europe we got to or never got to; and Yehune always out there in front, using nothing but his mouth and the cheek he was born with to get us the best deal every time. And afterwards, well OK, he was down. You'd have to expect that. Only, he was *down* all right, deep down and out-of-it... which again if you take it that way and give yourself the benefit of not doubting what it was that Mairi...

or even just to entertain yourself, to take it to an extreme, seeing it her way, *if* she was right... it could mean more than that. And then, God, you'd have to go on to *post*-ulate that the mix that had gone to make him so tough wasn't quite such a successful cocktail. All the constant pushing from behind. Always looking for a way to get somewhere, while at the same time sliding out from under it, that way he had, to merriment and bastardry. And then later on when he hooked in to what might have seemed a *rebel* way, at the same time happening to fulfil all the success-win-fuck conditioning they'd laid on him; and then, well, then....

Before I stepped out, I looked straight up through twisting blackberry to where the creek cut through the grass bank and disappeared under a fenceline. Rubbish there. A broken piece of plastic moulding. You could see straight up to the house with the double roof, and to the angled-away beginning of Lyars Road which was really the A198. I looked around for him, that old Yehune, running spiked at the head along pathways through the grass; and looked and looked, scanned over hillocks, fields, green countries, tufts and rising peaks in all the grazed-down scrubland of the Longniddry roadside. And didn't see him.

Or Else

And if just for a moment you could conjure up a world where what she said was true, looking back and forward again across the run of sections, sequences, stripes marked out in sand, then first you'd have to think of him not as the instigator even when everything looked like turning on actions or decisions of his. Like when we first came out to Edinburgh, when he would have had to have been picking up wordless comments, glances, flicks of an eyelid, from that inanimate vomiter laid out behind Celestine's sofa; and let's face it that's what humans always do in any case, take stock of all the possible flavours of opinion in the humans round about them before seeming to gather the threads and take the initiative and hurl the unamenable tangle of fate off in a new direction. So then it's nothing, and you'd have to take it further still, re-read the grain of living memory, trace it back and further back, to where we became *artists* – how, why? Which is beyond us to see in detail; we can only catch it in single moments, footsteps. Then... taking one moment... how about that evening in Bondi, the escape from Australia, continuation of flight, where he'd come in breathing fast out of the action and lights of King's Cross and stood there in the room and lit a fag over my prostrate body and said, among other things, what was it he said,

'Shit, we'll have to get a car, though. Can't run a life without one, in Sydney.'

'... A car?'

and it's no mystery that for some people the mere flatness of a voice can be enough to carry across a message, something along the lines of, Cars are for people who are going to *live* here. Which would be to assume more sensitivity to the thoughts of others than I'd ever really imagined in Yehune, but that, well, that in itself....

And then you remember he asked me whether I wanted to come out and I said, 'Oh yeah, I would have,' and started to witter on at random about something that was in my head at the time, tired as I was to the point of floating backwards into dreams. What was it? My work, and old Peter giving the Maori names to the trees, and then about leaves, about something I'd seen in a leaf, held it up to the light. And you could see through it. Go to skeletons; there's usually quite a few on the ground after the... skip it. But it makes, I don't know how to say it, a picture in your head, something you can suddenly understand, like a spark in a plug.

Which was when I've always supposed Yehune began to have doubts of me, looking around at the walls in the bedroom of the house in Bondi and not actually listening to what I was saying, hearing instead something underneath it, some whisper of self-absorbed contentment, like the voice of someone able to live and breathe and drink and look at leaves all in the harsh-baked air of a country not three good hours away across the Tasman. A stayer – or something. Something of the sort. Or else...

  or else

Through all this, Yehune hadn't made a noise, nor had he really been watching his friend. The words Mel was coming out with were something he recognised, a strain of enquiry beyond the outward faces of things that he himself didn't go in for, though he could single it out perfectly well in someone else. In fact, over time it had become the subject of a deliberate study for him, followed up more closely than anything in his years at school or university. He couldn't let one word of the man's half-conscious rambling pass him without searching for some clue behind it. A clue, for him, to block procedures – since he *had* chosen to share the high, the inexact aim. At the same time – 'we're not even that far away' – Peter and the trees – a message was coming through to him beyond Mel's capacity to express, as he lay there dirtying the bedspread (because whether he knew it or not, small flakes and dustings of dried brown mud had fallen off his boots and were spreading just beyond the area covered by the Sydney Herald). Move on, it said. If said openly, proclaimed from any mountaintop by any force on earth or elsewhere, it might have been the one thing that Yehune in his self-certainty would have decided not to do. Here, though, it became a spirit guide, the voice of the oracle accurately pinned through sleep or hallucinogens, seeming, just maybe, to offer him a blueprint for the pursuit of his profession.

'Fuck it,' he'd said. And again, 'Fuck it.'

And then it had been *him*, Yehune had been the one who'd gone over to the drawer and started to rummage violently through wads of travel pamphlets.

And still, that's just a moment; and who can isolate and revise the ever-accreting moments of years and years of life, award new values, chart the rise and fall? It's like a weather system, usual enough in people, and something I'd already noticed: one gives, the other takes, and the next day maybe the other way around. The more hyperactive Yehune was, the more gone and sleepy Mel, and vice versa. Or, you could say as well, the more effort the guy had put into some new manipulation of the reality around him, the greater the slump afterwards – Russian train. His moroseness at the window. Rising fly – the dark invading geist. Which is all it is. Unless, of course… unless you could go on to postulate a touch more complexity, self-awareness, something more than the picture I've got of the unreflective guy from Matamata. Imbalances, and a perpetual striving to correct them, and the sort of sneaking and back-handed adaptability I'd so often seen or suspected. Using that as a tool, adjusting and rebuilding himself. Which could have led him into all the blacker gaps. How *conscious* was he…?

How conscious – conscious? And then, out of the whole series, what would you say stands out? The Refectory, Yehune's crossing of the floor. An epiphany, in the accident of filtered lights, to be interpreted now and forever after in terms of Russian heroic sculpture. Now I'd always seen that as the exercise of a magnificent caprice, and pretty obviously done from a position of strength – how could it not have been? However important anyone thinks marks are, they're not tries in a rugby game. And so you can see that sudden swerve of life-direction must have been done just like that; not any fruit of long consideration, no. Far from it. Because to do it that way, see the position, judge the gap, to have it all worked out beforehand, that would have argued not power, but a sense of insecurity, and a good deal more awareness of the pitfalls of the future than I would have expected from Yehune....

There was a sign somewhere among the varied houses and buildings: 'Members of the public should feel free to enter and enjoy the University Grounds'. Yehune considered it. Enter, enter and enjoy. What it must be to be a member of the public. The University Grounds, here, were no immemorial lawns with facings of ancient stone; cars ground their way down Symonds Street past buildings that were either relics of old Auckland or grey concrete monstrosities. He heard Mr Rigellan yelling at them up ahead, pulling them together into a herd.

By his side was Thoroughwell, dark-skinned, a focussed look around his eyes from some part of his ethnic mix.

'Don' think much of this, eh,' he said. 'Fuckin' poncey-land. An' it's nearly time for lunch.'

Yehune silently agreed. None of it had anything to do with him, and the whole tedious officialdom of it somehow emphasised the fact. It made him feel tired. That sign: University Grounds. I saw a sign, that said, bbb.... Beeblie the beautiful, is dead, is dead. ... English poetry.

A short way down Grafton Road, where big shade trees stood among houses that were teaching centres for obscure languages, a girl walking near them was the first to spot a young man or boy teetering dangerously at an open window. 'Hey, what's he doing?' she cooed out, and voices from the street overlapped her. 'Look,' 'Look, over there.' It was a very thin student – presumably a student – in an orange tee-shirt, climbing with care out through a high second-storey window. Yehune put his head up, watched him turning round, and then he saw the reason for the slowness. His face was bisected by a dark blindfold.

'He's gonna jump!' shouted someone.

There was something just a bit too self-conscious, light-hearted in the boy's movements. He was waving to one side and the other. From just behind the heads of cronies appeared, yelling to the street below, 'Jump, jump!' 'He's gonna suicide!' So it seemed it was all a prank, a piece of lovable student horseplay. But by then the mass of the sixth formers was losing cohesion, some spilling out, turning to jabber. Even the teacher had found a passing adult to talk to, possibly part of the University staff. … Laughter, and what might have been the breaking of a bottle, made abstract ripples over all the other noise.

Yehune broke away. He strode quickly towards the rear. No-one was likely to miss him, he thought.

Thoroughwell's voice came from just behind him,

'Where y' goin'?'

'Back to base.'

They were nearly to the crossing now, Yehune hoping their blue sixth-form uniforms wouldn't be spotted among so many strollers.

'Why?'

He said nothing. There was some depth in his mind, a cooler darker space, far away from buildings, signs and all the mechanics of life to come. It was getting on for lunchtime.

No-one brought up under the influence of Brigitte and Andrew Trent could fail to be aware of the *value* of university. It was a sort of pin you wore on your chest, making doors open, so they said, wherever you went. For some time, though, Yehune had known in a general way that it wasn't going to happen for himself. He justified himself inwardly, while at the same time looking for a way out, taking up the old accomplishments and turning them over one by one, music? maths? or… what else? Rugby was the cool, the roughneck way; and led to nothing but a job in a back-street garage repairing other people's cars. Unless you were great. He thought of tricks he'd learned, shortcuts, and the way he had to allow for certain weaknesses of his stocky body.

Now Rhat had joined them from somewhere. Together they burst in the door of the temporary refectory, on an upper floor of the Student Union building. Where he could just hear some hard fast music, but not where they were. They came into a curtained half-darkness, which over the next few minutes expanded in richness and contrast to a new world of downtoned light.

The stay-ins, the unsporty ones, users of chairs, were congregated there as he'd expected, with a teacher or two behind a trestle to keep an eye on them.

Mr Peele glanced sharply towards Yehune and his friends as they arrived, flung down bags, and took positions sprawled on the floor at the back of the room. Mickey and one other were already there.

'Y' seen their sports block here?' Mickey asked. 'Slack, eh?'

'Wha'? Why?'

'Play fuckin' *squash*.'

'Oh gorrr.'

Seuchar and a few of the other marks getters, Alan Templeton and the built girl Kathleen, were upright on the top of the largest table, others seated or crouched around them, and most of the chairs below were occupied. Funny the teachers let 'em. But – there you have it. He glanced sideways at Rhat, who was picking at bits of his lunch. His shirt was hanging out, dull blond hair harbouring some mud or leaves he'd managed to pick up.

Ugly, but staunch. Tenacious in battle – he meant, on the field.

'Sheesies fuck,' muttered the Rhat, pulling out a mess of destroyed sandwich filling.

Yehune's own sandwiches were cut perfectly in two deep triangles, a tight sculpture. Motherly care.

When he looked up to the table over by the window, he saw a carefully-composed group of statues. Strange... well, not strange for that place and the peculiar properties of the light. On and around their table, Mel Seuchar and his friend Templeton and some of the other academic successes, the girl Bicklespear, others, along with a few hangers-on like Locke and Timothy Castor, stood in the banded, luminous jut and shadow of filtered and refiltered sun's rays; some, like Seuchar and his friend, actually raised up on chairs or the tabletop so that they formed slim masts, a sort of irregular summit to the array; others flanking them, stilled for just that moment in supporting attitudes. There was something striking about the accidental contrast of dark and light, visible to him from where he leaned against the facing of the wall, different, he supposed, from any other angle – upward spars, imposition of light-haloes – and the word occurred to him: 'alphas'. This was just a sampling, Seuchar and Templeton,

Kathleen Bicklespear too; the swots, the goodlets; but the ones who he supposed in the course of things would go on to dominate the social pack.

In a way it was a nuisance, the fact that Thoroughwell and Rhat had tagged along. It made this more in the nature of a public statement. However... he stood up, leaving his bag and lunchbox where they lay.

'Trent!' said someone just in the door.

He did experience that small sway of perspectives as he drew up closer to the table sculpture, where the composition changed from moment to moment, but never lost its heroic or mock-heroic overtones. Something glassy there as well; hard to break into. Half-tones of light were passing him, like successive veils that laid themselves over schoolbags, faces, and the concrete moulding of the edge of a wall.

Cas looked round, sitting on a chair at the periphery.

'Cas,' Yehune said.

'Oh hi, Yehune. How's it goin'?'

'All right.'

(Above their heads he could make out short clips of what sounded like a technical discussion,

'No, no, it's like, these girders all over everything, you know... Soviet Constructivist?'

was it Mel? Mel Seuchar, or....) He seized on a chair, pulled it up with careless brutality, and sat astride it.

A few more words with Cas followed. But Yehune was impatient. He didn't bother to wait for a gap in Mel's conversation,

'So, Mel! Hey, Mel. Ahh-m... what sort of stuff are you thinkin' of taking in university, then?'

The features of Mel Seuchar appeared above. Spare, eyes close together, the jawline sculpted and a bit prolonged.

'Oh, Trent. Don't know yet, I haven't got the Calendar.'

'You mean you're not doing English?'

'English, why English?' Mel let his eyes turn back to Templeton in apology for the distraction. Templeton's face was even more chiselled, his framework taller, as he stepped down to the tableside.

Mel went on, 'Oh well... no, I doubt it. You don't take English if you're...'

He looked away into space for a moment, then said,

'You know... Solzhenitsyn said the best thing he ever did was not getting a literary education.'

'Oh. Soldier Nitsin said that?'

Yehune's thoughts, if any, on the subject of Nitsin were interrupted by another chair-sitter, 'Orr, hey, Y'une, can't believe the way you played in the rugby, it was *mighty*. Ran like a hairy goat.... Two tries!'

He answered automatically. But in the meantime he kept on thinking and taking clues. Apparently some of them here at the upper end of up were in a position to cast doubt on the different shadings of higher education. It boosted him, gave a lift to his resolve. Bullshit, maybe; but it was a sort of bullshit he could file away and use.

In the meantime, Templeton had started a conversation with the Bicklespear girl; Mel had snagged out a crushed Woolly's supermarket bag that must have had his lunch in it.

Yehune caught his eye again.

'What about you,' Mel asked, 'you going on to the seventh form?'

'I'm not charging straight on in here, if that's what you mean.'

'No, I just didn't know if you.... Maths was your thing, wasn't it?'

'Used to be. Now it's music. You know, ah, piano – bit of composition.'

He knew he was reaching. But he could feel every tone under control, like in some small comedy act where punchlines are delayed.

He said, 'Remember when you used to write essays for me and I'd slip you all the maths answers?'

'Oh yeah... I can vaguely remember scribbling some stuff.'

'Right. So now I can give your music the old master-touch too.'

Mel laughed. 'There isn't any.'

Which would seem to finish that. A commotion in the back part of the room made him look over, to see a bustle of movement, Thoroughwell and Rhat with Mickey all straggling away with their bags and racquets towards the door. About to be offsided.... What was more, the pause was drawing out.

He prompted, 'Come on, you must listen to *music*.'

310

'Well, you know, only rock, and a bit of blues… is that the kind of music you…?'

Yehune was looking with guilty fascination at the half-squashed and unappetising lump of food Mel had extracted from the Woolly's bag.

'You like Zappa, the Mothers of Invention?'

'Ah, I think so… I usually listen to older stuff though. You know, Clapton and Led Zeppelin and that.'

'Oh, right. "In Through the Out Door".'

Mel's voice came muffled by food,

'That's the last one… I haven't actually heard it yet.'

'I've got it at home,' he said. 'Come round and listen to it some time, if you can be bothered.'

'Wouldn't mind.'

So there it was: the invitation. Come to nothing as it probably would. He was aware of his position, there and then, one of three or four sitting on the refectory table at the top of that fluid and ever-revolving stack.

At that moment, a very loud voice crowed out from somewhere near them,

'Bugger my arse, they're married!'

He could have spat. Brought into public. Looked around to see who he had to deal with. Mel had reacted as well… probably as aware as he was….

And he picked out Templeton and the girl Kathleen, walking together towards the door like a procession down an aisle.

… So, all right then, it could have been that. A matter of connections – could be we were seeing not the great Yehunian spontaneity, but something out of the lexicon of Brigitte and Andrew Trent, because in bohemianism as well as professionalism, you isolate the players, rub shoulders, infiltrate, acquire. How had Yehune even survived so long? By always taking the back way. And so in this case he was doing nothing but building up contacts – *I* was his contact.

And we can assume then that internally he was conscious enough;

like anyone, he was what he made himself, visualised in the silence of the inner skull and then imperfectly, doggedly, repetitively put into practice. Which was a process I could never see, no-one could have seen, packed in as it was under that burnished and immaculate outer casing, his concern for appearances. No-one would ever have suspected a crack. And all the time, I'm beginning to realise, he was looking for something else, a way past, a way through, under the aegis of a contact beyond any he could have found on earth: he was looking for what was outside himself

———————

a thaka-thunna a thaka-thunna a thaka-thunna tun tun t

railway girders or a ghost of the operation of falling blocks as if an overbridge or standing post for an overhead light in the last few moments of arrested motion of the carriage underneath had buckled lost balance and fallen forward slow-seeming in the slipped descent to crash through the sheet metal and plastic roof of the train and skewer at random the warm meat of bodies gesturing and breathing in the seats *rische rische* ants of tower legs breaking skulls like shells at the merest touch in an abrupt and centred image of every match around me splintered at onceit is imperative to observe manufacturers' load tables as re distance between welded K-jointswhich in an explosive one-shot cancels that last thought merest touch

Yehune's Thing

Music – there was music everywhere, a looping and unpredictable series of any old notes, dancing along an inch or so above the junk landscapes on the floor of their flat, grabbing their attention while they worked or lay in bed or walked along a dirty street side, or hiding, sometimes, in the coloured thickets of shop displays, among the feebler strains of commercial Muzak, to leap out at them suddenly, stitch zigzag lines across the inner spaces of their heads like strings of eccentric party decorations. Neither Mel nor Yehune could help it, they were constantly humming small motifs; or it might have been the motifs that worked on them and harried them and refused to leave them alone. Just now, it was mostly the trumpet solo. Yehune worked on it with a feverish energy, hurrying over to the piano at any hour of the day or night to try out new permutations, trying to make his little plastic keyboard produce something like a trumpet tone, programming it to play back an endless loop of the latest version, and filling binbag after binbag with crumpled-up music paper. But it wasn't the only source; any other passage from Yehune's Swing Sonata, sections of other pieces he might be working on, and in fact anything in the whole Ensemble repertoire, could make a playground of their heads. Mel had already given up trying to distinguish them from the general musical culture all around them: to remember, on the spur of any moment, whether whatever little snatch of notes was driving him crazy was of a Trent or non-Trent origin.

Everything was working up to the concert at the Masons', which was going to reverse all their fortunes. Mel couldn't help overhearing some of Yehune's conversations; off the phone, the cracked and angry voices of band members asking about the promised trips to Italy and Denmark, or where all their money had gone; on it, monotonously repeated, the only answer he ever gave, beginning: 'Wait for the Masons' '. He was upbeat, as an entrepreneur has to be, and expected no less from any other member. There'd be no apologies, no returns.

313

Instead of complaining, everyone had better work hard, practise and practise, and if there were any questions about the latest update of the music, he, or failing him Andrew, was always on the line to answer them. And in times when they weren't practising, there were posters to hang, streets to walk, doorbells to push, workplaces to inform of the coming aesthetic treat, marriage of bebop and Berlioz, no less than the creation of a musical language for the coming age on a single occasion in a medium-sized venue in West Edinburgh. Which was the point of it all. ... Wasn't it?

Whether or not it was, all the activity had at least had the effect of nailing Yehune down to what he ought to be thinking about: music, and what he was trying to create. Mel didn't know what quick-switching light shows might have been going on among the wires in his head, but it was certain that his direction had changed time and time again. Now the goateed Bandmaster with the cropped-down hair seemed committed enough, though it didn't make his temper any sunnier. He was restless, frustrated, inwardly and outwardly raging. But that could have had just as much to do with their finances and the pressures operating on them from every direction. Which, Mel freely admitted, were more his worry than Yehune's. Their lack of money had reached crisis point. Though he bought the cheapest possible food, obsessively comparing prices from shop to shop, and designed their meals around dry soy protein that he lumped home in sacks, there was only barely enough money left over to pay the household bills. If not for Mairi's cheques, they would have had to give up on living where they were.

As for Yehune's extracurricular activities, they gave every sign of going on as before, though you could never be absolutely sure. In fact, the insistency of females other than Mairi was one of the things that contributed to the man's general rush and irritability. Certain girls, like Francine (whom Yehune explained as the girlfriend of Tub the set drummer) and Siobhan (explained as Francine's friend), would knock on the door of the flat and either invite him out with them or else bounce in and start making cups of tea for themselves, while Yehune told them how busy he was, loudly banged the piano, and was only barely civil. Mel had long ceased to have any doubts about Yehune's guilt as a historical fact; it would have been obvious just from Francine's body-language when she kissed him on her way in and out. But whether that fling was still current was another question. In any case, he didn't feel like bringing it up. Yehune wasn't shy, he would have told him all about it if he wanted to; in the same way as, long ago and in another country, he'd boasted about getting his hands up two girls' skirts at once.

Knock, knock, knock!

'Fuckin', will you get that Mel?'

'I think it's for you. Those girls, Francine…'

'OK, OK.' He waved his hand towards the door.

(Opens.)

'Oh, hell-*ooo*. I can see Yehune's busy so we won't stay very long. Hi Yoonie! Me'n Siobhan just dropped by to see if you want to come out to the Kar Krash.'

'No. Thanks. I'm working. I'll see you girls later on.'

'*Oh,* well then. It looks like it's Yehune's flat for just now…'

'No – I'm really in the middle of something, Francine, it's not a good time. Come back later. Jus' tryin' to think… Thursday?'

'But can't we at least make ourselves a cup of *tea*?' The girls were already in, adding the bustle of two bodies and the flounce of skirts and fringed bags to the overcluttered space inside. Francine picked her way over the floor to where Yehune sat on the piano stool, and gave him a long, smooching kiss on the cheek. Then, for good measure, one on the mouth.

Yehune: 'Francine, think of Tub.'

An incredulous look, a long giggle. Siobhan joining in.

Mel was hunkered down, trying to pull out the big black rubbish bag he and Yehune kept their dirty washing in.

'Mel, you're not going out?' Yehune protested.

'Yeah, gotta get to the laundrette. Have you got any other clothes?'

'Um, hang on a sec…'

Along the back wall, on the other side from the wall-bed, a long, chipped, seventies-style breakfast bar walled off a kitchen space. Siobhan was already behind it,

'Where are the *tea*-bags?'

Mel said, 'Got none. Loose tea these days, I get it at Real Foods. You'll have to use the teapot.'

'Oh. … That's rough.'

Of the two, Mel found Siobhan the more attractive, well-formed at thighs and hips, though her face was built around a great prow of a nose (so what? a European thing), and he couldn't ignore a slightly gaping expression. Siobhan was generally stuck fast to Francine's arm, and Francine had plainly staked a claim on Yehune. Now, the notes of the trumpet solo cracked gong-like into the limited space, louder than Mel had ever heard it played, Yehune's voice audible in the gaps muttering about the 'tones'. ('Tones'? Acoustic pianos apparently had these 'tones', Mel had been told, which could be improved by the sort of weight the pianist brought to bear or by the curlicues he described with his hands and arms; a revelation to him, when it all sounded like a harsh 'dunk' and quick degradation of several pitches aspiring to be the same but never quite making it, like a singing of high powerlines over a basis of dark mud.) He was down by the table leg, trying to get a sock out from under it. Francine's symmetrical bottom in skirt fabric was nearly in his face; Siobhan's off somewhere else. There y'are. Everything comes in twos. The trumpet solo rose up to a high *bi-bi-bi-bi* that was a syncopated jazz-cum-Stravinskyesque thing Yehune did sometimes, now definitely an injury to the ears. He could have wished the guy's fingers off.

Try finding two socks the same, ever. Not a – f'king – chance.

But he managed to get the thing free, caked in dust and twisted up inside itself. One sock. Single. Holding the rubbish bag open with his left hand, he started to whip it straight, thrashing and thrashing the heavy knot of wool violently into space.

Siobhan hummed, 'Mm, h-hmm, h-hmm,' as she clanked the teapot in the sink.

'Fuckin', bloody, ass-head, sock bastard…'

'Mel?' Yehune stopped playing.

'Gotta get this…'

They were all staring at him, Siobhan openly, Francine covertly, Yehune's face beginning to open to the sun.

'Mel… hey,' he said. 'Leave off. I think it's dead.'

As for Yehune's relations with Mairi, they seemed to have gone through some readjustment. Nobody but themselves could have known the details. But Mel imagined he could see it working in the barest trifles: the tone one of them used to answer the other one, a turn of Mairi's head and an expression fleetingly caught, or the angle of her neck and upper body as Yehune bent to kiss her on the cheek at one moment in a café. If he hadn't known anything about tissues, notes, or the contents of his friend's pockets, he would have missed it completely... or else his expectations would have missed creating it.

Naturally, he'd never said a word to Yehune about tissues or handkerchiefs. How could he, without confessing to everything that had happened? And he didn't tell Mairi anything either – having, when it came down to it, nothing to tell. He already had the feeling that whenever he met her eye, too much passed between them. Knowledge was unwipable; you could never begin again. ... But in any case, neither of them would have referred to the subject even if they'd found themselves alone for the odd few minutes. Rather than dwell on old mistakes, all three of them, Yehune, Mairi and Mel, were each in their own way directed towards the future, willing it with every nerve to amount to some sort of success, while the date of the concert at the Masons' came closer and closer.

Saturday night at the Scottish Masonic Hall on Palmerston Place. The night was fresh, poised and breathless, or so Mel felt it, remembering other clear nights outside the same old smudged facade when there'd been nothing more in prospect than a ceilidh for foreigners and beginners. What surprised him, even though he himself had been involved in advertising the event, was the number of people trickling towards the door; such a crowd of coat-and-scarf-wearing figures (he couldn't help thinking) as you might expect for a *real* concert. He and Mairi turned up together, Yehune having been there since four o'clock to supervise the setting up of the hall. At a small table inside, Eber's wife Sadie sat collecting people's cash. Mel paid his five fifty, while Mairi exchanged a few words with somebody she knew behind the table. A moment later, she joined him. But not before he'd noticed her paying, when she was supposed to be exempt; carefully shielding her hands with her body in case anybody saw her.

The moderate-sized hall hadn't been used for any Masonic purpose for some time, but was still called by the old name by virtue of the crusty old lettering set into the stonework outside. Bucket-seats in fixed rows had been introduced into a venerable panelled interior, stained with age and tobacco smoke, which hadn't been properly refurbished in all its years of use as a casual venue. Modern blue plastic clashed with the varnished wood and high straight windows. It has to be said that Yehune's Ensemble, set on a raised stage at the front, only added to the incongruity. It wasn't an orchestra, nor a big band, but an eclectic collection of instruments both modern and orchestral, arranged in a shallow curve to face the audience. There was a whole section of guitarists standing and sitting, including (Mel had been told) one of each of the different sorts of guitar: folk, classical, slide, bass, semi-acoustic and solid body electric and so on. Beside that, a cut-down wind section out of an orchestra, heavy on the brass. Saxophonists had been added in a tidy row. There were even a few strings, coyly hidden at one edge of the percussion section, which was big and varied and included ethnic drums Mel had never seen before in his life. A bank of amplifiers stood in a block on either side of the stage, and on the left side, slotted in front-to-back so as to make more room, was a full-sized concert piano. Yehune was at the front from the start, hovering between the piano stool and the main microphone, sounding an A for everyone to tune up to, and fielding organisational questions.

The whole effect must have been a bit bizarre to the concert-goers. But that could have been what they'd come there to experience; none of the posters or flyers Mel had seen had laid any stress on the *conventional*. What struck him most, as a member of the audience, was a strange disparity of atmosphere. He'd been at most of the Ensemble's little concerts at churches and chapels throughout the city – now here was the same whimsical, frankly experimental band, facing up to what was beginning to look like a serious concert audience. The hall was getting near full, and people still hadn't stopped filing in.

318

Mel and Mairi found seats on the left side and about three quarters of the way up. The audience gave him the impression of being made up of distinct groups or factions, slotted together uneasily; he could imagine how some of the string players might have invited just their mums or boyfriends, a drummer or two given out mass invitations to all his friends at the pub... some people were already leaning over seatbacks talking to each other, while whole rows sat stolidly saying nothing. Mairi pointed out a man three rows ahead of them with white hair and a Roman-emperor nose, 'That's Auchterinver.' 'Aucha-who?' 'You know, the conductor.' Oh, right? Did you ever. The dark-suited backs on all sides of the head gave the strong impression of a bodyguard, but more likely belonged to violinists and music journalists and people of that sort.

Yehune presently started things off; he came up to the microphone and began to say a few words about himself and the Ensemble. He spoke breezily enough, trying to put the audience at their ease. Among more prosaic subjects (difficulties of funding, the peaks and troughs of the history of the Ensemble until then) he did let a hint of his sense of mission show through – The World and The Future were mentioned, and the burning zeal of the innovative composer barely sketched, in a way that might have been a bit too grandiose for some people at that early stage of the evening. The more excitable sections of the audience rustled their programmes and muttered among themselves.

'Then, without further ado...' he proclaimed.

He looked thoroughly competent and in control as he turned towards the musicians and raised his arms. That might have been the last good impression the audience had, the single, definitive moment before all confidence failed. His arms came down (Yehune never used a baton) and a loud noise burst out. Even to a non-musician, it was quickly obvious that at least two different timings and sets of notes were being played. Many of the Ensemblists, the merest beginners, stopped playing straight away, so that the sound thinned and nearly died; others doggedly stuck to their scripts as they'd been taught. In the lull in the noise, Yehune called out, 'Pavane, Pavane!' He tapped a few bars with his foot, and ducked over to the piano, where he began to thump out the slower of the two rhythms with as much emphasis as possible.

Looking down at his programme, Mel saw that the name of the first number had been changed: the original printing had been scored out and 'Black Rage Pavane' written above it in ballpoint pen. It seemed that not all the musicians had been informed of the change, or else they'd been doing something else at the time; now there was a desperate scrabbling among the music sheets, and almost everyone found their way to the right piece of music. A lot of them began at the beginning, not knowing where else to come in. An electric guitarist standing at one end of his group stretched for a sheet of paper passed by another guitarist (steel acoustic) near the other end, and lost his balance, and fell over the row with a *crrr-rump* and wail of tortured strings. One of the percussionists, relatively free at the front, left a waist-high drum and ran out across the stage to help him up.

Through all of this, Mairi sat completely motionless. Mel, on the other hand, couldn't help flicking his eyes here and there over the assembled rows of people. He saw a tall man in a formal jacket beside the Classical conductor turn and give an insinuating smile to someone in the row behind him. A particularly excitable group at front right were mostly laughing, some of them waving their arms to and fro as if at a football game, others standing or craning to talk to other people. Most of the right-hand side further back was taken up by a large glum contingent, not so well-dressed, who just sat there as if waiting for their execution. The music crashed, and piped, and bleated on, Yehune having managed to drive the players together towards the final bars, but by that time hardly a musical note was being produced – some players were heroically overblowing to try and get their companions back on the track, others had gone so tentative as to produce nothing more than a weak noise, like a whistle in a downpipe.

Three bare chords finished it off, missing all the ornamental licks that should have come from the electric guitarist. The noise from the audience afterwards – not clapping, except for a brief period of sarcastic slow claps started by unseen people to the left and behind – almost rivalled the efforts of the band; it might have qualified for a number in its own right. The companions of the Classical gentleman were animated, laughing and joking among themselves, and the right front was plainly roaring. Even some of the glum brigade had begun to perk up.

Mel was making an effort to keep it in perspective. But he was worried about what Mairi might be thinking; and he murmured to her under the cloak of the noise,

'Just a little hitch, sort of thing.'

'I think some of them were still playing the old opening piece.'

'Yeah. I thought so too.'

It was true, this kind of setback would have been fairly common in the earlier Ensemble concerts; the difference was only context. In those small church halls, they would have been lucky if the first three pews had been filled. He looked out on the high darkness of the windows, and the line after line after line of heterogeneous heads (and bodies, in the sections that were standing): people who'd made their way to the hall on purpose that night and paid £5.50 at the door.

Yehune himself looked stubborn and unflappable. It was true that he wasn't smiling. To Mel, the only sign that he'd even noticed a problem was an extra nonchalance in the way he moved, rattled his music stand and leaned over for a word or two with Andrew. The 'fuck you' attitude could still be useful, apparently, even when it was your own success or failure that was at stake. But most of the other musicians on the stage weren't so well shielded, and already their confidence had taken a knock; the gravity of the occasion and the disastrousness of failing to live up to it were beginning to come home to them. For all that, the next two pieces were brought off nearly successfully, allowing some leeway for tension and fumbling lips and fingers. Interestingly, the audience reacted to that with impatience, as if they couldn't wait for a really juicy catastrophe, and there was shouting and catcalling in the intervals over the sound of clapping. The Classical conductor showed no expression on his own account; he left that to his flankers, like a sort of human field or aura around him. Mostly, they projected jocular contempt.

And so the time came for Yehune's first-half set piece, the Swing Sonata.

It was true that some faster, more spectacular pieces were being kept for the second half, some even with tunes in them that people might have known. But to Mel the Sonata was the real focus, either because he knew how much labour had been expended on it, or else because little fragments of it made up the bulk of the music that had been dancing in his head for so many weeks past. The idea itself was simple enough, and had no doubt been done many times before. It was a brazen contrast of styles: Classicism alternating with swinging jazz rhythms, usually joined together by a short solo by some instrument or other. The trumpet solo was the high point, where the whole struggle was repeated or encapsulated in a single line of notes, which developed it and took it higher, higher, towards... nothing that could be described in words, but something removed, a culmination of some kind; after which the band's concluding passage was just a single step downwards into silence. It was in parts of that solo that Mel felt Yehune might possibly have hit on something; something small, quirkish maybe, but in the end, something of his own that didn't rely on formulae or copied styles. But then again... how could he tell? He wasn't musical. And he knew that familiarity alone could make things resonate, calling up answering motions out of a person's hidden psyche, clarifying dormant memories, until it seemed to tell him about other lifetimes never lived but which were suddenly a step away, across a sort of creeping integument the colour of water. ... To get to that, you only had to play something over and over again.

Before they started, Yehune gave the Ensemble a quiet pep-talk. Here the restlessness of the audience actually worked for him: whatever he might have been saying, it never came up above the rumble and resurgence of different layers of noise. In any case, when the music began, it was the right music. Mel thought some of the high notes sounded pretty good, comparing them with Classical things he'd heard in the past. But it was obvious that the instrumentalists weren't quite up to realising Yehune's intentions. There was a sort of bricked-in misunderstanding of the rhythm common to whole sections, plain enough to anyone who knew Yehune's piano version. The guitar players were having difficulty getting the notes played quickly enough; wind instruments had a tendency to come in just a moment too late. But the audience, he thought hopefully, couldn't know how the thing was *supposed* to sound. The first formal section seemed reasonably together, and the solo that led it all into jazziness was carried off all right – despite departures from the straight route due to nervousness or forgetfulness – by one of the clarinettists. There was a full, big-band swing passage to follow, and a short and funky intermezzo by the piano. And then, suddenly, Mel could hear the rhythms as they were supposed to be heard, all the real expression of the composer... of course, since he was the one who was playing it. But it was the almost absent-minded certainty of it, as if some people grew up walking black-and-white keyboards with their fingers instead of walking the planet's surface on their feet, that impressed him. And here came the figure that would repeat and shift and bring it all down to Classicism again; a tink-le *tink,* a tink-le *tink,* a tink-*le* tink tink, a tink-*le* tink tink, like that, over and over, and....

There. Entry of the band. *That* wasn't so bad.

He looked round him again, and noticed that Mairi's eyes were fixed unwaveringly ahead. The crowd was quiet, on pause, waiting its chance. The Classical conductor turned his head to whisper to the next person in line, and he could see all the contours of the cheek and the prominent beak – undulation to a headland – a coastline photographed from space.

Next, Andrew the trumpet stood up. And for the second time the audience was presented with a thorough master of his craft; the notes were clear and precise, and the long body of the trumpeter showed no more tension than if he'd been standing talking to someone. In fact, he gave that impression, as if he were just speaking in some brassily-singing native language of his own. Now Mel heard sounds that actually surpassed Yehune's idealised version, especially in the matter of tone. Not that the identification was obvious. There had plainly been more last-minute changes than he'd known about; for a moment Andrew hit a high note and wavered and wavered on it, something Mel couldn't remember from all the repetitions on piano and electric beep and sometimes haphazard voice that had crowded his head for so long. And – weren't some of the theme-y bits missing?

323

The first clue he had that Andrew was going it alone, making it up as he went along, was when Yehune slipped over to the piano stool and started playing corrections, small tinkling runs and single motifs, trying to get him on the right track again. Now, it must have been obvious enough to the composer-director that this kind of musical prompting could be a bit transparent to an audience, so he started interweaving his suggestions with the rising and falling trumpet noise in a way he might possibly have thought was subtle. From the beginning, he was at a disadvantage, since Andrew had the floor and could do what he liked – by this time the man was plainly hot-dogging, lipping through fast random finger-movements, wavering high, wavering higher, wavering ear-piercingly shrill, in a standard syncopated style that had absolutely nothing to do with that or any Sonata. Yehune seemed to give up at that point, and stood up to bring the massed instruments in over him.

Andrew refused to stand down. What was more, only about half of the remaining musicians responded to Yehune's gesture; a proportion did nothing; and to make matters worse another maverick stood up just then, a saxophonist, impatient for a turn. A trumpet solo protracted so far could become a sort of brassy tincture of the air, abrading the senses but hardly really noticed any more, like slow lightning weaving among the darkest crannies of the ceiling while ordinary life went on somewhere else. This one of Andrew's had long ago left music behind and was given to virtuoso display. Richard, the man behind the saxophone, obviously thought he could do better; he was a stooped-over man with a bowl haircut who some time during his life had mastered a style of fluid Dixieland improvisation. And on they went – neither could be tamed – neither even attempted to fit in with the other, or with the general shape of the piece, which was still being belted out by a few musicians.

Then came a surprise, or a reversal. Andrew, whose lip must have been needing a rest by then, half-turned in his place and dipped his trumpet once, and the silent portion of the band launched into a jazz or boogie theme that wasn't in the Sonata and wasn't even by Yehune. Richard, surprised and hurt, stopped in mid-riff. Such a thing couldn't have happened without forethought, at least one rehearsal, a whole weft of collusion and deceit. Some proportion of the audience might have understood that, and scented blood. Certainly nobody there was in any mood for musical appreciation, even if there'd been any music worth appreciating. By now most people on the floor were standing, some to scoff and laugh and flail their arms, others to shout or boo. Certain members of the dour section on the right had linked arms in the aisle and begun a strange, primitive, wobble-bottomed dance; something Mel had never seen, but he guessed was maybe an allusion to some TV show.

The rebel players were loud and aggressive enough, but still couldn't keep together very well. Tub, the set drummer, seemed inspired, or rather possessed, rattling and cymballing out the rhythm for the insurrectionists with far more abandon than he'd shown all evening. Eber backed him up on a pair of woodblocks. By this time, the Sonata proper should have been winding down; and in fact it never really did finish, the loyal musicians being too rattled to stick to their notes. But once their musical resistance was over, they started to show a more physical indignation. Some of them stood up to push or shout at the ones who were still playing. A drum fell over with a loud crash; a tuba- and a trombone-player started wrestling arm to arm in the back row; the strings sat looking around them like a herd of nervous deer. Yehune was standing off a bit by then, his hands dangling at his sides.

Andrew sensed his triumph, and stilled the music with a cut of the hand. The crowd noise roared on. He strode over and took up the microphone... and found it turned off, as anyone might have expected.

So he shouted at the top of his voice, *'Ladies and Gentlemen!'*

His voice sounded hoarse and weak, not a patch on his trumpet playing.

'What you have just witnessed is not a diss-*olution, but an* ev-*olution, the birth of something new out of the ground base of proletarian, er, um... discontentment. How long have we struggled under the tyranny of this so-called conductor, this piano player, this Yehune Trent? I say too long, too long...'* He seemed inclined to make a chant of it, but thought better of it, seeing Yehune coming towards him. He tried to finish off,

'The time has come for every thinking musician to stand together and split off, and I hereby announce the...'

Past a group of bodies, the companions of the Classical man, Mel witnessed the short struggle between Yehune and the far taller Andrew. Yehune was furious and not nearly as civilised a fighter, and Andrew was trying to protect his trumpet. In another moment, Yehune had the microphone and the trumpeter was staggering away to one side. Behind them, the Ensemble was now in open war, the loudest shouts being reserved for damage or the threat of damage to their instruments. (... But a few had had enough, and were quietly slipping away to one side of the stage and the other.)

Yehune must have had the secret of the microphone. In any case, it was suddenly turned on, and barked out harshly over the noise,

'I apologise for the interruption by this Andrew, who's a disruptive influence, and assure you that normal performance will continue as soon as him and his whole circus have been thrown out of here...'

But Andrew had gathered his strength and come back. Both directors were holding the microphone in one fist each as he yelled towards it, creating a shriek of feedback to shatter ears and bleed up towards the ceiling,

('... the formation of the And-) *drew Barris Jazz Combo!'*

Yehune made a menacing forward motion of the head, forcing the renegade to duck back. Looking like a purposeful dwarf, he lowered the microphone onto the floor, and left it there whistling while he followed Andrew back into his nest among the wasteland of fallen chairs and music stands. Back there, the balance of power was no longer really in question. Most of the Jazz Combo-ists, seeing the rout of their leader, jostled and screamed at by the loyalists all around them, had picked up their instruments and were filing out, or trying to file out wherever they could get past.

The audience had gone almost quiet, as if acknowledging the superior level of mayhem up on the stage. Hardly anyone was sitting down any more. Some, like Mel and Mairi, just stood and watched, others argued among themselves, and most of the primitive dancers (who were they? What Ensemble member had them for friends?) were now clapping rhythmically in support of some faction or other.

Only the conductor's small group was still active, gesturing and shouting out for more; but their actions gave the impression of being somehow mechanical, worn down and falsely buoyant.

Andrew must have been intending a sweeping stage coup, after which he could have played his own second half to the concert. As things were, the only musicians left among the seating (some of which was still being picked up and disentangled from wires and music stands) were on Yehune's side; and there were few enough of those. The noise of stage and floor seemed to come to an equilibrium as the last Combo members trailed away, and the public paused to see what would happen next.

Yehune walked out to the front and picked up the microphone. He held it away from him until it stopped shrieking.

He said, 'Well, sorry about that, mates – I mean, music lovers. It can go that way sometimes. And no, it wasn't all arranged beforehand, even my orchestrations aren't that subversive…'

He turned to take a quick tally of the people left behind him. There were a few: brass players mainly, and the electric and the slide guitarist, and three of the burlier drummers. Enough to go on with any sort of concert? Mel was pretty sure it wasn't. But Yehune still seemed to be considering it; and he talked to pad out the moment,

'Before we go on, I'd like to just give a few personal impressions of this whole business of writing music and trying to direct it…'

For a wonder, whole sections of the audience sat down again after a few minutes. That was a tribute to Yehune's naturalness of tone, and also to what most of them there no doubt took to be a flippant treatment of his subject. Only comedy, at that stage, would have done any good; and his talk was full of wild exaggerations, burlesque anecdotes, what seemed like the extremest expressions of the most cynical possible view of the music scene. There were interruptions, certainly; a raucous cry or two from the more fun-loving, and some guttural swearwords. At one point Tub the drummer rushed the stage trying to regain control of his toppled drumset, and was walked away, shouting personal abuse. But people waited even through that. A speech was only a speech; but the programming of convention told them they should at least sit still for it.

327

Only Mel, and possibly Mairi, could have seen the difference between the speaker's intention and the way his words were being taken. Mel knew enough about him to understand that his friend was deadly serious, speaking, as much as he ever did, from the heart; the apparent jokiness was a side-effect of his usual way of forming phrases. The exaggerations to him were no exaggerations at all.

So it went on for a while, but as Yehune ran out of new ideas, began to repeat himself in other words and with more extravagant examples, changing the names of the characters on some ad hoc basis every time he mentioned them, ranting, obsessing, whether for comic effect or not, restlessness began to build up again. It was that fatal misunderstanding of tone that, from the audience's point of view, stopped him winding it all up in the way it should be wound up; with a short joke, or a reference to the ignominious failure of the evening.

Behind him, what musicians were left stared unseeingly in front of them, fidgeted and examined their mouthpieces. Yehune's views and opinions seemed to fall into a well-worn hole in their apprehension of life. At the high murky windows, rain had begun to rattle in short bursts.

'Ah, well, I've gotta say,' Yehune admitted reluctantly, 'I can't very well play a concert without any musicians... thanks, everyone, for coming, for your patience... you deserve a medal every one of you. And while I'm at it I'd like to thank some of the heroes of the recent combat, Douglas there on the tam-tam and big Steve, and all our fallen comrades, God knows where they've got to...'

The audience was stirring again, some starting to catcall and demand their money back, but most thinking of nothing but getting away before the bottleneck at the door squashed them all into a solid body. The Classical conductor, turning to leave, met Mairi's eye and mumbled a greeting, 'Miss MacFar...'mm.'

Mairi took the opportunity. She said bravely, hardly having to raise her voice to be heard,

'He really can play, you know... Classical music.'

The conductor's head was a mountain. White chalk cliffs extended through cols and archways and fissures to the overhang of the brow;

above that was a great sweep of snow carved freely by the wind. Three shuffling figures got between them, desperate to reach the end of their row, and that seemed to be the end of it.

It was only when his own current in the mass of people came close to them again that Auchterinver mumbled a second time,

'You see, Miss MacFarlane, so many people *think* they can play… *Classical* music.'

Mel was standing looking past them. On the stage, as if in accidental illustration of one or the other idea, Yehune had gravitated to the piano as the most natural place to rest, and again naturally had let his fingers begin to produce sounds on it. A slight wisp of bluish-white cigarette smoke hung in the air somewhere over his head, or over the keyboard, as his hands started a progression of very even chords, mutating, ending in a trickle of falling water, pausing, and starting again. Growing to a rush or torrent, droplets released like a perfectly radiating splash; and then four notes, descending, to a stop. It was nothing like any of the sounds that had been heard there that night, very un-Yehune; and though Mel had no idea what it was (later he found out from his friend that it was one of Beethoven's late somethings, some Bechstein or Wurlitzer and a row of letters and numbers), he was taken with it, very taken, in the aftermath of all the action and emotion. The crowd were treating it as music to file out to, and shouted and boomed above it. But Mel's own opinion was that those sounds were worth the whole five fifty they'd paid for the evening. And on it went, rising and falling, shifting in speed and mood, past the time when the field was finally clear enough for him and Mairi to file back against the current and rejoin the pianist on the stage, where they started to help the Ensemble faithfuls put some order into the devastated stands and seating. … But back there on the floor, the circumstances so perfectly illustrated what Mairi had said and (as Mel saw it) the snob's arrogant reply, that he'd watched the white hair away in its slow glide towards the door. Willing it to show a reaction.

And was rewarded, just before the conductor followed his cronies into the anteroom. Auchterinver did glance back, with a look of repudiation and weary disgust.

(… And Mel was thinking, Context, it's context again, and if he'd heard those notes somewhere in some festival or competition he might have responded; here his mind was made up even before the fingers started to trek along the rows and ridges and fire sparks into the overloaded space of here and now and stitch his old skull with familiarities and differences never to be assimilated at a go; and it's all because I know Yehune, Mairi knows Yehune, his creativity's a living thing to us, to Auchter-ochter he's just another face among too many faces and his music's another mess of cold spaghetti forced onto his plate and it's all too much and why not just sit safe in the knowledge he has and shove it all away…)

His mouth could only say,

'God, where does he get off, that bloody wanker? "Not just *anyone* can play… *Claah-sical* music."'

They were stacking chairs in heaps at the time, and picking up the litter on the stage, while Yehune thundered on through the headlong downhill rush of the final section.

Mairi was slow to answer.

'I don't know… I suppose he was just responding to what he'd heard.'

'Oh right. If you ask me, he and his loudmouth friends came here on purpose just to take the piss.'

She was trying to sort out sheaves of photocopied parts for Yehune compositions, which might or might not ever be used again. She looked at him.

'Mel…'

And the obvious occurred to him. He paused with two chairs in his hand, and a flush began at his ears and started to spread slowly out across his cheeks. Mairi had decently turned away, and Beethoven continued to speak from the nine-foot grand in tones that no-one who'd been at that concert would ever have seriously expected of it.

He didn't know how he could be so dense. Why had he not seen straight away that Auchterinver was Mairi's secret contribution, that she'd invited him there to be the influential witness of Yehune's moment of triumph? And he'd so nearly shouted 'Bollocks' straight in his face. On reflection, maybe better that he hadn't.

'Yeah, it's not a bad piano, that,' was Yehune's response when Mel told him, the next morning at the flat, how much he'd enjoyed his playing at the end. Which was of a piece with the heroic way he passed the whole incident off, skirting realities and their implications, not letting himself be drawn into discussion or any sort of direct statement just on the idle probing of whoever was talking to him. He moved – as he'd moved on the stage when he eventually rejoined the rest of them – with insouciant bravado. By his first small comments at the time, he'd managed to give the impression that he felt it hadn't gone too badly, all things considered: there'd been (so far) no mass demand for the return of the door takings, and he was well rid of Andrew and what he called the 'scum' who backed him up. Every organisation needed a clearout of its rotten elements every now and then. He'd averred that in his opinion they weren't *progressive*, only wanted to play the same tired old j'zzz-zzz. Also that Andy might find it not all smooth sailing when he started trying to pick up the old baton himself. But that was his problem – guy was out of his hair. His fingers strayed idly up to his own hair, almost too curtailed to get a grip on. And he didn't resist when Mairi gave him a quick squeeze indicating sympathy and support. ... But to Mel, there was still a look on his face, cracked, unnatural, like a patina of old egg spread and dried in the area of his eyes, only noticeable when the artificial light beamed obliquely across the brow and cheekbones and the straight nose; something that belied all the neatness of his goatee beard and designer shirt.

Neither he nor Yehune nor Mairi wasted a word on the Ensemble, which just possibly didn't exist as a body any more. But the next morning, while seeming to talk about anything but that, Yehune gave out that he was going to stand by the real spirit of the entrepreneur. He'd do it all again, this time the way it should be done. Because to him, the key was action – that things were moving and changing. Change would always go both ways. You just had to wait. And having casually announced himself, he'd sloped off to the piano and started playing stray chords and figures, for the hour and a half before Mel had to go out and meet his first pupil.

After the concert, Yehune had disappeared with Mairi, no doubt hitting a bar or two, and hadn't come in again till morning. So he must have spent the night at hers. Mel couldn't help hoping that something positive at least had come out of it all: that it might have served to bring them closer together. As for the future of Yehune's artistic aspirations, it wasn't for him to say. But he could sort of picture to himself a far smaller group of musicians, more fluid, meeting now and then to play one-off compositions. Something new – possibly minimalist? Minimally composed, supported, attended... but that was OK. The guy'd be still be writing, wouldn't he?

As he sat there sipping tea, the finger exercises kept riding on upwards, clashing and jangling in the higher registers, managing to bring out the more unpleasant aspects of the acoustics of the ceiling plaster.

So Mel went for his bag, said a word or two, and left. He was even lightly whistling to himself on his way down Gardner's Crescent onto Fountainbridge. Of course, at that time he hadn't been in possession of all the facts. He knew nothing about the debt-ridden Ensemble finances, didn't know that the takings from the Masons', after adjustments, hadn't even covered the cost of hiring the hall, or that Yehune had been relying completely on the stream of concerts that were bound to be booked once the group had made its name.

Derek Again

And he came in the door carrying two plastic bags and on into the scuffed rectangular landing and a bright-yellow football skipped in and ricocheted and barely missed him and bounded and rebounded from wall to wall, as down a short flight of stairs their own door shot open and Derek staggered out attached to Yehune's arms, Yehune himself following on, and there was shouting in more than one voice and he looked back at the three kids one in a football stripe chattering and trying to elbow their way past. 'Muster, gi's th' ba', wu ye?' 'Aw, Muster.' '*Eh!* C'mon Archie, we'r goin' tae...' And he was seeing Yehune there down the stairs and only hearing scraps of the shouted exchange as yells entwined cascaded until the time when Derek looked up, and seeing him seemed to deflate, feeling someone's eyes on him, stumbled up towards him weaving a bit as he shouted back, and knocked it aside with a foot, bigger than head size, all but run to a stop, and it bounced and landed neatly in Yehune's two hands.

Who dropped it straight away.

'Aw, *Muster,* w'ye...'

'No more you go! Now remember!' shouted Derek, and something probably in Slovak, '*To je...* (whatsit).' And he thought, Interesting, not like Russian. Still have a copula. The man pushed past him, spreading a taint of whisky, and past at least one smaller body, which gave out a squeal and viciously jabbed back. 'Uh!' And Derek had left the building.

Yehune was sagging down against the door. 'So what's all this?' Mel asked him curiously. Just as one of his bags was knocked out of his hand by the boldest of the three street footballers, who ducked in between them for the yellow. Damn and shit. Anything breakable in there?... Good training for them: artful dodgers. Yehune looked up.

And so from the few words he'd heard flying there at the end, and from Yehune's bare words of explanation, he was able to piece together what must have happened.

Now, the outer door was on a buzzer. Derek wasn't the man to be held up by such a small obstacle. Whether or not he pressed their button, whether or not he tried every other button in the plastic-mounted column in the hope that someone would get impatient and buzz him in, would never be known; only as it happened the girl Elsa (whose flat was on the third floor up the stairs) was going out at just that time, weighed down by three plastic bags full of something-or-other and an umbrella. Derek would have stood aside, in his courtly but somehow intrusive way offered to help – she would have looked at him, eyes not confiding under the brown hair, slightly shaken her head, and by natural courtesy let his shoe take the strain of the open door as her shoulder let it go.

Once in, Derek would have stridden with a no-nonsense air across the grimy bay of the stairs towards the short downward flight on the far left. Maybe he heard muffled notes from a piano. If so, they were nothing coherent. There were no scales and exercises here, no practising loops, not even that fumbling after an elusive blush or colour in an onward run of intervals that you might expect from a composer. Three skips, and he was down at the door, and thumping powerfully in a way that back in his home country was known to get results.

And what was Yehune doing? Just at that moment, sitting on the piano stool, which was lopsided and had to be propped up with music books under three of its legs. Existing there as he had been all day with nothing much to do, he'd allowed the soft sounds his fingers had made on the keyboard to lull him into a sort of semi-conscious daze, an appreciation, you could say, of the state of being Yehune, or of the accidental hatches and figures of his life in the moment of his living it. His mind rode on splinters of glasslike colour-fall; and the booming energetic depths of musical timbres barely decayed in memory; along with some far more prosaic scraps of thought about broken lightbulbs, what they were having for dinner that night, and the genital equipment of girls. Maybe because it was sound that had plunged him into it, the sound of that determined battery at the door was more than enough to shatter his mood, almost to startle him awake. But not to make him move especially quickly.

He cursed mildly, and stood up. He stepped to the centre of the room, choosing where to put his feet. He stretched. Renewed pounding. '*Eaaaaauuuu-uuugh.* Mmm-hmm.'

He looked around him once, even as the voice of the door became frantic, belligerent, unignorable; and after a while decided on a trip in its direction.

He stepped over the telephone, turned the key and opened the door. He looked up into the face of Derek. There was usually something out-of-true about the way Derek held himself; now he was hanging there looking downwards like something on a gibbet.

'Derek,' Yehune said.

The other said nothing, only glared at him.

'Surprise to see you here,' said Yehune. No answer. But the Slovakian business high-flyer gave the impression of not being all that contented with the world.

'I don't suppose you'd like to come in, or...?'

Derek was still silent, but walked straight in, to find that any sort of quick movement became impossible about two yards in the door, where the tidal swamp of Yehune and Mel's possessions covered all the available floor-space. More slowly, he pushed on, treading down clothes and papers and cardboard boxes with an indifference that might have been pointed. He came to a stop beyond the breakfast bar.

'So how's things in the old Pan-European whatsit?' Yehune asked politely. He'd already realised this must be more than a social call, which suddenly gave the boring old amenities a new potential for humour. Partly for his own enjoyment, but also to resist the emotional pall Derek was trying to cast, Yehune went through them one by one. He'd invited him in; now he offered him a cup of tea, and suggested he take a seat – 'there's probably some over there by the table.' He even brushed by him to go through the gap of the breakfast bar and begin to put the kettle on.

He was well aware of the sort of person Derek was; dynamic,

confident, thrusting a straight track forward through the world. Probably a formidable opponent in any sort of hostilities. And so he might have been bracing himself, though what that would imply in the case of Yehune was doubtful; nothing that would have been visible on the surface. In any case, it was probably enough to wake up the counter-resources in him – his spirit of mischief – a ready lack of scruple in using anything and everything that came to hand.

Having set the kettle going, he came round the end again, for all the world as if he expected to find his guest perched on top of one of the heaps of random possessions that made every one of their chairs unusable.

And here, before Derek speaks his first words, we have to stop. Before the account of any battle great or small, it's important to give the readers a general picture of the terrain. Mel and Yehune's one-roomed or 'studio' flat was more a subterranean dugout than a room, half below and half above ground level; which made the high half-windows seem scanty, dark and slitlike. It was a small space bounded by scarred and battered walls, which instead of being repaired had been plastered over in a wholesale way with blue-and-white wallpaper. The unfashionable breakfast bar walled off a basic bench and sink. Once upon a time, there had been a bathroom; but in the interests of making this seem a place a person might conceivably live in, or, more to the point, pay rent for, the separating wall had been knocked down and a new miniature shower-toilet installed in what had been the flat's only cupboard. So there was a badly-matched extra rectangle gaping out to the right, with a full-sized mirror added. That was to give a sense of space, which was something the room certainly needed. Unfortunately, though, most of the liberated area was taken up by boxes of soap, toilet paper, flannels and toothbrushes and everything else you might expect to be in a bathroom, since the cupboard was only big enough for one moderate-sized person.

Yehune's piano and a tangle of musical gear stood against the innermost wall; on the left-hand side was the big makeshift wardrobe. In the middle of the room, a sea of temporarily-placed junk washed in very slow motion. Clothes were heaped or draped everywhere, forever changing position as they were picked up and flung down again on top of household necessities, curiosities, and relics of old enthusiasms, all of which competed for space by an obscure law of precedence only an inanimate object would have understood. Yehune's stereo was in there somewhere, and a variety of radios, shavers and lamps, wired up by a complex mess of flexes dividing and intersecting. There were thermoses, parts of dismantled bicycles, an electric heater, books, boxes and papers, and an ironing board floating casually on top of cardboard boxes of irregular heights. A curved surface of the vacuum-cleaner (or 'hoover', as they'd been taught to call it) peeked out from among the bathroom things, grey with a layer of dust.

Of course, since this was a studio flat with two people living in it, beds had to be put down from time to time in or on top of the general mulch. The regular clearing of spaces for Mel's thin mattress and Yehune's wall-bed (which was just inside the door) only tended to mix the different grades of objects all the more hopelessly together – so that whatever impulse either of them might have had to get some order into the chaos was killed before it was born.

Derek broke silence,

'You are aware why I have come.'

It was Yehune's turn then. He said nothing, but looked a question.

'No? But you are aware I know Mairi.'

'Hm? Who's that then?'

'Ah. I can see we are to play some games. Then I shall spell it out. You – have been having relationships, liaisons, affairs, with other women than Mairi.'

Yehune was on his way to the piano stool, which was his preferred place to perch. 'You interest me strangely,' he remarked.

'Strange, perhaps, but the interest is plain to see,' snapped Derek, having, possibly, not completely understood. But he was quick to get back to his point,

'I am here to tell you that Mairi is a person and not to be played with.'

Yehune smiled distantly at some thought. '... Played with. Quite right.'

'So you acknowledge it?'

Now Yehune was sitting on the stool, with his head on a slant.

337

'Acknowledge what? So far I've heard all about a little game you've made up in your head involving this imaginary character who fucks other broads. It all seems to be going pretty much to your satisfaction. So now, if you *don't* want a cup of tea, I'll be having one anyway.' He got up and wove his way back in the direction of the bar.

Derek blocked his way, deliberately powering down his feet to crush any sensitive items that might be between them and the floor. He said more heatedly,

'You will not slip out of it. Your behaviour is not so... successfully secretive. You cannot deny this.'

'Oh, bollocks. You know Derek, I kind of think in the traditional scenario you're supposed to bring in this weeping and very-pregnant female to back you up. Or whatever – a list of names. Signed statements. Something.'

'You are getting me very angry.'

'Tough. Why don't you turn around again and walk out that door, since you've obviously gone off half-cocked. Then just maybe we'll have forgotten all about it by the next time we meet.'

The Slovak stomped down viciously, aiming for a plastic radio, which managed to trickle lightly out of reach of his foot.

'No! You are more slippery than I thought,' he said. 'I can see talk is useless. Only a thrashing can teach you anything.'

'Out with the knout, eh?'

'I will show you how you have to treat a lady!'

'... Come on then, you puffed-up wanker.'

Derek lunged forward. Yehune sidestepped, referring without knowing it to a kind of mental map, kept constantly updated, of where everything was in relation to everything else. All this would have been nothing more than a bit of manoeuvring, a feeling out of each other's defences, if what had looked like a bulky heap of clothes just beyond Yehune's right leg hadn't in fact been a cover of jackets and tracksuit tops over a stack of heavy bicycle gears. Derek's shin struck it hard, and he sprawled onwards. The ironing board, delicately balanced on its boxes like a kind of oversized ouija-board, and possibly just as receptive to psychic zephyrs, slid the inch or so forward that made it impossible that Derek's chin should miss it. After that impact, he careered on, knocking against one strut of the wardrobe. Now, from the instant Derek had forged so carelessly into the room, a hostile spirit must have risen up against him in the complex hive-mind of its true inhabitants, the things and objects, silent representatives of the great Inanimate. The wardrobe, though generally peaceful, faithful (though badly balanced) to its calling of storing a top-heavy bulk of clothes and camping equipment, saw its duty at this point, ponderously toppled forward, and caught Derek a glancing blow on the left side of his neck. Its uppermost edge just missed cudgelling the piano, and did knock the piano stool sideways and ringingly topple Yehune's lamp. Which luckily had a broken bulb already.

'Oh shit,' said Yehune, when the noise had stopped and everything settled into a new equilibrium. 'Hey man, are you OK? ... We'll get you sat down.'

'No! Off!' Derek shouted as Yehune tried to get near. Yehune ignored his vehemence, taking it to be a side-effect of pain and surprise. He did manage to pull several objects off the sprawled body, bring it somehow to its feet, and act as a human crutch to get it over to the table. And Derek let it happen, though under protest.

'I do not sit down in this house,' he said, impressively but incorrectly, as Yehune swept a heavy pile of TEFL periodicals off the nearest chair and bent the Slovak in such a way as to seat him on it.

While all this went on, the kettle had added a noise like a muffled drum-roll to the general sound effects, blown to a climax, and subsided again. After Yehune had tried and failed for nearly a minute to get a look at Derek's neck, he remembered it, and started to pick his way back behind the bar. But once there, he had a better thought. He kept going, and hooked a litre bottle of Famous Grouse down from a cupboard.

He poured some into two big water glasses, and came back to the table.

'Whisky. Drink,' he said.

Which Derek did. Yehune had to heave piles of clutter from place to place to make room for the bottle and himself.

'No really, how's your neck?' he asked him. 'That looked nasty.'

Derek had fallen back on silence. He applied himself to his whisky. Further approaches by Yehune – telling him he was actually lucky, he hated to think what would have happened if the whole thing had landed on him – wondering whether he oughtn't to look in at a hospital just to get it checked – were given the same treatment. And yet he was still sitting there. Why, Yehune wondered? In shock? A secret alcoholic, for whom a glass of Grouse outweighed any moral consideration? ... For himself, he was already feeling happier. To his mind, Derek had seriously failed to live up to his persona, the supposed formidability of the man who knew how to get things done. If he'd been just a tiny bit more interested in human motives and interaction, he might have asked the question why he was here at all – what, in fact, Derek's interest in all this was in the first place.

As it was, time passed. He refilled the man's glass, and his own, once and then again. A sense of borderless space, duration without limit, had been oppressing him; and now suddenly here was someone to talk to, neutralised as an opponent by having accepted bread and salt, or in this case, forty-percent malt and grain liquor. Those detachable splinters of his personality that had circled and circled him in the time of endless twilight, the age before Derek had knocked, had long ago begun to form themselves into words, into thoughts pulled randomly out of the air... some relevant to the subject at hand, others not very....

'Things, y'know, are hard to *judge*,' he said, 'if you don't know the *details*. Details, everything happens in the details.' (A pause to drink.) 'Notes. Which notes? It's all very well to say, "I'm going to do this amazing thing." But you've got – pieces of paper, you've got a room without too much fucking light, yourself, and of course the old out-of-tune banger – pianos're always out of tune. Lot of people don't know that. 'S impossible for them to *be* in tune...'

As he talked on about pianos and their difficulties, Derek supplying not even a grunt in response, he was feeling more and more at his ease. The massive slugs of Grouse he was dispensing had already brought the bottle to the halfway mark, where it had started out nearly full. Each note on the piano, as Derek probably knew, had three strings to it – most of them, anyhow – all supposedly tuned to the same pitch. But because of various kinks and imperfections a lot of them ended up wavering a bit, and so the tuner was forced to tune all three to slightly *different* pitches, to set up beats to cancel out the beats, if Derek saw what he meant. And not only that. The length of a string could actually be *right* or *wrong* for a given fundamental pitch. Now, the bass strings in an upright were too short, it went without saying, and so the upper overtones were way out of tune with the fundamental. Which meant they clashed with the corresponding note higher up on the piano, so the tuner had to tune that note a little bit *wrong* to stop the whole thing sounding totally horrendous to a human ear – which was a very different thing, he reminded Derek, from some precision vibration-counter. He'd seen a table in an article. (A slurp of Grouse; a bout of coughing). *Scientific American*, he thought it was. (A more cautious slurp.) This Model A Steinway that had been tuned by, like, the best tuner in the world, had been measured on some computerised setup they had and the results put on a, whatsit, a graph – and he just wouldn't *believe* how the whole thing flattened out in the upper.... And so on.

The pitches of the walls, as well, were altered. Colours of things either mumbled down in the background, or, more often, leapt out to slap you violently in the eye, as if to prove to you that you'd never seen them properly in your life. The flat seemed so homey, despite the minor devastation at the wardrobe-and-piano end, now that the resonances of another human body had been brought in to inhabit, yes, to bless it. Yehune was feeling friendly, almost loving, towards this fellow human occupying the other chair. He leaned over and sloshed another tenth into his glass out of sincere consideration. Now that Derek (by the evidence of his silence and his acceptance of whisky) had completely given up hostilities, Yehune was left with a nagging feeling that he owed him something. Even the least hint that he was bringing up the subject formerly under discussion would, of course, have been disastrous. But he felt sure that the man *could* understand. It would all have to be kept very, very general. But that was a height which Yehune felt, sitting there inspired at the foldable table, that he might even be able to attain to:

'You're inside there,' he started out, 'in among the wires and

341

hammers, darknesses, wood blocks shifting forwards and back, colossal *whack* of the percussion, sort of thing, doing shit knows what to you, you don't even know yourself. And suddenly – ah, something happens. A little glint of light, like, I don't know, the lid seems to open a micrometre. What do most guys do? It's not as if it involves any actual decision. … And afterwards – I mean, given that such a thing might ever actually occur – the situation'll be the same, you're still in there with all the exact same stresses, all those little bits of darkness everywhere. Although to the guy standing off and looking at the fake walnut side panels' (here he nodded towards Derek), 'it's easy to imagine that something in there's mysteriously *changed*. I mean, when you think about it…'

Although speaking in generalities wasn't Yehune's forte, he might have thought he was safe enough at that moment. The man on the other end would have had to be far more alert than Derek, who was slumped down on the table and only rousing himself now and then to take a swallow, to gather any sort of admission from what he was saying. More than that, he would have to be actually listening. And it was true that Derek didn't immediately rise up from the table and point a finger of denunciation. As Yehune went on in ever more Baroque analogies, hopefully beyond the ability of the canniest corporate whizzkid to take even a general sense from them, the Slovak's head did straighten up, allowing deep-set eyes to fix themselves on the browner ones under the woolly pate of hair, just above the nose that no-one had ever been able to see as Jewish. Derek adjusted his weight and sat up a bit, as if he were casting around for a more comfortable position. For possibly twenty minutes, half an hour – time had become uncertain, ticking in slow phrases, bound up with the speed of beats of the vibrations in the buzzing, gold-tinged air – he hadn't said a word.

Now he levered himself right up to a standing position. Yehune paused.

'Ha! Now I giff – give you what you deserve.'

'Careful, you'll knock your…'

But Derek didn't care about the glass, which in any case held only a shallow amber lens; and by a sort of irony it was Yehune's that went flying as the Slovak's big hands caught him sidelong around the neck and shoulders. The intention was obviously to pull him up by force. But the concept of 'up', in their new and resonating world, had become uncertain. It may or may not have been that the whole flat was swaying on a pivot like one of those trick rooms made for early movies; in any case it felt as if the laws of nature had strangely slipped. Yehune, complete with chair, came more out than up, his weight at the last moment falling against Derek's right midriff in such a way that they were both in danger of going over. But luckily, it seemed that life had been woken in things not usually alive... as if all the timbres and vibrations in their Grouse-washed sinuses really amounted to the hum of warm machinery in airline bags, digital alarm clocks, and abandoned clothing all around the room. The chair clattered out of the way, and the table actually managed to nudge one corner in under Yehune's sprawled elbow, giving him some support at the last moment. Derek, as well, was being attended to, but in a way that wasn't quite so benevolent. He was wrapped with the python of a white spiral extension cord, pulled back up to his feet by a pair of skeletal grilles: a music stand on one hand, an indoor clothes-hanging rack on the other. The turmoil of noise came partly from their own inner ears, partly from the kettle, which had impossibly begun again to chuckle and sing over behind the bench, and more than anything from the body of cups, folders, notebooks, displaced and neglected objects of all kinds, which were now finding their secret voices, having waited so long for a chance to express themselves. Quite a lot of them were flying, sent precariously up into the air to occupy the gaps in the room's three dimensions – or was it four by now, or five? Not only that, but Yehune felt that just for the moment he was flying too; his feet had left the floor, the table had refolded itself behind him into some sort of ingenious exoskeleton. Lampreys, snakes, were more the lot of Derek; the diabolical element was embodied mainly in long and bendable things: in covers and tapes and strings, a lost sheet hoaching with dust-mummies, and most of all the electric wiring, squirming and tangling in air that prickled with a smell of burning. Though he struggled and punched out, Derek couldn't move very far in any direction chosen by himself. The colours around them were vibrant greens and reds and deep yellows, eternal and unfading, like the memory of certain iridescent toys from childhood; that is, unless Yehune's senses were so altered that he was synthesising the colours out of shadow. Derek still hadn't given up, caught up and soaring, head strained back. 'No more you go to Mairi's! No more!' he bawled in a self-immolating ecstasy, or it could just as well have been agony. He was plainly visible, moving slowly, his shoes two and a half feet above the floor, and he rotated as Yehune watched him to a bent-back position where his shoulders were within reach. At the same time, Yehune's own angelic – or you might say more robotic – supports had delivered him to the perfect place from which he could apply the two-armed necklock, something he remembered well from his years at school.

The kettle, climaxing again, repeated and repeated, in a looped regurgitation something like a slow-motion cackle. Yehune couldn't remember the flat ever being so lurid, or so alive.

He took a few moments to steady himself, and said to the side of Derek's neck-locked head,

'Now hold on. … Y'come into my place, drink m' wh'sky, I'm tryin' to tell you how it is. An' this is how you – you know.' He thought about it a bit. 'I think it's time for you to…'

Derek didn't want to cooperate. He nearly managed to squirm out of the hold. But neither he nor anyone could have resisted the sudden compulsive rush of every current in the room towards the door. Such an imperative had arisen that the atmosphere itself drew books and papers and pens and a stray electric heater like elongated streaks towards and past the end of the bench, and Yehune felt not so much a rushing wind, or a corridor of sound and light, as an effect of riding easily along in colours, drawn out impossibly fine, like a speed-mark in a cartoon. Derek's voice was now deep, now squeaky, as he shouted and protested. Insults in English lost themselves in nests of Central European syllables: 'Nie! Nerob, ty sviňa! Bastard! Nechaj ma tak!' Though Yehune didn't have to wrestle him in the right direction, just keep a general grip around his neck and shoulders, he did find it nearly impossible to get the door open at the same time. In one moment, he glimpsed the mirror on the right-hand wall, and saw that it reflected nonsense, distortions, or a version of reality so close up or far away that it had nothing to do with the shapes he would have expected to see. In another, he was gazing at the red welt on Derek's rear-left neck between his own fingers, strained pink and white. Then the door was open, and they were pouring out of it, into other light, a new vaulted universe of sound and colour, the common staircase rising above, someone looking over from the landing, and the dry-skipping noise of a ball that dashed from wall to wall,

and the boy in the football stripe brushed past Mel's leg and nearly trampled the fallen bag as he dived out again, shouting, '*Yeaaaaah!* Tek a pass!', and down at the door Yehune said a word or two more as he stood aside and Mel caught his first angle past the door-jamb on the wholesale wreck inside, where by the look of it everything had been flung around and broken except the piano and the fucking mirror (and how had *that* escaped?), and he turned to his friend and asked him another question, but by that time the man was slumped back and drawing breath and complaining that that thieving bugger had drunk up all their Grouse and Mel'd have to go out again and get to an off-licence and buy some more if he wanted to get where *he* was. And Mel was already beginning to form some idea of the sequence of events, by some distant alchemy based on Yehune's slurred words and the state of each uprooted and destroyed item in the flat, leaving him not exactly enlightened, but enmythed, as he pulled in the two shopping bags and started to do what he could to straighten the odd thing out. Thinking all the time that the mess underneath it all was beginning to be unstraightenable.

At that point, Yehune seemed to have dried up, just sitting there bonelessly on the one upright chair and smoking as Mel pottered around him. That might have been because his usual process of telling and retelling any recent incident until it was word-swollen, heroicised, changed out of recognition, wouldn't have worked here, bringing in as it would certain subjects and causes that were all too close to home. Mel did notice some extra frustration in every movement of his stocky body, almost as if all this were no more than a symptom of something larger, some demon of the ineffectual that was beginning to make itself felt at every level of his life. An encounter that hadn't been resolved; that couldn't possibly ever have been resolved. … And so it was left to Mel to bully together the version given here, and to draw what further conclusions there were to be drawn about Derek, Derek's interest in the subject, and what, taking one thing with another, Derek was likely to do next.

It wasn't until later that they found out one possible result. As it turned out, it wasn't Yehune, but Derek who gave up all his visits to Mairi's father's flat in Spottiswoode Street. Some matter or other, business or personal, made the Slovak resource manager leave Edinburgh not long afterwards; and if any of them saw him again, it was long after the period this story is concerned with.

A Long Long Way

Waking, for the second time that morning waking up out of confused dreams, he seemed to see a tiny spool of film running out in front of him on which everything in his life was written in miniature, and he ran after it, catching sight of places and faces and events bent round and strangely foreshortened, until it grew and expanded and he was drawn in with it, waving to all the people around: Mairi, and Alice, and Pom. That was how it came back to him. Edinburgh, he remembered. The wash of the darkened streets, the seethed-potato smell of the breweries. And himself, Mel Seuchar. In his late twenties now... full-length and unestablished. His real eyes were seeing the shaded edge of a sheet and the table leg disappearing upwards. But back there, just for a moment, it had been as if he could have chosen this or something else; he'd felt himself floating detached and all-powerful at the centre not only of every rung of time, but of all the countless possible selves.

Where's Y'une? ... Oh, right. Gone.

He rolled across something angular under his back, slightly tipped backwards, and balanced his body up. Already he was trying to work out his pupil times, checking that he didn't have any that morning. Gerhard, or Briet? No. Just as well, 'cause he'd have missed them. As he wadded his sheet and duvet up under one arm and picked the old mattress up off the floor, he felt the flat around him like a second limit to his head, set at a slight remove. Fragile, like an eggshell. He picked his way over to the corner to stow his bedding behind an upright clothes rack. And as he did, he had the fleeting and irrational impression that just beyond that wall was the most spacious of countries, hovering out of sight – the uneven bit of lawn, the trees, the high wailing seabirds, of the Maeraki clifftop he'd lived on all his life.

But there was no cliff here. Just the street bay of Gardner's Crescent.

It was ten days since Yehune had taken off, leaving no note. Neither he nor Mairi had any clue as to where the guy had gone, when or even whether he'd be back. Mel checked times with himself as he stumbled over to the cupboard-bathroom. His own birthday had been eight days ago; he'd just turned twenty-seven. Now it was – first of August?

He went into the cupboard, and a second or two later came out again. No bugging toilet paper. Looked into the cardboard box, and hooked out the last solitary roll.

Not long afterwards, he was weaving around the room picking up one article of clothing after another, and noticed the way his possessions and Yehune's were drifting. There was something like a cleared space now around the general centre of the floor, where he usually put his mattress down, and Yehune's things were beginning to be pushed up towards the piano and the wardrobe. Yehune: Yehune's stuff. Giving way to Mel's. Change, and still more change. Without his friend to consider, it was almost as if some tenuous connection of invisibilities that held him down to the ground, to this dingy flat, had been lost.

He saw his bills and accounts and statements, an untidy fan of papers, lying out of their plastic bag in a cleared space on the table. July-August; tax time.

The faint *brrrrr* of an entry phone in some other flat seemed to jog his memory. Statement for February? Should've got here. He'd lost the original, and ordered another one from the bank at a cost of £5.

He went over to the edge of the breakfast bar, already able to see it, or some white oblong shape, on the cracked darkness of the floorboards just under the letter-slot.

Amazing. Incredible. It's *it*. And another letter under it, a real one, girl's hand, who…?

He knew who it was from, and even the basic contents, before tearing off a corner and inserting his forefinger to break the upper edge. *Leanne's* handwriting was so much her own that it was as if he were looking into her face: looping o's and a fat low t, and an a that looked like print. He was seeing her face, the tiny bulge at her lower cheeks, as she told him all about it in her conventional phrases, with 'dears' and 'darlings', as if she were just gossiping to fill the time. In fact, none of it came as a surprise to Mel. He'd heard about it already, from that jovial-cheeked guy in the Language School, Doug, or was it Duncan? She was planning to get married, it seemed, to someone he'd never met. Someone who ran his own business. Good going – so that was it. He knew now that the news hadn't been real to him, never completely registered, until the fluent and chatty phrases from her own pen sealed it somehow into the space behind his eyes.

Leanne: he saw her moving, turning once, with the single lift of her hair like the side of a piece of paper. Sunshine; people standing there.

So it had been nothing after all – just a kind of comfortable flirting.

He planed the letter sideways towards the table, but it flipped in the air and dropped onto a heap of bags and dusty newspaper clippings. For some reason, the quality of light inside the flat had changed, migrated a bit lower in the spectrum. It wasn't so much that he'd lost that person. But ties were being snatched away from him, leaving him momentarily without a base.

He looked around him again. What was it that was holding him here…?

If he was levitating for a moment, logic came in to remind him, to nail his feet down to the floor. Naturally, Yehune would turn up again sooner or later. And there was still Mairi – Mairi was left. She was the only one he could talk to. As he worked through it all, took himself back over the same questions and answers, he was automatically collecting things together and packing them down in his bag.

Tax papers – *gaaachk*. The Teal bag: corners of diary notebooks; a fire-lighter. Get something to eat? Na….

It was almost as if he hadn't noticed one thing falling away in him; the decaying of a single strut, an imperative that had ruled him ever since he'd come to that city. That was the idea of supporting Yehune while he tried to be an artist. If the guy could take off, just like that, without a word…. The sense of his obligation was possibly no less, but slowly and surely it was sinking back into the past. People would take their own paths. He would; Yehune would. None of this came very near the front of his mind. But there were impulses that had already begun to stir further towards the back.

As he swung his bag onto his back, checked for his keys, and took a look at his watch, his eyes were unusually open. The flat behind him seemed more densely populated than before. Yehune's departure hadn't subtracted a figure, it seemed, but added new ones out of the reservoir of his own mind, drawing in heads and bodies from all sides. The key crunched in the lock, and he could see them everywhere: heads, formed up around him, moving alongside him, diverting, absorbing, insubstantial – people from his dreams, people from his imagination, from real life, from Auckland and Maeraki, and from the great repository of living memory he carried with him back to his earliest childhood.

'What did she say about him in her letter?'

'Leanne? – oh, nothing much. She didn't describe the guy or anything.'

'She didn't?'

'It was like she was pretending I knew him. Maybe she thought I did.'

Mairi looked over. 'But she must have said *something*.'

'Oh yeah.' He gave a small laugh. 'She wrote very warmly about him.'

The habits of his old life had barely had time to fade away before new ones sprang up to take their place. He was in the back seat of Pom's flash BMW, with Mairi on the opposite side. This was only his third outing to Longniddry, to Pom and Alice's rented haven and the beach; but it was already starting to feel to him like something he couldn't have done without. Each time, it let a slanting ray of light into his life, as if a corridor had been broken open on the sky.

It occurred to him that to anyone reading this story as a narrative, everything would have changed. No Yehune – and Pom and Alice, who're they? Two small, ragged pictures came into being, over a background of yellow-white sand worn flat by the wind. Pom: massive and scruffy-haired in a loose-weave jersey. His wife Alice, who was far more colourfully New Age, with three painted stars on her forehead. And depths of background opening inwards – Alice, swaying lightly as she walked, offering him a drink in a diminutive voice, but smiling at the corners of her eyes as if it was all a bit of a joke to her. Or another time, Pom sitting off with Yehune, answering a question about how he'd first come across Mairi,

'Derek,' he'd said in his rustic English accent. 'Derek was the one who got to me first. Hunted my head.' He framed his large head comically between two hands.

'Oh, right. From Derek, to Mairi's dad, to Mairi.'

'That's it.'

'But what did he want from you?'

'Oh, I held the import licence for a particular item they thought they needed for their corporation. So Derek tried to employ me. Of course, I wasn't having any of that.'

'What happened?'

'They had to buy it from me – quite lucrative, that turned out to be.' He had a humorous, majestic set of the face when it wasn't in repose; he let it move towards the light of the open window, emphasising lines scored deeply from around his eyes down nearly to the jawbone.

Now, from the seat behind, Mel was presented with the back of Pom's grey-brown hair, half-hidden by the driver's headrest. In the passenger seat he could see Robbie, an older friend of Pom's who was sharing their lift home – or it might be better to say they were sharing his.

'At least she didn't invite me to the fucking wedding,' he growled over to Mairi.

'Which would have made you the old family friend?'

'You got it.'

The two of them were separated by an empty seat; Mairi was at the left-hand window. The colours outside were still strong as they drove along the coastal road through Prestonpans and Musselburgh, slowing to a crawl in the towns, where they watched children in queues for ice-cream, women leading small parties while pushing prams ahead of them. Every few yards they had to stop, either for a snarl-up of cars or a crossing or a traffic light.

Thank God for Mairi, Mel was thinking. Her presence there did a lot to counteract the edgy feeling he was getting these days from lifts and car-rides of any kind.

At just that moment, they were stopped again. He waited and stared up at a red circle. Waited, and thought; and instead of getting impatient (though it was there, that shading of sharp intolerance, pushed back and balanced out of sight), he let himself dive back into the time when they were on the beach, playing over colours and impressions in his head....

...

Mairi had stopped. She'd thrown down her towel. She proceeded to peel the smooth fawn jeans she wore down her even smoother legs. Her bikini was dark, nearly black, underneath, in a style which was modest enough for the time; but Mel had to look away, let his eyes fall into the pale-blue wash of the sky ahead of them. Gaps of cloud up there. … Of course, Alice had stripped to her swimsuit as well, and it had done nothing for him. Good thing too. The lady's hair was a shade of darkened blonde, usually tied in interesting knots, though now it streamed free.

Alice stepped away, tracking right to avoid the meandering of the beach creek that came out under the road. 'Wait just a second,' Mairi said, but too softly. The wind made sudden rushes, tearing at the bays of their ears. 'Aren't you *freezing*?' she called out louder.

But Alice had walked down the coarse sand and through some small breakers, and in a matter-of-fact movement crouched down into the sea.

Mairi followed, leaving the towels. In two dark bands, her limbs dancing. She gave a few high whoops when she reached the water. Mel was looking out across it, not where the girls were but further over, at a container-ship moving slowly along the Firth of Forth, and the hugeness of the sky and open air.

He walked straight off into the wind. He wasn't intending to go for a swim (though calls sounded after him, pretend-sweet: 'Come on in Mel, it's *beautiful*. It's warm as toast.') Past standing plants he half-recognised, hadn't had the time to look up. Tiny, tiny dandelion-like things, and a white buttercup on a spiked stem with an opposed leaf pattern… what could that be? Dog-rose and blackberry were overgrowing the creek bed. To his left, the speeding cars seemed to form a translucent force-field in front of the golf course.

Over on his side of the road, a pensioner carrying a golf-club stood looking uncertainly out to sea. On towards the Give Way sign. That wasn't oleaster…?

Beyond a labyrinthine bush of thorns standing in scrub grass was a seawall, something that couldn't fail to remind him of Maeraki, Thompsons Beach and all the other Auckland beaches he knew so well. Each time he'd come here he'd visited it. Then he supposed it was the beach he came for, more than the smoke-filled interior of the guest house where Pom's friends sat and played their music. At the moment, the wind was strong and buffeting. It had been calmer last time. Then why was he...?

When you took a closer look, it wasn't all that similar. But... a beach was a beach. In this hemisphere, all the plants and bushes seemed beaten down, sky bleached out by gales, and every tree was bent away from the prevailing wind. It was as if the waves themselves were subdued by it, not caught up to the epic breaker-past-breaker of some of the beaches he remembered. Back home, he meant. Muriwai; Rapahoe. For some days or weeks, evocations had been coming back to him out of what seemed a former life, vistas opening up to him in the bay of a street, and the personalities of people he'd known in New Zealand appearing suddenly in front of him, shifting and exchanging traits. This beach view with its grainy rocks and huge white-out of sky was nothing but a catalyst, it seemed, for forces which were already pushing their way to the surface. He could see stories... oh yeah. Stories and situations, working themselves out again in memory, under the barest of membranes: this beach and the present.

The wind – God, it was absolutely shrieking at him when he stood at this angle, at the edge of the bank. No more protected than one of those signposts. He tried turning his head into it, and saw Alice and Mairi like bobbing nests of limbs, further away in the water than he'd have expected.

Should he take his shoes off, do a run along the sand? – No. He imagined broken bottles; shrapnel-twists of metal sticking up.

Instead, he turned the other way, and walked up and down tracks through the tussock grass. He had flashes of memory of the Torrance kids; of a time of sand fortresses and fighting up and down Thompsons Beach. With the splintered remains of wharves. Was that Mandy with them? God, they must've been crazy. Strangely enough (he'd noticed), it wasn't even the full events that played themselves through in his head. It was as if the details all existed there, under some cowl or sequestered lid higher up in the hierarchies of memory. He could have replayed it moment after moment; but in the event, he didn't have to. Instead, those small clips, pictures, went flashing in his mind, each carrying all the meaning and significance of a strand of life lived. Manipulable, like beads. That was how he referred to them, experimented with them, seeing them flow and part in patterns, as if the wind itself were pushing them here and there.

And, he thought expansively, it was the same with everything. Pom and Alice, all the ebb and flow of time that had brought him to this point. It existed… all of it existed… under the cowl.

Now seabird voices were calling; dying away. He'd hesitated, hovering over a grassless lip of the bank, and gazed out into a volume of air that looked perfectly empty….

…

Mairi turned to look at something. Wheels rolling again; the shouts of kids outside the window, '*I* wanna…'

She asked him, 'How are you feeling about it?'

'What – Leanne?' He was taken a bit off guard. 'Oh, all right. I mean, it was nothing really serious.'

He added, 'More to the point, how are *you* feeling?'

'Oh, you mean…. I'm fine.' The smooth note of the engine rose and fell. 'I'm expecting him back any day.'

For a while, neither of them said anything. Then Mel asked, 'How was the water, back there?'

'Cold. It was fun though. Alice says she goes in every day when they're up there.' She cast a glance towards Pom's head, but he was talking away to Robbie.

Mel remarked, 'She read the runes for me.'

'Did she?'

There was a note of amusement in Mairi's voice. It was so typically Alice, to read the runes. The couple both had a New Age hippie streak that didn't seem to have been affected by Pom's business success.

'… How did it come out?' Mairi asked.

He made sure his voice was low enough. 'Oh, just… some total bullshit that confirms what I've always thought about it.'

She looked across the car seat at him.

'Well – ' he began, 'it comes up with something she called "Fehu", which means "wealth".'

'Uh-huh?'

'Wealth. I mean, come on. Isn't that the hilariousest thing out? I mean, even my tax bill comes to about nothing. Why bother, they must be thinking.' He laughed.

Mairi didn't see it. 'But isn't it supposed to mean something else? Richness. I don't know – something about character?'

'Oh.'

The car had been slowing; now it came smoothly to a halt in a pretty, absolutely standard residential district. The houses neatly stuccoed, always joined at some point or another to the next, like Siamese twins, as if it wasn't possible for humans to live too far from one another. Robbie, thin and white-haired, slipped out the door,

'An' so 'e says to me... eh, like 'e's standin' jus' there...'

'Richness', Mel thought. He hadn't seen it that way. Then it should have been drawn for Mairi, he told himself fiercely – which meant that it was still the most essential bullshit. Better not say that, though.

Robbie was coughing out more words. Mel tried to work out some other interpretations. *Fehu,* that must be, what, Gothic? *Fé* in Norse, genitive *fjár.* Which meant not only money to them, but their livestock. So I'm a sheep, a cow. Mo-o-o-o-uuuuhh. Which means that like any word you could come up with for anybody, you can take it in such a way that it seems to apply. Which is us, which is everyone....

At the same time, something in the clarity of the actual scene, Robbie's characteristic turns of phrase, was making him experience a sort of double vision. How would you depict this? And by the way, what was it the guy reminded him of? A busy meat-market – men standing in natty tartan suits. And something more, a taste, or a smell, coming in over the in-car smell of leather upholstery. Something acrid... blue-metal gun barrel?

'A'll be seein' yas around. Mairi an' ... mm. Pure delight, it was, t' meet y's. Pom, thanks, till the next time...'

Robbie made the sounds, and disappeared with his instrument case towards the sculpted residential door. The car motor purred on, no more than a vibration. Just then, the sides of houses looked perfectly frozen in the delicate, falling light of the evening. Single birdcalls stood out like lucid drops. Robbie turned and waved. Pom revved the motor; and just at the same moment Mairi leaned forward to say something.

How would you say this, how could you ever, Mel thought – using what rags, what twine, what upward-balanced triangle to the level of the street lights?

As he crashed in the door and swivelled his wrist to look at his watch, he saw the armchair in an upper halo of his eye: good one, new armchair. Better'n the... 3:25, a bit after. Mairi's coming at *3:30*. Got here, fuck it, now to flop. Or no, start making coffee, she always has coffee when she....

Under the simple verbal idiocies that ran through his mind, he felt elements shifting, fields. Like great block universe-segments converging into each other. The outside, the huge all-involving vault under the sky, that he'd just been in; and now the inside, shaded with lines. He made his way in behind the breakfast bar and started to fill the kettle. The back of his hand accidentally knocked against a bowl on the cluttered surface, which pushed a frying pan nearly to the brink. Phew. Lucky that didn't.... For a moment, he was reminded strangely of a rowlock of his father's old clinkerbuilt dinghy.

He reached up to a high shelf for the coffee, missed getting a grip on it, and it toppled. An instant later it was spread out around his feet. *Shit,* I've spilled....

A rich, dark aroma expanded across the spaces of the flat. He thought: Mairi'll love that.

He started looking around for a cloth to wipe it up. All the while, he could feel the orientating sweep of time behind him, like the coloured rush of a waterfall, pinning him in place on that Sunday mid-afternoon. He'd just come hurrying back from the Language School, the small stair among shopfronts on George IV Bridge, where he'd met a few ex-colleagues who had admin to do or nowhere else to go. Then he'd suddenly realised the time, and come pounding back through the uncrowded streets. Though he hadn't been expecting much, he'd felt the King's English kids were grudging with their words, as if for some reason they didn't want to be seen talking to him. Maybe because he wasn't with Leanne any more. ... So could be that was the end of all that?

With the result that he'd gone back to an old idea, while cutting the corners of streets – seeing faces frozen in the moment – a green windmill-clock in a shop window. What was keeping him here? He could just take off. The flat was a drain; and his private pupils... well, he could get pupils somewhere else. If Yehune had done it, why couldn't he? Three times, in the thirteen minutes before he reached his own door, he'd reasoned it through, sold up and moved on, each time to a different country; but each time a few sparse threads of logic pulled him back.

There was Mairi, first of all. And Yehune, of course. Was he still supposed to be waiting for him? – The guy had been gone for a month now; one day over.

He'd left the street door open for Mairi. He started thinking about what he could be doing while he waited. There was his project, which he felt as one more thread on him, another reason for staying where he was. A grid of pictures, framed inside a wicker head and shoulders. Of *text* and pictures. A massive piece of cartridge paper.

He mixed himself a cup of lime juice, and moved himself into the big square armchair that took up a section of floor side-on to the piano. 'New', he'd called it, but it was second-hand, a relic of the seventies, with a broad seat and big chunky arms that came in handy for balancing things on. Behind him, Yehune's possessions had been piled up around the piano and the wardrobe, and what lay out on the floor was mainly Mel's. He had no trouble finding and extracting his different-sized bits of paper and a fistful of pens and pencils.

Mairi? – still hadn't knocked. Well, of course. He'd been thinking 3:30 was 3:30.

He felt a mild excitement, unrolling the big piece of paper. I've *started – started*. But that was quickly damped when he looked it over. It was obvious to him how unsatisfactory it was. Everything was just barely sketched in with pencil, the banks of rectangles ragged and unsteady. Only the frame had any substance, the head and shoulders of a huge wicker man that stood outside and contained the whole thing. He'd drawn that in with a black felt pen. He told himself that it didn't matter, that this page was just for scribble and ideas taking shape. He should throw the outlines boldly together, then chuck the whole thing away and start again.

... He didn't, just then. He picked up a pencil, and started to cajole a bit of definition into some of the lines.

He'd made a decision not to use words alone. He had reservations about them, useful as they were as building blocks, as a sort of narrative sticking-plaster. Admittedly he fooled with them constantly, strung them together inside notebooks, and filled his planning sheets with words and more words. Words were strange things, he'd found. They could kill an idea stone dead. He wasn't sure that he had it in him to handle them, at least not in anything large-scale. Better to fall back on pictures, frames, collages. (Though he'd just realised, as a side-effect of his survey a moment before, that he couldn't draw.)

He turned to the right chair-arm and took a mouthful of lime juice out of his plastic cup. The swingeing, green-chemical Ships. *Ahhhh* – veesh. Ough.

The big hand stood at well past the half hour. He should have remembered Mairi wasn't exactly noted for being on time. Had to be out of there by 5:30 – hadn't he told her that?

The big piece of paper was hard to hold open; it was always wanting to spring together and roll up. His thumbs must have been relaxing – with a sudden rattle, the whole page flipped off him and onto the floor. It skittered away, coming to rest against the side of a cardboard box. Well... OK. The characters, think about them instead. He had them all sketched and partly described on a series of A4 sheets. Rattray, Toaster. Sometimes, you know, draw them as a little rat and toaster. And there was Florence, his superwoman, in fashion-perfect jeans, wearer of hats. ... After that, Jessie, a friend of Florence's. She shouldn't turn out to be *Toaster's* love-interest, as Florence was *Rattray's*. No no. That'd be too obvious.

He read through notes in his own handwriting, and squinted critically at his picture of Florence. Then looked around for his blue highlighter to put a bit of shading into some of the lines.

... Couldn't find the damn thing. Hadn't he been using it yesterday?

He moved around in his chair, wondering whether he should get the coffee over. Started without you, sort of thing. The hands of his watch were moving so slowly, it might as well have been stopped. ... Mairi, come *on*.

Anyway, he didn't need coffee. And the characters seemed to have gone mysteriously dead for him. What could he do then? Letterings? He started to toy with the idea of developing a sort of presentation handwriting; you could probably get a book about it in the library.

Thinking about books, he experienced a peculiar effect. Suddenly every book in the flat – and there were quite a few – was pointed out in radiant colours, magically desirable, whispering to him in a voice of its own about fabulous worlds he could enter just by breaking open its covers. His image of them was all bound up with the shape and heft of the word itself, 'book'. He could get a book. Or a magazine, which at that moment had become almost as beautiful. The wandering eye of his mind found comparisons in the m and the z with exotic words: *Mazarin, Mazeppa*. Look at a mg-g-i-z-z-z.... Look at one. They were all over the place in there.

Quickly as it had arisen, he forced the idea down again. Fuck it. Grab no books. No magazines either; least of all that. His project should be as *little* as possible like a bloody magazine. It had to be stark – grainy – sharp-edged.

He got out of the armchair, and picked up a paperback lying nearby. *The Trial,* Kafka. His eyes fell on it with a sort of injured incredulity: how had it managed to be what a moment ago it was? Now, it was only yellowing page-edges and a cardboard cover. He stood still, looking out in the direction of Yehune's wardrobe.

He couldn't understand it. What could be keeping her? He knew that under the excitement, the novelty of finally working at something of his own, his deepest desire was for Mairi to turn up and rescue him from it. He could see himself from outside himself, sitting in that chair, making marks on bits of A4 paper. Which in turn couldn't fail to remind him of Yehune: his woolly head, bent over sheets of staves, making his dots and dashes. ... Or, far more often, not.

Mel was perfectly well aware of the difficulties of doing anything of the sort. But hadn't experienced them for himself quite so vividly before, in just that place; so that he seemed to see into the guy's mental processes with an eerie self-identification.

You had to hope, he supposed....

You hoped there'd come a moment, there *had* to come a moment, when under all the cultural commonplaces, all the words and shapes

absorbed out of the world of the senses, some voice would speak…
the *me*, the *this*… the raw, aesthetic – underlay –

Andale. Andale. Meksikanski, a broad-brimmed hat. Spread out
of wicker. Burn it. Turn and say hello.

Oh God, what was that? He must be tired. That was the reason
for his total lack of connection with what he should be doing. And
of course there was the waiting too. (Mairi, where've you *got* to?) He
could feel a tightening in him despite the tiredness, every sense in
him straining for what was supposed to, what didn't happen, so that
he was a centre point for cables under load. Somewhere in his skull
behind the eyeballs he was aware of a dim and foggy region, where
the bead, the cutting edge of his thought ought to be. It should be –
what? Hard, purposeful. Not that damn candy-floss. Come *on*.

For want of anything else in the room to interest him, but with a
feeling of being dragged back into prison, he flopped down into the
chair again.

Picked up his papers. Florence this time looked to him so poised
and unreflecting, so without devices (though, he admitted, not quite
in proportion), that he wondered what he'd ever wanted with a
highlighter. He began to doodle different versions of her, seen from
one angle and another. They still didn't seem to get near what he was
after. That invisible dusting, that almost oppressive sense of mystique
– in films, he thought, they tried to do it by casting actors who were
too beautiful to be real.

What was it, anyway, about that configuration, that flare at the
hips, complementary delicacy of forms above it…?

Now he was beginning to sketch in a few accessories. He had an
idea of showing Florence sometimes in completely different shapes,
but with one small thing to identify her. An earring? A skull, a horse-
head, a stylised cross. Huge or tiny, depending on the angle.

He was dotting in the shadings. If you did it with a pen and not
a machine, hell, it was practically pointillisme. Her face, now; not
totally symmetrical. Like a fruit, something you could cup in your
hands. And what was it about…? The way she could be both childlike
and unapproachable, exacting and irrational at the same time.

Just as he happened to think that, a moment from Longniddry

flashed through his mind – brown thigh-tops, the tight swimsuit material.

Mairi; that was Mairi. Oh Gord. I'll have to keep *her* away from Florence. *Lontana da Firenze.* It was an accident, of course; two completely different subjects. But here he was, stuck inside, waiting for her, and so....

It had been some time near the beginning of their acquaintance, back in Paris, that Mel had first come to the realisation that Mairi, curvy as she was, attractive as she must have been to other people, was not his type. He remembered the moment when he'd seen it: she'd been leaning over the sofa at Celestine's offering him a crêpe, was it, or some café delicacy in a plastic pot. He'd looked at her face, sculpted by the light, and decided then that no matter what happened she'd always be a friend and only a friend to him. He'd imagined the two of them forced together in an isolation tank for a period of years or centuries, and nothing ever happening between them. (As he touched on that picture, there was Yehune in it too, leaning jovially up against the tank wall.)

He went in behind the bar after all, and started pottering around with the coffee things. Coffee-making: that was something that took time. Yehune... outside there ... smoking a fag. Shapes were falling through his head: a filter holder, half a packet of bread, and the face of his Seiko watch with its Roman numerals, ticking off seconds. Surprising. Serendipitous. The stim... stim....

He'd set the kettle and was waiting for it to boil, when another memory shone out from the toppling array. It was a story Yehune had said he was writing, or was thinking of writing, Mel wasn't sure which. It had sounded interesting, in a way. And it was probably in there somewhere. If he could find it – couldn't he get something from it, some reference, which he could slip into his own project somehow? Not, of course, to steal from the guy. To honour him.

Having something concrete to do gave him a burst of energy, and almost straight away he was across the room, looking into the compacted mess around the wardrobe.

Yehune was interested in clothes, and had left a lot behind in the wardrobe they both used. Mel had decided the easiest thing was to take his own stuff out, fill the space with Yehune's possessions and some heavy music folders, and seal it all off for the day when the guy came back. Now he moved boxes and large items away from the base of the wardrobe. He dug in, scattering objects, shaving kits, a torch and an isolated screwdriver, past the small keyboard that lay with legs folded in on itself. He was surprised how little there was when you crammed it all together.

Of course, it would all come out again when Yehune came back. *If* he came back.

Ah, what's this – exercise books?

He squatted there, opening the battered covers one after another. He didn't find much writing inside, only functional scribbles, or the occasional name and phone number in someone else's hand. Lines, shapes, shadings. A few paragraphs of spiel for the Ensemble. He turned another page.

There, spread across two leaves, was a large, detailed pen drawing of an outlandish-looking structure, something which reminded Mel of the crownlike top of St Giles' Cathedral in the High Street. But it was indescribably askew, twisted back on itself, with tendrils snaking out from it in every direction, branching and multiplying and tangling one behind the other. What *was* this? There was something weird about it. Spectral, white-light tubes, snaking out through space, then looping around again and plunging back into the whole. It wasn't well-drawn; Yehune had no more control over a pen than he did.

Mel just sat there staring at it for a minute or two. Could he use something like that? Well, of course he could, as some kind of design motif. But there was something there that put him off. It was way outside any intention he might have had for his own project – or, better said, he wanted to keep it outside. He clapped the book shut.

He creaked to his feet and started to pack a few things back into boxes. He supposed it was nothing; some doodle the guy had unconsciously done while he blathered on the phone to one of his girlfriends. But suddenly, he wasn't too happy about the idea of fossicking around in Yehune's things.

Drawings in five dimensions. St Giles… with wormholes… a wrenched-back topknot.

All in all, the experience had made Mel even tireder. He went back to the armchair, fell into it with a drawn-out sigh, and looked at his watch. Why couldn't he *do* anything...?

It was nearly 4:30 now. There'd been no sign of Mairi, no message. What could she be doing? His thoughts were like an objective cloud in him, cruising wherever they liked, and he had no defence against them. He saw her face, the soft lines, the fineness of proportion, all lightly distorted with the effect of some secret malice. A contempt for other people's suffering, or even – who knew? – a joy in it. How could she do this to him? She was a torturer, no more, no less. He fitted together words, working out how he'd tell her off when she did, finally, turn up. He could just imagine it. Mairi, floating in carelessly with some story about people she knew at seven removes, along with the life-history of every one of them. What about her *real* friends? he'd rage at her. Didn't they deserve anything but casual – callous – neglect? He was saying the words out loud, persuasively, forcefully, with gestures. Hadn't he told her that he had to be out of there at *5:30*? That was for the Spanish conversation class, and he might not have needed half an hour to get there; but she didn't know that. To just not turn up... without even....

In the next instant, he was faced round on himself, watching. Some extraneous objectivity had fallen on him, how or from where he didn't know. He realised several things. He could see his disproportionate rage, the strength of his emotion... along with its cause, which was nothing but the extreme value he was putting on seeing her. Yehune peeped furtively in again; not Yehune his friend, but Yehune Mairi's... you know. Mel had stood up, and was standing in one place, turning one way and another. He found himself ticking off details of her in his mind's eye: qualities of the exact curve of one side of her neck and its relation to the chin. The spearing blaze of the eyes, behind dark makeup like crusts of old fires. Everything was magnified and intensified. If he tried to picture her as a whole, it was somehow a different image that came to him every time... streaked with bright colours, feverish, outré.

Oh, what? He laughed at the ceiling. Surely I'm not... for God's sake.

He could see it perfectly objectively. These were the opening stages of some obsession. Of course, it was only sex – how could it not be? He would never, could never have felt anything like this for a friend, an old crone, someone's mum. He *needed, needed,* to be in her presence. It would make everything new, point out every object with bales of heaven-dusting radiance… well, of course. But more than that, it would be a simple release of tension. Everything else was a straining towards it, a pulling emptiness, like hawsers strung through space. Everything that wasn't her – the uniqueness of her, the way she expressed herself, the ideas she had about opening other people's letters, the way *she* opened a letter, standing side-on, self-deprecating, slicing it with a brass knife of her father's. It was neither taste, nor colour, but a building up and peaking of vast atmospheric clouds, moving in and engulfing all his senses, focussed forever on that single personality… tripping some tragic power….

Stop. No. Stop it. He could almost laugh at himself, feeling the phenomena as they happened, since he had no intention of letting them happen. He didn't want to be dragged into the toils of Mairi's sexual mystique. Or 'fall in love'… as they called it. What could he do? Think about Leanne; think about some film star; anything. He told himself over and over that it was just sex. Though he'd already demonstrated that to his own satisfaction, it felt like anything but; it sent feelers into the deepest parts of him, evoking things he thought he'd long forgotten, stirring them together into a dizzying flux.

He'd chosen a track across the floor, and was pacing on it, from the bathroom boxes to the table and back again. The reasoning, he thought, was clear enough. This was just a side-effect of the situation he was in. Isolated, short on resources, and Mairi the only one who understood. They had a common subject, which was Yehune. It was all because of Yehune. And yet, Yehune was the reason he couldn't…. No. No. He was being hysterical. She wasn't his type….

None of these mental escape-routes had any effect on his emotion. He stopped walking, simply because it made the drying rack, the ironing board, the wardrobe structure in the corner of his eye, seem to move. There was an effect of subliminal movement – everything gathering together to pull him into the surge. His sense of desperation, of the impossibility of giving it up, giving *her* up, connected him suddenly with every time in the past when he'd been lost or helpless in some way. And the objects, sidelong shapes and colours, were catching him, drawing him along with them, building like a wave, and sweeping him... sweeping him....

If he were writing it, he'd have to say 'to a brink'. ... What brink?

He plunged along, feeling a kind of brittle alertness. He would have tried ringing her number, if he'd thought she'd be home. But some small, calculating part of him didn't want to put her parents on their guard. While he thought that, looked at the phone – tried to connect ideas – he could feel his eyes literally beginning to close on him. Hardly thinking what he was doing, he wavered over to pull his worn mattress and sheets out from behind the drying rack. He shoved the armchair over to one side, not bothering to clear away pens and papers.

He could remember times... when, you could say, a brink had been reached....

He flopped down on the mattress. Before he fell asleep, he saw one fleeting image. It was as if the surge and lift of the flat's inanimate objects were carrying him on and through the wall, out onto the irregular lawn of the house at Maeraki – and on – and on, despite him, horrifyingly, into the empty blue of the sky, over the worn-down cliff's edge no-one had ever thought to fence off.

Straight away, he seemed to be falling, but not past the rocky margin of a cliff. He fell in and out of scenes that he didn't so much see as inhabit, as if the distinction between observer and observed had been lifted away. Grey ends of ridges; monster crickets crawling out of holes in a bank; and a complicated palace at the very end of long flights of forest stair. He experienced a fugue of downward-slipping thoughts, of momentary states of being, each of them another level in his slow descent into the deeper well of the dream. In the end he paused beside a muddy pond with a crenellation of ice around the edges, which must have been in some industrial suburb; he was aware of a plan of vertical and horizontal streets that built and grew and stretched up and down forever to take in the whole extension and curve of the earth.

He came to rest.

Now the suburb had become a school, or there was a school in the suburb. He was walking up and down pathways and quadrangles. All the buildings were deserted. He stepped over the coloured lines of games courts painted on the asphalt. This was obviously a New Zealand coastal school, of the sort he'd gone to as a boy; but something in him, some instinct, told him that he was still on the other side. In fact (here the scene darkened, not because any sun was covered) he became aware that this was the central TEFL building for the whole of Britain. Windows with bars receded into a murk of nothing he could make out. He stood there, thumping on the doors, and in the end he picked up a rough stone and tried rapping on the window glass. He shouted and shouted to get in. But his words turned into little many-legged creatures which seemed to run away along the seams of the world, meaning nothing to anyone who might be listening.

He could remember walking on for some time more – remember it without experiencing it – until the ground must have begun to break and rise. Up, up he'd gone, on a track that got narrower and narrower, until, now, he was crawling on his hands and knees along a ledge beside a vertical drop. A friend was there with him, crawling on behind – sometimes it seemed to be Cas, the flyer, sometimes that beetle-browed kid from Weimar Road. The ledge was becoming slighter and slighter, and his job of balancing harder. He could hardly move for the fear of falling. At one stage he heard a small sound behind him, a noise of effort made in the throat. He forced his head round, and there was no-one there. Then turning back he could see the path ahead of him somehow paved or overlapped with panels, grey-white and corrugated, like the huge wings of a moth.

Things changed again, without rhyme or reason, as they do in a dream. He was further down the same or a different hill. A baby had appeared out of nowhere – a *baby*. That was a strange thing: babies had no real part in his thinking. This one came accompanied by a flotilla of oversized bees, with dazzling black-and-yellow stripes. Mel had to look around him to discover that he was walking or running up a path through head-high foliage, everything flooded with patterns of sunlight. It was the foot track up the side of Arthur's Seat, the one that began on the Salisbury Crags side. But verdant, far more verdant, the brush and gorse sprung out and flowering. The small boy floated beside him, unaffected by gravity. It sang and chattered to itself. It was tiny. Why wasn't it in a cradle? He knew nothing at all about babies. But he sort of enjoyed its company, muttering words back to it from time to time.

For all that, the scene was far from gentle or idyllic. Everything was tinged with anxiety, as virulently-coloured insects droned around them. He was unnaturally aware of every object that passed his eye, no matter how fleetingly, and there was always a sense of hidden danger – to one or both of them – like the awareness of stings under yellow fuzz.

His eyes opened. That last effect, the stripes of black and yellow and the tight anxiety, survived his transition to the waking world. He gasped for air. He realised, first with something like blankness, then relief, that there was no baby, no path, nothing to worry about. As the awareness of himself filtered back (he was deeper into the room this time, so that his eyes opened to the discoloured paintwork of the ceiling edge), he could see the dream receding behind him like a discrete shape, a long corridor of narrative, swelling out near the end into a great organ-climax of image and atmosphere.

God, he thought – the *colours*.

Who was it – Jim or someone – who'd told him once categorically that humans didn't dream in colour?

There were some noises from just outside the door, then three sharp knocks, just as he was getting to his feet. Ow – God – slept with my lenses in. He looked down along himself to check he was fully dressed, not thinking yet about who it might be.

So when he opened the door to Mairi, he was actually surprised.

'Hi! So you got here.'

'You weren't waiting on me, were you?'

'Ah, well… since 3:30.' He looked at his watch again, which showed a bit after 5:30.

'I'm sorry about that,' she said indistinctly. 'I got held up. What have you been doing?'

Drawing back into the room, he realised that the mattress with its rucked-up off-white sheets was lying in the middle of the floor, like the signature of squalor. It was too late to do anything about it. Mairi was immaculate in her dark skirt and jacket and an orangey-pink blouse; she walked past him, carrying a small backpack.

'Oh, just scribbling some… I mean, nothing. I crashed out for a bit.'

'Writing – oh. So you've started?'

That impressed him. He hadn't known Mairi was aware of any aspirations he might or might not have.

'I mean, it's just a few ideas,' he mumbled. 'You weren't working, on a Sunday?'

'Oh yes. Some of the Festival accounts badly needed sorted. Pascuale was there. And Sheena… I don't know. She just wanted me to stay on.'

In the meantime, Mel had taken her jacket and showed her into the new armchair, in which she looked strangely undersized, like a perfectly-dressed scale model of a person.

'For company?' he guessed.

'Well, she's scared of him, a bit.'

'Of *Pascuale*?' (he pronounced it as Italianly as humanly possible). 'You're not, are you?'

She didn't answer. She said,

'Look, I'm really needing a shower. I meant to get one in the gym, but we had to work through. Will I best go home just now, and…?'

'No no no!'

But stripes lay behind it. In some distant version of reality, Mel was actually aware that that might be the best idea for both of them. So of course, he fought against it with all his might. Hadn't lived through that, waited two hours, just to watch her buzzing away into the distance.…

'No no no! Is that a change of clothes you've got? Look, you can have one here.'

He opened the door of their cupboard-bathroom to show her.

'Can I really?'

'I'll just start the water heating. You'll have coffee, won't you?'

'Well, OK… thanks… thanks.'

He moved around, clearing away all the evidence of his nap, of which he felt ashamed for some reason. According to his previous plan, he ought to be away by now. To a conversation class. Amazing. He went in behind the breakfast bar and started clattering with the kettle and cups.

'So, what are you working on?' she asked.

'Oh, just one idea. I have lots of them. This is probably a stupid one. But I thought I might just do it this time – I've got some big bits of paper.'

'So you have,' she said, looking over.

He felt embarrassed talking about it. The characters and devices of his half-baked graphic novel made a strange clash with the reality there in the flat, and especially with her. Dibs and Rattray – idiotic names. Mairi in her silk blouse sat in the chair, occupying a spectrum absolutely apart.

He still sensed some kind of constraint in her. He made a guess, 'Does he come on to you, this *Pascuale* guy?'

'Och, he's got this patriarchal way with him. As if everyone's the admiring… you know. He wasn't bad today, it just goes with his mood.'

'But he must know you're spoken for?'

'I think he's got his spies…. In fact…'

She looked around the room. Though she didn't especially single out the places crammed with ex-Yehune possessions, he saw immediately what she might mean.

'I suppose you've told a few people about Yehune taking off?'

'Only everyone I know.'

They only had a one-cup filter. Mairi's cup was just about ready. There was a *zzt*, quickly, of irrelevant bee noise in a space inward from his temple – what it must be to be rich. And: fuck these insects.

Mairi had passed on to the subject of Yehune, going over facts she must surely have known already:

'He took his rucksack with him, didn't he?' she asked. 'And a lot of clothes, you said?'

'Mm-hmm. Bivvy-bag, camping stuff. Quite a bit.'

'Is there anything, really, he'd have to come back for?'

'I don't know.'

But he felt she needed reassuring. He went on, 'You know, it's nothing to worry about, this is just what he does. It's the way he works things out.'

'But for a *month*?'

'Well – not normally.'

'What's the longest he's been away?'

He paused. 'It's usually no more than a few days.'

'Would he come back for the piano? To get it sold, or something?'

Mel's view from behind the bench was of the armchair, a bit forward and to the right, Mairi sitting side-on in it, and behind that the rectangular piano in light-brown wood. He thought, if he didn't come back for *her*, would he come back for...?

She said softly, 'No...'

Now his own coffee had almost run through. The aroma, the dark and bitter resin, was everywhere in the air. Harsher than he'd expected, when he'd seen it as just an aerosol added for effect.

Mairi got up for hers. She started to walk around, with her hands loosely round the cup.

'Sheena's got these parents, I think they're her main problem. I got to know quite a lot about her and the people she...'

As she moved and talked, he watched her. The perfect human system: complementary masses, everything centred perfectly and circling against its opposite. That incredible design, a girl. At the same time, he had the disturbing impression that he'd never seen her looking like this before. There was something charmed in the line of her face in profile, a sort of youthfulness that he thought of as American, out of films; but weighed with a deliberation that was serious as houses. Nothing like the usual waif-pictures he applied to her. There was a line of reflected light at about the longitude of her cheekbone, extending to the line of her jaw. It disappeared as her head turned round again. He noticed her hair was managed, cut to contour, with a hazing of lighter stripes towards the ends. She went on talking, going into more and more detail about her workmate's friends, until they began to brush on stories Mel had heard from her before, people's names he remembered, places in Glasgow and on the West Coast, and he was lost.

She stopped, passing his big sheet of paper, and picked it up from beside the cardboard box.

'Is this what you've been doing? Oh… wow, it's…'

'Oh no. Hey, don't look at that. Sit down, sit down.'

She hesitated as she put the paper down. 'But isn't this your own special chair?'

Mel laughed. 'I've got a chair.' And he pulled a wooden one over from the side of the table.

So they both sat down again, where the objects on the floor allowed, on an angle to each other and at a respectable distance. She said,

'It's good that you're doing something of your own. Things are a bit different now… mm.' She added thoughtfully, 'Sometimes you've got to get what *you* want.'

Only then it struck him that she might have been deliberately limiting her own life to fit in with Yehune's. She might have been living somewhere else by now; branched out; even had some money to spend on herself.

He asked her, 'What about you?'

She made a brushing motion, like a shrug done with just one hand. Poised – slim-fingered – no rings.

'Look how much room there is,' she remarked, measuring from her middle to the arm of the chair. 'I bet we could both fit in.'

'Easily.'

Putting his cup down on the floor, going to her chair and carefully insinuating himself into it, was the obvious thing to do just then. But his body was shaken by regular thumps; he was all too aware that this could be thought of as a decisive moment. The colours in the dimly-lit flat were showing sharper contrasts, bending towards the red. Her cheekline, so near, was like a contour in old porcelain.

She commented, 'It's a bit tight. I should get my shower first.'

'Water takes about an hour to heat.'

'I must be mingin'.'

'No you're not.'

She picked up his hand. 'Look. Your hands are all pen.'

'So they are.'

There were marks of black and red there from the drawing he'd been doing. How funny. Funnier was the feeling of softness, the contrast of sizes, the utter femininity of every gesture her hand could make, though it was nearly the same shape as his. And the rise of her hip in the dark skirt: necessary, so that his legs could fit in as well. Had she tried to take her hand back? Any movement she made was so slight that he could hardly tell it had happened. But he wanted to keep that hand. Of course, it felt as if all the facets of her personality were suddenly concentrated there, and it was her he was touching, her at the breast, her at the self. It was certainly doing something to him.

It was Mel who eventually moved his hand to touch somewhere else, behind the shoulder where her ornamental sleeve met the blouse. She made a small sound, 'e...'

Their legs had had to twine in with each other to make the best use of the space. He brought his face closer in, and kissed her on the lips, which quickly lost their pure detachment. A slight taste of coffee. Even more her than the hands. Bars, bright and dark, were printed in the hidden space behind his eyelids.

Some more time passed. They talked a bit, inconsequentially. Otherwise they didn't do much more than sit up tight against each other.

She said at one point, catlike, 'This is nice.'

His mind was a little bit adrift. The darkness of her skin at the visible points. Even in the past, he'd noticed she could be darker or lighter in skin-tone, depending on how recently she'd gone to the Continent. Now his own hand looked whiter and bonier by contrast. And then it seemed the chair was something drawing them along, a kind of bicycle, out of control, wheeling away to who-knew-where, unstoppable even if they'd wanted to stop it. A tandem. Their two skins. Together, in.

He said involuntarily, '...tan.'

Mairi looked amused.

'Everything goes on inside, doesn't it? Inside there.' She pressed the knuckles of one hand to his head.

'Oh, not really,' he said conversationally. 'You should see me when I'm on my own. Just can't stop talking to myself, I shout and rave away...'

'I didn't see it, not till I got to know you properly.'

Inside. He let the back of his left-hand fingers trail along the silky, orange-blancmange material of her blouse.

Something occurred to him, 'Yehune didn't give you this?'

'No. My dad. For my Christmas.'

Straight away, he wished he hadn't said it. Vibrations from the false note wavered away on the air; he assumed she was as aware of them as he was. He rearranged himself, untwining his legs from hers, to get up out of the chair.

His mind turned to what was in the cupboards. After all, they'd have to have some sort of dinner. He went over to the kitchen area, thinking it'd at least give him something to do while she waited for the water to heat up.

It was hard for him to look at the patch of foreground where she sat in the armchair. The colours there were too bright, the shadings too dark. Her face hovered over it like a symbol in his mind's eye. The image he saw was of one of their Scottish black-faced sheep, presented in negative – a pale face, and hair like black wool.

He put some music on: a live concert of The Doors. In the meantime he threw together his own version of spaghetti bolognese, using whatever he had in the cupboard.

Later, when he'd half-cleared the table and they'd sat down, Mairi ate almost nothing. But she did say,

'We should have some wine with this.'

So out he went to get the wine, while Mairi got ready for her shower. Not that it was really necessary for him to leave her alone. But in any case, it gave him an excuse to get away and think about things. Some demon seemed to have got into him, a demon of *inconsistency*. He wasn't sure what he was doing any more. He hadn't expected things to turn out this way. The fact that Mairi seemed to be accepting it all, letting things happen, was one more puzzling factor in what was becoming, for him, an impossible equation. What could *she* be thinking? He only wished her inner thoughts were a manuscript put down in front of him, in whatever obscure language you cared to name. He would have deciphered it. As it was....

He walked out of the small bay in Gardner's Crescent and down towards Fountainbridge, past two yellow skips and the deserted building site on his right. The traffic was light at that time of the day. 'Mecca' met his eye as he turned the corner, a white classical portico... the Bingo palace. He wondered what sort of wine he should try and get. French, Mairi liked French wine. How much cash did he have...?

'Hae-God, Hae-A' ' was set in relief on an old stone crest on the tenement. Under it, two men turned their shoulders to him, huddled over some scrap or envelope.

He told himself that it was his own thinking he had to justify, not hers. He had to iron it all out somehow in his head. And yet – when you thought about it, what was there to justify? What had they done? They'd sat in a chair, and kissed, and touched each other's hands. It was nothing. To him, the whole problem seemed to float on a pocket of air somewhere up above the asphalt and the grubby window ledges, unconnected with anything real. His own small game of scruples.

Just then, he was walking past Fat Sam's at the corner of Semple Street. Fat Sam seemed to leer out invitingly at him: a cartoon painted on the building-side.

By the time he was at the traffic islands, hopping from one to the other, a whole train of logic had come together, seeming to give him a basis for what he was already feeling. Loyalty to Yehune (Yehune, who might or might not ever come back) was great. It was the highest impulse he could have. But, he thought, in some extreme cases, there could be something even more important. His feelings for Mairi had changed completely; that was something he'd discovered over the course of the afternoon. If they were paramount, overmastering? He laid down a rule for himself, one which he was going to stick to whether he liked it or not. Only if he thought that this might be *the one thing* – the full, monogamous relationship for life – could he let himself go on.

... And there was the question. Was it?

At the corner with Lothian Road was a big barnlike chemist's. There was something he'd thought of getting. But he let it go, put off by the desolate look of the aisles through frosted glass.

A smaller chemist's came up on the left. Closed. A few doors up was Thresher's, the wine shop. That turned out to be closed as well.

Of course, you idiot. Sunday night. He could see the square spire of St John's against the luminous sky, somewhere off to the north.

So he turned left again at the corner with the MGM cinema, formerly the Cannon. It looked like it had to be the full loop. He knew of an Evening News outlet that might still be open, and a pub, if he remembered, a little bit beyond that.

Was it? he asked himself again. Or – was there a chance for them, for him and Mairi? He put his mind to it, imagining spending his life with her. And found out he could imagine it very easily. But he told himself that was stupid thinking. Fragile, conditional. A spider trail of blue-tinted smoke stood in the western part of the sky, diaphanous, hardly there. Of course, it was no more than the slightest possibility. But didn't that mean it could, conceivably, actually happen... the miracle could come to pass?

On the other side of the road, a drunken fight was going on outside a bookmaker's shop. It brought back a picture he'd known in his boyhood – cheaply coloured – Jesus clearing the Temple.

At the dog-leg the roads made with Morrison Street, he came to Gardner's Crescent from the other end, and the small shop, 'News 2 U', that could generally be relied on to be open. A 'clink!' in his ear as he went in. He stood in front of a few small shelves of wine, and in the end reached down a white box from the top shelf. Mouton-Cadet, £5.95. He could remember hearing something about it. He paid the man behind the counter, and took careful stock of what change he had left.

Then he went on to the pub. That didn't look very open either, but a door was ajar and there were backs milling inside. He snuck into the toilets, and inserted money into a vending machine for three condoms. He had to face down a few people who looked at him curiously, him and his white box. The place stank differently in different places, of urine, used alcohol and some sort of perfume or disinfectant. A bitch to be in. But you've got to provide for the conditional. Prepare for the accident of miracles. Someone shouted something at him, loud and argotic, just as he was going out again.

'The Oisin' stood on the sign outside. Bloody names keep changing. All-Irish, brewed under licence. Oisin and his nose.

The argument with himself went on all the way down Gardner's Crescent. He crossed the West Approach Road to the place where the house fronts opened out in a wide semicircle. Right now, this evening, now, he was about to do what he might regret forever. If Mairi was up for it. If she wasn't – that was fine, there was no decision to make. But he wasn't going to let himself off so easily. It was up to him to decide what *he* wanted. He'd lost that proud, magisterial confidence he'd had in himself before anything like this had actually happened to him.

His memory wasn't quite of Jim's girlfriend Jodie. But he had a feeling of no fixed ground, the cuddy of a boat, and yellow cloth spread out over a squab.

Oh no. No, no, no. That sort of thing could rob you. You'd never get yourself back again. He went over all the words he'd schooled into himself just in case something of the sort ever seemed likely to happen again. And went on arguing it as he walked down his own street. On one side (a dip to his right past the fence and low buildings) was a sense of seasickness, the humping of thighs inside a tied-up yacht. On the other (trees, the curved porticos of houses that had once been grand), the very particular circumstances. Mairi – who could be expecting something of him? And the thing he'd worked out: that this could be, just might be, what everything so far had been leading up to, the relationship that had in some way been intended....

He came to the end of the fenced walk. There was a big brick lump on his right, Rosemount Buildings, looking like a converted prison. Your soul in a box. Oh Jodie, sweetheart – whispering snatches of bullshit in her ear, taking the offered ride. No, there was no way he could justify this. Yehune was away; that didn't stop him being Yehune. As for himself, he was either a person who learned from his mistakes… or.

One of the Edinburgh street bins stood on the corner, with a rubbish bag or two leaned up beside it. He fished for the condoms in his pocket, and brought them up within an inch of the dark opening. But he stopped himself at the last moment. He was too poor to go throwing away money.

In any case, it made no difference, none at all. His mind was completely made up as he crossed the muddy floor of the stair and juggled with the keys. He was even a bit embarrassed about the way he'd been thinking – assuming Mairi's part in some mad fantasy of his own.

Inside the flat, everything was different. He had an impression of quickly-fleeting stripes as he passed the bench and set the white box down. Mairi was dressed in jeans and a brown frilly top, standing by the sink drying a few dishes. The air in there was still and cloistered, and the course of things seemed somehow laid out in advance. He couldn't help glancing over at her, admiring the way her jeans curved backwards and gathered in exactly the right places. She was real. She was Mairi. She was....

From then on, it was as if all the decisions worth making had already been made in the minds of both of them.

He ducked into the cupboard, first, and hurriedly washed himself all over in cold water. When he was dressed again, he went to the bench and poured the wine into two glasses. He took one sip. It tasted harsh and metallic. Mairi didn't even touch hers. They sort of gravitated to a random point of the floor, physically nudging together, as if they wanted to stand inside each other.

'S'posed to be reliable, someone told me,' he apologised.

'It will be. It just needs to breathe a bit.'

Her hand was at the nape of his neck. 'Your hair used to be longer,' she said thoughtfully.

They had another conversation about each other's height, while they fitted themselves together front-to-front, finding that parts of them came to different levels than you might have expected. A strange business, till you got used to it.

'... I've only got this damned mattress,' he whispered.

'The one I saw when I came in? It seemed all right.'

In fact, it was a lot less than all right. But it still seemed better to them than the alternative, which would have been to lie on Yehune's fold-down bed. Mel had never slept on it; he'd cleared off the sheets at some point and straightened it up, so that it reverted to a loose-looking panel to the left of the door. He must have been aware that Mairi had spent whole nights on it; but he pushed the thought aside into a sort of willed darkness in his head.

He threw off his jeans and tee-shirt while getting the mattress and bedding ready. Mairi's undressing proved trickier. By that time, they were locked together, magnetised, not wanting to let even one limb get out of their common possession. Mel had brought her wineglass down to the floor for her; they had to work around it. The jeans girls wore these days, he thought, would have taken at least two strong men to pull them off. Maybe he'd started out with the wrong technique?... In the end, by combining forces, they managed it.

It was simpler after that. She undid her bra, and he could see the lines of white and dark, the perfect outline of a bikini in paler skin. They left the light on so as to be able to appreciate each other. Mairi had put some music on, turned down until it wasn't much more than a bassy thump.

So everything was hands and arms, tongues and lips, in the partial draping of sheets. He couldn't believe how complete she was, in a size that was very slightly miniature. He tried to make himself acquainted with every inch of her. As for him, the swivelling club attached to him at the thighs tended to get in the way when they repositioned their bodies. She cradled it in one hand, helping it from place to place. Though he'd taken care to clear all the rubbish from under the mattress, that had gone completely flat in places, bumping parts of them down against the bare floor no matter what position they were in. So they didn't keep to any one for long.

A quick conversation about protection revealed that Mairi wasn't, at that time, on the pill; Mel did have condoms; but Mel was deeply dubious of using them as their only defence. His father (a medical researcher) had once told him a few percentages, and advised him always to use two forms at once.

380

'But there are still all sorts of amazing things we can do.'

'Oh, I know. But…'

There was a lot in that 'but'. An inaudible burring of wings. A flurry of expectations, her expectations and his, which were being short-changed by their holding back. Her hands expressed it, a sort of manual consideration, a gentleness made physical, at a point when words had ceased to be much use to them. They did do all sorts of amazing things. Without the real freedom to act, they took it all out on each other's bodies, in drawn-out, cyclic repetition, always steering clear of the fateful coupling. And over all of it, Yehune seemed to hover (didn't hover) snickering and advising (all nonsense), or stared down at Mel out of whatever object happened to be in his eye. The chair – an alarm clock – the rigid upper lip of the piano keyboard. The room had got colder. There was no music any more; the tape had clicked off and neither of them had thought of putting another one on. Mel decided it was this light: it was too clinical for him at this time of the night. He untwined himself from the sheets, and stepped over to turn it off – getting a shamefaced 'Mel…' at his priapic double-outline.

That did make things easier. More hours passed, in which orgasm was a tantalising ghostlight just removed. They both seemed to take a strange delight in avoiding it. They lay and drowsed for a while, facing the same direction, Mairi in front – and she mentioned to him that he never stayed still. Meaning that one part of him. By then, she was ready to light things up again, and writhed and danced with every curve of her. All a matter of *experience,* Mel thought confusedly. He lost tumescence for a while, and later on got it back again, and then it was as if it would never go away. The fact of the situation was what enchanted him, as well as stretching his belief beyond its limits. It was as if, there in the dark, in the apparent teeming of particles his eyes made out of blankness, anything could happen, and was happening, moment by moment, without the need for sleep, and bringing with it every single sexual feeling short of release.

Some time in the early hours, they whispered together again, and came to a different understanding. His father's advice, he realised now, had never been the point. There was another reason for his reluctance; and under the titanic rusting cities the darkness built on either side, he'd found such things could be confronted after all. She slipped the condom on him with her own hands, touching it, dandling it, as if his whole sexual apparatus was a small animal with no connection to either of them. It was this: in the twilight places, while he wasn't sleeping, the world had turned over and back on him like a wave. The justification he'd agonised over had come to seem obvious. She *was* the one; he *could* spend his life. ... I mean, of course. And she was superb, and ready. And in any case, he thought they must have established their togetherness by that time.

Wrung along, caressed along, on imaginary pillows in the dark. She was slick to receive him, tight to hold him, and any movement they made took them both aside, for glorious tactile moments, from the day-to-day world of flats and finances and stultifying places of work. It could be managed, held back – excruciatingly, wonderfully – while the other person breathed full in your face. The bodies, held like objects, receded into a gentle liquorice continuity of the senses, which was chewed by them continuously at the hips... tug, tug. At the same time there were all the rhythms of their heartbeats and their breathing and their insistent motion, like a battering of drumbeats out of synch. He seemed to hear, somewhere on the borders of his mind or in the complexity of his inner ear, a swarm of voices wailing. After all that time holding off, this act had been carried above itself. It had become something extraordinary. He wanted it to last forever, he wasn't willing to let it end even with a climax. The condom helped him there, limiting feeling to the point where he was able to keep himself in bounds, while his living recognition of the fact of what was happening kept him hard enough. Either by a sort of telepathy, or by the total willingness of each to fit in with the other, they decided on new positions, and gymnastically took them up without a withdrawal. It was a dance, all right – motion within motion, cycling and oscillation of bodies. And she was some dancer. He experienced the closeness with her in a way he'd never felt it; with her, the girl, so near that he seemed to encompass her all ways round with his body and arms and thighs; just for this time, there was a chemical magic sending him out of his brain and out of the room and into an effigy of her, of her as rising sun, an expression of light, no Mel, no Mairi, no names any more. Strips of yellow sunlight stood apart on black. The bars, the bees… the bales. The physical part of them dwindled away below them, and it was as if some insubstantial glow or centre was released to fly away, pyrelike, on fragile wings of sheets, in the raging throat of an indescribable music; and they were both of them caught up, carried onwards, out of themselves, and out of themselves, and ah, and ah, and ah….

It wasn't much later in the morning when Mairi picked her watch up from the floor, looked at it, and returned to normal life. She ran naked to the bathroom and ran taps for a while. Later Mel was treated to the sight of her dressing hurriedly in the middle of the floor. Every gesture of her body held some quintessential charm for him.

He got up as well. He caught at her.

'Got to go… wait – I've got some lipstick.'

She allowed a kiss before she went over to apply it, briskly, staring into her own face in the big wall mirror.

'I'll see you soon, then?'

'Of course.'

'Tonight?'

She smiled at him, and was about to say something, but barely avoided kicking over the full wineglass he'd left there on the floor.

After she'd gone, he absently picked the glass up and took a sip. He was surprised by the taste. It was as rich as plumcake, smooth as the slide of an oyster. Overnight, the 'breathing' must have happened; it was all transformed.

Return

approximately 50 seconds before failure observers to a distance of 4.5 (14' 9.16") were clearly subjected to high axial force and low resonance combination being a direct function of strand slipclearly able to verify visually and audially the progress of a gross crack from bottom to top of the visible web which continued notwithstanding the fibre reinforcement to lead to an unstable behaviour in the gullet of the ant where falling tower track toppled starts to call into question the effective ductility factor of the truss-girder framing system tested at or around 1.7being a direct function of sudden sideways displacement of the vertebral column given the dramatically reduced stiffness where block. where block. block.

When you were as far away from home as you could possibly be, there was a dread associated with night phonecalls. They screamed away with the voices of everyone you knew back there. Especially parents, brothers, sisters, went brittle as glass in the mechanical trill, their lives already blowing past you. So after ten or twenty rings you forced yourself up and went to pick up the phone. Usually to hear the 'click' as whoever it was rang off.

Only a few days later, very early in the morning, Mel was jarred out of sleep by the bell of the telephone. He lay letting the rings build up. If they didn't get as far as eight... but they got to eight. He took to interposing a swearword after every ring, till the count was eighteen. Then he pulled himself up from the squashed old mattress.

'Hello?'

'Oh – ah – man. It's just…. Sorry it's so fucking early.'

'Jesus!… Yehune.'

'Hrrf hrrf, one or th'other, yeah, yeah.'

'Um, I mean, where are you? What's going on?'

'Where? Here. Well, I mean in the airport.'

'Edinburgh airport? So you're… oh, right. … Would you like, I don't know, someone to come and pick you up?'

'Ahm-hm.'

'Mairi. Have you rung Mairi?'

'Mm… na.'

'Because she's got a car.'

'Mm.'

'So where have you been?'

'Here and there.'

'Fuck man, you sound spaced out. Look, if you give Mairi a call we can maybe both come. It's ages till her work starts.'

'Ah, well, I wasn't sure how things… you know. … Don't s'pose you could ring her for me?'

'What? Sure. I'll ring you back, or… no, I can't. Look, tell you what, you ring me back in about ten minutes, OK?'

'Uh-huh.'

'Are you all right? Have you got enough money?'

'Money. Ah. Got… 57… no, one pound seven, right here.'

'Holy shit. Call me back then, don't forget.'

'Right. Right.'

He didn't immediately dial Mairi's number. He righted a chair that lay on its side near the mattress, and sat on it. He took a handful of his own hair. Then he went over to pick up a pair of old black jeans that were lying sprawled beside the table leg. He felt he had to be dressed for this.

Surprisingly, Mairi answered the phone, though it was so early. She hardly said a word. But she told him she'd be there to pick him up in twenty-five minutes.

In which time, while he waited for Yehune to ring back, Mel had to go to the loo, see to general necessities, get dressed for going out, pick up some money, and revise all his assumptions about the state of his life. He thought he did well in the last bit; in everything else he was a model of fumbling incompetence.

Mairi buzzed a few minutes earlier than she'd said.

'Hi Mel.'

'Mairi. He hasn't rung back yet.'

'Do you think he will?'

There was a bilious sort of overcast, defeating most of the early-morning light. Mairi looked as pale as paste. A tiny, dispassionate woman's face, grafted on a back-and-white sepulchral background. This was Mairi, he reminded himself. Her eyes looked the same to him, but the mouth was someone else's.

They drove out via Fountainbridge and Grove Street to Haymarket and the road west. Unusually for Mairi, she said almost nothing.

Eventually he came out with,

'So what do you think? Not breathing a word?'

She threw him a genuinely frightened look. 'Of course.'

'Ah – huh.'

She said, 'This... I didn't know he was going to...'

'No. You and me both.'

But Mel was busy thinking. He knew very well the two of them wouldn't have a chance to discuss anything after the car-ride. And arrangements were looming, everything was poised on the brink of taking another path.

'You know the thing at Pom and Alice's?' he said. 'We'll have to cancel it. Very quietly.'

'Oh – yes. We'll just ring and tell them Yehune's come back.'

'Anyway, they didn't know anything. It's not like we were going around being a couple.'

But of course, that was what it would have been for, the weekend coming, when in Pom and Alice's hired place in Longniddry they would have made the gestures, tipped the wink to a chosen group of people... Mel supposed. He'd no idea how it had all been arranged, Mairi had seen to that.

Only about now, still long before Mairi's work began, the lanes in the other direction were beginning to fill up as they drew near their turnoff from the Glasgow Road.

386

She said, 'Mel, you know what this is, don't you? … It's just the way things happen.'

'Yeah.' He mentally gathered his forces. 'But we're going to have to be careful how we let them happen. I mean, from now on. We'll have to agree on exactly what we're going to say.'

She breathed, 'There's nothing to say.'

'Oh, there's always plenty to say,' he replied heartily enough. 'People don't realise they're talking when they don't know it, with their eyes, their bodies, their tones of voice when they're saying something completely different…'

'Mm. … I hope he's all right. How did he sound on the phone?'

'Um, wasted. A bit vague.'

'I'm just wondering what made him…' She paused. 'Vague – and he never rang back.'

'I'm absolutely sure he's all right. He often sounds that way.'

'Did he ask to be picked up? He knows I've got the car.'

He didn't answer. But all the time he was thinking: talk with their bodies, people talk with their bodies. Sometimes they even dance with their bodies. Out of the corner of his eye he could see her legs in tights, built to fall together, moving under soft musculature as she changed down. My dancer. But could that have really…?

Yes, it had really. But that dance was all in the past.

Edinburgh Turnhill wasn't what you might call a proper airport. It was a splinter of that universal space linking point to point on the world's surface, an annexe of the great impersonal, with the same general air of 'Sorry, we can't help you'. They left the Renault in the short-term carpark and came in through automatic doors. Mel only hoped Yehune would still be there. It was an hour after the phonecall, and his imagination built strange movements of fate: the traveller getting impatient, meeting someone, taking off somewhere, this time never to be seen again.

The place was small, at least. If it had been Heathrow or even Stanstead, they might have gone on searching for days. Mel chose the first direction, heading for International Arrivals. He found it all but deserted, only four or five people there busily filling the space with smoke. A whiff of Yehune already – he realised he'd got out of the habit of adapting himself to perpetual cigarette smoke.

On their first pass up the length of the building, Mairi saw something, and was suddenly gone from his line of sight. Mel looked over. He'd seen it too, a man sitting on a squashed-down pack facing away from them. He didn't have a fag, and his hair looked somehow whitish, as if lightly impregnated with dust – Mel had taken him for someone much older.

'*Yehune!*' Mairi called out. His head turned, and Mel could see his eyes, strained and weary.

He said, 'Mairi. I'm... oh wow.'

The goatee beard had gone, and he was wearing clothes that Mel had never seen before. Scuffed old chino trousers, a worn-out pale-coloured fleece over tartan shirttails. Even his good boots were replaced by some odd grey shoes. Mel found the whole effect out of character for Yehune, and tried to justify himself, no wonder he hadn't....

It made no difference. The prodigal was back, making a lot of Mairi, holding her off to look at her from her hair to her smart work shoes, even twirling her round to catch a back view. He wasn't answering her questions, but chatted away at random. Then he went over to Mel.

He hugged him. Mel felt a hard grip on him.

'Shit man,' Mel babbled, 'where have you *been*? Don't go taking off into the blue like that again, huh?'

'Yeah, right, ah... shit. I'm here now.'

But his eyes had lost focus again. Before they left, he had to go up the escalator and buy three packets of Marlboros with some money he borrowed from Mairi.

Their talk on the way back was more to do with immediate things, Mairi's work time, what they were going to do that evening, than where or for what reason Yehune had gone. Mel picked up the general impression that he'd covered some Northern European countries that they hadn't got to before, after scooting here and there around Scotland. But Yehune was too tired, his speech was disjointed, and he gave the impression that he didn't want to talk about himself. There was plenty of time; plenty of time for all that. But not for Mairi to get to her work. At the door of the Gardner's Crescent flat Yehune hugged her fondly, while Mel did the job of lugging the pack to the door. He had a strange sensation of interchangeability.

Once inside, Yehune seemed taken aback by the new arrangement of objects, but even more concerned to get his bed down. He was grumpy until Mel found him sheets and a duvet; then he collapsed in the folding bed without saying another word.

In streets and cafés that day, unselfed, ungirled, Mel tried to see himself in terms of the completely altered nuts and bolts of things around him. An opportunity, a flight above the level of the normal, had barely begun, and been chopped off again as quickly. He could find nothing in the decoration of a café interior to fasten himself on. Waitresses, cool and irrelevant, moved in his eye. He could remember worse losses he'd had in the past – on the whole, he thought he was taking it pretty well.

Mairi called in after work, woke Yehune up, and took him out on a compulsory clothes-buying expedition. In Norway (he'd hinted with the minimum of coherent speech) he'd had his clothes stolen; he might even have been robbed twice. The flat was empty when Mel got back from his second lesson. But before long Mairi and Yehune burst in, loaded down with bags, seemingly chatting as gaily as ever before. Then they were all due to go off to the Kar Krash.

At the Kar Krash club, Mel was surprised to find another girl with them, sitting where they sat, involved in everything they did, someone called Tessa. She was dumpy, had dyed hair that tended to fall over half of her face, and was perfectly nice on casual acquaintance. He didn't have much to say to her. Only after the third drink did it dawn on him that she was Mairi's cover, his own 'date'. He possibly hadn't played up very well. It occurred to him that if Mairi had introduced her to him, a man recently entangled, in some kind of emotional shock, she couldn't have had a very high esteem for this friend of hers.

'So, where'd you go?'
'Told you. Arrhh… starting with Scotland. Here 'n' there.'

The next morning, Mel was already up and dressed; they idled around the flat while Yehune took his time getting into brand-new casual clothes. Mel didn't have any lessons, and Yehune, naturally, didn't have anything in particular to do. He was playing some music he'd brought back, something he called German Thrash. It frenziedly worried at their ears. And that old atmosphere was back; Yehune was chain-smoking as they talked.

'… Here 'n' there.'

'OK. But where, mainly?'

'Mainly round the north – yeah, I s'pose. An' then…'

'…?'

'Not quite to Oc. Oc. Thurso, not to Ock-ney.' Yehune laughed. 'An' then, ah, from Inverness, got a ticket…'

He was staring into the wall mirror. Mel had mixed a cup of lime juice, and was hovering in the kitchen bay.

'Oh right. To the Continent, you mean?'

'Yeah, *exactly*. To, ah, Edinburgh-some bloody place.'

'What are you saying? You got a ticket from Edinburgh?'

'Uh-huh. Raced myself to get down here. You shoulda seen me. … Well, you actually might have, given that I had to go right through the centre. God knows what you and, and…'

'Mairi.'

'… Did make it though. Which I almost didn't.'

He wasn't quite the same. Unless it was that perspectives are altered in memory, after the gap of over a month the model picture Mel carried in his head had peeled lightly away from the edges of the real. After the first day, two moderate sleeps, he might have expected his friend to lose that effect of drifting semi-functionality, as if he was only erratically connected with what was going on around him. But Yehune seemed… how *did* he seem? It was hard to say. Any symptom you could point to always turned out to be a well-attested trait in him stretching back for years. It didn't help that Mel was under a constraint as well: he couldn't let his best friend know even the general shape of what he'd been doing lately. The whole thing left him feeling edgy, uncertain of himself, as if he was bouncing at random along the hard stream of the Thrash.

Now Yehune had each of his two feet balanced on a different pile of objects, searching for some small item in the wardrobe.

'Why'd you go an' shove all my stuff together like this?' he moaned. 'Fuck knows it'll be a job to sort it all out. I dunno, I leave for a few days and find myself... embalmed...'

'Uh. ... So you got to the Continent – where'd you end up?'

'Oh that. Frankfurt or somewhere, and then round all those little countries... Lick'nstein... Scowwegia, you know.'

'Didn't you say you got robbed?'

'*Did* I get robbed. Am'sh'dam. Amster-*damn*.'

'I thought you said it was Norway?'

'Uh-huh.'

With his trousers on, he started again. 'Gods... so I was walking down this street – *fuck*, those bastards. I was dumb enough to flash a wad. This guy in a doorway was, ah, *begging alms*, so I bring out what bills I got. Sees it, pulls a knife, and whaddaya know if not he's got a good ol' friend just behind the corner and they want me to strip off never mind give 'em all my. So I show the slightest... er... unkeenness at all this, gonna do it though, and they start pounding into me, wake up a bit later, haah haah. *Kkkuuuuoorgh.*'

He hawked, looked round, and couldn't find anywhere to spit. He bit punitively on his fag, and started telling it again in a different way. Eventually he ran down.

'How'd you get more money, then?'

'Oh, I got it.' And added, 'Working... managed to...'

He was over near the stereo; he turned up his music very loud.

'But they didn't take your pack?'

'My what? Pack?' He waved his hand, '... Left luggage.'

'What is that music anyway?' Mel shouted. 'I kind of like it.'

'What? Oh yeah, 's good, eh? This one's, ah, Atomreaktor, 'think.'

For the next two weeks or so until the pub crawl, Mel kept trying and trying to put his finger on it. Though Yehune's trip had left him more languorous, beat, it hadn't exactly mellowed him: he was more protean than ever, so that the Yehune you dealt with in the morning might be a different person from the one you came back to during the day. There was something mooching, inactive about the set of his shoulders… except, that is, when he was going hyperactive in the streets, or fell into one of his inarticulate rages. Then shoulders, head and upper torso were rooster-erect, and seemed to radiate peaks of melody, a broken, razor-invasive music never to be realised on any instrument. If they were at home, Mel headed for the door, taking care to close it quietly behind him.

In ancient times, in the era of 'think together', Mel would never have suspected any conscious control behind the changing faces. And even now, it wasn't any lack of sincerity he half-intuited – filtered out through the flickering hints, expressions, giveaways – more a feeling of experiment, as if the man wasn't quite sure which persona to fit himself into any more.

Back on that Thursday morning, he'd felt it was still allowable to hassle for explanations. He turned the volume down himself, and said,

'Anyway, how did it go? I mean, was it all worth it?'

'It was… yeah…. It was great. I found something. Found that thing.'

An isolated comment. Yehune was sitting now, taking a deep drag on his fag; but Mel knew that if he waited long enough he'd get a fuller story.

Sure enough, eventually,

'I get the impression… well, you know, you remember there's *something outside,* I've always told you that…'

'Uh-huh.'

'Well, I got onto something more. You can almost see them, you know? I mean, they can even talk to you… dictate. In certain states. In the states of… uuh. Well, I could just…'

Yehune trailed off, looking at the cigarette in his hand, which sent a white wisp fuming upwards, petering out towards the deep-stained upper wallpaper of the room.

'You could just?'

'I mean, it was one time I was bicycling in the hills, managed to – hire – a bike, you see, and I hurt my hand, bashed it on a fence post… well, I was trying to open a gate on this trail… um, God, there was this great purple fucking, I dunno, great hemisphere… sum'ing…

spreading into my hand from the east or rightward side…'

'Oh yeah?'

'Yeah, goddamn, and then I heard something sort of talking. I didn't *hear* it, but you know…'

'But you heard it?'

'Ah… not that that matters a shit… actually there was this other time…'

Yehune hadn't dropped in on a very eventful period in their lives. In the two weeks, two and a half, before their famous pub crawl along the Royal Mile, things seemed to evolve rather than really occur; Mel trying to build up his pupil-base, the flat and their life-surroundings becoming gradually scrappier and more decrepit as the days went by. He'd had the idea of tutoring younger pupils for the school English exams, which of course he could do from the parents' houses. Back at the flat, statutory notices had begun appearing on the walls and doorways, nothing much for the moment, but promising trouble to come. And relations with their neighbours in the stair were at an all-time low. When Mel came in from the day's teaching appointments there was more often than not someone lurking behind a door or in a corner of the main stair, ready to start complaining at him. Never, even at the height of Yehune's composing fervour for the Ensemble, had things been so bad. The noise, they said – and seemed vague about causes, but if pressed would sometimes mention the piano. It made Mel wonder what Yehune did as soon as he was away – start dancing in hobnailed boots on the piano keyboard? Or turn some noise-maker up high, throw on a jacket and take off in the other direction?

As for relations between Yehune and Mairi, they seemed to have picked up where they left off. With the small difference that now, all three of them were rarely together at the same time. It might have been coincidence, an accident of timing; more likely it was a kind of involuntary shying away in one or two of them from a situation they might not be able to deal with.

So Mel didn't see Mairi very often. And yet, she was somehow always present – Mairi would arise – like a potent, all-altering stamp across every aspect of the world they saw.

One time in Cockburn Street, for example, a bit less than a week later....

The two New Zealanders were together on the sickle-shaped descending street with its rows of trendy shops. 'Gotta get so' more clothes,' Yehune had drawled out to him, and Mel mentally filled in, 'Mairi said I've...'

The brightly-decorated jeans shops looked halfway inviting in the early autumn sun, clear and almost warm around the beginning of September. But Yehune wasn't paying them much attention. At that moment, he was halfway up a lamp post, in full sight of the public, loudly calling personal references down to Mel. He yelled out something about Freemans Bay and the Trumps. There were no Trumps here: only a subfusc half-limousine sailing past sedately, and the stream of pedestrians, who seemed to be using all their British taste and discretion not to notice. It was a bitch, Yehune had told him, to get up those free-standing poles, but he'd found one right beside a green electrical box and managed to struggle up from there.

'Hey man, can't you gi's a leg up?'

Mel had refused.

'Peter! Peter!' the climber had shouted in a strained, satirical voice.

'Who's Peter?' Mel asked far more quietly.

'I can see your house from here!'

What put a stop to the game was no policeman, no deputation from surrounding shops, but a row of gawking roughnecks who'd gathered to watch and spit their own commentaries, and who looked all too ready to join in.

So a little later they were wandering again along the line of shops. Jewellery, New Age clothing, and the jeans-and-accessories. Yehune exploded laughing at a one-piece orange lycra jumpsuit with flashing sequins, quite obviously designed for a man and not a woman.

'Ah, yeah, that one in the window – orange. Y'can't miss it.' His deadpan to the polite salesperson was transparent to Mel, only it seemed this game had to be played through to the end.

'Ah, d'y' think it'll wash? What? Label? What label? ... Oh yeah, that wincy one right down there...'

He bought it with a fistful of free notes, without even enquiring about the size. As a sort of joke, apparently. At a decent distance from the shopfront Mel couldn't help starting in on him,

'So where'd you get all that money, to go buying that?'

'Oh – seemed to have it.'

'What the fuck is that supposed to *be*? What do you want with it? If you've got the cash to go arsing around buying things out of a misplaced sense of, I dunno...'

'I thought it might set me off.'

Mairi was there, all right, she was prominent in that exchange, because Mel suspected it was Mairi's money Yehune was wasting, just like that, pissing away in the street. Where else could he have got it from? It was that that made Mel lose it for a while, shouting and raging at Yehune in front of everyone passing by. Mel could go on and on with the best of them. Verbal invention, on the old, loose, self-repetitive level, never flagged. Yehune said nothing, he just stood there. But in the end when the tirade was beginning to wind down he turned his face away, and across the bulky shoulder Mel surprised a look in him. A furtive gleam of triumph... unless it was some accident of the light.

A little bit later, walking home, Yehune remarked to him mildly, 'See, y'can take these things back.'

And it occurred to Mel that none of his would-be objectivity was any use, the researcher was muddying the field – he was managing to set up a loop of reaction between the two of them that would spoil any chance of coming near the truth.

The prodigal would still discuss things, particularly art. But there was a closed self-absorption about him as if he was talking to himself. Mel told him the news about the flat while he was in just one of those states, going on about his private methods... or it could be theoretical ideals... which in the end seemed to amount to a kind of mystical-practical Dadaism.

Yehune's face was monumental, blank, like the face of a mountain, as he talked about it, planes of light cutting down from the grubby window to form roughly geometrical shapes, the edges falling away in progressive wrinkles like the broad continuation of the range.

'An' I mean, like, where does it all come from? Y'see? Y'see what I mean? So then it'll...'

'You know we have to find another place to live?' Mel butted in. 'Landlord's letter.'

'Something that's like out of space, so it's really just a matter of finding an outlet like the whosit inter-what, which means – mm – it might actually...'

'They're selling this whole building to a development corporation.'

'... *help* to be...'

'Letter's been lying on the snackbar for a couple of days.'

'Oh, ah...' Yehune's track had been changed, by that or something else.

'Reminds me,' he said. 'Meaning to ask, have you still got any of those short stories you did way back when, I mean before we left...?'

To look at him just then you'd think you were seeing the sharpest dial of an investigative lawyer you could imagine, but out of touch, clouded by a patina of time or distance. Mel had given up trying to tell anything from the face. He could only guess at undercurrents, frustration, anxiety, symptoms of something or anything, by the smallest twitches in the intonation of the words themselves.

He gave up, then, stood and stretched, and went over to put on a cassette before Yehune could think of doing the same.

This one was a compilation of Beethoven piano sonatas that he'd found in the Central Library. It had been in the house of one of his pupils that he'd heard something of the sort playing, something that reminded him of the thing Yehune had played at the last Concert. Of course, it was about as far from the new Thrash as you could possibly get. And yet... there was something in it, he'd thought; something in that limpid simplicity, the formalised storm....

Yehune's face did wake up then. Every line of it registered *satirical indulgence*:

'Shit, man,' he muttered, 'used t' listen to those sorta stuff when o's about twelve.'

About six days or a week before the pub crawl, Mel came in in the late afternoon to find the flat perfectly dark and quiet. Even the stair had been empty; for once the mousey-haired woman from Flat One hadn't laid into him with her 'Oh Mr *Seuchar*... Mr *Seuchar*!' He chucked his bag, stretched, and was about to hit the light switch, when through the complex shadow-world of scattered possessions he made out an extra lump on the stool facing the piano. Yehune? ... Sure enough, it was him, sitting there silent and unconnected.

For a few moments the body didn't move or answer greetings. Then, 'Oh... shit... I must've...'

And he laboriously started to turn around. As if he were apologising for falling asleep, but his eyes had been open all the time.

Mel thought at first that he could just pick up a few periodicals and go out again. He had another pupil later on. But Yehune seemed to be in a strange state, subdued and listless, with the vulnerability of something emerging from a cocoon. He'd hardly said a coherent word. ... Regressed to childhood? Lost his language?

The pianist staggered up from his stool and launched himself in the direction of the kitchen, then apparently forgot what he'd gone there for.

'I guess... y'might be wonderin',' he started. He fumbled for a fag from his top pocket, realised that shirt didn't have any pockets, and started searching in other places while he continued,

'Why I wen' off? Y'know... been thinkin'.'

Now he was striking a match. He drew a breath. Oracular, he uttered,

'I think... it was. Um. I think I just, you know, had the feelin'. That I had to be on the road.'

Mel received that information and considered it carefully. A few years before, it might have seemed the complete explanation to both of them. 'On the road' – the nomad generation – brave-sounding seventies and eighties cool.

'What does that actually mean?' he asked.

'Fff. *Mean*. It's a feeling. Felt. Feel.'

More time passed, as Mel found and leafed through a few glossy publications. In the meantime, Yehune had fumbled with cassettes and put one on at half-volume – this time one of the grotesquer varieties from Sweden. Eventually he wended his way back to the piano stool.

'So you've got no real idea at all?' Mel ventured to ask. 'I mean, why you went away?'

The other seemed to be busy listening. One song was just ending and a new one beginning.

'Thi's a good one.'

He was rolling his burned-out fag-end in his hand, endlessly squashing and reconstituting it. After an interval, he said,

'Why... why?'

as if he was thinking more about the shape or status of the word itself than any application it might have to the conversation. There was no ashtray; he flicked the fag-end towards a dirty saucer lying on the floor. Mumbling,

'... Know you don't like that.'

That was all there was to it. Mel thought about it afterwards – the significance of small gestures. Just then, at the time, he'd been thinking about something else, and the slowness of the process of realisation struck him: touch – spark – percussion, like the audible lag of one of those early matchlocks. Know you don't like that, Yehune had said. But when had Mel ever told him he didn't like it? He hadn't. Not ever. He wasn't guessing; it was something he knew.

Difficult as it had been for him to remould his own psychology into a state where he could exist full-time in the smell of burning cigarettes, Mel had always taken it as a point of pride not to let Yehune know anything about it. He'd done a job on himself, secretly casting himself in the role of a smoker at second hand, revelling in the smell of the things in other people's hands, managing to induce a sense of disappointment in himself when his friend *didn't* have a fag on the go. And it had worked fairly well. So the single tiny thing that had survived to annoy him – the man's habit of cosseting his fag-ends, rolling and caressing them between his forefinger and the side of his thumb – would never have been dragged out of him (so he thought) by men or horses. Well... yes, all right... he'd said himself that people talked with their bodies (the perfect example being, maybe, that flick by Yehune of a pummelled and distorted fag-end down towards a saucer that had recently been used for toast – what was more, he missed). But as it happened, it was hardly even worth considering whether anything might have got through to Yehune by means of body-reading or guesswork or parallel thought processes in the two of them. There was a far more obvious way he might have found out: Mel *had* written about it in a diary.

So far, the thought carried no real danger. Mel could see the passage clearly in his mind's eye, beginning on a recto or odd-numbered page about five eighths of the way down, written in the colour of ink called 'wild blue', not by any design but by the accident of what pen happened to be lying around at the time. There, he'd ranted on about it to his own satisfaction, in the cause of bile or humour putting the case more vividly than was absolutely necessary, certainly more strongly than he would have put it if he'd suspected anyone was going to actually *read* it. Now, as Yehune smoked, talked desultorily, began to hump himself around the flat putting together a peanut butter sandwich, and even, a bit later, started to roll another fag-end between his fingers while handling the jars and knives, Mel sat and let his eyes wander around the complex topography of the room, searching for the old Teal bag he kept his diaries in. The piano... wardrobe... new mix of their combined possessions, built on electrical leads and the dusty hoover, topped with scraps of clothing. Dirty cups balanced on a pile of magazines. A single piece of music paper, strange chicken-tracks wavering across it that completely ignored the lines. He made out something dark-blue in the shadows of a corner, and tried to interpret it as a crumpled edge of the bag.

What else had been in it? he wondered. Well, there'd been bits of camping equipment, Dimp, fire-lighters, travel soap-containers....

Dimp – that was it. Dimp, the standard New Zealand insect repellent, which had never noticeably worked against the great Scottish midge, but which Yehune would surely have looked for if he even had the vaguest intention of going near the north of Scotland. That would have taken him to the bag. So it seemed that Yehune had had a look into his diaries. A natural enough thing for any flatmate to do, especially one who'd known him for as long as he had. But the question was, the point that froze Mel's faculties with a sense of danger immediate yet time-delayed, not in any way pressing, long ago done or not-done, was this: what else, what secret and inadmissible things might he have written about in those diaries?

He tried to review it all from memory. Anything about Mairi? Their first meeting, what he'd thought of her? How she looked that night at Tiger Jim's? Her character, vagueness, gregarious nature, personal curvature...? He couldn't think of anything special, in fact he came out almost convinced that there was nothing really compromising in any of the diaries *before the one he carried with him*. Which he'd already made the decision to pull apart and burn at the earliest opportunity.

There was a solid block of notebooks numbered 1-32, kept together in a home-made cardboard box wrapped up with a rubber band, existing in some imaginary velvety darkness inside the Teal bag. Mel could picture them clearly, but not get a hand or an eye to them, not until Yehune went out. And there was a problem – Yehune seemed to have taken it into his head not to go out at all.

He waited, and waited and waited, for Yehune to leave the flat. Over the next two days, the freelance tutor was forced to go out several times to meet with pupils, but there was no particular reason why the other shouldn't be in all the time. Whenever Mel came back, there was Yehune. Hanging his compact stockiness in one corner or another, smoking, playing Thrash and Death Metal, tinkering with the electronic keyboard which had broken down yet again, or making short, cacophonic assaults on the piano. Asking Mel whether he could just run down to Andrews Electrical for some connectors. Enquiring whether he, Mel, wasn't wasting his time hanging around the flat all day, not without an implication that he was cramping his style. Mel had no idea what his friend might be doing while he was away. There wasn't any indication that he ever applied himself, either to composition or anything else. Nor could he really be sure that he never left the flat. It was the timing, the hellish timing of it all.... Mel's abiding hope, his exasperated, nervous prayer, was that some time while he was in Yehune would run out of cigarettes.

That happened, late on Thursday morning, and Mel was finally alone in the flat. He felt as if his hands were someone else's, his procedures cunning, careful, un-Mel-like, as he unearthed the bag (which turned out to be crushed under the ironing board on the opposite side of the room from the pile he'd been obsessing on). The diaries were in order. Well, OK, they would be. Dimp? Not there. Either he'd put it back in the wrong place, or Yehune had taken it with him on his trip.

He quickly discovered that skimming his own crabbed handwriting wasn't enough to give him the answers he wanted. There was far too much of it. He couldn't find the passage he remembered; there wasn't time to go through systematically and prove that he *hadn't* written anything about Mairi. Expecting Yehune back any moment, he took the whole box and jammed it into his work satchel, so that he could go out and read and read in some café, preferably one where Yehune wasn't likely to come bouncing in on him.

It took him days to find the comment about the fag-rolling. He reviewed dozens of jocular observations about Yehune, life, girls, Mairi and Mairi's parents and hangers-on, and the Ensemble, and the Concert. And ended up as uncertain as before. There was nothing in there, he thought, that couldn't be taken in good part by an open-minded Kiwi joker who knew perfectly well that it hadn't been written for his eyes. Or was there? Nothing much about Mairi, nothing *admiring*. ... But the account of that piercing consummation, that bout on a mattress, transcendent vintaging, violation and shame, he tore to pieces and burned on a waste piece of ground beside the Union Canal towpath.

Right up until the evening before, Mel tended to be somewhere else whenever Mairi might be likely to drop in. That night, he happened to know she was away at a conference. So it came as a surprise to him, as he walked in tired after his last pupil on Rosebery Crescent, to see a compact young woman approaching their entrance along the other footpath, arriving there just ahead of him. The sudden drop at the

401

pit of his stomach, the reasonable arguments for the impossibility of it being Mairi while at the same time some other voice begged for it to be her, for them to meet, exchange words, begged to be catapulted again into the heart of life where things would happen then and in the next instant and the next, no matter how painful those things might turn out to be – all of it would have been familiar to anyone who'd been in love.

Not that he was, of course. Oh no. Wasn't his type.

'Mairi!' he said. 'I thought you… weren't you supposed to be off in Nottingham?'

'Oh aye… yes. It's tomorrow, I'm taking an early train.'

'… From Waverley?'

He already had his key ready, but the buzzer sounded from indoors at the same time, and Mairi pushed in the outer door.

'Are you coming out with us to the Amphitheatre?' she asked.

'Um… dunno… who you going with?'

She was in a mauve-coloured short dress under her jacket, dressed for going out. The chiselled clarity of her face must have been from some extra-subtle makeup. They both hung back in the darkened recess of the stairwell base, neither of them apparently wanting to go on to the three downward steps and the door.

'How does he seem to you?' she began in a hushed voice. 'I mean, his health?'

'Ah, not bad… why?'

He damned himself for the habit of speaking without giving any information. Mairi looked around carefully in the echo-chamber of the stair.

'Because of that doctor's line he's trying to get… you know.'

'Oh right.' He knew nothing about any doctor's line.

'Well, it doesn't matter. I just wondered.'

'You mean, like… for some sort of benefit?'

'Yes. Surely you knew about it?'

'But can you do that, up here…?'

They were already at the numbered flat door; any more hesitation might have seemed unjustified either to the buzzer of the entry phone or to themselves. He looked at her. There was a moment when her eyes moved towards him as well, as if they were about to connect in sympathy; but she must have felt the danger at the last moment. Her eye twitched away, in two quick movements, her head turning with it away from Mel and the door.

Which was pulled open from the inside. Yehune was there, bulking to fit the lower half of the doorway. His shirt was open, a fag smoked in his hand.

'Fuck, guys,' he said, 'y'*can* come in.'

Old Town Evening

In Caffè Fiorentino
  'Forren-teeno. Uh-huh. Yellow one. Sunflowers.'
earlier in the day
  'Ah, 'fore lunchtime, a bit. I was there with…'

> *In Caffè Fiorentino*
> *Earlier in the day;*
> *In Caffè Fiorentino,*
> *Not a helluva way away*

Words fell together into lines, mumbled and repeated, endlessly shuffled and reshuffled in the head, while street scenes in Teviot Place and Forrest Road presented themselves and changed and fled past and flashed up again in different colours. It was all so resonant, full of an almighty resonance. 'Mighty', yeah boy.

'Yehune, you're talking about today, right?'

'Na well… yeah.'

'Today, the morning. Of which it's now the evening.'

'You got a point?'

'Um, yeah, that Fiorentino's on some side street just off the Royal Mile, and now we've decided to do a pub crawl right along there.'

'Yeah?'

Mel said nothing more. Yehune just stomped alongside, the top of his head clearly visible from just above. And feathered arclights, stroking past the Unibuildings.

'Max pubs f' th' distance. What else d'you want?'

> *In Caffè Fiorentino*
> *It wasn't quite so keeno*
> *For Yehune in that fucking scene-o*
> *Not a million miles…*

The words of layabouts cut into the line, high ecstatic noises male and female, and a guttural voice sounding out, *'Yech yech!'*

Yech yech, yep-yep, here in the University surrounds on a Saturday night that was the noise that synapsed, he meant synopsed it all. Where groups of tall and brutal-voiced young Lochinvars escorted their ladies-love past shopfronts closed and delicately lit-lit-lit on top of the lighting by spheres and ambits of a thousand bulbs.

Yech; and we're no better. Only three along so far. A corniced premises pointed out ahead, a well between shop and shop.

'Oddfellas there,' Mel pronounced. 'We bother?'

'Na. Fa' the cat... the hat... the Crappit Hen.'

Alcoves. He could remember alcoves there. And small drinks, little drinks're better, easier to get down you than a gassy great half pint. They went they strung along they strang along the road that led to the long unfolding bay of the Grassmarket with its other pubs; not there; not yet to Greyfriars Bobby on the corner.

Fioren, Forren-teeno.

Mel was able to imagine the earlier scene in the café, to build coloured transparencies of fact-after-the-event that floated out of synch above and through their alcove in the Crappit Hen. A drink was in front of him, Yehune across from him. But back there behind the yellowy shopfront on St Giles Street – how different! Well, I mean, it is different, it looks different. And as he saw it over again, tweaked and reinvented it, the clanks and bangs and straying voicetracks of the Hen went clucking crappitly in his ears, not dispelling the illusion but in some way maybe even helping it along....

Yehune comes in with Murphy. Now, Murphy's an ex-Ensemble member; might've met him in the street soon after seeing Mairi off at the train. And they sit. In the first of two rooms, would you say, Yehune facing outwards? There at a table topped with a minuscule parquet of wooden squares, all settled in and looking out like eyes – two heads; two yellow sunflowers.

In the background, reflections of trays and tables in the window glass. A noisy throng of people in the next room, among which, strangely pointed out (though Yehune hasn't seen them yet), Pom and his wife Alice, his bulky form frozen in a gesture over a forkful of cake.

Three figures move in. With subdued blaze of trumpets. Two

stretch across the small tabletop, while the other occupies Murphy in a counter-conversation. Three unknowns, hovering grey-black as kites....

'Who were they, exactly?' Mel asked now, 'These guys that came looking for you?'

'Oh, Perce... from the Ensemble. He was in Andrew's split group. The other two I don' remember seeing.'

Yehune shifted his weight in the woodtone darkness. 'Might be... dunno. Could have been some of the ones who came...'

'Came what?'

'Ah, one of the ones who only came once or twice... always end up thinking I owe them money.' And he turned up big eyes. 'Imagine that. *I* owe *them*. God, they'd better look out for a better-heeled prospect.'

'... So you mean they were asking for their money *back*?'

'Could've been, could've been.'

All of the three are serious in the face. Two lean, one fat in a multi-coloured cardigan. One of the leaner ones in a brown suede jacket, with a beaklike nose and disappearing chin. Inclined across the table to Yehune, while Murphy shamefacedly stands.

Yehune: 'Fucking wanna go... I'm not interested in all this stuff. Let me...'

Beak nose: 'You'll just stay where y'are. *Perce,* hold him, will you?'

And here there's what you might call a minor disturbance, attracting disapproving glances from other café-goers sitting or standing. Clash of cutlery in the intercut, and a rustle of voices. The table, then, must be far enough out from the wall for fatboy to move in behind and get a grip on Yehune's shoulders. He squirms. He calls on Murphy, but that one's been led aside and is involved in another exchange, with righteous intonations, pound signs glinting from under the fuzz like blue-silver medallions.

One result is that a Fiorentino staff member forges out from behind the counter, to calm down or chuck out, not that he looks too ecstatic about it personally. Bustling the queueing bodies. Not quite managing to get through; because at just that moment *Pom* appears with a chunky hand held up, to have a word or two…. Wild woodnote tones. A sough in the café air.

Pom says, 'What's all this about?'

The interlopers naturally ignore him. Awfully rude it is, up here, to break in on a private conversation.

But 'Excuse me,' he begins again, with all the presence of his six-four 16 stone-odd, 'this is a friend of mine. I've just come over to tell him it's time to go.' And to Yehune, 'Come on.'

'You've got some bloody strange friends then,' says the cardigan. 'Look, we've got something to talk about to this conman. He owes us money.'

Suede jacket: 'Hands off 'im. *Come* on, get your…'

But Pom by then has prised himself in between wall and tableside. Fights a quick engagement with the rival pair of hands; takes Yehune by the shoulders and all but hoists him in full body out of the chair,

'You can talk later. Right now, we're going.'

'Fucking leave off… I'm not letting you go now, Trent.'

And various shouts, 'Just mind your own…', 'Keep out of this…'.

Where's Murphy by now, and Alice? Nowhere to be seen. The ex-Ensemble party has deserted his leader, possibly for the second time; the third man's gone with him; and now something of a channel's opened in the distribution of clients to give any malcontents a free path to the door, should they choose to avail themselves, bla bla. Cardigan's left at the table. But before Pom and his friend quite get there, the one in the suede jacket (nose protruding like a submarine) just touches his arm, and Pom turns, yes?

'I'll be remembering you.'

Pom's face opens, and humorously, in his slow West Country voice,

'Much good may it do you.'

While back here in the Hen, in the barnyard clack of bottles,

'Gods, can't believe old Pom… of all people. Been thinking he'd sort of disappeared into the…'

'But he lifted you out.'

'*Lifted* me all right. Can still feel it, eh, he must have clicked a neck muscle… whaddayacallit.'

Rubbing his neck. Under the eyes of wall posters, drinks there in front, the two of them alone again in the absence of Mairi were constantly checking each other out in eye and profile. She was away in *Nottingham* – Nottingham. Bizarre. … For some reason, the conversation of those two world-wanderers turned around very older days; the early forms of things in a country of beaches and strong sunlight; going to school in compounds of painted weatherboard.

That is, until Yehune was on the point of moving out. But ducked back quickly behind an ornamental wooden edge,

'Holy – bloody – shit. Hide me man.'

'Whaddaya mean? It's…'

'One of them – I recognise 'im.'

Mel's head turning. Drinks centred, as before, on the tabletop, each a perfect rounded stadium floating on liquid rings.

Said, 'It's not like anyone can see you right in here.'

'Shh… kee' quiet. Don't get up.' Yehune shuffled nimbly past him and hunkered half down behind the well-worn tabletop. 'Jus' go on talking without saying anything – tell me when they're…'

'Oh right. Well…'

In Mel's pocket, under trailing fingers, a scurf of lint, two tissues. He began to heel the tongue at random catching the moment's squall, to talk about them: tissues as a phenomenon; as a socio-economic icon; their takeover from the handkerchief; concept of waste; of forest regeneration; tissues from their own point of view; what a shit life it must be to be a tissue; squashed into the middle of someone's face only to be cast aside afterwards, as you might say, like a used tissue; or else shoved into a pocket to fester until you're taken out and snorted on again. For his part he had to say he abhorred the practice….

… While down in the seatrace, face of old Yehune. How old it seemed. Washed-out and colourless in the remnants of smoke wafting in from his own cigarette, those tired fretful features not far over the level of the table behind which (as someone not sympathetic to the man would have said) he cowered, waiting body folded, one arm and shoulder still out of the mix and slight-lifted straight across the edge of the brink of the. Not quite enough room to get right down. So he had to accommodate his thick body and limbs to some invisible arrangement of corner and rustic bench-struts; he was blotchy, indistinct, the lower face with its darkening of stubble looking to the talker like a clown's mouth smudged.

Mel had a peculiar vision then. Seeing, side-on, that old familiar face in the instant faced by another, the same again, but divisional, a clearer brighter spectre forming in the air: of a Y a Yune far younger, the hair a woolly gloss, eyes aspark with devilry and humour. Now with two aerials, fizzing biactionary wands that cut up into the air one side and the other as if sending receiving messages on the aether – split lightnings – afloat on two drifting densities of smoke.

Cut across. Like a swift, a sudden mental shaving. Face to face. God that's

Str

… and back in time, Mel craned his neck around the edge. Kept talking, even though he might have been losing the thread a bit, as he searched the visible through and across and back again. For what could be cruising. Swimming in circles lazily for the kill.

At the bar, he saw an ordinary human figure, in a humped brown jacket that might have been suede or might not, doing something with a drink and talking to some others.

'Parker'. A quick association with that word. Something in the back and understated chin and forward-thrusting submarine of a nose. Could that be relevant? Help, at all, like in a description? … No.

So he pulled back to face a Yehune who was factual and unmirrored,

'Saw 'im at the bar. Seems to be on the point of leaving.' He craned his head again, and, 'Going… going… no no, hang on.'

The exit of Parker turned out to be the slowest event in human history, fraught with setbacks and false starts and re-engagements and elaborate farewells, and beginning all over again whenever anyone there brought up a new subject; none of which is worth much going into, while Yehune sat there or rather crouched, not even drinking but just endured, existed, as much a part of the furniture as the framed display of wine labels a metre or so above his head. Cracked side of a cabinet under glass. Colour: archaic yellow. *Stamps of Australia.*

And when the group had wended its way to the door and finally trickled through it one by one, he pulled himself up to seat level. Even then, he didn't seem in a hurry to leave.

'We should get going,' Mel commented. 'Could come back – never know.'

'Shit… just settling in. I mean, look at my…' A finger crooked at his glass.

Stamps of

Mel leaned over the table, grabbing Yehune's shirtfront, taking the gin glass in the other hand, and made as if to tip it down his throat.

'Hey!' the man said. 'Don't touch the shirt…. Bloody half-arses before already creased me up.'

But gave in, drank it down, and wiped his mouth. 'Aaaaahh.'

So they were out in the street again, gazing at luminosities man-made and natural in the sky now dark and aching cobalt overhead, and around and in front of them, lights, lines, pavement and shadows, all swinging as they turned and tic by tic regressing as the two together propelled themselves along the roadside. Everyone was there, or it seemed so, either squatting in a doorway with an ash-muzzled dog or arms-around-the-shoulders swaggering and singing on the sidewalk, boys with girls, girls with girls, and their own version; and they hesitated for a moment before plunging all the way down Candlemaker and scouting, Maggie's? Milligan's? Last Drop, there? and looking in and deciding for or against, and kept breaking off on different tacks whenever the memory of a licensed premises happened to occur to one or the other of them. Seething at the head with words, singly or in phrases, apparently falling in from nowhere – so that it felt to him to Mel as if a stitched and ragged hem of language wandered away in front of them across the ground, threading roadsides, pavements, selected doors and entrances, which his feet invariably followed, pitch or hesitate or retrace his steps as he would: words fine-printed or handwritten or blocked in thick headlines, future-harbingers, reeling and weaving from concrete to asphalt to the rough parquet and back again.

…

410

At a hearth unreasonably crowded, smoke and fire, The Jolly Judge, the words came back into their mouths. So they must have made their way all the way up Vic Street and over the Mile, gone nosing in among the Closes. They stood uncomfortably, looking for something in each other or themselves like a great pre-dating of all their troubles – back to school days, where their eyes were dazzlingly open, time was half-begun.

Yehune, head strained upright: 'Fuck, feel I'm throbbing... like, here on my back and shoulder.'

Mel: 'Still? C'mon, let me tickle it up a bit for you.'

'No fuckin' – once was enough.'

'Oh yeah... d'you still remember that? In the Geog class, fourth form, was it? I really gave you a good, ah, bash – then old Hodgey turns round, knows something's happened but he's not sure what...'

'God, that hurt. You fucking bastard.'

'You were jabbing me with, whatsit, compasses. Anyway I couldn't feel my hand for an hour or so afterwards.'

'And no-one told 'im. No-one said a word.'

'Dumb insolence.'

'Well, I think I saw Jim looking a bit stuffy.'

'Was he there?'

The Jolly Judge was the smallest bar of all, so someone'd said. No seats were to be had, and they'd propped themselves on a bar-edge, choking lightly in the unnecessary smudge-fire from the hearth. Jim, he was the third of them; now Mel couldn't even remember –

'Can't even remember why we called him the Excise.'

'Customs and. You know, on account of he w's always so straight?'

Mel aspirated towards the ceiling, 'Fff. In *those* days.'

...

And walking down the Mile was not long after when the sky, painted in jazz of dark and light, beckoned to him with an upright finger and a Coca-Cola smile that was born, somehow, out of broken shouts and snatches of sound effect, and sense melting into sense, and the numbness like a frozen muzzle over your face. The talk between them straggled on, jumping episodes from their history without benefit of fill-in: they were walking side by side on the Great

Wall Badaling, Mel stopping to sketch the shape of the ramparts; dossing in Belorusski; later with Geoff and his wife Jenny, when all the trouble had begun. Sort of a legend, that was. Like all the words foreseen and retroseen. Always been trouble, y'know, an' always will be. Which Mel attempted to explain now in human language, crossing over a street from which two teenage girls and a Scotty dog in tartan advanced in a bright slick colour-world of their own; Yehune was heeling to the left....

Oh, St Giles Street? He was sliding towards it. Reeling away, like a planet on a woozy orbit.

Wooze a million miles away

Mel: 'Hey you're nudging me.'

In Caffè Fio-Fio-Fio

'Hey, we're...' (Laughed.) 'That's actual Caffè Fiorentino. Not goin' in *there*.'

'Na, mean, there's a bar. Some place upstairs.'

'You cracked? You don't mean the one right over the café?'

'Fuck yeah.'

'Fucking *no*, Yehune. You're further gone than I even thought.'

'But I...'

Forcefully, Mel forced against the flow. He directed Yehune like one of those lopsided electronic balls, spinning aconcentrically, reconnecting somehow with a line that led off and away from there. Stitches in the grass. Well, asphalt, more.

Yehune mumbling all the time, protesting, in one bar of which Mel caught a word '(lightning)', which was then repeated punitively in his ear,

'Lightning.'

Never strikes twice, of course, which is another bloody legend. Surprising such a sensible chap, or maybe not really when you think about it. Some scraps of their old connection seemed to be resurfacing, so that Yehune felt free to discuss things to do with his art, whether real or off the top of his head was hard to say; as they found their way one by one through the doors of the major pubs they'd come to sample, Alba Bar and Mitre and Royal and World's End, Waverley,

Tass, with a brief excursion sideways down along Cockburn Street to another three on wha'wasit Market Street below. The wandering put Yehune onto the subject of wandering; he mumbled something-or-other about 'Us Jews', or was it 'Us t'choose'?

At the time Mel was busy trying to balance the amount of change left in his pockets with the number of drinks they'd had; it came out that they'd gone through a whole lot more than he'd ever allowed for.

Yehune was blasé,

'It's just the 'quiv'lent of drinkin' a bottle of gin.'

'Each?' said Mel.

From time to time Yehune allowed him precious glimpses into a brand-new work-in-prospect,

'Yeah, so, like, it's this great idea, can't have come from me, you know everything I think up's sort of, um, I dunno; that's why I think it must have been visited on me, or that's not *why*, I just noticed in a sort of moment somewhere along the line how things seem to work...'

It was all crammed together in a hurry, as if he only had a few minutes to describe the remarkable landscape of his future vision.

And though the lightning didn't really ever strike, or anyway not in exactly that way, they had amazing encounters in mid-High Street with people they couldn't anyhow have expected to meet, as when a pram pushed on by a dogged young woman just missed crushing Yehune's rear foot, Mel glimpsed at the same time two faces approaching,

Said, 'Hi.'

No response. Until just as they were passing one of the pair elbowed her escort,

'Oh, *look* Fabio, it's your old English teacher.'

'Ah – ah yes... Mr Malv.' Her gentleman had to pause and put out his hand.

'Hi-hi. How you doing?'

Waved the other arm, embarrassed, 'Well – as you see...'

The girl put in insinuatingly, 'He gets all his English lessons from *me* now.'

While in the meantime Mel was catching vibrations of speech

413

between Yehune and the pram-driver,

'Emma. I'm Emma. You know. Roberts-that-was.'

'M... m'God. How's, uh, Nicky these days?'

and on it went, a mess of two half-conversations, obbligato, chewing and rechewing the relics of scrap histories. Six people and a vehicle formed a tangle on the pavement other people found it hard to get round; loud swearwords fell in as they tried. In the end it did break up, and off they wove, hoping not to run into anyone else. Nice to hear old Nicky's. His heel: not hardly pulverised. ... What was she fucking doing walking there with a *pram*?

Now further down on the Canongate the evening was rumbling well, *yech yech*; and among quick dislocated descriptions of Yehune's new idée fixe Mel began to have an idée of his own, which was, why not tell all? Get it off his chest. Ah, by the way mate – something I've been meaning to tell you. You know when you took off that time, left me in a private huddle with Mairi without the least fucking idea when or if you'd be back... well, actually, sorry and all that, but. It was so easy: the gin and ambient lights sucked up and engulfed the meanings, cruising fireflies, just as soon as they got out of the dream-mouth, assimilating them into the directionless rampage of shooting stars that was the real world of Saturday night in Edinburgh's Old Town. He was well enough aware Yehune would react. He'd beat his head in, then murder him; no doubt get up to even more; never forgive him either, not if he knew his own best mate; Mel would be homeless and friendless and cast adrift in a city he had no real reason to be in; but just now on the corkscrew of some momentary self-disgust it only made the idea seem more attractive.

Yehune was still talking, saying what? Train of thought elusive, as usual. As if he harped on a subject with some part of his mind on the basis of currents you might call hidden, interstitial. – Stish, stish, stish'l. – Yeah, nice sound.

And Mel was actually opening his mouth, he was about to begin. Ah, Yehune, you know when...? Ah, Yehune.... When suddenly and belatedly, he realised why he couldn't; a woman's face flashed past him in painted stripes, chuckling of girls' voices at the street sides. It

414

came as a shock to him. When did he get so dumb? Naturally there was Mairi to think of; if he confessed he'd be confessing for her as well.

For some reason he stopped and started to turn in a sort of stumbling circle. Yehune lumbered on for ten or twenty paces before noticing,

'Ah, mm, an' I've been thinking a lot about water, like if you put your head up under the shower you know there's this kinda…'

And then, to the last site of the evening – if it was the last. But this is the way it goes with pub crawls, when after all that brave unhampered motion through the streets the fingers of the drug begin to snake their way into the neural pathways, people look round for a seat, surroundings cease to shift, and everyone starts to try to gather hisis'er forces for the big walk home. They'd got as far as B. A. R, the ground floor of a modern stucco building on the last slope on the left as you go down. B. A. R. being 'bar', but also standing for whatever words you might care to choose to put to it. Barometric Appurtenances are Rare. Bloody Anal Wreck. No, that's a W. Bending Ancient Roo-gooouu… no word came. In the meantime the two of them were engulfed, in a civilised enough way, in the strategic shadowing of the venue, where not much could be seen but what the management wanted you to see – heads bobbing under a shiny disco globe; the bar, lit up in glowworms of bright blue and indigo.

They found a place at a two-chair table under one wall. Diagonally behind them, a row of masks in peculiar shapes, cunningly lit. A New York skyline. Human-simian mix. A noseless face, faintly ghastly in the interplay of colour and cast light. Yehune looked back; then, presently, across. There was a line of girls moving endlessly past them between the dance floor and the bar, mostly obscured behind the bodies of their escorts.

He pulled himself up to go and get drinks. Mel was left behind, imagining what rats, webs, man-eating plants might be lurking in the smudges between the lighty bits. No-one there he knew? Nope, not a. Now, if Mairi had been there *(if Mairi had been there…)* – she would have discovered and collared and talked to at least four different people out of the stream of passing heads. But not, 'cause she wasn't. Nottingham... she was in a kingdom of old battlements, pennants flying off the tops of towers. He saw it, reasonless, and straight away started wanting to be in a place like that, or at least look at it, apprehend through windows passing. Notice, no f'k'ng windows. Or they don't work, funny thing that, about a bar.

Later a while, Yehune being back, the conversation did flow well enough, without rhyme or reason, beginning or end, except when he took it into his head to go on a bit about his idea. They tapped on the table, complained about the music (Yehune did inane vocalisations), slurred out words, took up new slumping or decayed positions on their chairs. Yehune made a thing of fitting his lighted fag in one of the designer holes in the chairbacks, or in a branching support under the table, or one of the wall-ornaments.

Mel said, 'Shit. Feel like changing.'

'Drinks? ... Wouldn't.'

Some spiked-hair marvel in a yellow-and-black shirt stumbled on the back of Yehune's chair, and stood peering into his face,

' 'S at you, Barry?'

Yehune by then seemed to have loosened up completely; he was more than willing to talk about any detail that occurred to him,

'It's a sort of, looking into the place it might have *come* from, imaginativ-ly I mean; if you can hear all those voices jabbering and all that you can at least thinkofa sort of place where it all, you know. And that's my subject. See it, you know, like a sort of cavemouth, opens inwards, and there's water there, definitely lots of water, singing water, *tinkling* water, all that bloody incredible South Island beech forest outside the entrance where you can see the light breaking through like, um. It's a pool, there's a pool inside, I think, or could be'm sure...'

So much, in fact, that Mel began to doubt that the project had even existed before the accidental slips and runnels of thought of this particular evening. Or might it have? ... He didn't have the impression Yehune did anything at all, left in there all day.

Shyly, he tried out,

'So how's things goin', these days?'

Yehune gave an upbeat answer, all about how this new idea was going to *revolutionise* everything, which was a word he'd used a few times already. Everything was a rev, a rev-rev. At a table nearby, further into a localised light-pool, a healthy girl rose up suddenly in indignation, shouting words at her table partners, and flounced out into the crowd in a gorgeously-embroidered skirt. Yehune's head followed her.

He let it slump back, talking about the flat now, how it drove him crazy, what a filthy little claustrophobic hole it was – how it seemed to eat time – *drink* time – conversationally, his eyes hunting about the ceiling.

'Yeah, well,' Mel commented, 'we're going to have to move soon anyway.'

'Right-right. ... Why?'

'You know. Landlord. Eviction order. They're going to pull the place down.'

'Oh... huh.'

... 'We haven't been anywhere for a while, have we?'

'Whassat?'

'I mean, you have. Might've been forgetting, or...' and stopped, and started again. 'Shit, it's an idea though, isn't it? We could just, bop on. Why not? Get out of here again. Well, we...'

'Yehn' what'd we use for money?'

'Ahm, hmm. Well, s'pose it can be got.' A pause. 'If you could maybe find yourself some sort of job...'

'A jo-, jo-, jijo-jo-jo.'

Yehune's face didn't change at all. But it was straight away obvious, all too obvious, God, what, that it was a betrayal of everything he was doing or trying to do and all his pretensions to you know artisthood, didn't mean that or not in that way really, I meant just get a grip, above all stop living off Mairi

...

The next thing that happened was *the noise*. Nothing else was different, Yehune was saying something, when such a catastrophic and murderous discord of wreck and simultaneous jangling counterwaves rang out around them that Mel wanted to lie on the floor with his

417

hands over his ears, couldn't believe that everyone there hadn't stood stock-still, rocked to one side, fallen with ruptured blood-vessels; it was like a sudden single collision of what could have been metal machinery and something structural, as if the whole building next to theirs had been demolished, like that, at a blow. Yehune was

'Look at that guy up there, thinks he can dance. S'many guys think they can dance. Don't tend to and at least I know I can't, not even in the old days like in the rugby. But it makes me wonder, an'…'

when it came, with a

CARROOOuuuughhrasscccchhha gggeeaorbaa*aaghhesithasitha* feefeeafeefrifrifi mentenanceofstressesonthe thak a tak a thun thu chordsmusttrussbeorientedfractionfractalfracc peganmaskincursion-memmemm a bum a bumthunathunthun*thuntuntunta* flectcracking-creasedirrecslipcapacnecstabstablitycontoolrevorttracAAcapalbucklA OOAAV**AWEAAAIIIAkkhkkkrraiklbuurorummbll**

An accident, a terrible accident; crane fallen on a building, aeroplane driven into one, this one right here that they were sitting in; still it was as if no-one else appeared to notice or care; small silvery crowd of heads still bobbing on the dance floor, waiters sailing to and fro, even Yehune he was just talking on as if he didn't realise everything he said had been finally and definitively wiped across –

'… girls.'

Mel stumbled out in the still the stillness

'God – I've got speakers – in my fucking *ears*. Anything come across as unbearably loud, to you?'

Beginning to hear music

'Hrrrf hrrf hrrf,' Yehune laughed wheezily. 'Somethin' broke.'

…

A long while later, Yehune moved on his chair. Taking his time, like an enterprising sloth.

'What about you then, what're *you* doin'?'

Mel, succumbing to an inward stillness, painfully sparked into by flints of motion and noise:

'Can't do anythin'. Just write diaries.'

'Diaries, oh yeah, your diaries,' he said affectionately, reminiscently. Then, 'So what about all those fuckin' bollockin' great bits of paper?'

'That's just somethin' I started.'

'Might as well, eh,' he began at random. 'Fuckin' might as well. In fact you better had. Not me, I'm... not really. It's the other thing. Where y'goin'?'

... 'So what's this project of yours?'

Now, although Yehune opened a jaw shaded with hairs and started talking, it wasn't the sort of talk that could even be remembered afterwards, giving no picture, focussing on nothing, but rolling on and away among the hard high fragments of chipped impression that were Barland in the specific moments it was happening. A girl's face, reddened like clay under her multi-dyed hair. Two bouncers shouting chat without a soundtrack. Angular wall-extensions, could be for candles. Mel tried out a question or two, interested in finding out at least what medium Yehune was talking about: words? music? static installation?... quickly coming to realise it wasn't a question he even cared about. It was a location, not much more; some New Zealand forest-and-cave apotheosis he'd once been in or dreamed about or seen in a picture; and all these words and words weren't so much an opening up or any attempt to communicate anything as a smokescreen, a detrack, action in absentia, a long-line mumble accompanying some thought process hidden behind the mask that well-worn face was starting to resemble. Human-simian mix. Skyscape reliefs. Impassively running backwards, through history to pre-history. ... Not so much the ears. Those you could sometimes catch something from: a setting, hints of an expression.

'Wan' a... wan' another gin?'

Yehune did. Mel had already made up his mind to sit this one out. He was thinking of going soon.

In some sort of cacophony of repeating loops he forced himself up out of his chair and into the swim, bathing backwards with his arms to help himself through to the bar. Dry-shouting into a roar. Barman wheeling, taking orders; beyond him how he could even hear a word. Mel waited, picked up a single glass, shouldered his way back without spilling it, just. Someone was standing there arguing about the vacant chair. Mel took possession, trying to avoid making it into a fight. He sat. Started talking vaguely about plans, the past the future. Not Mairi, which he couldn't do; though he would have done. Would have done. If not for, fu-u-u-u. Nor any idea of a job. But what were they thinking of doing now, given that their lease was up? Yehune seemed to listen, and agreed to everything. But his head was down, he looked nearly gone. Best not bring anything up, not now when the guy was revving at an all-time low....

About ten minutes later, though, the Yehune head rose again. With mischief and ill intent, eyeing the skirts of girls passing them by. Seeing through and through. Some oriental-type confection, wrapped tight like a robe. One white mini, clean lined above the clean milk-coloured tights.

'You goin'?' he asked.

'Ah, yeah... I'm feelin' a bit, you know...'

'OK then. Get out, 'n leave me here. I want to pick somethin' up.'

'... I wouldn' do that.'

'No-no-no. G'out. L'me. I want... *hrrrhmm,*' he cleared his throat, shook himself at the shoulders, 'I wanna ride tonight.'

Mel had stood up; he was looking down at the tight-curled head top. So what had made him why'd he think there was any sort of moral question about this or that or anything when the tone was just about this?

'Wish you luck.'

The last impression he had was of Yehune's head dropped down again, talking about his project.

'... A pool among rock edges... maybe... pool among limestone.'

That was all.

What happened next was a different kind of reconstruction. Yehune must have been in the bar for about another quarter of an hour, not nearly enough to pick anyone up. The next sighting was by a taxi driver, at about twenty-five to eleven: Yehune had been in the High Street with a backpack he'd somehow acquired, probably already containing a large bottle of water he'd bought in a shop. He'd taken the taxi to Spottiswoode Street. There, he'd buzzed Mairi's parents (it wasn't too late yet), and with all sorts of sweet talk and apologies prevailed on them to let him use their loo. He didn't appear especially drunk, but smelled strongly of alcohol and cigarette smoke. He was polite and well-behaved; he'd asked after Mairi, used the toilet, and left. Neither of them had noticed that his bag was bulkier when he left than when he'd come in. It was only the next morning that they discovered their medicine cupboard, which had been bursting with all the medications and quack remedies either of them had had occasion to try over the last ten years or more, was empty of everything but cotton buds and tampons.

No clue has been found to the form of transport that brought him to the Queensferry Road leading north; but there, by the reconstructed story, he hitched a lift with a lorry driver over the Forth Road Bridge and out on the M90, then the A9. The report came in some time later that he'd seemed sleepy. And that after a while he'd said he was desperate for a leak, and asked the driver to let him off somewhere before Dunkeld, where there were plenty of covering bushes.

He must have wandered around there for some time, taken all the pills he hadn't already taken, and found them slow to have the desired effect. In any case he was some distance away, near Birnam, when he found an old stone bridge and climbed up onto the side, then either lost his balance or threw himself down onto the ground below.

Death and Elsa

A few stray scraps, blowing through his mind like torn-off bookmarks. Around them there was a sort of darkness, lightly reflecting, neither brown nor black, like the funereal look of certain bricks he'd seen – where was it? His memories of that whole period were uncertain, almost as if some objective event could have the power to send shockwaves in through his nose and ears and eyes and affect the working of the mind behind them. He had a confused impression of trips here and there, to chapels, auctioneers', and municipal offices. The telephone ringing on and on; and having to pull the jack out of the wall to get a quarter of an hour's rest.

But of course, nothing was irrecoverable. It was all in there somewhere, and you could sort it out again, organise it into separate headings and maybe write them down on a bit of paper.

The next morning, the Sunday, he had to go out and give three lessons. Yehune wasn't back yet; but he hadn't expected him to be.

It was about two thirty when he got back to Gardner's Crescent. There were various people milling in the stairwell. He saw Elsa-up-the-stair just disappearing round the corner of the banister.

A neighbour he barely knew came up to him,

'The police called for you,' he announced in an English-accented bark.

Mel turned round to see the man straining his mouth back in a parody of a smile. He was wearing an old Barbour jacket and trousers that bagged at the knees.

'There were two of them,' he said, 'one a police-*woman*. They were knocking for quite a time. You might find a note? In there, under the door.'

Mel by that time was trying to get the key to turn in his lock. The man fell into a string of insinuations and 'a word to the wise', only cut off when Mel shut the door on him.

He found the note. Rang the number. Was switched from

department to department by official-sounding voices, and then put on hold for a while while they tried to find the right person for him to talk to.

It was a strange conversation, partly because this particular policeman was trying to juggle two roles. He wanted information, but at the same time he was forced to be the bearer of tidings. A body had been found near Birnam, it seemed, with nothing on it to identify it except a small address-book, which contained a name, Y. Trent, and that address. Mel's reaction was a wave of relief and a momentary sense of security: it was so obviously a mistake. Yehune's address-book had naturally been stolen or gone astray somehow. He told the policeman that a Y. Trent did live there, but that he'd been with him the night before, and neither of them had been anywhere out of Edinburgh. The other took note of that, and told him two officers would come round to question him the next day. A pity he hadn't been in when they'd called. Mainly, he needed to know the next of kin.

As the words went back and forth, Mel began to feel an awful suspicion, which crept nearer and nearer to a certainty as the details built up. A body under a bridge, a bag and some empty pill bottles. No actual addresses in the address-book, only a lot of scribbled calculations, possibly meant to be pounds and pence. That was why they knew nothing so far about Mairi, or Mairi's parents, or the national origin of this 'Y. Trent'. What did the body look like? Thick-set, with dark and curly hair.

To start with, he was hit by a sort of wall, lifted out on a darkness of incongruities. No systematic thinking could have unravelled it. It was mainly the swinging away of an entire four-dimensional life, leaving nothing for his feet to stand on. Then everything flooded in, the most selfish thoughts to the fore – a sense of being abandoned, realising he'd never have a chance now to get things right between the two of them, and the quick readjustment of an imaginary balance sheet of win-and-loss. Worse was a sort of tragic scenario of himself receiving the news. And worst of all, a sneaking thought that just slipped in before any of his filters could stop it: that now Mairi would be free.

The whole thing, the wave, the breathless clips, was something he'd experienced before. Which didn't help him in any way. The policeman's routine phrases, regret the this, sorry to give the that, hardly registered on his mind. For a while Mel's lower face seemed to hold up the conversation without any participation from him.

'Next of kin... ah... I don't know. His parents? But they live in New Zealand.'

The result was that it was Mel who was asked, or ordered, to go and identify the body.

'We'll send a car,' the policeman told him.

'What's that? ... Um, look, where is it?'

'The city mortuary. It's OK, we'll be at your house in ten minutes.'

'No. No lifts,' he said. ' – If you don't mind. Where is the city mortuary?'

'297 Cowgate.'

'Cowgate – OK. Right. I can walk there in... half an hour?'

'Whatever you like. But bring the parents' address and phone number.'

To find the address of the Trents in New Zealand was a harder job than you might have expected. Mel stood there surrounded by the clutter of Yehune's present life, looking at shirts discarded before the pub crawl last night, an open Swiss Army knife he might have used to fix a light fitting. After a while, he couldn't stand it any more; he went to get his jacket and keys instead. Address or no address, he had to get himself moving.

He must have walked down to the Fountainbridge end, across to the Lloyds TSB, and on towards the brow of the hill. There, old red buildings with pyramid-edged roofs made a new level, plunging downwards towards the Grassmarket. Colours – a yellow TV aerial van lumbered towards him – were so normal he could hardly believe in them. He could see other, brighter colours, heat-hazed in the distance, and the kerbs that swung in endless sideways pan from his father's car. Back through to childhood, looking out through car windows, where the world streaked fast in lines like grains of treetrunks, or turned, homelike and beautiful, in the light of his open eyes.

...

In Auckland nearly five years before, his mother had been lying in hospital after a series of setbacks in her health. It had begun with some transient ischaemic attacks, progressing to a full stroke which invited tests, and she'd had a double operation on her carotid arteries which had seemed to be successful. Then came the massive stroke that hit her between the recovery room and the ward. After that, most people were expecting her to die. But instead she rallied and started to recover. For a week, then, she'd been slowly recovering, and could get up and walk as far as the door. Mel felt as if he and his dad were living in the hospital; Geoff had come back as well, and Mandy was up from Napier. So Geoff and Mandy had stayed with his mother when, in the heat of the February day, his father had driven him to his appointment with the optician to be fitted for new contact lenses. It had seemed reasonable enough at the time. The streets of Auckland City were dull and deathly functional on the way out; then on the way back, focussed to a diamond point. All the colours and street bustle tearing past with the blank of an inevitable process, something learned, drilled deeply into the brain. Reforming themselves in their immediate proportions at the lights. The hum of the engine, almost unnoticeable against other engines, and the milling of small crowds. The constricted feeling of their surroundings, where both of them sat strapped in and unable to move very far. Slow pace of in-car conversation. Negotiating the judder-bars into the carpark, looking round for a space. And finding his mother and Mandy gone from their place, Geoff hanging back to give them the news.

In the funeral home, he'd been offered a chance to 'view the body'. He hadn't taken it. Never in his life had he dreamed of anything like that being necessary. What was the point of it, he asked himself; what would be the earthly point? Afterwards, when it was too late, he'd had second thoughts about that.

...

With Yehune, or whoever these human remains were, it appeared he wasn't going to be given a choice. High walls towered over him on every side. Of course, he'd scribbled the street number down. But when he took it out and looked at it, he discovered he couldn't read his own writing. So he had to guess at the general level of the Cowgate he was looking for. Streams of sunlight fled in from the steep streets to the side, and were lost in the deep of the road. Shadows followed them, carrying a swirl of rain. He passed the first bridge, black and dripping, which made a tunnel effect around his head and ears. Through to... to nothing, to the street again. But it was like a different street, somehow, and then the next bridge came. In the spaces underneath, old slime had built up in corners, obviously never washed or regarded. How far was he going to have to walk? The third bridge came while the sky rumbled, dark as lead, and he came out again, and walked on, further and further and further down into an illusory bay of rain and shadow.

He'd nearly gone past before he noticed a building on the other side that surely had to be a mortuary. Designed by some literalist architect to look like a many-times-baked stone out of an Auschwitz oven, it broadcast the official face of death. The bricks it was built from were dark, neither brown nor really black, and lightly glazed, so that they gave out a blinking, deceptive pallor.

He had to negotiate stout security fences to get to the door. There were some people inside who let him in. But to get any further, he had to give them a name.

The attendant couldn't find it anywhere.

'So it's a Y – Chin, y'say?' he said, flipping through the pages of his book.

'No. I said Trent.'

'Oh, *Trr-ên*. In the T's then – Y. Trent.'

'Oh aye, that's the suicide,' said a helpful porter passing by.

A little bit later came one of the images that stood out from all the confusion. A thing lying on a slim table, looking surely shorter than a male human could be. And when the cloth was lifted back, it had Yehune's head – or rather, not his head. The features were starker, stronger in contrasts, drained of everything that could be said to have made him himself. The jowl lifted from cheekbones like a matter-of-fact bulge in a range of hills; looking, Mel supposed, the way it must

426

have looked every day he'd known him. A bit of purple bruising crept high on the neck in one place. The rest of it could have been about the right size if you measured it carefully with your eye. But even later, in his worst nightmares or daylight fancies, Mel never imagined it sitting up and flipping him a confidential wink. Instead he had a picture of some papier-mâché artist walking in another door as soon as he was gone, taking the head off and walking away with it under his arm.

He pronounced it 'Y. Trent', and spent some time in an office filling in forms.

What came next? It must have been ringing Mairi. He had to get hold of her at that anonymous conference down in Nottingham. He couldn't just ring her parents – not really. So he dug for a phone number, through papers and accumulations of the most recent junk, which created a sense of overlapping realities that was precise and cruel. Yehune had just gone out for a moment – he'd fiddled with this wiring, scribbled on this pad the night before. Mel was light-headed with it. Not to think about the body was impossible: it blazed out in his mind in all its macabre colours.

Mairi's reaction on the phone turned out to be completely different from his. She left out the incredulous phase, and burst into helpless tears after a very short time. After that she started blaming herself. Then stopped, possibly realising even then, in that extremity, that some of it threw a certain sidelight of blame on Mel as well. And so she went on vaguely about coaches or flights or train times, not able at the moment to work out how she was going to get back.

'Ah, you know, Mairi… there's actually no hurry.'

She went incoherent again, and he realised how badly he'd expressed himself.

When he did ring Mairi's parents, they were cool and matter-of-fact enough. They gave him what details they knew about the previous night. Then he rang the police, when he'd finally unearthed an address (but no phone number) for Andrew and Brigitte Trent from a confusion of Yehune's scribbled notes.

The next morning, Waverley Station. Meeting the 8:45 a.m. train.

Crowds were streaming out of the doors. He'd already decided Mairi wasn't on it when she appeared at his elbow, looking smaller to him than he'd ever seen her – reduced, he fancied for a moment, to slip half-invisible between the hulking bodies of travellers.

They hugged, but only gently. A determined-looking businessman almost ploughed into them. But they stood there, until Mairi made a deep inhalation of breath that grated somehow like a snore.

'It's OK,' he murmured, meaninglessly, and let her go.

Coming through into the flat, Mel had the strong impression of a tropical diorama. 'Steamy,' he thought, and didn't laugh. She was walking in ahead of him, able to be seen and summed up, a little heavy in the forms of flank and haunch, brushing past long-leafed plants. An aspidistra there – no, it really was. And something more exotic that he didn't know the name of, and behind that, vagued-out, something like the green unmoving texture of a forest.

She turned round to him. 'Coffee'll take a wee while,' she said, 'the machine's broken.'

There was the interview with the policemen, which he didn't remember much about. They were suspicious; told him Yehune was there illegally, soaked up his information blank-faced. The next thing that made much impression on his memory was when he found himself with Mairi again in her sitting room in Spottiswoode Street.

It was so different from the last time he'd been in there. Mairi might have been much the same in a physical way. But it was as if they were both inhabiting a frame of reference which was darker, supported on other links, moving at about two thirds of light-speed in a different direction.

'What happened?' Mairi wanted to know.

'I don't know. You know we were on that pub crawl. We just went from one pub to another, and he was talking about some new thing he was starting on.'

'What was the new thing? Did you get an impression... he might have meant...?'

'Mairi. Don't.'

She took some time to control herself. Her face had a look as if she was straining for breath.

'I can't work out *why*,' she said. 'If I'd only been there. Maybe, then, do you think…?'

'I just don't know. Anything's possible. How are we supposed to know how it was when he didn't leave a note?'

'But something must have come across. Wasn't there anything obvious?'

'If there was then it sure wasn't obvious to me. I couldn't get a thing out of him.'

'Is that why you went away?'

Why you went away – Mel had foreseen this problem. Of course, he'd gone off on his own because Yehune had pretended to want to pick up another chick. Equally of course, he couldn't say anything like that to Mairi.

'It was just… it's just how it went. I'd had enough to drink and I had pupils in the morning, would've liked him to come with me, but…'

'Don't think I'm blaming you.'

There was an absolution. But it was obvious to him where the blame had been put.

'It's most *certainly* not bloodywell your fault. For being away in Nottingham?'

'That… and.'

He took a moment. 'You can't think he knew about us?'

'No. Do you?'

'I think he can't have.'

She was standing up, walking one way and the other in front of the fireplace. She seemed to be thinking about it. A brush of sunlight made a relief map out of her woollen jersey.

After a while, she said, 'I can't answer for you or me or any of us. We've all done so many things, and… they pull everything one way, and this time it led to Yehune taking my mum's pills and jumping off a bridge.'

Mel stood up then. 'OK, right. We'll take it systematically. What are the *possible* times he might have guessed anything about it from you? Then from me. There was one time in the stair…'

'No, that time he just thought you and I were plotting about him behind his back.'

'Well then… I can't think of a single solitary thing. 'Course I wrote about it in my diary, but there's no way…'

'Your diary?'

Her face was clarified by surprise as she looked at him; the light of it almost hurt his eyes. So slowly, link by link, Mel explained why it was impossible that Yehune could have worked anything out from his diaries. How he'd gone through every page, taking days to do it; how the only relevant notebook had been with him all the time and then he'd ripped it up and burned it down by the towpath.

After that, she seemed to eject the whole subject forcibly from her mind. Instead she started going into detail about the evening they'd spent together. The men after him for money. How he'd seemed. What he'd said. The new project he talked about. The suggestion Mel had made about going travelling, and about getting a job. She kept coming back to the bit at the end,

'He wanted you to leave that bar. Didn't he? Did he – eh – think of something to get rid of you?'

'No, I just… it was like I said.'

'And then he took a taxi straight here. Because he knew my mum and dad had the pills.'

It seemed that anything in there could be an answer, or nothing. They sat down again, and just looked at each other.

Eventually, Mairi started asking about Mel instead.

'Are you not having to move out soon?'

'Oh yeah. I've been kind of too busy to think about it. But I've been going through Yehune's things.'

'That can't be fun.'

'No – it's a weird feeling.'

'I'm sure my parents would be happy for you to stay here, just for a while. You need – eh – some support.'

'*You* need some support.'

430

She was sitting on the sofa again, where they were separated by about the width of a human body. From just where he was sitting he couldn't see the mirror in the hall. But the room itself was enough to remind him of the handkerchief, and his first mistake. 'Arm around the shoulder'. Though this conversation plainly held no promise for them, though he wasn't looking at those tapering upper legs in trousers as something to be desired, he would have liked to be able to reassure her.

There was a noise from outside the door, and it was obvious that one or both parents had come back. He quickly moved over for the conventional quarter-hug, done more with arms than bodies. And in that moment, a sense of *horror* passed through him – instantaneous, like the shiver of a leaf, and reflected back to him, he thought, in the involuntary movement of her arm and shoulder.

That was when he decided he had to leave right away, and at the same time that there was no prospect of his ever staying at Mairi's, either for a longer or a shorter time. He only had to go to the toilet and he'd be out of their way.

In the bathroom, he curiously examined the white wooden cupboard that had had all the pills in it. Going over the directions of the grain with the tips of his fingers.

When he came out, he caught the eye of Mairi's mother in the hall outside. And she must have looked straight through him,

'Aye, we'll no be keeping so much in *there* from now on.'

She, Elsa, moved so placidly that she hardly made an impact on the long, slow self-absorption of her sitting room. The heating must have been turned up high for the plants. She'd taken her blouse off, with movements so normal and unenticing that they were almost hypnotic, and went on making coffee in her jeans and a violet-coloured bra. Mel kept looking around him, comparing this with their own flat. It was huge here, but he noticed the kitchen was still part of the sitting room. And of course, there was a separate bedroom. Ceremoniously, he took

431

a cup from her, wondering whether he'd have a chance to disturb her when the motions were gone through.

Mel's home life was strange and chaotic. He'd begun to clear the floor and pile up everything Yehune had owned against the back wall by the piano. It gave the space a hollow effect, and sounds began to echo again as they'd done when the room was empty. Into that hole, phonecalls fell continually, from Yehune's friends (Jim from Miami, Alice the wife of Pom), his enemies (two separate groups of Yehune's creditors had got hold of his number and rang it at every opportunity), and his mother in New Zealand, who'd been put in charge of the funeral arrangements.

Brigitte Trent was hard to deal with. Her first call was nothing but an incoherent rant in which she all but accused Mel of taking her 'Johann' away and killing him. Later, she rang again, and was icily controlled. She gave Mel orders about the selling of her son's effects. She proclaimed that the funeral would be held in New Zealand, they'd pay to have the body airlifted back, and any memorial service anywhere else was of no interest to her or the family.

But afterwards, it turned out that the body had to be kept on ice until the inquest – so both services were deprived of the presence of that thing under the sheet.

After some of Yehune's ex-acquaintances had tried their hardest to get in, Mel started to keep the flat's high half-windows covered during the day. He'd reduced his teaching hours, but there was still never enough time to get things done. He had to organise sales of things like the piano and Yehune's keyboard, and sort out a pile of stuff to be freighted back to New Zealand. There were still a few weeks before he had to move out. But he'd done nothing at all about finding another place. He had the sense of things winding down, of time uncontrollably running away behind him.

One evening while the auctioneers were moving the piano out, Mel met his neighbour Elsa coming in the door of the stair. She had to move back against the wall to let them get past her. Mel, of course, apologised to her.

'No harm done,' she smiled back. 'I only wish I was that organised.'

'Oh – you mean the piano?'

'Yes. I haven't even started to think about removals.'

'You're talking about the eviction order, aren't you?'

'Uh-huh. Isn't that why you're getting things moved out?'

So a conversation started up between them in the stairwell. Mel had to admit he hadn't thought about another place to live yet. The piano had belonged to his friend, or what-do-you-call-it, flatmate, who was… recently deceased.

'Oh! I'm so sorry to hear that.'

'Ah, yeah. Thanks.'

'Was it… something you were expecting? Are you all right?'

She leant on the contoured end-piece of the banister. Mel was standing off a bit. He found her easy to talk to; she was good at projecting sympathy, and wasn't at all embarrassed at the turn the conversation had taken.

Like Mairi, she was dark-haired and probably in her twenties. But there all resemblance ended. Elsa was a bit taller and quite a bit fuller-bodied. The jeans she had on, below a stylish cutaway waistcoat coloured purple, were so different from Mairi's jeans, differently fitted, smoother at the creases, rounder and broader and less backwardly-angled, that Mel found it hard to believe both these people were female. Her face, as well, was as different as it could be; a very human face, not looking at all as if it was made out of porcelain. Her eyes were actually blue, though a dark blue; her cheeks were broad and slightly flabby, and little clusters of spots or freckles were positioned near her cheekbone on one side. It was a good face, an attractive face; but one that was hard to read to the depths, not one to betray every passing shade of emotion.

They stood there and talked together in a neighbourly way, until they got tired of the curious glances of other residents brushing past. The auctioneer's van was gone; all the forms were filled in. And so they gravitated to a pub down the road in Fountainbridge, where they went on talking.

Elsa was like blotting-paper. She soaked up everything he said, and generally said only what she had to to keep him going. He found it unusual to be able to trust himself so much in conversation. She didn't drink anything alcoholic; he had two beers and then another half to finish with. By closing time, it occurred to him that he still didn't know very much about her. He'd picked up that she was half-Scottish, half-Scandinavian of some kind (which might have accounted for the eye colour), and she'd been living with someone up there in her third-floor flat who wasn't with her any more.

She invited him up to her flat, 'for coffee'. Her movements ahead of him were slow, shiplike, built on a spacious articulation at hip and haunch. And she did make coffee, laboriously because of the broken machine; and in the course of taking off her jacket and getting comfortable discarded her blouse as well. The air in there was very warm. Other than that, there was no come-on at all on her part. Mel did all the guessing and took the chances; he went up to her and touched her on the bare shoulder.

They ended up in her bedroom, in a real bed, without clothes, and without second thoughts or thin mattresses or wineglasses on the floor. Later Mel would think of the whole thing as something bestial, gonad-driven, maybe because neither of them seemed to expect any relationship to come out of it. She was ultimately passive, which at that time tended to stir him up to the opposite extreme; his movements grew more forceful and energetic, you could even say demanding. And she seemed to expect it. For him, it was a one-off moment, a hard flailing to a consummation.

The picture that stood out for him was from later in the night, where she lay motionless, a statue of dusky feminine curvatures, and he humped and pumped his skinny arse on top of her with an energy that appeared – when he looked back – more furious than sexual.

In a room of different-textured darknesses, sultry and closed in, the ticking of time fled backwards, forwards, or allowed quick cutouts to drop in out of other stories told. Half-diaphanous webs of shading cloth were draped across the windows, but in any case it was full night outside. Moisture naturally built up at their pores. Language, as well as coherence, had deserted them, but occasionally a small sound was audible from one throat or the other. The plants watched, creaking. There was a sense of fecund vegetable growth, and in that atmosphere he moved on her, and moved, and moved, like some great insect overstimulated in the seething of the tropical heat.

Three floors below, in his own flat, the phone was ringing.

'Where were you when I rang?' asked Mairi.

She'd appeared at Gardner's Crescent the next morning. They were off to see the minister of King's Kirk Tollcross, where the British memorial service was going to be held. She might have been got up specially for minister-interviews, in a natural linen-coloured skirt and matching jacket.

'Where were you when I rang?'

'Um, what time was it? – I was probably at the pub.'

'Well, anyway. It was about Pom and Alice – you know they take all those rooms in the B and B?'

'Of course.'

'Well, they've asked you to come and stay with them when you move out, in case you haven't got anything... eh...'

'My God,' said Mel, and looked at her profile floating beside him. 'That's so nice of them.'

'I don't think there's a time limit, except when they move back home themselves. That could be... around the beginning of December?'

'Thanks. Thanks a lot. You didn't put the idea into their heads yourself?'

She said nothing to that. But later, as they walked on,

'Were you away all night? I rang you again quite late.'

'Oh. Yeah. Actually I was with Elsa – you know Elsa, up my stair?'

'I don't know.'

'Well, she lives in a flat like mine, she's going to have to move out too, so naturally we sort of got talking.'

'And you went to the pub with her. And stayed with her?'

'Ah – just the one night.'

She paused. 'And does she know that?'

'Well, I think…. You know, Mairi, it wasn't anything…'

'Mel. I really don't want to know.'

They were on their way down Ponton Street, coming to the corner with West Tollcross. 'But I meant to say…'

'Please.' She turned her face to him above the dull-coloured collar. He could see a twitching strain-line that he hadn't noticed before, just bringing in the edge of an upper eyelid, and started to wonder whether he should have been quite so open, or whether the conclusions he'd drawn about Mairi and himself had been quite so all-knowing.

The memorial service itself came soon afterwards, and should have made little impression on him, meaningless and badly-attended as it was. Ex-Ensemble members had been carefully kept out of the loop. Mel sat there beside Mairi, who was dressed this time in a purple that might have been the closest thing she had to black, and listened to the minister weave fantasies of Yehune's life on the basis of some tags of information he'd provided himself. And they would all be resurrected. And they would all meet again some happy day. There was an elaborate panelling in the dark, varnished wood behind the pulpit: beaded lines like arches soaring up and up, to diverge by some design intricacy at the top. His eyes fled up the sides of the curving seams, up again, and up again, in the echoing clash of voices, as he thought how little any of this had to do with Yehune. Even the flowers looked false, like tiny sculptures of dust. Two old ladies dozed in a pew further back: habitués.

Up, and up, and up, to the peak of the arch… and slide apart.

The effect must have been stronger than he thought. Because it was as if he saw those seams again, high and dark and bifurcating, when Mairi rang him to say she had some time off work and was leaving for the Continent that Friday. She didn't seem to know when she was getting back, and he got the impression she might not even be coming back at all. By which time he was caught up in a different seam or process, channelled away, as he started to pack his things together for the move to Pom and Alice's retreat in Longniddry by the beach.

THREE

And I took the steps three steps it was from the fluffed corroding edge over the plank semi-submerged and then I was springing over on the other side; only felt the unsolidity an instant too late when my feet were skittering down in the sand again. Ahead of me was that big hollow plain which had somehow set into me by now. Diagonally to my right, a field of decaying seaweed. Thinking by now that it all seemed to fit, it did make sense, what Mairi had said, and certainly it went further than I'd taken it myself. So that granite statue of him I'd been carrying in my head was only that, he was both more complex and more aware of himself, flawed at heart and head, and hell-bent spinning off for something whether it was what actually happened or some other damned God-imagined thing. Here, on the far side of the creek, it was all run through and nothing could be taken back. Yet at the same time strangely it felt as if I was making it, re-envisaging it in the roll of every footstep. Ruddered on vision, tricks of motion. It all depended on the way you walked.

I'd started to wander on, higher up from a long extra loop of the creek that ran parallel for a while before the rock level and the sea-edge. Grey, or transparent, or silver, depending how the light fell on it.

I was then I thought I was hearing wavering runs of notes or an aimless sort of chorus in the roar of unpitched noise behind, which for sure must be the wind. But it was louder and louder, till it came above the everlasting moan of the weather. Just then, parallel on the road above the bank, a bus appeared, a double-decker. Now I was seeing it double; to me it was overrun with a whole unruly orchestra of people drunk and shouting and blaring into instruments; their red red faces; bawling out from the frame of the old bus that ground its way progressively past one sign and the other down the line of the coast.

437

Which was only the beginning of worse things; it seemed everything was out in front of me, running away, like a headlong rush of objects static in themselves but animated with a thousand different motions, drawing me on with them until I hurtled out into the throat of the bay with them and over the edge, over it again – bookcases, wall tacks, mounted fish, a chest of drawers mountainous and careening – shooed onwards by more than the wind to what, an edge was edging, fallen out of phase, or any foot or handhold, to the cliff's edge;

to the edge of what in sand and lustred sand no not sa

(But then again why did it matter, why should it even matter what happened to me, which is what I thought long ago about 15 or 16 when everything seemed not much more than what might happen to a character in a novel so long as other people's eyes were off it, well now I was seeing it differently I couldn't help it)

and glanced over to the left, I fixed my eyes deliberately to the left. To the sack of the old sea, bucket to damp the world. ... And for a moment, I could imagine all of it happening again under there, in the vaulted blue and silence.

Those two ships were on the surface of the water. Still divided. Would have thought by now they'd be merged into one, but no, they were only just keeping pace in the perspective. Apart from that, there was nothing. And so it struck me then that I was alone, they'd all gone, her and her and Yehune as well, so it didn't matter what my eyes fell on or didn't. Because isn't everything in yourself? The whole of it contained in you, might have to think so; in which case the Outside isn't even outside. Switching my glance, then, over the long half-scythe that was left and a stranded log above on my right and the bank again, I screwed my eyes together, and tried with all my might to see him walking.

... Forced it just. – Greyish abiding puzzle of the air over grass.

In the hollow. In the holl hall, metal, a kind of bitter taint. And signs there written. But – no. It's not just me, or at least it doesn't feel like it; and the reasoning's this. What did I do? What did *we* do? We chose the old mattress with a wineglass standing beside us on the floor. Where suddenly in a moment's slip and duck of mouths the skein of all perspective was defeated, run behind, and suddenly under us there was no basis, flying across water to the spring of the plank and split the moment hanging, yellow-and-black, with the sting of some other knowledge flown around us but never looked at, and it was clear and transparent and running and flowing. To the, you know. To the top, to the heart of light, that turned out specious, that sting or bale that could have been the burr of tiny flies here over in the forest of dried black seaweed spun out to the side of me. Fermenting; done. That was it, or it was how I was seeing it now, and it was something we chose, only because we couldn't see, or not as far as the carpark. No-one can....

And it happened that at just that moment, he was back. To my right past the slightly-brown edge of a clump of standing grass I could make him out, gesticulating, large as life. Only he was different now, built out of mainly rectangles with a hexagon high on the left like the momentary beading in a camera lens; his face was all furrows and had no expression I could read. Colours – grey, amber, purple burning out to violet. Not a statue, because the arms at right angles swung here and there in semaphore, always at right angles. Meant to mean something. All the strange geometry of it suddenly recentred and reborn in different figures, as he turned side-on, ready to run again.

Keep up, man

Keep up, whatever you are. I keep asking myself why you did it, and whether we can see; can we ever? Is there enough in common...?

Here to the left there was nothing but the bare sand, creek having run away to join the ocean. A few birds squalling up above. And cold. Poor bastards, only feathers. ... Where I looked out and saw or seemed to see

A man passing our table. Dressed in a green striped shirt past masks, wall-hangings in the selective light. Heard, *sort of a job*. The one the words were addressed to broad-set and slumped over portions of the chair and struts, not but finally conversationally responding with a jitter to the voice; *ji-ji-ji-jo*. But that was nothing the man would have dwelt on, whose need just then was to negotiate his way with several drinks held perfectly upright to a farther corner where his Gemma or Germa waited to resume a crepuscular somehow promising conversation over other people's forearms. But jumped a bit – *CRRR-AAA-SSHH* – and shit oh damn, I've spilt

So off you slip to the side, that can happen; or happens to me, does it happen to you? And then then you might see

Yehune, once, looking up from a folder in which he dashed down ideas and pothooked notes on five lines extended to infinity, at his best friend a certain Mel Seuchar and Mairi, faces gently angled to each other, in the inside light of a 100-watt pearl bulb, or arms lightly around each other's backs beaming down on him complacently with a look well-grazed on oysters.

And another time, Yehune reading in his very unconcerted way page after close-written page of deathless Seuchar rabbiting on about life and the days' events and anything else that fell into his head, but *meaning* supposedly something, carrying some message, obliterated now in the transit of hemisphere to hemisphere of hardly-related skulls. Simultaneously, in the same diary-cover, a pattern yellowish and involved of squares in the eyes' run magnifying – wine labels – Stamps of Australia.

Till he moves away, wily and evasive, he exits the room or club in a way that causes least disturbance past the skirts of girls pure-white against a leg. Secure your avenues of retreat. Looks back at me with something like a smile, or was it, enigmatic lift of the corner of a mouth already turned. His corner-hair connected by hairfine wires into everything; flash of a jagged re-outline of shoulders broad enough to carry any and all of us surely and the flesh built up around the chin

but here, here, racing on the grass mounds to the right where more substantial bushes have come into sight, he's drawing off again, run far away in an instant, japing in light-fall crazy weaving out towards the hills which are low here and weather-ground but still far away enough; so I'm the one couldn't keep up; dancing under the hills, split now, light-encapsuled, turning and falling away to the planes away from plane which is where she is he's gone out of the light in the

lightning. the lightning cut. which is knowledge of difference in the run of time and flick of what we don't know raved away beyond us mustbe bottomless   gone   and going on regardless

...

So you close your eyes, you open them again. Seeing nothing but the bled-dry cut of the world vanishing on ahead with a leftwards curl. A few rocks isolated to the side, greener with that old slime. A logic. You try and measure it.

The steps and levels, that *character,* organic as the slime, you have to say in logic it exists; I, what?, I see words violently arrayed and striped; I like a comfy armchair; don't go all out for status; I have my little ways and tics, which are and always were different from him and his. Though skewed through time and the view through past and present, time being...? Manner of perception. You're folded away in the present but you don't see them as gone exactly, in the way of not to think about, in fact a sort of depth comes in standing for an answer to what's already or seems concluded, in the cept pre cept, in the productionary act of walking –

Hey there! Hi, old tatters, relics of the deeper studied and unfelt, hi, you *traits,* you backs in jackets,

hi, on an evening I met Mairi and there was Stewart the Festival Theatre Productions Manager with her and we stayed for a moment in the vestibule and I he I had to see to a few issues of ticketing and correspondence and went on to give her a lift out to the flat, in the back seat the other one with the air of a friend more than a lover, took them in to the hairy old tweedy expanse of the indoors and offered them both a sherry out of my 18th-century decanter, perfect facets above the polished wood of the sideboard, and observed her only from the side, in a muted violet tweed skirt which did suit my favourite space but her body I'm not quite sure, if only I didn't have Loretta. So we pretended not to care, I suppose much to the comfort of Mal the interloper who was too tall for his girth and apart from that nothing at all, but there's time, I've always found there's time; already I was looking forward to the immediate future when they'd be gone and I could sit back and put on the new blue-sided Wagner

or Pas-cuaaaa-le, hi, really as much of a Scot as they all of them are and only happening to have got hold of a habit of connection that's all it is and the example of my dear Aunt Clemenza; seeing a bauble, walking lick of graces, in my own establishment and knowing all about her and her boyfriend a composer and her private life from A to Z right down to the colour of today's knickers as I do about any employee for whom I might show an a-*vunc*-ular affection or regard, looking out of a window one day pensive about cigarette cards and the stacking of a small deck and happening to see her

seeing him, out of the side of a rain cape she was putting on, where she felt not slyly but in a way instinctive or unspoken the lidded *sexual* intention of it, not of course invited by herself, but you could say in the moment's fatal being-as-it-is relished mildly from the other side, in the other way, sub-glaze of the thick and stubby energy of dominance in a part below conscious thought... slip out... slide down and farther

...

As much as his face I see the hands. Why do they keep coming back to me? They were big enough in the bones but more than that they had all that sensitivity and could reach out to you. Not Mr Pascuale's which had three rings on them one a turquoise and they were brown and smaller and he would have liked to touch me with but not to touch me. But I wasn't having any. Hands for the office, hands of a sort of power. Only direct and open and not betraying, except for what the rings told you. A red sportscar right behind me in the lane, he's right up close, sorry, I'm sorry. I'll change as soon as I can. Something peculiar about them when they have the top up and the windscreen seems to go flat opaque. What do I mean by that because none of it can be open, what can reach towards you out of a dismal and soulless place can go to other girls as well and show that same care and consideration only not to me but to Polly or Francine or Annabelle just before the hump ahead and trees over a rise. I'm sorry, see there, I'm pulling over. And now he's got the lane to himself and he doesn't want to go. I can't believe it. Nothing can make me believe it, when

442

I can see that little tip of his eye and mouth that changes all the shape and makes his eyeline ripple in with mine, only in memory now, seen through the thrown-up spray of the wheels of a lorry in the inside lane. Swerving a bit unstable from side to side. While at the same time the sporty red's taken his chance, he's going – going. I can't, I never can believe he's gone. But that's not the reason, not, or not just that, it's the way things happened and how they worked out, and now because of it....

Thinking of Celestine and Celestine's flat, I think I told her most of it, only she might not have been absolutely listening because of her *préocc*. Distrait, moving a wee bit in the distance even while she was telling me to try the Île again that we tried to visit on the last trip but never ever made it, but I can still remember the first time. *Île de lumière*, the light that sort of like shimmers whenever the sun's out. Can you imagine a more perfect place, and least likely to come across him especially now right outside the season. Mainly Parisians and from Marennes. Of course she couldn't come, she's had a hard time of it. It can't help either to have a friend from Scotland staying for a week when she has those money troubles and her father's off drunk most of the time while she's trying to do this course, and she didn't ever say that he was paying for it, but now the mother's dead it might have been put in trust. Either way I think she feels it. How can you not? You have to feel it. As far away as you can get and that's four hours down from Paris now the knowledge follows again like a whisper and a touch of the hand behind the ear sometimes when you think your hair. It's hard to see from here, will I best change lanes again? That's the trouble with the right-hand drive, you can never properly see. Here goes, and now I've passed him. F Poiret, Hypométrique. *Salut, F Poiret. Salut, Monsieur…* no, don't say. Hurry and touch wood.

I'm getting on to Blois, and the rain's so steady it seems to have set in for ever and ever. Will I stay there, given I know a place? You come straight down off the hill from the autoroute with the rain pouring down and the heads of buildings grey under it and the slow pattern the windscreen wipers are making from side to side. Singing a song, whee-*wick* whee-*wick* whee-*wick*. Remember the time we had to go into a café here to go to the loo and they were on their lunch break sitting around a table with wine and wouldn't let us, Celestine and me, but then we bought a bottle of their rosé which turned out to be the worst in the whole universe and the man went suddenly galant and they let us through. Later we poured it out in a gutter by the campsite. Camping's available even out of season in Les Huttes. But now I'm thinking of here and now and no car phantoms pulling you around and off your seat. I can see the end of the coast and the bridge you drive over with the beds all around you and below you and the salty fishy smell, *cabines* painted orange and blue. But now, in Blois, coming into forests of signs. What could we do, I mean I do there? *I* do. We did the worst we could, and it's right that I can't rely on it now for any sort of safety. It didn't turn out, it never will now since what happened and where I've gone, and in a way that only makes it less complicated. Just on my own I can't imagine it. Beachcombing, living in one of their chalets at the campground. Signs here everywhere showing arrows that twist back and forth and under themselves, and I'm trying all the time to decide and then decide again....

See hair, for the beachcomber. Tawny in the sun like the Dittmers, or you could say like Xavier though his was just a shade darker. Yes you'd need someone else there so you would if you didn't want it to go to dust and ashes... don't say. The shoulders so brown. Only of course he was just a student in those days with Jean-Pierre and Jean-Marc who was the littler of the two, and I think, what was her name? Diving like a seal – blue swimsuit. Now here's the same hill, has it gone darker for the rain? I can't remember which café. Do you need the loo, Cel? There's a forest of them somewhere on the sixth floor of the *immeuble* in Nice where Xavier and the others used to live out most of their lives in the early morning. I think I've still got his address, have I? Derek said when I told him about it that he was only after me, I mean my, you know. But now anyway I bet he's got a girlfriend or might even be married, and what about it, what do I want from him? Another life, living torso. Or words and chatter to drown out the voice in me that it was all my fault in some way, which is a bit silly because how could it not have been? Lights take so long to change in the rain behind that's falling. It's right over in the other direction, all the way to the bottom of France, on the other coastline, Méditerranée. Remember that old town he lives in Gresse or Grasse where he told me there was that *vieille dame* who helped look after the house I think it was his parents', if only I can find the address, I can remember taking all the papers off the dresser and throwing them in the bag. Big green bag. Reorganised in Celestine's. And I'll have to look out the map book as well – maps, and no-one there this time to help me match the little wiggly lines to turnings in the real. Rain's falling on and on like dimpled specks all over the side windows, and just there, a touch of sun, look how the sunlight spilled out of that direction glints on them progressively and all of a sudden everything's remade in colours. In the green bag, back in the boot under the suit-carrier. There's a gendarme now redirecting everyone into the far lane where there's a P sign, standing there in a blue cape, thank you, thanks, and I'll take the totie slip road off to the right and stop and maybe have a bite to eat. And then start up again over the hill to get on the route across and down, how far can I get, because I'll have to find a hotel before nightfall, because when you think there's nothing to stop me now or hold me back except....

...Nothing, except, it's nothing, except. All right. That's strange. How did it happen, or could I catch...?

Catch what? Not that, not that seeing through Mairi. But only the questions, all the questions. ... What makes the mind connect under the table, brings us out of our skin? Fruits of knowing – and the single smash of intuition which is, more than fragments, whole.

We're so much in the process of making ourselves that nothing will be nothing can be sealed. No item carried. Yet if in the process of all time those imprints repeat to give us just… a direction, tendency?

So he was. Rocks in a swept line. Undermachinery of vast earth movements in the rock that grumbles makes dark fissures. By disappointments, pushing him to excel; go for it, Yipman. In a light that's bent from the way he might have, though he didn't. So then there are the undercreatures, knobs of waiting, hollows in the sheet… below which then we come to the terms and logic; lizard-mind, or the stuff of the new-born beyond which under which

Rocks, here, in a long line. Just before. What's it…? There's something on the edge, in the vanishing point like a creep of pixels, rain. If you can only burn to where you lose your memory blank back to that time and be what always underneath you were, so there's no distance, are of the am and open-eyed. What is it? Stirring in the contact point, fold out of which all, looks like, cattle? some… or buffaloes, a jostle-range of humps. Or plunging horses. No they're…

bulls, they're bulls, with the high backs black-and-brown, great heads tossing and heaving *toro* and a rumble under hearing for the plunge of them the legs *te toroloro* that tiny edge-shape, bend out into vision somewhere before beach and carpark seem to begin, distant, far distant, but wheeling up. *Taralara taralara taralara* there's the movement in the ground, the trickle of it, underlying thunder. Where I stand. They're coming out of the distance, drawing closer, hooves chumping into the wet sand surface and chucked-up sand in clouds, driven by who, by what? can't see anyone, and the great expanded nostrils and the eyes hell-gleaming frantic and every one those spikes at the corners of the head, now bending belting hurtling down the sandfall four or is it five I can't I fall to a knee but there're too many cover too broad a field and instinct in the wealth and intricacy of the building of a haunch a foreleg is the thought-made-truth the blank or silence gnarled up to this fuck better move man or in a sec you'll be plenty blank yourself but there's nowhere to *tararara te toroanamoana ana ana* fuck o spears of horns

I   I   I 'll   be   what   she   what   not   then   another
stumble   you   thu   integre   that   I   I   or

and then   was rising up above the bulls and surface of the beach
that beach or any flipped for a moment in the local node of sun reflected
under cloud so all of it could run of elongated backs paunched out at the
sides a different size for different colours and the map of the seaweeds
from up here broken black to brown-and-violet smoothed lost roughness
in the minutes was it hours when   was seeing or seeming to see past toss
and upthrust through and through white stables over land as if   was in
a lens a something magnifying nodal small dilation all across the sight
and still the noise out there of the climax of impact heard long-drawn
like a vooooo-ooooooooor of daydream caught at shock and   could spy
down on the earth but under sky,   gazed down on us, could apprehend
rashwork of stars like features of a face dissolved and dying frankly into
a stranger set one set which is the inchoate blind impress which is for one
untuned for all which was a movement of the being of the what is being
you   am you he art no we are they arethey not but textured side-on at a
reading lamp or table stall under motions caught or is and turning slowly
slowly saw   saw till boned again from slips of sun they line up hairy in
convoy like a fleet of ships bovine to the underbending lights port light
where he when   was what's the catch when three's a multitude nothing's
more than one in the uneroded gleam or inner spark which is where lights
*   of what's being human turning still   'm turning the bulls regressed*
now half a length away or any sign of bodies torn limbs not a thing except
the humps in stippled lines and hooffall drawn on losing wake   seem to
catch and turn   seeming to see what 's 's

... Fell! and I'd fallen, stretched out on the mounded grains,
felt then that I was upright, steadied myself with one step to the
side. And paused, and looked back. Saw nothing. Nothing, not a
bull's hind quarters dunged and ragged, no reversed stampede; not
anything; I looked straight down into the eye of the light behind and
felt the wind's cold slap and what was what was
... that I almost had it then. Really, I nearly. What was behind

447

me? Nothing. Or rather something, through the meshes of the blue-green-golden shock of a small sun horizontal almost seen. It looked like the thinnest graveclothes spilt into the air, greyed down and circling, reeled out lost behind me. Dipped and pirouetted as I watched like a soiled cloth whirling among vague impress of figures… maybe? All away. What was it? Lost, just lost it, blown back in dearth of ending out towards the power station, done dissolved against the wind the wind's

In the Beach House

Slats and slates, and panes of glass in a heap. The wind, toned down
here by walls and hedges, blowing straight through a gap in the glass
surrounding. Mel Seuchar as he sat there remembered pausing one
more time on the sand, looking ahead to the low headland with
parked cars, until a moment came when something seemed to pull
him away from it, back along the line of the shore towards the place
where the creek flowed out. It could have been the sense of passing
time; the policemen like dark-uniformed lead toys drawing everything
into them. So the end of the curve was unachieved. Instead, he'd
plodded back along a line of seaweed, water moving to the right of
him, and up onto the tilted bank where the grass lay trampled. Still
blackberries there, wild rose, and the dead sticks of thistles. Up to the
meeting with the foot track, and on along to the point of a gatepost
set with a hanging rubbish tin, just before the road; and over the
road, crossing there regardless while the wind gave back car noise and
jet noise and the voices of all creatures. Taking his chance between
the bright whisks of cars. Then walking up along Lyars Road, parallel
to the stone wall under the trees. Turning right into Gosford Road,
and again where the driveway made a break in the white wall.

Their 'beach house', Pom and Alice called it. No mere B and B.
He'd come in the smaller door on the left side of the house, and just
paused in the corridor. He could make out voices from inside the
offset lounge. So Pom must still be in there with the cops. Alice?
He didn't know. With the racing of the wind in him just then and
the living movement of his blood, he somehow couldn't bear the
thought of his bedroom, and so he'd walked out again and in at
another door, into the draughty, roofless space of the conservatory
under construction.

Looking for planks to sit on. There were only a few long rods of
wood or plastic leaning against the outer wall of the house... but he
found something better: a trampled wooden step set up on blocks.

449

Why not, since it wasn't raining? A part of him might have been trying to preserve the feel, the unrepeatable mental signature of that series of moments not long before when he'd wandered freely along the Longniddry shoreline.

Time flows – forms eddies – gathers in great instants; so they tell us. But from wherever you happen to be standing, it seems to be stopped. A light tiredness had fallen on him, now that his energy levels were beginning to fall back to an idle. Mingled a bit with worry. A race of images, flicked back through in memory – and stop. Jerk ahead – and stop. … And here he was again, arrested, pulled to a halt beside the jacket he'd just taken off. His ears still numb from the wind. Seeing, if he cared to look through the glass panes edged with new putty, the coast. The golf course. Pine windbreaks, not quite blocking the view of Cockenzie and the bump of Arthur's Seat.

He knew now that the stop, the essential vantage-point for him, was and would always be that point of all perception on the beach by the line of rocks, when the bulls had seemed to charge and toss him over their heads. What had he seen? Words failed to bring him near it. But he could still see a shape, like a fortuitous imprint squeezed out of coloured paints. Being in a mind, which was all minds – no, minds carved away from the distinctions of characteristic – was it? He'd almost caught it, had been on the very brink of catching it. Now, it was receding from him: he couldn't expect that clarity, that apparently perfect knitting of detail to detail, again. Especially not now, when his metabolic speed was falling off, other things were coming in to distract him. The cops, what could they be wanting from him? Cops – the mortuary – Yehune dead. Which left him here among heaps of builder's junk, trying to remember something. Tumbling slowly, over and over, in the limitless space beyond the cliff's edge.

He stood up. He was looking pilot-like through a single pane of glass, which gave out on the rows of pines and the distant skyline. At times of great stress or grief – it seemed – whole regions and ages out of the subconscious could suddenly rise up and invade you, leaving you helpless in the grip of an unveiled emotional force. Moments out of the past, broad sections of your life, all run through, swept together and juxtaposed. And now something was suddenly obvious to him. The Work – the thing he'd always been aspiring to – couldn't it be this? Instead of snips of writing and drawing and cuttings and fabrics arranged on a page, couldn't it amount to what he'd just lived through – a matter of fifteen or twenty minutes wandering along a beach? Those violent encroaching narratives of the lives of himself and other people, coming close, so close, to the moment of real understanding... it could all be gathered up, held seamless here in the mind. The patchwork Sail that he'd always seen driving him forward: wasn't it this, this very patchwork? A seeing through the eyes of selves related, and through them, onward, to something else... and all the details, they were life....

Noises were breaking out in the house, pulling his thoughts away. Voices, sounding and answering each other. He half-turned. His knee knocked against a protruding slate, and the whole stack of them just missed toppling down.

Shit and damn. He managed to steady it with one hand. The view through the pane of glass was gone and forgotten.

'*Muuuu-oo,*' came another faint shout. ... Couldn't they be *quiet* for two seconds?

He tried to get his mind back onto the same track. But more than distractions, the tiredness was burdening him, making him disconsolate, shifting the sense of what he'd seen. 'The Work', oh yeah. That's great. Some kind of final experience. Could you still have those...? It had all the hallmarks of a grand theory. But he'd had moments of what seemed definitive insight before, and gone on to modify or forget them, over the course of time, in the prison of his ever-shifting series of moods.

And speaking of time – how long was it since he'd left the house? Three quarters of an hour? It had all just barely happened....

'Mel!' the shout was clearer now. It might have been in Alice's voice.

They were calling for *him*. He remembered the police, but now as no more than an extra irritation. They couldn't bother him now. He looked distractedly around, seeing the bones of a half-glazed room open on the sky.

But it seemed they could. Pom appeared bulkily from the inside doorway.

'Oh, here you are. Cops want you.'

'Ah – thanks.'

Mel made an enquiry with his eyebrows and the tilt of his head. He got back a small shrug of the shoulder: it's nothing.

He picked up the jacket lying beside him, and had various thoughts about what he was wearing just then – the horrendousness of his old jersey and death's-head tee-shirt – whether he should stick his jacket back on to cover it.

And so, the whole question was taken away from him. Never worked through, it was somehow perpetuated in his mind, enacted by a simple decision rather than any fine weighing up of arguments.

When he came into the small lounge he met the eyes of two of the three policemen. Where was the other...? They stood up for Pom to make the introductions. Only one was in uniform; the other wore a dark suit – he was a squat man with bushy black hair, black eyebrows, and tangled black thickets in his ears and nostrils.

Mel took a seat, and the sandy-haired constable pronounced,

'First thing is to reassure you that the stories of all concerned have been provis'n'ly confirmed. The lorry driver who picked up Mr Trent on Queensferry Street on the ninth of September has come forward, a Mr Guthrie – Robert Guthrie, of Perthshire. Mr Trent was dropped off in the vicinity of Dunkeld. Accordingly, you might say, the order of events leading to his death is reason'bly well established.'

'Oh,' Mel said. He looked around. Dirty teacups were placed around the room, one on a tiny round occasional table.

'You understand that this seems to rid those closest to Mr Trent of a certain oä-nus of suspicion?'

'Uh-huh.'

'Well then. That's that. The detective sergeant has a few questions to ask you on another subject.'

And the uniformed one sat down, vaguely searching his surroundings for another biscuit or a sip or two of tea.

'Mr Seuchar,' the man in mufti began with apparent friendliness. 'Is that a Scottish name? You don't sound Scottish.'

'Oh no, I'm from New Zealand. It's my father who's Scottish.'

'And he lives down there?'

'Yes.'

'Right... right.' He looked down, and up again. 'Eh... you might recall Mr Trent suggesting that some people were after him, something to do with money he might have owed?'

'Ah. – I'm not sure which ones you...'

'I think, earlier on the same day the accident occurred.'

'Oh, that's right. Some people from the Ensemble. Yehune told me they'd cornered him in *Caffè Fiorentino*.'

'Beg pardon?'

'I mean, Forren-teeno – off the High Street. In fact, now that I think, Pom and Alice were there at the time.'

'Exactly so. I can see you're putting two and two together. I can tell you, without naming any names, that one of the parties involved is now wanted for other reasons. So the CID's interested in tracing his activities on that night. Now, I believe you and Mr Trent stopped at a variety of venues later that same evening? – And we're informed, of course at second hand, that the, eh, party in question might have reappeared, looking for Mr Trent?'

'Oh, right. Yeah, that happened in the Crappit Hen. Yehune ducked down in the alcove and told me to keep a lookout.'

'Thank you, Mr Seuchar.' The small man, looking in his suit more like a stockbroker or an off-duty funeral director than a policeman, leaned forward. 'Now, the question is, what did he look like to you?'

Mel could see the uniformed man holding a notebook, poised to write down anything he said. He brought his mind back to his recollections of that night. They were intense, atmospheric, making a unique imprint on his mind; he saw the glowing dark of the alcove, Yehune cowering down to hide under the table surface. And the wandering shark – or the one Mel had assumed was him – he'd had a protruding nose, a weak chin, bringing the word 'Parker' out of some irrelevant alcove in his subconscious. He'd seen him all right; a shape moving in and out of other shapes.

Or then again – was it the jacket alone that had suggested

'Parker'? And had the face been a kind of lightning reconstruction, fitted up to go with the coat...?

'The man I saw – I *think* it was the right one – had a brown jacket on.'

'Yes?'

Mel struggled with his memory. He had to be careful, here, not to mistake some fabrication of his own for fact.

'How tall was he?' asked the detective. 'And did you manage to catch sight of his face?'

'Ah... I think... that is, Yehune told me...'

'Let's stick to what you saw yourself, shall we?' he snapped.

'Oh, yeah. Of course. Ah...' He thought for a while, then told him candidly, 'Tell the truth, I can't be sure how much I'm really remembering.'

'Of course,' said the other, with a stretch of his mouth that was more world-weary than humorous. 'You can't be sure.'

And sat back, at the same time giving a very small shake of the head to the man with the notebook.

'Mr Seuchar... what was your *per*-sonal involvement with the finances of Mr Trent's Ensemboe?'

A whole series of questions followed that were obviously aimed at implicating Mel in Yehune's financial problems. There even seemed to be hints that he might have something to do with unknown actions later by 'Parker'. He denied everything patiently, exhaustively, and went on denying it. But now the detective was hot on his trail. Sometimes he shot the same question twice in quick succession, or suddenly again when the subject seemed to have been changed. The constable sat silently glaring, seeming to repeat each question with his eyes. ... Had Mel had any part in an agreement between Ensemble members and the other parties for the collection of moneys owed? ... Had he been approached or threatened by any individuals? ... How much had Mr Trent owed *him*?

For the tenth or twentieth time, Mel protested that he didn't have anything to do with Yehune's money affairs. Then, with an expression of triumphant shrewdness, the detective asked about

454

how the two of them lived – wasn't it true that Mr Trent had done no work, and lived on money that he, Mel, earned?

This conversation, or interrogation, went on for some time. In the end, it was judged that not much more could be got out of it. They told Mel he could go. Four hard eyes followed him out of the room, searing new holes (he imagined) in the back of his old jersey.

Gods Chriss, he thought. That was what you got for a habit of imagining things. ... And other thoughts visited him, harsher ones, about the *un*-imaginative mindset.

His best exit route was towards the front of the house. Out there on the driveway, Alice was leaned on a rough abutment of two walls, chatting merrily to the second uniformed policeman. The two of them seemed to have found an affinity. The police car was bright and garish on the gravel not far away, the orange and blue and yellow stripes almost incandescent under the pale sky. Mel struggled his jacket back on. Free, for the moment....

He did toy with the idea of going out again, walking somewhere else, or even returning to the beach, wandering around there and trying to see it all again. But by then he knew he wouldn't. Something in the weariness of his body had built a new sensitivity to low temperatures; he couldn't take any more of that beating wind.

He waved to Alice, then turned back towards the door. He thought he might go back to his room after all, hole up there for a while, maybe even hit the pillow. He had a picture of himself doing nothing, just lying back and closing his eyes. Lying back, and dreaming maybe, dreaming their lives again – the lives of him and Yehune and Mairi and all the rest of them – reimagined, retouched, and perfected.

Going On

When he first came to the Beach House, Mel had thought of it as a very small universe standing parallel to the real one. It was fully life-supporting, but not quite complete. Across the water from the series of sweeping curves that were one beach and the next and the next, Edinburgh lay like a mainland; and it was as if a floor and a few roof slats had been cut away from it, removed by several miles, and provided by some mechanism with food and drink and people flowing in and rubbish bags and cloacae and people in their cars flowing out. Every time he stood at the shoreline – and he did it often – looking back over a corner of the Firth of Forth to the city he'd lived in for three and a half years, he felt himself to be as much divided and reduced. There, over there, was his life with Yehune and Mairi and the rest of them, with all its violent energy and colour, set apart from him now by the wide blue gulf of time. It was as if he could actually see it, but couldn't get to it.

Pom and Alice were very hospitable. They gave him a tiny room with a sloping roof under the stairs, provided meals if he happened to be in, and refused any sort of payment. Pom even became a bit growly when he mentioned it. Under normal circumstances, his host didn't have much to do with him; he was kept busy coordinating one small event after another in the sort of mini-folk festival that went on there all through the summer months. Alice gave him more attention; she seemed to have decided to take him under her wing. Both of them were careful never to mention Mairi, who, when it came down to it, was their real friend.

Edinburgh came to have a magnetic attraction for him. He spent a lot of time walking the streets, sitting in parks, looking into travel agents'. He changed his ideas about what he might do next with every passing day. He always tended to leave out the more southern European destinations, involuntarily seeing them as belonging to Mairi; but anything in the north was all right, or there was New

Zealand, or Asia again. Or anywhere, really. He no longer had any pupils to keep him where he was. Alice was always arranging lifts for him with people going in and out of the city; otherwise he got the bus. But in the Beach House itself, things were

acrosstheboundary and a

more edgy; he didn't really know what to do with himself. He was always more at home walking the streets, haunting the old places, as if he could somehow have fallen back in with the mental tags and paraphernalia of his former life, or even, as he turned some windy corner, met himself coming back the other way.

There were peanuts in a shallow bowl on the arm of one chair. The problem was, the chair was occupied. Mel parked himself on the edge of a big black amplifier, which put it within easy arm's reach, and chewed on a handful of peanuts. Behind him people were talking and laughing and fiddling with different musical instruments.

'Excuse me,' said a young woman in purple flowery leggings and a wrap-around skirt. She bent awkwardly over the amplifier, stretching out her arm and hand to an elongated guitar-like object that leant back against the chair. Her bottom, half exposed as the skirt rode up, seemed to wink at him with a quizzical expression. Mm-*hmm*? it said. Off-centre, cute-cheeked. The seat of human character.

Mel had got up, and slowly, deliberately, with circumspection, backed into a tweedy older man standing just behind him.

'Careful,' the man said, and steadied him at one shoulder.

The woman was upright, and was looking at Mel with something that bordered on suspicion. But I just.

He said, 'Sorry,' to all and sundry. And to the man,

'She was just getting her guitar.'

The man looked at him tolerantly. 'Isn't it a dulcimer?'

Now the woman had moved away, and was standing with her

457

back to him beside another, whose broader posterior in jeans put him in mind of old puddings. Expressive, they can be, as faces. The undercover study. *Les culs des autres.*

The peanuts were all gone now. It was obvious to Mel that everyone here knew each other; also, everything seemed to be gearing up for something. He scanned around for Pom or Alice. Nowhere. Just then, a sudden wail from behind his ear

composite action was set up between the primary beam components (joist members) initiated mostly by

gave
him a quick memory, forlorn and close as a heartbeat, of the endless dribbles of sound Yehune had trailed around him when he was still alive.

Standing up, he still wasn't sure which way he wanted to move. He told himself that what he'd been needing was something to eat, and started to thread his way through thickets of upright people, aiming approximately for the door through to the hall and then the kitchen. And just in time; the amp he'd chosen for a seat and a dozen other sources all exploded without warning, burdening the common sitting room – or eating, milling, and main performance room – with howling peaks of noise.

Out in the hall, there was a bit less of it.

Mel went on to the kitchen opening, and saw Robbie in there, the friend of Pom's.

'Y'all right?' Robbie asked him.

Mel nodded and smiled. 'Yep. You?'

'Haein' a drink wi' me?'

'Oh, no thanks. I just came in to get something to eat.'

There was a tray of various drinks laid out with glasses and plastic beer-mugs on the bench. Pom's hospitality was unflagging. Mel had to be careful not to let himself take too much advantage of it, or he would have ended up sozzled all day and night.

'I mind,' said Robbie suddenly, 'you're Mairi's friend.'

Mel admitted it.

'I heard her other friend had – ehm – an accident?'

'Committed suicide.'

'Aye, tha's right.'

Nothing shook Robbie's confidence; he was just as happy to call a spade a spade. He asked whether Mel had any recent news from Mairi.

'Not really. I think she's travelling on the Continent. France?'

'Oh aye. … A fine lady, tha'.'

It was obviously true. Mel looked into the weatherbeaten face under cropped white hair; etched with character, lines of meaning; and for some reason shirked the chance of engaging with it more closely.

He got together a few things, bread and some leftover battered fish from the fridge. By that time Robbie had gone out, and a few more people he didn't know had tottered in, looking for the drinks. One younger man played a game with his eyes, not sure if he knew him. Then they all went on with their lively conversation.

Mel finished quickly, and retreated to his bedroom under the staircase.

of the top chords leading to significant flexural cracking at the girder base just above the bearing

The westward-facing cubby hole under the stairs had wallpaper like a tessellation of icing, coloured dull aquamarine. The pattern of white dots ran in all directions. Everywhere, dot dot dot…. From where he sat on the bed, he could see most of his worldly possessions in one cardboard suitcase and a backpack. A few things – Yehune's fat music folder, a travel pamphlet – were spilled out on top of a skimpy tower of shelves.

To his left was a window with a gauze curtain. On the wall opposite him there seemed to be another window opening into the wall; but it was only a framed print of a muddy-coloured hotel front, labelled 'Chamonix'.

He picked up his book, a paperback *Anna Karenina*, and

found his place in it. He wasn't sure whether he was going to be able to read it; someone's radio was blaring so loudly from a contiguous room that he could clearly hear the individual words.

Normally, he had the gift of losing himself completely in whatever he was reading, so that his surroundings ceased to exist. Now, with the interruption of phrases out of some news programme – 'Alan Bristow comments'; 'End of her political career' – he was constantly brought up with a jerk, each time making one of those lightning involuntary scans of his inner self and the moment's state of play. Everything away – fled back around him – nobody and nothing in prospect. And he tried to focus on the words again. But they were reduced to brash, blind meanings, and individual syllables that glared up at him, making bloody colours. *Frame. Sal. Bears.* Where was he, anyway? Or where was Yehune, or Mairi, or Geoff or Mandy, or…?

He let his eyes flick around the room again. A single glance was enough to take it in. He'd already got rid of most of his possessions, including everything he'd written, big sheets or small, except for his block of diaries. Even the book he was reading was borrowed. The same with Yehune's things; he'd made a clean sweep. And so he was left… where? Swept, unimaged, un-himself.

His eyes were half-resting on the word 'Karenin', and at the same time a phrase sounded through the wall: '… said that the effect of *Perestroika* on the Soviet…'. He saw the word, gleaming, solid, enigmatic, in its Cyrillic letters: Пере-

There was a knock at the door.

'Hi,' he called out, and corrected himself, 'Come in.'

Alice appeared. She was wearing a green linen shawl, a long yellowish dress with faded patterns of girders, and a heap of varied scarves. Two moons painted on one cheek gave her a gypsy look.

'Hi,' she said. 'I've got some haricot soup. I don't know if you've eaten anything?'

She wasn't actually carrying anything, so he said,

'Oh, yeah, thanks. I did have something, just now, in the kitchen.'

'That's all right then. Because you didn't get back for dinner, so I just thought…'

'I'm fine, thanks.'

She stepped in. She seemed enormous between the walls.

'How are you, otherwise?'

'Oh, you know. – I'm good.'

She looked around. 'This room is so *tiny*. We'll have to see about getting you put somewhere else.'

'No, I like it here.' And in a lower tone, 'Damn lucky to have it, if you ask me.'

'Don't think that way. We… I mean, Pom and I…'

She stopped, and swayed around the room, touching things.

Her hand brushed over his glasses, lying in a case beside the bed. She was clearly amused.

'Are these your glasses?'

'Uh-huh. They're pretty old now. Brought them from New Zealand.'

'Do you miss New Zealand?' she asked him, but automatically, as if it was just something to say.

The next thing was that Alice sat down on the bed beside him. She made a careful scrutiny of his face.

'You know, you're a good-looking boy. You shouldn't ever wear anything like these.'

'Old-fashioned?'

'I can see you in a big floppy cardigan, with your hair a bit longer. With everything to match, of course. … You may not think it matters at all?'

'Oh, I dunno.'

She stood up again. 'Looks are important wherever you go.' She laughed. 'I could be your look consultant.'

Mel said, 'I s'pose they set the expectations.'

'That's right.'

Now she was on the move again. She'd found Yehune's big lever arch file, out of which various loose pieces of paper were spilling. She gathered the excess pages together in her slim, ring-covered fingers, and started to square them off. (And: Get off! Leave that alone! he yelled uncontrollably in himself, while on the surface nothing showed.)

But she finished, and left it on the top of the shelves again, put right.

And that was Alice's visit done. She turned vaguely for the door.

'Oh, I remember,' she said before she went. 'Pom said the police called, wanted to interview us about... the night, I mean, when Yehune. First us, then you. It's the day after tomorrow. So – you know? – they'd rather you didn't go off anywhere.'

'Oh right.'

'Well, ta-ta for now. I'm *so* glad to see you're doing well.'

After she'd gone, he suddenly noticed the radio again. How strange – that he hadn't heard it all that time. It was playing music now, some strident military tune. And there was something else he felt, as strong as the whelming up of brassy voices in a radio speaker. There was no doubt about it: Alice was doing so much for him, and Pom as well. They were incredibly generous. It was the force of their expectations he felt, pushing, pushing on some invisible array of settings down inside him. In any case, he knew that was the way things worked: disembodied voices made their claim on you, and in some part of you, unnoticing, you applied the correction. They thought it was about time he started functioning normally. And Mel agreed with them. In any case he would have liked to do something, anything, to pay them back. It was just that... that he didn't. That he couldn't.

He'd stood up and walked the few steps over to Yehune's blue folder on top of the shelves, the one Alice had tidied up. What had caused that moment of panic, what had made him so protective? A picture of sunny Tajikistan from the Flight Centre, Edinburgh, lay perfectly symmetrically on the top. In moving it off, he accidentally let it flutter down onto the floor.

He smoothed his hand over the textures in the folder's stained cover.

That folder should by rights have been shipped back to Yehune's parents in New Zealand, along with all his other personal effects in two tea chests. Mel actually had included quite a bulk of papers, a lot of which were musical: photocopies, illegible sheets crumpled and torn, and band parts laboriously written out. These were just the ones he'd saved. In his thorough musical ignorance, he'd gone through and guessed which bits had been intended to be anything like an original work. There were a few pages from Yehune's stories there as well (most had disappeared), and that twisted, tormented picture of a building top. Mel just couldn't bring himself to send them back. To be burned, no doubt, long before the body of their creator came to the same end. Brigitte Trent was reputed never to have said a positive word about her son's art.

Mel idly opened the cover and looked inside; he saw whirls and little tadpoles all over the page on top. Nothing he understood himself. But for Yehune, this was the final result, the end of all those expectations and the silent processes of the soul. Mel himself had sealed it off, making decisions about which pages to keep and which to discard. He was responsible for it, then, in a way no-one else could ever be. Who else even cared? … One other person, maybe, and she was far away.

No expectations there. The expectations were all carried over to the living.

A party of tipsy revellers paused outside his door; one tried out a drumbeat on the panels while another one started whistling to it on some sort of pipe. A *ra-ra-ra-ra-ra-ra-raaaaat*. They went on for some time. He didn't burst out and interrupt them. But in a strange way it scrambled his train of thought, made subjects loom up and fall back like shrouded bodies.

Something was coming back to him: it was something Alice had said. The police coming to interview them. When? …

He thought she'd said the day after tomorrow; that would be Friday.

And afterwards…

Nothing especially changed. In the Beach House folk music was perpetually in his ears, new people kept arriving and departing again, he inhabited the lounge, or squatted in his bedroom, or sat in cars going in and out, or, more often, stood waiting for the single bus to carry him back along the coast. The tape of time was running out; the moment in early December when all this would magically dissolve kept drawing closer. There was nothing in the intense compacted experience he'd had on Friday – that moment's astonished trajectory over sharpened horns – to make any physical dent in the world around him. But every direction of a thought in him was somehow altered, he was convinced of that; and that, of course, was enough to bring change inching and sparking and welling out into the flow of time, affecting him at the level of the tiniest decisions, building to take in the whole of him, and from there, inevitably, spreading on into the reactions and movements and habits of other people.

Who can chart it? What furtive logics can be found for it? ... Since the beach, such questions seemed to have come alive for him again.

The décor of Café Lucien, on the other side of the street from the King's English, was clean and glassy, reflecting chrome stanchions, seeming with its big light-breaking windows to include all the passers-by outside. Faces kept looking into his. Every now and then, someone he half-knew would go hurrying past, and either twitch a greeting or not.

Could he go another coffee? He felt for coins in his pocket.

Then Annette was standing by the next high chair, saying, 'Hello Mel,' and scouting around for a waitress. The brown portmanteau she put down looked brand-new from the luggage shop.

'Hi Annette. How's th'old teaching?'

She made a face. 'If you're going to make nasty jokes to me I'll sit somewhere else.'

'OK. Piss off.'

It might have been his robust Southern Hemisphere turn of phrase that had made some of his workmates wary of him. Annette was at least surprised enough to laugh. When the waitress came up, he ordered another *bol* for himself as well.

'I haven't seen you around for a while,' she said.

'Oh, I've been here and there. Living in Longniddry just now.'

'Oh, have you moved?'

Now there was a strange thing. He felt so comfortable with the wide set of her face, where the cheek structure was flattened out with regular indents, with the orange-to-blonde hair combed and parted, and her pauseless way of talking, that he didn't feel any need to explain in detail. He talked about her, and the present timetabling and other Language School shop. It was like a moment of comfortable unawareness.

With the result that, when it was time for her to go, he decided to go with her; drop in again to the dingy staircase and well-known rooms in the School across the road.

Annette had a class to go to straight away. But Pete and Jonathan were there, two teachers he knew from the old days, and he got chatting with them. He found out Leanne had quit a few weeks before she was married. Then he drifted on to their personal histories. He tried to pump them as much as he could about the CTEFLA courses they'd done, without giving away the fact that he'd never done one himself. What cities were they in? How long had it taken? ... With all their ingrained politeness, they couldn't bring themselves to the point of asking him what the hell he was even doing there.

Which (Mel thought) is the way we move. We circle, feinting and riposting. On stilts, reaching out long artificial arms, touching and fading back again. We move together; utterly apart.

This time, wandering into the Beach House kitchen, he brushed past Robbie going out, who acknowledged him with a humorous twitch of the mouth. Inside the kitchen was Pom. Like a mountain of discarded wool-remnants over by the left-hand bench, fiddling with bottles and things on a tray.

Mel muttered a greeting.

'Escaped arrest, then?' Pom rumbled down in his chest.

'Uh-huh. Just barely.'

'Something to drink?'

The glasses and bottles were exposed to Mel's line of sight as Pom turned aside from them to face him. He saw Bailey's Irish Cream, and asked for that.

Pom seemed more disposed to talk than usual, possibly because of a lull in the endless round of jams and performances.

'Robbie's telling me he thinks you need something to do.'

'Me? Oh, I'm OK.' Mel had the usual casual simultaneity of thought processes; he was wondering what Robbie's interest was, while at the same time thinking again that we were all ambulatory sexual organs under our clothes, and looking at a seahorse-shaped nick in one cupboard by the door, and wondering whether a noise in the background might have been Alice's clàrsach.

'Actually I was thinking about staying here –' he said. And laughed, 'I mean, getting a flat again.'

'Oh? This is new.'

Mel sipped brown creaminess. The seahorse had transmuted into a bell, which brought back the rusty old cowbell his mum had once kept under the house.

'Yeah, see, the thing about private teaching is that if you stop for a few weeks, you haven't got any pupils any more. So it struck me – ah – I should maybe go and do the course.'

'What course is that?'

'A CTEFLA is what I need. I mean, I already needed it... only I was just sort of letting on I had it.'

'Mm. Good. ... That's a good idea.' Pom looked straight at his eyes. 'And you can do this in Edinburgh?'

'I think so, I'm almost sure. There used to be a place up in the New Town.'

'Because funnily enough, I was just talking to Rob, and he was actually going to offer you a job.'

'Wow. Nice of him. Ah... doing what?'

Pom's big face looked as if he was relishing a secret joke.

'Bit of this, bit of that. Mr Tologh's not the one for job descriptions.'

Mel thought about that, let his hand fall back against the sink, and took a larger mouthful of Bailey's, which he swirled back and forth a bit before swallowing it. Not the one for job descriptions – Pom was practically telling him it was something criminal. He glimpsed a forking path, some porpoise-shaped skein of possibilities falling back and under him: something he might have barely skirted by deciding what he'd decided.

Pom said suddenly, 'Tell you what, why don't you leave it with me? I'll find out about the CTEFLA. Cost, accommodation, conditions. … It's the sort of thing I like to do.'

And he smiled, showing more warmth than Mel had felt from him since the day he'd turned up, Mairi-less, in his private kingdom.

'Oh – thanks! Thanks a lot.'

'And don't forget, we're happy to have you here. Don't feel any need to rush away.'

Two other people bustled in then, Phil and Marie, who were closer to Pom's age and were often seen in conference with him. But for the moment, the man's eyes didn't leave Mel's. Who felt honoured by the reassurance. Though he knew, as Pom did, that they really only had three more weeks there, four at the outside.

Pascuale, Pascuale, how could you escape Pascuale? Mel tried to do it by starting out at the extreme opposite end, with the punters, the audiences, those unsuspecting lovers of the arts who milled around in bars during the intervals or spilled out into the street in populous schools after the show was done; he joined them, mixed in with them, studied their currents and characteristics. Again and again he went to venues and paid his money and sat through performances that were mostly ultra-modern, some far-fetched; by wind bands that broke out into fairly melodious whistling or string quartets that knocked on their instruments with hammers or (one time) a group that brought in a recording of a busy building site to clang and rattle over them while they played. Which was probably supposed to bring up questions not about the sound itself, but the framing of it: the phenomenon of this performance which by virtue of being conducted on a stage was supposed to be raised above the level of everything around it, with the subtext, 'this is art'. All right. In something like the same spirit, Mel's concern was more with what happened off the stage than on it. He was really only waiting for the main event, which was the brief formation of a crowd somewhere on the premises or on the pavement just outside. That was his hunting ground. There, he'd try and insinuate himself into whatever group of talkers and music specialists presented itself to his eye, starting conversations out of nothing, interrupting meetings of old friends, constantly talking into the faces of people he didn't know and who seemed to have less than no desire to know him, always holding the carefully-chosen sample pages he'd extracted from Yehune's blue folder and clipped together in a plastic presentation sleeve.

The response he got could have been easily predicted: he was cut off, fobbed off, or (a bit less often than he might have expected) abused. A woman in a purple coat with a frizz of greying hair made interested noises, small cooing sounds like 'oh' and 'aah', but really just to humour him; a stocky market-gardener type in striped shirtsleeves suggested he might want to join his own musical appreciation group run under the auspices of the Fife Council; a few bony university students started a fairly inventive rave about how some people had no idea of social distances or what a private conversation was and'd be spinning ratchets and yelling out their sales pitches on the steps to the fucking Pearly Gates. Of the people who looked at the presentation sleeve, most only extended their hands in order to fend it off, which threatened at times to taint its shop-new smoothness. The fact that an actual page of music was visible through the front panel made the situation worse if anything; there'd been no way for Mel to make the manuscripts look more finished than they were, and the quarry saw nothing but grubby pencil marks on some cheap-quality music paper, startling them, horrifying them.

If anyone ever made a positive suggestion, it was to apply to the concert organiser. Occasionally Mel did go to the trouble of tracing it back, through organisations and departments and committees and companies run by other companies, and always ended up with the name Pascuale.

Pascuale – he wasn't the one he wanted to talk to about this, for the reason of some grudging inner awkwardness he couldn't even explain to himself. Instead, he took his quest a level up, to the musicians who were doing the actual performing. Why not, he thought? Why shouldn't he find an answering chord in them, the tenuous entering brightness of a sense of sympathy for someone who in life had maybe had aspirations not a million miles removed from theirs, who'd produced notes, scraped or blown or sung and listened with concentration to the results and tried to preserve them on bits of stave-lined paper? He got to know the back doors, the practice and preparation rooms when there were any, or the remnant-scattered stages when there weren't. He was hardly ever challenged; everyone always thought he was a friend of someone else's. If a conductor or public spieler got wind of him, the game was up; but then he took a positive pleasure in scattering his seed on stony ground, praising Yehune's musical genius with all the more sincerity when he was sure it was the last thing anyone wanted to hear.

He came on a bald lead-cellist whose name was Julian, standing by a stack of music stands other people were trying to add to past his elbow. Julian was unguarded enough to take the clear plastic sleeve in his hands and look at it, and so he couldn't really get away; he had to listen until Mel had gone through his whole pitch, even while another musician, flip-haired, carrying a smaller case, was doing his best to get his attention. And the cellist seemed a little bit interested, he did; all the more when he understood that the composer in question was newly dead. He couldn't make out much from a first glance, he told Mel, or even work out whether the notes were written for strings. He couldn't find many of a thing called 'clefs' on the pages, and the deceased composer had only displayed the 'key signature', it seemed, when he felt like it. The other musician was getting insistent, calling 'Julian!' with a little upward whine of the voice; so the cellist suggested Mel leave what he had with him and come and see him in his office in a week.

Julian's office. It was in a subterranean level of a building in South College Street long associated with the University of Edinburgh, which must have been where he had his day job. There (after being offered white wine out of a cardboard box), Mel was told that Julian had been able to work out, on the basis of one small sample of four lines barred together, that some of the music had been intended for a four-part ensemble, quite possibly a string quartet. Only it

469

might take a bit of deductive reasoning to work out which notes were meant. Now, Julian knew of a man who did that sort of work for people, and (confidentially) was a bit hard up just now and so probably wouldn't charge him much. His name was Pendell, and Julian had his name and address on a card, he wasn't sure where. On a card... there somewhere.

While Julian searched the nooks and crannies of his desk and the surrounding shelves for the card, Mel was opening up his backpack, in which he'd crammed the big blue folder with the rest of Yehune's music. On some pages the scrawled notes seemed to wind off in approximate trails at a distance to the groups of five lines, like the accidental paw-marks of a wandering cat, or something written by someone whose eyes were closed.

'What about these?' he asked. 'Can you make anything of them at all?'

Julian looked cursorily at a page or two, and said,

'Pendell'll write up all of this into string quartets if you like. It depends how much money you want to spend.'

And that, Mel began to understand, was as far as he was going to get with the methods he was using. At the very end of every slow descent there was a deeper well, blocked off, with a pound sign painted across it. He didn't even resent the scam, or not very much. In fact, he recognised it as just the sort of thing Yehune might have got into himself given the connections in musical circles this Pendell obviously had.

So after all that trouble, he was forced to go and see Pascuale after all. Mel prepared it like an expedition, buying and setting up a new red plastic folder, considering all his avenues of approach, while at the same time being careful not to tip the target off by making any sort of enquiry beforehand. He knew that Pascuale's organisation was based in a palatial New Town block, which he strode into at one o'clock one weekday afternoon. There was a separate reception for each company in the building, and so they were easy enough to bypass; in fact, the difficult thing was to retain any orientation at all among the archaic lifts and staircases. Mel got lost, and ended up having to ask the representatives of a Belgian arbitration company on the third floor how to open their exit door – which was fixed by some system of brass rods and catches he'd never seen the like of.

And so it went on. After a few more false starts, he found himself face-to-face with the great man's secretary.

The secretary was in the middle of telling him he'd have to wait at least a month for an appointment, when Pascuale himself, strong-boned, impeccable and a little bit overweight in a light fawn suit with subtly-shaded accessories, walked out of a different door, closely followed by the conductor Auchterinver. Pale and nearly unstrung with nervousness, Mel went up to him and saluted him politely, not waiting for any sort of gap in Auchterinver's flow of words, and asked him whether he'd mind having a look at the work of an exciting new composer who'd just died in that city. The secretary broke in, apologising and saying something about appointments. But the millionaire already had the plastic folder in his hands, and was looking at it as if he didn't know how to get rid of it. Auchterinver, waspish just then, and looking quite a lot shorter with his hair combed smooth, asked the composer's name. Mel told him. He laughed without humour, and murmured something in Pascuale's ear. Pascuale advised Mel in a voice smooth as a cello-note to make an appointment, and swept in with Auchterinver at the door behind the outer desk. Mel went straight round after them, and started violently thumping on the door panels, having realised the arts boss still had the folder with him, which contained not photocopies, but samples from the originals of what he'd judged to be Yehune's most legible-looking compositions. The secretary told him she was calling Security. He said he wanted his folder back. But she didn't seem to be listening, and so he yelled with pronounced Antipodean vowels through the door, 'Hey! Gimme back my folder!', and thankfully, at the very last instant before two impressive men dressed in a thin parody of policemen's uniforms came to grab him under the arms, the door did open, and the conductor dangled the folder out to him pinched between two fingers.

That was all the help he got from Pascuale. But at least he'd got his folder back; and the security men even relieved him of the pressure of their grips about one floor further down, when it became obvious to everyone he didn't want to go anywhere else but out.

Alice asked, 'Well, shall I leave you two alone?'

'Um, I think I've basically seen...' said Mel.

And Ed, the landlord: 'I've already got – ah – Mel's details, and I can get back to you if there's anything else I need to know.'

'Oh, but I know you'll want some time to have a bit of a chat. Discover common interests, that sort of thing?' Alice made a flighty movement of her hand and arm, and checked in the floppy linen bag that dangled down by her side. 'Now, I'm just going to drop in on someone, and maybe look at a shop or two, I'll come back at... oh, half four?'

'Or I could just get the bus,' Mel suggested.

'OK. I'll come back anyway and pick you up if you're still here.'

'I mean, don't go to any trouble...'

'No trouble at all. What's a car for?'

And she sailed out, leg-motions invisible, in a long skirt reaching down to her bare feet. Mel was left with Ed, the owner of the house, a man young enough, but with a stripe of baldness marring the head of dark hair, and something upwardly-compacted about the chin and jaw that hinted at moodiness.

They looked at each other across Ed's sitting room. It was sparsely furnished, with rectangularly-patterned curtains and ethnic wooden chairs and sofa, and various sporting accessories arranged around the walls. A real man's room, all right. Which should have suited both of them.

'Ah... cup of tea? Coffee, som'ing like that?' Ed asked.

'No, I'm fine, thanks.'

As the days wore on through late November, Mel's flat-hunting had become more active and desperate. But nothing he could do was enough to counteract the principle he remembered Yehune stating once upon a time: No-one wants a single male flatmate. Interview after interview went by, some of them quite promising, where he met people with similar attitudes, all sorts of interesting lifestyles, and a strongly-professed sympathy for Australians or whatever Mel exactly was. But no phonecall ever resulted. Alice was keeping a finger on the pulse, and had to bear disappointment after disappointment with him.

Then, by a stroke of luck, a room had come up in her friend Ed's house in Portobello. This time Alice insisted on doing all the negotiations herself.

'So... you particularly want to stay in Portobello?' Ed asked guardedly.

'Ah, not really. I've been looking at shared flats all over Edinburgh.'

'And where were you before?'

'It was Gardner's Crescent. You know, a bit off Lothian Road.'

'Didn't like it there?'

'Oh yeah. But it died – that is, the property was condemned.'

Ed said nothing. Mel could see he was managing to give an impression that he was two steps away from destitution.

'You play golf?' he asked suddenly, seeing a large set of clubs leaning against the wall.

'Yep. You?'

'No.'

There was another pause. Everything Mel said since he arrived seemed to have fallen into a gaping hole in Ed's opinions and beliefs. The two of them sat there, Mel on the sofa, Ed on a chair, contemplating each other while their eyes strayed off in different directions into the room.

'Well...' Ed said, 'I've got some work to do... feel free to look around at anything you like.'

'Right, OK.'

Ed went out into the D-shaped hallway, heading, probably, for the small bedroom-cum-office Mel had seen in the course of his tour.

So there Mel was, in an alien sitting room in Portobello, in travois, somehow juddering along on the threadbare shirttails of a sense of obligation. It was pretty obvious to him that nothing was going to come of this. He had to keep reminding himself that it was a matter of principle to show Alice he'd given it all he'd got. If that meant

473

hanging around until 4:30 – a generous 45 minutes away – then that's what he'd do.

He went over to the window, and admired the view of a car-parking space enclosed by an ancient wall. The curtains, printed with red and blue rectangles. He turned back into the room, and noticed a set of black iron weights tucked coyly in a corner behind a stereo speaker. So Ed was a body builder? Ah-huh. He repeated it deliberately to himself: he'd be there when Alice came back again. Which was how long…? A clock standing on the mantelpiece made a regular tic – tic every second. It was whitish and square, the hands like straight black beams.

A sense of strangeness fluttered strangely down out of the ceiling corners. To be standing here, in this interior that no doubt meant so much to another person – black-jowled, brown-eyed Ed – but in which every individual element was so extraneous to him. Just think of the gulf between them. And more than that, the bareness, the phenomenon of being placed outside the familiar, to squirm and hesitate mentally and try to keep his grip on a sense of self. *Tic* – the clock sounded once. Then a gap. The gap – the solidity of the total loss of a connection, the broken skein of life. *Tic.* Of lives, he meant. Where one was always parted from another. Where was the tic, now? Coming. Almost here. It….

Frames moved, the photography of the endlessly-stuttering eye, which jumped flealike over any surface to see it as a plane. At the moment he was staring at the lines of light near the edges of a pewter golf trophy. So far from any… TIC.

Some loud, shallow music suddenly started up, with an effect of something bouncing off plate tin. It was a girl-group, wailing something. Wa-wa-*waaaoooo*…. There was something unbearably saccharine, to him, about the choice of track, spilling ill-digested honey over everything in his eyes and mind. It must be coming from Ed's little office; he must have had a secondary system hidden back there. He actually couldn't stand the sense of rot the music smeared over everything he was thinking, or the interior he was stuck in, or his life; or the life of the other one, that dark-haired, offset presence in another room….

He called into the hall, 'Just going out. Be back in a while.' There was no response – the music made the walls palpitate with imaginary petulant and sweety-sweety waves – and he wondered whether he'd shouted loud enough.

He didn't care. He had to get out of there; right then; had to. There was a vague plan in his head of getting out and searching for sand.

So he came to the porch just before the front door, in which there were handy pegs each with some useful item hanging from it. Two jackets, a raincoat hanging higher. Underneath, a soft cloth bag with bits and pieces, a woolly hat... some clumsy charm or vulnerability in the arrangement did affect his mood for a passing instant, so that he almost saw Ed as he really was, from inside, beyond the clash of faces.

Then the music was dwindling, *wa-wa*-ing away into the air around him, and he felt the stickiness slowly lifting from his head as he walked away from the row of set-back houses and down towards the street end. A blank intersection of grey stone walls. He turned left at random. The wind was frustrated at one moment, the next blowing hard across him. He scanned the ranked facings for any access on Portobello Beach.

Henrietta

Diagonally to his right, the buildings fell away. He walked up until he came to some iron railings that imprisoned a small park. The light here had a bent effect, as if the air was strangely polished; he couldn't find the sun wherever he looked. But there was plenty of wind all right, rippling, cracking across him. He turned right and walked on, down a straight path through the park towards the beach, passing first a big stepped plinth, then a lump of sculpted stone – some olde Victorian drinking fountain?

Out he came onto the sand. This beach gave him the impression of being in some way quintessentially British; cold and windswept, with a promenade, and those long timber barriers that divided the sand into segments. *Groynes*, they were called... he repeated the word for its strangeness. When he looked back across the walkway he saw a row of proud brick and stone buildings, like the self-satisfied faces of burghers. But out here, there was a remoteness, a washed-out sadness, with falling notes from the gulls. The groynes looked somehow derelict, bringing up pictures of the broken bits of wooden jetties that had always littered the sand on Thompsons Beach.

In any case, this was about a million times better than being in Ed's lounge. He'd be back there by half past four, and Alice'd never know the difference.

Moving away to his left, he saw a man walking a tiny dog into the wind, and on an opposing course, a woman with a black Labrador. Sure enough, as they came together the dogs started barking and fighting and winding round frenetically on their leashes.

He looked around: what else was there? The wide wash of the sea. A few small figures playing in the waves. A group of women, who by coincidence were converging with the path he'd taken, so that in an instant or two they'd migrate from background to his real surroundings.

He heard a loud noise: one voice raised sharply. Then,

'… thought he was playing at the fountain. Yes, I…'

It was a large woman, wearing a skirt that blew shapelessly in the wind. One of the others answered,

'He couldn't have gone off with Eila's two?'

By then Mel was practically in among them, and couldn't help feeling like an intruder. A crisis seemed to be developing around him. A slim, dark-haired woman cast around in all directions; she wore a light-blue ski jacket. A fairer one in leggings was gazing back in the direction of the stone monument.

The fat one was the calmest by far; she was saying,

'No, he stayed. I tried to make him say bye-bye.'

'Oh, *Marjorie*,' said dark-hair. 'Didn't you notice whether he followed us down? He could be anywhere.'

'Hughie… Hughie,' the fair woman started to call.

'Come on, we'll have a look. If he's not there you can maybe chase after Eila… but…'

'Hughie!'

Now suddenly the dark-haired woman in the ski jacket, rebounding here and there like a free particle, happened to connect with Mel. She was polite enough, quite attractive, and blazing at the eyes with strong emotion. Impression of quicksilver… or was that the light blue?

'Oh, excuse me – we've lost a little boy – I thought he might be wandering along the beach somewhere.' With a constrained gesture, she indicated the whole broad space around them, and flashed a look back.

Mel was happy enough to get involved. 'Tell you what,' he suggested, 'I'll have a scout around just now, leave you free. What does he look like?'

'He's… he's three, and he was wearing a green jacket… blue corduroy trousers, and… Marjorie? was it a red scarf?'

'Scarlet and orange,' said the fat woman, Marjorie.

'OK,' he said, 'I'll see you back here in… oh, twenny minutes?'

'Thank you,' said the light-blue streak, already turning. 'Thanks – we'll see you.'

She hurried off after her friend. Marjorie followed more slowly.

That must be the mum. And seemed to care least of the three. The shouts of the two in front became antiphonal, and the wind caught them away, till it was hard to pick them out from the calls of the seabirds. 'Oo-eee… oo-eee.'

As he jogged away, Mel felt the relief of having something to do rather than nothing. He was already calculating the possibilities: small kid lost, hadn't followed its mother out onto the sand. The most likely thing was that it was back on the promenade, or, worse, had been caught in some pitfall of the darkening shorefront. Abducted…? But even as he was thinking that, he was heading in the opposite direction, down to the water's edge. It was for the real searchers to worry about that. He was Mel, the rearguard. Catcher for the remoter disasters… blocking off the back exits.

Quickly he scanned the paddlers and bathers up and down the line of blown-back surf. More than he'd have thought, given the cold. Of the youngest ones, most were girls, and those who weren't looked older than three. Further out, no flailing of tiny arms. Only a few bobbing heads. Could be he'd already…? Forget it then; go on.

On his right, the wooden barrier stood a fair distance away. But the one to the left was no closer. Which way – which way had 'Eila' gone? He made a quick decision to go as far as he could in one direction, then double back. To the east he could see a fat chimney, the strange antique fronts of the town, and then green hills receding.

He hurried off. Felt the stitching of his footfalls one by one by one on crumble-sand, among dog tracks, boot tracks, and the dried-out shells. Noting each human body. Birds were all around him, at a distance, chuckling and crying. Suddenly, the groyne. Just two bolted wooden beams clamped to a central palisade, with long stays reaching back. Two hops and he was over. To reveal another section just as long again, with a scattering of figures, dogs, abandoned diggings. Mel was running now, feeling the pounding of his legs and heart like two different gauges of drum. Asymmetrical beatings. A group over to the right, loitering at the shorefront. Three kids playing. Seemed at home. A woman in a very old-fashioned *maillot* looked hard at him, challenging him, till he was past. – So what? This once, on this occasion, he could forget about decorum, this strange behaviour in a public place. Do I dare to...? Just now, he was coming closer to two waddling strollers with a toddler supported between them.

Not really, he thought. Too well guarded; and not green.

That quality of greenness, in the cold, filtered light of the Portobello moment, had started to worry him. Green – but for how long? In just another ten minutes, quarter of an hour, it wouldn't be possible to make out the colour of a small jacket. Or to do much useful searching. He wondered whether those women had thought to alert the cops. And answered himself, yes, they would have – at least the dark-haired one. For a while she ran with him, seeing through his eyes, all agitation and near-panic. Blue-silver thwarted.

He came to the next wooden barrier, which was higher and deeper, so that he had to run up further on the white sand to make a crossing. Yet another section stretched onwards, the same as the one before it. He ran along, keeping his eyes mostly on the promenade. Any kids there? Walking, running, lost? He couldn't see any. He did take a moment to glance at his watch. Twenny, he'd told them – which left him piles of time for getting back to Alice.

He turned back then. Only his toes were touching the ground, on a crunchy, giving surface, as the general lack of any result began to tickle his sense of urgency. He hopped the groyne again, number two. Could see blue light with pools of sudden yellow, splashes from the prom-lights overhead. A shadow gulf howling with wind. Again, he picked out the loiterers by a short half-ramp, half-stair.

Mainly men, but there were two kids. No – one other, and a dog.

He changed course with no real hope, almost with the feeling that he had to use each moment to the fullest. None of the kids had a green jacket on. But his sense of mission gave him an excuse to break in on anything. We'll just make sure, eh? Ha ha. The smallest child was trying to play with a miniature dog, scruffy around the snout, which seemed to want nothing to do with him. The others were set apart, maybe seven or eight, one a girl.

As he came in close, he saw a small disturbance in the sand. A rucked surface of cloth. The jacket...?

' 'Scuse me,' he called out. And again, ' 'Scuse me.'

He didn't get much response. The men were cautious, huddling among themselves. Didn't they use words here? Of course they did: a radio commentary on a football game roared on and on in the background like audible wallpaper.

One head did half-turn towards him. Close-clipped fair hair, bold ridges of eyes.

'I was wondering if this child belonged to you,' said Mel, standing right beside the tiny boy, who had likewise turned to look. And didn't seem to like what he saw; he stood in an attitude of wonky wariness, while the dog sniffed around Mel's feet.

'Any of you?'

By which time all the heads, all six of them, were turned to him. Some removed fags. The fair-haired man spoke patiently, as if he'd been through all this before,

'Naw, a dinni think so. Y'can take 'im awa' wi' y' if y' really wantae.'

'Ay, and take the dug,' someone added.

Some laughter followed, until a man with a pronounced back to the head and a withered face snapped out,

'Y'll leave 'er aloän.'

While more quips went back and forth, Mel set about trying to persuade the child to go with him. But the small one was justifiably wary of total strangers, preferring to trust himself to the company of the dog. Good sense, thought Mel (while at the same time talking softly, hinting at treats, trying to tell him his mum was waiting). Hope it'll survive into adult life. However....

He took the boy up in his arms in the end, where he kicked and struggled for a while, then accommodated himself. Maybe coming to appreciate the improved view from a height. Surprisingly – heavy – Mel found. When he'd trudged up to the green jacket lying in the sand, he had to put the child down and start all over again.

Squashing along the beach with a burden took a lot longer than running up and down it, and after a while Mel set the three-year-old down on the sand and invited him to walk. The boy preferred to squat, for some reason Mel didn't want to know about. He did manage to cajole him as far as groyne number one, by which time he expected the women would be running demented.

And yet, he was before his meeting time. The light, the life had died out of the sky, leaving nothing but a glow that picked out the edges of the buildings in spectral flatness. The beach felt breathless, shocked: the last forgotten shore of civilisation. But there were a few figures here and there. He recognised the dark-haired woman, pacing outward on an angle, before he was anywhere near the fountain.

She came hurrying over,

'Oh, *thank* you, thank you so much,' she said. Her face was set very slightly sideways. 'I just can't tell you – where was he?'

'Over there – one partition away.'

'Hughie, is it you? Is it really? You've been a *bad* boy. Come to Hettie.'

The child came, and was clasped in an arm, murmuring, 'Bad boy. Bad boy.' He gazed around, at everything but the adults, with eyes like cold jewels.

Hettie called a message to the promenade, and before long Marjorie was there with them.

She turned out to be mostly concerned with the scarf,

'Wasn't it with him? Did you see it on the sand? Where was it you found him, exactly?'

When Marjorie started to question Hughie about his immediate excretory and alimentary status, Mel and Hettie moved away a bit. Then the mother did come out with some conventional thank-yous, though with an accusing undertone. She said that they, she and Hughie, were off to search for the scarf (scarlet and orange, he couldn't possibly have missed it), then to go and get Susan from the police station.

Mel was left with Hettie. Her eyes were wide awake, and she was inclined to talk.

'I was just *out of my mind* with worry,' she told him. 'I was thinking anything could have happened… all those things you hear.'

'It's the town you've got to worry about,' Mel suggested. 'I mean, more than the water.'

'I kept thinking all the time, why didn't I look round – why couldn't I have checked?'

Though free and clear, her eyes were haunted in that moment

481

with all the profound anxiety she'd felt, and they got a message across to Mel that no words could have done. To come to a turning point. Know that however much you wanted it, you'd never see that person again. He remembered how he'd been approaching the search, as a bit of a laugh, or something to distract him from the wait. Missed it, he thought. It should have been like trying to catch Yehune again; or the other one he'd lost.

'You're Hettie, aren't you?'

She said apologetically, 'It's short for Henrietta. What's your name?'

'Mel – Mel Seuchar.'

'Oh. You don't sound like you're from round here.'

'Na, I'm from New Zealand.'

They talked on for a bit, almost as a sort of social rounding-off. The quickness and energy had passed away from her; she appeared defensive in the way she stood, stiff around the shoulders, right hand supporting her left elbow. Neither her hair nor the shape of her face was particularly striking; the eyes were what did it all. He could catch every shift of emotion in them. Her physique: neat swelling of hips around the jacket's edge, where dark trousers began; the top of her head coming to about the level of his nose.

'I hardly ever come to this beach. This time I just came over with Susan, because she was going for a walk with Marjorie.'

'And the kid.'

'Yes, Hughie…. It's amazing what you'll do for them. I suppose in a way they're the point of everything, if there is any point. And when I think…'

It didn't take long for him to notice that she was guarding herself in conversation far less than he might have expected. She gave the impression that she was freely reacting, freely expressing what she thought, as if she were some floating foam particle that had bobbed up above the murky swim of prevarication and cross-intention that was most people's whole social field. And up here, too – where Mel had always found individuals less ready to open their mouths and let fly. But then, what did he know of the habits of different regions or villages in a country which had once been, he'd understood, a patchwork of separate kingdoms? She wasn't from Scotland, he could tell from her voice. Maybe somewhere in the north of England…? It was mainly when she speculated, hunted on the spur of the moment for an answer to some fresh new riddle, that it came across to him, where the currents of actual thought processes seemed to be reflected in the motions of her face; especially, he thought, the muscles round her large, dark-lustred eyes.

He talked a bit about travel, and thought he saw her quickening, ready to go either way: to appreciate or regret.

'So you've been all over?' she asked.

'Oh, not really. We just came up through China and the U.S.S.R., and we've gone round Europe a bit.'

'I've only ever been to Yugoslavia. For a trip at the end of school. I wish I'd done more now. You see so much *difference* in everything.'

'That's right. It's people – ways of thinking.'

'Ways of thinking? Then you could do it all…?' she laughed, and tapped the side of her head.

'Of course. The be-all and end-all. Primary telescope.'

They'd drifted for shelter closer in to the wall, a bit to the east of the fountain. Mel stood facing a smooth, backwards-curving wall and the edge of the first big building. Lights in the windows made an uncompleted grid. The wind had died down a bit, but the background was darker, blue-dark, and he could see the pallid glint of stars through a gap in the cloud.

'So, with all that travelling,' she said, '– I mean, what did you have in mind?'

'Oh, I dunno. Nothing much.'

'You mean you came here without a job, you haven't had any… continuity? Aren't you working towards something?'

'Well, I've got an aim, I suppose. But not something that'd thrill an employer too much.'

'What is it you want to do?'

'Ah, well,' he shuffled around, considered lamps and the ornate receding blocks of housing. 'I'm a sort of writer. I mean, an artist of some sort. I've been working, so it hasn't had a chance to develop into anything. But it's… mm. It's what I've decided to do.'

'God. So you want to write – what, books?'

'I don't know. I... want to do something original. With a combination of things?'

He was doing his best to reciprocate her openness, not tone everything down to fit in with what it was normal to say. But having brought the words out of him, seen them shining there in rows, he found them just as much an easy formula – one he'd once put together to explain himself to himself.

'No,' he trailed off. 'That's what I thought I wanted. But maybe it isn't true any more.'

'Did something happen? I mean, to change it?'

'Oh... a friend of mine died.'

It was dark, pure dark, on the beach; the wind had shifted and was doing its best to blow them away sideways.

'I'm so sorry to hear that. Did you know – the friend long?'

He didn't say anything. He just literally, truly, couldn't talk about it. He was mobile, turning a bit, trying to get between her and the wind, while she stayed planted.

After a while, he came back. 'What about you? What brought you to Edinburgh?'

She seemed to find it easy to switch tracks. She'd come up to get a flat with two friends who were doing the same secretarial course, and met a man the first day who'd later become her boyfriend. That had finished, her friends had drifted away, but by that time she'd managed to get a job as a legal secretary and a lot of new friends, and she didn't want to leave.... She liked it there.

All this time, he wasn't looking at his watch, but he knew he was past the time he should have met Alice. Thank God he'd left it open, he thought. Because in any case he would have missed it.

By now he couldn't see her eyes as eyes, they were only cavities left unlighted by the pale glow of the promenade lighting; and yet he could sense the life in there, dancing out to him. Even in this ritual exchange of information, he felt lifted up and out. All the time knowing that real communication was impossible. They'd met on a beach, for God's sake, they'd never see each other again. Despite that, he was moving, gesturing in her eyes, experiencing them all around him like two extra-complex windows; and he didn't want the conversation to end; he, she, he, were hardly masking their tendency to draw it out, to keep talking on and on about this and that and everything.

In the end, sharp splinters of rain started to sting them, sweeping out of the west. There was a sense of an undefeatable curtain, the underlying sadness of the darkened beach. It was Hettie who said,

'I suppose I'd better be getting on…'

'It was really great to meet you – almost worth old Hughie getting lost.'

'Oh, don't say that.'

'Be a pity if, you know, we never…'

She hesitated visibly. 'I *never* give my address or phone number to anyone.'

'Specially foreign weirdos you meet on the beach at night.'

'Exactly.'

She'd taken a scrap of paper out of her pocket; she had to ask him for a pen. She turned away from the rain to write something down.

It was something in the way she moved that made him wonder. He confirmed it out of the corner of his eye as they walked up again past the big stone lump and along the path, finally grasping that her hunched look hadn't been defensive, or due to any accidental positioning of the arms. Something was wrong with her left shoulder.

Pathos, like the beam of a searchlight that sweeps in horizontally, barely grazing the surface of the sand, pointing out every rill and hollow, blazing with harsh suddenness on the near faces of objects that lie here and there and everywhere along the length of the beach: the front of an antique armchair, a tennis racquet, and, tipped over and half-filled with sand, a little doll's-house photo studio. That was something like the picture, the effect, produced on him not then but some time later, when his first impression of her – some blue-cold, impetuous quickness expanding through prisms in the eyes – had grown to include a lot of unexpected aspects of her character. If she was a 'character' – if there was any unity about her at all. She was united by her body, by her name. And though Mel was aware that the real source of his interest must be that body, and the source of the pathos (which was indefensible, but went right on existing anyway) something that had happened to its left shoulder a matter of five years before on a mountain range in Wales; it wasn't enough to convince him that the real Hettie existed anywhere near the physical. In trying to come to an understanding of her, Henrietta Tarbet, born and brought up in Hull in north-east England, he found himself visualising planetary landscapes each of which held some truth about her, overlapping with others in a different kind of space, just as a picture held in the mind might seem for a moment to occupy the same coordinates as a coat or a cardboard box we see with our eyes. But by that time he was involved himself; the contradictions were his own; whatever vulnerabilities he might be seeing were common to him and her.

He'd left it a week before ringing her up. They went to a seafood place in Leith, and the outfit she wore was another defining point for him: a brown jacket and matching skirt that hugged the contours of her hips, and a black beret worn on one side. Hettie had a gift for talking. He wondered, remembering Leanne and others, whether she was more fluent with people she specially related to.

She did know what to order. She had a chicken something-or-other, while he dared the King Prawn Sambal which laid his stomach low for three days afterwards.

She told him all about the accident (and a month afterwards he got to see the scar on her upper back, so small, white and innocent-looking) – an equipment failure while rock climbing. But the injury had been the least part of it. An orthopedic surgeon had ordered her shoulder to be strapped up for a matter of months, possibly caring about nothing else except the perfect knitting of the bone. She'd never recovered proper mobility in her arm and shoulder; they were painful to move in certain directions, and there was a slight effect of hunching. So, she told him casually, she'd taken up tennis, and relied on her right arm for most things.

That subtle entering light, the grazing touch of sadness, provided him with a kind of mental access-point on the baffling country that was Hettie. A body defined her in space; and there were the superficial likes and dislikes printed on her over a 26-year lifetime in Hull and Edinburgh. An interest in sports, secretarial skills, and a gift for taking photographs from exactly the right angle. But the better he got to know her, the more every solid statement crumbled. An unembarrassed daring in social situations was set against long-term financial caution; an upbeat openness against a tendency to get low and doubt herself, or defer to the opinion of whoever she'd happened to speak to last. Artistic flair; a completely flat occupation. An equal acceptance, it seemed, of heartfelt protest and the social norms. In the process of feeling each other out, they tripped constantly over each other's inner pitfalls, sensitive spots or long-standing calluses, stumbled and argued and retreated to the wall before going in again.

He got to know her social circle. Susan turned out to be quite a good friend, while Marjorie was just a figure in the middle distance. One other habitué turned out to be far more significant for Mel; that was Ruaridh, an ex-boyfriend who still assumed privileges. Hettie never seemed to find it in herself to give him a serious talking-to or show him the door. Ruaridh was everywhere; Ruaridh sometimes ended up going along on a trip they'd intended for themselves alone. Mel was within a whisker of taking on the problem himself. Good sense, and his actual regard for the girl, were only just enough to keep him back. But then, gentlemen were hovering everywhere. Mel knew by that time that Hettie welcomed everyone; she'd never absolutely split from any of her former loves or crushes, and new acquaintances were turning up all the time.

By this time, Pom had come through for Mel, and he was fully informed on the subject of the CTEFLA course. Only he couldn't afford to pay his way into it. He managed to get a job in the Council offices checking people's eligibility for benefit. And by the usual stumbling, arse-backwards sequence of events, he found a shared flat in Abbeyhill, not far from Hettie's small house in Dumbledykes on the margin of Arthur's Seat.

As for her, she was never still; she was constantly looking out for something else. She kept saying she didn't know why she'd ever trained in secretarial work. Mel tried to put his weight behind an idea she'd had herself: of setting up as a professional photographer. If she could just take the plunge. He saw it glowing there in his mind's eye: a little white shopfront – a studio of the interplay of light and dark.

But she only laughed at him, at a different segment of the revolving wheel of ever-variable natures that was Hettie. You needed capital for a shop, she said. By then, she was looking around for courses in corporate computer systems.

ONE, TWO, THREE

Inside that strange archaic hall, with columns, arms of ironwork. A vast suspended inside-outside roof. Feat of Victorian engineering. Where crowds turn, weary, confused, their faces pale as lizards. Where the sun can never penetrate. Waverley. And there was a slight break or trickle of people trailing past me towards the barrier, and I took a chance, following their lead over to the one gate you could get through, under the eyes of British Rail officials. I tried to get my ticket into the slot, this way, then that way, then upside-down. Seeing a fat man looking haunted beside a suitcase. And broke through, into the murmuring hive, where the wind blew chill, among the blocks and beams and ends of tracks.

When you're tired, you feel that everything's a fag. Into the buzz and numbness of your self-absorption the stimuli come crashing, shocking, jarring. And yet, I could see it, easily see it for what it was. A blessing. Sudden pitch through of the sun above us, here where there was no sun to be seen.

Platform. Platform. Which platform? 13; oh yeah.

Hettie rang me at about six this evening, at just the moment when I'd got in the door and slung my bag and was putting the kettle on, after a long day at the course. In Great Stuart Street, the Edinburgh Fount of English Undefiled. You do dry runs and group exercises or sit there taking notes in huge unairy rooms, until the need for a few minutes to put your feet up builds up in you into something you can touch.

So the phone rings. Should I answer it, you think? Na leave it, probably for one of the flatmates.

Anneka ends up taking it, and hands it on with a look of sour uninterest,

' 'S for you.'

'Oh, Mel,' the receiver says, 'thank God I've caught you.'

Thank God. Thank God. Platform 13 had a train edging into it at that moment, gliding over the oily gravel down in the pit of the track. And people milling loosely, waiting for the nearest door to open.

Headphones, buzzing in false distance. *A huh, a huh-huh*

I said,

'You say you've *found* a car?'

'Well, we just came into Stirling for the day, and I passed this garage and there it was. Far cheaper than it'd be in Edinburgh. Just 40,000 miles on it.'

'Oh? Right. … That's…'

'So, could you come up and have a look at it? You know I'm not all that good with cars.'

'Come up there?'

'Yes. Oh, it's easy. You take any train from Waverley.'

'You mean right now? Or…'

'I don't mind waiting. They don't close until quite late, and I'm sure they'd stay open even longer.'

'Um. Waverley. OK. Waverley.'

'Oh Mel, that's fantastic. I wouldn't feel right about it if you hadn't looked it over. So I'll expect you in, oh, an hour and a half?'

Hettie had gone on, filling in the details, the name, Stirling Automotive, and how to get there, and what make of car it was, and how much it was and what we could do to afford it. A small Peugeot, she didn't know the model. … What *we* can do, she'd said. *Our* car. When it was all her; I was even more strapped than usual, having sprung all the money I'd been saving for the course.

So there it was. My life, in a standing nutshell. Given from above. Where struts soared overhead, unyielding metal curves. I was shuffling in among businessmen in mufti and a teenager or two, one with the headphones, to the gap beyond the flimsy carriage-side. Was this even the right train? It was hard to tell.

A year had passed already since the crisis of Hughie on the beach. Things had developed between Hettie and me to the point where we were thinking of getting married – or rightly, not thinking, but assuming. Taking as given. I couldn't remember any moment when I'd actually asked her the question. It had just… somehow…

490

appeared, like droplets in the hanging air. And hadn't gone away, despite any difficulties we might have had. Things hadn't gone absolutely smoothly for us. I'd had a job to hold Ruaridh off, as well as one or two others. Now that she was away for a week or two, on holiday with Sue and Bryant in a cottage at Loch Earn, now that I was sleeping in my own bed at the flat rather than staying over at hers, I was able to see it with more detachment.

Ba. Ba. Ba. The carriage rocked continuously to the throb of the engine. There were rows of cranebacked seats and spaces around tables, all quickly filling up. *A huh-huh.* Peculiarly enough, all of them were facing backwards, except for a few around the near end of a table. With tightly-controlled politeness, people arranged themselves around the tables, slapping sandwiches and periodicals down in front of them like section markers. I came parallel to an empty pair of seats and swung myself in.

Despite any difficulties. Which were probably my fault; probably mainly. A state of mind, or absence of mind. Paralysis, of a sort, after what had happened. But slowly, slowly, things were coming together. The CTEFLA course. And this car she'd seen – did she say green, or yellow?

Hettie and the car. I'd be seeing her in only an hour, or was it three quarters.

Despite the crush, no-one had taken the seat beside me. That was a principle, I supposed. The instinct of urban man to sit one to a pair of seats. My bag sat on it instead, crumpled, looking back at me. A sudden acceleration of noises, ba ba-ba-*bbbbbbbb,* and the whole train heaved into motion, heading for the edge of the cowl. A bright bale from somewhere. Then we were outside, in a wasteland of wires and overarching structures; and here was the sunlight, breaking through wedges of cloud. A big window beside me gave me a good view of the sky and the way we'd just come; on the other side there was a metal luggage rack.

It was only then that I started thinking, are we really going to Stirling? Or where are we going?

And here was the first tunnel. Too late to jump for it, then. Around me among the fuzzy purple seatbacks people were flopped, talking, or fussing with their bags and gear. I tried to listen in – the match; a Jubilee mug; the prices of things. Stirling? Go on, someone say Stirling.

I was in a little cubby of my own, with the bag like a pug on the seat beside me. In front of me, the purple seatback, with a lighter pattern that looked like bacilli on a slide. I couldn't get much sense of an undercarriage – no *drmmp-a-drmm... drmmp-a-drmm* of wheels on rails, or not unless I really thought about it. Maybe the locomotive was too close to us? Not like the long, long trains through China and the Steppes.

I had nothing to do but sit, watching scenes unfolding of carpet showrooms and the yards of an industrial suburb. Backwards, always streaming back the way we'd come. The engine note was a continuous *brrrr* sound vibrating in my head, which as I discovered made it impossible to read a book, practise my languages, or set imaginary problems in classroom management. Scenes kept changing, sometimes broad vistas to the hills, more often the closer banks or trees flashing past with bewildering speed. For a moment, seeing... seeing... gone! I had to admit, the variety was amazing. Nets over the stone walls – details of masonry underneath. Then suddenly, a back street running away on an angle. Railway paraphernalia; a radio tower. The whole thing was inexhaustible. I thought of it as a sort of sample bore driven through the back-yard life of Britain.

As the train slowed down, braking towards some station, I could just feel it down through the soles of my feet. *Thak*(ata) *thak*(ata) *thak*.... We stopped at a platform in a lonely bay under hills. No-one got in, no-one got out. Just brand-new walkways, handrails around an empty space.

And up we sped again, to the audible ratchet of the diesel, *rrrrrrrr*. And on, and on. I fell back on a sort of dream-world, lulled by motion, where the order of my thoughts fled on without control. Worried into a racing darkness, heaved up on plumes from side to side. The country outside the window brought New Zealand back to me, seen ragged and fleeting out of the windows of various cars. The powerlines. Telegraph poles that blipped past, lines your vision could glide along until the next black pattern of nodes. That sense of being drawn on, breathing dust out of the crack in the window-top. Into the future. One future. One. And that was how it was. All that bewildering potential, the possibilities around you, reduced to a single line. A railtrack, what else?

There was a restlessness in the idea; I kept shifting side-to-side in my seat. Some subliminal pain, as if my mind was constantly driving up against a point of awkwardness. I didn't know what it was. Relax, can't you? I tried to picture Hettie's house, and a bed to rest in. I made myself think about skin, through waking and sleeping, in a variety of soft planes under bedclothes.

And then for an instant the skin was darker and I remembered
      someone, something. Darkness blipped under the one cowl roof between two scenes unfurling backwards

    …

There was a commotion further down the carriage. I tried to tell what was happening by the sound and the shapes of light. Someone coming round. To collect the tickets? Over the vibrations I heard a small dog, wuffling and barking suddenly.

Now, from the muffled chamber of the seat, I found I was seeing my own life as something darkened, obscure. As if the teeming possibilities I'd seen in everything were all paid out, or had come to one thing despite me. Shadowed – with a glow from somewhere….

'Tickets… please.'

That was how she said it, with a distinct pause in the middle. I craned my neck a bit, and saw a blue sleeve of the woman conductor, blonde and fifty-something.

(And from further ahead, a small whine from the dog;

'I'm so sorry, he's moulting. I hope he's not…'

'Och, we'll jus' enjoy 'is company.')

Then the lady was beside me, slung round with a hefty ticket apparatus. Her hair was pulled up in green and orange clips. I fumbled my ticket out; she took it and scribbled a mark on it with a ballpoint pen.

'This is the train to Stirling, isn't it?' I asked.

'Dunblane.'

Oh, she had me going, yes she did. But then she smiled, the puffier of her eyes going to a slit,

'But Stirling's on oor way.'

'Oh… OK. That's a relief.'

And she passed on, a type of all ticket ladies. Obviously with a sense of humour. Someone clipped her one? A cutout, shape from someone's novel. Auntie Ness, Nell, Nellie.

And so I saw her, I thought, and would always see her – forever from the outside.

But why? I indulged myself in thinking. When you quite easily could go deeper. So…. Auntie Nell, Nellie, lives with her common-law husband *Terry* who does sometimes forget himself but only when he's drunk; keeps a flat in Clovenstone, with flower boxes on the bedroom windowsill which makes her feel safe when a storm's howling outside because she always insists on keeping the window open at night. I could see a little paint-scraped thumbcatch that opened outwards, like in Hettie's flat. Made up, all of it. And always getting closer and closer to the things *I* knew. But. There must be a way, a way in, surely, which would at least let you allow for what someone might be when their actual innerness skewed away from you. I used to think I could do that

(Just here, the engine was faltering, changing tone as we swept around a long corner: a *brumm* – ba-ba-ba…)

do that with something, placards on buildings, great charcoal marks on the Surf Club, arrangements of stones on the shore. I supposed it only drew you further in to yourself….

Speaking of which, there was another trap. Try writing about *yourself*. You had to shade it, limit it; there were so many things you weren't allowed to say. Or if you insisted on sticking to what was absolutely real, then it all flew off in scraps, irrelevancies, burgeoning out immensely far outside your own bounds or anyone else's. Then they'd bring in the craft on you. Tell you to cut it down, truncate it; who are all these people? make one of them do for six. These *characters*. Who's Jim, exactly, and Nicky, and Richard and Francine and Robbie and Alice and Pom…?

And there I went again. Always thinking about the way you'd *write* things. When I knew: the stones were set, the Surf Club graffitied, it had all been lived and seen and imagined – it had, one time in my own living memory. When the bulls came charging down at me, on Longniddry Beach by the power station. 'The Work', in a matter of fifteen or twenty minutes wandering along the sand. Which was the charge, the overglaze, the substance missing. Wasn't it? At least I could remember a time when I'd thought that. I found myself looking into a darkened plane of the luggage rack, where a mirror image of the scene outside sped forwards into itself. Face into face forever. With sound effects from the dog.

But – could anything ever be established; I meant, beyond doubt? Finished and underlined, outside the sudden slip and shuffle of times and moods and faces? And what would it look like, seen again? Through a layer, and another layer, and another. I thought that there was no now, or ever was, except the seeing through it from ahead, or the past's strong and quirked and astonishing light filtered back into the moments lived.

So, now, through then, I was sailing parallel to the ground of footpaths on the coast road at Longniddry, deciding to cross at the place where the hawthorn loomed up large. Registering small patterns of stones in the meeting with the road. Bizarrely, with these railway seats, people talking all around me. It was all in the way the layers fell, the split, division. A fork of two beaches, I was remembering, and something crackling at the corners of his head. Split of past to present. And now another world stretched over that. So I was almost falling out of it, walking impossibly horizontal over the spread of sand, and slowly, against inertia, drifting downwards, at the seawall there by the white bench

And the fork was on a beach, was in my mind

The fork was on a beach, fork was in my mind, hesitancy of sun-blazed electricity, crackle across of worlds, while I felt the settling of my heels into the backed-up sand of each step down a stone seawall

...

kind of protection against flurries of pebble artillery but didn't protect us much when the Torrances got into the game, with some story about those rocks belong to my dad's cousin. Seeing, seeing as I remember, corrugations in the sand in the hieroglyphs of sun reflected, giving a wordless message to whatever it was in our heads that was open and unregarded; the me; which you can't expect to last very long in the lift of the wind and the corridors of school and the treading and treading down into mud-scuffed floors; but that's where other things can happen, in the shuffle of everyone together you might come across some other. Right there walking along in parallel in the riven cut of one world and another. Go f'r it Yipman. Like a kind of shadow theatre when you think you're alone. The one who's once again a me and whispers in your ear and plays with sticks and always seems the one tower you can rely on, till something sails up over his head, single black fleck or a dark stone floating softly up into the sky, and I don't know I can't tell what that was. A flight of cinders as the car drives on, light haemorrhage, or lure in the focus of spoiled light. 'Outside yourself', well OK, now you've made it, see you in the shivering of a grass blade up there in the wind like a floater past my eye as I stop here for a moment and try to catch it all, turn around on myself a couple of times

And then go on, letting my feet fall one by one *with the sand in streaks slopes up from the low-tide*

...

Surroundings, they never quite cease to exist.   The top of the carriage, lightly domed, with two fluorescent strips to light us.   Rumble and rattle and clatter of every fixture against every other.   A girl's arm dangling limp against a seatrest seen through the long gulf of seat to seat that ran away in front of my eye.   The fading in and out of light from outside, where the sun shone now and then through banks of cloud cruising in tattered archipelagos over the fields.   Two haystacks, cylindrical, side by side.   A wire, or the shadow of a wire, which cut the viewpoint but never divided it, as it streamed on in an endless progress of what was already past.   A crack of voices from nearly across the aisle.

'Got a...?' 'It's...' And all the time I was there, I seemed to be there again, seeing and reconsidering things once barely glimpsed in the raw, wondering again about whatever point or aim or object there might have been and looking up out of the spare flat scythe of the shore's edge to see not headlands but

...

leaning away out of the shock of the wind

And wondering, wondering as I walked, what the world could have been like otherwise or where he would have gone to with all that running, where the long line of the beach made a flat curved blade in front of me and a seagull went crying *kark* ka-ka-ka-ka somewhere over my head. Where everything hollowed to a point, to know what the point was, whether it was trudging up the side of a hill to fall into a sky wrung out with tails of the still high Alpine cloud like the lip of God, the almost-telling, venture to the end of life and out of the world, or just the other thing; and just then I saw past a silver thrown-up branch a rock on the edge of the pool level that stood up split from top to base, and I thought of Mairi. Living on with Mairi, whether that could have been all it was for him, that old bipolar thing; or was it Mairi in the car asking a question that began to ravel up everything I'd thought about him; and on the bank above the monkey-man started to change, appear in startling facets, with the low sun winking behind him and I could see again the way behind the closing of an eye in childhood before sleep come the renewable colours of a cartoon behind your eyelids, unworn, unrepetitive. In the blunt stick beside a hunch in the tussock, dwarf by a telegraph pole. Red was all over, a half-bead of the metamorphosis of light, and there he was, charging towards me now through grass like a stapling of all appearances in one like you know a boy might see who hasn't had the nail-pared instant he needs to decide what it is he'll see. Moustache and goatee, running scams. When suddenly on my right side the uncombed grass bank dropped away

And she was there the river of her something that cut away from us that innocence if it was ever that and all at once in front of me the creek meandering down the sand from bushes and scrap brambles up towards the railing and the roadway and the house with the double roof. Remember thinking. Of the lips like softer pillows parting and turning us away from every quest and inquest of the real below us, till guilt and the knowledge drive us crazy and the tape of the way of thinking scrambles and gets lost, and I drew up to the stream where two big hillocks had been formed and patted down by the hands of someone. Small kids, playing on the beach. Stitched across with footprints. So it looked like I was playing there as well, playing on a beach, came past the corner seeing without seeing the dams we built across the creek

Building and rebuilding it as I came. Accepting it; all right, all right. And when I looked up that time I couldn't see him, because everything depends on the way you walk

...

Just there.   Hovering over the tops of houses: the strange fragile hat of Linlithgow Castle.   So far on already?   Gone now.   Clipped grass of a perfectly-kept graveyard, in the middle a dirty yellow skip.   All coming in through the big window rounded at the edges, like a colossal TV screen.   Stations, stops, and always on the other side another window running with another sequence altogether, low banks sprung with shadows.   Speed, the dreamlike uninvolving speed.   And in the middle this big reverberant cigar, barely holding together, and people sprawled all over.   Pale reflections of themselves.   Seeing outside: a heap of rusted rails, small railway palings round a row of Dalek-cases.   Could keep a man in that.   And spindling little skeleton towers of struts

... or run or walk or run and leave the tally of the marks behind you, forming pictures. Pictures are pictures of the lunch you had that day or maybe a battered sardine sandwich fifteen

498

years or so before. Turning time over, recycling everything you imagined, something like a wardrobe knocked up out of planks and shoved into a corner and running at you suddenly out of a percussion of dividing fires and never seen the same again, not ever, no matter how tired or dead or numb you are. To catch a glimpse, just one glimpse from the side of a guy with sandy hair wandering alone along the wet sand at Longniddry among seaweed and bits of string grazed by fingers of the sun horizontally behind, who stops for a moment before the plank. Thinks again. No Mel, no you, no me. And will he do it? Two ships out there forever unapproaching, make a small double blot on the limitless plane of the Firth of Forth. Oh shit shit down there underwater I'm seeing it all again. But we didn't know, that was the point, or couldn't see out to the cars on the headland parked at the end of distance, and it's the not knowing that makes you free, isn't that what someone told me? Dim-crystal currents, the surface up above like wrinkles in the entering glow. So it seems we fucked it up, laying a mattress under water, drinking gallon glasses under water, it's amazing how the eye changes it all, reseeing. A ji-jo-jo-job, and her and me and the mistakes we made and the reasons he might or might not have known about it, aerial receiver, not as dumb as he looks; or was it could it have been something else entirely? I can see him suddenly now in cubes like sparkles sun-appended shifts as ever I look again with real fire elements gushed to right and left of the head or upper part, and now he's spilled as if to walk with semaphore of arms, a bas-relief. Cut across, cut through, down here we're seeing all of it, and as I fall slowly as the seabed falls again into a depthless trench below me he's opened like an orange to the cut of the knife, and I can see him turning, beginning to run for the flat hills to the south of me in the low perpetual howl, dancing away at the foot of an embankment, Yehune, no, Yehune, wait a sec

Planes of light, falling down over the back of the seat. Something you gaze into while thinking about something else. But making echoes in the run of thought, gradually folding in with it.   Quick green and violet flushes, as the stripes of sunlight fell on the outside of the train.   The walls gone faint, irrelevant.   My eyes caught in pathways of the fuzz.   I hardly noticed what I was seeing, then I was lost in it.   Shouldering on, through thickets of the cheap pile.   A seat upholstery can become a forest.   Small dustmotes, plant-heads that catch the sun.   All on a crazy perpendicular – or more, an overhang.   Like down there in Fiordland. Tree avalanches. The moss and lichens grow up again from the bare granite, so someone said; make a place for the roots to grip on, watered by the torrential rainfall, in the land of rivers. And you push yourself on, through purple growths of carpet. Mud-caked against the sandflies. Keeping a lookout for hints of a track, an indication of anyone who's come this way before you. On the journey you know you have to make, if ever you want to reach, attain it. The near-impossible thing. Find *pounamu*. The weather's built by cloudscapes, great luminaries, moments of the passing of the edge of a shadow. You only shiver and keep on. And there in the seatback, or lower down, in the dark shade between the brink of the seat my own seat and the next high-towering pinnacle

a landscape was beginning to form. Something familiar, known so well and seen so seldom. I was looking out on mountains. A big wooded hump to the left of me, in the right foreground the sprawling bottomland that held the road and the hotel and tiny village. All across, the row of them, like a crown high above the water: what they call the Elephant and the Lion on the edge, nearly round the turn of the fiord, and then a bare white cap. I could see straight up the valley; next, two peaks of a ridge nearly juxtaposed, and part of a river topped by another ridge. What could be… Barren Peak? on the extreme right. So I must have been standing about halfway up the hills, with Sheerdown, at a guess, somewhere behind me. There were fragments of white cloud and wisps floating higher in the air, and everything was gigantic, never to be encompassed in one field of vision. Which is the effect that nobody can ever get across in pictures. Not that they haven't tried, and keep on trying; it's wherever you look, on postcards, placemats, chocolate boxes everywhere. And funnily enough it doesn't even matter. That's just something we did to it. It was here before us, that rank extremity of the earth's growth. An accident with glaciers. Where the ice was squeezed together by walls a hundred million years old, remnants of the ancient continent, and only drove down the harder for it, grinding out new hills and valleys in a voracious U.

It must have been one of the few days of the year when it wasn't raining. I could see the beeches drawn clearly, the waterfalls single and discrete like cuts of silver. And bearing right across the textures of near-perpendicular faces – what was that? Thought I saw. No, it's gone. Or is that it again? Something cruising in the air, higher than birds, too small to be an aircraft. Microlight? Drifting, disjunct, across the faces of the bush. And now the view jolts momentarily, shudders and starts to expand, as I or what-am-I seem to launch straight out into the depthless clarity of the air. Without any sense of falling. Thrown out, far out across the water, and the wind blast hits me from the east and I watch as the village creeps backwards, the smallest sliver of the Mitre peeks out behind a face of rock.

Can't tell what that is. But better hurry, it's moving fast, starting to drop below me now. As my eyes swing downwards, I can barely make out something even lower… a tiny occlusion on the face of the water…?

A tourboat. Droplet on the immensity of a lens.

As for what I'm chasing, I'm still not close enough. But catching up bit by bit. I can see it's got no wings, it's smaller than I thought. It floats on over the water and huge land-masses, and I can't tell much about it beyond a size. About monkey-size, human-size. Beside me, the standing peak's drawn out into a ridge, two pinnacles separating it on the other side, and I seem to be moving on down the neck of the fiord towards the opening to the sea. There's a cold blast in the high air. I flip and plunge down lower, trying to see. Elongate – a single clutch of light and shading. And then suddenly I swing past, so that for the barest instant two eyes stare out like bullseyes on a shore.

Now again you're rising. I can see you clearly enough, though I seem to have to imagine the details before they're fixed: you're dressed as ever in your blue Fairydown fleece and chino trousers, this time with no tramping boots. Your feet are bare, with a stain of something dark like railway oil. Your hair's still curly, a bit longer, maybe, than it was just there at the end; and I can tell you can't see me, eyes look out on space, on a gaugeless volume of the wind and cloud before the mountain line somewhere behind. We've come to the foot of the falls, Wai manu, where they drift downward to the sea from the bowl of the hanging valley. Don't you know I'm here? You begin to rise, turning more loosely on the air than any bird or cartoon Superman, and the Elephant on the left and the Lion, Hurateke, tower up among heads of cloud. Small sparkles in the air: it's raining. Every crease in your clothes, every bulge and wrinkle of your face, is just as it was. Now the falls are sinking out of sight, dark mountain arms receding as you climb, into air that's rarefied, sparkling with the reflections of drops, and thickening here and there in scuds of trailing mist. For a minute or two you're not facing me. As we go higher, the whole ice-chopped mountain floor drops down and beyond it is the South Pacific, past the sunken sill of the moraine. All the time I'm trying to speak, say something to you. It seems I can't. I'm beside and a bit below you, can't keep an even keel. As your head turns round again, the expression changes, with that contraction of the cheek and side of the lip that I remember, and it seems to me you've caught sight of something behind my back. Now I'm not sure what clothes you're wearing. Your body's starting to change for the last time. Your features cease to be Yehune, and modulate frameless into jackal-heads and ursine squashed-muzzle figures, and then to qualities of the light gone solid, built in partitions lightly coloured, reflected in and through themselves. I can hear a booming groan from somewhere, jangling on the ear, where before there was only wind noise. A *muuoooo-oooor*. You're drawing out, longer and longer, you're both there in front of me and gone, built out of the world, in cold brinks and reflections. The wind's gone hard, but I can't hear it under the roar; we're bearing further off to westward. All right then – that's it – this is where I have to leave you; go on man, float off into the incredible high air, like a kite collapsed or a hitch in the colours of the sunlight, into the place you must have left and now belong in, and I can finally work my lips, take my last chance to say it, unheard and unhearable anywhere up here, and feel them move again and again, Goodbye, my friend

---

That noise; brake noise. It was faster, louder, pulling me back to myself. A cacophonic graunch of metal. I was forced suddenly back against the seat, hearing the hubbub of passengers on three sides. I tried to crane my neck back looking out the window. My teeth gritted against a harder thrum and scream

I made out towering struts that flashed above us, girders linked in V's on something falling, slowly in the incremental moment sliced so fine toppling above me as the train ran on unable to stop itself in time and hurtling broken struts of crystallised metal through the side and roof of the carriage I was, we were all sitting in. Braking, I thought, sudden stop, something on the line; ahead was the dark brickwork of a tunnel but everything seen in flashes stilled while all through my mind were spears of steel constructions run apart to fall through roof and light and seating and ram the bodies of men and women core all things in blood and chaos; what's that fallin, other, nother bridge

Two shadows slash past quick as lightning a thaka-thunna a thaka-thunna thak thak *thak* ... **thak**

Structural stability inheres in the box truss surrounding proper of the overpass which intersecting at either side of the track with triangulated upright supports is subject to fatigue-induced cracking from the effects of wind and vibration of passing trains or on occasion small buckles preexisting as initial imperfections in the chords and struts resulting in an initially only moderate displacement of internal elements which in turn can create a global instability accompanied by elastic buckling exceeding allowable limits and introducing the risk of catastrophic collapsoccurred suddenly as severe local deformation of Member 5-7 initiated by a ruptured angle leg degraded the strength of the girder and introduced cracks in the angle nearest the top flange initiating fibre pullout which led to complete delamination of the web from bottom flange upwards in the high-stressed shear region with the result that forces were unable

a block. a block. a block. a block.

abrupt and unexpected loss of vertical

I was looking at a mess of steel bars, with clouds floating behind. All around me, blood and scattered body-parts, and some new crumpled strut-and-axle sculptures that had sprung up from the floor. The light of day was streaming through the rags of the roof. Strangely, the big window was still intact.

I felt a throbbing pain in one arm. I realised my right hand had gripped it at the muscle so hard that it was cutting off the blood. Relaxed my right hand.

Somewhere, the dog, making excitable noises, *bark*-ba, *bark*-ba.

So something had survived. And me...? About then I began to hear the smaller sound effects, like a murmur of voices fading in.

I half-raised myself to look around. I managed to establish that it wasn't as bad as I thought. Our carriage must have come off particularly well. I looked for blood, and could only see shadows on the floor and seating. No fingers, no bits of arms severed at the elbow. And where was the mangled ironmongery? The luggage rack, shiningly straight and perfect. One large man stood with his back to me, beside himself, shouting about something. I could see braces where his waistcoat failed to come down over the shirt.

When I dropped back into my seat, I couldn't help seeing the overbridge right in my eye, still up there. It was a rusting box of triangulated rods that guarded some large-gauge pipe. Another one was behind it, out of sight. I'd seen them flash by, one, two, in the moment of braking. Wheeling up against the light. But nothing had fallen. No false-celestial darts had dropped out of heaven, this time, to pierce the shoulders, heads and kidneys of the characters and characters and more characters jammed all together under this flimsy carriage roof.

Though they were shaken up, that was for sure. Now that some balance was re-establishing itself, I could hear it in the tones of voice, the bellowing objections of the thick man by my seat.

'Will y' shut that dog up?' he interrupted himself to say.

'Jock. Sh-sh,' in a plaintive woman's voice.

The dog responded again. Amidst the background noise I heard the phrase 'British Rail' repeated now and then like a swearword.

For a while, nothing much happened. I only noticed that the engine had still been going when it cut out, with a quick *br-b'*.

The man wandered over to join a heated discussion somewhere ahead. The reasons for the sudden stop. The question of the dog, with an implication by some that it would be better off anywhere but at their table.

I looked out, craning my neck to get a better view of where we were going, or would have been going. Immediately outside my window was a small working area for the railwaymen. There were stacks of concrete blocks. Two of those upright metallic boxes you saw everywhere. A metal mast. Some cables were stretched across the track further on, towards a broad stone wall facing us. There, I saw a complicated mechanism holding lights, something that I guessed must be the lip of a tunnel, and one red eye.

'Could at least tell us what's...' someone was saying.

A woman cradling an off-white, curly-haired dog was roaming up and down the seats now, as if looking for a home.

She made me think for a moment of Hettie, waiting on and on in the showroom in Stirling beside the green or yellow car. Possibly swearing to herself. What would she do, eventually? ... Consult train timetables, start ringing up the hospitals?

It struck me then, absurdly, that I'd been given a chance to live on. I felt my heart still beating fast in the aftermath of the shock. It had been nothing really; I'd mistaken an emergency stop for something more catastrophic. But the impression of collapsing girders – that instant of looking up, seeing steel cages toppling out of the air – had been real enough to me. It had shaken me to the very roots, subtly shifted my grasp on everything. As if it was actually *meant* to be the end. ... And now?

Now here I was, jittering in the fug of the carriage interior, looking out on the most inconsequential things. Feeling time passing. Listening to people arguing.

The woman (who was in her forties or more, with a flushed irregular skin) had ambled back the way she came. She paused against the luggage rack.

'Sit here, if you like,' I said to her.

She made a gesture, refusing. But I could see a sort of shy gratification that I'd even offered. Her dog just bared its teeth.

Now that people had given up waiting for it, an announcement rattled out suddenly through speakers:

'Ladies and gentlemen, there will be a slight delay due to conditions on the track.' Some coughs and static, and *'Thank you for travelling with British Rail.'*

'A slight delay', he said. The train felt inert, like the bones of a dinosaur. Outside, two workmen in orange tabards strolled out alongside the train, sat down, and deliberately lit up cigarettes.

So there was nothing we could do. It would either take half an hour or half the night. Strangely, though, I didn't feel bored; far from it. At just that moment, some powerful apprehension was creeping up on me, as if small dots and indications throughout the train-ride to that point were congealing into a huge and almost palpable mass around my head. The clanks, the noises – the looming struts and girders – the feel of thundering onwards – the big sweep of the dark whenever the sun went behind a cloud....

It wasn't something I'd dreamed up; I couldn't have held it off if I'd wanted to. Sitting there in the seat, I had a vision of life, my life, as a shadowed space like the inside of a Zeppelin, built on a massive metallic framework. Everywhere I looked the functional struts ran backwards, forwards, diagonally across, in every imaginable gauge and length. It was like staring upwards through the Eiffel Tower. Beyond that, stretched and corrugated, the material of the airship, like a contour of dark sails. All somehow delimited: strict and heaven-crushed. That was the outer edge; no moving outside that. And yet, somewhere I could make out something glowing – just there, by the nut of an iron staple. An entering radiance... fire, maybe, starting somewhere...?

So this was what it had come to. All the bars and framing struts of event that had brought me here. An inside-airship. I supposed it was an impression that had crept up on me while living in this hemisphere: half-dark in the daytime, the rows of tenements blackened by smuts from the breweries. The crushing, overwhelming shell of day. And the feel of a gradual narrowing down of possibilities… as if my single line and everybody else's had formed up into that huge, interdependent cage.

But. … I realised, almost with another small shock, that that needn't be all of it. Hadn't life been given back to me? Wasn't I sitting here, somehow repeated in the obscure mechanics of life and death, heart set beating again, when everything seemed to have ended? And things looked different enough from here, as if the individuals on seats and spilling out across the aisle were bared, skeletal, moving in manifest patterns. I could see myself as clearly, and the way I'd come. I'd been fastening myself on some idea, stopped, now, now; with only an illusion of forward motion. That I was an artist of some kind, maybe a writer. Now was the time, I understood, to give that up. It was Yehune who'd taken that forward – he'd actually created something. Written a pile of music. So now it was up to me to get it in front of people's eyes. I'd put his work out there somehow or other. It must be possible, if I tried hard enough. I swore it. There. And for the rest of it….

What were we, anyway? So much more than what they made us – these 'characters', milling together and grumbling words to each other, looking out the windows, some already breaking out packs of cards. Who could codify us, any one of us? Any little two-eyed human leaving? The complexity was too far beyond us, or beyond the capacity of words directly used – there was a point where any statement could be replaced with its opposite, and only the blank stood behind, staring back at us, charged and supercharged with the instant of life lived. The idea occurred to me that the only one who might ever come close to understanding – could be, in flashes – was someone who was in love. That flushed, anomalous state. That deadly truth-in-fever. Otherwise… what could we see?

Here, looking in from the other side of death, I seemed to watch us run on, run on, lumped together in some peculiar simultaneity that defied chronology. He and she and me and the one who bore me, faces staring out of the air or the dulled plastic fittings of the carriage, frozen, in moments of soaring or collapse. The 'when' was only relative – we looked out from a bundle of instants compassable in one. Stood at a vantage-point. As I was standing myself... on a blown-out shoreline, with lines of the beach vanishing ahead of me. Of course: Longniddry. As if my whole life had been shaped to get there. The sky was patterned with near-invisible seams, curled bicycle spokes that hemmed one cause to another. Bright silver streaks, flashing with colours of the past. I was toppling back and upwards, to my left a line of rocks. It was still, all at one instant, and we were there, we all....

I'm turning in my seat. I'm craning to look back, or rather, onwards, towards the reddish stone wall that probably flanks a tunnel. There's a row of dirty steps there, set into the stone and running down. Around me, echoes and fragments of things I'm hearing or have heard in the last half hour: bangs, barks, train noises, catches of conversation. Thinking, what will I do? Of course, I'll go on; make a run for the heart of light. Reject all the disconsolacies that could pull me down. I'll take up with Hettie, finish my course, get some sort of a job; get married if she'll have me. I might still scribble something; who knows? But it's not the point. We can maybe do what we've always talked about: go and have a look at Europe. She's always wanted to travel. I might finally get to see Norway. We, I should say, I mean Hettie and...

and now I'm actually seeing her, a medium-sized woman's figure, walking down the stone steps to the railway-side from the bridge up above. Or seeing someone. Can it really be...? Yes, there's that telltale bob at the shoulder. It's Hettie in every detail, drawn dark against the glow of the sun, hatless, soft at the edges of the hair. She's got a skirt on and a brown caftan top, she's stepping on medium high heels. Her face is in shadow; looks over from the handrail, hasn't seen me yet. I can't imagine how she got here. But there it is. Hettie! I even raise my hand to her through the window. The other self. So now there are two

and suddenly I'm seeing everything through this, as the streams of memory flow back from me in wings and fragments, scrapes and wordless noises; thinking, now, it's now; in a breathless moment all of it framed and caught. And not ending here, not for either of us, Hettie. I can see us running on regardless, rejecting the answers we've

509

been given, taking it all as new, trying not to falter despite anything they do to force us down, this time working always at the level of the earth… for life, that grows in frightening arms up above our heads, while we shoulder whatever burdens we have to, fossick out a way, not for words, or art, or aims, or any object that can be held in the hand – but for life – the earth, the human world – that vast metallic structure overradiated.

A Note About the Author

K. M. Ross was born in 1959 in Auckland, New Zealand, and grew up on the North Shore. He attended Rangitoto College, gained a Scholarship and entered the University of Auckland, where he completed a BA in languages. He went on to study for two piano performance diplomas while writing short stories and pursuing his enthusiasm for Italian motorcycles. In 1986 he travelled to Australia and Hong Kong, then overland via the Trans-Siberian Railway to Europe. He settled in Edinburgh, where he earned a living as a private music teacher while he worked on short stories and several novels. His novel *Falling Through the Architect* was published in 2005. He plays the bagpipes, and reads and speaks Icelandic among other languages.

OTHER BOOKS FROM WAYWISER

*Co-published with Picador